LES MISÉRABLES

VOLUME I

Victor Hugo

Introduction and Notes by
ROGER CLARK
University of Kent at Canterbury

The first of two volumes bound separately

WORDSWORTH CLASSICS

For my husband
ANTHONY JOHN RANSON
with love from your wife, the publisher.
Eternally grateful for your unconditional love.

Readers who are interested in other titles from
Wordsworth Editions are invited to visit our website at
www.wordsworth-editions.com

For our latest list and a full mail-order service, contact
Bibliophile Books, 5 Datapoint, South Crescent, London E16 4TL
TEL: +44 (0)20 7474 2474 FAX: +44 (0)20 7474 8589
ORDERS: orders@bibliophilebooks.com
WEBSITE: www.bibliophilebooks.com

This edition published 1994 by Wordsworth Editions Limited
8B East Street, Ware, Hertfordshire SG12 9HJ
Introduction and Notes added 2002

ISBN 978 1 85326 085 8

Text © Wordsworth Editions Limited 1994
Introduction and Notes © Roger Clark 2002

Wordsworth® is a registered trademark of
Wordsworth Editions Limited

Wordsworth Editions
is the company founded in 1987 by
MICHAEL TRAYLER

Typeset in Great Britain by Antony Gray
Printed and bound by Clays Ltd, St Ives plc

GENERAL INTRODUCTION

Wordsworth Classics are inexpensive editions designed to appeal to the general reader and students. We commissioned teachers and specialists to write wide ranging, jargon-free introductions and to provide notes that would assist the understanding of our readers rather than interpret the stories for them. In the same spirit, because the pleasures of reading are inseparable from the surprises, secrets and revelations that all narratives contain, we strongly advise you to enjoy this book before turning to the Introduction.

General Adviser
KEITH CARABINE
Rutherford College
University of Kent at Canterbury

HISTORICAL NOTE

Few novels are more historically specific than Victor Hugo's *Les Misérables*. Few deal with a more turbulent period in French (and indeed in European) history. And there is little doubt that Hugo wanted his novel to be read, in considerable part, as an historical novel, as a kind of modern follow-up to the medieval *Notre-Dame de Paris* (1831). The aim of the following note is to provide some of the information that will help the reader make sense of the historical background to *Les Misérables*. References to Hugo's text are to Part, Book and Chapter and are given thus: I, 1, i.

The events portrayed in *Les Misérables* span the period between October 1815 (Jean Valjean's arrival in Digne) and the summer of 1833 (the death of Valjean). But, to either side of these dates, there are flashbacks to the French Revolution of 1789 and to the Napoleonic Wars as well as flashforwards to the revolutionary events of 1848 and to the early days of Louis-Napoleon's Second Empire (1852–70). Hugo's belief is that the historical events underpinning his fiction can only be understood in terms of what preceded them; and in turn that subsequent developments, whether realised at the time of writing or projected into the future, are determined by the events represented in the narrative.

After Napoleon's defeat at Waterloo on 18 June 1815 (the subject of all of II, 1) and his subsequent abdication, the allied powers (chiefly England, Russia and

Prussia) agreed that the discredited Bourbon monarchy should be restored to the French throne. The period 1815–30 in French political history is accordingly known as the (Bourbon) Restoration. Louis XVIII (1755–1824), the grandson of Louis XV and the brother of the guillotined Louis XVI, was the first of two restored Bourbon kings. An elderly sixty when he returned to France from emigration, Louis XVIII was a sickly and physically somewhat grotesque individual; suffering from gout and other bodily unpleasantnesses, he was the butt of many scurrilous caricatures and lampoons. The Restoration (a vain attempt to return to the *status quo ante*) projected a visibly outdated and gerontocratic image (expressed in *Les Misérables* principally through the figure of old Gillenormand, Marius's grandfather), in sharp retrospective contrast with what was remembered, not always accurately, as the energy and youthfulness of Empire (these represented in the novel by recollections of Marius's father). Despite early signs of political realism and an apparent willingness to strike compromises (e.g. his acceptance, albeit reluctant, of a constitutional Charter with the French nation), Louis XVIII moved markedly to the right towards the end of his reign, especially after the assassination in February 1820 of the Duc de Berry, his nephew and the pretender to the French throne. At his death in 1824 he was succeeded by his brother the comte d'Artois (1757–1836), who reigned as Charles X, the last of the Bourbons. Part III, 3, iii provides a telling analysis of the early years of the Restoration and of its ideology.

Charles X, the standard-bearer of the diehard Royalists (known as the *Ultras*), was physically more attractive but considerably more stupid than his brother; he lacked Louis XVIII's political nous and willingness to contemplate the possibility of change. The product of his doctrinaire ultraroyalism, Charles X's already conservative policies, notably on religious and constitutional matters (e.g. the laws that he pushed through on sacrilege and on the indemnification of the *émigrés*), became increasingly reactionary in the late 1820s. Opposition protests at the growing illiberalism of successive government measures prompted the king to dissolve the Chamber of Deputies in May 1830. Charles X refused to accept the unfavourable results of the ensuing elections (July 1830), dissolved the Chamber once more, tinkered with the electoral laws and abolished press freedom (in what are known as the Four Ordinances). These measures triggered widespread protest movements which culminated in the overthrowing of the senior branch of the French royal family in the course of the July Revolution of 1830. Like his brother before him, Charles X was forced to flee France and to seek ignominious refuge abroad, in Edinburgh and Prague. The 'three glorious days' at the end of July 1830 (*les trois glorieuses*), immortalised by Delacroix in his *Liberty Leading the People*, thus effectively brought an end to the Bourbon Restoration. The best literary representation of France in the late 1820s is to be found in Stendhal's *Scarlet and Black* (1830). Hugo for his part provides an overall judgement on the Restoration, its politics and personalities, in IV, 1, i.

Charles X was succeeded by his cousin, Louis-Philippe, Duc d'Orléans (1773–1850), the representative of the younger Orléans branch of the French royal family. He was the son of the trouble-making Philippe-Egalité who had voted for the execution of Louis XVI in 1793, an act which however failed to save Philippe-Egalité himself from the guillotine. Determined to mark himself off from his Bourbon predecessors and to cut a resolutely middle-class appearance (he is said to have been fond of walking incognito around Paris carrying an umbrella), Louis-Philippe, the citizen king, reigned as king of the French (rather than of France, the nuance is important) until February 1848. With his pear-shaped head and with what was seen as his bourgeois caution and philistinism, Louis-Philippe and his entourage provided material for many caustic cartoons in the satirical press of the period (most notably in the magazines of Daumier and Philipon). The period from 1830 to 1848 in France is known as the July Monarchy (from the month of its inception); it is during this time that much of the action of *Les Misérables* takes place.

The July Revolution raised many liberal and republican hopes that were however rapidly disappointed. Although the new monarch accepted his constitutional status (there was no glorious coronation in Rheims, no extravagant royal living) and replaced the white Bourbon flag with the revolutionary tricolour, the revolution that had brought him to power rapidly came to be seen by many as a *révolution escamotée* (a 'squandered revolution'). The feeling of disenchantment that resulted, especially amongst the less well-off and the young, is a major constituent part of the Romantic malaise known as *mal du siècle* (analysed by Hugo in III, 4, i). Opposition to Louis-Philippe's moderation, to his *juste milieu* (middle-of the-road) policies, was not slow in manifesting itself. The Lyons silk workers rose up in protest against their living and working conditions in November 1831 whilst the funeral of the liberal general Lamarque in June 1832 triggered a violent demonstration and the erection of barricades across the streets of eastern Paris: the barricade stands as a permanent icon of French revolutionary activity, whether it be in 1789, 1830, 1848, 1871 or . . . 1968. The whole of IV, 10 is devoted to a long and highly allusive comparison between different forms of revolutionary activity (revolution, ambushes, insurrection, street fighting, rioting, etc.).

The insurrection around the funeral of General Lamarque and its eventual suppression provides the historical centrepiece of Hugo's novel. Further rumblings continued throughout the 1830s and 1840s as, despite its relative success in matters of foreign policy, dissatisfaction with the bourgeois regime grew. Desperate food shortages together with Louis-Philippe's reluctance to make concessions on electoral reform led the opposition to sponsor a series of liberal banquets (the so-called *campagne des banquets*) during the winter of 1847–8. The banning of one of these gatherings in January 1848 provided the spark that ignited the violent February uprising; this in turn precipitated the resignation of the citizen king. The February Revolution and its immediate aftermath provide part of the subject matter for Flaubert's *L'Education sentimentale* (1869) in which the novelist brilliantly interweaves his account of a crisis in French history with the story of the sentimental education of his hero, the somewhat limp Frédéric Moreau. Hugo's judgement on the overall significance of the July Monarchy and of Louis Philippe's contribution to French history is given in great detail in IV, 1, ii–v.

These are the historical events that provide the backdrop for the made-up story and invented characters that are to be encountered in *Les Misérables*. In this sense Hugo makes historical reality act as the guarantor of the verisimilitude of his fiction. References to these events, and to the real personalities involved, minor as well as major, are liberally sprinkled throughout the novel. But in addition, thanks to the hindsight and omniscience that are the privilege of the author, there are in *Les Misérables* allusions to events that postdate the closure of the narrative (1833). Hugo thus provides the reader with references to the February Revolution of 1848 and to the bloody workers uprising in June of the same year (V, 1, i). Furthermore, the Second Empire of Louis-Napoleon (Napoleon's nephew and Hugo's *Napoléon le petit*), when much of *Les Misérables* was written, appears as a ghostly watermark in the texture of Hugo's fiction. In this context Jean Valjean, permanently exiled and permanently striving to right the injustices of society, should be read as a transposition of the figure of the author, writing in exile on Guernsey from a position of unyielding opposition to the régime of Louis-Napoleon. There is in addition little doubt that much of Hugo's representation of the structures of Restoration and July-Monarchy France was intended to stand as a (barely) veiled critique of the organisation of what has come to be known by some as Louis-Napoleon's carnival empire.

INTRODUCTION

Arguably marking the apex of a writing career that spans over sixty years and of an *oeuvre* that runs to over thirty volumes in the most recent French edition, the one thousand or more pages of Victor Hugo's *Les Misérables* (1862) present a bewildering multitude of stories that solicit a variety of emotional responses. They tell in the first instance of M. Charles-François-Bienvenu Myriel, the Bishop of Digne and the 'upright man', whose story provides the moral and structural entrance into Hugo's monumental fiction. The reader will later be expected to weep when he reads of the fate of the miserable Fantine and of her illegitimate daughter Cosette. He will be required to hiss at the antics of the arch-villains of the piece, the despicable Thénardier ménage, but to feel sympathy for their children, chiefly for Eponine and Gavroche. He will experience a chill of apprehension each time he is confronted by the sinister but conscientious Inspector Javert, a distant forerunner of Simenon's Maigret. He will derive amusement from the adventures of Gavroche, the streetwise urchin of the middle sections of the novel, and feel the full injustice of his brutal death during the fighting on the Parisian barricades. Later still the reader will be asked to join in the celebrations around the marriage of the novel's Romantic protagonists, Cosette and Marius; he will be encouraged to participate in their happiness and to share the hopes for their future that colour the somewhat saccharine final episodes of the novel. And throughout Hugo's fiction the reader, his attitude veering between horror and admiration, will follow the vicissitudes of the career of Jean Valjean.

With its network of interwoven plot strands, not all of which have been mentioned above, its proliferation of characters taken from a wide range of professions and social categories, its exploration of a multiplicity of themes and subjects, Hugo's novel may be seen to function as a metaphor for the modern city. The book becomes in this sense a formal image of Paris, the capital city in which its action principally takes place and to which most of its characters gravitate. The organisations of city and novel reveal parallel complexities and are characterised by similar contrasts. Even before Haussmann's rebuilding, Hugo's Paris had its splendid boulevards but also its dingy and tortuous backwaters; his novel is a mix of high-flown Romanticism, lurid sensationalism, solemn didacticism and sometimes pedantic erudition. Paris's elegant parks, rectilinear avenues and reassuring monuments lie in close proximity to a maze of dangerous blind alleys and secret passageways; areas of calm and tranquillity abut districts dominated by lawlessness and anarchy. Similarly, in the novel, long meditative digressions on a variety of subjects (what Hugo terms 'parentheses') are juxtaposed with a tangle of chapters full of intense and melodramatic action. The seemingly organised structures of both worlds, fictional as well as urban, are under constant subterranean menace: the city from the germs and miasmas lurking in the labyrinthine sewers that lie just beneath the surface of its streets; the novel from the many subplots that threaten to disrupt the texture of the narrative by opening up reading expectations that frequently lead nowhere.

For the modern student the process of familiarisation with *Les Misérables* is an experience that strangely replicates what it must have been like to become acquainted with preHaussmannian Paris. The very length of Hugo's novel imposes an essentially ambulatory pattern upon the reader's journey of discovery. This is reinforced, beneath an apparently ordered architecture (thus the highly self-conscious division into Parts, Books and Chapters), by the fragmented nature of the book's narrative structure, by its atomisation into a swirl of generally short chapters. Halts in the reading process have to be made, rests need to be taken, sitdowns in cafés and visits to *vespasiennes* (urinals) become necessary. City and novel, the novel as city, are constructs in which the stroller-reader (the nineteenth-century *flâneur*) and the reader-stroller (the twentieth-century browser) need always to be on their guard. Both are environments from which one must learn to expect the unexpected, where not everything is as it appears, where few things are subject to logical explanation. Both worlds are ruled by chance and coincidence: they are places where the unforeseen (the *imprévu*) and the disquieting (the *insolite*) are constantly lurking, ready to leap out from every page of the narrative and from around every street corner. An equally inchoate vision of the city was being associated at much the same time with a very different but equally fragmenting literary genre (the prose poem) by one of the greatest of Hugo's contemporaries, the poet Charles Baudelaire. Baudelaire's ideal ('the miracle of a form of poetic prose') is born of a similar urban source to that that inspires *Les Misérables*:

> This obsessive ideal springs above all from frequent contacts with enormous cities, from the junction of their innumerable connections.

This vision will later underpin the reading of the modern capital promoted by the Surrealists, most notably by André Breton in *Nadja*, as well as by the critic Walter Benjamin. It will come as no surprise that both Baudelaire and the Hugo of *Les Misérables* feature prominently in Benjamin's jottings for his magisterial *Arcades Project*.

The structures of Hugo's novel and of its urban setting are however unified and bound together by the book's principal plot strand, the story of Jean Valjean. The organisation of Hugo's fiction revolves to a large extent around the figure of the ex-convict, around the sequence of events that befall him and that determine his development. Of all the novel's many characters Valjean is the only one to be present from beginning to end (a pattern that is strongly underlined by Hugo in the early drafts of the book); by contrast Cosette and Marius, Thénardier and Javert are introduced late on and are then allowed to drift in and out of the narrative. In this sense the story of Jean Valjean provides the novel with a clearly defined structural backbone. It is also Valjean who links together the individual stories of the other characters and bridges their separate dramas. Thus it is through Valjean's intervention, because of the promise he has made to Fantine, that Cosette is delivered out of the hellish world of the Thénardiers; without him Marius would not have fallen in love with and eventually married Cosette; and it is the ex-convict who is also indirectly responsible for the murder of Gavroche and very directly responsible for Javert's suicide.

Equally, in terms of the geography of *Les Misérables*, it is Valjean who connects the various settings, provincial as well as Parisian, in which the novel's action takes place. Valjean alone journeys from Digne to Montreuil, from Montreuil via Toulon to Montfermeil where the Thénardiers have their inn, eventually from Montfermeil to Paris. He is also the only character to have access to all of the novel's many Parisian settings, sewers as well as parks, east and west ends, and to the city's different social milieux: the criminal underworld (the world of thieves, swindlers, prostitutes and convicts), religious institutions (principally through the Petit-Picpus episode and the convent in which Valjean and Cosette temporarily find refuge), the increasingly irrelevant ultraroyalist establishment (chiefly represented by old Luc-Esprit Gillenormand, Marius's grandfather, and his circle of friends), as well as the republican opposition (the group of young Romantic radicals, the various members of the ABC secret society led by Enjolras). In this way Jean Valjean acts as the spider (a favourite Hugolian metaphor) at the heart of the novel's gigantic web of characters, locations and events. In that it tells the story of the fall and rise of an exemplary individual, the basic structure of Hugo's novel remains in essence quite simple. *Les Misérables* is in this sense very different from some other contemporary fictions with which it has been compared, chiefly Eugène Sue's *Mysteries of Paris* and Balzac's *Splendeurs et misères des courtisanes* (*A Harlot High and Low*). The influence of both is freely acknowledged by Hugo in the course of his novel (p. 669) but where Balzac and especially Sue (as is suggested by the titles of their books) are primarily interested in weaving and then unravelling a complicated storyline, Hugo subordinates the mechanisms of plot to the moral message of his novel.

It is a moral message to which Jean Valjean makes the most central of contributions. The theme of spiritual redemption, more generally of progress in all its forms, lies at the heart of *Les Misérables*; we shall see that the significance of Hugo's title derives to a large extent from this thematic preoccupation. Valjean's story is that of a man who finds himself, who discovers his true identity after discarding a multitude of disguises and false identities. As the account of someone who obtains salvation through the sacrifices he makes on behalf of others, *Les Misérables* tells in the first instance of the cleansing of an individual conscience. The opening episodes of the novel, in a section significantly entitled 'The Fall', the theft of Myriel's candelabra and even more reprehensibly of Petit-Gervais's coin firmly situate the character in a moral quagmire. Both events will haunt Valjean to the end of his life. But, through a series of magnanimous gestures, the character succeeds in raising himself out of the morass of his beginnings. As mayor of Montreuil (known, not by accident, as *le père* Madeleine) he is loved by all and sacrifices his personal well-being to the good of the community; later, in the complicated 'Champmathieu Affair' episode (Book 7 of Part 1), he discloses his true identity and compromises his freedom in order to save the falsely accused Champmathieu. In subsequent sections of the novel Valjean devotes himself unreservedly to the abandoned Cosette, becoming in effect a proxy father figure: there is much of Hugo's love for his daughter Léopoldine and of his pain at her death in Valjean's feelings towards Cosette. Valjean later immerses himself in good works on behalf of the Parisian down-and-outs, frees Javert and saves Marius's life before carrying him, like Saint Christopher with the boy Jesus on his shoulders or like Christ carrying His Cross, through and out of the sludge of the Parisian sewers. Mud in all its forms, physical as well as moral, is a key motif in the imagery of *Les Misérables*: Valjean's emergence out of the excremental mire of Paris counterpoints the character's moral regeneration and clearly signals the final stage of his rehabilitation.

The titles of the last three books of the novel ('The Last Drop in the Chalice', 'The Twilight Wane', 'Supreme Shadow, Supreme Dawn') have a distinctly Christian and resurrectional ring to them. They are intended to underline the regeneration of Valjean that is ultimately realised through his sacrifice of himself in death to the happiness of Cosette and Marius. The young man is quick to grasp the fullness of the ex-convict's rehabilitation and the sincerity of his conversion:

> In short, whatever this Jean Valjean might be, he had incontestably an awakened conscience. There was in him some mysterious regeneration begun; and, according to all appearances, for a long time already the scruple had been master of the man. Such paroxysms of justice and goodness do not belong to vulgar natures. An awakening of conscience is greatness of soul.
>
> [p. 951]

The climax and final part of *Les Misérables* (aptly entitled 'Jean Valjean') accumulates images that direct our reading of the central character as a proletarian Christ figure: 'He also bears his cross' is for instance the title of one of the chapters of Book 3. Valjean's deathbed confession, in the presence of Cosette and Marius (a clear echo here of old Goriot's death in Balzac's *Le Père Goriot*), is that of a man who has made peace with himself and with the world. The ex-convict can now bring himself to forgive those who have sought to harm him, even the odious Thénardiers. His last gesture is to give his blessing to the young couple beside him, to Cosette his adopted daughter but also to Marius who has stolen Cosette from him. Accordingly, and in sharp contrast with his entry into Hugo's novel and its world ('The Fall'), Valjean's exit is marked by a strongly upward movement:

> He had fallen backwards, the light from the candlestick fell upon him; his white face looked towards heaven, he let Cosette and Marius cover his hands with kisses; he was dead.
>
> The night was starless and very dark. Without doubt, in the gloom some mighty angel was standing, with outstretched wings, awaiting the soul.
>
> [p. 986]

Few novels are characterised by a greater degree of historical specificity than *Les Misérables*. The wealth of historical allusion that it contains may contribute in some measure to the difficulty that English (and even French) readers may experience in coming to terms with the novel: some familiarity with early nineteenth-century French history is essential for an understanding of Hugo's text and to this end a brief Historical Note precedes this Introduction. The various constituent parts of Les Misérables (the story of Valjean, the romance of Marius and Cosette, the demolition of the Thénardier family, digressions on a whole raft of more or less interesting topics) are inserted into an historical frame that is considerably more ornate and more detailed than those of other similar novels (e.g. the works of Balzac and Sue quoted earlier). The opening sections of Hugo's book thus firmly localise the plot at very precise moments in time: the novel's first words take the reader back to the hinge year 1815 (the year of Waterloo), the opening sentence of Book 2 narrows the chronological focus down to October 1815, Book 3 is entitled 'In the Year 1817' (as is its first chapter) and Book 4 moves us on to the spring of 1818. We are later given an extended and celebrated evocation of the Battle of Waterloo (Book 1 of Part 2, almost forty pages in the present edition) that would appear at first sight to have little to do with the novel's principal preoccupations. There are also long passages analysing the significance of the revolutions of 1789 and 1830. The insurrectional activity of June 1832 (not the July uprising of 1830 as is frequently thought) sparked by the funeral of the liberal General Lamarque provides the background to much of Parts 4 and 5 of the novel. In addition Les Misérables is studded with references to a vast range of historical events and figures, both major and minor. What, readers must ask themselves, is the value of these references? Why does Hugo go out of his way to provide his work with this enormously detailed (and perhaps potentially tiresome) historical background?

It is one of the implications of Hugo's title that his novel is not solely about certain individual characters (Valjean, Marius, Cosette, Javert, etc.) and their fictional dramas. The form of his title makes it clear that, beyond the stories of invented individuals, Hugo is also anxious to say something about a collection of beings (Les Misérables), about the French nation and, beyond these, about the human community at large. If Les Misérables deals with the progress of an exemplary figure (Valjean), it was intended in addition to say something about the progress, past and future, of the French national body. The novel charts the development of the nation from the revolution of 1789, through Napoleon's Empire and the Bourbon Restoration to the July Monarchy of Louis-Philippe and beyond. For Hugo, as omniscient narrator, takes his readers past the chronological boundary of his plot (1833) in order, by implication at least, to pass judgement on the early years of Louis-Napoleon's Second Empire (1852–70). This was precisely the historical context against which the concluding sections of Les Misérables were written: an appreciation of the novel's significance cannot accordingly be divorced from the timing of its composition. Hugo worked on his book over two clearly distinct periods. He began writing the novel (first called Jean Tréjean, later Les Misères) in the autumn of 1845 after gathering material throughout the 1830s. Composition was abruptly interrupted in February 1848 'for revolutionary reasons' and resumed after an interval of twelve years in late 1860. The novel (now with its definitive title) was completed in June 1861, revised and added to during the winter of 1861–2 and published between April and June of 1862. It should be borne in mind that publication of Les Misérables was in book form only: although it reflects some of the patterns and formulae of the roman-feuilleton (serial novel), Hugo's novel, unlike those of Balzac and Sue, was never intended for serialisation in a newspaper.

Hugo's historical thesis is that the modern France he sees emerging around him was born out of the trauma of the 1789 revolution; and more specifically, given its importance in his novel, out of the French defeat at Waterloo. He argues (correctly) that the restoration of a conservative Bourbon monarchy under Louis XVIII and then Charles X should be seen as a direct consequence of Waterloo; and that it is the conservative policies of successive Restoration and July Monarchy governments that have triggered the revolutionary surges of 1830, 1832 (the latter directly evoked in *Les Misérables*) and 1848. Besides providing a brilliant example of something Hugo knew he was very good at (epic description) and allowing the rather contrived introduction of Thénardier, the evocation of Napoleon's defeat at Waterloo becomes a necessary component of Hugo's historical argument in *Les Misérables*. According to this, what Enjolras stands for on the 1832 barricades can only be understood in terms of what happened to Napoleon on the 1815 battlefield. Hence the curiously interrogative chapter heading (curious at least for a Frenchman): 'Must we approve Waterloo?' (p. 237). It is a question that with the benefit of hindsight Hugo cautiously answers in the affirmative:

> Waterloo, by cutting short the demolition of European thrones by the sword, has had no other effect than to continue the revolutionary work in another way. The saberers have gone out, the time of the thinkers has come. The age which Waterloo would have checked has marched on and pursued its course. This inauspicious victory has been conquered by liberty. [p. 238]

The argument is reiterated a few paragraphs later in a passage that marvellously encapsulates the mood of Hugo's generation, the group of French Romantic writers and artists born around 1800 who followed Hugo on to the literary barricades:

> In presence of and confronting this ancient Europe made over, the lineaments of a new France began to appear. The future, the jest of the emperor, made its appearance. It had on its brow this star, Liberty. The ardent eyes of rising generations turned towards it. Strange to tell, men became enamoured at the same time of this future, Liberty, and of this past, Napoleon. [p. 239]

The notion of progress, whether individual or collective, lies at the heart of Hugo's worldview in *Les Misérables*. We have seen how the book charts Valjean's personal progress from damnation to redemption; it also tells of Cosette's growth from miserable orphan-girl to angelic bride and, in a different register, of Marius's potential for future intellectual development after the end of the novel (pp. 953–4). But *Les Misérables* is also about the progress of the nation towards a more just, less *misérable* society. Hugo looks towards a fairer social system, one of course that was realised neither at the time of the novel's setting nor (and perhaps even less so) at that of its composition. His ideal is one of a society that will seek to banish all forms of injustice, to erode distinctions based on wealth, class and gender. Specifically in the context of *Les Misérables* the writer pleads for a fairer penal system, for the abolition of the death penalty (this a permanent element in Hugo's thinking about the organisation of society), and for the eventual disappearance of all carceral institutions. The author *qua* social thinker thus has no qualms in interrupting the flow of his story-telling and in intruding into his narrative at one of its most nailbiting moments (the fighting on the barricades) in order to underline the moral point that is central to his novel. The book's medium (a narrative based on action, derring-do and suspense) here unambiguously takes second place to its message:

> Progress!
> This cry which we often raise is our whole thought; and, at the present point of this drama, the idea that it contains having still more than one ordeal to undergo, it is permitted us perhaps, if not to lift the veil from it, at least to let the light shine clearly through.
> The book which the reader has now before his eyes is, from one end to the other, in its whole and in its details, whatever may be the intermissions, the exceptions, or the defaults, the march from evil to good, from injustice to justice, from the false to the true, from night to day, from appetite to conscience, from rottenness to life, from brutality to duty, from Hell to Heaven, from nothingness to God. Starting point: matter; goal: the soul. Hydra at the beginning, angel at the end.   [p. 845]

In this context, the revolutionary upheavals of 1789 and 1830, the defeat at Waterloo and, centrally in *Les Misérables*, the insurrection on the barricades of June 1832 are to be read as 'convulsive movement[s] towards the ideal'. They are 'tragic epilepsies', interludes on the path to progress (p. 845).

What in conclusion should the reader make of the title of Hugo's novel? Who exactly are the eponymous *Misérables*? The term firstly and most obviously denotes those who are forced to live in physical misery, in ignorance and hunger, the poor and the destitute, those who exist on the fringes of respectability. The *misérables* are in general terms the down-and-outs, the pariahs and outcasts of society. They are those figures, 'the unfortunate and the infamous' (p. 508) who inhabit, both literally and metaphorically, the muddier reaches of the community and the squalid outer limits of the city. Thieves and prostitutes, pickpockets and footpads, they are in the novel those characters who live in the vicinity of the dilapidated Gorbeau hovel, the sinister leaders of the Patron-Minette gang with their strange names (Babet, Gueulemer, Claquesous and Montparnasse) and even stranger appearances, Thénardier's criminal companions. They make up what Hugo calls the subterranean 'third sub-stage of Paris' (p. 482), ectoplasmic spectres who lurk around the disused chalk quarries of Montmartre and Montrouge, creatures of the night who, like the perverse Mademoiselle Bistouri (Miss Scalpel) from Baudelaire's prose poem, haunt the outer boulevards and roam the scruffy suburban peripheries of the capital:

> Such men, when, towards midnight, on a lone boulevard, you meet them or catch a glimpse of them, are terrifying. They seem not men, but forms fashioned of the living dark; you would say that they are generally an integral portion of the darkness, that they are not distinct from it, that they have no other soul than the gloom, and that it is only temporarily and to live for a few minutes a monstrous life that they are disaggregated from the night.
>
> [p. 485]

This is a tribe, a distinct species within or rather beneath the overall population of Paris. It has its own language, its own customs and social organisation. Its members have taken over and made their own certain far-flung districts of the capital, chiefly its peripheral and subterranean sectors that are shunned by the city's more conventional inhabitants. Hugo's lengthy parenthesis on the Parisian argot (the whole of Book 7 in Part 4 of the novel) has a crucial contribution to make, both to his analysis of the capital's underclasses and to the meaning of his novel as a whole. Argot, the private and coded language of the *misérables*, is the pariah medium of a pariah population. In line with the didactic and moralising dimension of the book as well as with its sociological intent, Hugo argues that an understanding of the Parisian vernacular is indispensable if one is to understand the *misérables* who speak it. But, more menacingly, the writer sees the argot of the city as being characterised, like its speakers, by a frightening impenetrability; like them, and like the places they inhabit, it has an earthy energy and a cloacal vitality; all three (language, locations and speakers) are characterised by a virulent spirit of subversiveness. Slang and sewer, *argot* and *faubourg*, medium and locus, are thus permanently linked in the private mythology that underpins *Les Misérables*. Writing about the one, Hugo could equally well be writing about the other:

> Certainly, to go into the lowest depths of the social order, where the earth ends and the mire begins, to search in those thick waters, to pursue, to seize and to throw out still throbbing upon the pavement this abject idiom which streams with filth as it is thus drawn to the light, this pustulous vocabulary in which each word seems a huge ring from some monster of the slime and the darkness, is neither an attractive task nor an easy task. Nothing is more mournful than to contemplate thus bare, by the light of thought, the fearful crawl of argot. It seems indeed as if it were a species of horrible beast made for the night, which has just been dragged from its cesspool.   [p. 669]

The worlds of sewer and slang have a potential in common that threatens to undermine the etiolated veneer of social and verbal orthodoxies. The popular idiom, by absorbing the linguistic detritus scorned by 'correct' French, was seen to represent a threat that might pollute the integrity of the official register. Hence the endeavours by a variety of academic bodies, with the *Académie française* in the van, to police the language; hence also the shrieks of protest from conservative critics that greeted the publication of *Les Misérables* and of other novels in a similar vein. Most shocking as it carries the reader directly into the world of the sewer, from lexis to cesspit, was Hugo's shameless exploitation of General Cambronne's celebrated excremental expletive ('Merde!'). Hugo's vision of the Parisian cloaca possesses a metaphorical charge no less strong than that of its linguistic counterpart, slang. Underground viscera running just below the 'respectable' surface of the capital's street pattern, the sewers course with the variegated cast-offs of the well-to-do. Complementing the role of their above-ground cousins, the Parisian rag-pickers (the *chiffonnier* is another bugbear of *bien-pensant* society), the sewermen threaten at any moment to disgorge the most intimate secrets of the establishment.

The subterranean menace represented by the underclasses is hinted at, sometimes explicitly stated, throughout Hugo's novel. It is implied for example in the curious heading to the opening chapter of Part 3, Book 7, 'The mines and the miners'; the writer deals here not literally with mines and miners (the subject of another novel, Zola's *Germinal*) but metaphorically with the promise of subversion that is embedded in working-class realities. Given the iconoclastic quality of their private discourse and the threats that emanate from their mysterious habitats, one should not be surprised if much of Hugo's social vision in *Les Misérables* betrays a distinctly conservative quality. On the other hand the writer's sense of the potential for revitalisation that is contained within popular language and culture, his awareness of their picturesqueness and local colour (both key elements in the aesthetics of Romanticism), and his willingness to draw from them, trigger the self-conscious attempts Hugo makes to renew French literary diction through the incorporation of more popular elements: his boast of having crowned the official dictionary of the French language with the red bonnet of the revolution is well known. There is here a tension between fear and desire, a mixture of fascination and repulsion, that lies at the heart of the ambivalence of Hugo's representation of the Parisian working classes and of all that is associated with them.

But in the final analysis the meaning of Hugo's title should not be seen exclusively in terms of class or social groupings. The novel's focus extends beyond the narrow scope of what sociologists have identified as Paris's labouring and dangerous classes; nor does *Les Misérables* deal merely with the materially impoverished and the socially marginalised. For the French adjective *misérable* carries with it a much more all-embracing force than its English counterpart *miserable*: with its etymological sense (from the Latin *miserabilis*, worthy of pity), it refers to anyone who deserves to be pitied, irrespective of their position in society, of their profession or their financial worth. Accordingly we may all be *misérable* without necessarily being *miserable*: the two adjectives are in this sense what grammarians term 'false friends' (*faux amis*), words that look similar in the two languages but that carry very different meanings.

The full value of Hugo's title and its universalising implications are made very clear early in the novel, in the course of the Petit-Gervais episode; it is probably no coincidence that this occupies Chapter 13 of a Book entitled 'The Fall'. The episode is crucial to an understanding of Valjean's character and of his future career but also to the overall moral significance of Hugo's novel. After robbing the little Savoyard (Petit-Gervais) of his coin, Valjean is left in solitary contemplation in a night-time wilderness; its physical bareness acts as a reflection of the character's moral desperation. In a scene that is loaded with biblical echoes, the ex-convict is represented as being racked with guilt. Eventually Valjean breaks down:

> Again he murmured: 'Petit-Gervais!' but with a feeble, and almost inarticulate voice. That was his last effort; his knees suddenly bent under him, as if an invisible power overwhelmed him at a blow, with the weight of his bad conscience; he fell exhausted upon a great stone, his hands clenched in his hair, and his face on his knees, and exclaimed: 'What a wretch I am!'
>
> Then his heart swelled, and he burst into tears. It was the first time he had wept for nineteen years.   [p. 76]

In the original French text Valjean's final exclamation ('What a wretch I am!'), the climax of the episode and the catalyst of his moral rebirth, is rendered as 'Je suis un misérable!' Valjean is a *misérable* not just because he is poor, an outsider on the criminal fringes of society. More significantly in terms of the novel's moral message, his feeling of spiritual wretchedness, his guilty conscience and the consequent quest for redemption demand the label *misérable* and render Valjean worthy of the reader's pity.

Hugo's perception will be extended much later in the novel, in the Petit-Picpus episode. In the course of this long parenthesis on monastic life, author and character draw an extraordinary and sustained parallel (pp. 382–5, the final chapter of Part II) between two 'seats of slavery' (p. 385), between two places of exile both of which are situated outside the boundaries of conventional society, the prison and the convent. The juxtaposition of penitentiary and nunnery is reinforced in Hugo's narrative by the way in which Valjean's escape from prison is followed by his quest for refuge in the Petit-Picpus convent. It is a juxtaposition that is meant in the first instance to illustrate the writer's critique of the monastic way of life, an attitude that is inherited from eighteenth-century rationalism and from certain Enlightenment texts (e.g. Diderot's *The Nun*). Gaol and convent are places of sequestration, both institutions that imprison their inmates. Those who have willingly (if mistakenly according to Hugo) opted for captivity are seen as being in a situation that is little different from that of those who have been condemned to captivity. Yet, within the context of the Christian ethic that colours Hugo's novel, the feelings experienced by both groups are seen to be similar. Both are acutely aware of human fallibility, of the misery of sin, and of the consequent need for expiation:

> And, in these two places, so alike and yet so different, these two species of beings so dissimilar were performing the same work of expiation.   [p. 385]

The convict and the nun, figures from opposite ends of the moral spectrum, both fit Hugo's understanding of what it is to be a *misérable*. The behaviour of both is determined by an awareness of the misery (*misère*) of the human condition and by a desire to redeem it. The outsider's sense of pity, in the first place that of the writer and reader, is aroused by both: the one on account of the crimes he has committed (Hugo's contention would be that this is usually through no fault of his own); the other on account of the responsibility for the crimes of others that she has accepted to make her own (in sublime if misguided fashion according to Hugo). Somewhere between these two extremes, the rest of Hugo's fictional personnel finds its place: between Valjean the criminal and Mother Crucifixion the saint there is room for the inflexible Javert and the reptilian Thénardier, for the miserable Fantine and the sublime Eponine, for the parasitic Batambois and Enjolras the idealist, for old Gillenormand and young Gavroche, as well as for a host of other *Misérables*. And alongside Hugo's enormous cast of characters there are the readers of his vast fiction, in France and elsewhere: readers and characters alike, it is intended that we should all be seen as *misérables*.

NOTE ON THE MUSICAL
VERSION OF *LES MISÉRABLES*

Hugo's novel has over the years been the subject of a huge number of adaptations, for stage, screen and comic-strip (*bande dessinée*). Recently an apocryphal sequel has been produced (François Céresa's *Cosette or the Time of Illusions*), much to the consternation of the writer's descendants. Most famously *Les Misérables* has been adapted for the stage in the wildly successful musical version ('The Musical that swept the World') by Alain Boublil and Claude-Michel Schönberg with lyrics by Herbert Kretzner. Besides following the broad outlines of Hugo's narrative, the music and lyrics of the adaptation brilliantly capture the youthfulness, the colour and revolutionary fervour of Hugo's original. In particular the barricade scene, drawing from Delacroix as well as Hugo, provides an unforgettable theatrical experience.

The impossibility of compressing a one-thousand-page novel into a three-hour stage performance has however made certain cuts inevitable. There is thus no mention of Waterloo, of the Petit-Picpus (convent) episode, of Marius's Gillenormand family background. This results in the disappearance of some of the socio-political dimensions of the original, in particular of the clash between royalist gerontocrats and republican hotheads that is so central to Hugo's investigation of the French mood in the early part of the nineteenth century. This is something of which he had had personal experience in the course of the struggle for Romanticism in the early 1830s.

The musical version also makes certain telling alterations to the organisation of the novel's characters. Eponine's contribution to the story is thus considerably enhanced, much dramatic effect being obtained from her role as foil to Cosette and as competitor for the affection of Marius. Bizet had done something very similar in *Carmen* when he and his librettists invented Micaela (absent from the original novella by Merimée) as a rival to Carmen for the love of Don José. The musical does on the other hand present a highly sanitised version of the Thénardier *ménage*. In Hugo's novel Thénardier is the arch-villain of the piece. He is the only character whose *misère* appears to be irredeemable: it will be remembered in this context that at the end of *Les Misérables* he is despatched to the United States to embark on a career in the slave trade. In the musical on the other hand the Thénardiers are played largely for comic purposes – notably with their two show-stopping numbers, 'Master of the House' and 'Beggars at the Feast'. Finally, largely as a result of the disappearance of the Petit-Picpus episodes, the Valjean of the musical is a far less complex character than his counterpart in the novel: there is in him none of the tension that characterises Hugo's representation, none of the conflict between his fatherly feelings for Cosette and his growing jealousy as he watches Marius slowly fall in love with Fantine's daughter.

BIBLIOGRAPHY

There is a vast corpus of critical literature devoted to Hugo's life and work, in French, English and other languages. Listed below is a small selection of works in English that will help the reader with his or her understanding of *Les Misérables*.

Natalie Babel Brown, *Hugo and Dostoevsky*, Ardis, Ann Arbor 1978

Victor Brombert, *Victor Hugo and the Visionary Novel*, Harvard University Press, Cambridge (Massachusetts) and London 1984. Brombert's book provides by far the most compelling account in English of Hugo's fictions.

Richard B. Grant, *The Perilous Quest: Image, Myth and Prophecy in the Narratives of Victor Hugo*, Duke University Press, Durham 1968

Kathryn M. Grossman, *Figuring Transcendence in* Les Misérables, *Hugo's Romantic Sublime*, Southern Illinois University Press, Carbondale and Edwardsville 1994

Karen Masters-Wicks, *Victor Hugo's* Les Misérables *and the Novels of the Grotesque*, Peter Lang, New York 1994

Graham Robb, *Victor Hugo*, Picador, London 1997. By some distance the best biography of Hugo in English.

There are two good websites (www.geocities.com/stuartfernie and www.rural.escape.ca/wideman/hugo) that deal with Hugo's novel. In addition, there are a multitude of others that have to do with the musical adaptation.

CONTENTS

PART ONE: FANTINE

BOOK 1: AN UPRIGHT MAN

BOOK 2: THE FALL

BOOK 3: IN THE YEAR 1817

BOOK 4: TO ENTRUST IS SOMETIMES TO ABANDON

BOOK 5: THE DESCENT

BOOK 6: JAVERT

BOOK 7: THE CHAMPMATHIEU AFFAIR

BOOK 3: FULFILMENT OF THE PROMISE TO THE DEPARTED

BOOK 4: THE OLD GORBEAU HOUSE

BOOK 5: A DARK CHASE NEEDS A SILENT HOUND

BOOK 6: PETIT PICPUS

BOOK 2: THE GRAND BOURGEOIS

BOOK 3: THE GRANDFATHER AND THE GRANDSON

BOOK 4: THE FRIENDS OF THE ABC

BOOK 5: THE EXCELLENCE OF MISFORTUNE

BOOK 6: THE CONJUNCTION OF TWO STARS

The end of Volume One

PART FOUR: SAINT DENIS AND IDYLL
OF THE RUE PLUMET

BOOK 1: A FEW PAGES OF HISTORY

BOOK 2: ÉPONINE

BOOK 3: THE HOUSE IN THE RUE PLUMET

BOOK 4: AID FROM BELOW MAY BE AID FROM ABOVE

BOOK 5: THE END OF WHICH IS
UNLIKE THE BEGINNING

AUTHOR'S PREFACE

So long as there shall exist, by reason of law and custom, a social condemnation, which, in the face of civilisation, artificially creates hells on earth, and complicates a destiny that is divine, with human fatality; so long as the three problems of the age – the degradation of man by poverty, the ruin of woman by starvation, and the dwarfing of childhood by physical and spiritual night – are not solved; so long as, in certain regions, social asphyxia shall be possible; in other words, and from a yet more extended point of view, so long as ignorance and misery remain on earth, books like this cannot be useless.

HAUTEVILLE HOUSE, 1862

PART ONE: FANTINE

BOOK I: AN UPRIGHT MAN

1. *M. Myriel*

IN 1815, M. Charles François-Bienvenu Myriel was Bishop of D—. He was a man of seventy-five, and had occupied the bishopric of D— since 1806. Although it in no manner concerns, even in the remotest degree, what we have to relate, it may not be useless, were it only for the sake of exactness in all things, to notice here the reports and gossip which had arisen on his account from the time of his arrival in the diocese.

Be it true or false, what is said about men often has as much influence upon their lives, and especially upon their destinies, as what they do.

M. Myriel was the son of a counsellor of the Parliament of Aix; of the rank given to the legal profession. His father, intending him to inherit his place, had contracted a marriage for him at the early age of eighteen or twenty, according to a widespread custom among parliamentary families. Charles Myriel, notwithstanding this marriage, had, it was said, been an object of much attention. His person was admirably moulded; although of slight figure, he was elegant and graceful; all the earlier part of his life had been devoted to the world and to its pleasures. The revolution came, events crowded upon each other; the parliamentary families, decimated, hunted, and pursued, were soon dispersed. M. Charles Myriel, on the first outbreak of the revolution, emigrated to Italy. His wife died there of a lung complaint with which she had long been threatened. They had no children. What followed in the fate of M. Myriel? The decay of the old French society, the fall of his own family, the tragic sights of '93, still more fearful, perhaps, to the exiles who beheld them from afar, magnified by fright – did these arouse in him ideas of renunciation and of solitude? Was he, in the midst of one of the reveries or emotions which then consumed his life, suddenly attacked by one of those mysterious and terrible blows which sometimes overwhelm, by smiting to the heart, the man whom public disasters could not shake, by aiming at life or fortune? No one could have answered; all that was known was that when he returned from Italy he was a priest.

In 1804, M. Myriel was curé of B— (Brignolles). He was then an old man, and lived in the deepest seclusion.

Near the time of the coronation, a trifling matter of business belonging to his curacy – what it was, is not now known precisely – took him to Paris.

Among other personages of authority he went to Cardinal Fesch on behalf of his parishioners.

One day, when the emperor had come to visit his uncle, the worthy curé, who was waiting in the ante-room, happened to be on the way of his Majesty. Napoleon noticing that the old man looked at him with a certain curiousness, turned around and said brusquely:

'Who is this goodman who looks at me?'

'Sire,' said M. Myriel, 'you behold a good man, and I a great man. Each of us may profit by it.'

That evening the emperor asked the cardinal the name of the curé, and some time afterwards M. Myriel was overwhelmed with surprise on learning that he had been appointed Bishop of D—.

Beyond this, no one knew how much truth there was in the stories which passed current concerning the first portion of M. Myriel's life. But few families had known the Myriels before the revolution.

M. Myriel had to submit to the fate of every newcomer in a small town, where there are many tongues to talk, and but few heads to think. He had to submit, although he was bishop, and because he was bishop. But after all, the gossip with which his name was connected, was only gossip: noise, talk, words, less than words – *palabres*, as they say in the forcible language of the South.

Be that as it may, after nine years of episcopacy, and of residence in D—, all these stories, topics of talk, which engross at first petty towns and petty people, were entirely forgotten. Nobody would have dared to speak of, or even to remember them.

When M. Myriel came to D— he was accompanied by an old lady, Mademoiselle Baptistine, who was his sister, ten years younger than himself.

Their only domestic was a woman of about the same age as Mademoiselle Baptistine, who was called Madame Magloire, and who, after having been the servant of M. le curé, now took the double title of femme de chambre of Mademoiselle and housekeeper of Monseigneur.

Mademoiselle Baptistine was a tall, pale, thin, sweet person. She fully realised the idea which is expressed by the word 'respectable'; for it seems as if it were necessary that a woman should be a mother to be venerable. She had never been pretty; her whole life, which had been but a succession of pious works, had produced upon her a kind of transparent whiteness, and in growing old she had acquired what may be called the beauty of goodness. What had been thinness in her youth had become in maturity transparency, and this etherialness permitted gleams of the angel within. She was more a spirit than a virgin mortal. Her form was shadow-like, hardly enough body to convey the thought of sex – a little earth containing a spark – large eyes, always cast down; a pretext for a soul to remain on earth.

Madame Magloire was a little, white, fat, jolly, bustling old woman, always out of breath, caused first by her activity, and then by the asthma.

M. Myriel, upon his arrival, was installed in his episcopal palace with the honours ordained by the imperial decrees, which class the bishop next in rank to the field-marshal. The mayor and the president made him the first visit, and he, on his part, paid like honour to the general and the prefect.

The installation being completed, the town was curious to see its bishop at work.

2. *M. Myriel becomes Monseigneur Bienvenu*

THE BISHOP'S PALACE at D— was contiguous to the hospital: the palace was a spacious and beautiful edifice, built of stone near the beginning of the last century by Monseigneur Henri Pujet, a doctor of theology of the Faculty of Paris, abbé of Simore, who was bishop of D— in 1712. The palace was in truth a lordly dwelling: there was an air of grandeur about everything, the apartments of the bishop, the saloons, the chambers, the court of honour, which was very large, with arched walks after the antique Florentine style; and a garden planted with magnificent trees.

In the dining hall was a long, superb gallery, which was level with the ground, opening upon the garden; Monseigneur Henri Pujet had given a grand banquet on the 29th of July 1714, to Monseigneur Charles Brûlart de Genlis, archbishop, Prince d'Embrun, Antoine de Mesgrigny, capuchin, bishop of Grasse, Philippe de Vendôme, grand-prior de France, the Abbé de Saint Honoré de Lérins, François de Berton de Grillon, lord bishop of Vence, Cesar de Sabran de Forcalquier, lord bishop of Glandève, and Jean Soanen priest of the oratory, preacher in ordinary to the king, lord bishop of Senez; the portraits of these seven reverend personages decorated the hall, and this memorable date, July 29th, 1714, appeared in letters of gold on a white marble tablet.

The hospital was a low, narrow, one storey building with a small garden.

Three days after the bishop's advent he visited the hospital; when the visit was ended, he invited the director to oblige him by coming to the palace.

'Monsieur,' he said to the director of the hospital, 'how many patients have you?'

'Twenty-six, monseigneur.'

'That is as I counted them,' said the bishop.

'The beds,' continued the director, 'are very much crowded.'

'I noticed it.'

'The wards are but small chambers, and are not easily ventilated.'

'It seems so to me.'

'And then, when the sun does shine, the garden is very small for the convalescents.'

'That was what I was thinking.'

'Of epidemics we have had typhus fever this year; two years ago we had military fever, sometimes one hundred patients, and we did not know what to do.'

'That occurred to me.'

'What can we do, monseigneur?' said the director; 'we must be resigned.'

This conversation took place in the dining gallery on the ground floor.

The bishop was silent a few moments: then he turned suddenly towards the director.

'Monsieur,' he said, 'how many beds do you think this hall alone would contain?'

'The dining hall of monseigneur!' exclaimed the director, stupefied.

The bishop ran his eyes over the hall, seemingly taking measure and making calculations.

'It will hold twenty beds,' said he to himself; then raising his voice, he said:

'Listen, Monsieur Director, to what I have to say. There is evidently a mistake here. There are twenty-six of you in five or six small rooms: there are only three of us, and space for sixty. There is a mistake, I tell you. You have my house and I have yours. Restore mine to me; you are at home.'

Next day the twenty-six poor invalids were installed in the bishop's palace, and the bishop was in the hospital.

M. Myriel had no property, his family having been impoverished by the revolution. His sister had a life estate of five hundred francs, which in the vicarage sufficed for her personal needs. M. Myriel received from the government as bishop a salary of fifteen thousand francs. The day on which he took up his residence in the hospital building, he resolved to appropriate this sum once for all to the following uses. We copy the schedule then written by him.

SCHEDULE FOR THE REGULATION OF MY HOUSEHOLD EXPENSES

For the little seminary, fifteen hundred livres.

Mission congregation, one hundred livres.

For the Lazaristes of Montdidier, one hundred livres.

Congregation of the Saint-Esprit, one hundred and fifty livres.

Seminary of foreign missions in Paris, two hundred livres.

Religious establishments in the Holy Land, one hundred livres.

Maternal charitable societies, three hundred livres.

For that of Arles, fifty livres.

For the amelioration of prisons, four hundred livres.

For the relief and deliverance of prisoners, five hundred livres.

For the liberation of fathers of families imprisoned for debt, one thousand livres.

Additions to the salaries of poor schoolmasters of the diocese, two thousand livres.

Public storehouse of Hautes-Alpes, one hundred livres.

Association of the ladies of D— of Manosque and Sisteron for the gratuitous instruction of poor girls, fifteen hundred livres.

For the poor, six thousand livres.

My personal expenses, one thousand livres.

Total, fifteen thousand livres.

M. Myriel made no alteration in this plan during the time he held the see of D—; he called it, as will be seen, *the regulation of his household expenses.*

Mademoiselle Baptistine accepted this arrangement with entire submission: M. Myriel was to her at once her brother and her bishop, her companion by ties of blood and her superior by ecclesiastical authority. She loved and venerated him unaffectedly: when he spoke, she listened; when he acted, she gave him her co-operation. Madame Magloire, however, their servant, grumbled a little. The bishop, as will be seen, had reserved but a thousand francs; this, added to the income of Mademoiselle Baptistine, gave them a yearly independence of fifteen hundred francs, upon which the three old people subsisted.

Thanks, however, to the rigid economy of Madame Magloire, and the excellent management of Mademoiselle Baptistine, whenever a curate came to D—, the bishop found means to extend to him his hospitality.

About three months after the installation, the bishop said one day, 'With all this I am very much cramped.' 'I think so too,' said Madame Magloire: 'Monseigneur has not even asked for the sum due him by the department for his carriage expenses in town, and in his circuits in the diocese. It was formerly the custom with all bishops.'

'Yes!' said the bishop; 'you are right, Madame Magloire.'

He made his application.

Some time afterwards the conseil-général took his claim into consideration and voted him an annual stipend of three thousand francs under this head:

'Allowance to the bishop for carriage expenses, and travelling expenses for pastoral visits.'

The bourgeoisie of the town were much excited on the subject, and in regard to it a senator of the empire, formerly member of the Council of Five Hundred, an advocate of the Eighteenth Brumaire, now provided with a rich senatorial seat near D—,wrote to M. Bigot de Préameneu, Minister of Public Worship, a fault-finding, confidential epistle, from which we make the following extract:

'Carriage expenses! What can he want of it in a town of less than 4000 inhabitants? Expenses of pastoral visits! And what good do they do, in the first place; and then, how is it possible to travel by post in this mountain region? There are no roads; he can go only on horseback. Even the bridge over the Durance at Chateau-Arnoux is scarcely passable for ox-carts. These priests are always so; avaricious and miserly. This one played the good apostle at the outset: now he acts like the rest; he must have a carriage and post-chaise. He must have luxury like the old bishops. Bah! this whole priesthood! Monsieur le Comte, things will never be better till the emperor delivers us from these macaroni priests. Down with the pope! (Matters were getting embroiled with Rome.) As for me, I am for Cæsar alone,' etc., etc., etc.

This application, on the other hand, pleased Madame Magloire exceedingly. 'Good,' said she to Mademoiselle Baptistine; 'Monseigneur began with others, but he has found at last that he must end by taking care of himself. He has arranged all his charities, and so now here are three thousand francs for us.'

The same evening the bishop wrote and gave to his sister a note couched in these terms:

CARRIAGE AND TRAVELLING EXPENSES

For beef broth for the hospital, fifteen hundred livres.
For the Aix Maternal Charity Association, two hundred and fifty livres.
For the Draguignan Maternal Charity Association, two hundred and fifty livres.
For Foundlings, five hundred livres.
For Orphans, five hundred livres.
Total, three thousand livres.

Such was the budget of M. Myriel.

In regard to the official perquisites, marriage licences, dispensations, private baptisms, and preaching, consecrations of churches or chapels, marriages, etc., the bishop gathered them from the wealthy with as much exactness as he dispensed them to the poor.

In a short time donations of money began to come in; those who had and those who had not, knocked at the bishop's door; some came to receive alms and others to bestow them, and in less than a year he had become the treasurer of all the benevolent, and the dispenser to all the needy. Large sums passed through his hands; nevertheless he changed in no wise his mode of life, nor added the least luxury to his simple fare.

On the contrary, as there is always more misery among the lower classes than there is humanity in the higher, everything was given away, so to speak, before it was received, like water on thirsty soil; it was well that money came to him, for he never kept any; and besides he robbed himself. It being the custom that all bishops should put their baptismal names at the head of their orders and pastoral letters, the poor people of the district had chosen by a sort of affectionate instinct, from among the names of the bishop, that which was expressive to them, and they always called him Monseigneur Bienvenu. We shall follow their example and shall call him thus; besides, this pleased him. 'I like this name,' said he; 'Bienvenu counterbalances Monseigneur.'

We do not claim that the portrait which we present here is a true one; we say only that it resembles him.

3. *Good bishop – hard bishopric*

THE BISHOP, after converting his carriage into alms, none the less regularly made his round of visits, and in the diocese of D— this was a wearisome task. There was very little plain, a good deal of mountain; and hardly any roads, as a matter of course; thirty-two curacies, forty-one vicarages, and two hundred and eighty-five sub-curacies. To visit all these is a great labour, but the bishop went through with it. He travelled on foot in his own neighbourhood, in a cart when he was in the plains, and in a *cacolet*, a basket strapped on the back of a mule, when in the mountains. The two women usually accompanied him, but when the journey was too difficult for them he went alone.

One day he arrived at Senez, formerly the seat of a bishopric, mounted on an ass. His purse was very empty at the time, and would not permit any better conveyance. The mayor of the city came to receive him at the gate of the episcopal residence, and saw him dismount from his ass with astonishment and mortification. Several of the citizens stood near by, laughing. 'Monsieur Mayor,' said the bishop, 'and Messieurs citizens, I see what astonishes you; you think that it shows a good deal of pride for a poor priest to use the same conveyance which was used by Jesus Christ. I have done it from necessity, I assure you, and not from vanity.'

In his visits he was indulgent and gentle, and preached less than he talked. He never used far-fetched reasons or examples. To the inhabitants of one region he would cite the example of a neighbouring region. In the cantons where the necessitous were treated with severity he would say, 'Look at the people of Briançon. They have given to the poor, and to widows and orphans, the right to mow their meadows three days before anyone else. When their houses are in ruins they rebuild them without cost. And so it is a country blessed of God. For a whole century they have not had a single murderer.'

In villages where the people were greedy for gain at harvest time, he would say, 'Look at Embrun. If a father of a family, at harvest time, has his sons in the army, and his daughters at service in the city, and he is sick, the priest recommends him in his sermons, and on Sunday, after mass, the whole population of the village, men, women, and children, go into the poor man's field and harvest his crop, and put the straw and the grain into his granary.' To families divided by questions of property and inheritance, he would say, 'See the mountaineers of Devolny, a country so wild that the nightingale is not heard there once in fifty years. Well now, when the father dies, in a family, the boys go away to seek their fortunes, and leave the property to the girls, so that they may get husbands.' In those cantons where there was a taste for the law, and where the farmers were ruining themselves with stamped paper, he would say, 'Look at those good peasants of the valley of Queyras. There are three thousand souls there. Why, it is like a little republic! Neither judge nor constable is known there. The mayor does everything. He apportions the impost, taxes each one according to his judgement, decides their quarrels without charge, distributes their patrimony without fees, gives judgement without expense; and he is obeyed, because he is a just man among simple-hearted men.' In the villages which he found without a schoolmaster, he would again hold up the valley of Queyras. 'Do you know how they do?' he would say. 'As a little district of twelve or fifteen houses cannot always support a teacher, they have schoolmasters that are paid by the whole valley, who go around from village to village, passing a week in this place, and ten days in that, and give instruction. These masters attend the fairs, where I have seen them. They are known by quills which they wear in their hatband. Those who teach only how to read have one quill; those who teach reading and arithmetic have two; and those who teach reading, arithmetic, and Latin, have three; the latter are esteemed great scholars. But what a shame to be ignorant! Do like the people of Queyras.'

In such fashion would he talk, gravely and paternally; in default of examples he would invent parables, going straight to his object, with few phrases and many images, which was the very eloquence of Jesus Christ, convincing and persuasive.

4. *Words answering words*

HIS CONVERSATION was affable and pleasant. He adapted himself to the capacity of the two old women who lived with him, but when he laughed, it was the laugh of a schoolboy.

Madame Magloire usually called him *Your Greatness*. One day he rose from his armchair, and went to his library for a book. It was upon one of the upper shelves, and as the bishop was rather short, he could not reach it. 'Madame Magloire,' said he, 'bring me a chair. My greatness does not extend to this shelf.'

One of his distant relatives, the Countess of Lô, rarely let an occasion escape of enumerating in his presence what she called 'the expectations' of her three sons. She had several relatives, very old and near their death, of whom her sons were the legal heirs. The youngest of the three was to receive from a great-aunt a hundred thousand livres in the funds; the second was to take the title of duke from his uncle; the eldest would succeed to the peerage of his grandfather. The bishop commonly listened in silence to these innocent and pardonable maternal displays. Once, however, he appeared more dreamy than was his custom, while Madame de Lô rehearsed the detail of all these successions and all these 'expectations'. Stopping suddenly, with some impatience, she exclaimed, 'My goodness, cousin, what are you thinking about?' 'I am thinking,' said the bishop, 'of a strange thing which is, I believe, in St Augustine: "Place your expectations on him to whom there is no succession!"' On another occasion, when he received a letter announcing the decease of a gentleman of the country, in which were detailed, at great length, not only the dignities of the departed, but the feudal and titular honours of all his relatives, he exclaimed: 'What a broad back has death! What a wondrous load of titles will he cheerfully carry, and what hardihood must men have who will thus use the tomb to feed their vanity!'

At times he made use of gentle raillery, which was almost always charged with serious ideas. Once, during Lent, a young vicar came to D—, and preached in the cathedral. The subject of his sermon was charity, and he treated it very eloquently. He called upon the rich to give alms to the poor, if they would escape the tortures of hell, which he pictured in the most fearful colours, and enter that paradise which he painted as so desirable and inviting. There was a retired merchant of wealth in the audience, a little given to usury, M. Géborand, who had accumulated an estate of two millions in the manufacture of coarse cloths and serges. Never, in the whole course of his life, had M. Géborand given alms to the unfortunate; but from the date of this sermon it was noticed that he gave regularly, every Sunday, a penny to the old beggar women at the door of the cathedral. There were six of them to share it. The bishop chanced to see him one day, as he was performing this act of charity, and said to his sister, with a smile, 'See Monsieur Géborand, buying a pennyworth of paradise.'

When soliciting aid for any charity, he was not silenced by a refusal; he was at no loss for words that would set the hearers thinking. One day, he was receiving alms for the poor in a parlour in the city, where the Marquis of Champtercier, who was old, rich, and miserly, was present. The marquis managed to be, at the same time, an ultra-royalist and an ultra-Voltairian, a species of which he was not the only representative. The bishop coming to him in turn, touched his arm and said, 'Monsieur le Marquis, you must give me something.' The marquis turned and answered drily, 'Monseigneur, I have my own poor.' 'Give them to me,' said the bishop.

One day he preached this sermon in the cathedral:

'My very dear brethren, my good friends, there are in France thirteen hundred and twenty thousand peasants' cottages that have but three openings; eighteen hundred and seventeen thousand that have two, the door and one window; and finally, three hundred and forty-six thousand cabins, with only one opening – the door. And this is in consequence of what is called the excise upon doors and windows. In these poor families, among the aged women and the little children, dwelling in these huts, how abundant is fever and disease? Alas! God gives light to men; the law sells it. I do not blame the law, but I bless God. In Isère, in Var, and in the Upper and the Lower Alps, the peasants have not even wheelbarrows, they carry the manure on their backs; they have no candles, but burn pine knots, and bits of rope soaked in pitch. And the same is the case all through the upper part of Dauphiné. They make bread once in six months, and bake it with the refuse of the fields. In the winter it becomes so hard that they cut it up with an axe, and soak it for twenty-four hours, before they can eat it. My brethren, be compassionate! behold how much suffering there is around you.'

Born a Provençal, he had easily made himself familiar with all the patois of the south. He would say, '*Eh, bé! moussu, sès sagé?*' as in Lower Languedoc; '*Onté anaras passa?*' as in the Lower Alps; '*Puerte un bouen moutou embe un bouen froumage grase,*' as in Upper Dauphiné. This pleased the people greatly, and contributed not a little to giving him ready access to their hearts. He was the same in a cottage and on the mountains as in his own house. He could say the grandest things in the most common language; and as he spoke all dialects, his words entered the souls of all.[1]

Moreover, his manners with the rich were the same as with the poor.

He condemned nothing hastily, or without taking account of circumstances. He would say, 'Let us see the way in which the fault came to pass.'

Being, as he smilingly described himself, an *ex-sinner*, he had none of the inaccessibility of a rigorist, and boldly professed, even under the frowning eyes of the ferociously virtuous, a doctrine which may be stated nearly as follows:

'Man has a body which is at once his burden and his temptation. He drags it along, and yields to it.

'He ought to watch over it, to keep it in bounds; to repress it, and only to obey it at the last extremity. It may be wrong to obey even then, but if so, the fault is venial. It is a fall, but a fall upon the knees, which may end in prayer.

'To be a saint is the exception; to be upright is the rule. Err, falter, sin, but be upright.

'To commit the least possible sin is the law for man. To live without sin is the dream of an angel. Everything terrestrial is subject to sin. Sin is a gravitation.'

When he heard many exclaiming, and expressing great indignation against anything, 'Oh! oh!' he would say, smiling, 'It would seem that this is a great crime, of which they are all guilty. How frightened hypocrisy hastens to defend itself, and to get under cover.'

He was indulgent towards women, and towards the poor, upon whom the weight of society falls most heavily; and said: 'The faults of women, children, and servants, of the feeble, the indigent, and the ignorant, are the faults of their husbands, fathers, and masters, of the strong, the rich, and the wise.' At other times, he said, 'Teach the ignorant as much as you can; society is culpable in not providing instruction for all, and it must answer for the night which it produces. If the soul is left in darkness, sins will be committed. The guilty one is not he who commits the sin, but he who causes the darkness.'

As we see, he had a strange and peculiar way of judging things. I suspect that he acquired it from the Gospel.

In company one day he heard an account of a criminal case that was about to be tried. A miserable man, through love for a woman and for the child she had borne him, had been making false coin, his means being exhausted. At that time counterfeiting was still punished with death. The woman was arrested for passing the first piece that he had made. She was held a prisoner, but there was no proof against her lover. She alone could testify against him, and convict him by her confession. She denied his guilt. They insisted, but she was obstinate in her denial. In this state of the case, the *procureur du roi* devised a shrewd plan. He represented to her that her lover was unfaithful, and by means of fragments of letters skilfully put together, succeeded in persuading the unfortunate woman that she had a rival, and that this man had deceived her. At once exasperated by jealousy, she denounced her lover, confessed all, and proved his guilt. He was to be tried in a few days, at Aix, with his accomplice, and his conviction was certain. The story was told, and everybody was in ecstasy at the adroitness of the officer. In bringing jealousy into play, he had brought truth to light by means of anger, and justice had sprung from revenge. The bishop listened to all this in silence. When it was finished he asked:

'Where are this man and woman to be tried?'

'At the Assizes.'

'And where is the *procureur du roi* to be tried?'

A tragic event occurred at D—. A man had been condemned to death for murder. The unfortunate prisoner was a poorly educated, but not entirely ignorant man, who had been a juggler at fairs, and a public letter-writer. The people were greatly interested in the trial. The evening before the day fixed for the execution of the condemned, the almoner of the prison fell ill. A priest was needed to attend the prisoner in his last moments. The curé was sent for, but he refused to go, saying, 'That does not concern me. I have nothing to do with such drudgery, or with that mountebank; besides, I am sick myself; and moreover it is not my place.' When this reply was reported to the bishop, he said, 'The curé is right. It is not his place, it is mine.'

He went, on the instant, to the prison, went down into the dungeon of the 'mountebank', called him by his name, took him by the hand, and talked with him. He passed the whole day with him, forgetful of food and sleep, praying to God for the soul of the condemned, and exhorting the condemned to join with him. He spoke to him the best truths, which are the simplest. He was father, brother, friend; bishop for blessing only. He taught him everything by encouraging and consoling him. This man would have died in despair. Death, for him, was like an abyss. Standing shivering upon the dreadful brink, he recoiled with horror. He was not ignorant enough to be indifferent. The terrible shock of his condemnation had in some sort broken here and there that wall which separates us from the mystery of things beyond, and which we call life. Through these fatal breaches, he was constantly looking beyond this world, and he could see nothing but darkness; the bishop showed him the light.

On the morrow when they came for the poor man, the bishop was with him. He followed him, and showed himself to the eyes of the crowd in his violet camail, with his bishop's cross about his neck, side by side with the miserable being, who was bound with cords.

He mounted the cart with him, he ascended the scaffold with him. The sufferer, so gloomy and so horror-stricken in the evening, was now radiant with hope. He felt that his soul was reconciled, and he trusted in God. The bishop embraced him, and at the moment when the axe was about to fall, he said to him, 'whom man kills, him God restoreth to life; whom his brethren put away, he findeth the Father. Pray, believe, enter into life! The Father is there.' When he descended from the scaffold, something in his look made the people fall back. It would be hard to say which was the most wonderful, his paleness or his serenity. As he entered the humble dwelling which he smilingly called his *palace*, he said to his sister, 'I have been officiating pontifically.'

As the most sublime things are often least comprehended, there were those in the city who said, in commenting upon the bishop's conduct, that it was affectation, but such ideas were confined to the upper classes. The people, who do not look for unworthy motives in holy works, admired and were softened.

As to the bishop, the sight of the guillotine was a shock to him, from which it was long before he recovered.

The scaffold, indeed, when it is prepared and set up, has the effect of a hallucination. We may be indifferent to the death penalty, and may not declare ourselves, yes or no, so long as we have not seen a guillotine with our own eyes. But when we see one, the shock is violent, and we are compelled to decide and take part, for or against. Some admire it, like Le Maistre; others execrate it, like Beccaria. The guillotine is the concretion of the law; it is called the Avenger; it is not neutral, and does not permit you to remain neutral. He who sees it quakes with the most mysterious of tremblings. All social questions set up their points of interrogation about this axe. The scaffold is vision. The scaffold is not a mere frame, the scaffold is not a machine, the scaffold is not an inert piece of mechanism made of wood, of iron, and of ropes. It seems a sort of being which had some sombre origin of which we can have no idea; one would say that this frame sees, that this machine understands, that this mechanism comprehends; that this wood, this iron, and these ropes, have a will. In the fearful reverie into which its presence casts the soul, the awful apparition of the scaffold confounds itself with its horrid work. The scaffold becomes the accomplice of the executioner; it devours, it eats flesh, and it drinks blood. The scaffold is a sort of monster created by the judge and the workman, a spectre which seems to live with a kind of unspeakable life, drawn from all the death which it has wrought.

Thus the impression was horrible and deep; on the morrow of the execution, and for many days, the bishop appeared to be overwhelmed. The almost violent calmness of the fatal moment had disappeared; the phantom of social justice took possession of him. He, who ordinarily looked back upon all his actions with a satisfaction so radiant, now seemed to be a subject of self-reproach. By times he would talk to himself, and in an undertone mutter dismal monologues. One evening his sister overheard and preserved the following: 'I did not believe that it could be so monstrous. It is wrong to be so absorbed in the divine law as not to perceive the human law. Death belongs to God alone. By what right do men touch that unknown thing?'

With the lapse of time these impressions faded away, and were probably effaced. Nevertheless it was remarked that the bishop ever after avoided passing by the place of execution.

M. Myriel could be called at all hours to the bedside of the sick and the dying. He well knew that there was his highest duty and his greatest work. Widowed or orphan families had no need to send for him; he came of himself. He would sit silent for long hours by the side of a man who had lost the wife whom he loved, or of a mother who had lost her child. As he knew the time for silence, he knew also the time for speech. Oh, admirable consoler! he did not seek to drown grief in oblivion, but to exalt and to dignify it by hope. He would say, 'Be careful of the way in which you think of the dead. Think not of what might have been. Look steadfastly and you shall see the living glory of your well-beloved dead in the depths of heaven.' He believed that faith is healthful. He sought to counsel and to calm the despairing man by pointing out to him the man of resignation, and to transform the grief which looks down into the grave by showing it the grief which looks up to the stars.

5. *How Monseigneur Bienvenu made his cassock last so long*

THE PRIVATE LIFE of M. Myriel was full of the same thoughts as his public life. To one who could have seen it on the spot, the voluntary poverty in which the Bishop of D— lived, would have been a serious as well as a pleasant sight.

Like all old men, and like most thinkers, he slept but little, but that little was sound. In the morning he devoted an hour to meditation, and then said mass, either at the cathedral, or in his own house. After mass he took his breakfast of rye bread and milk, and then went to work.

A bishop is a very busy man; he must receive the report of the clerk of the diocese, ordinarily a prebendary, every day; and nearly every day his grand vicars. He has congregations to superintend, licences to grant, all ecclesiastical bookselling to examine, parish and diocesan catechisms, prayer-books, etc., charges to write, preachings to authorise, curés and mayors to make peace between, a clerical correspondence, an administrative correspondence, on the one hand the government, on the other the Holy See, a thousand matters of business.

What time these various affairs and his devotions and his breviary left him, he gave first to the needy, the sick, and the afflicted; what time the afflicted, the sick, and the needy left him, he gave to labour. Sometimes he used a spade in his garden, and sometimes he read and wrote. He had but one name for these two kinds of labour; he called them gardening. 'The spirit is a garden,' said he.

Towards noon, when the weather was good, he would go out and walk in the fields, or in the city, often visiting the cottages and cabins. He would be seen plodding along, wrapt in his thoughts, his eyes bent down, resting upon his long cane wearing his violet doublet, wadded so as to be very warm, violet stockings and heavy shoes, and his flat hat, from the three corners of which hung the three golden grains of spikenard.

His coming made a fête. One would have said that he dispensed warmth and light as he passed along. Old people and children would come to their doors for the bishop as they would for the sun. He blessed, and was blessed in return. Whoever was in need of anything was shown the way to his house.

Now and then he would stop and talk to the little boys and girls – and give a smile to their mothers. When he had money his visits were to the poor; when he had none, he visited the rich.

As he made his cassock last a very long time, in order that it might not be perceived, he never went out into the city without his violet doublet. In summer this was rather irksome.

On his return he dined. His dinner was like his breakfast.

At half-past eight in the evening he took supper with his sister, Madame Magloire standing behind them and waiting on the table. Nothing could be more frugal than this meal. If, however, the bishop had one of his curés to supper, Madame Magloire improved the occasion to serve her master with some excellent fish from the lakes, or some fine game from the mountain. Every curé was a pretext for a fine meal; the bishop did not interfere. With these exceptions, there was rarely seen upon his table more than boiled vegetables, or bread warmed with oil. And so it came to be a saying in the city, 'When the bishop does not entertain a curé, he entertains a Trappist.'

After supper he would chat for half an hour with Mademoiselle Baptistine and Madame Magloire, and then go to his own room and write, sometimes upon loose sheets, sometimes on the margin of one of his folios. He was a well-read and even a learned man. He has left five or six very curious manuscripts behind him; among them is a dissertation upon this passage in Genesis: *In the beginning the spirit of God moved upon the face of the waters.* He contrasts this with three other versions; the Arabic, which has: *the winds of God blew;* Flavius Josephus, who says: *a wind from on high fell upon all the earth;* and finally the Chaldean paraphrase of Onkelos, which reads: *a wind coming from God blew upon the face of the waters.* In another dissertation, he examines the theological works of Hugo, Bishop of Ptolemais, a distant relative of the writer of this book,[2] and proves that sundry little tracts, published in the last century under the pseudonym of Barleycourt, should be attributed to that prelate.

Sometimes in the midst of his reading, no matter what book he might have in his hands, he would suddenly fall into deep meditation, and when it was over, would write a few lines on whatever page was open before him. These lines often have no connection with the book in which they are written. We have under our own eyes a note written by him upon the margin of a quarto volume entitled: '*Correspondance du Lord Germain avec les généraux Clinton, Cornwallis, et les amiraux de la Station de l'Amérique. A Versailles, chez Poincot, Libraire, et à Paris, chez Pissot, Quai des Augustins.*'

And this is the note:

'Oh Thou who art!

'Ecclesiastes names thee the Almighty; Maccabees names thee Creator; the Epistle to the Ephesians names thee Liberty; Baruch names thee Immensity; the Psalms name thee Wisdom and Truth; John names thee Light; the book of Kings names thee Lord; Exodus calls thee Providence; Leviticus, Holiness; Esdras, Justice; Creation calls thee God; man names thee Father; but Solomon names thee Compassion, and that is the most beautiful of all thy names.'

Towards nine o'clock in the evening the two women were accustomed to retire to their chambers in the second storey, leaving him until morning alone upon the lower floor.

Here it is necessary that we should give an exact idea of the dwelling of the Bishop of D—.

6. How he protected his house

THE HOUSE which he occupied consisted, as we have said, of a ground floor and a second storey; three rooms on the ground floor, three on the second storey, and an attic above. Behind the house was a garden of about a quarter of an acre. The two women occupied the upper floor; the bishop lived below. The first room, which opened upon the street, was his dining-room, the second was his bedroom, and the third his oratory. You could not leave the oratory without passing through the bedroom, and to leave the bedroom you must pass through the dining-room. At one end of the oratory there was an alcove closed in, with a bed for occasions of hospitality. The bishop kept this bed for the country curés when business or the wants of their parish brought them to D—.

The pharmacy of the hospital, a little building adjoining the house and extending into the garden, had been transformed into a kitchen and cellar.

There was also a stable in the garden, which was formerly the hospital kitchen, where the bishop now kept a couple of cows, and invariably, every morning, he sent half the milk they gave to the sick at the hospital. 'I pay my tithes,' said he.

His room was quite large, and was difficult to warm in bad weather. As wood is very dear at D—, he conceived the idea of having a room partitioned off from the cow-stable with a tight plank ceiling. In the coldest weather he passed his evenings there, and called it his *winter parlour.*

In this winter parlour, as in the dining-room, the only furniture was a square white wooden table, and four straw chairs. The dining-room, however, was furnished with an old sideboard stained red. A similar sideboard, suitably draped with white linen and imitation-lace, served for the altar which decorated the oratory.

His rich penitents and the pious women of D— had often contributed the money for a beautiful new altar for monseigneur's oratory; he had always taken the money and given it to the poor. 'The most beautiful of altars,' said he, 'is the soul of an unhappy man who is comforted and thanks God.'

In his oratory he had two prie-dieu straw chairs, and an armchair, also of straw, in the bedroom. When he happened to have seven or eight visitors at once, the prefect, or the general, or the major of the regiment in the garrison, or some of the pupils of the little seminary, he was obliged to go to the stable for the chairs that were in the winter parlour, to the oratory for the prie-dieu, and to the bedroom for the armchair; in this way he could get together as many as eleven seats for his visitors. At each new visit a room was stripped.

It happened sometimes that there were twelve; then the bishop concealed the embarrassment of the situation by standing before the fire if it were winter, or by walking in the garden if it were summer.

There was another chair in the stranger's alcove, but it had lost half its straw, and had but three legs, so that it could be used only when standing against the wall. Mademoiselle Baptistine had also, in her room, a very large wooden easy-chair, that had once been gilded and covered with flowered silk, but as it had to be taken into her room through the window, the stairway being too narrow, it could not be counted among the movable furniture.

It had been the ambition of Mademoiselle Baptistine to be able to buy a parlour lounge, with cushions of Utrecht velvet, roses on a yellow ground, while the mahogany should be in the form of swans' necks. But this would have cost at least five hundred francs, and as she had been able to save only forty-two francs and ten sous for the purpose in five years, she had finally given it up. But who ever does attain to his ideal?

Nothing could be plainer in its arrangements than the bishop's bed-chamber. A window, which was also a door, opening upon the garden; facing this, the bed, an iron hospital-bed, with green serge curtains; in the shadow of the bed, behind a screen, the toilet utensils, still betraying the elegant habits of the man of the world; two doors, one near the chimney, leading into the oratory, the other near the bookcase, opening into the dining-room. The bookcase, a large closet with glass doors, filled with books; the fireplace, cased with wood painted to imitate marble, usually without fire; in the fireplace, a pair of andirons ornamented with two vases of flowers, once plated with silver, which was a kind of episcopal luxury; above the fireplaace, a copper crucifix, from which the silver was worn off, fixed upon a piece of threadbare black velvet in a wooden frame from which the gilt was almost gone; near the window, a large table with an inkstand, covered with confused papers and heavy volumes. In front of the table was the straw armchair, and before the bed, a prie-dieu from the oratory.

Two portraits in oval frames hung on the wall on either side of the bed. Small gilt inscriptions upon the background of the canvas indicated that the portraits represented, one, the Abbé de Chaliot, bishop of Saint Claude, the other, the Abbé Tourteau, vicar-general of Agde, abbé of Grandchamps, order of Citeaux, diocese of Chartres. The bishop found these portraits when he succeeded to the hospital patients in this chamber, and left them untouched. They were priests, and probably donors to the hospital – two reasons why he should respect them. All that he knew of these two personages was that they had been named by the king, the one to his bishopric, the other to his living, on the same day, the 27th of April 1785. Madame Magloire having taken down the pictures to wipe off the dust, the bishop had found this circumstance written in a faded ink upon a little square piece of paper, yellow with time, stuck with four wafers on the back of the portrait of the Abbé of Grandchamps.

He had at his window an antique curtain of coarse woollen stuff, which finally became so old that, to save the expense of a new one, Madame Magloire was obliged to put a large patch in the very middle of it. This patch was in the form of a cross. The bishop often called attention to it. 'How fortunate that is,' he would say.

Every room in the house, on the ground floor as well as in the upper storey, without exception, was white-washed, as is the custom in barracks and in hospitals.

However, in later years, as we shall see by and by, Madame Magloire found, under the wall paper, some paintings which decorated the apartment of Mademoiselle Baptistine. Before it was a hospital, the house had been a sort of gathering-place for the citizens, at which time these decorations were introduced. The floors of the chambers were paved with red brick, which were scoured every week, and before the beds straw matting was spread. In all respects the house was kept by the two women exquisitely neat from top to bottom. This was the only luxury that the bishop would permit. He would say, '*That takes nothing from the poor.*'

We must confess that he still retained of what he had formerly, six silver dishes and a silver soup ladle, which Madame Magloire contemplated every day with new joy as they shone on the coarse, white, linen tablecloth. And as we are drawing the portrait of the Bishop of D— just as he was, we must add that he had said, more than once, 'It would be difficult for me to give up eating from silver.'

With this silverware should be counted two large, massive silver candlesticks which he inherited from a great-aunt. These candlesticks held two wax-candles, and their place was upon the bishop's mantel. When he had anyone to dinner, Madame Magloire lighted the two candles and placed the two candlesticks upon the table.

There was in the bishop's chamber, at the head of his bed, a small cupboard in which Madame Magloire placed the six silver dishes and the great ladle every evening. But the key was never taken out of it.

The garden, which was somewhat marred by the unsightly structures of which we have spoken, was laid out with four walks, crossing at the drain-well in the centre. There was another walk round the garden, along the white wall which enclosed it. These walks left four square plats which were bordered with box. In three of them Madame Magloire cultivated vegetables; in the fourth the bishop had planted flowers, and here and there were a few fruit trees. Madame Magloire once said to him with a kind of gentle reproach: 'Monseigneur, you are always anxious to make everything useful, but yet here is a plat that is of no use. It would be much better to have salads there than bouquets.' 'Madame Magloire,' replied the bishop, 'you are mistaken. The beautiful is as useful as the useful.' He added, after a moment's silence, 'perhaps more so.'

This plat, consisting of three or four beds, occupied the bishop nearly as much as his books. He usually passed an hour or two there, trimming, weeding, and making holes here and there in the ground, and planting seeds. He was as much averse to insects as a gardener would have wished. He made no pretensions to botany, and knew nothing of groups or classification; he did not care in the least to decide between Tournefort and the natural method; he took no part, either for the utricles against the cotyledons, or for Jussieu against Linnæus. He did not study plants, he loved flowers. He had much respect for the learned, but still more for the ignorant; and, while he fulfilled his duty in both these respects, he watered his beds every summer evening with a tin watering-pot painted green.

Not a door in the house had a lock. The door of the dining-room which, we have mentioned, opened into the cathedral grounds, was formerly loaded with bars and bolts like the door of a prison. The bishop had had all this iron-work taken off, and the door, by night as well as by day, was closed only with a latch. The passer-by, whatever might be the hour, could open it with a simple push. At first the two women had been very much troubled at the door being never locked; but Monseigneur de D— said to them: 'Have bolts on your own doors, if you like.' They shared his confidence at last, or at least acted as if they shared it. Madame Magloire alone had occasional attacks of fear. As to the bishop, the reason for this is explained, or at least pointed at in these three lines written by him on the margin of a Bible: 'This is the shade of meaning; the door of a physician should never be closed; the door of a priest should always be open.'

In another book, entitled *Philosophie de la Science Medicale*, he wrote this further note: 'Am I not a physician as well as they? I also have my patients; first I have theirs, whom they call the sick; and then I have my own, whom I call the unfortunate.'

Yet again he had written: 'Ask not the name of him who asks you for a bed. It is especially he whose name is a burden to him, who has need of an asylum.'

It occurred to a worthy curé, I am not sure whether it was the curé of Couloubroux or the curé of Pomprierry, to ask him one day, probably at the instigation of Madame Magloire, if monseigneur were quite sure that there was not a degree of imprudence in leaving his door, day and night, at the mercy of whoever might wish to enter, and if he did not fear that some evil would befall a house so poorly defended. The bishop touched him gently on the shoulder, and said:* *'Nisi Dominus custodierit domum, in vanum vigilant qui custodiunt eam.'*

And then he changed the subject.

He very often said: 'There is a bravery for the priest as well as a bravery for the colonel of dragoons.' 'Only,' added he, 'ours should be quiet.'

7. *Cravatte*

THIS IS THE PROPER PLACE for an incident which we must not omit for it is one of those which most clearly shows what manner of man the Bishop of D— was.

After the destruction of the band of Gaspard Bès,[3] which had infested the gorges of Ollivolles, one of his lieutenants, Cravatte, took refuge in the

---

* Unless God protects a house, they who guard it, watch in vain.

mountains. He concealed himself for some time with his bandits, the remnant of the troop of Gaspard Bès, in the county of Nice, then made his way to Piedmont, and suddenly reappeared in France in the neighbourhood of Barcelonnette. He was first seen at Jauziers, then at Tuiles. He concealed himself in the caverns of the Joug de l'Aigle, from which he made descents upon the hamlets and villages by the ravines of Ubaye and Ubayette.

He even pushed as far as Embrun, and one night broke into the cathedral and stripped the sacristy. His robberies desolated the country. The gendarmes were put upon his trail, but in vain. He always escaped; sometimes by forcible resistance. He was a bold wretch. In the midst of all this terror, the bishop arrived. He was making his visit to Chastelar. The mayor came to see him, and urged him to turn back. Cravatte held the mountains as far as Arche, and beyond; it would be dangerous, even with an escort. It would expose three or four poor gendarmes to useless danger.

'And so,' said the bishop, 'I intend to go without an escort.'

'Do not think of such a thing,' exclaimed the mayor.

'I think so much of it, that I absolutely refuse the gendarmes, and I am going to start in an hour.'

'To start?'

'To start.'

'Alone?'

'Alone.'

'Monseigneur, you will not do it.'

'There is on the mountain,' replied the bishop, 'a humble little commune, that I have not seen for three years; and they are good friends of mine, kind and honest peasants. They own one goat out of thirty that they pasture. They make pretty woollen thread of various colours, and they play their mountain airs upon small six-holed flutes. They need someone occasionally to tell them of the goodness of God. What would they say of a bishop who was afraid? What would they say if I should not go there?'

'But, monseigneur, the brigands?'

'True,' said the bishop, 'I am thinking of that. You are right. I may meet them. They too must need someone to tell them of the goodness of God.'

'Monseigneur, but it is a band! a pack of wolves!'

'Monsieur Mayor, perhaps Jesus has made me the keeper of that very flock. Who knows the ways of providence?'

'Monseigneur, they will rob you.'

'I have nothing.'

'They will kill you.'

'A simple old priest who passes along muttering his prayer? No, no; what good would it do them?'

'Oh, my good sir, suppose you should meet them!'

'I should ask them for alms for my poor.'

'Monseigneur, do not go. In the name of heaven! you are exposing your life.'

'Monsieur Mayor,' said the bishop, 'that is just it. I am not in the world to care for my life, but for souls.'

He would not be dissuaded. He set out, accompanied only by a child, who offered to go as his guide. His obstinacy was the talk of the country, and all dreaded the result.

He would not take along his sister, or Madame Magloire. He crossed the mountain on a mule, met no one, and arrived safe and sound among his 'good friends' the shepherds. He remained there a fortnight, preaching, administering the holy rites, teaching and exhorting. When he was about to leave, he resolved to chant a Te Deum with pontifical ceremonies. He talked with the curé about it. But what could be done? there was no episcopal furniture. They could only place at his disposal a paltry village sacristy with a few old robes of worn-out damask, trimmed with imitation-galloon.

'No matter,' said the bishop. 'Monsieur le curé, at the sermon announce our Te Deum. That will take care of itself.'

All the neighbouring churches were ransacked, but the assembled magnificence of these humble parishes could not have suitably clothed a single cathedral singer.

While they were in this embarrassment, a large chest was brought to the parsonage, and left for the bishop by two unknown horsemen, who immediately rode away. The chest was opened; it contained a cope of cloth of gold, a mitre ornamented with diamonds, an archbishop's cross, a magnificent crosier, all the pontifical raiment stolen a month before from the treasures of Our Lady of Embrun. In the chest was a paper on which were written these words: '*Cravatte to Monseigneur Bienvenu.*'

'I said that it would take care of itself,' said the bishop. Then he added with a smile: 'To him who is contented with a curé's surplice, God sends an archbishop's cope.'

'Monseigneur,' murmured the curé, with a shake of the head and a smile, 'God – or the devil.'

The bishop looked steadily upon the curé, and replied with authority: 'God!'

When he returned to Chastelar, all along the road, the people came with curiosity to see him. At the parsonage in Chastelar he found Mademoiselle Baptistine and Madame Magloire waiting for him, and he said to his sister, 'Well, was I not right? the poor priest went among those poor mountaineers with empty hands; he comes back with hands filled. I went forth placing my trust in God alone; I bring back the treasures of a cathedral.'

In the evening before going to bed he said further: 'Have no fear of robbers or murderers. Such dangers are without, and are but petty. We should fear ourselves. Prejudices are the real robbers; vices the real murderers. The great dangers are within us. What matters it what threatens our heads or our purses? Let us think only of what threatens our souls.'

Then turning to his sister: 'My sister, a priest should never take any precaution against a neighbour. What his neighbour does, God permits. Let us confine ourselves to prayer to God when we think that danger hangs over us. Let us beseech him, not for ourselves, but that our brother may not fall into crime on our account.'

To sum up, events were rare in his life. We relate those we know of; but usually he passed his life in always doing the same things at the same hours. A month of his year was like an hour of his day.

As to what became of the 'treasures' of the Cathedral of Embrun, it would embarrass us to be questioned on that point. There were among them very fine things, and very tempting, and very good to steal for the benefit of the unfortunate. Stolen they had already been by others. Half the work was done; it only remained to change the course of the theft, and to make it turn to the side of the poor. We can say nothing more on the subject. Except that, there was found among the bishop's papers a rather obscure note, which is possibly connected with this affair, that reads as follows: '*The question is, whether this ought to be returned to the cathedral or to the hospital.*'

8. *After-dinner philosophy*

THE SENATOR heretofore referred to was an intelligent man, who had made his way in life with a directness of purpose which paid no attention to all those stumbling-blocks which constitute obstacles in men's path, known as conscience, sworn faith, justice, and duty; he had advanced straight to his object without once swerving in the line of his advancement and his interest. He had been formerly a *procureur*, mollified by success, and was not a bad man at all, doing all the little kindnesses that he could to his sons, sons-in-law, and relatives generally, and even to his friends; having prudently taken the pleasant side of life, and availed himself of all the benefits which were thrown in his way. Everything else appeared to him very stupid. He was sprightly, and just enough of a scholar to think himself a disciple of Epicurus, while possibly he was only a product of Pigault-Lebrun.[4] He laughed readily and with gusto at infinite and eternal things, and at the 'crotchets of the good bishop'. He laughed at them sometimes, with a patronising air, before M. Myriel himself, who listened.

At some semi-official ceremony, Count — (this senator) and M. Myriel remained to dinner with the prefect. At dessert, the senator, a little elevated, though always dignified, exclaimed:

'Parbleu, Monsieur Bishop; let us talk. It is difficult for a senator and a bishop to look each other in the eye without winking. We are two augurs. I have a confession to make to you; I have my philosophy.'

'And you are right,' answered the bishop. 'As one makes his philosophy, so he rests. You are on a purple bed, Monsieur Senator.'

The senator, encouraged by this, proceeded:

'Let us be good fellows.'

'Good devils, even,' said the bishop.

'I assure you,' resumed the senator, 'that the Marquis d'Argens, Pyrrho, Hobbes, and M. Naigeon are not rascals. I have all my philosophers in my library, gilt-edged.'

'Like yourself, Monsieur le Comte,' interrupted the bishop. The senator went on:

'I hate Diderot; he is an idealogist, a demagogue, and a revolutionist, at heart believing in God, and more bigoted than Voltaire. Voltaire mocked at Needham, and he was wrong; for Needham's eels prove that God is useless. A drop of vinegar in a spoonful of flour supplied the *fiat lux*. Suppose the drop greater and the spoonful larger, and you have the world. Man is the eel. Then what is the use of an eternal Father? Monsieur Bishop, the Jehovah hypothesis tires me. It is good for nothing except to produce people with scraggy bodies and empty heads. Down with this great All, who torments me! Hail, Zero! who leaves me quiet. Between us, to open my heart, and confess to my pastor, as I ought, I will confess that I have common sense. My head is not turned with your Jesus, who preaches in every cornfield renunciation and self-sacrifice. It is the advice of a miser to beggars. Renunciation, for what? Self-sacrifice, to what? I do not see that one wolf immolates himself for the benefit of another wolf. Let us dwell, then, with nature. We are at the summit, and let us have a higher philosophy. What is the use of being in a higher position if we can't see further than another man's nose? Let us live gaily; for life is all we have. That man has another life, elsewhere, above, below, anywhere – I don't believe a single word of it. Ah! I am recommended to self-sacrifice and renunciation, that I should take care what I do; that I must break my head over questions of good and evil, justice and injustice, over the *fas* and the *nefas*. Why? Because I shall have to render an account for my acts. When? After death. What a fine dream! After I am dead it will take fine fingers to pinch me. I should like to see a shade grasp a handful of ashes. Let us who are initiated, and have raised the skirt of Isis, speak the truth; there is neither good nor evil; there is only vegetation. Let us seek for the real; let us dig into everything. Let us go to the bottom. We should scent out the truth, dig in the earth for it, and seize upon it. Then it gives you exquisite joy; then you grow strong, and laugh. I am firmly convinced, Monsieur Bishop, that the immortality of man is a will-o'-the-wisp. Oh! charming promise. Trust it if you will! Adam's letter of recommendation! We have souls, and are to become angels, with blue wings to our shoulders. Tell me, now, isn't it Tertullian who says that the blessed will go from one star to another? Well, we shall be the grasshoppers of the skies. And then we shall see God. Tut tut tut. All these heavens are silly. God is a monstrous myth. I shouldn't say that in the *Moniteur*, of course, but I whisper it among my friends. *Inter pocula*. To sacrifice earth to paradise is to leave the substance for the shadow. I am not so stupid as to be the dupe of the Infinite. I am nothing; I call myself Count Nothing, senator. Did I exist before my birth? No. Shall I, after my death? No. What am I? A little dust, aggregated by an organism. What have I to do on this earth! I have the choice to suffer or to enjoy. Where will suffering lead me? To nothing. But I shall have suffered. Where will enjoyment lead me? To nothing. But I shall have enjoyed. My choice is made. I must eat or be eaten, and I choose to eat. It is better to be the tooth than the grass. Such is my philosophy. After which, as I tell you, there is the gravedigger – the pantheon for *us* – but all fall into the great gulf – the end; *finis;* total liquidation. This is the vanishing point. Death is dead, believe me. I laugh at the idea that there is anyone there that has anything to say to me. It is an invention of nurses: Bugaboo for children; Jehovah for men. No, our morrow is night. Beyond the tomb are only equal nothings. You have been Sardanapalus, or you have been Vincent de Paul – that amounts to the same nothing. That is the truth of it. Let us live, then, above all things; use your personality while you have it. In fact, I tell you, Monsieur Bishop, I have my philosophy, and I have my philosophers. I do not allow myself to be entangled with nonsense. But it is necessary there should be something for those who are below us, the bare-foots, knife-grinders, and other wretches. Legends and chimeras are given them to swallow, about the soul, immortality, paradise, and the stars. They munch that; they spread it on their dry bread. He who has nothing besides, has the good God – that is the least good he can have. I make no objection to it, but I keep Monsieur Naigeon for myself. The good God is good for the people.'[5]

The bishop clapped his hands.

'That is the idea,' he exclaimed. 'This materialism is an excellent thing, and truly marvellous; reject it who will. Ah! when one has it, he is a dupe no more; he does not stupidly allow himself to be exiled like Cato, or stoned like Stephen, or burnt alive like Joan of Arc. Those who have succeeded in procuring this admirable materialism have the happiness of feeling that they are irresponsible, and of thinking that they can devour everything in quietness – places, sinecures, honours, power rightly or wrongly acquired, lucrative recantations, useful treasons, savoury capitulations of conscience, and that they will enter their graves with their digestion completed. How agreeable it is! I do not say that for you, Monsieur Senator. Nevertheless, I cannot but felicitate you. You great lords have, you say, a philosophy of your own, for your special benefit – exquisite, refined, accessible to the rich alone; good with all sauces, admirably seasoning the pleasures of life. This philosophy is found at great depths, and brought up by special search. But you are good princes, and you are quite willing that the belief in the good God should be the philosophy of the people, much as goose with onions is the turkey with truffles of the poor.'

9. *The brother portrayed by the sister*

To AFFORD an idea of the household of the Bishop of D—, and the manner in which these two good women subordinated their actions, thoughts, even their womanly instincts, so liable to disturbance, to the habits and projects of the bishop, so that he had not even to speak, in order to express them; we cannot do better than to copy here a letter from Mademoiselle Baptistine to Madame la Viscontesse de Boischevron, the friend of her childhood. This letter is in our possession:

D—, DEC. 16TH, 18—

MY DEAR MADAME: Not a day passes that we do not speak of you; that is customary enough with us; but we have now another reason. Would you believe that in washing and dusting the ceilings and walls, Madame Magloire has made some discoveries? At present, our two chambers, which were hung with old paper, white-washed, would not disparage a chateau in the style of your own. Madame Magloire has torn off all the paper: it had something underneath. My parlour, where there is no furniture and which we use to dry clothes in, is fifteen feet high, eighteen feet square, and has a ceiling, once painted and gilded, with beams like those of your house. This was covered over with canvas during the time it was used as a hospital; and then we have wainscoting of the time of our grandmothers. But it is my own room which you ought to see. Madame Magloire has discovered beneath at least ten thicknesses of paper some pictures, which, though not good, are quite endurable. Telemachus received on horseback, by Minerva, is one; and then again, he is in the gardens – I forget their name; another is where the Roman ladies resorted for a single night. I could say much more; I have Romans, men and women [here a word is illegible], and all their retinue. Madame Magloire has cleaned it all, and this summer she is going to repair some little damages, and varnish it, and my room will be a veritable museum. She also found in a corner of the storehouse two pier tables of antique style; they asked two crowns of six livres to regild them, but it is far better to give that to the poor; besides that they are very ugly, and I much prefer a round mahogany table.

I am always happy: my brother is so good: he gives all he has to the poor and sick. We are full of cares: the weather is very severe in the winter, and one must do something for those who lack. We at least are warmed and lighted, and you know those are great comforts.

My brother has his peculiarities; when he talks he says that a bishop ought to be thus. Just think of it that the door is never closed. Come in who will, he is at once my brother's guest; he fears nothing, not even in the night; he says that is his form of bravery.

He wishes me not to fear for him, nor that Madame Magloire should; he exposes himself to every danger, and prefers that we should not even seem to be aware of it; one must know how to understand him.

He goes out in the rain, walks through the water, travels in winter, he has no fear of darkness, or dangerous roads, or of those he may meet.

Last year he went all alone into a district infested with robbers. He would not take us. He was gone a fortnight, and when he came back, though we had thought him dead, nothing had happened to him, and he was quite well. He said: "See, how they have robbed me!" And he opened a trunk in which he had the jewels of the Embrun Cathedral which the robbers had given him.

Upon that occasion, on the return, I could not keep from scolding him a little, taking care only to speak while the carriage made a noise, so that no one could hear us.

At first I used to say to myself, he stops for no danger, he is incorrigible. But now I have become used to it. I make signs to Madame Magloire that she shall not oppose him, and he runs what risks he chooses. I call away Madame Magloire; I go to my room, pray for him, and fall asleep. I am calm, for I know very well that if any harm happened to him, it would be my death: I should go away to the good Father with my brother and my bishop. Madame Magloire has had more difficulty in getting used to what she calls his imprudence. Now the thing is settled: we pray together; we are afraid together, and we go to sleep. Should Satan even come into the house, no one would interfere. After all, what is there to fear in this house? There is always One with us who is the strongest: Satan may visit our house, but the good God inhabits it.

That is enough for me. My brother has no need now even to speak a word. I understand him without his speaking, and we commend ourselves to Providence.

It must be so with a man whose soul is so noble.

I asked my brother for the information which you requested respecting the Faux family. You know how well he knows about it, and how much he remembers, for he was always a very good royalist, and this is really a very old Norman family, of the district of Caen. There are five centuries of a Raoul de Faux, Jean de Faux, and Thomas de Faux, who were of the gentry, one of whom was a lord of Rochefort. The last was

Guy Etienne Alexandre, who was a cavalry colonel, and held some rank in the light horse of Brittany. His daughter Marie Louise married Adrien Charles de Gramont, son of Duke Louis de Gramont, a peer of France, colonel of the Gardes Françaises, and lieutenant-general of the army. It is written Faux, Fauq, and Faouq.

Will you not, my dear madame, ask for us the prayers of your holy relative, Monsieur le Cardinal? As to your precious Sylvanie, she has done well not to waste the short time that she is with you in writing to me. She is well, you say; studies according to your wishes, and loves me still. That is all I could desire. Her remembrance, through you, reached me, and I was glad to receive it. My health is tolerably good; still I grow thinner every day.

Farewell: my paper is filled and I must stop. With a thousand good wishes,

BAPTISTINE

P.S. – Your little nephew is charming; do you remember that he will soon be five years old? He saw a horse pass yesterday on which they had put knee-caps, and he cried out: 'What is that he has got on his knees?' The child is so pretty. His little brother drags an old broom about the room for a carriage, and says, hi!

As this letter shows, these two women knew how to conform to the bishop's mode of life, with that woman's tact which understands a man better than he can comprehend himself. Beneath the gentle and frank manner of the Bishop of D— which never changed, he sometimes performed great, daring, even grand acts, without seeming to be aware of it himself. They trembled, but did not interfere. Sometimes Madame Magloire would venture a remonstrance beforehand: never at the time, or afterwards; no one ever disturbed him by word or token in an action once begun. At certain times, when he had no need to say it, when, perhaps, he was hardly conscious of it, so complete was his artlessness, they vaguely felt that he was acting as bishop, and at such periods they were only two shadows in the house. They waited on him passively, and if to obey was to disappear, they disappeared. With charming and instinctive delicacy they knew that obtrusive attentions would annoy him; so even when they thought him in danger they understood, I will not say his thought, but his nature rather, to the degree of ceasing to watch over him. They entrusted him to God's keeping.

Besides, Baptistine said, as we have seen, that his death would be hers. Madame Magloire did not say so, but she knew it.

10. *The bishop in the presence of an unknown light*[6]

A LITTLE WHILE before the date of the letter quoted in the preceding pages, the bishop performed an act, which the whole town thought far more perilous than his excursion across the mountains infested by the bandits.

In the country near D—, there was a man who lived alone. This man, to state the startling fact without preface, had been a member of the National Convention. His name was G—.

The little circle of D— spoke of the conventionist with a certain sort of horror. A conventionist, think of it; that was in the time when folks thee-and-thoued one another, and said 'citizen'. This man came very near being a monster; he had not exactly voted for the execution of the king, but almost; he was half a regicide, and had been a terrible creature altogether. How was it, then, on the return of the legitimate princes, that they had not arraigned this man before the provost court? He would not have been beheaded, perhaps, but even if clemency were necessary he might have been banished for life; in fact, an example, etc. etc. Besides, he was an atheist, as all those people are. Babblings of geese against a vulture!

But was this G— a vulture? Yes, if one should judge him by the savageness of his solitude. As he had not voted for the king's execution, he was not included in the sentence of exile, and could remain in France.

He lived about an hour's walk from the town, far from any hamlet or road, in a secluded ravine of a very wild valley. It was said he had a sort of resting-place there, a hole, a den. He had no neighbours or even passers-by. Since he had lived there the path which led to the place had become overgrown, and people spoke of it as of the house of a hangman.

From time to time, however, the bishop reflectingly gazed upon the horizon at the spot where a clump of trees indicated the ravine of the aged conventionist, and he would say: 'There lives a soul which is alone.' And in the depths of his thought he would add, 'I owe him a visit.'

But this idea, we must confess, though it appeared natural at first, yet, after a few moments' reflection, seemed strange, impracticable, and almost repulsive. For at heart he shared the general impression, and the conventionist inspired him, he knew not how, with that sentiment which is the fringe of hatred, and which the word 'aversion' so well expresses.

However, the shepherd should not recoil from the diseased sheep. Ah! but what a sheep!

The good bishop was perplexed: sometimes he walked in that direction, but he returned.

At last, one day the news was circulated in the town that the young herdsboy who served the conventionist G— in his retreat, had come for a doctor; that the old wretch was dying, that he was motionless, and could not live through the night. 'Thank God!' added many.

The bishop took his cane, put on his overcoat, because his cassock was badly worn, as we have said, and besides the night wind was evidently rising, and set out.

The sun was setting; it had nearly touched the horizon when the bishop reached the accursed spot. He felt a certain quickening of the pulse as he drew near the den. He jumped over a ditch, cleared a hedge, made his way through a brush fence, found himself in a dilapidated garden, and after a bold advance across the open ground, suddenly, behind some high brushwood, he discovered the retreat.

It was a low, poverty-stricken hut, small and clean, with a little vine nailed up in front.

Before the door in an old chair on rollers, there sat a man with white hair, looking with smiling gaze upon the setting sun.

The young herdsboy stood near him, handing him a bowl of milk.

While the bishop was looking, the old man raised his voice.

'Thank you,' he said, 'I shall need nothing more;' and his smile changed from the sun to rest upon the boy.

The bishop stepped forward. At the sound of his footsteps the old man turned his head, and his face expressed as much surprise as one can feel after a long life.

'This is the first time since I have lived here,' said he, 'that I have had a visitor. Who are you, monsieur?'

'My name is Bienvenu-Myriel,' the bishop replied.

'Bienvenu-Myriel? I have heard that name before. Are you he whom the people call Monseigneur Bienvenu?'

'I am.'

The old man continued half-smiling. 'Then you are my bishop?'

'Possibly.'

'Come in, monsieur.'

The conventionist extended his hand to the bishop, but he did not take it. He only said:

'I am glad to find that I have been misinformed. You do not appear to me very ill.'

'Monsieur,' replied the old man, 'I shall soon be better.'

He paused and said:

'I shall be dead in three hours.'

Then he continued:

'I am something of a physician; I know the steps by which death approaches; yesterday my feet only were cold; today the cold has crept to my knees, now it has reached the waist; when it touches the heart, all will be over. The sunset is lovely, is it not? I had myself wheeled out to get a final look at nature. You can speak to me; that will not tire me. You do well to come to see a man who is dying. It is good that these moments should have witnesses. Everyone has his fancy; I should like to live until the dawn, but I know I have scarcely life for three hours. It will be night, but what matters it: to finish is a very simple thing. One does not need morning for that. Be it so: I shall die in the starlight.'

The old man turned towards the herdsboy:

'Little one, go to bed: thou didst watch the other night: thou art weary.'

The child went into the hut.

The old man followed him with his eyes, and added, as if speaking to himself: 'While he is sleeping, I shall die: the two slumbers keep fit company.'

The bishop was not as much affected as he might have been: it was not his idea of godly death; we must tell all, for the little inconsistencies of great souls should be mentioned; he who had laughed so heartily at 'His Highness', was still slightly shocked at not being called monseigneur, and was almost tempted to answer 'citizen'. He felt a desire to use the brusque familiarity common enough with doctors and priests, but which was not customary with him.

This conventionist after all, this representative of the people, had been a power on the earth; and perhaps for the first time in his life the bishop felt himself in a humour to be severe. The conventionist, however, treated him with a modest consideration and cordiality, in which perhaps might have been discerned that humility which is befitting to one so nearly dust unto dust.

The bishop, on his part, although he generally kept himself free from curiosity, which to his idea was almost offensive, could not avoid examining the conventionist with an attention for which, as it had not its source in sympathy, his conscience would have condemned him as to any other man; but a conventionist he looked upon as an outlaw, even to the law of charity.

G—, with his self-possessed manner, erect figure, and vibrating voice, was one of those noble octogenarians who are the marvel of the physiologist. The revolution produced many of these men equal to the epoch: one felt that here was a tested man. Though so near death, he preserved all the appearance of health. His bright glances, his firm accent, and the muscular movements of his shoulders seemed almost sufficient to disconcert death. Azrael, the Mahometan angel of the sepulchre, would have turned back, thinking he had mistaken the door. G— appeared to be dying because he wished to die. There was freedom in his agony; his legs only were paralysed; his feet were cold and dead, but his head lived in full power of life and light. At this solemn moment G— seemed like the king in the oriental tale, flesh above and marble below. The bishop seated himself upon a stone near by. The beginning of their conversation was *ex abrupto*:

'I congratulate you,' he said, in a tone of reprimand. 'At least you did not vote for the execution of the king.'

The conventionist did not seem to notice the bitter emphasis placed upon the words 'at least'. The smiles vanished from his face, and he replied:

'Do not congratulate me too much, monsieur; I did vote for the destruction of the tyrant.'

And the tone of austerity confronted the tone of severity.

'What do you mean?' asked the bishop.

'I mean that man has a tyrant, Ignorance. I voted for the abolition of that tyrant. That tyrant has begotten royalty, which is authority springing from the False, while science is authority springing from the True. Man should be governed by science.'

'And conscience,' added the bishop.

'The same thing: conscience is innate knowledge that we have.'

Monsieur Bienvenu listened with some amazement to this language, novel as it was to him.

The conventionist went on:

'As to Louis XVI: I said no. I do not believe that I have the right to kill a man, but I feel it a duty to exterminate evil. I voted for the downfall of the tyrant; that is to say, for the abolition of prostitution for woman, of slavery for man, of night for the child. In voting for the republic I voted for that: I voted for fraternity, for harmony, for light. I assisted in casting down prejudices and errors: their downfall brings light! We caused the old world to fall; the old world, a vase of misery, reversed, becomes an urn of joy to the human race.'

'Joy alloyed,' said the bishop.

'You might say joy troubled, and, at present, after this fatal return of the blast which we call 1814 joy disappeared. Alas! the work was imperfect I admit; we demolished the ancient order of things physically, but not entirely in the idea. To destroy abuses is not enough; habits must be changed. The windmill has gone, but the wind is there yet.'

'You have demolished. To demolish may be useful, but I distrust a demolition effected in anger!'

'Justice has its anger, Monsieur Bishop, and the wrath of justice is an element of progress. Whatever may be said matters not, the French revolution is the greatest step in advance taken by mankind since the advent of Christ; incomplete it may be, but it is sublime. It loosened all the secret bonds of society, it softened all hearts, it calmed, appeased, enlightened; it made the waves of civilisation to flow over the earth; it was good. The French revolution is the consecration of humanity.'

The bishop could not help murmuring: 'Yes, '93!'

The conventionist raised himself in his chair with a solemnity well nigh mournful, and as well as a dying person could exclaim, he exclaimed:

'Ah! you are there! '93! I was expecting that. A cloud had been forming for fifteen hundred years; at the end of fifteen centuries it burst. You condemn the thunderbolt.'

Without perhaps acknowledging it to himself, the bishop felt that he had been touched; however, he made the best of it, and replied:

'The judge speaks in the name of justice, the priest in the name of pity, which is only a more exalted justice. A thunderbolt should not be mistaken.'

And he added, looking fixedly at the conventionist; 'Louis XVII?'

The conventionist stretched out his hand and seized the bishop's arm.

'Louis XVII.' Let us see! For whom do you weep? – for the innocent child? It is well; I weep with you. For the royal child? I ask time to reflect. To my view the brother of Cartouche, an innocent child, hung by a rope under his arms in the Place de Grève till he died, for the sole crime of being the brother of Cartouche, is no less sad sight than the grandson of Louis XV, an innocent child, murdered in the tower of the Temple for the sole crime of being the grandson of Louis XV.'

'Monsieur,' said the bishop, 'I dislike this coupling of names.'

'Cartouche or Louis XV; for which are you concerned?'

There was a moment of silence; the bishop regretted almost that he had come, and yet he felt strangely and inexplicably moved.

The conventionist resumed: 'Oh, Monsieur Priest! you do not love the harshness of the truth, but Christ loved it. He took a scourge and purged the temple; his flashing whip was a rude speaker of truths; when he said '*Sinite parvulos*,' he made no distinctions among the little ones. He was not pained at coupling the dauphin of Barabbas with the dauphin of Herod. Monsieur, innocence is its own crown! Innocence has only to act to be noble! She is as august in rags as in the fleur-de-lis.'

'That is true,' said the bishop, in a low tone.

'I repeat,' continued the old man; 'you have mentioned Louis XVII. Let us weep together for all the innocent, for all the martyrs, for all the children, for the low as well as for the high. I am one of them, but then, as I have told you, we must go further back than '93, and our tears must begin before Louis XVII. I will weep for the children of kings with you, if you will weep with me for the little ones of the people.'

'I weep for all,' said the bishop.

'Equally,' exclaimed G—, 'and if the balance inclines, let it be on the side of the people: they have suffered longer.'

There was silence again, broken at last by the old man. He raised himself upon one elbow, took a pinch of his cheek between his thumb and his bent forefinger, as one does mechanically in questioning and forming an opinion, and addressed the bishop with a look full of all the energies of agony. It was almost an anathema.

'Yes, Monsieur, it is for a long time that the people have been suffering, and then, sir, that is not all; why do you come to question me and to speak to me of Louis XVII? I do not know you. Since I have been in this region I have lived within these walls alone, never passing beyond them, seeing none but this child who helps me. Your name, has, it is true, reached me confusedly, and I must say not very indistinctly, but that matters not. Adroit men have so many ways of imposing upon this good simple people. For instance I did not hear the sound of your carriage. You left it doubtless behind the thicket, down there at the branching of the road. You have told me that you were the bishop, but that tells me nothing about your moral personality. Now, then, I repeat my question – Who are you? You are a bishop, a prince of the church, one of those men who are covered with gold, with insignia, and with wealth, who have fat livings – the see of D—, fifteen thousand francs regular, ten thousand francs contingent, total twenty-five thousand francs – who have kitchens, who have retinues, who give good dinners, who eat moor-hens on Friday, who strut about in your gaudy coach, like peacocks, with lackeys before and lackeys behind, and who have palaces, and who roll in your carriages in the name of Jesus Christ who went bare-footed. You are a prelate; rents, palaces, horses, valets, a good table, all the sensualities of life, you have these, like all the rest, and you enjoy them like all the rest; very well, but that says too much or not enough; that does not enlighten me as to your intrinsic worth, that which is peculiar to yourself, you who come probably with the claim of bringing me wisdom. To whom am I speaking? Who are you?'

The bishop bowed his head and replied, '*Vermis sum.*'

'A worm of the earth in a carriage!' grumbled the old man.

It was the turn of the conventionist to be haughty, and of the bishop to be humble.

The bishop replied with mildness:

'Monsieur, be it so. But explain to me how my carriage, which is there a few steps behind the trees, how my good table and the moor-fowl that I eat on Friday, how my twenty-five thousand livres of income, how my palace and my lackeys prove that pity is not a virtue, that kindness is not a duty, and that '93 was not inexorable?'

The old man passed his hand across his forehead as if to dispel a cloud.

'Before answering you,' said he, 'I beg your pardon. I have done wrong, monsieur; you are in my house, you are my guest. I owe you courtesy. You are discussing my ideas; it is fitting that I confine myself to combating your reasoning. Your riches and your enjoyments are advantages that I have over you in the debate, but it is not in good taste to avail myself of them. I promise you to use them no more.'

'I thank you,' said the bishop.

G— went on:

'Let us get back to the explanation that you asked of me. Where were we? What were you saying to me? that '93 was inexorable?'

'Inexorable, yes,' said the bishop. 'What do you think of Marat clapping his hands at the guillotine?'

'What do you think of Bossuet chanting the Te Deum over the dragonnades?'[8]

The answer was severe, but it reached its aim with the keenness of a dagger. The bishop was staggered, no reply presented itself; but it shocked him to hear Bossuet spoken of in that manner. The best men have their fetishes, and sometimes they feel almost crushed at the little respect that logic shows them.

The conventionist began to gasp; the agonising asthma which mingles with the latest breath, made his voice broken: nevertheless, his soul yet appeared perfectly lucid in his eyes. He continued:

'Let us have a few more words here and there – I would like it. Outside of the revolution which, taken as a whole, is an immense human affirmation, '93, alas! is a reply. You think it inexorable, but the whole monarchy, monsieur? Carrier is a bandit; but what name do you give to Montrevel? Fouquier-Tainville is a wretch; but what is your opinion of Lamoignon Bâville? Maillard is frightful, but Saulx Tavannes, if you please? Le père Duchêne is ferocious, but what epithet will you furnish me for Le père Letellier? Jourdan-Coupe-Tête is a monster, but less than the Marquis of Louvois. Monsieur, monsieur, I lament Marie Antoinette, archduchess and queen, but I lament also that poor Huguenot woman who, in 1685, under Louis le Grand, monsieur, while nursing her child, was stripped to the waist and tied to a post, while her child was held before her; her breast swelled with milk, and her heart with anguish; the little one, weak and famished, seeing the breast, cried with agony; and the executioner said to the woman, to the nursing mother, "Recant!" giving her the choice between the death of her child and the death of her conscience. What say you to this Tantalus torture adapted to a mother? Monsieur, forget not this; the French revolution had its reasons. Its wrath will be pardoned by the future; its result is a better world. From its most terrible blows comes a caress for the human race. I must be brief. I must stop. I have too good a cause; and I am dying.'

And, ceasing to look at the bishop, the old man completed his idea in these few tranquil words:

'Yes, the brutalities of progress are called revolutions. When they are over, this is recognised: that the human race has been harshly treated, but that it has advanced.'

The conventionist thought that he had borne down successively one after the other all the interior entrenchments of the bishop. There was one left, however, and from this, the last resource of Monseigneur Bienvenu's resistance, came forth these words, in which nearly all the rudeness of the exordium reappeared.

'Progress ought to believe in God. The good cannot have an impious servitor. An atheist is an evil leader of the human race.'

The old representative of the people did not answer. He was trembling. He looked up into the sky, and a tear gathered slowly in his eye. When the lid was full, the tear rolled down his livid cheek, and he said, almost stammering, low, and talking to himself, his eye lost in the depths:

'O thou! O ideal! thou alone dost exist!'

The bishop felt a kind of inexpressible emotion.

After brief silence, the old man raised his finger towards heaven, and said:

'The infinite exists. It is there. If the infinite had no *me*, the *me* would be its limit; it would not be the infinite; in other words, it would not be. But it is. Then it has a *me*. This *me* of the infinite is God.'

The dying man pronounced these last words in a loud voice, and with a shudder of ecstasy, as if he saw someone. When he ceased, his eyes closed. The effort had exhausted him. It was evident that he had lived through in one minute the few hours that remained to him. What he had said had brought him near to him who is in death. The last moment was at hand.

The bishop perceived it, time was pressing. He had come as a priest; from extreme coldness he had passed by degrees to extreme emotion; he looked upon those closed eyes, he took that old, wrinkled, and icy hand, and drew closer to the dying man.

'This hour is the hour of God. Do you not think it would be a source of regret, if we should have met in vain?'

The conventionist reopened his eyes. Calmness was imprinted upon his face, where there had been a cloud.

'Monsieur Bishop,' said he, with a deliberation which perhaps came still more from the dignity of his soul than from the ebb of his strength, 'I have passed my life in meditation, study, and contemplation. I was sixty years old when my country called me, and ordered me to take part in her affairs. I obeyed. There were abuses, I fought them; there were tyrannies, I destroyed them; there were rights and principles, I proclaimed and confessed them. The soil was invaded, I defended it; France was threatened, I offered her my breast. I was not rich; I am poor. I was one of the masters of the state, the vaults of the bank were piled with specie, so that we had to strengthen the walls or they would have fallen under the weight of gold and of silver; I dined in the Rue de l'Arbre-Sec at twenty-two sous for the meal. I succoured the oppressed, I solaced the suffering. True, I tore the drapery from the altar; but it was to staunch the wounds of the country. I have always supported the forward march of the human race towards the light, and I have sometimes resisted a progress which was without pity. I have, on occasion, protected my own adversaries, your friends. There is at Peteghem in Flanders, at the very place where the Merovingian kings had their summer palace, a monastery of Urbanists, the Abbey of Sainte Claire in Beaulieu, which I saved in 1793; I have done my duty according to my strength, and the good that I could. After which I was hunted, hounded, pursued, persecuted, slandered, railed at, spat upon, cursed, proscribed. For many years now, with my white hairs, I have perceived that many people believed they had a right to despise me; to the poor, ignorant crowd I have the face of the damned, and I accept, hating no man myself, the isolation of hatred. Now I am eighty-six years old; I am about to die. What have you come to ask of me?'

'Your benediction,' said the bishop. And he fell upon his knees.

When the bishop raised his head, the face of the old man had become august. He had expired.

The bishop went home deeply absorbed in thought. He spent the whole night in prayer. The next day, some persons, emboldened by curiosity, tried to talk with him of the conventionist G—; he merely pointed to Heaven.

From that moment he redoubled his tenderness and brotherly love for the weak and the suffering.

Every allusion to 'that old scoundrel G—', threw him into a strange reverie. No one could say that the passage of that soul before his own, and the reflex of that grand conscience upon his own had not had its effect upon his approach to perfection.

This 'pastoral visit' was of course an occasion for criticism by the little local coteries of the place.

'Was the bedside of such a man as that the place for a bishop? Of course he could expect no conversion there. All these revolutionists are backsliders. Then why go there? What had he been there to see? He must have been very curious to see a soul carried away by the devil.'

One day a dowager, of that impertinent variety who think themselves witty, addressed this sally to him. 'Monseigneur, people ask when your Grandeur will have the red bonnet.' 'Oh! ho! that is a high colour,' replied the bishop. 'Luckily those who despise it in a bonnet, venerate it in a hat.'

11. *A qualification*

WE SHOULD BE very much deceived if we supposed from this that Monseigneur Bienvenu was 'a philosopher bishop', or 'a patriot curé'. His meeting, which we might almost call his communion with the conventionist G—, left him in a state of astonishment which rendered him still more charitable; that was all.

Although Monseigneur Bienvenu was anything but a politician, we ought here perhaps to point out very briefly his position in relation to the events of the day, if we may suppose that Monseigneur Bienvenu ever thought of having a position.

For this we must go back a few years.

Sometime after the elevation of M. Myriel to the episcopacy, the emperor made him a baron of the empire, at the same time with several other bishops. The arrest of the pope took place, as we know, on the night of the 5th of July 1809, on that occasion, M. Myriel was called by Napoleon to the synod of the bishops of France and Italy, convoked at Paris. This synod was held at Notre Dame, and commenced its sessions on the 15th of June 1811, under the presidency of Cardinal Fesch. M. Myriel was one of the ninety-five bishops who were present. But he attended only one sitting, and three or four private conferences. Bishop of a mountain diocese, living so near to nature, in rusticity and privation, he seemed to bring among these eminent personages ideas that changed the temperature of the synod. He returned very soon to D—. When asked about this sudden return, he answered: '*I annoyed them. The free air went in with me. I had the effect of an open door.*'

Another time, he said: '*What would you have? Those prelates are princes. I am only a poor peasant bishop.*'

The fact is, that he was disliked. Among other strange things, he had dropped the remark one evening when he happened to be at the house of one of his colleagues of the highest rank: 'What fine clocks! fine carpets! fine liveries! This must be very uncomfortable. Oh! how unwilling I should be to have all these superfluities crying for ever in my ears: "There are people who hunger! there are people who are cold! there are poor! there are poor!"'

We must say, by the way, that the hatred of luxury is not an intelligent hatred. It implies a hatred of the arts. Nevertheless, among churchmen, beyond their rites and ceremonies, luxury is a crime. It seems to disclose habits which are not truly charitable. A wealthy priest is a contradiction. He ought to keep himself near the poor. But, who can be in contact continually, by night as well as day, with all distresses, all misfortunes, all privations, without taking upon himself a little of that holy poverty, like the dust of a journey? Can you imagine a man near a fire, who does not feel warm? Can you imagine a labourer working constantly at a furnace, who has not a hair burned, nor a nail blackened, nor a drop of sweat, nor a speck of ashes on his face? The first proof of charity in a priest, and especially a bishop, is poverty.

That is doubtless the view which the Bishop of D— took of it.

It must not be thought, however, that he took part in the delicate matters which would be called 'the ideas of the age'. He had little to do with the theological quarrels of the moment, and kept his peace on questions where the church and the state were compromised; but if he had been pressed, he would have been found rather Ultramontane than Gallican. As we are drawing a portrait, and can make no concealment, we are compelled to add that he was very cool towards Napoleon in the decline of his power. After 1813, he acquiesced in, or applauded all the hostile manifestations. He refused to see him as he passed on his return from the island of Elba, and declined to order in his diocese public prayers for the emperor during the Hundred Days.

Besides his sister, Mademoiselle Baptistine, he had two brothers; one, a general, the other, a prefect. He wrote occasionally to both. He felt a coolness towards the first, because, being in a command in Provence, at the time of the landing at Cannes, the general placed himself at the head of twelve hundred men, and pursued the emperor as if he wished to let him escape. His correspondence was more affectionate with the other brother, the ex-prefect, a brave and worthy man, who lived in retirement at Paris, in the Rue Cassette.

Even Monseigneur Bienvenu then had his hour of party spirit, his hour of bitterness, his clouds. The shadow of the passions of the moment passed over this great and gentle spirit in its occupation with eternal things. Certainly, such a man deserved to escape political opinions. Let no one misunderstand our idea; we do not confound what are called 'political opinions' with that grand aspiration after progress, with that sublime patriotic, democratic, and human faith, which, in our days, should be the very foundation of all generous intelligence. Without entering into questions which have only an indirect bearing upon the subject of this book, we simply say: it would have been well if Monseigneur Bienvenu had not been a royalist, and if his eyes had never been turned for a single instant from that serene contemplation where, steadily shining, above the fictions and the hatreds of this world, above the stormy ebb and flow of human affairs, are seen those three pure luminaries, Truth, Justice, and Charity.

Although we hold that it was not for a political function that God created Monseigneur Bienvenu, we could have understood and admired a protest in the name of right and liberty, a fierce opposition, a perilous and just resistance to Napoleon when he was all-powerful. But what is pleasing to us towards those who are rising, is less pleasing towards those who are falling. We do not admire the combat when there is no danger; and in any case, the combatants of the first hour have alone the right to be the exterminators in the last. He who has not been a determined accuser during prosperity, ought to hold his peace in the presence of adversity. He only who denounces the success at one time had a right to proclaim the justice of the downfall. As for ourselves, when providence intervened and struck the blow, we took no part; 1812 began to disarm us. In 1813, the cowardly breach of silence on the part of that taciturn Corps Legislatif, emboldened by catastrophe, was worthy only of indignation, and it was base to applaud it; in 1814, from those traitorous marshals, from that senate passing from one baseness to another, insulting where they had deified, from that idolatry recoiling and spitting upon its idol, it was a duty to turn away in disgust; in 1815, when the air was filled with the final disasters, when France felt the thrill of their sinister approach, when Waterloo could already be dimly perceived opening before Napoleon, the sorrowful acclamations of the army and of the people to the condemned of destiny, were no subjects for laughter; and making every reservation as to the despot, a heart like that of the Bishop of D— ought not perhaps to have refused to see what was august and touching, on the brink of the abyss, in the last embrace of a great nation and a great man.

To conclude: he was always and in everything just, true, equitable, intelligent, humble, and worthy, beneficent, and benevolent, which is another beneficence. He was a priest, a sage, and a man. We must say even that in those political opinions which we have been criticising, and which we are disposed to judge almost severely, he was tolerant and yielding, perhaps more than we, who now speak. The doorkeeper of the City Hall had been placed there by the emperor. He was an old subaltern officer of the Old Guard, a legionary of Austerlitz, and as staunch a Bonapartist as the eagle. This poor fellow sometimes thoughtlessly allowed words to escape him which the law at that time defined as *seditious matters*. Since the profile of the emperor had disappeared from the Legion of Honour, he had never worn his badge, as he said, that he might not be compelled to bear his cross. In his devotion he had himself removed the imperial effigy from the cross that Napoleon had given him; it left a hole, and he would put nothing in its place. '*Better die*,' said he, '*than wear the three toads over my heart.*' He was always railing loudly at Louis XVIII.[9] '*Old gouty-foot with his English spatterdashes!*' he would say, '*let him go to Prussia with his goat's-beard*,' happy to unite in the same imprecation the two things that he most detested, Prussia and England. He said so much that he lost his place. There he was without bread, and in the street with his wife and children. The bishop sent for him, scolded him a little, and made him doorkeeper in the cathedral.

In nine years, by dint of holy works and gentle manners, Monseigneur Bienvenu had filled the City of D— with a kind of tender and filial veneration. Even his conduct towards Napoleon had been accepted and pardoned in silence by the people, a good, weak flock, who adored their emperor, but who loved their bishop.

12. *Solitude of Monseigneur Bienvenu*

THERE IS ALMOST ALWAYS a squad of young abbés about a bishop as there is a flock of young officers about a general. They are what the charming St Francis de Sales somewhere calls 'white-billed priests'. Every profession has its aspirants who make up the cortège of those who are at the summit. No power is without its worshippers, no fortune without its court. The seekers of the future revolve about the splendid present. Every capital, like every general, has its staff. Every bishop of influence has his patrol of undergraduates, cherubs who go the rounds and keep order in the episcopal palace, and who mount guard over monseigneur's smile. To please a bishop is a foot in the stirrup for a sub-deacon. One must make his own way; the apostolate never disdains the canonicate.

And as there are elsewhere rich coronets so there are in the church rich mitres. There are bishops who stand well at court, rich, well endowed, adroit, accepted of the world, knowing how to pray, doubtless, but knowing also how to ask favours; making themselves without scruple the viaduct of advancement for a whole diocese; bonds of union between the sacristy and diplomacy; rather abbés than priests, prelates rather than bishops. Lucky are they who can get near them. Men of influence as they are, they rain about them, upon their families and favourites, and upon all of these young men who please them, fat parishes, livings, archdeaconates, almonries, and cathedral functions – steps towards episcopal dignities. In advancing themselves they advance their satellites; it is a whole solar system in motion. The rays of their glory empurple their suite. Their prosperity scatters its crumbs to those who are behind the scenes, in the shape of nice little promotions. The larger the diocese of the patron, the larger the curacy for the favourite. And then there is Rome. A bishop who can become an archbishop, an archbishop who can become a cardinal, leads you to the conclave; you enter into the rota, you have the pallium, you are auditor, you are chamberlain, you are monseigneur, and from grandeur to eminence there is only a step, and between eminence and holiness there is nothing but the whiff of a ballot. Every cowl may dream of the tiara. The priest is, in our days, the only man who can regularly become a king; and what a king! the supreme king. So, what a nursery of aspirations is a seminary. How many blushing chorus boys, how many young abbés, have the ambitious dairymaid's pail of milk on their heads! Who knows how easily ambition disguises itself under the name of a calling, possibly in good faith, and deceiving itself, saint that it is!

Monseigneur Bienvenu, an humble, poor, private person, was not counted among the rich mitres. This was plain from the entire absence of young priests about him. We have seen that at Paris 'he did not take'. No glorious future dreamed of alighting upon this solitary old man. No young ambition was foolish enough to ripen in his shadow. His canons and his grand-vicars were good old men, rather common like himself, and like him immured in that diocese, from which there was no road to promotion, and they resembled their bishop, with this difference, that they were finished, and he was perfected. The impossibility of getting on under Monseigneur Bienvenu was so plain, that as soon as they were out of the seminary, the young men ordained by him procured recommendations to the Archbishop of Aix or of Auch, and went immediately to present them. For, we repeat, men like advancement. A saint who is addicted to abnegation is a dangerous neighbour; he is very likely to communicate to you by contagion an incurable poverty, an anchylosis of the articulations necessary to advancement, and, in fact, more renunciation than you would like; and men flee from this contagious virtue. Hence the isolation of Monseigneur Bienvenu. We live in a sad society. Succeed; that is the advice which falls drop by drop, from the overhanging corruption.

We may say, by the way, that success is a hideous thing. Its counterfeit of merit deceives men. To the mass, success has almost the same appearance as supremacy. Success, that pretender to talent, has a dupe – history. Juvenal and Tacitus only reject it. In our days, a philosophy which is almost an official has entered into its service, wears its livery, and waits in its antechamber. Success; that is the theory. Prosperity supposes capacity. Win in the lottery, and you are an able man. The victor is venerated. To be born with a caul is everything. Have but luck, and you will have the rest; be fortunate, and you will be thought great. Beyond the five or six great exceptions, which are the wonder of their age, contemporary admiration is nothing but shortsightedness. Gilt is gold. To be a chance comer is no drawback, provided you have improved your chances. The common herd is an old Narcissus, who adores himself, and who applauds the common. That mighty genius, by which one becomes a Moses, an Æschylus, a Dante, a Michaelangelo, or a Napoleon, the multitude assigns at once and by acclamation to whoever succeeds in his object, whatever it may be. Let a notary rise to be a deputy; let a sham Corneille write *Tiridate*; let a eunuch come into the possession of a harem; let a military Prudhomme accidentally win the decisive battle of an epoch; let an apothecary invent pasteboard soles for army shoes, and lay up, by selling this pasteboard instead of leather for the army of the Sambre-et-Meuse, four hundred thousand livres in the funds; let a pack-pedlar espouse usury and bring her to bed of seven or eight millions, of which he is the father and she the mother; let a preacher become a bishop by talking through his nose; let the steward of a good house become so rich on leaving service that he is made Minister of Finance; – men call that Genius, just as they call the face of Mousqueton, Beauty, and the bearing of Claude, Majesty.[10] They confound the radiance of the stars of heaven with the radiations which a duck's foot leaves in the mud.

13. *What he believed*

WE NEED NOT examine the Bishop of D— from an orthodox point of view. Before such a soul, we feel only in the humour of respect. The conscience of an upright man should be taken for granted. Moreover, given certain natures, and we admit the possible development of all the beauties of human virtues in a faith different from our own.

What he thought of this dogma or that mystery, are secrets of the interior faith known only in the tomb where souls enter stripped of all externals. But we are sure that religious difficulties never resulted with him in hypocrisy. No corruption is possible with the diamond. He believed as much as he could. *Credo in Patrem*, he often exclaimed; and, besides, he derived from his good deeds that measure of satisfaction which meets the demands of conscience, and which says in a low voice, 'thou art with God'.

We think it our duty to notice that, outside of and, so to say, beyond his faith, the bishop had an excess of love. It is on that account, *quia multum amavit*, that he was deemed vulnerable by 'serious men', 'sober persons', and 'reasonable people'; favourite phrases in our sad world, where egotism receives its keynote from pedantry. What was this excess of love? It was a serene benevolence, overflowing men, as we have already indicated, and, on occasion, extending to inanimate things. He lived without disdain. He was indulgent to God's creation. Every man, even the best, has some inconsiderate severity which he holds in reserve for animals. The Bishop of D— had none of this severity peculiar to most priests. He did not go as far as the Brahmin, but he appeared to have pondered over these words of Ecclesiastes: 'who knows whither goeth the spirit of the beast?' Ugliness of aspect, monstrosities of instinct, did not trouble or irritate him. He was moved and afflicted by it. He seemed to be thoughtfully seeking, beyond the apparent life, for its cause, its explanation, or its excuse. He seemed at times to ask changes of God. He examined without passion, and with the eye of a linguist decyphering a palimpsest, the portion of chaos which there is yet in nature. These reveries sometimes drew from him strange words. One morning, he was in his garden, and thought himself alone; but his sister was walking behind him; all at once he stopped and looked at something on the ground: it was a large, black, hairy, horrible spider. His sister heard him say: 'Poor thing! it is not his fault.'

Why not relate this almost divine childlikeness of goodness? Puerilities, perhaps, but these sublime puerilities were those of St Francis of Assisi and of Marcus Aurelius. One day he received a sprain rather than crush an ant.

So lived this upright man. Sometimes he went to sleep in his garden, and then there was nothing more venerable.

Monseigneur Bienvenu had been formerly, according to the accounts of his youth and even of his early manhood, a passionate, perhaps a violent, man. His universal tenderness was less an instinct of nature than the result of a strong conviction filtered through life into his heart, slowly dropping in upon him, thought by thought; for a character, as well as a rock, may be worn into by drops of water. Such marks are ineffaceable; such formations are indestructible.

In 1815, we think we have already said, he attained his seventy-sixth year, but he did not appear to be more than sixty. He was not tall; he was somewhat fleshy, and frequently took long walks that he might not become more so; he had a firm step, and was but little bowed; a circumstance from which we do not claim to draw any conclusion. Gregory XVI, at eighty years, was erect and smiling, which did not prevent him from being a bad bishop. Monseigneur Bienvenu had what people call 'a fine head', but so benevolent that you forgot that it was fine.

When he talked with that infantile gaiety that was one of his graces, and of which we have already spoken, all felt at ease in his presence, and from his whole person joy seemed to radiate. His ruddy and fresh complexion, and his white teeth, all of which were well preserved, and which he showed when he laughed, gave him that open and easy air which makes us say of a man: he is a good fellow; and of an old man: he is a good man. This was, we remember, the effect he produced on Napoleon. At the first view, and to one who saw him for the first time, he was nothing more than a good man. But if one spent a few hours with him, and saw him in a thoughtful mood, little by little the goodman became transfigured, and became ineffably imposing; his large and serious forehead, rendered noble by his white hair, became noble also by meditation; majesty was developed from this goodness, yet the radiance of goodness remained; and one felt something of the emotion that he would experience in seeing a smiling angel slowly spread his wings without ceasing to smile. Respect, unutterable respect, penetrated you by degrees, and made its way to your heart; and you felt that you had before you one of those strong, tried, and indulgent souls, where the thought is so great that it cannot be other than gentle.

As we have seen, prayer, celebration of the religious offices, alms, consoling the afflicted, the cultivation of a little piece of ground, fraternity, frugality, self-sacrifice, confidence, study, and work, filled up each day of his life. Filled up is exactly the word; and in fact, the Bishop's day was full to the brim with good thoughts, good words, and good actions. Nevertheless it was not complete if cold or rainy weather prevented his passing an hour or two in the evening, when the two women had retired, in his garden before going to sleep. It seemed as if it were a sort of rite with him, to prepare himself for sleep by meditating in presence of the great spectacle of the starry firmament. Sometimes at a late hour of the night, if the two women were awake, they would hear him slowly promenading the walks. He was there alone with himself, collected, tranquil, adoring, comparing the serenity of his heart with the serenity of the skies, moved in the darkness by the visible splendours of the constellations, and the invisible splendour of God, opening his soul to the thoughts which fall from the Unknown. In such moments, offering up his heart at the hour when the flowers of night inhale their perfume, lighted like a lamp in the centre of the starry night, expanding his soul in ecstasy in the midst of the universal radiance of creation, he could not himself perhaps have told what was passing in his own mind; he felt something depart from him, and something descend upon him; mysterious interchanges of the depths of the soul with the depths of the universe.

He contemplated the grandeur, and the presence of God; the eternity of the future, strange mystery; the eternity of the past, mystery yet more strange; all the infinities deep-hidden in every direction about him; and, without essaying to comprehend God; he was dazzled by the thought. He reflected upon these magnificent unions of atoms which give visible forms to Nature, revealing forces in establishing them, creating individualities in unity, proportions in extension, the innumerable in the infinite, and through light producing beauty. These unions are forming and dissolving continually; thence life and death.

He would sit upon a wooden bench leaning against a broken trellis, and look at the stars through the irregular outlines of his fruit trees. This quarter of an acre of ground, so poorly cultivated, so cumbered with shed and ruins, was dear to him, and satisfied him.

What was more needed by this old man who divided the leisure hours of his life, where he had so little leisure, between gardening in the day time, and contemplation at night? Was not this narrow enclosure, with the sky for a background, enough to enable him to adore God in his most beautiful as well as in his most sublime works? Indeed, is not that all, and what more can be desired? A little garden to walk, and immensity to reflect upon. At his feet something to cultivate and gather; above his head something to study and meditate upon; a few flowers on the earth, and all the stars in the sky.

14. *What he thought*

A FINAL word.

As these details may, particularly in the times in which we live, and to use an expression now in fashion, give the Bishop of D— a certain 'pantheistic' physiognomy, and give rise to the belief, whether to his blame or to his praise, that he had one of those personal philosophies peculiar to our age, which sometimes spring up in solitary minds, and gather materials and grow until they replace religion, we insist upon it that no one who knew Monseigneur Bienvenu would have felt justified in any such idea. What enlightened this man was the heart. His wisdom was formed from the light that came thence.

He had no systems; but many deeds. Abstruse speculations are full of headaches; nothing indicates that he would risk his mind in mysticisms. The apostle may be bold, but the bishop should be timid. He would probably have scrupled to sound too deeply certain problems, reserved in some sort for great and terrible minds. There is a sacred horror in the approaches to mysticism; sombre openings are yawning there, but something tells you, as you near the brink – enter not. Woe to him who does!

There are geniuses who, in the fathomless depths of abstraction and pure speculation – situated, so to say, above all dogmas, present their ideas to God. Their prayer audaciously offers a discussion. Their worship is questioning. This is direct religion, full of anxiety and of responsibility for him who would scale its walls.

Human thought has no limit. At its risk and peril, it analyses and dissects its own fascination. We could almost say that, by a sort of splendid reaction, it fascinates nature; the mysterious world which surrounds us returns what it receives; it is probable that the contemplators are contemplated. However that may be, there are men on the earth – if they are nothing more – who distinctly perceive the heights of the absolute in the horizon of their contemplation, and who have the terrible vision of the infinite mountain. Monseigneur Bienvenu was not one of those men: Monseigneur Bienvenu was not a genius. He would have dreaded those sublimities from which some very great men even like Swedenborg and Pascal, have glided into insanity. Certainly, these tremendous reveries have their moral use; and by these arduous routes there is an approach to ideal perfection. But for his part, he took the straight road, which is short – the Gospel.

He did not attempt to make his robe assume the folds of Elijah's mantle; he cast no ray of the future upon the dark scroll of events; he sought not to condense into a flame the glimmer of things; he had nothing of the prophet and nothing of the magician. His humble soul loved; that was all.

That he raised his prayer to a superhuman aspiration, is probable; but one can no more pray too much than love too much; and, if it was a heresy to pray beyond the written form, St Theresa and St Jerome were heretics.

He inclined towards the distressed and the repentant. The universe appeared to him like a vast disease; he perceived fever everywhere, he auscultated suffering everywhere, and, without essaying to solve the enigma, he endeavoured to staunch the wound. The formidable spectacle of created things developed a tenderness in him; he was always busy in finding for himself, and inspiring others with the best way of sympathising and solacing; the whole world was to this good and rare priest a permanent subject of sadness seeking to be consoled.

There are men who labour for the extraction of gold; he worked for the extraction of pity. The misery of the universe was his mine. Grief everywhere was only an occasion for good always. *Love one another;* he declared that to be complete; he desired nothing more, and it was his whole doctrine. One day, this man, who counted himself 'a philosopher', this senator before mentioned, said to the bishop: 'See now, what the world shows; each fighting against all others; the strongest man is the best man. Your *love one another* is a stupidity.' '*Well,*' replied Monseigneur Bienvenu, without discussion, '*if it be a stupidity, the soul ought to shut itself up in it, like the pearl in the oyster.*' And he shut himself up in it, he lived in it, he was satisfied absolutely with it, laying aside the mysterious questions which attract and which dishearten, the unfathomable depths of abstraction, the precipices of metaphysics – all those profundities, to the apostle converging upon God, to the atheist upon annihilation; destiny, good and evil, the war of being against being, the conscience of man, the thought-like dreams of the animal, the transformation of death, the recapitulation of existences contained in the tomb, the incomprehensible engrafting of successive affections upon the enduring *me*, the essence, the substance, the Nothing, and the Something, the soul, nature, liberty, necessity; difficult problems, sinister depths, towards which are drawn the gigantic archangels of the human race; fearful abyss, that Lucretius, Manou, St Paul, and Dante contemplate with that flaming eye which seems, looking steadfastly into the infinite, to enkindle the very stars.

Monseigneur Bienvenu was simply a man who accepted these mysterious questions without examining them, without agitating them, and without troubling his own mind with them; and who had in his soul a deep respect for the mystery which enveloped them.

BOOK 2: THE FALL

1. *The night of a day's tramp*

AN HOUR BEFORE SUNSET, on the evening of a day in the beginning of October 1815, a man travelling afoot entered the little town of D—. The few persons who at this time were at their windows or their doors, regarded this traveller with a sort of distrust. It would have been hard to find a passer-by more wretched in appearance. He was a man of middle height, stout and hardy, in the strength of maturity; he might have been forty-six or seven. A slouched leather cap half hid his face, bronzed by the sun and wind, and dripping with sweat. His shaggy breast was seen through the coarse yellow shirt which at the neck was fastened by a small silver anchor; he wore a cravat twisted like a rope; coarse blue trousers, worn and shabby, white on one knee, and with holes in the other; an old ragged grey blouse, patched on one side with a piece of green cloth sewed with twine: upon his back was a well-filled knapsack, strongly buckled and quite new. In his hand he carried an enormous knotted stick: his stockingless feet were in hobnailed shoes; his hair was cropped and his beard long.

The sweat, the heat, his long walk, and the dust, added an indescribable meanness to his tattered appearance.

His hair was shorn, but bristly, for it had begun to grow a little, and seemingly had not been cut for some time. Nobody knew him; he was evidently a traveller. Whence had he come? From the south – perhaps from the sea; for he was making his entrance into D— by the same road by which, seven months before, the Emperor Napoleon went from Cannes to Paris. This man must have walked all day long; for he appeared very weary. Some women of the old city which is at the lower part of the town, had seen him stop under the trees of the boulevard Gassendi, and drink at the fountain which is at the end of the promenade. He must have been very thirsty, for some children who followed him, saw him stop not two hundred steps further on and drink again at the fountain in the market-place.

When he reached the corner of the Rue Poichevert he turned to the left and went towards the mayor's office. He went in, and a quarter of an hour afterwards he came out.

The man raised his cap humbly and saluted a gendarme who was seated near the door, upon the stone bench which General Drouot mounted on the fourth of March, to read to the terrified inhabitants of D— the proclamation of the *Golfe Juan.*

Without returning his salutation, the gendarme looked at him attentively, watched him for some distance, and then went into the city hall.

There was then in D—, a good inn called *La Croix de Colbas;* its host was named Jacquin Labarre, a man held in some consideration in the town on account of his relationship with another Labarre, who kept an inn at Grenoble called *Trois Dauphins,* and who had served in the Guides. At the time of the landing of the emperor there had been much noise in the country about this inn of the *Trois Dauphins.* It was said that General Bertrand, disguised as a wagoner, had made frequent journeys thither in the month of January, and that he had distributed crosses of honour to the soldiers, and handfuls of Napoleons to the country-folks. The truth is, that the emperor when he entered Grenoble, refused to take up his quarters at the prefecture, saying to the monsieur, after thanking him, '*I am going to the house of a brave man, with whom I am acquainted,*' and he went to the *Trois Dauphins.* This glory of Labarre of the *Trois Dauphins* was reflected twenty-five miles to Labarre of the *Croix de Colbas.* It was a common saying in the town: '*He is the cousin of the Grenoble man!*'

The traveller turned his steps towards this inn, which was the best in the place, and went at once into the kitchen, which opened out of the street. All the ranges were fuming, and a great fire was burning briskly in the chimney-place. Mine host, who was at the same time head cook, was going from the fireplace to the sauce-pans, very busy superintending an excellent dinner for some wagoners who were laughing and talking noisily in the next room. Whoever has travelled knows that nobody lives better than wagoners. A fat marmot, flanked by white partridges and goose, was turning on a long spit before the fire; upon the ranges were cooking two large carps from Lake Lauzet, and a trout from Lake Alloz.

The host, hearing the door open, and a newcomer enter, said, without raising his eyes from his ranges:

'What will monsieur have?'

'Something to eat and lodging.'

'Nothing more easy,' said mine host, but on turning his head and taking an observation of the traveller, he added, 'for pay.'

The man drew from his pocket a large leather purse, and answered,

'I have money.'

'Then,' said mine host, 'I am at your service.'

The man put his purse back into his pocket, took off his knapsack and put it down hard by the door, and holding his stick in his hand, sat down on a low stool by the fire. D— being in the mountains, the evenings of October are cold there.

However, as the host passed backwards and forwards, he kept a careful eye on the traveller.

'Is dinner almost ready?' said the man.

'Directly,' said mine host.

While the newcomer was warming himself with his back turned, the worthy innkeeper, Jacquin Labarre, took a pencil from his pocket, and then tore off the corner of an old paper which he pulled from a little table near the window. On the margin he wrote a line or two, folded it, and handed the scrap of paper to a child, who appeared to serve him as lackey and scullion at the same time. The innkeeper whispered a word to the boy, and he ran off in the direction of the mayor's office.

The traveller saw nothing of this.

He asked a second time: 'Is dinner ready?'

'Yes; in a few moments,' said the host.

The boy came back with the paper. The host unfolded it hurriedly, as one who is expecting an answer. He seemed to read with attention, then throwing his head on one side, thought for a moment. Then he took a step towards the traveller, who seemed drowned in troublous thought.

'Monsieur,' said he, 'I cannot receive you.'

The traveller half rose from his seat.

'Why? Are you afraid I shall not pay you, or do you want me to pay in advance? I have money, I tell you.'

'It is not that.'

'What then?'

'You have money – '

'Yes,' said the man.

'And I,' said the host; 'I have no room.'

'Well, put me in the stable,' quietly replied the man.

'I cannot.'

'Why?'

'Because the horses take all the room.'

'Well,' responded the man, 'a corner in the garret; a truss of straw: we will see about that after dinner.'

'I cannot give you any dinner.'

This declaration, made in a measured but firm tone, appeared serious to the traveller. He got up.

'Ah, bah! but I am dying with hunger. I have walked since sunrise; I have travelled twelve leagues. I will pay, and I want something to eat.'

'I have nothing,' said the host.

The man burst into a laugh, and turned towards the fireplaace and the ranges.

'Nothing! and all that?'

'All that is engaged.'

'By whom?'

'By those persons, the wagoners.'

'How many are there of them?'

'Twelve.'

'There is enough there for twenty.'

'They have engaged and paid for it all in advance.'

The man sat down again and said, without raising his voice: 'I am at an inn. I am hungry, and I shall stay.'

The host bent down to his ear, and said in a voice which made him tremble: 'Go away!'

At these words the traveller, who was bent over, poking some embers in the fire with the iron-shod end of his stick, turned suddenly around, and opened his mouth, as if to reply, when the host, looking steadily at him, added in the same low tone: 'Stop, no more of that. Shall I tell you your name? your name is Jean Valjean, now shall I tell you *who* you are? When I saw you enter, I suspected something. I sent to the mayor's office, and here is the reply. Can you read?' So saying, he held towards him the open paper, which had just come from the mayor. The man cast a look upon it; the innkeeper, after a short silence, said: 'It is my custom to be polite to all: Go!'

The man bowed his head, picked up his knapsack, and went out.

He took the principal street; he walked at random, slinking near the houses like a sad and humiliated man: he did not once turn around. If he had turned, he would have seen the inn-keeper of the *Croix de Colbas*, standing in his doorway with all his guests, and the passers-by gathered about him, speaking excitedly, and pointing him out; and from the looks of fear and distrust which were exchanged, he would have guessed that before long his arrival would be the talk of the whole town.

He saw nothing of all this: people overwhelmed with trouble do not look behind; they know only too well that misfortune follows them.

He walked along in this way some time, going by chance down streets unknown to him, and forgetting fatigue, as is the case in sorrow. Suddenly he felt a pang of hunger; night was at hand, and he looked around to see if he could not discover a lodging.

The good inn was closed against him: he sought some humble tavern, some poor cellar.

Just then a light shone at the end of the street; he saw a pine branch, hanging by an iron bracket, against the white sky of the twilight. He went thither.

It was a tavern in the Rue Chaffaut.

The traveller stopped a moment and looked in at the little window upon the low hall of the tavern, lighted by a small lamp upon a table, and a great fire in the chimney-place. Some men were drinking, and the host was warming himself; an iron pot hung over the fire seething in the blaze.

Two doors lead into this tavern, which is also a sort of eating-house – one from the street, the other from a small court full of rubbish.

The traveller did not dare to enter by the street door; he slipped into the court, stopped again, then timidly raised the latch, and pushed open the door.

'Who is it?' said the host.

'One who wants supper and a bed.'

'All right: here you can sup and sleep.'

He went in, all the men who were drinking turned towards him; the lamp shining on one side of his face, the firelight on the other, they examined him for some time as he was taking off his knapsack.

The host said to him: 'There is the fire; the supper is cooking in the pot; come and warm yourself, comrade.'

He seated himself near the fireplace and stretched his feet out towards the fire, half dead with fatigue: an inviting odour came from the pot. All that could be seen of his face under his slouched cap assumed a vague appearance of comfort, which tempered the sorrowful aspect given him by long-continued suffering.

His profile was strong, energetic, and sad; a physiognomy strangely marked: at first it appeared humble, but it soon became severe. His eye shone beneath his eyebrows like a fire beneath a thicket.

However, one of the men at the table was a fisherman who had put up his horse at the stable of Labarre's inn before entering the tavern of the Rue de Chaffaut. It so happened that he had met, that same morning, this suspicious-looking stranger travelling between Bras d'Asse and – I forget the place, I think it is Escoublon. Now, on meeting him, the man, who seemed already very much fatigued, had asked him to take him on behind, to which the fisherman responded only by doubling his pace. The fisherman, half an hour before, had been one of the throng about Jacquin Labarre, and had himself related his unpleasant meeting with him to the people of the *Croix de Colbas*. He beckoned to the tavern-keeper to come to him, which he did. They exchanged a few words in a low voice; the traveller had again relapsed into thought.

The tavern-keeper returned to the fire, and laying his hand roughly on his shoulder, said harshly:

'You are going to clear out from here!'

The stranger turned round and said mildly,

'Ah! Do you know?'

'Yes.'

'They sent me away from the other inn.'

'And we turn you out of this.'

'Where would you have me go?'

'Somewhere else.'

The man took up his stick and knapsack, and went off. As he went out, some children who had followed him from the *Croix de Colbas*, and seemed to be waiting for him, threw stones at him. He turned angrily and threatened them with his stick, and they scattered like a flock of birds.

He passed the prison: an iron chain hung from the door attached to a bell. He rang.

The grating opened.

'Monsieur Turnkey,' said he, taking off his cap respectfully, 'will you open and let me stay here tonight?'

A voice answered:

'A prison is not a tavern: get yourself arrested and we will open.'

The grating closed.

He went into a small street where there are many gardens; some of them are enclosed only by hedges, which enliven the street. Among them he saw a pretty little one-storey house, where there was a light in the window. He looked in as he had done at the tavern. It was a large whitewashed room, with a bed draped with calico, and a cradle in the corner, some wooden chairs, and a double-barrelled gun hung against the wall. A table was set in the centre of the room; a brass lamp lighted the coarse white tablecloth; a tin mug full of wine shone like silver, and the brown soup-dish was smoking. At this table sat a man about forty years old, with a joyous, open countenance, who was trotting a little child upon his knee. Near by him a young woman was suckling another child; the father was laughing, the child was laughing, and the mother was smiling.

The traveller remained a moment contemplating this sweet and touching scene. What were his thoughts? He only could have told: probably he thought that this happy home would be hospitable, and that where he beheld so much happiness, he might perhaps find a little pity.

He rapped faintly on the window.

No one heard him.

He rapped a second time.

He heard the woman say, 'Husband, I think I hear someone rap.'

'No,' replied the husband.

He rapped a third time. The husband got up, took the lamp, and opened the door.

He was a tall man, half peasant, half mechanic. He wore a large leather apron that reached to his left shoulder, and formed a pocket containing a hammer, a red handkerchief, a powderhorn, and all sorts of things which the girdle held up. He turned his head; his shirt, wide and open, showed his bull-like throat, white and naked; he had thick brows, enormous black whiskers, and prominent eyes; the lower part of the face was covered, and had withal that air of being at home which is quite indescribable.

'Monsieur,' said the traveller, 'I beg your pardon; for pay can you give me a plate of soup and a corner of the shed in your garden to sleep in? Tell me; can you, for pay?'

'Who are you?' demanded the master of the house.

The man replied: 'I have come from Puy-Moisson; I have walked all day; I have come twelve leagues. Can you, if I pay?'

'I wouldn't refuse to lodge any proper person who would pay,' said the peasant; 'but why do you not go to the inn?'

'There is no room.'

'Bah! That is not possible. It is neither a fair nor a market-day. Have you been to Labarre's house?'

'Yes.'

'Well?'

The traveller replied hesitatingly: 'I don't know; he didn't take me.'

'Have you been to that place in the Rue Chaffaut?'

The embarrassment of the stranger increased; he stammered: 'They didn't take me either.'

The peasant's face assumed an expression of distrust: he looked over the newcomer from head to foot, and suddenly exclaimed, with a sort of shudder: 'Are you the man!'

He looked again at the stranger, stepped back, put the lamp on the table, and took down his gun.

His wife, on hearing the words, '*are you the man*', started up, and, clasping her two children, precipitately took refuge behind her husband; she looked at the stranger with affright, her neck bare, her eyes dilated, murmuring in a low tone: '*Tso maraude!*'*

All this happened in less time than it takes to read it; after examining the man for a moment, as one would a viper, the man advanced to the door and said:

'Get out!'

'For pity's sake, a glass of water,' said the man.

'A gun shot,' said the peasant, and then he closed the door violently, and the

---

*Patois of the French Alps: *Chat de maraude* – rascally marauder man heard two heavy bolts drawn. A moment afterwards the window-shutters were shut, and noisily barred.

Night came on apace; the cold Alpine winds were blowing; by the light of the expiring day the stranger perceived in one of the gardens which fronted the street a kind of hut which seemed to be made of turf; he boldly cleared a wooden fence and found himself in the garden. He neared the hut; its door was a narrow, low entrance; it resembled, in its construction, the shanties which the road-labourers put up for their temporary accommodation. He, doubtless, thought that it was, in fact, the lodging of a road-labourer. He was suffering both from cold and hunger. He had resigned himself to the latter; but there at least was a shelter from the cold. These huts are not usually occupied at night. He got down and crawled into the hut. It was warm there, and he found a good bed of straw. He rested a moment upon this bed motionless from fatigue; then, as his knapsack on his back troubled him, and it would make a good pillow, he began to unbuckle the straps. Just then he heard a ferocious growling, and looking up saw the head of an enormous bulldog at the opening of the hut.

It was a dog-kennel!

He was himself vigorous and formidable; seizing his stick, he made a shield of his knapsack, and got out of the hut as best he could, but not without enlarging the rents of his already tattered garments.

He made his way also out of the garden, but backwards; being obliged, out of respect to the dog, to have recourse to that kind of manoeuvre with his stick, which adepts in this sort of fencing call *la rose couverte*.

When he had, not without difficulty, got over the fence, he again found himself alone in the street without lodging, roof, or shelter, driven even from the straw-bed of that wretched dog-kennel. He threw himself rather than seated himself on a stone, and it appears that someone who was passing heard him exclaim, 'I am not even a dog!'

Then he arose, and began to tramp again, taking his way out of the town, hoping to find some tree or haystack beneath which he could shelter himself. He walked on for some time, his head bowed down. When he thought he was far away from all human habitation he raised his eyes, and looked about him inquiringly. He was in a field: before him was a low hillock covered with stubble, which after the harvest looks like a shaved head. The sky was very dark; it was not simply the darkness of night, but there were very low clouds, which seemed to rest upon the hills, and covered the whole heavens. A little of the twilight, however, lingered in the zenith; and as the moon was about to rise these clouds formed in mid-heaven a vault of whitish light, from which a glimmer fell upon the earth.

The earth was then lighter than the sky, which produces a peculiarly sinister effect, and the hill, poor and mean in contour, loomed out dim and pale upon the gloomy horizon: the whole prospect was hideous, mean, lugubrious, and insignificant. There was nothing in the field nor upon the hill, but one ugly tree, a few steps from the traveller, which seemed to be twisting and contorting itself.

This man was evidently far from possessing those delicate perceptions of intelligence and feeling which produce a sensitiveness to the mysterious aspects of nature; still, there was in the sky, in this hillock, plain, and tree, something so profoundly desolate, that after a moment of motionless contemplation, he turned back hastily to the road. There are moments when nature appears hostile.

He retraced his steps; the gates of D— were closed. D—, which sustained sieges in the religious wars, was still surrounded, in 1815, by old walls flanked by square towers, since demolished. He passed through a breach and entered the town.

It was about eight o'clock in the evening: as he did not know the streets, he walked at hazard.

So he came to the prefecture, then to the seminary; on passing by the Cathedral square, he shook his fist at the church.

At the corner of this square stands a printing-office; there were first printed the proclamations of the emperor, and the Imperial Guard to the army, brought from the island of Elba, and dictated by Napoleon himself.

Exhausted with fatigue, and hoping for nothing better, he lay down on a stone bench in front of this printing-office.

Just then an old woman came out of the church. She saw the man lying there in the dark, and said:

'What are you doing there, my friend?'

He replied harshly, and with anger in his tone:

'You see, my good woman, I am going to sleep.'

The good woman, who really merited the name, was Madame la Marquise de R—.

'Upon the bench?' said she.

'For nineteen years I have had a wooden mattress,' said the man; 'tonight I have a stone one.'

'You have been a soldier?'

'Yes, my good woman, a soldier.'

'Why don't you go to the inn?'

'Because I have no money.'

'Alas!' said Madame de R—, 'I have only four sous in my purse.'

'Give them then.' The man took the four sous, and Madame de R— continued:

'You cannot find lodging for so little in an inn. But have you tried? You cannot pass the night so. You must be cold and hungry. They should give you lodging for charity.'

'I have knocked at every door.'

'Well, what then?'

'Everybody has driven me away.'

The good woman touched the man's arm and pointed out to him, on the other side of the square, a little low house beside the bishop's palace.

'You have knocked at every door?' she asked.

'Yes.'

'Have you knocked at that one there?'

'No.'

'Knock there.'

2. *Prudence commended to wisdom*

THAT EVENING, after his walk in the town, the Bishop of D— remained quite late in his room. He was busy with his great work on Duty, which unfortunately is left incomplete. He carefully dissected all that the Fathers and Doctors have said on this serious topic. His book was divided into two parts: First, the duties of all: Secondly, the duties of each, according to his position in life. The duties of all are the principal duties; there are four of them, as set forth by St Matthew: duty towards God (Matt. vi.); duty towards ourselves (Matt. v. 29, 30); duty towards our neighbour (Matt. vii. 12); and duty towards animals (Matt. vi. 20, 25). As to other duties the bishop found them defined and prescribed elsewhere; those of sovereigns and subjects in the Epistle to the Romans: those of magistrates, wives, mothers, and young men, by St Peter; those of husbands, fathers, children, and servants, in the Epistle to the Ephesians; those of the faithful in the Epistle to the Hebrews; and those of virgins in the Epistle to the Corinthians. He collated with much labour these injunctions into a harmonious whole, which he wished to offer to souls.

At eight o'clock he was still at work, writing with some inconvenience on little slips of paper, with a large book open on his knees, when Madame Magloire, as usual, came in to take the silver from the panel near the bed. A moment after, the bishop, knowing that the table was laid, and that his sister was perhaps waiting, closed his book and went into the dining-room.

This dining-room was an oblong apartment, with a fireplace, and with a door upon the street, as we have said, and a window opening into the garden.

Madame Magloire had just finished placing the plates.

While she was arranging the table, she was talking with Mademoiselle Baptistine.

The lamp was on the table, which was near the fireplace, where a good fire was burning.

One can readily fancy these two women, both past their sixtieth year: Madame Magloire, small, fat, and quick in her movements; Mademoiselle Baptistine, sweet, thin, fragile, a little taller than her brother, wore a silk puce colour dress, in the style of 1806, which she had bought at that time in Paris, and which still lasted her. To borrow a common mode of expression, which has the merit of saying in a single word what a page would hardly express, Madame Magloire had the air of a peasant, and Mademoiselle Baptistine that of a lady. Madame Magloire wore a white funnel-shaped cap: a gold *jeannette* at her neck, the only bit of feminine jewellery in the house, a snowy fichu just peering out above a black frieze dress, with wide short sleeves, a green and red checked calico apron tied at the waist with a green ribbon, with a stomacher of the same pinned up in front; on her feet, she wore coarse shoes and yellow stockings like the women of Marseilles. Mademoiselle Baptistine's dress was cut after the fashion of 1806, short waist, narrow skirt, sleeves with epaulettes, and with flaps and buttons. Her grey hair was hid under a frizzed front called *à l'enfant*. Madame Magloire had an intelligent, clever, and lively air; the two corners of her mouth unequally raised, and the upper lip projecting beyond the under one, gave something morose and imperious to her expression. So long as monseigneur was silent, she talked to him without reserve, and with a mingled respect and freedom; but from the time that he opened his mouth as we have seen, she implicitly obeyed like mademoiselle. Mademoiselle Baptistine, however, did not speak. She confined herself to obeying, and endeavouring to please. Even when she was young, she was not pretty; she had large and very prominent blue eyes, and a long pinched nose, but her whole face and person, as we said in the outset, breathed an ineffable goodness. She had been fore-ordained to meekness, but faith, charity, hope, these three virtues which gently warm the heart, had gradually sublimated this meekness into sanctity. Nature had made her a lamb; religion had made her an angel. Poor, sainted woman! gentle, but lost souvenir.

Mademoiselle Baptistine has so often related what occurred at the bishop's house that evening, that many persons are still living who can recall the minutest details.

Just as the bishop entered, Madame Magloire was speaking with some warmth. She was talking to *Mademoiselle* upon a familiar subject, and one to which the bishop was quite accustomed. It was a discussion on the means of fastening the front door.

It seems that while Madame Magloire was out making provision for supper, she had heard the news in sundry places. There was talk that an ill-favoured runaway, a suspicious vagabond, had arrived and was lurking somewhere in the town, and that some unpleasant adventures might befall those who should come home late that night; besides, that the police was very bad, as the prefect and the mayor did not like one another, and were hoping to injure each other by untoward events; that it was the part of wise people to be their own police, and to protect their own persons; and that everyone ought to be careful to shut up, bolt, and bar his house properly, and *secure his door thoroughly*.

Madame Magloire dwelt upon these last words; but the bishop, having come from a cold room, seated himself before the fire and began to warm himself, and then, he was thinking of something else. He did not hear a word of what was let fall by Madame Magloire, and she repeated it. Then Mademoiselle Baptistine, endeavouring to satisfy Madame Magloire without displeasing her brother, ventured to say timidly:

'Brother, do you hear what Madame Magloire says?'

'I heard something of it indistinctly,' said the bishop. Then turning his chair half round, putting his hands on his knees, and raising towards the old servant his cordial and good-humoured face, which the firelight shone upon, he said: 'Well, well! what is the matter? Are we in any great danger?'

Then Madame Magloire began her story again, unconsciously exaggerating it a little. It appeared that a bare-footed gypsy man, a sort of dangerous beggar, was in the town. He had gone for lodging to Jacquin Labarre, who had refused to receive him; he had been seen to enter the town by the boulevard Gassendi, and to roam through the street at dusk. A man with a knapsack and a rope, and a terrible-looking face.

'Indeed!' said the bishop.

This readiness to question her encouraged Madame Magloire; it seemed to indicate that the bishop was really well-nigh alarmed. She continued triumphantly: 'Yes, monseigneur; it is true. There will something happen tonight in the town: everybody says so. The police is so badly organised (a convenient repetition). To live in this mountainous country, and not even to have street lamps! If one goes out, it is dark as a pocket. And I say, monseigneur, and mademoiselle says also – '

'Me?' interrupted the sister; 'I say nothing. Whatever my brother does is well done.'

Madame Magloire went on as if she had not heard this protestation:

'We say that this house is not safe at all; and if monseigneur will permit me, I will go and tell Paulin Musebois, the locksmith, to come and put the old bolts in the door again; they are there, and it will take but a minute. I say we must have bolts, were it only for tonight; for I say that a door which opens by a latch on the outside to the first comer, nothing could be more horrible: and then monseigneur has the habit of always saying "Come in," even at midnight. But, my goodness! there is no need even to ask leave – '

At this moment there was a violent knock on the door.

'Come in!' said the bishop.

3. *The heroism of passive obedience*

THE DOOR opened.

It opened quickly, quite wide, as if pushed by someone boldly and with energy.

A man entered.

That man, we know already; it was the traveller we have seen wandering about in search of a lodging.

He came in, took one step, and paused, leaving the door open behind him. He had his knapsack on his back, his stick in his hand, and a rough, hard, tired, and fierce look in his eyes, as seen by the firelight. He was hideous. It was an apparition of ill omen.

Madame Magloire had not even the strength to scream. She stood trembling with her mouth open.

Mademoiselle Baptistine turned, saw the man enter, and started up half alarmed; then, slowly turning back again towards the fire, she looked at her brother, and her face resumed its usual calmness and serenity.

The bishop looked upon the man with a tranquil eye.

As he was opening his mouth to speak, doubtless to ask the stranger what he wanted, the man, leaning with both hands on his club, glanced from one to another in turn, and without waiting for the bishop to speak, said in a loud voice:

'See here! My name is Jean Valjean. I am a convict; I have been nineteen years in the galleys. Four days ago I was set free, and started for Pontarlier, which is my destination; during those four days I have walked from Toulon. Today I have walked twelve leagues. When I reached this place this evening I went to an inn, and they sent me away on account of my yellow passport, which I had shown at the mayor's office, as was necessary. I went to another inn; they said: "Get out!" It was the same with one as with another; nobody would have me. I went to the prison, and the turnkey would not let me in. I crept into a dog-kennel, the dog bit me, and drove me away as if hc had been a man; you would have said that he knew who I was. I went into the fields to sleep beneath the stars: there were no stars; I thought it would rain, and there was no good God to stop the drops, so I came back to the town to get the shelter of some doorway.

There in the square I lay down upon a stone; a good woman showed me your house, and said: "Knock there!" I have knocked. What is this place? Are you an inn? I have money; my savings, one hundred and nine francs and fifteen sous which I have earned in the galleys by my work for nineteen years. I will pay. What do I care? I have money. I am very tired – twelve leagues on foot, and I am so hungry. Can I stay?'

'Madame Magloire,' said the bishop, 'put on another plate.'

The man took three steps, and came near the lamp which stood on the table. 'Stop,' he exclaimed; as if he had not been understood, 'not that, did you understand me? I am a galley-slave – a convict – I am just from the galleys.' He drew from his pocket a large sheet of yellow paper, which he unfolded. 'There is my passport, yellow as you see. That is enough to have me kicked out wherever I go. Will you read it? I know how to read, I do. I learned in the galleys. There is a school there for those who care for it. See, here is what they have put in the passport: "Jean Valjean, a liberated convict, native of —," you don't care for that, "has been nineteen years in the galleys; five years for burglary; fourteen years for having attempted four times to escape. This man is very dangerous." There you have it! Everybody has thrust me out; will you receive me? Is this an inn? Can you give me something to eat, and a place to sleep? Have you a stable?'

'Madame Magloire,' said the bishop, 'put some sheets on the bed in the alcove.'

We have already described the kind of obedience yielded by these two women. Madame Magloire went out to fulfil her orders.

The bishop turned to the man:

'Monsieur, sit down and warm yourself: we are going to take supper presently, and your bed will be made ready while you sup.'

At last the man quite understood; his face, the expression of which till then had been gloomy and hard, now expressed stupefaction, doubt, and joy, and became absolutely wonderful. He began to stutter like a madman.

'True? What! You will keep me? you won't drive me away? a convict! You call me *Monsieur* and don't say, "Get out, dog!" as everybody else does. I thought that you would send me away, so I told first off who I am. Oh! the fine woman who sent me here! I shall have a supper! a bed like other people with mattress and sheets – a bed! It is nineteen years that I have not slept on a bed. You are really willing that I should stay? You are good people! Besides I have money: I will pay well. I beg your pardon, Monsieur Innkeeper, what is your name? I will pay all you say. You are a fine man. You are an innkeeper, aren't you?'

'I am a priest who lives here,' said the bishop.

'A priest,' said the man. 'Oh, noble priest! Then you do not ask any money? You are the curé, aren't you? the curé of this big church? Yes, that's it. How stupid I am; I didn't notice your cap.'

While speaking, he had deposited his knapsack and stick in the corner, replaced his passport in his pocket, and sat down. Mademoiselle Baptistine looked at him pleasantly. He continued:

'You are humane, Monsieur Curé; you don't despise me. A good priest is a good thing. Then you don't want me to pay you?'

'No,' said the bishop, 'keep your money. How much have you? You said a hundred and nine francs, I think.'

'And fifteen sous,' added the man.

'One hundred and nine francs and fifteen sous. And how long did it take you to earn that?'

'Nineteen years.'

'Nineteen years!'

The bishop sighed deeply.

The man continued: 'I have all my money yet. In four days I have spent only twenty-five sous which I earned by unloading wagons at Grasse. As you are an abbé, I must tell you, we have an almoner in the galleys. And then one day I saw a bishop; monseigneur, they called him. It was the Bishop of Majore from Marseilles. He is the curé who is over the curés. You see – beg pardon, how I bungle saying it, but for me, it is so far off! you know what we are. He said mass in the centre of the place on an altar; he had a pointed gold thing on his head, that shone in the sun; it was noon. We were drawn up in line on three sides, with cannons and matches lighted before us. We could not see him well. He spoke to us, but he was not near enough, we did not understand him. That is what a bishop is.'

While he was talking, the bishop shut the door, which he had left wide open.

Madame Magloire brought in a plate and set it on the table.

'Madame Magloire,' said the bishop, 'put this plate as near the fire as you can.' Then turning towards his guest, he added: 'The night wind is raw in the Alps; you must be cold, monsieur.'

Every time he said this word monsieur, with his gently solemn, and heartily hospitable voice, the man's countenance lighted up. *Monsieur* to a convict, is a glass of water to a man dying of thirst at sea. Ignominy thirsts for respect.

'The lamp,' said the bishop, 'gives a very poor light.'

Madame Magloire understood him, and going to his bedchamber, took from the mantel the two silver candlesticks, lighted the candles, and placed them on the table.

'Monsieur Curé,' said the man, 'you are good; you don't despise me. You take me into your house; you light your candles for me, and I haven't hid from you where I come from, and how miserable I am.'

The bishop, who was sitting near him, touched his hand gently and said: 'You need not tell me who you are. This is not my house; it is the house of Christ. It does not ask any comer whether he has a name, but whether he has an affliction. You are suffering; you are hungry and thirsty, be welcome. And do not thank me; do not tell me that I take you into my house. This is the home of no man, except him who needs an asylum. I tell you, who are a traveller, that you are more at home here than I; whatever is here is yours. What need have I to know your name? Besides, before you told me, I knew it.'

The man opened his eyes in astonishment:

'Really? You knew my name?'

'Yes,' answered the bishop, 'your name is my brother.'

'Stop, stop, Monsieur Curé,' exclaimed the man. 'I was famished when I came in, but you are so kind that now I don't know what I am; that is all gone.'

The bishop looked at him again and said:

'You have seen much suffering?'

'Oh, the red blouse, the ball and chain, the plank to sleep on, the heat, the cold, the galley's crew, the lash, the double chain for nothing, the dungeon for a word – even when sick in bed, the chain. The dogs, the dogs are happier!

Nineteen years! and I am forty-six, and now a yellow passport. That is all.'

'Yes,' answered the bishop, 'you have left a place of suffering. But listen, there will be more joy in heaven over the tears of a repentant sinner, than over the white robes of a hundred good men. If you are leaving that sorrowful place with hate and anger against men, you are worthy of compassion; if you leave it with goodwill, gentleness, and peace, you are better than any of us.'

Meantime Madame Magloire had served up supper; it consisted of soup made of water, oil, bread, and salt, a little pork, a scrap of mutton, a few figs, a green cheese, and a large loaf of rye bread. She had, without asking, added to the usual dinner of the bishop a bottle of fine old Mauves wine.

The bishop's countenance was lighted up with this expression of pleasure, peculiar to hospitable natures. 'To supper!' he said briskly, as was his habit when he had a guest. He seated the man at his right. Mademoiselle Baptistine, perfectly quiet and natural, took her place at his left.

The bishop said the blessing, and then served the soup himself, according to his usual custom. The man fell to, eating greedily.

Suddenly the bishop said: 'It seems to me something is lacking on the table.'

The fact was, that Madame Magloire had set out only the three plates which were necessary. Now it was the custom of the house, when the bishop had anyone to supper, to set all six of the silver plates on the table, an innocent display. This graceful appearance of luxury was a sort of childlikeness which was full of charm in this gentle but austere household, which elevated poverty to dignity.

Madame Magloire understood the remark; without a word she went out, and a moment afterwards the three plates for which the bishop had asked were shining on the cloth, symmetrically arranged before each of three guests.

4. *Some account of the dairies of Pontarlier*

Now, IN ORDER TO GIVE an idea of what passed at this table, we cannot do better than to transcribe here a passage in a letter from Mademoiselle Baptistine to Madame de Boischevron, in which the conversation between the convict and the bishop is related with charming minuteness.

This man paid no attention to anyone. He ate with the voracity of a starving man. After supper, however, he said:

'Monsieur Curé, all this is too good for me, but I must say that the wagoners, who wouldn't have me eat with them, live better than you.'

Between us, the remark shocked me a little. My brother answered:

'They are more fatigued than I am.'

'No,' responded this man; 'they have more money. You are poor, I can see. Perhaps you are not a curé even. Are you only a curé? Ah! if God is just, you well deserve to be a curé.'

'God is more than just,' said my brother.

A moment after he added:

'Monsieur Jean Valjean, you are going to Pontarlier?'

'A compulsory journey.'

I am pretty sure that is the expression the man used. Then he continued:

'I must be on the road tomorrow morning by daybreak. It is a hard journey. If the nights are cold, the days are warm.'

'You are going,' said my brother, 'to a fine country. During the revolution, when my family was ruined, I took refuge at first in Franche-Comté, and supported myself there for some time by the labour of my hands. There I found plenty of work, and had only to make my choice. There are papermills, tanneries, distilleries, oil-factories, large clock-making establishments, steel manufactories, copper foundries, at least twenty iron foundries, four of which, at Lods, Châtillion, Audincourt, and Beure, are very large.'

I think I am not mistaken, and that these are the names that my brother mentioned. Then he broke off and addressed me:

'Dear sister, have we not relatives in that part of the country?'

I answered:

'We had; among others Monsieur Lucenet, who was captain of the gates at Pontarlier under the old régime.'

'Yes,' replied my brother, 'but in '93, no one had relatives; everyone depended upon his hands. I laboured. They have, in the region of Pontarlier, where you are going, Monsieur Valjean, a business which is quite patriarchal and very charming, sister. It is their dairies, which they call *fruitières.*'

Then my brother, while helping this man at table, explained to him in detail what these *fruitières* were; – that they were divided into two kinds: the *great barns,* belonging to the rich, and where there are forty or fifty cows, which produce from seven to eight thousand cheeses during the summer; and the associated *fruitières,* which belong to the poor; these comprise the peasants inhabiting the mountains, who put their cows into a common herd, and divide the proceeds. They hire a cheesemaker, whom they call a *grurin;* the *grurin* receives the milk of the associates three times a day, and notes the quantities in duplicate. Towards the end of April – the dairy work commences, and about the middle of June the cheese-makers drive their cows into the mountains.

The man became animated even while he was eating. My brother gave him some good Mauves wine, which he does not drink himself, because he says it is too dear. My brother gave him all these details with that easy gaiety which you know is peculiar to him, intermingling his words with compliments for me. He dwelt much upon the good condition of a *grurin,* as if he wished that this man should understand, without advising him directly, and abruptly, that it would be an asylum for him. One thing struck me. This man was what I have told you. Well! my brother, during the supper, and during the entire evening, with the exception of a few words about Jesus, when he entered, did not say a word which could recall to this man who he himself was, nor indicate to him who my brother was. It was apparently a fine occasion to get in a little sermon, and to set up the bishop above the convict in order to make an impression upon his mind. It would, perhaps, have appeared to some to be a duty, having this unhappy man in hand, to feed the mind at the same time with the body, and to administer reproof, seasoned with morality and advice, or at least a little pity accompanied by an exhortation to conduct himself better in future. My brother asked him neither his country nor his history; for his crime lay in his history, and my brother seemed to avoid everything which could recall it to him. At one time, as my brother was speaking of the mountaineers of Pontarlier, who have *a pleasant labour near heaven, and who,* he added, *are happy, because they are innocent,* he stopped short, fearing there might have been in this word which had escaped him something which could wound the feelings of this man. Upon reflection, I think I understand what was passing in my brother's mind. He thought, doubtless, that this man, who called himself Jean Valjean, had his wretchedness too constantly before his mind; that it was best not to distress him by referring to it, and to make him think, if it were only for a moment, that he was a common person like anyone else, by treating him thus in the ordinary way. Is not this really understanding charity? Is there not, dear madame, something truly evangelical in this delicacy, which abstains from sermonising, moralising, and making allusions, and is it not the wisest sympathy, when a man has a suffering point, not to touch upon it at all? It seems to me that this was my brother's inmost thought. At any rate, all I can say is, if he had all these ideas, he did not show them even to me: he was, from beginning to end, the same as on other evenings, and he took supper with this Jean Valjean with the same air and manner that he would have supped with Monsieur Gédéon, the provost, or with the curé of the parish.

Towards the end, as we were at dessert, someone pushed the door open. It was mother Gerbaud with her child in her arms. My brother kissed the child, and borrowed fifteen *sous* that I had with me to give to mother Gerbaud. The man, during this time, paid but little attention to what passed. He did not speak, and appeared to be very tired. The poor old lady left, and my brother said grace, after which he turned towards this man and said: 'You must be in great need of sleep.' Madame Magloire quickly removed the cloth. I understood that we ought to retire in order that this traveller might sleep, and we both went to our rooms. However, in a few moments afterwards, I sent Madame Magloire to put on the bed of this man a roebuck skin from the Black Forest, which is in my chamber. The nights are quite cold, and this skin retains the warmth. It is a pity that it is quite old, and all the hair is gone. My brother bought it when he was in Germany, at Totlingen, near the sources of the Danube, as also the little ivory-handled knife, which I use at table.

Madame Magloire came back immediately, we said our prayers in the parlour which we use as a drying-room, and then we retired to our chambers without saying a word.

5. *Tranquillity*

AFTER HAVING SAID GOOD-NIGHT to his sister, Monseigneur Bienvenu took one of the silver candlesticks from the table, handed the other to his guest, and said to him:

'Monsieur, I will show you to your room.'

The man followed him.

As may have been understood from what has been said before, the house was so arranged that one could reach the alcove in the oratory only by passing through the bishop's sleeping chamber. Just as they were passing through this room Madame Magloire was putting up the silver in the cupboard at the head of the bed. It was the last thing she did every night before going to bed.

The bishop left his guest in the alcove, before a clean white bed. The man set down the candlestick upon a small table.

'Come,' said the bishop, 'a good night's rest to you: tomorrow morning, before you go, you shall have a cup of warm milk from our cows.'

'Thank you, Monsieur l'Abbé,' said the man.

Scarcely had he pronounced these words of peace, when suddenly he made a singular motion which would have chilled the two good women of the house with horror, had they witnessed it. Even now it is hard for us to understand what impulse he obeyed at that moment. Did he intend to give a warning or to throw out a menace? Or was he simply obeying a sort of instinctive impulse, obscure ever to himself? He turned abruptly towards the old man, crossed his arms, and casting a wild look upon his host, exclaimed in a harsh voice:

'Ah, now, indeed! You lodge me in your house, as near you as that!'

He checked himself, and added, with a laugh, in which there was something horrible;

'Have you reflected upon it? Who tells you that I am not a murderer?'

The bishop responded:

'God will take care of that.'

Then with gravity, moving his lips like one praying or talking to himself, he raised two fingers of his right hand and blessed the man, who, however, did not bow; and without turning his head or looking behind him, went into his chamber.

When the alcove was occupied, a heavy serge curtain was drawn in the oratory, concealing the altar. Before this curtain the bishop knelt as he passed out, and offered a short prayer.

A moment afterwards he was walking in the garden, surrendering mind and soul to a dreamy contemplation of these grand and mysterious works of God, which night makes visible to the eye.

As to the man, he was so completely exhausted that he did not even avail himself of the clean white sheets; he blew out the candle with his nostril, after the manner of convicts, and fell on the bed, dressed as he was, into a sound sleep.

Midnight struck as the bishop came back to his chamber.

A few moments afterwards all in the little house slept.

6. Jean Valjean

TOWARDS THE MIDDLE of the night, Jean Valjean awoke.

Jean Valjean was born of a poor peasant family of Brie. In his childhood he had not been taught to read: when he was grown up, he chose the occupation of a pruner at Faverolles. His mother's name was Jeanne Mathieu, his father's Jean Valjean or Vlajean, probably a nickname, a contraction of *Voilà Jean*.

Jean Valjean was of a thoughtful disposition, but not sad, which is characteristic of affectionate natures. Upon the whole, however, there was something torpid and insignificant, in the appearance at least, of Jean Valjean. He had lost his parents when very young. His mother died of malpractice in a milk-fever: his father, a pruner before him, was killed by a fall from a tree. Jean Valjean now had but one relative left, his sister, widow with seven children, girls and boys. This sister had brought up Jean Valjean, and, as long as her husband lived, she had taken care of her young brother. Her husband died, leaving the eldest of these children eight, the youngest one year old. Jean Valjean had just reached his twenty-fifth year: he took the father's place, and, in his turn, supported the sister who reared him. This he did naturally, as a duty, and even with a sort of moroseness on his part. His youth was spent in rough and ill-recompensed labour: he never was known to have a sweetheart; he had not time to be in love.

At night he came in weary and ate his soup without saying a word. While he was eating, his sister, Mère Jeanne, frequently took from his porringer the best of his meal; a bit of meat, a slice of pork, the heart of the cabbage, to give to one of her children. He went on eating, his head bent down nearly into the soup, his long hair falling over his dish, hiding his eyes, he did not seem to notice anything that was done. At Faverolles, not far from the house of the Valjeans, there was on the other side of the road a farmer's wife named Marie Claude; the Valjean children, who were always famished, sometimes went in their mother's name to borrow a pint of milk, which they would drink behind a hedge, or in some corner of the lane, snatching away the pitcher so greedily one from another, that the little girls would spill it upon their aprons and their necks; if their mother had known of this exploit she would have punished the delinquents severely. Jean Valjean, rough and grumbler as he was, paid Marie Claude; their mother never knew it, and so the children escaped.

He earned in the pruning season eighteen sous a day: after that he hired out as reaper, workman, teamster, or labourer. He did whatever he could find to do. His sister worked also, but what could she do with seven little children? It was a sad group, which misery was grasping and closing upon, little by little. There was a very severe winter; Jean had no work, the family had no bread; literally, no bread, and seven children.

One Sunday night, Maubert Isabeau, the baker on the Place de l'Eglise, in Faverolles, was just going to bed when he heard a violent blow against the barred window of his shop. He got down in time to see an arm thrust through the aperture made by the blow of a fist on the glass. The arm seized a loaf of bread and took it out. Isabeau rushed out; the thief used his legs valiantly; Isabeau pursued him and caught him. The thief had thrown away the bread, but his arm was still bleeding. It was Jean Valjean.

All that happened in 1795, Jean Valjean was brought before the tribunals of the time for 'burglary at night, in an inhabited house'. He had a gun which he used as well as any marksman in the world, and was something of a poacher, which hurt him, there being a natural prejudice against poachers. The poacher, like the smuggler, approaches very nearly to the brigand. We must say, however, by the way, that there is yet a deep gulf between this race of men and the hideous assassin of the city. The poacher dwells in the forest, and the smuggler in the mountains or upon the sea; cities produce ferocious men, because they produce corrupt men; the mountains, the forest, and the sea, render men savage; they develop the fierce, but yet do not destroy the human.

Jean Valjean was found guilty: the terms of the code were explicit; in our civilisation there are fearful hours; such are those when the criminal law pronounces shipwreck upon a man. What a mournful moment is that in which society withdraws itself and gives up a thinking being for ever. Jean Valjean was sentenced to five years in the galleys.

On the 22nd April 1796, there was announced in Paris the victory of

Montenotte, achieved by the commanding-general of the army of Italy, whom the message of the Directory, to the Five Hundred, of the 2nd Floréal, year IV, called Buonaparte; that same day a great chain was riveted at the Bicêtre. Jean Valjean was a part of this chain. An old turnkey of the prison, now nearly ninety, well remembers this miserable man, who was ironed at the end of the fourth plinth in the north angle of the court. Sitting on the ground like the rest, he seemed to comprehend nothing of his position, except its horror: probably there was also mingled with the vague ideas of a poor ignorant man a notion that there was something excessive in the penalty. While they were with heavy hammer-strokes behind his head riveting the bolt of his iron collar, he was weeping. The tears choked his words, and he only succeeded in saying from time to time: '*I was a pruner at Faverolles.*' Then sobbing as he was, he raised his right hand and lowered it seven times, as if he was touching seven heads of unequal height, and at this gesture one could guess that whatever he had done, had been to feed and clothe seven little children.

He was taken to Toulon, at which place he arrived after a journey of twenty-seven days, on a cart, the chain still about his neck. At Toulon he was dressed in a red blouse, all his past life was effaced, even to his name. He was no longer Jean Valjean: he was Number 24,601. What became of the sister? What became of the seven children? Who troubled himself about that? What becomes of the handful of leaves of the young tree when it is sawn at the trunk?

It is the old story. These poor little lives, these creatures of God, henceforth without support, or guide, or asylum; they passed away wherever chance led, who knows even? Each took a different path, it may be, and sank little by little into the chilling dark which engulfs solitary destinies; that sullen gloom where are lost so many ill-fated souls in the sombre advance of the human race. They left that region; the church of what had been their village forgot them; the stile of what had been their field forgot them; after a few years in the galleys, even Jean Valjean forgot them. In that heart, in which there had been a wound, there was a scar; that was all. During the time he was at Toulon, he heard but once of his sister; that was, I think, at the end of the fourth year of his confinement. I do not know how the news reached him: someone who had known him at home had seen his sister. She was in Paris, living in a poor street near Saint Sulpice, the Rue du Geindre. She had with her but one child, the youngest, a little boy. Where were the other six? She did not know herself, perhaps. Every morning she went to a bindery, No. 3 Rue du Sabot, where she was employed as a folder and book-stitcher. She had to be there by six in the morning, long before the dawn in the winter. In the same building with the bindery, there was a school, where she sent her little boy, seven years old. As the school did not open until seven, and she must be at her work at six, her boy had to wait in the yard an hour, until the school opened – an hour of cold and darkness in the winter. They would not let the child wait in the bindery, because he was troublesome, they said. The workmen, as they passed in the morning, saw the poor little fellow sometimes sitting on the pavement nodding with weariness, and often sleeping in the dark, crouched and bent over his basket. When it rained, an old woman, the portress, took pity on him; she let him come into her lodge, the furniture of which was only a pallet bed, a spinning-wheel, and two wooden chairs; and the little one slept there in a corner, hugging the cat to keep himself warm. At seven o'clock the school opened and he went in. That is what was told Jean Valjean. It was as if a window had suddenly been opened, looking upon the destiny of those he had loved, and then all was closed again, and he heard nothing more for ever. Nothing more came to him; he had not seen them, never will he see them again! and through the remainder of this sad history we shall not meet them again.

Near the end of this fourth year, his chance of liberty came to Jean Valjean. His comrades helped him as they always do in that dreary place, and he escaped. He wandered two days in freedom through the fields; if it is freedom to be hunted, to turn your head each moment, to tremble at the least noise, to be afraid of everything, of the smoke of a chimney, the passing of a man, the baying of a dog, the gallop of a horse, the striking of a clock, of the day because you see, and of the night because you do not; of the road, of the path, the bush, of sleep. During the evening of the second day he was retaken; he had neither eaten nor slept for thirty-six hours. The maritime tribunal extended his sentence three years for this attempt, which made eight. In the sixth year his turn of escape came again; he tried it, but failed again. He did not answer at rollcall, and the alarm cannon was fired. At night the people of the vicinity discovered him hidden beneath the keel of a vessel on the stocks; he resisted the galley guard which seized him. Escape and resistance. This the provisions of the special code punished by an addition of five years, two with the double chain. Thirteen years. The tenth year his turn came round again; he made another attempt with no better success. Three years for this new attempt. Sixteen years. And finally, I think it was in the thirteenth year, he made yet another, and was retaken after an absence of only four hours. Three years for these four hours. Nineteen years. In October 1815, he was set at large: he had entered in 1796 for having broken a pane of glass, and taken a loaf of bread.

This is a place for a short parenthesis. This is the second time, in his studies on the penal question and on the sentences of the law, that the author of this book has met with the theft of a loaf of bread as the starting-point of the ruin of a destiny. Claude Gueux stole a loaf of bread;[11] Jean Valjean stole a loaf of bread; English statistics show that in London starvation is the immediate cause of four thefts out of five.

Jean Valjean entered the galleys sobbing and shuddering: he went out hardened; he entered in despair: he went out sullen.

What had been the life of this soul?

7. The depths of despair

LET US ENDEAVOUR to tell.

It is an imperative necessity that society should look into these things: they are its own work.

He was, as we have said, ignorant; but he was not imbecile. The natural light was enkindled in him. Misfortune, which has also its illumination, added to the few rays that he had in his mind. Under the whip, under the chain, in the cell, in fatigue, under the burning sun of the galleys, upon the convict's bed of plank, he turned to his own conscience, and he reflected.

He constituted himself a tribunal.

He began by arraigning himself.

He recognised, that he was not an innocent man, unjustly punished. He acknowledged that he had committed an extreme and a blamable action; that the loaf perhaps would not have been refused him, had he asked for it; that at all events it would have been better to wait, either for pity, or for work; that it is not altogether an unanswerable reply to say: 'could I wait when I was hungry?' that, in the first place, it is very rare that anyone dies of actual hunger; and that, fortunately or unfortunately, man is so made that he can suffer long and much, morally and physically, without dying; that he should, therefore, have had patience; that that would have been better even for those poor little ones; that it was an act of folly in him, poor, worthless man, to seize society in all its strength, forcibly by the collar, and imagine that he could escape from misery by theft; that that was, at all events, a bad door for getting out of misery by which one entered into infamy; in short, that he had done wrong.

Then he asked himself:

If he were the only one who had done wrong in the course of his fatal history? If, in the first place, it were not a grievous thing that he, a workman, should have been in want of work; that he, an industrious man, should have lacked bread. If, moreover, the fault having been committed and avowed, the punishment had not been savage and excessive. If there were not a greater abuse, on the part of the law, in the penalty, than there had been, on the part of the guilty, in the crime. If there were not an excess of weight in one of the scales of the balance – on the side of the expiation. If the discharge of the penalty were not the effacement of the crime; and if the result were not to reverse the situation, to replace the wrong of the delinquent by the wrong of the repression, to make a victim of the guilty, and a creditor of the debtor, and actually to put the right on the side of him who had violated it. If that penalty, taken in connection with its successive extensions for his attempts to escape, had not at last come to be a sort of outrage of the stronger on the weaker, a crime of society towards the individual, a crime which was committed afresh every day, a crime which had endured for nineteen years.

He questioned himself if human society could have the right alike to crush its members, in the one case by its unreasonable carelessness, and in the other by its pitiless care; and to keep a poor man for ever between a lack and an excess, a lack of work, an excess of punishment.

If it were not outrageous that society should treat with such rigid precision those of its members who were most poorly endowed in the distribution of wealth that chance had made, and who were, therefore, most worthy of indulgence.

These questions asked and decided, he condemned society and sentenced it.

He sentenced it to his hatred.

He made it responsible for the doom which he had undergone, and promised himself that he, perhaps, would not hesitate someday to call it to an account. He declared to himself that there was no equity between the injury that he had committed and the injury that had been committed on him; he concluded, in short, that his punishment was not, really, an injustice, but that beyond all doubt it was an iniquity.

Anger may be foolish and absurd, and one may be irritated when in the wrong; but a man never feels outraged unless in some respect he is at bottom right. Jean Valjean felt outraged.

And then, human society had done him nothing but injury; never had he seen anything of her, but this wrathful face which she calls justice, and which she shows to those whom she strikes down. No man had ever touched him but to bruise him. All his contact with men had been by blows. Never, since his infancy, since his mother, since his sister, never had he been greeted with a friendly word or a kind regard. Through suffering on suffering he came little by little to the conviction, that life was a war; and that in that war he was the vanquished. He had no weapon but his hate. He resolved to sharpen it in the galleys and to take it with him when he went out.

There was at Toulon a school for the prisoners conducted by some not very skilful friars, where the most essential branches were taught to such of these poor men as were willing. He was one of the willing ones. He went to school at forty and learned to read, write, and cipher. He felt that to increase his knowledge was to strengthen his hatred. Under certain circumstances, instruction and enlightenment may serve as rallying-points for evil.

It is sad to tell; but after having tried society, which had caused his misfortunes, he tried Providence which created society, and condemned it also.

Thus, during those nineteen years of torture and slavery, did this soul rise and fall at the same time. Light entered on the one side, and darkness on the other.

Jean Valjean was not, we have seen, of an evil nature. His heart was still right when he arrived at the galleys. While there he condemned society, and felt that he became wicked; he condemned Providence, and felt that he became impious.

It is difficult not to reflect for a moment here.

Can human nature be so entirely transformed from top to bottom? Can man, created good by God, be made wicked by man? Can the soul be changed to keep pace with its destiny, and become evil when its destiny is evil? Can the heart become distorted and contract deformities and infirmities that are incurable, under the pressure of a disproportionate woe, like the vertebral column under a too heavy brain? Is there not in every human soul; was there not in the particular soul of Jean Valjean, a primitive spark, a divine element, incorruptible in this world, immortal in the next, which can be developed by good, kindled, lit up, and made resplendently radiant, and which evil can never entirely extinguish.

Grave and obscure questions, to the last of which every physiologist would probably, without hesitation, have answered *no*, had he seen at Toulon, during the hours of rest, which to Jean Valjean were hours of thought, this gloomy galley-slave, seated, with folded arms, upon the bar of some windlass, the end of his chain stuck into his pocket that it might not drag, serious, silent, and thoughtful, a pariah of the law which views man with wrath, condemned by civilisation which views heaven with severity.

Certainly, we will not conceal it, such a physiologist would have seen in Jean Valjean an irremediable misery; he would perhaps have lamented the disease occasioned by the law; but he would not even have attempted a cure; he would have turned from the sight of the caverns which he would have beheld in that soul; and, like Dante at the gate of Hell, he would have wiped out from that existence the word which the finger of God has nevertheless written upon the brow of every man – *Hope!*

Was that state of mind which we have attempted to analyse as perfectly clear to Jean Valjean as we have tried to render it to our readers? Did Jean Valjean distinctly see, after their formation, and had he distinctly seen, while they were forming, all the elements of which his moral misery was made up? Had this rude and unlettered man taken accurate account of the succession of ideas by which he had, step by step, risen and fallen, till he had reached that mournful plane which for so many years already had marked the internal horizon of his mind? Had he a clear consciousness of all that was passing within him, and of all that was moving him? This we dare not affirm; we do not, in fact, believe it. Jean Valjean was too ignorant, even after so much ill fortune, for nice discrimination in these matters. At times he did not even know exactly what were his feelings. Jean Valjean was in the dark; he suffered in the dark; he hated in the dark; we might say that he hated in his own sight. He lived constantly in this darkness, groping blindly and as in a dream. Only, at intervals, there broke over him suddenly, from within or from without, a shock of anger, an overflow of suffering, a quick pallid flash which lit up his whole soul, and showed all around him, before and behind, in the glare of a hideous light, the fearful precipices and the sombre perspectives of his fate.

The flash passed away; the night fell, and where was he? He no longer knew.

The peculiarity of punishment of this kind, in which what is pitiless, that is to say, what is brutalising, predominates, is to transform little by little, by a slow stupefaction, a man into an animal, sometimes into a wild beast. Jean Valjean's repeated and obstinate attempts to escape are enough to prove that such is the strange effect of the law upon a human soul. Jean Valjean had renewed these attempts, so wholly useless and foolish, as often as an opportunity offered, without one moment's thought of the result, or of experience already undergone. He escaped wildly, like a wolf on seeing his cage-door open. Instinct said to him: 'Away!' Reason said to him: 'Stay!' But before a temptation so mighty, reason fled; instinct alone remained. The beast alone was in play. When he was retaken, the new severities that were inflicted upon him only made him still more fierce.

We must not omit one circumstance, which is, that in physical strength he far surpassed all the other inmates of the prison. At hard work, at twisting a cable, or turning a windlass, Jean Valjean was equal to four men. He would sometimes lift and hold enormous weights on his back, and would occasionally act the part of what is called a *jack*, or what was called in old French an *orgeuil*, whence came the name, we may say by the way, of the Rue Montorgeuil near the Halles of Paris. His comrades had nicknamed him Jean the Jack. At one time, while the balcony of the City Hall of Toulon was undergoing repairs, one of Puget's admirable caryatides, which support the balcony, slipped from its place, and was about to fall, when Jean Valjean, who happened to be there, held it up on his shoulder till the workmen came.

His suppleness surpassed his strength. Certain convicts, always planning escape, have developed a veritable science of strength and skill combined, – the science of the muscles. A mysterious system of statics is practised throughout daily by prisoners, who are eternally envying the birds and flies. To scale a wall, and to find a foot-hold where you could hardly see a projection, was play for Jean Valjean. Given an angle in a wall, with the tension of his back and his knees, with elbows and hands braced against the rough face of the stone, he would ascend, as if by magic, to a third storey. Sometimes he climbed up in this manner to the roof of the galleys.

He talked but little, and never laughed. Some extreme emotion was required to draw from him, once or twice a year, that lugubrious sound of the convict, which is like the echo of a demon's laugh. To those who saw him, he seemed to be absorbed in continually looking upon something terrible.

He was absorbed, in fact.

Through the diseased perceptions of an incomplete nature and a smothered intelligence, he vaguely felt that a monstrous weight was over him. In that pallid and sullen shadow in which he crawled, whenever he turned his head and endeavoured to raise his eyes, he saw, with mingled rage and terror, forming, massing, and mounting up out of view above him with horrid escarpments, a kind of frightful accumulation of things, of laws, of prejudices, of men, and of acts, the outlines of which escaped him, the weight of which appalled him, and which was no other than that prodigious pyramid that we call civilisation. Here and there in that shapeless and crawling mass, sometimes near at hand, sometimes afar off, and upon inaccessible heights, he distinguished some group, some detail vividly clear, here the jailer with his staff, here the gendarme with his sword, yonder the mitred archbishop; and on high, in a sort of blaze of glory, the emperor crowned and resplendent. It seemed to him that these distant splendours, far from dissipating his night, made it blacker and more deathly. All this, laws, prejudices, acts, men, things, went and came above him, according to the complicated and mysterious movement that God impresses upon civilisation, marching over him and crushing him with an indescribably tranquil cruelty and inexorable indifference. Souls sunk to the bottom of possible misfortune, and unfortunate men lost in the lowest depths, where they are no longer seen, the rejected of the law, feel upon their heads the whole weight of that human society, so formidable to him who is without it, so terrible to him who is beneath it.

In such a situation Jean Valjean mused, and what could be the nature of his reflections?

If a millet seed under a millstone had thoughts, doubtless it would think what Jean Valjean thought.

All these things, realities full of spectres, phantasmagoria full of realities, had at last produced within him a condition which was almost inexpressible.

Sometimes in the midst of his work in the galleys he would stop, and begin to think. His reason, more mature, and, at the same time, perturbed more than formerly, would revolt. All that had happened to him would appear absurd; all that surrounded him would appear impossible. He would say to himself: 'It is a dream.' He would look at the jailer standing a few steps from him; the jailer would seem to be a phantom; all at once this phantom would give him a blow with a stick.

For him the external world had scarcely an existence. It would be almost true to say that for Jean Valjean there was no sun, no beautiful summer days, no radiant sky, no fresh April dawn. Some dim window light was all that shone in his soul.

To sum up, in conclusion, what can be summed up and reduced to positive results, of all that we have been showing, we will make sure only of this, that in the course of nineteen years, Jean Valjean, the inoffensive pruner of Faverolles, the terrible galley-slave of Toulon, had become capable, thanks to the training he had received in the galleys, of two species of crime; first, a sudden, unpremeditated action, full of rashness, all instinct, a sort of reprisal for the wrong he had suffered; secondly, a serious, premeditated act, discussed by his conscience, and pondered over with the false ideas which such a fate will give. His premeditations passed through the three successive phases to which natures of a certain stamp are limited – reason, will, and obstinacy. He had as motives, habitual indignation, bitterness of soul, a deep sense of injuries suffered, a reaction even against the good, the innocent, and the upright, if any such there are. The beginning as well as the end of all his thoughts was hatred of human law; that hatred which, if it be not checked in its growth by some providential event, becomes, in a certain time, hatred of society, then hatred of the human race, and then hatred of creation, and reveals itself by a vague and incessant desire to injure some living being, it matters not who. So, the passport was right which described Jean Valjean as *a very dangerous man*.

From year to year this soul had withered more and more, slowly, but fatally. With this withered heart, he had a dry eye. When he left the galleys, he had not shed a tear for nineteen years.

8. *The waters and the shadow*

A MAN overboard!

What matters it! the ship does not stop. The wind is blowing, that dark ship must keep on her destined course. She passes away.

The man disappears, then reappears, he plunges and rises again to the surface, he calls, he stretches out his hands, they hear him not; the ship, staggering under the gale, is straining every rope, the sailors and passengers see the drowning man no longer; his miserable head is but a point in the vastness of the billows.

He hurls cries of despair into the depths. What a spectre is that disappearing sail! He looks upon it, he looks upon it with frenzy. It moves away; it grows dim; it diminishes. He was there but just now, he was one of the crew, he went and came upon the deck with the rest, he had his share of the air and of the sunlight, he was a living man. Now, what has become of him? He slipped, he fell; and it is finished.

He is in the monstrous deep. He has nothing under his feet but the yielding, fleeing element. The waves, torn and scattered by the wind, close round him hideously; the rolling of the abyss bears him along; shreds of water are flying about his head; a populace of waves spat upon him; confused openings half swallow him; when he sinks he catches glimpses of yawning precipices full of darkness; fearful unknown vegetations seize upon him, bind his feet, and draw him to themselves; he feels that he is becoming the great deep; he makes part of the foam; the billows toss him from one to the other; he tastes the bitterness; the greedy ocean is eager to devour him; the monster plays with his agony. It seems as if all this were liquid hate.

But yet he struggles.

He tries to defend himself; he tries to sustain himself; he struggles; he swims. He – that poor strength that fails so soon – he combats the unfailing.

Where now is the ship? Far away yonder. Hardly visible in the pallid gloom of the horizon.

The wind blows in gusts; the billows overwhelm him. He raises his eyes, but sees only the livid clouds. He, in his dying agony, makes part of this immense insanity of the sea. He is tortured to his death by its immeasurable madness. He hears sounds, which are strange to man, sounds which seem to come not from earth, but from some frightful realm beyond.

There are birds in the clouds, even as there are angels above human distresses, but what can they do for him? They fly, sing, float, while he is gasping.

He feels that he is buried at once by those two infinites, the ocean and the sky; the one is a tomb, the other a pall.

Night descends, he has been swimming for hours, his strength is almost exhausted; that ship, that far-off thing, where there were men, is gone; he is alone in the terrible gloom of the abyss; he sinks, he strains, he struggles, he feels beneath him the shadowy monsters of the unseen; he shouts.

Men are no more. Where is God?

He shouts. Help! help! He shouts incessantly.

Nothing in the horizon. Nothing in the sky.

He implores the blue vault, the waves, the rocks; all are deaf. He supplicates the tempest; the imperturbable tempest obeys only the infinite.

Around him are darkness, storm, solitude, wild and unconscious tumult, the ceaseless tumbling of the fierce waters; within him, horror and exhaustion. Beneath him the engulfing abyss. No resting-place. He thinks of the shadowy adventures of his lifeless body in the limitless gloom. The biting cold paralyses him. His hands clutch spasmodically, and grasp at nothing. Winds, clouds, whirlwinds, blasts, stars, all useless! What shall he do? He yields to despair; worn out, he seeks death; he no longer resists; he gives himself up; he abandons the contest, and he is rolled away into the dismal depths of the abyss for ever.

O implacable march of human society! Destruction of men and of souls marking its path! Ocean, where fall all that the law lets fall! Ominous disappearance of aid! O moral death!

The sea is the inexorable night into which the penal law casts its victims. The sea is the measureless misery.

The soul drifting in that sea may become a corpse. Who shall restore it to life?

9. New griefs

WHEN THE TIME for leaving the galleys came, and when there were sounded in the ear of Jean Valjean the strange words: *You are free!* the moment seemed improbable and unreal; a ray of living light, a ray of the true light of living men, suddenly penetrated his soul. But this ray quickly faded away. Jean Valjean had been dazzled with the idea of liberty. He had believed in a new life. He soon saw what sort of liberty that is which has a yellow passport.

And along with that there were many bitter experiences. He had calculated that his savings, during his stay at the galleys, would amount to a hundred and seventy-one francs. It is proper to say that he had forgotten to take into account the compulsory rest on Sundays and holydays, which, in nineteen years, required a deduction of about twenty-four francs. However that might be, his savings had been reduced, by various local charges, to the sum of a hundred and nine francs and fifteen sous, which was counted out to him on his departure.

He understood nothing of this, and thought himself wronged, or, to speak plainly, robbed.

The day after his liberation, he saw before the door of an orange flower distillery at Grasse, some men who were unloading bags. He offered his services.

They were in need of help and accepted them. He set at work. He was intelligent, robust, and handy; he did his best; the foreman appeared to be satisfied. While he was at work, a gendarme passed, noticed him, and asked for his papers. He was compelled to show the yellow passport. That done, Jean Valjean, resumed his work. A little while before, he had asked one of the labourers how much they were paid per day for this work, and the reply was: *thirty sous*. At night, as he was obliged to leave the town next morning, he went to the foreman of the distillery, and asked for his pay. The foreman did not say a word, but handed him fifteen sous. He remonstrated. The man replied: '*That is good enough for you.*' He insisted. The foreman looked him in the eyes and said: '*Look out for the lock-up!*'

There again he thought himself robbed.

Society, the state, in reducing his savings, had robbed him by wholesale. Now it was the turn of the individual, who was robbing him by retail.

Liberation is not deliverance. A convict may leave the galleys behind, but not his condemnation.

This was what befell him at Grasse. We have seen how he was received at D—.

10. *The man awakes*

As THE CATHEDRAL clock struck two, Jean Valjean awoke.

What awakened him was, too good a bed. For nearly twenty years he had not slept in a bed, and, although he had not undressed, the sensation was too novel not to disturb his sleep.

He had slept something more than four hours. His fatigue had passed away. He was not accustomed to give many hours to repose.

He opened his eyes, and looked for a moment into the obscurity about him, then he closed them to go to sleep again.

When many diverse sensations have disturbed the day, when the mind is preoccupied, we can fall asleep once, but not a second time. Sleep comes at first much more readily than it comes again. Such was the case with Jean Valjean. He could not get to sleep again, and so he began to think.

He was in one of those moods in which the ideas we have in our minds are perturbed. There was a kind of vague ebb and flow in his brain. His oldest and his latest memories floated about pell mell, and crossed each other confusedly, losing their own shapes, swelling beyond measure, then disappearing all at once, as if in a muddy and troubled stream. Many thoughts came to him, but there was one which continually presented itself, and which drove away all others. What that thought was, we shall tell directly. He had noticed the six silver plates and the large ladle that Madame Magloire had put on the table.

Those six silver plates took possession of him. There they were, within a few steps. At the very moment that he passed through the middle room to reach the one he was now in, the old servant was placing them in a little cupboard at the head of the bed. He had marked that cupboard well: on the right, coming from the dining-room. They were solid; and old silver. With the big ladle, they would bring at least two hundred francs, double what he had got for nineteen years' labour. True; he would have got more if the '*government*' had not '*robbed*' him.

His mind wavered a whole hour, and a long one, in fluctuation and in struggle. The clock struck three. He opened his eyes, rose up hastily in bed, reached out his arm and felt his haversack, which he had put into the corner of the alcove, then he thrust out his legs and placed his feet on the ground, and found himself, he knew not how, seated on his bed.

He remained for some time lost in thought in that attitude, which would have had a rather ominous look, had anyone seen him there in the dusk – he only awake in the slumbering house. All at once he stooped down, took off his shoes, and put them softly upon the mat in front of the bed, then he resumed his thinking posture, and was still again.

In that hideous meditation, the ideas which we have been pointing out, troubled his brain without ceasing, entered, departed, returned, and became a sort of weight upon him; and then he thought, too, he knew not why, and with that mechanical obstinacy that belongs to reverie, of a convict named Brevet, whom he had known in the galleys, and whose trousers were only held up by a single knit cotton suspender. The checked pattern of that suspender came continually before his mind.

He continued in this situation, and would perhaps have remained there until daybreak, if the clock had not struck the quarter or the half-hour. The clock seemed to say to him: 'Come along!'

He rose to his feet, hesitated for a moment longer, and listened; all was still in the house; he walked straight and cautiously towards the window, which he could discern. The night was not very dark; there was a full moon, across which large clouds were driving before the wind. This produced alternations of light and shade, out-of-doors eclipses and illuminations, and indoors a kind of glimmer. This glimmer, enough to enable him to find his way, changing with the passing clouds, resembled that sort of livid light, which falls through the window of a dungeon before which men are passing and repassing. On reaching the window, Jean Valjean examined it. It had no bars, opened into the garden, and was fastened, according to the fashion of the country, with a little wedge only. He opened it; but as the cold, keen air rushed into the room, he closed it again immediately. He looked into the garden with that absorbed look which studies rather than sees. The garden was enclosed with a white wall, quite low, and readily scaled. Beyond, against the sky, he distinguished the tops of trees at equal distances apart, which showed that this wall separated the garden from an avenue or a lane planted with trees.

When he had taken this observation, he turned like a man whose mind is made up, went to his alcove, took his haversack, opened it, fumbled in it, took out something which he laid upon the bed, put his shoes into one of his pockets, tied up his bundle, swung it upon his shoulders, put on his cap, and pulled the vizor down over his eyes, felt for his stick, and went and put it in the corner of the window, then returned to the bed, and resolutely took up the object which he had laid on it. It looked like a short iron bar, pointed at one end like a spear.

It would have been hard to distinguish in the darkness for what use this piece of iron had been made. Could it be a lever? Could it be a club?

In the day-time, it would have been seen to be nothing but a miner's drill. At that time, the convicts were sometimes employed in quarrying stone on the high hills that surround Toulon, and they often had miners' tools in their possession. Miners' drills are of solid iron, terminating at the lower end in a point, by means of which they are sunk into the rock.

He took the drill in his right hand, and holding his breath, with stealthy steps, he moved towards the door of the next room, which was the bishop's, as we know. On reaching the door, he found it unlatched. The bishop had not closed it.

11. *What he does*

JEAN VALJEAN listened. Not a sound.

He pushed the door.

He pushed it lightly with the end of his finger, with the stealthy and timorous carefulness of a cat. The door yielded to the pressure with a silent, imperceptible movement, which made the opening a little wider.

He waited a moment, and then pushed the door again more boldly.

It yielded gradually and silently. The opening was now wide enough for him to pass through; but there was a small table near the door which with it formed a troublesome angle, and which barred the entrance.

Jean Valjean saw the obstacle. At all hazards the opening must be made still wider.

He so determined, and pushed the door a third time, harder than before. This time a rusty hinge suddenly sent out into the darkness a harsh and prolonged creak.

Jean Valjean shivered. The noise of this hinge sounded in his ears as clear and terrible as the trumpet of the Judgement Day.

In the fantastic exaggeration of the first moment, he almost imagined that this hinge had become animate, and suddenly endowed with a terrible life; and that it was barking like a dog to warn everybody, and rouse the sleepers.

He stopped, shuddering and distracted, and dropped from his tiptoes to his feet. He felt the pulses of his temples beat like trip-hammers, and it appeared to him that his breath came from his chest with the roar of wind from a cavern. It seemed impossible that the horrible sound of this incensed hinge had not shaken the whole house with the shock of an earthquake: the door pushed by him had taken the alarm, and had called out; the old man would arise; the two old women would scream, help would come; in a quarter of an hour the town would be alive with it, and the gendarmes in pursuit. For a moment he thought he was lost.

He stood still, petrified like the pillar of salt, not daring to stir. Some minutes passed. The door was wide open; he ventured a look into the room, nothing had moved. He listened. Nothing was stirring in the house. The noise of the rusty hinge had wakened nobody.

This first danger was over, but still he felt within him a frightful tumult. Nevertheless he did not flinch. Not even when he thought he was lost had he flinched. His only thought was to make an end of it quickly. He took one step and was in the room.

A deep calm filled the chamber. Here and there indistinct, confused forms could be distinguished; which by day, were papers scattered over a table, open folios, books piled on a stool, an armchair with clothes on it, a prie-dieu, but now were only dark corners and whitish spots. Jean Valjean advanced, carefully avoiding the furniture. At the further end of the room he could hear the equal and quiet breathing of the sleeping bishop.

Suddenly he stopped: he was near the bed, he had reached it sooner than he thought.

Nature sometimes joins her effects and her appearances to our acts with a sort of serious and intelligent appropriateness, as if she would compel us to reflect. For nearly a half hour a great cloud had darkened the sky. At the moment when Jean Valjean paused before the bed the cloud broke as if purposely, and a ray of moonlight crossing the high window, suddenly lighted up the bishop's pale face. He slept tranquilly. He was almost entirely dressed, though in bed, on account of the cold nights of the lower Alps, with a dark woollen garment which covered his arms to the wrists. His head had fallen on the pillow in the unstudied attitude of slumber; over the side of the bed hung his hand, ornamented with the pastoral ring, and which had done so many good deeds, so many pious acts. His entire countenance was lit up with a vague expression of content, hope, and happiness. It was more than a smile and almost a radiance. On his forehead rested the indescribable reflection of an unseen light. The souls of the upright in sleep have vision of a mysterious heaven.

A reflection from this heaven shone upon the bishop.

But it was also a luminous transparency, for this heaven was within him; this heaven was his conscience.

At the instant when the moonbeam overlay, so to speak, this inward radiance, the sleeping bishop appeared as if in a halo. But it was very mild, and veiled in an ineffable twilight. The moon in the sky, nature drowsing, the garden without a pulse, the quiet house, the hour, the moment, the silence, added something strangely solemn and unutterable to the venerable repose of this man, and enveloped his white locks and his closed eyes with a serene and majestic glory, this face where all was hope and confidence – this old man's head and infant's slumber.

There was something of divinity almost in this man, thus unconsciously august.

Jean Valjean was in the shadow with the iron drill in his hand, erect, motionless, terrified, at this radiant figure. He had never seen anything comparable to it. This confidence filled him with fear. The moral world has no greater spectacle than this; a troubled and restless conscience on the verge of committing an evil deed, contemplating the sleep of a good man.

This sleep in this solitude, with a neighbour such as he, contained a touch of the sublime, which he felt vaguely but powerfully.

None could have told what was within him, not even himself. To attempt to realise it, the utmost violence must be imagined in the presence of the most extreme mildness. In his face nothing could be distinguished with certainty. It was a sort of haggard astonishment. He saw it; that was all. But what were his thoughts; it would have been impossible to guess. It was clear that he was moved and agitated. But of what nature was this emotion?

He did not remove his eyes from the old man. The only thing which was plain from his attitude and his countenance was a strange indecision. You would have said he was hesitating between two realms, that of the doomed and that of the saved. He appeared ready either to cleave this skull, or to kiss this hand.

In a few moments he raised his left hand slowly to his forehead and took off his hat; then, letting his hand fall with the same slowness, Jean Valjean resumed his contemplations, his cap in his left hand, his club in his right, and his hair bristling on his fierce-looking head.

Under this frightful gaze the bishop still slept in profoundest peace.

The crucifix above the mantelpiece was dimly visible in the moonlight, apparently extending its arms towards both, with a benediction for one and a pardon for the other.

Suddenly Jean Valjean put on his cap, then passed quickly, without looking at the bishop, along the bed, straight to the cupboard which he perceived near its head; he raised the drill to force the lock; the key was in it; he opened it; the first thing he saw was the basket of silver, he took it, crossed the room with hasty stride, careless of noise, reached the door, entered the oratory, took his stick, stepped out, put the silver in his knapsack, threw away the basket, ran across the garden, leaped over the wall like a tiger, and fled.

12. The bishop at work

THE NEXT DAY, at sunrise, Monseigneur Bienvenu was walking in the garden. Madame Magloire ran towards him quite beside herself.

'Monseigneur, monseigneur,' cried she, 'does your greatness know where the silver basket is?'

'Yes,' said the bishop.

'God be praised!' said she, 'I did not know what had become of it.'

The bishop had just found the basket on a flower-bed. He gave it to Madame Magloire and said: 'There it is.'

'Yes,' said she, 'but there is nothing in it. The silver?'

'Ah!' said the bishop, 'it is the silver then that troubles you. I do not know where that is.'

'Good heavens! it is stolen. That man who came last night stole it.'

And in the twinkling of an eye, with all the agility of which her age was capable, Madame Magloire ran to the oratory, went into the alcove, and came back to the bishop. The bishop was bending with some sadness over a cochlearia des Guillons, which the basket had broken in falling. He looked up at Madame Magloire's cry:

'Monseigneur, the man has gone! the silver is stolen!'

While she was uttering this exclamation her eyes fell on an angle of the garden where she saw traces of an escalade. A capstone of the wall had been thrown down.

'See, there is where he got out; he jumped into Cochefilet lane. The abominable fellow! he has stolen our silver!'

The bishop was silent for a moment, then raising his serious eyes, he said mildly to Madame Magloire:

'Now first, did this silver belong to us?'

Madame Magloire did not answer; after a moment the bishop continued:

'Madame Magloire, I have for a long time wrongfully withheld this silver; it belonged to the poor. Who was this man? A poor man evidently.'

'Alas! alas!' returned Madame Magloire. 'It is not on my account or mademoiselle's; it is all the same to us. But it is on yours, monseigneur. What is monsieur going to eat from now?'

The bishop looked at her with amazement:

'How so! have we no tin plates?'

Madame Magloire shrugged her shoulders.

'Tin smells.'

'Well, then, iron plates.'

Madame Magloire made an expressive gesture.

'Iron tastes.'

'Well,' said the bishop, 'then, wooden plates.'

In a few minutes he was breakfasting at the same table at which Jean Valjean sat the night before. While breakfasting, Monseigneur Bienvenu pleasantly remarked to his sister who said nothing, and Madame Magloire who was grumbling to herself, that there was really no need even of a wooden spoon or fork to dip a piece of bread into a cup of milk.

'Was there ever such an idea?' said Madame Magloire to herself, as she went backwards and forwards: 'to take in a man like that, and to give him a bed beside him; and yet what a blessing it was that he did nothing but steal! Oh, my stars! it makes the chills run over me when I think of it!'

Just as the brother and sister were rising from the table, there was a knock at the door.

'Come in,' said the bishop.

The door opened. A strange, fierce group appeared on the threshold. Three men were holding a fourth by the collar. The three men were gendarmes; the fourth Jean Valjean.

A brigadier of gendarmes, who appeared to head the group, was near the door. He advanced towards the bishop, giving a military salute.

'Monseigneur!' said he:

At this word Jean Valjean, who was sullen and seemed entirely cast down, raised his head with a stupefied air:

'Monseigneur!' he murmured, 'then it is not the curé!'

'Silence!' said a gendarme, 'it is monseigneur, the bishop.'

In the meantime Monsieur Bienvenu had approached as quickly as his great age permitted:

'Ah, there you are!' said he, looking towards Jean Valjean, 'I am glad to see you. But! I gave you the candlesticks also, which are silver like the rest, and would bring two hundred francs. Why did you not take them along with your plates?'

Jean Valjean opened his eyes and looked at the bishop with an expression which no human tongue could describe.

'Monseigneur,' said the brigadier, 'then what this man said was true? We met him. He was going like a man who was running away, and we arrested him in order to see. He had this silver.'

'And he told you,' interrupted the bishop, with a smile, 'that it had been given him by a good old priest with whom he had passed the night. I see it all. And you brought him back here? It is all a mistake.'

'If that is so,' said the brigadier, 'we can let him go.'

'Certainly,' replied the bishop.

The gendarmes released Jean Valjean, who shrank back:

'Is it true that they let me go?' he said in a voice almost inarticulate, as if he were speaking in his sleep.

'Yes! you can go. Do you not understand?' said a gendarme.

'My friend,' said the bishop, 'before you go away, here are your candlesticks; take them.'

He went to the mantelpiece, took the two candlesticks, and brought them to Jean Valjean. The two women beheld the action without a word, or gesture, or look, that might disturb the bishop.

Jean Valjean was trembling in every limb. He took the two candlesticks mechanically, and with a wild appearance.

'Now,' said the bishop, 'go in peace. By the way, my friend, when you come again, you need not come through the garden. You can always come in and go out by the front door. It is closed only with a latch, day or night.'

Then turning to the gendarmes, he said:

'Messieurs, you can retire.' The gendarmes withdrew.

Jean Valjean felt like a man who is just about to faint.

The bishop approached him, and said, in a low voice:

'Forget not, never forget that you have promised me to use this silver to become an honest man.'

Jean Valjean, who had no recollection of this promise, stood confounded. The bishop had laid much stress upon these words as he uttered them. He continued, solemnly:

'Jean Valjean, my brother: you belong no longer to evil, but to good. It is your soul that I am buying for you. I withdraw it from dark thoughts and from the spirit of perdition, and I give it to God!'

13. *Petit Gervais*

JEAN VALJEAN went out of the city as if he were escaping. He made all haste to get into the open country, taking the first lanes and bypaths that offered, without noticing that he was every moment retracing his steps. He wandered thus all the morning. He had eaten nothing, but he felt no hunger. He was the prey of a multitude of new sensations. He felt somewhat angry, he knew not against whom. He could not have told whether he were touched or humiliated. There came over him, at times, a strange relenting which he struggled with, and to which he opposed the hardening of his past twenty years. This condition wearied him. He saw, with disquietude, shaken within him that species of frightful calm which the injustice of his fate had given him. He asked himself what should replace it. At times he would really have liked better to be in prison with the gendarmes, and that things had not happened thus; that would have given him less agitation. Although the season was well advanced, there were yet here and there a few late flowers in the hedges, the odour of which, as it met him in his walk, recalled the memories of his childhood. These memories were almost insupportable, it was so long since they had occurred to him.

Unspeakable thoughts thus gathered in his mind the whole day.

As the sun was sinking towards the horizon, lengthening the shadow on the ground of the smallest pebble, Jean Valjean was seated behind a thicket in a large reddish plain, an absolute desert. There was no horizon but the Alps. Not even the steeple of a village church. Jean Valjean might have been three leagues from D——. A bypath which crossed the plain passed a few steps from the thicket.

In the midst of this meditation, which would have heightened not a little the frightful effect of his rags to anyone who might have met him, he heard a joyous sound.

He turned his head, and saw coming along the path a little Savoyard, a dozen years old, singing, with his hurdygurdy at his side, and his marmot box on his back.

One of those pleasant and gay youngsters who go from place to place, with their knees sticking through their trousers.

Always singing, the boy stopped from time to time, and played at tossing up some pieces of money that he had in his hand, probably his whole fortune. Among them there was one forty-sous piece.

The boy stopped by the side of the thicket without seeing Jean Valjean, and tossed up his handful of sous; until this time he had skilfully caught the whole of them upon the back of his hand.

This time the forty-sous piece escaped him, and rolled towards the thicket, near Jean Valjean.

Jean Valjean put his foot upon it.

The boy, however, had followed the piece with his eye, and had seen where it went.

He was not frightened, and walked straight to the man.

It was an entirely solitary place. Far as the eye could reach there was no one on the plain or in the path. Nothing could be heard, but the faint cries of a flock of birds of passage, that were flying across the sky at an immense height. The child turned his back to the sun, which made his hair like threads of gold, and flushed the savage face of Jean Valjean with a lurid glow.

'Monsieur,' said the little Savoyard, with that childish confidence which is made up of ignorance and innocence, 'my piece?'

'What is your name?' said Jean Valjean.

'Petit Gervais, monsieur.'

'Get out,' said Jean Valjean.

'Monsieur,' continued the boy, 'give me my piece.'

Jean Valjean dropped his head and did not answer.

The child began again:

'My piece, monsieur!'

Jean Valjean's eye remained fixed on the ground.

'My piece!' exclaimed the boy, 'my white piece! my silver!'

Jean Valjean did not appear to understand. The boy took him by the collar of his blouse and shook him. And at the same time he made an effort to move the big, iron-soled shoe which was placed upon his treasure.

'I want my piece! my forty-sous piece!'

The child began to cry. Jean Valjean raised his head. He still kept his seat. His look was troubled. He looked upon the boy with an air of wonder, then reached out his hand towards his stick, and exclaimed in a terrible voice: 'Who is there?'

'Me, monsieur,' answered the boy, 'Petit Gervais! me! me! give me my forty sous, if you please! Take away your foot, monsieur, if you please!' Then becoming angry, small as he was, and almost threatening:

'Come, now, will you take away your foot? Why don't you take away your foot?'

'Ah! you here yet!' said Jean Valjean, and rising hastily to his feet, without releasing the piece of money, he added: 'You'd better take care of yourself!'

The boy looked at him in terror, then began to tremble from head to foot, and after a few seconds of stupor, took to flight and ran with all his might without daring to turn his head or to utter a cry.

At a little distance, however, he stopped for want of breath, and Jean Valjean in his reverie heard him sobbing.

In a few minutes the boy was gone.

The sun had gone down.

The shadows were deepening around Jean Valjean. He had not eaten during the day; probably he had some fever.

He had remained standing, and had not change his attitude since the child fled. His breathing was at long and unequal intervals. His eyes were fixed on a spot ten or twelve steps before him, and seemed to be studying with profound attention the form of an old piece of blue crockery that was lying in the grass. All at once he shivered; he began to feel the cold night air.

He pulled his cap down over his forehead, sought mechanically to fold and button his blouse around him, stepped forward and stooped to pick up his stick.

At that instant he perceived the forty-sous piece which his foot had half buried in the ground, and which glistened among the pebbles. It was like an electric shock. 'What is that?' said he, between his teeth. He drew back a step or two, then stopped without the power to withdraw his gaze from this point which his foot had covered the instant before, as if the thing that glistened there in the obscurity had been an open eye fixed upon him.

After a few minutes, he sprang convulsively towards the piece of money, seized it, and, rising, looked away over the plain, straining his eyes towards all points of the horizon, standing and trembling like a frightened deer which is seeking a place of refuge.

He saw nothing. Night was falling, the plain was cold and bare, thick purple mists were rising in the glimmering twilight.

He said: 'Oh!' and began to walk rapidly in the direction in which the child had gone. After some thirty steps, he stopped, looked about, and saw nothing.

Then he called with all his might, 'Petit Gervais! Petit Gervais!'

And then he listened.

There was no answer.

The country was desolate and gloomy. On all sides was space. There was nothing about him but a shadow in which his gaze was lost, and a silence in which his voice was lost.

A biting norther was blowing, which gave a kind of dismal life to everything about him. The bushes shook their little thin arms with an incredible fury. One would have said that they were threatening and pursuing somebody.

He began to walk again, then quickened his pace to a run, and from time to time stopped and called out in that solitude, in a most desolate and terrible voice:

'Petit Gervais! Petit Gervais!'

Surely, if the child had heard him, he would have been frightened, and would have hid himself. But doubtless the boy was already far away.

He met a priest on horseback. He went up to him and said:

'Monsieur curé, have you seen a child go by?'

'No,' said the priest.

'Petit Gervais was his name?'

'I have seen nobody.'

He took two five-franc pieces from his bag, and gave them to the priest.

'Monsieur curé, this is for your poor. Monsieur curé, he is a little fellow, about ten years old, with a marmot, I think, and a hurdygurdy. He went this way. One of these Savoyards, you know?'

'I have not seen him.'

'Petit Gervais? Is his village near here? Can you tell me?'

'If it be as you say, my friend, the little fellow is a foreigner. They roam about this country. Nobody knows them.'

Jean Valjean hastily took out two more five-franc pieces, and gave them to the priest.

'For your poor,' said he.

Then he added wildly:

'Monsieur abbé, have me arrested. I am a robber.'

The priest put spurs to his horse, and fled in great fear.

Jean Valjean began to run again in the direction which he had first taken.

He went on in this wise for a considerable distance, looking around, calling and shouting, but met nobody else. Two or three times he left the path to look at what seemed to be somebody lying down or crouching; it was only low bushes or rocks. Finally, at a place where three paths met, he stopped. The moon had risen. He strained his eyes in the distance, and called out once more 'Petit Gervais! Petit Gervais! Petit Gervais!' His cries died away into the mist, without even awakening an echo. Again he murmured: 'Petit Gervais!' but with a feeble, and almost inarticulate voice. That was his last effort; his knees suddenly bent under him, as if an invisible power overwhelmed him at a blow, with the weight of his bad conscience; he fell exhausted upon a great stone, his hands clenched in his hair, and his face on his knees, and exclaimed: 'What a wretch I am!'

Then his heart swelled, and he burst into tears. It was the first time he had wept for nineteen years.

When Jean Valjean left the bishop's house, as we have seen, his mood was one that he had never known before. He could understand nothing of what was passing within him. He set himself stubbornly in opposition to the angelic deeds and the gentle words of the old man, 'You have promised me to become an honest man. I am purchasing your soul, I withdraw it from the spirit of perversity, and I give it to God Almighty.' This came back to him incessantly. To this celestial tenderness, he opposed pride, which is the fortress of evil in man. He felt dimly that the pardon of this priest was the hardest assault, and the most formidable attack which he had yet sustained; that his hardness of heart would be complete, if it resisted this kindness; that if he yielded, he must renounce that hatred with which the acts of other men had for so many years filled his soul, and in which he found satisfaction; that, this time, he must conquer or be conquered, and that the struggle, a gigantic and decisive struggle, had begun between his own wickedness, and the goodness of this man.

In view of all these things, he moved like a drunken man. While thus walking on with haggard look, had he a distinct perception of what might be to him the result of his adventure at D—? Did he hear those mysterious murmurs which warn or entreat the spirit at certain moments of life? Did a voice whisper in his ear that he had just passed through the decisive hour of his destiny, that there was no longer a middle course for him, that if, thereafter, he should not be the best of men, he would be the worst, that he must now, so to speak, mount higher than the bishop, or fall lower than the galley slave; that, if he would become good, he must become an angel; that, if he would remain wicked, he must become a monster?

Here we must again ask those questions, which we have already proposed elsewhere: was some confused shadow of all this formed in his mind? Certainly, misfortune, we have said, draws out the intelligence; it is doubtful, however, if Jean Valjean was in a condition to discern all that we here point out. If these ideas occurred to him, he but caught a glimpse, he did not see; and the only effect was to throw him into an inexpressible and distressing confusion. Being just out of that misshapen and gloomy thing which is called the galleys, the bishop had hurt his soul, as a too vivid light would have hurt his eyes on coming out of the dark. The future life, the possible life that was offered to him thenceforth, all pure and radiant, filled him with trembling and anxiety. He no longer knew really where he was. Like an owl who should see the sun suddenly rise, the convict had been dazzled and blinded by virtue.

One thing was certain, nor did he himself doubt it, that he was no longer the same man, that all was changed in him, that it was no longer in his power to prevent the bishop from having talked to him and having touched him.

In this frame of mind, he had met Petit Gervais, and stolen his forty sous. Why? He could not have explained it, surely; was it the final effect, the final effort of the evil thoughts he had brought from the galleys, a remnant of impulse, a result of what is called in physics *acquired force*? It was that, and it was also perhaps even less than that. We will say plainly, it was not he who had stolen, it was not the man, it was the beast which, from habit and instinct, had stupidly set its foot upon that money, while the intellect was struggling in the midst of so many new and unknown influences. When the intellect awoke and saw this act of the brute, Jean Valjean recoiled in anguish and uttered a cry of horror.

It was a strange phenomenon, possible only in the condition in which he then was, but the fact is, that in stealing this money from that child, he had done a thing of which he was no longer capable.

However that may be, this last misdeed had a decisive effect upon him; it rushed across the chaos of his intellect and dissipated it, set the light on one side and the dark clouds on the other, and acted upon his soul, in the condition it was in, as certain chemical re-agents act upon a turbid mixture, by precipitating one element and producing a clear solution of the other.

At first, even before self-examination and reflection, distractedly, like one who seeks to escape, he endeavoured to find the boy to give him back his money; then, when he found that that was useless and impossible, he stopped in despair. At the very moment when he exclaimed: 'What a wretch I am!' he saw himself as he was, and was already so far separated from himself that it seemed to him that he was only a phantom, and that he had there before him, in flesh and bone, with his stick in his hand, his blouse on his back, his knapsack filled with stolen articles on his shoulders, with his stern and gloomy face, and his thoughts full of abominable projects, the hideous galley slave, Jean Valjean.

Excess of misfortune, we have remarked, had made him, in some sort, a visionary. This then was like a vision. He veritably saw this Jean Valjean, this ominous face, before him. He was on the point of asking himself who that man was, and he was horror-stricken by it.

His brain was in one of those violent, and yet frightfully calm, conditions where reverie is so profound that it swallows up reality. We no longer see the objects that are before us, but we see, as if outside of ourselves, the forms that we have in our minds.

He beheld himself then, so to speak, face to face, and at the same time, across that hallucination, he saw, at a mysterious distance, a sort of light which he took at first to be a torch. Examining more attentively this light which dawned upon his conscience, he recognised that it had a human form, and that this torch was the bishop.

His conscience weighed in turn these two men thus placed before it, the bishop and Jean Valjean. Anything less than the first would have failed to soften the second. By one of those singular effects which are peculiar to this kind of ecstasy, as his reverie continued, the bishop grew grander and more resplendent in his eyes; Jean Valjean shrank and faded away. At one moment he was but a shadow. Suddenly he disappeared. The bishop alone remained.

He filled the whole soul of this wretched man with a magnificent radiance.

Jean Valjean wept long. He shed hot tears, he wept bitterly, with more weakness than a woman, with more terror than a child.

While he wept, the light grew brighter and brighter in his mind – an extraordinary light, a light at once transporting and terrible. His past life, his first offence, his long expiation, his brutal exterior, his hardened interior, his release made glad by so many schemes of vengeance, what had happened to him at the bishop's, his last action, this theft of forty sous from a child, a crime the meaner and the more monstrous that it came after the bishop's pardon, all this returned and appeared to him, clearly, but in a light that he had never seen before. He beheld his life, and it seemed to him horrible; his soul, and it seemed to him frightful. There was, however, a softened light upon that life and upon that soul. It seemed to him that he was looking upon Satan by the light of Paradise.

How long did he weep thus? What did he do after weeping? Where did he go? Nobody ever knew. It is known simply that, on that very night, the stage-driver who drove at that time on the Grenoble route, and arrived at D— about three o'clock in the morning, saw, as he passed through the bishop's street, a man in the attitude of prayer, kneeling upon the pavement in the shadow, before the door of Monseigneur Bienvenu.

BOOK 3: IN THE YEAR 1817

1. *The year 1817* [12]

THE YEAR 1817 was that which Louis XVIII, with a certain royal assumption not devoid of stateliness, styled the twenty-second year of his reign. It was the year when M. Bruguière de Sorsum was famous. All the hairdressers' shops, hoping for the return of powder and birds of Paradise, were bedizened with azure and fleurs-de-lis. It was the honest time when Count Lynch sat every

Sunday as churchwarden on the official bench at Saint Germain des Prés, in the dress of a peer of France, with his red ribbon and long nose, and that majesty of profile peculiar to a man who has done a brilliant deed. The brilliant deed committed by M. Lynch was that, being mayor of Bordeaux on the 12th of March 1814, he had surrendered the city a little too soon to the Duke of Angoulême. Hence his peerage. In 1817 it was the fashion to swallow up little boys from four to six years old in great morocco caps with ears, strongly resembling the chimney-pots of the Eskimo. The French army was dressed in white after the Austrian style; regiments were called legions, and wore, instead of numbers, the names of the departments. Napoleon was at St Helena, and as England would not give him green cloth, had had his old coats turned. In 1817, Pellegrini sang; Mademoiselle Bigottini danced; Potier reigned; Odry was not yet in existence. Madame Saqui succeeded to Forioso. There were Prussians still in France. M. Delalot was a personage. Legitimacy had just asserted itself by cutting off the fist and then the head of Pleignier, Carbonneau, and Tolleron. Prince Talleyrand, the grand chamberlain, and Abbé Louis, the designated minister of the finances, looked each other in the face, laughing like two augurs; both had celebrated the mass of the Federation in the Champ-de-Mars on 14th of July 1790, Talleyrand had said it as bishop, Louis had served him as deacon. In 1817, in the cross-walks of this same Champ-de-Mars, were seen huge wooden cylinders, painted blue, with traces of eagles and bees, that had lost their gilding, lying in the rain, and rotting in the grass. These were the columns which, two years before, had supported the estrade of the emperor in the Champ-de-Mai. They were blackened here and there from the bivouac-fires of the Austrians in barracks near the Gros-Caillou. Two or three of these columns had disappeared in the fires of these bivouacs, and had warmed the huge hands of the kaiserlics. The Champ-de-Mai was remarkable from the fact of having been held in the month of June, and on the Champ-de-Mars. In the year 1817, two things were popular – Voltaire-Touquet and Chartist snuff-boxes. The latest Parisian sensation was the crime of Dautun, who had thrown his brother's head into the fountain of the Marché-aux-Fleurs. People were beginning to find fault with the minister of the navy for having no news of that fated frigate, *La Méduse*, which was to cover Chaumareix with shame, and Géricault with glory. Colonel Selves went to Egypt, there to become Soliman-Pacha. The palace of the Thermes, Rue de la Harpe, was turned into a cooper's shop. On the platform of the octagonal tower of the Hôtel de Cluny, the little board shed was still to be seen, which had served as observatory to Messier, the astronomer of the navy under Louis XVI. The Duchess of Duras read to three or four friends, in her boudoir, furnished in sky-blue satin, the manuscript of *Ourika*. The N's were erased from the Louvre. The bridge of Austerlitz abdicated its name, and became the bridge of the Jardin-du-Roi, an enigma which disguised at once the bridge of Austerlitz and the Jardin-des-Plantes. Louis XVIII, absently annotating Horace with his finger-nail while thinking about heroes that had become emperors, and shoemakers that had become dauphins, had two cares, Napoleon and Mathurin Bruneau. The French Academy gave as a prize theme, *The happiness which Study procures*. M. Bellart was eloquent, officially. In his shadow was seen taking root the future Attorney-General, de Broë, promised to the sarcasms of Paul Louis Courier. There was a counterfeit Chauteaubriand called Marchangy, as there was to be later a counterfeit Marchangy called d'Arlincourt.

Claire d'Albe and *Malek Adel* were masterpieces; Madame Cottin was declared
the first writer of the age. The Institute struck from its list the academician,
Napoleon Bonaparte. A royal ordinance established a naval school at Angoulême,
for the Duke of Angoulême being Grand Admiral, it was evident that the town
of Angoulême had by right all the qualities of a seaport, without which the
monarchical principle would have been assailed. The question whether the
pictures, representing acrobats, which spiced the placards of Franconi, and drew
together the blackguards of the streets, should be tolerated, was agitated in the
cabinet councils. M. Paër, the author of *L'Agnese*, an honest man with square
jaws and a wart on his cheek, directed the small, select concerts of the
Marchioness de Sassenaye, Rue de la Ville-l'Evêque. All the young girls sang
l'Ermite de Saint Avelle, words by Edmond Géraud. The *Nain jaune* was
transformed into the *Miroir*. The Café Lemblin stood out for the emperor in
opposition to the Café Valois, which was in favour of the Bourbons. A marriage
had just been made up with a Sicilian princess for the Duke of Berry, who was
already in reality regarded with suspicion by Louvel. Madame de Staël had been
dead a year. Mademoiselle Mars was hissed by the bodyguards. The great
journals were all small. The form was limited, but the liberty was large. *Le
Constitutionnel* was constitutional; *La Minerve* called Chateaubriand, *Chateaubriant*.
This excited great laughter among the citizens at the expense of the great writer.

In purchased journals, prostituted journalists insulted the outlaws of 1815;
David no longer had talent, Arnault no longer had ability, Carnot no longer had
probity, Soult had never gained a victory; it is true that Napoleon no longer had
genius. Everybody knows that letters sent through the post to an exile rarely
reach their destination, the police making it a religious duty to intercept them.
This fact is by no means a new one; Descartes complained of it in his
banishment. Now, David having shown some feeling in a Belgian journal at not
receiving the letters addressed to him, this seemed ludicrous to the royalist
papers, who seized the occasion to ridicule the exile. To say, *regicides* instead of
voters, *enemies* instead of *allies*, *Napoleon* instead of *Buonaparte*, separated two men
more than an abyss. All people of common sense agreed that the era of
revolutions had been for ever closed by King Louis XVIII, surnamed 'The
immortal author of the Charter'. At the terreplain of the Pont Neuf, the word
Redivivus was sculptured on the pedestal which awaited the statue of Henri IV.
M. Piet at Rue Thérèse, No. 4, was sketching the plan of his cabal to consolidate
the monarchy. The leaders of the Right said, in grave dilemmas, 'We must write
to Bacol.' Messrs Canuel O'Mahony and Chappedelaine made a beginning, not
altogether without the approbation of Monsieur, of what was afterwards to
become the 'conspiracy of the Bord de l'Eau'. L'Epingle Noire plotted on its
side; Delaverderie held interviews with Trogoff; M. Decazes, a mind in some
degree liberal, prevailed. Chateaubriand, standing every morning at his window
in the Rue Saint Dominique, No. 27, in stocking pantaloons and slippers, his
grey hair covered with a Madras handkerchief, a mirror before his eyes, and a
complete case of dental instruments open before him, cleaned his teeth, which
were excellent, while dictating *La Monarchie selon la Charte* to M. Pilorge, his
secretary. The critics in authority preferred Lafon to Talma. M. de Féletz
signed himself A.; M. Hoffman signed himself Z. Charles Nodier was writing
Thérèse Aubert. Divorce was abolished. The lyceums called themselves colleges.
The students, decorated on the collar with a golden fleur-de-lis, pommelled

each other over the King of Rome. The secret police of the palace denounced to her royal highness, Madame, the portrait of the Duke of Orleans, which was everywhere to be seen, and which looked better in the uniform of colonel-general of hussars than the Duke of Berry in the uniform of colonel-general of dragoons – a serious matter. The city of Paris regilded the dome of the Invalides at its expense. Grave citizens asked each other what M. de Trinquelague would do in such or such a case; M. Clausel de Montals differed on sundry points from M. Clausel de Coussergues; M. de Salaberry was not satisfied. Comedy-writer Picard, of the Academy to which comedy-writer Molière could not belong, had *Les deux Philiberts* played at the Odeon, on the pediment of which, the removal of the letters still permitted the inscription to be read distinctly: THÉÂTRE DE L'IMPERATRICE. People took sides for or against Cugnet de Montarlot. Fabvier was factious; Bavoux was revolutionary. The bookseller Pelicier published an edition of Voltaire under the title, *Works of Voltaire*, of the French Academy. 'That will attract buyers,' said the naïve publisher. The general opinion was that M. Charles Loyson would be the genius of the age; envy was beginning to nibble at him, a sign of glory, and the line was made on him –

Même quand Loyson vole, on sent qu'il a despattes.

Cardinal Fesch refusing to resign, Monsieur de Pins, Archbishop of Amasie, administered the diocese of Lyons. The quarrel of the Vallée des Dappes commenced between France and Switzerland by a memorial from Captain, afterwards General Dufour. Saint-Simon, unknown, was building up his sublime dream. There was a celebrated Fourier in the Academy of Sciences whom posterity has forgotten, and an obscure Fourier in some unknown garret whom the future will remember. Lord Byron was beginning to dawn; a note to a poem of Millevoye introduced him to France as a *certain Lord Baron*. David d'Angers was endeavouring to knead marble. The Abbé Caron spoke with praise, in a small party of Seminarists in the cul-de-sac of the Feuillantines, of an unknown priest, Félicité Robert by name, who was afterwards Lamennais. A thing which smoked and clacked on the Seine, making the noise of a swimming dog, went and came beneath the windows of the Tuileries, from the Pont Royal to the Pont Louis XV; it was a piece of mechanism of no great value, a sort of toy, the day-dream of a visionary inventor, a Utopia – a steamboat. The Parisians looked upon the useless thing with indifference. Monsieur Vaublanc, wholesale re-former of the Institute by royal ordinance and distinguished author of several academicians, after having made them, could not make himself one. The Faubourg Saint-Germain and the Pavillon Marsan desired Monsieur Delaveau for prefect of police, on account of his piety. Dupuytren and Récamier quarrelled in the amphitheatre of the Ecole de Médicine, and shook their fists in each other's faces, over the divinity of Christ. Cuvier, with one eye on the book of Genesis and the other on nature, was endeavouring to please the bigoted reaction by reconciling fossils with texts and making the mastodons support Moses. Monsieur François de Neufchâteau, the praiseworthy cultivator of the memory of Parmentier, was making earnest efforts to have *pomme de terre* pronounced *parmentière*, without success. Abbé Grégoire, ex-bishop, ex-member of the National Convention, and ex-senator, had passed to the condition of the 'infamous Grégoire', in royalist polemics. The expression which we have just employed, 'passed to the condition', was denounced as a neologism by Monsieur Royer-Collard. The new stone could still be distinguished by its whiteness under the third arch of the bridge of Jena, which, two years before, had been used to stop up the entrance of the mine bored by Blücher to blow up the bridge. Justice summoned to her bar a man who had said aloud, on seeing Count d'Artois entering Notre-Dame, 'Sapristi! I regret the time when I saw Bonaparte and Talma entering the Bal-Sauvage, arm in arm.' Seditious language. Six months' imprisonment.

Traitors showed themselves stripped even of hypocrisy; men who had gone over to the enemy on the eve of a battle made no concealment of their bribes, and shamelessly walked abroad in daylight in the cynicism of wealth and dignities; deserters of Ligny and Quatre-Bras, in the brazenness of their purchased shame, exposed the nakedness of their devotion to monarchy, forgetting the commonest requirements of public decency.

Such was the confused mass of events that floated pell-mell on the surface of the year 1817, and is now forgotten. History neglects almost all these peculiarities, nor can it do otherwise; it is under the dominion of infinity. Nevertheless, these details, which are wrongly called little – there are neither little facts in humanity nor little leaves in vegetation – are useful. The physiognomy of the years makes up the face of the century.

In this year, 1817, four young Parisians played 'a good farce'.

2. Double quatuor

THESE PARISIANS WERE, one from Toulouse, another from Limoges, the third from Cahors, and the fourth from Montauban; but they were students, and to say student is to say Parisian; to study in Paris is to be born in Paris.

These young men were remarkable for nothing; everybody has seen such persons ; the four first comers will serve as samples; neither good nor bad, neither learned nor ignorant, neither talented nor stupid; handsome in that charming April of life which we call twenty. They were four Oscars; for at this time, Arthurs were not yet in existence. *Burn the perfumes of Arabia in his honour*, exclaims the romance. *Oscar approaches! Oscar, I am about to see him!* Ossian was in fashion, elegance was Scandinavian and Caledonian; the pure English did not prevail till later, and the first of the Arthurs, Wellington, had but just won the victory of Waterloo.

The first of these Oscars was called Félix Tholomyès, of Toulouse; the second, Listolier, of Cahors; the third, Fameuil, of Limoges; and the last, Blacheville, of Montauban. Of course each had his mistress. Blacheville loved Favourite, so called, because she had been in England; Listolier adored Dahlia, who had taken the name of a flower as her *nom de guerre*; Fameuil idolised Zéphine, the diminutive of Josephine, and Tholomyès had Fantine, called *the Blonde*, on account of her beautiful hair, the colour of the sun. Favourite, Dahlia, Zéphine, and Fantine were four enchanting girls, perfumed and sparkling, something of workwomen still, since they had not wholly given up the needle, agitated by love-affairs, yet preserving on their countenances a remnant of the serenity of labour, and in their souls that flower of purity, which in woman survives the first fall. One of the four was called the child, because she was the youngest; and another was called the old one – the Old One was twenty-three. To conceal nothing, the three first were more experienced, more careless, and better versed in the ways of the world than Fantine, the Blonde, who was still in her first illusion.

Dahlia, Zéphine, and Favourite especially, could not say as much. There had been already more than one episode in their scarcely commenced romance, and the lover called Adolphe in the first chapter, was found as Alphonse in the second, and Gustave in the third. Poverty and coquetry are fatal counsellors; the one grumbles, the other flatters, and the beautiful daughters of the people have both whispering in their ear, each on its side. Their ill-guarded souls listen. Thence their fall, and the stones that are cast at them. They are overwhelmed with the splendour of all that is immaculate and inaccessible. Alas! was the Jungfrau ever hungry?

Favourite, having been in England, was the admiration of Zéphine and Dahlia. She had had at a very early age a home of her own. Her father was a brutal, boasting old professor of mathematics, never married, and a rake, despite his years. When young, he one day saw the dress of a chambermaid catch in the fender, and fell in love through the accident. Favourite was the result. Occasionally she met her father, who touched his hat to her. One morning, an old woman with a fanatical air entered her rooms, and asked, 'you do not know me, mademoiselle?' – 'No.' – 'I am your mother.' – The old woman directly opened the buffet, ate and drank her fill, sent for a bed that she had, and made herself at home. This mother was a devotee and a grumbler; she never spoke to Favourite, remained for hours without uttering a word, breakfasted, dined and supped for four, and went down to the porter's lodge to see visitors and talk ill of her daughter.

What had attracted Dahlia to Listolier, to others perhaps, to indolence, was her beautiful, rosy finger-nails. How could such nails work! She who will remain virtuous must have no compassion for her hands. As to Zéphine, she had conquered Fameuil by her rebellious yet caressing little way of saying 'yes, sir'.

The young men were comrades, the young girls were friends. Such loves are always accompanied by such friendships.

Wisdom and philosophy are two things; a proof of which is that, with all necessary reservations for these little, irregular households, Favourite, Zéphine, and Dahlia, were philosophic, and Fantine was wise.

'Wise!' you will say, and Tholomyès? Solomon would answer that love is a part of wisdom. We content ourselves with saying that the love of Fantine was a first, an only, a faithful love.

She was the only one of the four who had been petted by but one.

Fantine was one of those beings which are brought forth from the heart of the people. Sprung from the most unfathomable depths of social darkness, she bore on her brow the mark of the anonymous and unknown. She was born at M— on M—. Who were her parents? None could tell, she had never known either father or mother. She was called Fantine – why so? because she had never been known by any other name. At the time of her birth, the Directory was still in existence. She could have no family name, for she had no family; she could have no baptismal name, for then there was no church. She was named after the pleasure of the first passer-by who found her, a mere infant, straying barefoot in the streets. She received a name as she received the water from the clouds on her head when it rained. She was called little Fantine. Nobody knew anything more of her. Such was the manner in which this human being had come into life. At the age of ten, Fantine left the city and went to service among the farmers of the suburbs. At fifteen, she came to Paris, to 'seek her fortune'. Fantine was beautiful and remained pure as long as she could. She was a pretty blonde with fine teeth. She had gold and pearls for her dowry; but the gold was on her head and the pearls in her mouth.

She worked to live; then, also to live, for the heart too has its hunger, she loved.

She loved Tholomyès.

To him, it was an amour; to her a passion. The streets of the Latin Quarter, which swarm with students and grisettes, saw the beginning of this dream. Fantine, in those labyrinths of the hill of the Pantheon, where so many ties are knotted and unloosed, long fled from Tholomyès, but in such a way as always to meet him again. There is a way of avoiding a person which resembles a search. In short, the eclogue took place.

Blacheville, Listolier, and Fameuil formed a sort of group of which Tholomyès was the head. He was the wit of the company.

Tholomyès was an old student of the old style; he was rich, having an income of four thousand francs – a splendid scandal on the Montagne Sainte-Geneviève. He was a good liver, thirty years old, and ill preserved. He was wrinkled, his teeth were broken, and he was beginning to show signs of baldness, of which he said, gaily: '*The head at thirty, the knees at forty.*' His digestion was not good, and he had a weeping eye. But in proportion as his youth died out, his gaiety increased; he replaced his teeth by jests, his hair by joy, his health by irony, and his weeping eye was always laughing. He was dilapidated, but covered with flowers. His youth, decamping long before its time, was beating a retreat in good order, bursting with laughter, and displaying no loss of fire. He had had a piece refused at the Vaudeville; he made verses now and then on any subject; moreover, he doubted everything with an air of superiority – a great power in the eyes of the weak. So, being bald and ironical, he was the chief. Can the word *iron* be the root from which irony is derived?

One day, Tholomyès took the other three aside, and said to them with an oracular gesture:

'For nearly a year, Fantine, Dahlia, Zéphine, and Favourite have been asking us to give them a surprise; we have solemnly promised them one. They are constantly reminding us of it, me especially. Just as the old women at Naples cry to Saint January, "*Faccia gialluta, fa o miracolo,* yellow face, do your miracle," our pretty ones are always saying: "Tholomyès, when are you going to be delivered of your surprise?" At the same time our parents are writing for us. Two birds with one stone. It seems to me the time has come. Let us talk it over.'

Upon this, Tholomyès lowered his voice, and mysteriously articulated something so ludicrous that a prolonged and enthusiastic giggling arose from the four throats at once, and Blacheville exclaimed: 'What an idea!'

An ale-house, filled with smoke, was before them; they entered, and the rest of their conference was lost in its shade.

The result of this mystery was a brilliant pleasure party, which took place on the following Sunday, the four young men inviting the four young girls.

3. *Four to four*

IT IS DIFFICULT to picture to oneself, at this day, a country party of students and grisettes as it was forty-five years ago. Paris has no longer the same environs; the aspect of what we might call circum-Parisian life has completely changed in half a century; in place of the rude, one-horse chaise, we have now the railroad car; in place of the pinnace, we have now the steamboat; we say Fécamp today, as we then said Saint Cloud. The Paris of 1862 is a city which has France for its suburbs.

The four couples scrupulously accomplished all the country follies then possible. It was in the beginning of the holidays, and a warm, clear summer's day. The night before, Favourite, the only one who knew how to write, had written to Tholomyès in the name of the four: 'It is lucky to go out early.' For this reason, they rose at five in the morning. Then they went to Saint Cloud by the coach, looked at the dry cascade and exclaimed: 'How beautiful it must be when there is any water!' breakfasted at the *Tête Noire*, which Castaing had not yet passed, amused themselves with a game of rings at the quincunx of the great basin, ascended to Diogenes' lantern, played roulette with macaroons on the Sèvres bridge, gathered bouquets at Puteaux, bought reed pipes at Neuilly, ate apple puffs everywhere, and were perfectly happy.

The young girls rattled and chattered like uncaged warblers. They were delirious with joy. Now and then they would playfully box the ears of the young men. Intoxication of the morning of life! Adorable years! The wing of the dragonfly trembles! Oh, ye, whoever you may be, have you memories of the past? Have you walked in the brushwood, thrusting aside the branches for the charming head behind you? Have you glided laughingly down some slope wet with rain, with the woman of your love, who held you back by the hand, exclaiming: 'Oh, my new boots! what a condition they are in!'

Let us hasten to say that that joyous annoyance, a shower, was wanting to this good-natured company, although Favourite had said, on setting out, with a magisterial and maternal air: 'The snails are crawling in the paths. A sign of rain, children.'

All four were ravishingly beautiful. A good old classic poet, then in renown, a good man who had an Eléanore, the Chevalier dc Labouïsse, who was walking that day under the chestnut trees of Saint Cloud, saw them pass about ten o'clock in the morning, and exclaimed, thinking of the Graces: 'There is one too many!' Favourite, the friend of Blacheville, the Old One of twenty-three, ran forward under the broad green branches, leaped across ditches, madly sprang over bushes, and took the lead in the gaiety with the verve of a young faun. Zéphine and Dahlia, whom chance had endowed with a kind of beauty that was heightened and perfected by contrast, kept together through the instinct of coquetry still more than through friendship, and, leaning on each other, affected English attitudes; the first *keepsakes* had just appeared, melancholy was in vogue for women, as Byronism was afterwards for men, and the locks of the tender sex were beginning to fall dishevelled. Zéphine and Dahlia wore their hair in rolls. Listolier and Fameuil, engaged in a discussion on their professors, explained to Fantine the difference between M. Delvincourt and M. Blondeau.

Blacheville seemed to have been created expressly to carry Favourite's dead-leaf coloured shawl upon his arm on Sunday.

Tholomyès followed, ruling, presiding over the group. He was excessively gay, but one felt the governing power in him. There was dictatorship in his joviality; his principal adornment was a pair of nankeen pantaloons, cut in the elephant-leg fashion, with under-stockings of copper-coloured braid; he had a huge rattan, worth two hundred francs, in his hand, and as he denied himself nothing, a strange thing called cigar in his mouth. Nothing being sacred to him, he was smoking.

'This Tholomyès is astonishing,' said the others, with veneration. 'What pantaloons! what energy!'

As to Fantine, she was joy itself. Her splendid teeth had evidently been endowed by God with one function – that of laughing. She carried in her hand rather than on her head, her little hat of sewed straw, with long, white strings. Her thick, blonde tresses, inclined to wave, and easily escaping from their confinement, obliging her to fasten them continually, seemed designed for the flight of Galatea under the willows. Her rosy lips babbled with enchantment. The corners of her mouth, turned up voluptuously like the antique masks of Erigone, seemed to encourage audacity; but her long, shadowy eyelashes were cast discreetly down towards the lower part of her face as if to check its festive tendencies. Her whole toilette was indescribably harmonious and enchanting. She wore a dress of mauve barege, little reddish-brown buskins, the strings of which were crossed over her fine, white, open-worked stockings, and that species of spencer, invented at Marseilles, the name of which, *canezou*, a corruption of the words *quinze août* in the Canebière dialect, signifies fine weather, warmth, and noon. The three others, less timid as we have said, wore low-necked dresses, which in summer, beneath bonnets covered with flowers, are full of grace and allurement; but by the side of this daring toilette, the canezou of the blonde Fantine, with its transparencies, indiscretions, and concealments, at once hiding and disclosing, seemed a provoking godsend of decency; and the famous court of love, presided over by the Viscountess de Cette, with the sea-green eyes, would probably have given the prize for coquetry to this canezou, which had entered the lists for that of modesty. The simplest is sometimes the wisest. So things go.

A brilliant face, delicate profile, eyes of a deep blue, heavy eyelashes, small, arching feet, the wrists and ankles neatly encased, the white skin showing here and there the azure arborescence of the veins; a cheek small and fresh, a neck robust as that of Ægean Juno, the nape firm and supple, shoulders modelled as if by Coustou, with a voluptuous dimple in the centre, just visible through the muslin; a gaiety tempered with reverie, sculptured and exquisite – such was Fantine, and you divined beneath this dress and these ribbons a statue, and in this statue a soul.

Fantine was beautiful, without being too conscious of it. Those rare dreamers, the mysterious priests of the beautiful, who silently compare all things with perfection, would have had a dim vision in this little work-woman, through the transparency of Parisian grace, of the ancient sacred Euphony. This daughter of obscurity had race. She possessed both types of beauty – style and rhythm. Style is the force of the ideal, rhythm is its movement.

We have said that Fantine was joy; Fantine also was modesty.

For an observer who had studied her attentively would have found through all this intoxication of age, of season, and of love, an unconquerable expression of reserve and modesty. She was somewhat restrained. This chaste restraint is the shade which separates Psyche from Venus. Fantine had the long, white, slender fingers of the vestals that stir the ashes of the sacred fire with a golden rod. Although she would have refused nothing to Tholomyès, as might be seen but too well, her face, in repose, was in the highest degree maidenly; a kind of serious and almost austere dignity suddenly possessed it at times, and nothing could be more strange or disquieting than to see gaiety vanish there so quickly, and reflection instantly succeed to delight. This sudden seriousness, sometimes strangely marked, resembled the disdain of a goddess. Her forehead, nose, and chin presented that equilibrium of line, quite distinct from the equilibrium of proportion, which produces harmony of features; in the characteristic interval which separates the base of the nose from the upper lip, she had that almost imperceptible but charming fold, the mysterious sign of chastity, which enamoured Barbarossa with a Diana, found in the excavations of Iconium.

Love is a fault; be it so. Fantine was innocence floating upon the surface of this fault.

4. *Tholomyès is so merry that he sings a Spanish song*

THAT DAY was sunshine from one end to the other. All nature seemed to be out on a holiday. The parterres of Saint Cloud were balmy with perfumes; the breeze from the Seine gently waved the leaves; the boughs were gesticulating in the wind; the bees were pillaging the jessamine; a whole crew of butterflies had settled in the milfoil, clover, and wild oats. The august park of the King of France was invaded by a swarm of vagabonds, the birds.

The four joyous couples shone resplendently in concert with the sunshine, the flowers, the fields, and the trees.

And in this paradisaical community, speaking, singing, running, dancing, chasing butterflies, gathering bindweed, wetting their open-worked stocking in the high grass, fresh, wild, but not wicked, stealing kisses from each other indiscriminately now and then, all except Fantine, who was shut up in her vague, dreary, severe resistance, and who was in love. 'You always have the air of being out of sorts,' said Favourite to her.

These are true pleasures. These passages in the lives of happy couples are a profound appeal to life and nature, and call forth endearment and light from everything. There was once upon a time a fairy, who created meadows and trees expressly for lovers. Hence comes that eternal school among the groves for lovers, which is always opening, and which will last so long as there are thickets and pupils. Hence comes the popularity of spring among thinkers. The patrician and the knife-grinder, the duke and peer, and the peasant, the men of the court, and the men of the town, as was said in olden times, all are subjects of this fairy. They laugh, they seek each other, the air seems filled with a new brightness; what a transfiguration is it to love! Notary clerks are gods. And the little shrieks, the pursuits among the grass, the waists encircled by stealth, that jargon which is melody, that adoration which breaks forth in a syllable, those cherries snatched from one pair of lips by another – all kindle up, and become transformed into celestial glories. Beautiful girls lavish their charms with sweet prodigality. We fancy that it will never end. Philosophers, poets, painters behold these ecstasies and know not what to make of them. So dazzling are they. The departure for Cythera! exclaims Watteau; Lancret, the painter of the commonalty, contemplates his bourgeois soaring in the sky; Diderot stretches out his arms to all these loves, and d'Urfé associates them with the Druids.[13]

After breakfast, the four couples went to see, in what was then called the king's square, a plant newly arrived from the Indies, the name of which escapes us at present, and which at this time was attracting all Paris to Saint Cloud: it was a strange and beautiful shrub with a long stalk, the innumerable branches of which, fine as threads, tangled, and leafless, were covered with millions of little, white blossoms, which gave it the appearance of flowing hair, powdered with flowers. There was always a crowd admiring it.

When they had viewed the shrub, Tholomyès exclaimed, 'I propose donkeys,' and making a bargain with a donkey-driver, they returned through Vanvres and Issy. At Issy, they had an adventure. The park, Bien-National, owned at this time by the commissary Bourguin, was by sheer good luck open. They passed through the grating, visited the mannikin anchorite in his grotto, and tried the little, mysterious effects of the famous cabinet of mirrors – a wanton trap, worthy of a satyr become a millionaire, or Turcaret metamorphosed into Priapus. They swung stoutly in the great swing, attached to the two chestnut trees, celebrated by the Abbé de Bernis. While swinging the girls, one after the other, and making folds of flying crinoline that Greuze would have found worth his study, the Toulousian Tholomyès, who was something of a Spaniard – Toulouse is cousin to Tolosa – sang in a melancholy key, the old *gallega* song, probably inspired by some beautiful damsel swinging in the air between two trees.

> Soy de Badajoz.
> Amor me llama.
> Toda mi alma
> Es en mi ojos
> Porque enseñas
> A tus piernas.

Fantine alone refused to swing.

'I do not like this sort of airs,' murmured Favourite, rather sharply.

They left the donkeys for a new pleasure, crossed the Seine in a boat, and walked from Passy to the Barrière de l'Etoile. They had been on their feet, it will be remembered, since five in the morning, but *bah! there is no weariness on Sunday*, said Favourite; *on Sunday fatigue has a holiday*. Towards three o'clock, the four couples, wild with happiness, were running down to the Russian mountains, a singular edifice which then occupied the heights of Beaujon, and the serpentine line of which might have been perceived above the trees of the Champs Elysées.

From time to time Favourite exclaimed:

'But the surprise? I want the surprise.'

'Be patient,' answered Tholomyès.

5. At Bombarda's

THE RUSSIAN MOUNTAINS exhausted, they thought of dinner, and the happy eight, a little weary at last, stranded on Bombarda's, a branch establishment, set up in the Champs Elysées by the celebrated restaurateur, Bombarda, whose sign was then seen on the Rue de Rivoli, near the Delorme Arcade.

A large but plain apartment, with an alcove containing a bed at the bottom (the place was so full on Sunday that it was necessary to take up with this lodging-room); two windows from which they could see, through the elms, the quay and the river; a magnificent August sunbeam glancing over the windows; two tables; one loaded with a triumphant mountain of bouquets, interspersed with hats and bonnets, while at the other, the four couples were gathered round a joyous pile of plates, napkins, glasses, and bottles; jugs of beer and flasks of wine; little order on the table, and some disorder under it.

Says Molière:

> Ils faisaient sous la table,
> Un bruit, un trique-trac epouvantable.*

Here was where the pastoral, commenced at five o'clock in the morning, was to be found at half-past four in the afternoon. The sun was declining, and their appetite with it.

The Champs Elysées, full of sunshine and people, was nothing but glare and dust, the two elements of glory. The horses of Marly, those neighing marbles, were curveting in a golden cloud. Carriages were coming and going. A magnificent squadron of bodyguards, with the trumpet at their head, were coming down the Avenue of Neuilly; the white flag, faintly tinged with red by the setting sun, was floating over the dome of the Tuileries. The Place de la Concorde, then become Place Louis XV again, was overflowing with pleased promenaders. Many wore the silver fleur-de-lis suspended from the watered white ribbon which, in 1817, had not wholly disappeared from the buttonholes. Here and there in the midst of groups of applauding spectators, circles of little girls gave to the winds a Bourbon doggerel rhyme, intended to overwhelm the Hundred Days, and the chorus of which ran:

> Rendez-nous notre père de Gand,[14]
> Rendez-nous notre père.†

Crowds of the inhabitants of the faubourgs in their Sunday clothes, some-times even decked with fleurs-de-lis like the citizens, were scattered over the great square and the square Marigny, playing games and going around on wooden horses; others were drinking; a few, printer apprentices, had on paper caps; their laughter resounded through the air. Everything was radiant. It was a time of undoubted peace and profound royal security; it was the time when a

---

* And under the table they beat   † Give us back our *Père de Gand*.
  A fearful tattoo with their feet.   Give us back our sire.

private and special report of Prefect of Police Anglès to the king on the faubourgs of Paris, ended with these lines: 'Everything considered, sire, there is nothing to fear from these people. They are as careless and indolent as cats. The lower people of the provinces are restless, those of Paris are not so. They are all small men, sire, and it would take two of them, one upon the other, to make one of your grenadiers. There is nothing at all to fear on the side of the populace of the capital. It is remarkable that this part of the population has also decreased in stature during the last fifty years; and the people of the faubourgs of Paris are smaller than before the Revolution. They are not dangerous. In short, they are good canaille.'

That a cat may become changed into a lion, prefects of police do not believe possible; nevertheless, it may be, and this is the miracle of the people of Paris. Besides, the cat, so despised by the Count Anglès, had the esteem of the republics of antiquity; it was the incarnation of liberty in their sight, and, as if to serve as a pendant to the wingless Minerva of the Piræus, there was, in the public square at Corinth, the bronze colossus of a cat. The simple police of the Restoration looked too hopefully on the people of Paris. They are by no means such good canaille as is believed. The Parisian is among Frenchmen what the Athenian was among Greeks. Nobody sleeps better than he, nobody is more frankly frivolous and idle than he, nobody seems to forget things more easily than he; but do not trust him, notwithstanding; he is apt at all sorts of nonchalance, but when there is glory to be gained, he is wonderful in every species of fury. Give him a pike, and he will play the tenth of August; give him a musket, and you shall have an Austerlitz. He is the support of Napoleon, and the resource of Danton. Is France in question? he enlists; is liberty in question? he tears up the pavement. Beware! his hair rising with rage is epic; his blouse drapes itself into a chlamys about him. Take care! At the first corner, Grenétat will make a Caudine Forks. When the tocsin sounds, this dweller in the faubourgs will grow; this little man will arise, his look will be terrible, his breath will become a tempest, and a blast will go forth from his poor, frail breast that might shake the wrinkles out of the Alps. Thanks to the men of the Paris faubourgs, the Revolution infused into armies, conquers Europe. He sings, it is his joy. Proportion his song to his nature, and you shall see! So long as he had the Carmagnole[15] merely for his chorus, he overthrew only Louis XVI; let him sing the Marseillaise, and he will deliver the world.

Writing this note in the margin of the Anglès report, we will return to our four couples. The dinner, as we have said, was over.

6. *A chapter of self-admiration*

TABLE TALK and lovers' talk equally elude the grasp; lovers' talk is clouds, table talk is smoke.

Fameuil and Dahlia hummed airs; Tholomyès drank, Zéphine laughed, Fantine smiled. Listolier blew a wooden trumpet that he had bought at Saint Cloud. Favourite looked tenderly at Blacheville, and said:

'Blacheville, I adore you.'

This brought forth a question from Blacheville:

'What would you do, Favourite, if I should leave you?'

'Me!' cried Favourite. 'Oh! do not say that, even in sport! If you should leave me, I would run after you, I would scratch you, I would pull your hair, I would throw water on you, I would have you arrested.'

Blacheville smiled with the effeminate foppery of a man whose self-love is tickled. Favourite continued:

'Yes! I would cry watch! No! I would scream, for example: rascal!'

Blacheville, in ecstasy, leaned back in his chair, and closed both eyes with a satisfied air.

Dahlia, still eating, whispered to Favourite in the hubbub:

'Are you really so fond of your Blacheville, then?'

'I detest him,' answered Favourite, in the same tone, taking up her fork. 'He is stingy; I am in love with the little fellow over the way from where I live. He is a nice young man; do you know him? Anybody can see that he was born to be an actor! I love actors. As soon as he comes into the house, his mother cries out: "Oh, dear! my peace is all gone. There, he is going to hallo! You will split my head;" just because he goes into the garret among the rats, into the dark corners, as high as he can go, and sings and declaims – and how do I know that they can hear him below! He gets twenty sous a day already by writing for a pettifogger. He is the son of an old chorister of Saint-Jacques du Haut-Pas! Oh, he is a nice young man! He is so fond of me that he said one day, when he saw me making dough for pancakes: "Mamselle, make your gloves into fritters and I will eat them." Nobody but artists can say things like these; I am on the high road to go crazy about this little fellow. It is all the same, I tell Blacheville that I adore him. How I lie! Oh, how I lie!'

Favourite paused, then continued:

'Dahlia, you see I am melancholy. It has done nothing but rain all summer; the wind makes me nervous and freckles me. Blacheville is very mean; there are hardly any green peas in the market yet, people care for nothing but eating; I have the spleen, as the English say; butter is so dear! and then, just think of it – it is horrible! We are dining in a room with a bed in it. I am disgusted with life.'

7. *The wisdom of Tholomyès* [16]

MEANTIME, while some were singing, the rest were all noisily talking at the same time. There was a perfect uproar. Tholomyès interfered.

'Do not talk at random, nor too fast!' exclaimed he; 'we must take time for reflection, if we would be brilliant. Too much improvisation leaves the mind stupidly void. Running beer gathers no foam. Gentlemen, no haste. Mingle dignity with festivity, eat with deliberation, feast slowly. Take your time. See the spring; if it hastens forward, it is ruined; that is, frozen. Excess of zeal kills peach and apricot trees. Excess of zeal kills the grace and joy of good dinners. No zeal, gentlemen! Grimod de la Reynière is of Talleyrand's opinion.'

'Tholomyès, let us alone,' said Blacheville.

'Down with the tyrant!' cried Fameuil.

'Bombarda, Bombance, and Bamboche!' exclaimed Listolier.

'Sunday still exists,' resumed Listolier.

'We are sober,' added Fameuil.

'Tholomyès,' said Blacheville, 'behold my calmness [*mon calme*].'

'You are its marquis,' replied Tholomyès.

This indifferent play on words had the effect of a stone thrown into a pool. The Marquis de Montcalm was a celebrated royalist of the time. All the frogs were silent.

'My friends!' exclaimed Tholomyès, in the tone of a man resuming his sway. 'Collect yourselves. This pun, though it falls from heaven, should not be welcomed with too much wonder. Everything that falls in this wise is not necessarily worthy of enthusiasm and respect. The pun is the dropping of the soaring spirit. The jest falls, it matters not where. And the spirit, after freeing itself from the folly, plunges into the clouds. A white spot settling upon a rock does not prevent the condor from hovering above. Far be it from me to insult the pun! I honour it in proportion to its merits – no more. The most august, most sublime, and most charming in humanity and perhaps out of humanity, have made plays on words. Jesus Christ made a pun on St Peter, Moses on Isaac, Æschylus on Polynices, Cleopatra on Octavius. And mark, that this pun of Cleopatra preceded the battle of Actium, and that, without it, no one would have remembered the city of Toryne, a Greek name signifying dipper. This conceded, I return to my exhortation. My brethren, I repeat, no zeal, no noise, no excess, even in witticisms, mirth, gaiety and plays on words. Listen to me; have the prudence of Amphiaraüs, and the boldness of Cæsar. There must be a limit, even to rebuses; *Est modus in rebus*. There must be a limit even to dinners. You like apple-puffs, ladies; do not abuse them. There must be, even in puffs, good sense and art. Gluttony punishes the glutton. Gula punishes Gulax. Indigestion is charged by God with enforcing morality on the stomach. And remember this: each of our passions, even love, has a stomach that must not be overloaded. We must in everything write the word *finis* in time; we must restrain ourselves, when it becomes urgent; we must draw the bolt on the appetite, play a fantasia on the violin, then break the strings with our own hand.

'The wise man is he who knows when and how to stop. Have some confidence in me. Because I have studied law a little, as my examinations prove, because I know the difference between the *question mue* and the *question pendante*, because I have written a Latin thesis on the method of torture in Rome at the time when Munatius Demens was quæstor of the Parricide; because I am about to become doctor, as it seems, it does not follow necessarily that I am a fool. I recommend to you moderation in all your desires. As sure as my name is Félix Tholomyès, I speak wisely. Happy is he, who, when the hour comes, takes a heroic resolve, and abdicates like Sylla or Origenes.'

Favourite listened with profound attention. 'Félix!' said she, 'what a pretty word. I like this name. It is Latin. It means prosperous.'

Tholomyès continued:

'*Quirites*, gentlemen, *caballeros, mes amis*, would you feel no passion, dispense with the nuptial couch and set love at defiance? Nothing is easier. Here is the recipe: lemonade, over exercise, hard labour; tire yourselves out, draw logs, do not sleep, keep watch; gorge yourselves with nitrous drinks and ptisans of water-lilies; drink emulsions of poppies and agnuscastus; enliven this with a rigid diet, starve yourselves, and add cold baths, girdles of herbs, the application of a leaden plate, lotions of solutions of lead and fomentations with vinegar and water.'

'I prefer a woman,' said Listolier.

'Woman!' resumed Tholomyès, 'distrust the sex. Unhappy is he who surrenders himself to the changing heart of woman! Woman is perfidious and tortuous. She detests the serpent through rivalry of trade. The serpent is the shop across the way.'

'Tholomyès,' cried Blacheville, 'you are drunk.'

'The deuce I am!' said Tholomyès.

'Then be gay,' resumed Blacheville.

'I agree,' replied Tholomyès.

Then, filling his glass, he arose.

'Honour to wine! *Nunc te, Bacche, canam.* Pardon, ladies, that is Spanish. And here is the proof, *señoras*; like wine-measure, like people. The arroba of Castile contains sixteen litres, the cantaro of Alicante twelve, the almuda of the Canaries twenty-five, the cuartin of the Baleares twenty-six, and the boot of Czar Peter thirty. Long live the czar, who was great, and long live his boot, which was still greater! Ladies, a friendly counsel! deceive your neighbours, if it seems good to you. The characteristic of love is to rove. Love was not made to cower and crouch like an English housemaid whose knees are callused with scrubbing. Gentle love was made but to rove gaily! It has been said to err is human; I say, to err is loving. Ladies, I idolise you all. O Zéphine, or Josephine, with face more than wrinkled, you would be charming if you were not cross. Yours is like a beautiful face, upon which someone has sat down by mistake. As to Favourite, oh, nymphs and muses, one day, as Blacheville was crossing the Rue Guerin-Boisseau, he saw a beautiful girl with white, well-gartered stockings, who was showing them. The prologue pleased him, and Blacheville loved. She whom he loved was Favourite. Oh, Favourite! Thou hast Ionian lips. There was a Greek painter, Euphorion, who was surnamed painter of lips. This Greek alone would have been worthy to paint thy mouth. Listen! before thee, there was no creature worthy the name. Thou wert made to receive the apple like Venus, or to eat it like Eve. Beauty begins with thee. I have spoken of Eve; she was of thy creation. Thou deservest the patent for the invention of beautiful women. Oh, Favourite, I cease to thou you, for I pass from poetry to prose. You spoke just now of my name. It moved me; but, whatever we do, let us not trust to names, they may be deceitful. I am called Félix, I am not happy. Words are deceivers. Do not blindly accept the indications which they give. It would be a mistake to write to Liege for corks or to Pau for gloves. Miss Dahlia, in your place, I should call myself Rose. The flower should have fragrance, and woman should have wit. I say nothing of Fantine, she is visionary, dreamy, pensive, sensitive; she is a phantom with the form of a nymph, and the modesty of a nun, who has strayed into the life of a grisette, but who takes refuge in illusions, and who sings, and prays, and gazes at the sky without knowing clearly what she sees nor what she does, and who, with eyes fixed on heaven, wanders in a garden among more birds than exist there. Oh, Fantine, know this: I, Tholomyès, am an illusion – but she does not even hear me – the fair daughter of chimeras! Nevertheless, everything on her is freshness, gentleness, youth, soft, matinal clearness. Oh, Fantine, worthy to be called Marguerite or Pearl, you are a jewel of the purest water. Ladies, a second counsel, do not marry; marriage is a graft; it may take well or ill. Shun the risk. But what do I say? I am wasting my words. Women are incurable on the subject of weddings, and all that we wise men can say will not hinder vestmakers and gaiter-binders from dreaming about husbands loaded with diamonds. Well, be it so; but, beauties, remember this: you eat too much sugar. You have but one fault, oh, women! it is that of nibbling sugar. Oh, consuming sex, the pretty, little white teeth adore sugar. Now, listen attentively! Sugar is a salt. Every salt is desiccating. Sugar is the most desiccating of all salts. It sucks up the liquids from the blood through the veins; thence comes the coagulation, then the solidification of the blood; thence tubercles in the lungs; thence death. And this is why diabetes borders on consumption. Crunch no sugar, therefore, and you shall live! I turn towards the men: gentlemen, make conquests. Rob each other without remorse of your beloved. Chassez and cross over. There are no friends in love. Wherever there is a pretty woman, hostility is open. No quarter; war to the knife! A pretty woman is a *casus belli;* a pretty woman is a *flagrans delictum.* All the invasions of history have been determined by petticoats. Woman is the right of man. Romulus carried off the Sabine women; William carried off the Saxon women; Cæsar carried off the Roman women. The man who is not loved hovers like a vulture over the sweetheart of others; and for my part, to all unfortunate widowers, I issue the sublime proclamation of Bonaparte to the army of Italy, 'Soldiers, you lack for everything. The enemy has everything.'

Tholomyès checked himself.

'Take breath, Tholomyès,' said Blacheville.

At the same time, Blacheville, aided by Listolier and Fameuil, with an air of lamentation hummed one of those workshop songs, made up of the first words that came, rhyming richly and not at all, void of sense as the movement of the trees and the sound of the winds, and which are borne from the smoke of the pipes, and dissipate and take flight with it. This is the couplet by which the group replied to the harangue of Tholomyès:

> Les pères dindons donnèrent
> De l'argent à un agent
> Pour que mons Clermont-Tonnerre
> Fût fait pape à la Saint-Jean;
> Mais Clermont ne put pas être
> Fait pape, n'étant pas prêtre;
> Alors leur agent rageant
> Leur rapporta leur argent.[17]

This was not likely to calm the inspiration of Tholomyès; he emptied his glass, filled it, and again began:

'Down with wisdom! forget all that I have said. Let us be neither prudes, nor prudent, nor prud'hommes! I drink to jollity; let us be jolly. Let us finish our course of study by folly and prating. Indigestion and the Digest. Let Justinian be the male, and festivity the female. There is joy in the abysses. Behold, oh, creation! The world is a huge diamond! I am happy. The birds are marvellous. What a festival everywhere! The nightingale is an Elleviou gratis. Summer, I salute thee. Oh, Luxembourg! Oh, Georgics of the Rue Madame, and the Allée de l'Observatoire! Oh, entranced dreamers! The pampas of America would delight me, if I had not the Arcades of the Odeon. My soul goes out towards virgin forests and savannahs. Everything is beautiful; the flies hum in the sunbeams. The humming-birds whizz in the sunshine. Kiss me, Fantine!'

And, by mistake, he kissed Favourite.

8. *Death of a horse*

'THE DINNERS are better at Édon's than at Bombarda's,' exclaimed Zéphine.

'I like Bombarda better than Édon,' said Blacheville 'There is more luxury. It is more Asiatic. See the lower hall. There are mirrors [*glaces*] on the walls.'

'I prefer ices [*glaces*] on my plate,' said Favourite.

Blacheville persisted.

'Look at the knives. The handles are silver at Bombarda's, and bone at Édon's. Now, silver is more precious than bone.'

'Except when it is on the chin,' observed Tholomyès.

He looked out at this moment at the dome of the Invalides, which was visible from Bombarda's windows.

There was a pause.

'Tholomyès,' cried Fameuil, 'Listolier and I have just had a discussion.'

'A discussion is good,' replied Tholomyès, 'a quarrel is better.'

'We were discussing philosophy.'

'I have no objection.'

'Which do you prefer, Descartes or Spinoza?'

'Désaugiers,' said Tholomyès.

This decision rendered, he drank, and resumed:

'I consent to live. All is not over on earth, since we can yet reason falsely. I render thanks for this to the immortal gods. We lie, but we laugh. We affirm, but we doubt. The unexpected shoots forth from a syllogism. It is fine. There are men still on earth who know how to open and shut pleasantly the surprise boxes of paradox. Know, ladies, that this wine you are drinking so calmly, is Madeira from the vineyard of Coural das Frerras, which is three hundred and seventeen fathoms above the level of the sea. Attention while you drink! three hundred and seventeen fathoms! and M. Bombarda, this magnificent restaurateur, gives you these three hundred and seventeen fathoms for four francs, fifty centimes.'

Fameuil interrupted again.

'Tholomyès, your opinions are law. Who is your favourite author?'

'Ber – '

'Quin?'

'No. Choux.'

And Tholomyès continued.

'Honour to Bombarda! he would equal Munophis of Elephanta if he could procure me an almée and Thygelion of Chæronea if he could bring me a hetaïra! for, oh, ladies, there were Bombardas in Greece and Egypt; this Apuleius teaches us. Alas! always the same thing and nothing new. Nothing more unpublished in the creation of the Creator! *Nil sub sole novum,* says Solomon; *amor omnibus idem,* says Virgil; and Carabine mounts with Carabin in the galliot at Saint Cloud, as Aspasia embarked with Pericles on the fleet of Samos. A last word. Do you know who this Aspasia was, ladies? Although she lived in a time when women had not yet a soul, she was a soul; a soul of a rose and purple shade, more glowing than fire, fresher than the dawn. Aspasia was a being who touched the two extremes of woman, the prostitute goddess. She was Socrates, plus Manon Lescaut.

Aspasia was created in case Prometheus might need a wanton.'

Tholomyès, now that he was started would have been stopped with difficulty, had not a horse fallen down at this moment on the quay. The shock stopped short both the cart and the orator. It was an old, meagre mare, worthy of the knacker, harnessed to a very heavy cart. On reaching Bombarda's, the beast, worn and exhausted, had refused to go further. This incident attracted a crowd. Scarcely had the carman, swearing and indignant, had time to utter with fitting energy the decisive word, '*mâtin!*' backed by a terrible stroke of the whip, when the hack fell, to rise no more. At the hubbub of the passers-by, the merry auditors of Tholomyès turned their heads, and Tholomyès profited by it to close his address by this melancholy strophe:[18]

> Elle était de ce monde où coucous et carrosses
> Ont le même destin;
> Et, rosse, elle a vécu ce que vivent les rosses,
> L'espace d'un matin!

'Poor horse!' sighed Fantine.

Dahlia exclaimed:

'Here is Fantine pitying horses! Was there ever anything so absurd?'

At this moment, Favourite, crossing her arms and turning round her head, looked fixedly at Tholomyès and said:

'Come! the surprise?'

'Precisely. The moment has come,' replied Tholomyès. 'Gentlemen, the hour has come for surprising these ladies. Ladies, wait for us a moment.'

'It begins with a kiss,' said Blacheville.

'On the forehead,' added Tholomyès.

Each one gravely placed a kiss on the forehead of his mistress; after which they directed their steps towards the door, all four in file, laying their fingers on their lips.

Favourite clapped her hands as they went out.

'It is amusing already,' said she.

'Do not be too long,' murmured Fantine. 'We are waiting for you.'

9. *Joyous end of joy*

THE GIRLS, left alone, leaned their elbows on the window sills in couples, and chattered together, bending their heads and speaking from one window to the other.

They saw the young men go out of Bombarda's, arm in arm; they turned round, made signals to them laughingly, then disappeared in the dusty Sunday crowd which takes possession of the Champs-Elysées once a week.

'Do not be long!' cried Fantine.

'What are they going to bring us?' said Zéphine.

'Surely something pretty,' said Dahlia.

'I hope it will be gold,' resumed Favourite.

They were soon distracted by the stir on the water's edge, which they distinguished through the branches of the tall trees, and which diverted them greatly. It was the hour for the departure of the mails and diligences. Almost all the stage-coaches to the south and west, passed at that time by the Champs-Elysées. The greater part followed the quay and went out through the Barrière Passy. Every minute some huge vehicle, painted yellow and black, heavily loaded, noisily harnessed, distorted with mails, awnings, and valises, full of heads that were constantly disappearing, grinding the kerbstones, turning the pavements into flints, rushed through the crowd, throwing out sparks like a forge, with dust for smoke, and an air of fury. This hubbub delighted the young girls. Favourite exclaimed:

'What an uproar; one would say that heaps of chains were taking flight.'

It so happened that one of these vehicles which could be distinguished with difficulty through the obscurity of the elms, stopped for a moment, then set out again on a gallop. This surprised Fantine.

'It is strange,' said she. 'I thought the diligences never stopped.'

Favourite shrugged her shoulders:

'This Fantine is surprising; I look at her with curiosity. She wonders at the most simple things. Suppose that I am a traveller, and say to the diligence; "I am going on; you can take me up on the quay in passing." The diligence passes, sees me, stops and takes me up. This happens every day. You know nothing of life, my dear.'

Some time passed in this manner. Suddenly Favourite started as if from sleep.

'Well!' said she, 'and the surprise?'

'Yes,' returned Dahlia, 'the famous surprise.'

'They are very long!' said Fantine.

As Fantine finished the sigh, the boy who had waited at dinner entered. He had in his hand something that looked like a letter.

'What is that?' asked Favourite.

'It is a paper that the gentlemen left for these ladies,' he replied.

'Why did you not bring it at once?'

'Because the gentlemen ordered me not to give it to the ladies before an hour,' returned the boy.

Favourite snatched the paper from his hands. It was really a letter.

'Stop!' said she. 'There is no address; but see what is written on it:

THIS IS THE SURPRISE.'

She hastily unsealed the letter, opened it, and read (she knew how to read):

'OH, OUR LOVERS!

Know that we have parents. Parents – you scarcely know the meaning of the word, they are what are called fathers and mothers in the civil code, simple but honest. Now these parents bemoan us, these old men claim us, these good men and women call us prodigal sons, desire our return and offer to kill for us the fatted calf. We obey them, being virtuous. At the moment when you read this, five mettlesome horses will be bearing us back to our papas and mammas. We are pitching our camps, as Bossuet says. We are going, we are gone. We fly in the arms of Laffitte, and on the wings of Caillard. The Toulouse diligence snatches us from the abyss, and you are this abyss, our beautiful darlings! We are returning to society, to duty and order, on a full trot, at the rate of three leagues an hour. It is necessary to the country that we become, like everybody else, prefects, fathers of families, rural guards, and councillors of state. Venerate us. We sacrifice ourselves. Mourn for us rapidly, and replace us speedily. If this letter rends you, rend it in turn. Adieu.

For nearly two years we have made you happy. Bear us no ill will for it.

Signed: BLANCHEVILLE
FAMEUIL
LISTOLIER
FÉLIX THOLOMYÈS

P.S. The dinner is paid for.'[19]

The four girls gazed at each other.

Favourite was the first to break silence.

'Well!' said she, 'it is a good farce all the same.'

'It is very droll,' said Zéphine.

'It must have been Blacheville that had the idea,' resumed Favourite. 'This makes me in love with him. Soon loved, soon gone. That is the story.'

'No,' said Dahlia, 'it is an idea of Tholomyès. This is clear.'

'In that case,' returned Favourite, 'down with Blacheville, and long live Tholomyès!'

'Long live Tholomyès!' cried Dahlia and Zéphine.

And they burst into laughter.

Fantine laughed like the rest.

An hour afterwards, when she had re-entered her chamber, she wept. It was her first love, as we have said; she had given herself to this Tholomyès as to a husband, and the poor girl had a child.

BOOK 4:   TO ENTRUST IS SOMETIMES
TO ABANDON

1. *One mother meets another*

THERE WAS, during the first quarter of the present century, at Montfermeil, near Paris, a sort of chop-house: it is not there now. It was kept by a man and his wife, named Thénardier, and was situated in the Lane Boulanger. Above the door, nailed flat against the wall, was a board, upon which something was painted that looked like a man carrying on his back another man wearing the heavy epaulettes of a general, gilt and with large silver stars; red blotches typified blood; the remainder of the picture was smoke, and probably represented a battle. Beneath was this inscription: TO THE SERGEANT OF WATERLOO.

Nothing is commoner than a cart or wagon before the door of an inn; nevertheless the vehicle, or more properly speaking, the fragment of a vehicle which obstructed the street in front of the Sergeant of Waterloo one evening in the spring of 1815, certainly would have attracted by its bulk the attention of any painter who might have been passing.

It was the fore-carriage of one of those drays for carrying heavy articles, used in wooded countries for transporting joists and trunks of trees: it consisted of a massive iron axle-tree with a pivot to which a heavy pole was attached, and which was supported by two enormous wheels. As a whole, it was squat, crushing, and misshapen: it might have been fancied a gigantic gun-carriage.

The roads had covered the wheels, felloes, limbs, axle, and the pole with a coating of hideous yellow-hued mud, similar in tint to that with which cathedrals are sometimes decorated. The wood had disappeared beneath mud; and the iron beneath rust.

Under the axle-tree hung festooned a huge chain fit for a Goliath of the galleys.

This chain recalled, not the beams which it was used to carry, but the mastodons and mammoths which it might have harnessed; it reminded one of the galleys, but of cyclopean and superhuman galleys, and seemed as if unriveted from some monster. With it Homer could have bound Polyphemus, or Shakespeare Caliban.

Why was this vehicle in this place in the street, one may ask? First to obstruct the lane, and then to complete its work of rust. There is in the old social order a host of institutions which we find like this across our path in the full light of day, and which present no other reasons for being there.

The middle of the chain was hanging quite near the ground, under the axle; and upon the bend, as on a swinging rope, two little girls were seated that evening in exquisite grouping, the smaller, eighteen months old, in the lap of the larger, who was two years and a half old.

A handkerchief carefully knotted kept them from falling. A mother, looking upon this frightful chain, had said: 'Ah! there is a plaything for my children!'

The radiant children, picturesquely and tastefully decked, might be fancied two roses twining the rusty iron, with their triumphantly sparkling eyes, and their blooming, laughing faces. One was a rosy blonde, the other a brunette; their artless faces were two ravishing surprises; the perfume that was shed upon the air by a flowering shrub nearby seemed their own out-breathings; the smaller one was showing her pretty little body with the chaste indecency of babyhood. Above and around these delicate heads, moulded in happiness and bathed in light, the gigantic carriage, black with rust and almost frightful with its entangled curves and abrupt angles, arched like the mouth of a cavern.

The mother, a woman whose appearance was rather forbidding, but touching at this moment, was seated on the sill of the inn, swinging the two children by a long string, while she brooded them with her eyes for fear of accident with that animal but heavenly expression peculiar to maternity. At each vibration the hideous links uttered a creaking noise like an angry cry; the little ones were in ecstasies, the setting sun mingled in the joy, and nothing could be more charming than this caprice of chance which made of a Titan's chain a swing for cherubim.

While rocking the babes the mother sang with a voice out of tune a then popular song:

'Il le faut, disait un guerrier.'

Her song and watching her children prevented her hearing and seeing what was passing in the street.

Someone, however, had approached her as she was beginning the first couplet of the song, and suddenly she heard a voice say quite near her ear:

'You have two pretty children there, madame.'

'A la belle et tendre Imogine,'

answered the mother, continuing her song; then she turned her head.

A woman was before her at a little distance; she also had a child, which she bore in her arms.

She was carrying in addition a large carpet-bag, which seemed heavy.

This woman's child was one of the divinest beings that can be imagined: a little girl of two or three years. She might have entered the lists with the other little ones for coquetry of attire; she wore a head-dress of fine linen; ribbons at her shoulders and Valenciennes lace on her cap. The folds of her skirt were raised enough to show her plump fine white leg: she was charmingly rosy and healthful. The pretty little creature gave one a desire to bite her cherry cheeks. We can say nothing of her eyes except that they must have been very large, and were fringed with superb lashes. She was asleep.

She was sleeping in the absolutely confiding slumber peculiar to her age. Mothers' arms are made of tenderness, and sweet sleep blesses the child who lies therein.

As to the mother, she seemed poor and sad; she had the appearance of a working woman who is seeking to return to the life of a peasant. She was young, – and pretty? It was possible, but in that garb beauty could not be displayed. Her hair, one blonde mesh of which had fallen, seemed very thick, but it was severely fastened up beneath an ugly, close, narrow nun's head-dress, tied under the chin. Laughing shows fine teeth when one has them, but she did not laugh. Her eyes seemed not to have been tearless for a long time. She was pale, and looked very weary, and somewhat sick. She gazed upon her child, sleeping in her arms, with that peculiar look which only a mother possesses who nurses her own child. Her form was clumsily masked by a large blue handkerchief folded across her bosom. Her hands were tanned and spotted with freckles, the forefinger hardened and pricked with the needle; she wore a coarse brown delaine mantle, a calico dress, and large heavy shoes. It was Fantine.

Yes, Fantine. Hard to recognise, yet, on looking attentively, you saw that she still retained her beauty. A sad line, such as is formed by irony, had marked her right cheek. As to her toilette – that airy toilette of muslin and ribbons which seemed as if made of gaiety, folly, and music, full of baubles and perfumed with lilacs – that had vanished like the beautiful sparkling hoarfrost, which we take for diamonds in the sun; they melt, and leave the branch dreary and black.

Ten months had slipped away since 'the good farce'.

What had passed during these ten months? We can guess.

After recklessness, trouble. Fantine had lost sight of Favourite, Zéphine, and Dahlia; the tie, broken on the part of the men, was unloosed on the part of the women; they would have been astonished if anyone had said a fortnight afterwards they were friends; they had no longer cause to be so. Fantine was left alone. The father of her child gone – Alas! such partings are irrevocable – she found herself absolutely isolated, with the habit of labour lost, and the taste for pleasure acquired. Led by her liaison with Tholomyès to disdain the small business that she knew how to do, she had neglected her opportunities, they were all gone. No resource. Fantine could scarcely read, and did not know how to write. She had only been taught in childhood how to sign her name. She had a letter written by a public letter-writer to Tholomyès, then a second, then a third. Tholomyès had replied to none of them. One day, Fantine heard some old women saying as they saw her child: 'Do people ever take such children to heart? They only shrug their shoulders at such children!' Then she thought of Tholomyès, who shrugged his shoulders at his child, and who did not take this innocent child to heart, and her heart became dark in the place that was his. What should she do? She had no one to ask. She had committed a fault; but, in the depths of her nature, we know dwelt modesty and virtue. She had a vague feeling that she was on the eve of falling into distress, of slipping into the street. She must have courage; she had it, and bore up bravely. The idea occurred to her of returning to her native village M— sur M—, there perhaps someone would know her, and give her work. Yes, but she must hide her fault. And she had a confused glimpse of the possible necessity of a separation still more painful than the first. Her heart ached, but she took her resolution. It will be seen that Fantine possessed the stern courage of life. She had already valiantly renounced her finery, was draped in calico, and had put all her silks, her gewgaws, her ribbons, and laces on her daughter – the only vanity that remained, and that a holy one. She sold all she had, which gave her two hundred francs; when her little debts were paid, she had but about eighty left. At twenty-two years of age, on a fine spring morning, she left Paris, carrying her child on her back. He who had seen the two passing, must have pitied them. The woman had nothing in the world but this child, and this child had nothing in the world but this woman. Fantine had nursed her child; that had weakened her chest somewhat, and she coughed slightly.

We shall have no further need to speak of M. Félix Tholomyès. We will only say here, that twenty years later, under King Louis Philippe, he was a fat provincial attorney, rich and influential, a wise elector and rigid juryman; always, however, a man of pleasure.

Towards noon, after having, for the sake of rest, travelled from time to time at a cost of three or four cents a league, in what they called then the Petites Voitures of the environs of Paris, Fantine reached Montefermeil, and stood in Boulanger Lane.

As she was passing by the Thénardier chop-house, the two little children sitting in delight on their monstrous swing, had a sort of dazzling effect upon her, and she paused before this joyous vision.

There are charms. These two little girls were one for this mother.

She beheld them with emotion. The presence of angels is a herald of paradise. She thought she saw above this inn the mysterious 'HERE' of Providence. These children were evidently happy: she gazed upon them, she admired them, so much affected that at the moment when the mother was taking breath between the verses of her song, she could not help saying what we have been reading.

'You have two pretty children there, madame.'

The most ferocious animals are disarmed by caresses to their young.

The mother raised her head and thanked her, and made the stranger sit down on the stone step, she herself being on the door-sill: the two women began to talk together.

'My name is Madame Thénardier,' said the mother of the two girls: 'we keep this inn.'

Then going on with her song, she sang between her teeth;

> 'Il le faut, je suis chevalier,
> Et je pars pour la Palestine,'

This Madame Thénardier was a red-haired, brawny, angular woman, of the soldier's-wife type in all its horror, and, singularly enough, she had a lolling air which she had gained from novel-reading. She had a masculine lackadaisicalness. Old romances impressed on the imaginations of mistresses of chop-houses have such effects. She was still young, scarcely thirty years old. If this woman, who was seated stooping, had been upright, perhaps her towering form and her broad shoulders, those of a movable colossus, fit for a market-woman, would have dismayed the traveller, disturbed her confidence, and prevented what we have to relate. A person seated instead of standing; fate hangs on such a thread as that.

The traveller told her story, a little modified.

She said she was a working woman, and her husband was dead. Not being able to procure work in Paris she was going in search of it elsewhere; in her own province; that she had left Paris that morning on foot; that carrying her child she had become tired, and meeting the Villemomble stage had got in; that from Villemomble she had come on foot to Montfermeil; that the child had walked a little, but not much, she was so young; that she was compelled to carry her, and the jewel had fallen asleep.

And at these words she gave her daughter a passionate kiss, which wakened her. The child opened its large blue eyes, like its mother's, and saw – what? Nothing, everything, with that serious and sometimes severe air of little children, which is one of the mysteries of their shining innocence before our shadowy virtues. One would say that they felt themselves to be angels, and knew us to be human. Then the child began to laugh, and, although the mother restrained her, slipped to the ground, with the indomitable energy of a little one that wants to run about. All at once she perceived the two others in their swing, stopped short, and put out her tongue in token of admiration.

Mother Thénardier untied the children and took them from the swing, saying:

'Play together, all three of you.'

At that age acquaintance is easy, and in a moment the little Thénardiers were playing with the newcomer, making holes in the ground to their intense delight.

This newcomer was very sprightly: the goodness of the mother is written in the gaiety of the child, she had taken a splinter of wood, which she used as a spade, and was stoutly digging a hole fit for a fly. The gravedigger's work is charming when done by a child.

The two women continued to chat.

'What do your call your brat?'

'Cosette.'

For Cosette read Euphrasie. The name of the little one was Euphrasie. But the mother had made Cosette out of it, by that sweet and charming instinct of mothers and of the people, who change Joséfa into Pepita, and Françoise into

Sillette. That is a kind of derivation which deranges and disconcerts all the science of etymologists. We knew a grandmother who succeeded in making from Theodore, Gnon.

'How old is she?'

'She is going on three years.'

'The age of my oldest.'

The three girls were grouped in an attitude of deep anxiety and bliss; a great event had occurred; a large worm had come out of the ground; they were afraid of it, and yet in ecstasies over it.

Their bright foreheads touched each other: three heads in one halo of glory.

'Children,' exclaimed the Thénardier mother; 'how soon they know one another. See them! One would swear they were three sisters.'

These words were the spark which the other mother was probably awaiting. She seized the hand of Madame Thénardier and said:

'Will you keep my child for me?'

Madame Thénardier made a motion of surprise, which was neither consent nor refusal.

Cosette's mother continued:

'You see I cannot take my child into the country. Work forbids it. With a child I could not find a place there; they are so absurd in that district. It is God who has led me before your inn. The sight of your little ones, so pretty, and clean, and happy, has overwhelmed me. I said: there is a good mother; they will be like three sisters, and then it will not be long before I come back. Will you keep my child for me?'

'I must think over it,' said Thénardier.

'I will give six francs a month.'

Here a man's voice was heard from within:

'Not less than seven francs, and six months paid in advance.'

'Six times seven are forty-two,' said Thénardier.

'I will give it,' said the mother.

'And fifteen francs extra for the first expenses,' added the man.

'That's fifty-seven francs,' said Madame Thénardier, and in the midst of her reckoning she sang indistinctly:

'Il le faut, disait un guerrier.'

'I will give it,' said the mother; 'I have eighty francs. That will leave me enough to go into the country if I walk. I will earn some money there, and as soon as I have I will come for my little love.'

The man's voice returned:

'Has the child a wardrobe?'

'That is my husband,' said Thénardier.

'Certainly she has, the poor darling. I knew it was your husband. And a fine wardrobe it is too, an extravagant wardrobe, everything in dozens, and silk dresses like a lady. They are there in my carpet-bag.'

'You must leave that here,' put in the man's voice.

'Of course I shall give it to you,' said the mother; 'it would be strange if I should leave my child naked.'

The face of the master appeared.

'It is all right,' said he.

The bargain was concluded. The mother passed the night at the inn, gave her money and left her child, fastened again her carpet-bag, diminished by her child's wardrobe, and very light now, and set off next morning, expecting soon to return. These partings are arranged tranquilly, but they are full of despair.

A neighbour of the Thénardiers met this mother on her way, and came in, saying:

'I have just met a woman in the street, who was crying as if her heart would break.'

When Cosette's mother had gone, the man said to his wife:

'That will do me for my note of 110 francs which falls due tomorrow; I was fifty francs short. Do you know I should have had a sheriff and a protest? You have proved a good mousetrap with your little ones.'

'Without knowing it,' said the woman.

2. First sketch of two equivocal faces

THE CAPTURED MOUSE was a very puny one, but the cat exulted even over a lean mouse.

What were the Thénardiers?

We will say but a word just here; by and by the sketch shall be completed.

They belonged to that bastard class formed of low people who have risen, and intelligent people who have fallen, which lies between the classes called middle and lower, and which unites some of the faults of the latter with nearly all the vices of the former, without possessing the generous impulses of the workman, or the respectability of the bourgeois.

They were of those dwarfish natures, which, if perchance heated by some sullen fire, easily become monstrous. The woman was at heart a brute; the man a blackguard: both in the highest degree capable of that hideous species of progress which can be made towards evil. There are souls which, crab-like, crawl continually towards darkness, going back in life rather than advancing in it; using what experience they have to increase their deformity; growing worse without ceasing, and becoming steeped more and more thoroughly in an intensifying wickedness. Such souls were this man and this woman.

The man especially would have been a puzzle to a physiognomist. We have only to look at some men to distrust them, for we feel the darkness of their souls in two ways. They are restless as to what is behind them, and threatening as to what is before them. They are full of mystery. We can no more answer for what they have done, than for what they will do. The shadow in their looks denounces them. If we hear them utter a word, or see them make a gesture, we catch glimpses of guilty secrets in their past, and dark mysteries in their future.

This Thénardier, if we may believe him, had been a soldier, a sergeant he said; he probably had made the campaign of 1815, and had even borne himself bravely according to all that appeared. We shall see hereafter in what his bravery consisted. The sign of his inn was an allusion to one of his feats of arms. He had painted it himself, for he knew how to do a little of everything – badly.

It was the time when the antique classical romance, which, after having been *Clelié* sank to *Lodoïska*, always noble, but becoming more and more vulgar, falling from Mdlle. de Scuderi to Madame Bournon-Malarme, and from Madame de Lafayette to Madame Barthélemy-Hadot, was firing the loving souls of the portresses of Paris, and making some ravages even in the suburbs. Madame Thénardier was just intelligent enough to read that sort of book. She fed on them. She drowned what little brain she had in them; and that had given her, while she was yet young, and even in later life, a kind of pensive attitude towards her husband, a knave of some calibre; a ruffian, educated almost to the extent of grammar; at once coarse and fine, but so far as sentimentalism was concerned, reading Pigault Lebrun, and in 'all which related to the sex', as he said in his jargon, a correct dolt without adulteration. His wife was twelve or fifteen years younger than he. At a later period, when the hair of the romantic weepers began to grow grey, when Mégère parted company with Pamela, Madame Thénardier was only a gross bad woman who had relished stupid novels.[20] Now, people do not read stupidities with impunity. The result was, that her eldest child was named Eponine, and the youngest, who had just escaped being called Gulnare, owed to some happy diversion made by a novel of Ducray Duminil, the mitigation of Azelma.

However, let us say by the way, all things are not ridiculous and superficial in this singular epoch to which we allude, and which might be termed the anarchy of baptismal names. Besides this romantic element which we have noticed, there is the social symptom. Today it is not unfrequent to see herdsboys named Arthur, Alfred and Alphonse, and viscounts – if there be any remaining – named Thomas, Peter or James. This change, which places the 'elegant' name on the plebeian and the country appellation on the aristocrat, is only an eddy in the tide of equality. The irresistible penetration of a new inspiration is there as well as in everything else: beneath this apparent discordance there is a reality grand and deep – the French Revolution.

3. *The Lark*

TO BE WICKED does not ensure prosperity – for the inn did not succeed well.

Thanks to Fantine's fifty-seven francs, Thénardier had been able to avoid a protest and to honour his signature. The next month they were still in need of money, and the woman carried Cosette's wardrobe to Paris and pawned it for sixty francs. When this sum was spent, the Thénardiers began to look upon the little girl as a child which they sheltered for charity, and treated her as such. Her clothes being gone, they dressed her in the cast-off garments of the little Thénardiers, that is in rags. They fed her on the orts and ends, a little better than the dog, and a little worse than the cat. The dog and cat were her messmates. Cosette ate with them under the table in a wooden dish like theirs.

Her mother, as we shall see hereafter, who had found a place at M— sur M— wrote, or rather had someone write for her, every month, inquiring news of her child. The Thénardiers replied invariably:

'Cosette is doing wonderfully well.'

The six months passed away: the mother sent seven francs for the seventh month, and continued to send this sum regularly month after month. The year was not ended before Thénardier said: 'A pretty price that is. What does she expect us to do for her seven francs?' And he wrote demanding twelve francs.

The mother, whom he persuaded that her child was happy and doing well, assented, and forwarded the twelve francs.

There are certain natures which cannot have love on one side without hatred on the other. This Thénardier mother passionately loved her own little ones: this made her detest the young stranger. It is sad to think that a mother's love can have such a dark side. Little as was the place Cosette occupied in the house, it seemed to her that this little was taken from her children, and that the little one lessened the air hers breathed. This woman, like many women of her kind, had a certain amount of caresses, and blows, and hard words to dispense each day. If she had not had Cosette, it is certain that her daughters, idolised as they were, would have received all, but the little stranger did them the service to attract the blows to herself; her children had only the caresses. Cosette could not stir that she did not draw down upon herself a hailstorm of undeserved and severe chastisements. A weak, soft little one who knew nothing of this world, or of God, continually ill-treated, scolded, punished, beaten, she saw beside her two other young things like herself, who lived in a halo of glory!

The woman was unkind to Cosette, Eponine and Azelma were unkind also. Children at that age are only copies of the mother; the size is reduced, that is all.

A year passed and then another.

People used to say in the village:

'What good people these Thénardiers are! They are not rich, and yet they bring up a poor child, that has been left with them.'

They thought Cosette was forgotten by her mother.

Meantime Thénardier, having learned in some obscure way that the child was probably illegitimate, and that its mother could not acknowledge it, demanded fifteen francs a month, saying 'that the "creature" was growing and eating,' and threatening to send her away. 'She won't humbug me,' he exclaimed, 'I will confound her with the brat in the midst of her concealment. I must have more money.' The mother paid the fifteen francs.

From year to year the child grew, and her misery also.

So long as Cosette was very small, she was the scapegoat of the two other children; as soon as she began to grow a little, that is to say, before she was five years old, she became the servant of the house.

Five years old, it will be said, that is improbable. Alas! it is true, social suffering begins at all ages. Have we not seen lately the trial of Dumollard, an orphan become a bandit, who, from the age of five, say the official documents, being alone in the world, 'worked for his living and stole!'

Cosette was made to run of errands, sweep the rooms, the yard, the street, wash the dishes, and even carry burdens. The Thénardiers felt doubly authorised to treat her thus, as the mother, who still remained at M— sur M—, began to be remiss in her payments. Some months remained due.

Had this mother returned to Montfermeil, at the end of these three years, she would not have known her child. Cosette, so fresh and pretty when she came to that house, was now thin and wan. She had a peculiar restless air. Sly! said the Thénardiers.

Injustice had made her sullen, and misery had made her ugly. Her fine eyes only remained to her, and they were painful to look at, for, large as they were, they seemed to increase the sadness!

It was a harrowing sight to see in the wintertime the poor child, not yet six years old, shivering under the tatters of what was once a calico dress, sweeping the street before daylight with an enormous broom in her little red hands and tears in her large eyes.

In the place she was called the Lark. People like figurative names and were pleased thus to name this little being, not larger than a bird, trembling, frightened, and shivering, awake every morning first of all in the house and the village, always in the street or in the fields before dawn.

Only the poor Lark never sang.

BOOK 5: THE DESCENT

1. *History of an improvement in jet-work*

WHAT had become of this mother, in the meanwhile, who, according to the people of Montfermeil, seemed to have abandoned her child? where was she? what was she doing?

After leaving her little Cosette with the Thénardiers, she went on her way and arrived at M— sur M—.

This, it will be remembered, was in 1818.

Fantine had left the province some twelve years before, and M— sur M— had greatly changed in appearance. While Fantine had been slowly sinking deeper and deeper into misery, her native village had been prosperous.

Within about two years there had been accomplished there one of those industrial changes which are the great events of small communities.

This circumstance is important and we think it well to relate it, we might even say to italicise it.

From time immemorial the special occupation of the inhabitants of M— sur M— had been the imitation of English jets and German black glass trinkets. The business had always been dull in consequence of the high price of the raw material, which reacted upon the manufacture. At the time of Fantine's return to M— sur M— an entire transformation had been effected in the production of these 'black goods'. Towards the end of the year 1815, an unknown man had established himself in the city, and had conceived the idea of substituting gum-lac for resin in the manufacture; and for bracelets, in particular, he made the clasps by simply bending the ends of the metal together instead of soldering them.

This very slight change had worked a revolution.

This very slight change had in fact reduced the price of the raw material enormously, and this had rendered it possible, first, to raise the wages of the labourer – a benefit to the country – secondly, to improve the quality of the goods – an advantage for the consumer – and thirdly, to sell them at a lower price even while making three times the profit – a gain for the manufacturer.

Thus we have three results from one idea.

In less than three years the inventor of this process had become rich, which was well, and had made all around him rich, which was better. He was a stranger in the Department. Nothing was known of his birth, and but little of his early history.

The story went that he came to the city with very little money, a few hundred francs at most.

From this slender capital, under the inspiration of an ingenious idea, made fruitful by order and care, he had drawn a fortune for himself, and a fortune for the whole region.

On his arrival at M— sur M— he had the dress, the manners, and the language of a labourer only.

It seems that the very day on which he thus obscurely entered the little city of M— sur M—, just at dusk on a December evening, with his bundle on his back, and a thorn stick in his hand, a great fire had broken out in the town-house. This man rushed into the fire, and saved, at the peril of his life, two children, who proved to be those of the captain of the gendarmerie, and in the hurry and gratitude of the moment no one thought to ask him for his passport. He was known from that time by the name of Father Madeleine.

2. *Madeleine* [21]

HE WAS A MAN of about fifty, who always appeared to be preoccupied in mind, and who was good-natured; this was all that could be said about him.

Thanks to the rapid progress of this manufacture, to which he had given such wonderful life, M— sur M— had become a considerable centre of business. Immense purchases were made there every year for the Spanish markets, where there is a large demand for jet-work, and M— sur M—, in this branch of trade, almost competed with London and Berlin. The profits of Father Madeleine were so great that by the end of the second year he was able to build a large factory, in which there were two immense workshops, one for men and the other for women: whoever was needy could go there and be sure of finding work and wages. Father Madeleine required the men to be willing, the women to be of good morals, and all to be honest. He divided the workshops, and separated the sexes in order that the girls and the women might not lose their modesty. On this point he was inflexible, although it was the only one in which he was in any degree rigid. He was confirmed in this severity by the opportunities for corruption that abounded in M— sur M—, it being a garrisoned city. Finally his coming had been a beneficence, and his presence was a providence. Before the arrival of Father Madeleine, the whole region was languishing; now it was all alive with the healthy strength of labour. An active circulation kindled everything and penetrated everywhere. Idleness and misery were unknown. There was no pocket so obscure that it did not contain some money and no dwelling so poor that it was not the abode of some joy.

Father Madeleine employed everybody; he had only one condition, 'Be an honest man!' 'Be an honest woman!'

As we have said, in the midst of this activity, of which he was the cause and the pivot, Father Madeleine had made his fortune, but, very strangely for a mere man of business, that did not appear to be his principal care. It seemed that he thought much for others, and little for himself. In 1820, it was known that he had six hundred and thirty thousand francs standing to his credit in the banking-house of Laffitte; but before setting aside this six hundred and thirty thousand francs for himself, he had expended more than a million for the city and for the poor.

The hospital was poorly endowed, and he made provision for ten additional beds. M— sur M— is divided into the upper city and the lower city. The lower city, where he lived, had only one schoolhouse, a miserable hovel which was fast going to ruin; he built two, one for girls, and the other for boys, and paid the two teachers, from his own pocket, double the amount of their meagre salary from the government; and one day, he said to a neighbour who expressed surprise at this: 'The two highest functionaries of the state are the nurse and the schoolmaster.' He built, at his own expense, a house of refuge, an institution then almost unknown in France, and provided a fund for old and infirm labourers. About his factory, as a centre, a new quarter of the city had rapidly grown up, containing many indigent families, and he established a pharmacy that was free to all.

At first, when he began to attract the public attention, the good people would say: 'This is a fellow who wishes to get rich.' When they saw him enrich the country before he enriched himself, the same good people said: 'This man is ambitious.' This seemed the more probable, since he was religious and observed the forms of the church, to a certain extent, a thing much approved in those days. He went regularly to hear mass every Sunday. The local deputy, who scented rivalry everywhere, was not slow to borrow trouble on account of Madeleine's religion. This deputy, who had been a member of the Corps Legislatif of the Empire, partook of the religious ideas of a Father of the Oratory, known by the name of Fouché, Duke of Otranto, whose creature and friend he had been. In private he jested a little about God. But when he saw the rich manufacturer, Madeleine, go to low mass at seven o'clock, he foresaw a possible candidate in opposition to himself, and he resolved to outdo him. He took a jesuit confessor, and went both to high mass and to vespers. Ambition at that time was, as the word itself imports, of the nature of a steeplechase. The poor, as well as God, gained by the terror of the honourable deputy, for he also established two beds at the hospital, which made twelve.

At length, in 1819, it was reported in the city one morning, that upon the recommendation of the prefect, and in consideration of the services he had rendered to the country, Father Madeleine had been appointed by the king, Mayor of M— sur M—. Those who had pronounced the newcomer 'an ambitious man', eagerly seized this opportunity, which all men desire, to exclaim:

'There! what did I tell you?'

M— sur M— was filled with the rumour, and the report proved to be well founded, for, a few days afterwards, the nomination appeared in the *Moniteur*. The next day Father Madeleine declined.

In the same year, 1819, the results of the new process invented by Madeleine had a place in the Industrial Exhibition, and upon the report of the jury, the king named the inventor a Chevalier of the Legion of Honour. Here was a new rumour for the little city. 'Well! it was the Cross of the Legion of Honour that he wanted.' Father Madeleine declined the Cross.

Decidedly this man was an enigma, and the good people gave up the field, saying, 'After all, he is a sort of an adventurer.'

As we have seen, the country owed a great deal to this man, and the poor owed him everything; he was so useful that all were compelled to honour him, and so kind that none could help loving him; his workmen in particular adored him, and he received their adoration with a sort of melancholy gravity. After he became rich, those who constituted 'society' bowed to him as they met, and, in the city, he began to be called Monsieur Madeleine; – but his workmen and the children continued to call him *Father Madeleine*, and at that name his face always wore a smile. As his wealth increased, invitations rained in on him. 'Society' claimed him. The little exclusive parlours of M— sur M—, which were carefully guarded, and in earlier days, of course, had been closed to the artisan, opened wide their doors to the millionaire. A thousand advances were made to him, but he refused them all.

And again the gossips were at no loss. 'He is an ignorant man, and of poor education. No one knows where he came from. He does not know how to conduct himself in good society, and it is by no means certain that he knows how to read.'

When they saw him making money, they said, 'He is a merchant.' When they saw the way in which he scattered his money, they said, 'He is ambitious.' When they saw him refuse to accept honours, they said, 'He is an adventurer.' When they saw him repel the advances of the fashionable, they said, 'He is a brute.'

In 1820, five years after his arrival at M— sur M—, the services that he had rendered to the region were so brilliant, and the wish of the whole population was so unanimous, that the king again appointed him mayor of the city. He refused again; but the prefect resisted his determination, the principal citizens came and urged him to accept, and the people in the streets begged him to do so; all insisted so strongly that at last he yielded. It was remarked that what appeared most of all to bring him to this determination, was the almost angry exclamation of an old woman belonging to the poorer class, who cried out to him from her door-stone, with some temper:

'A good mayor is a good thing. Are you afraid of the good you can do?'

This was the third step in his ascent. Father Madeleine had become Monsieur Madeleine, and Monsieur Madeleine now became Monsieur the Mayor.

3. *Moneys deposited with Laffitte*

NEVERTHELESS he remained as simple as at first. He had grey hair, a serious eye, the brown complexion of a labourer, and the thoughtful countenance of a philosopher. He usually wore a hat with a wide brim, and a long coat of coarse cloth, buttoned to the chin. He fulfilled his duties as mayor, but beyond that his life was isolated. He talked with very few persons. He shrank from compliments, and with a touch of the hat walked on rapidly; he smiled to avoid talking, and gave to avoid smiling. The women said of him: 'What a good bear!' His pleasure was to walk in the fields.

He always took his meals alone with a book open before him in which he read. His library was small but well selected. He loved books; books are cold but sure friends. As his growing fortune gave him more leisure, it seemed that he profited by it to cultivate his mind. Since he had been at M— sur M— it was remarked from year to year that his language became more polished, choicer, and more gentle.

In his walks he liked to carry a gun, though he seldom used it. When he did so, however, his aim was frightfully certain. He never killed an inoffensive animal, and never fired at any of the small birds.

Although he was no longer young, it was reported that he was of prodigious strength. He would offer a helping hand to anyone who needed it, help up a fallen horse, push at a stalled wheel, or seize by the horns a bull that had broken loose. He always had his pockets full of money when he went out, and empty when he returned. When he passed through a village the ragged little youngsters would run after him with joy, and surround him like a swarm of flies.

It was surmised that he must have lived formerly in the country, for he had all sorts of useful secrets which he taught the peasants. He showed them how to destroy the grain-moth by sprinkling the granary and washing the cracks of the floor with a solution of common salt, and how to drive away the weevil by hanging up all about the ceiling and walls, in the pastures, and in the houses, the flowers of the orviot. He had recipes for clearing a field of rust, of vetches, of moles, of dog-grass, and all the parasitic herbs which live upon the grain.

He defended a rabbit warren against rats, with nothing but the odour of a little Barbary pig that he placed there.

One day he saw some country people very busy pulling up nettles; he looked at the heap of plants, uprooted, and already wilted, and said: 'This is dead; but it would be well if we knew how to put it to some use. When the nettle is young, the leaves make excellent greens; when it grows old it has filaments and fibres like hemp and flax. Cloth made from the nettle is worth as much as that made from hemp. Chopped up, the nettle is good for poultry; pounded, it is good for horned cattle. The seed of the nettle mixed with the fodder of animals gives a lustre to their skin; the root, mixed with salt, produces a beautiful yellow dye. It makes, however, excellent hay, as it can be cut twice in a season. And what does the nettle need? very little soil, no care, no culture; except that the seeds fall as fast as they ripen, and it is difficult to gather them; that is all. If we would take a few pains, the nettle would be useful; we neglect it, and it becomes harmful. Then we kill it. How much men are like the nettle!' After a short silence, he added: 'My friends, remember this, that there are no bad herbs, and no bad men; there are only bad cultivators.'

The children loved him yet more, because he knew how to make charming little playthings out of straw and coconuts.

When he saw the door of a church shrouded with black, he entered: he sought out a funeral as others seek out a christening. The bereavement and the misfortune of others attracted him, because of his great gentleness; he mingled with friends who were in mourning, with families dressing in black, with the priests who were sighing around a corpse. He seemed glad to take as a text for his thoughts these funereal psalms, full of the vision of another world. With his eyes raised to heaven, he listened with a sort of aspiration towards all the mysteries of the infinite, to these sad voices, which sing upon the brink of the dark abyss of death.

He did a multitude of good deeds as secretly as bad ones are usually done. He would steal into houses in the evening, and furtively mount the stairs. A poor devil, on returning to his garret, would find that his door had been opened, sometimes even forced, during his absence. The poor man would cry out: 'Some thief has been here!' When he got in, the first thing that he would see would be a piece of gold lying on the table. 'The thief' who had been there was Father Madeleine.

He was affable and sad. The people used to say: 'There is a rich man who does not show pride. There is a fortunate man who does not appear contented.'

Some pretended that he was a mysterious personage, and declared that no one ever went into his room, which was a true anchorite's cell furnished with hour-glasses, and enlivened with death's heads and crossbones. So much was said of this kind that some of the more mischievous of the elegant young ladies of M— sur M— called on him one day and said: 'Monsieur Mayor, will you show us your room? We have heard that it is a grotto.' He smiled, and introduced them on the spot to this 'grotto.' They were well punished for their curiosity. It was a room very well fitted up with mahogany furniture, ugly as all furniture of that kind is, and the walls covered with shilling paper. They could see nothing but two candlesticks of antique form that stood on the mantel, and appeared to be silver, 'for they were marked,' a remark full of the spirit of these little towns.

But none the less did it continue to be said that nobody ever went into that chamber, and that it was a hermit's cave, a place of dreams, a hole, a tomb.

It was also whispered that he had 'immense' sums deposited with Laffitte, with the special condition that they were always at his immediate command, in such a way, it was added, that Monsieur Madeleine might arrive in the morning at Laffitte's, sign a receipt and carry away his two or three millions in ten minutes. In reality these 'two or three millions' dwindled down, as we have said, to six hundred and thirty or forty thousand francs.

4. *Monsieur Madeleine in mourning*

NEAR the beginning of the year 1821, the journals announced the decease of Monsieur Myriel, Bishop of D—, 'surnamed *Monseigneur Bienvenu*,' who died in the odour of sanctity at the age of eighty-two years.

The Bishop of D—, to add an incident which the journals omitted, had been blind for several years before he died, and was content therewith, his sister being with him.

Let us say by the way, to be blind and to be loved, is in fact, on this earth where nothing is complete, one of the most strangely exquisite forms of happiness. To have continually at your side a woman, a girl, a sister, a charming being, who is there because you have need of her, and because she cannot do without you, to know you are indispensable to her who is necessary to you, to be able at all times to measure her affection by the amount of her company that she gives you, and to say to yourself: she consecrates to me all her time, because I possess her whole heart; to see the thought instead of the face; to be sure of the fidelity of one being in the eclipse of the world; to imagine the rustling of her dress the rustling of wings; to hear her moving to and fro, going out, coming in, talking, singing, and to think that you are the centre of those steps, of those words, of that song; to manifest at every minute your personal attraction; to feel yourself powerful by so much the more as you are the more infirm; to become in darkness, and by reason of darkness, the star around which this angel gravitates; few happy lots can equal that. The supreme happiness of life is the conviction that we are loved; loved for ourselves – say rather, loved in spite of ourselves; this conviction the blind have. In their calamity, to be served, is to be caressed. Are they deprived of anything? No. Light is not lost where love enters. And what a love! a love wholly founded in purity. There is no blindness where there is certainty. The soul gropes in search of a soul, and finds it. And that soul, so found and proven, is a woman. A hand sustains you, it is hers; lips lightly touch your forehead, they are her lips; you hear one breathing near you, it is she. To have her wholly, from her devotion to her pity, never to be left, to have that sweet weakness which is your aid, to lean upon that unbending reed, to touch Providence with your hands and be able to grasp it in your arms; God made palpable, what transport! The heart, that dark but celestial flower, bursts into a mysterious bloom. You would not give that shade for all light! The angel-soul is there, for ever there; if she goes away, it is only to return; she fades away in dream and reappears in reality. You feel an approaching warmth, she is there. You overflow with serenity, gaiety, and ecstasy; you are radiant in your darkness. And the thousand little cares! The nothings which are enormous in this void. The most unspeakable accents of the womanly voice employed to soothe you, and making up to you the vanished universe! You are caressed through the soul. You see nothing, but you feel yourself adored. It is a paradise of darkness.

From this paradise Monseigneur Bienvenu passed to the other.

The announcement of his death was reproduced in the local paper of M— sur M—. Monsieur Madeleine appeared next morning dressed in black with crape on his hat.

This mourning was noticed and talked about all over the town. It appeared to throw some light upon the origin of Monsieur Madeleine. The conclusion was that he was in some way related to the venerable bishop. '*He wears black for the Bishop of D—,*' was the talk of the drawing-rooms; it elevated Monsieur Madeleine very much, and gave him suddenly, and in a trice, marked consideration in the noble world of M— sur M—. The microscopic Faubourg Saint Germain of the little place thought of raising the quarantine for Monsieur Madeleine, the probable relative of a bishop. Monsieur Madeleine perceived the advancement that he had obtained, by the greater reverence of the old ladies, and the more frequent smiles of the young ladies. One evening, one of the dowagers of that little great world, curious by right of age, ventured to ask him: 'The mayor is doubtless a relative of the late Bishop of D—?'

He said: 'No, madame.'

'But,' the dowager persisted, 'you wear mourning for him?'

He answered: 'In my youth I was a servant in his family.'

It was also remarked that whenever there passed through the city a young Savoyard who was tramping about the country in search of chimneys to sweep, the mayor would send for him, ask his name and give him money. The little Savoyards told each other, and many of them passed that way.

5. *Vague flashes on the horizon*

LITTLE BY LITTLE in the lapse of time all opposition had ceased. At first there had been, as always happens with those who rise by their own efforts, slanders and calumnies against Monsieur Madeleine, soon this was reduced to satire, then it was only wit, then it vanished entirely; respect became complete, unanimous, cordial, and there came a moment, about 1821, when the words Monsieur the Mayor were pronounced at M— sur M— with almost the same accent as the words Monseigneur the Bishop at D— in 1815. People came from thirty miles around to consult Monsieur Madeleine. He settled differences, he prevented lawsuits, he reconciled enemies. Everybody, of his own will, chose him for judge. He seemed to have the book of the natural law by heart. A contagion of veneration had, in the course of six or seven years, step by step, spread over the whole country.

One man alone, in the city and its neighbourhood, held himself entirely clear from this contagion, and, whatever Father Madeleine did, he remained indifferent, as if a sort of instinct, unchangeable and imperturbable, kept him awake and on the watch. It would seem, indeed, that there is in certain men the veritable instinct of a beast, pure and complete like all instinct, which creates antipathies and sympathies, which separates one nature from another for ever, which never hesitates, never is perturbed, never keeps silent, and never admits itself to be in the wrong; clear in its obscurity, infallible, imperious, refractory under all the counsels of intelligence, and all the solvents of reason, and which, whatever may be their destinies, secretly warns the dog-man of the presence of the cat-man, and the fox-man of the presence of the lion-man.

Often, when Monsieur Madeleine passed along the street, calm, affectionate, followed by the benedictions of all, it happened that a tall man, wearing a flat hat and an iron-grey coat, and armed with a stout cane, would turn around abruptly behind him, and follow him with his eyes until he disappeared, crossing his arms, slowly shaking his head, and pushing his upper with his under lip up to his nose, a sort of significant grimace which might be rendered by: 'But what is that man? I am sure I have seen him somewhere. At all events, I at least am not his dupe.'

This personage, grave with an almost threatening gravity, was one of those who, even in a hurried interview, command the attention of the observer.

His name was Javert, and he was one of the police.

He exercised at M— sur M— the unpleasant, but useful, function of inspector. He was not there at the date of Madeleine's arrival. Javert owed his position to the protection of Monsieur Chabouillet, the secretary of the Minister of State, Count Anglès, then prefect of police at Paris. When Javert arrived at M— sur M— the fortune of the great manufacturer had been made already, and Father Madeleine had become Monsieur Madeleine.

Certain police officers have a peculiar physiognomy in which can be traced an air of meanness mingled with an air of authority. Javert had this physiognomy, without meanness.

It is our conviction that if souls were visible to the eye we should distinctly see this strange fact that each individual of the human species corresponds to some one of the species of the animal creation; and we should clearly recognise the truth, hardly perceived by thinkers, that, from the oyster to the eagle, from the swine to the tiger, all animals are in man, and that each of them is in a man; sometimes even, several of them at a time.

Animals are nothing but the forms of our virtues and vices, wandering before our eyes, the visible phantoms of our souls. God shows them to us to make us reflect. Only, as animals are but shadows, God has not made them capable of education in the complete sense of the word. Why should he? On the contrary, our souls being realities and having their peculiar end, God has given them intelligence, that is to say, the possibility of education. Social education, well attended to, can always draw out of a soul, whatever it may be, the usefulness that it contains.

Be this said, nevertheless, from the restricted point of view of the apparent earthly life, and without prejudice to the deep question of the anterior or ulterior personality of the beings that are not man. The visible *me* in no way authorises the thinker to deny the latent *me*. With this reservation, let us pass on.

Now, if we admit for a moment that there is in every man some one of the species of the animal creation, it will be easy for us to describe the guardian of the peace, Javert.

The peasants of the Asturias believe that in every litter of wolves there is one dog, which is killed by the mother, lest on growing up it should devour the other little ones.

Give a human face to this dog son of a wolf, and you will have Javert.

Javert was born in a prison. His mother was a fortune-teller whose husband was in the galleys. He grew up to think himself without the pale of society, and despaired of ever entering it. He noticed that society closes its doors, without pity, on two classes of men, those who attack it and those who guard it; he could choose between these two classes only; at the same time he felt that he had an indescribable basis of rectitude, order, and honesty, associated with an irrepressible hatred for that gypsy race to which he belonged. He entered the police. He succeeded. At forty he was an inspector.

In his youth he had been stationed in the galleys at the South. Before going further, let us understand what we mean by the words human face, which we have just now applied to Javert.

The human face of Javert consisted of a snub nose, with two deep nostrils, which were bordered by large bushy whiskers that covered both his cheeks. One felt ill at ease the first time he saw those two forests and those two caverns. When Javert laughed, which was rarely and terribly, his thin lips parted, and showed, not only his teeth, but his gums; and around his nose there was a wrinkle as broad and wild as the muzzle of a fallow deer. Javert, when serious, was a bulldog; when he laughed, he was a tiger. For the rest, a small head, large jaws, hair hiding the forehead and falling over the eyebrows, between the eyes a permanent central frown, a gloomy look, a mouth pinched and frightful, and an air of fierce command.

This man was a compound of two sentiments, very simple and very good in themselves, but he almost made them evil by his exaggeration of them: respect for authority and hatred of rebellion; and in his eyes, theft, murder, all crimes, were only forms of rebellion. In his strong and implicit faith he included all who held any function in the state, from the prime minister to the constable. He had nothing but disdain, aversion, and disgust for all who had once overstepped the bounds of the law. He was absolute, and admitted no exceptions. On the one hand he said: 'A public officer cannot be deceived; a magistrate never does wrong!' And on the other he said: 'They are irremediably lost; no good can come out of them.' He shared fully the opinion of those extremists who attribute to human laws an indescribable power of making, or, if you will, of determining, demons, and who place a Styx at the bottom of society. He was stoical, serious, austere: a dreamer of stern dreams; humble and haughty, like all fanatics. His stare was cold and as piercing as a gimlet. His whole life was contained in these two words: waking and watching. He marked out a straight path through the most tortuous thing in the world; his conscience was bound up in his utility, his religion in his duties, and he was a spy as others are priests. Woe to him who should fall into his hands! He would have arrested his father if escaping from the galleys, and denounced his mother for violating her ticket of leave. And he would have done it with that sort of interior satisfaction that springs from virtue. His life was a life of privations, isolation, self-denial, and chastity: never any amusement. It was implacable duty, absorbed in the police as the Spartans were absorbed in Sparta, a pitiless detective, a fierce honesty, a marble-hearted informer, Brutus united with Vidocq.

The whole person of Javert expressed the spy and the informer. The mystic school of Joseph de Maistre,[22] which at that time enlivened what were called the ultra journals with high-sounding cosmogonies, would have said that Javert was a symbol. You could not see his forehead which disappeared under his hat, you could not see his eyes which were lost under his brows, you could not see his chin which was buried in his cravat, you could not see his hands which were drawn up into his sleeves, you could not see his cane which he carried under his coat. But when the time came, you would see spring all at once out of this shadow, as from an ambush, a steep and narrow forehead, an ominous look, a threatening chin, enormous hands, and a monstrous club.

In his leisure moments, which were rare, although he hated books, he read; wherefore he was not entirely illiterate. This was perceived also from a certain emphasis in his speech.

He was free from vice, we have said. When he was satisfied with himself, he allowed himself a pinch of snuff. That proved that he was human.

It will be easily understood that Javert was the terror of all that class which the annual statistics of the Minister of Justice include under the heading: *People without a fixed abode*. To speak the name of Javert would put all such to flight; the face of Javert petrified them.

Such was this formidable man.

Javert was like an eye always fixed on Monsieur Madeleine; an eye full of suspicion and conjecture. Monsieur Madeleine finally noticed it, but seemed to consider it of no consequence. He asked no question of Javert, he neither sought him nor shunned him, he endured this unpleasant and annoying stare without appearing to pay any attention to it. He treated Javert as he did everybody else, at ease and with kindness.

From some words that Javert had dropped, it was guessed that he had secretly hunted up, with that curiosity which belongs to his race, and which is more a matter of instinct than of will, all the traces of his previous life which Father Madeleine had left elsewhere. He appeared to know, and he said sometimes in a covert way, that somebody had gathered certain information in a certain region about a certain missing family. Once he happened to say, speaking to himself: 'I think I have got him!' Then for three days he remained moody without speaking a word. It appeared that the clue which he thought he had was broken.

But, and this is the necessary corrective to what the meaning of certain words may have presented in too absolute a sense, there can be nothing really infallible in a human creature, and the very peculiarity of instinct is that it can be disturbed, followed up, and routed. Were this not so it would be superior to intelligence, and the beast would be in possession of a purer light than man.

Javert was evidently somewhat disconcerted by the completely natural air and the tranquillity of Monsieur Madeleine.

One day, however, his strange manner appeared to make an impression upon Monsieur Madeleine. The occasion was this.

6. *Father Fauchelevent*

MONSIEUR MADELEINE was walking one morning along one of the unpaved alleys of M— sur M—; he heard a shouting and saw a crowd at a little distance. He went to the spot. An old man, named Father Fauchelevent, had fallen under his cart, his horse being thrown down.

This Fauchelevent was one of the few who were still enemies of Monsieur Madeleine at this time. When Madeleine arrived in the place, the business of Fauchelevent, who was a notary of long-standing, and very well-read for a rustic, was beginning to decline. Fauchelevent had seen this mere artisan grow rich, while he himself, a professional man, had been going to ruin. This had filled him with jealousy, and he had done what he could on all occasions to injure Madeleine. Then came bankruptcy, and the old man, having nothing but a horse and cart, as he was without family, and without children, was compelled to earn his living as a carman.

The horse had his thighs broken, and could not stir. The old man was caught between the wheels. Unluckily he had fallen so that the whole weight rested upon his breast. The cart was heavily loaded. Father Fauchelevent was uttering doleful groans. They had tried to pull him out, but in vain. An unlucky effort, inexpert help, a false push, might crush him. It was impossible to extricate him otherwise than by raising the wagon from beneath. Javert, who came up at the moment of the accident, had sent for a jack.

Monsieur Madeleine came. The crowd fell back with respect.

'Help,' cried old Fauchelevent. 'Who is a good fellow to save an old man?'

Monsieur Madeleine turned towards the bystanders:

'Has anybody a jack?'

'They have gone for one,' replied a peasant.

'How soon will it be here?'

'We sent to the nearest place, to Flachot Place, where there is a blacksmith; but it will take a good quarter of an hour at least.'

'A quarter of an hour!' exclaimed Madeleine.

It had rained the night before, the road was soft, the cart was sinking deeper every moment, and pressing more and more on the breast of the old carman. It was evident that in less than five minutes his ribs would be crushed.

'We cannot wait a quarter of an hour,' said Madeleine to the peasants who were looking on.

'We must!'

'But it will be too late! Don't you see that the wagon is sinking all the while?'

'It can't be helped.'

'Listen,' resumed Madeleine, 'there is room enough still under the wagon for a man to crawl in, and lift it with his back. In half a minute we will have the poor man out. Is there nobody here who has strength and courage? Five louis d'ors for him!'

Nobody stirred in the crowd.

'Ten louis,' said Madeleine.

The bystanders dropped their eyes. One of them muttered: 'He'd have to be devilish stout. And then he would risk getting crushed.'

'Come,' said Madeleine, 'twenty louis.'

The same silence.

'It is not willingness which they lack,' said a voice.

Monsieur Madeleine turned and saw Javert. He had not noticed him when he came.

Javert continued:

'It is strength. He must be a terrible man who can raise a wagon like that on his back.'

Then, looking fixedly at Monsieur Madeleine, he went on emphasising every word that he uttered:

'Monsieur Madeleine, I have known but one man capable of doing what you call for.'

Madeleine shuddered.

Javert added, with an air of indifference but without taking his eyes from Madeleine:

'He was a convict.'

'Ah!' said Madeleine.

'In the galleys at Toulon.'

Madeleine became pale.

Meanwhile the cart was slowly settling down. Father Fauchelevent roared and screamed:

'I am dying! my ribs are breaking! a jack! anything! oh!'

Madeleine looked around him:

'Is there nobody, then, who wants to earn twenty louis and save this poor old man's life?'

None of the bystanders moved. Javert resumed:

'I have known but one man who could take the place of a jack; that was that convict.'

'Oh! how it crushes me!' cried the old man.

Madeleine raised his head, met the falcon eye of Javert still fixed upon him, looked at the immovable peasants, and smiled sadly. Then, without saying a word, he fell on his knees, and even before the crowd had time to utter a cry, he was under the cart.

There was an awful moment of suspense and of silence.

Madeleine, lying almost flat under the fearful weight, was twice seen to try in vain to bring his elbows and knees nearer together. They cried out to him: 'Father Madeleine! come out from there!' Old Fauchelevent himself said: 'Monsieur Madeleine! go away! I must die, you see that; leave me! you will be crushed too.' Madeleine made no answer.

The bystanders held their breath. The wheels were still sinking and it had now become almost impossible for Madeleine to extricate himself.

All at once the enormous mass started, the cart rose slowly, the wheels came half out of the ruts. A smothered voice was heard, crying: 'Quick! help!' It was Madeleine, who had just made a final effort.

They all rushed to the work. The devotion of one man had given strength and courage to all. The cart was lifted by twenty arms. Old Fauchelevent was safe.

Madeleine arose. He was very pale, though dripping with sweat. His clothes were torn and covered with mud. All wept. The old man kissed his knees and called him the good God. He himself wore on his face an indescribable expression of joyous and celestial suffering, and he looked with tranquil eye upon Javert, who was still watching him.

7. *Fauchelevent becomes a gardener at Paris*

FAUCHELEVENT had broken his knee-pan in his fall. Father Madeleine had him carried to an infirmary that he had established for his workmen in the same building with his factory, which was attended by two sisters of charity. The next morning the old man found a thousand franc bill upon the stand by the side of the bed, with this note in the handwriting of Father Madeleine: *I have purchased your horse and cart.* The cart was broken and the horse was dead. Fauchelevent got well, but he had a stiff knee. Monsieur Madeleine, through the recommendations of the sisters and the curé, got the old man a place as gardener at a convent in the Quartier Saint Antoine at Paris.

Sometime afterwards Monsieur Madeleine was appointed mayor. The first time that Javert saw Monsieur Madeleine clothed with the scarf which gave him full authority over the city, he felt the same sort of shudder which a bulldog would feel who should scent a wolf in his master's clothes. From that time he avoided him as much as he could. When the necessities of the service imperiously demanded it, and he could not do otherwise than come in contact with the mayor, he spoke to him with profound respect.

The prosperity which Father Madeleine had created at M— sur M—, in addition to the visible signs that we have pointed out, had another symptom which, although not visible, was not the less significant. This never fails. When the population is suffering, when there is lack of work, when trade falls off, the tax-payer, constrained by poverty, resists taxation, exhausts and overruns the delays allowed by law, and the government is forced to incur large expenditures in the costs of levy and collection. When work is abundant, when the country is rich and happy, the tax is easily paid and costs the state but little to collect. It may be said that poverty and public wealth have an infallible thermometer in the cost of the collection of the taxes. In seven years, the cost of the collection of the taxes had been reduced three-quarters in the district of M— sur M—, so that that district was frequently referred to especially by Monsieur de Villèle, then Minister of Finance.

Such was the situation of the country when Fantine returned. No one remembered her. Luckily the door of M. Madeleine's factory was like the face of a friend. She presented herself there, and was admitted into the workshop for women. The business was entirely new to Fantine; she could not be very expert in it, and consequently did not receive much for her day's work; but that little was enough, the problem was solved; she was earning her living.

8. *Madame Victurnien spends thirty francs on morality*

WHEN FANTINE REALISED how she was living, she had a moment of joy. To live honestly by her own labour; what a heavenly boon! The taste for labour returned to her, in truth. She bought a mirror, delighted herself with the sight of her youth, her fine hair and her fine teeth, forgot many things, thought of nothing save Cosette and the possibilities of the future, and was almost happy. She hired a small room and furnished it on the credit of her future labour; a remnant of her habits of disorder.

Not being able to say that she was married, she took good care, as we have already intimated, not to speak of her little girl.

At first, as we have seen, she paid the Thénardiers punctually. As she only knew how to sign her name she was obliged to write through a public letter-writer.

She wrote often; that was noticed. They began to whisper in the women's workshop that Fantine 'wrote letters', and that 'she had airs'. For prying into any human affairs, none are equal to those whom it does not concern. 'Why does this gentleman never come till dusk?' 'Why does Mr So-and-so never hang his key on the nail on Thursday?' 'Why does he always take the by-streets?' 'Why does madame always leave her carriage before getting to the house?' 'Why does she send to buy a quire of writing-paper when she has her portfolio full of it?' etc. etc. There are persons who, to solve these enigmas, which are moreover perfectly immaterial to them, spend more money, waste more time, and give themselves more trouble than would suffice for ten good deeds; and that gratuitously, and for the pleasure of it, without being paid for their curiosity in any other way than by curiosity. They will follow this man or that woman whole days, stand guard for hours at the corners of the street, under the entrance of a passage-way, at night, in the cold and in the rain, bribe messengers, get hack-drivers and lackeys drunk, fee a chambermaid, or buy a porter. For what? for nothing. Pure craving to see, to know, and to find out. Pure itching for scandal. And often these secrets made known, these mysteries published, these enigmas brought into the light of day, lead to catastrophes, to duels, to failures, to the ruin of families, and make lives wretched, to the great joy of those who have 'discovered all' without any interest, and from pure instinct. A sad thing.

Some people are malicious from the mere necessity of talking. Their conversation, tattling in the drawing-room, gossip in the antechamber, is like those fireplaces that use up wood rapidly; they need a great deal of fuel; the fuel is their neighbour.

So Fantine was watched.

Beyond this, more than one was jealous of her fair hair and of her white teeth.

It was reported that in the shop, with all the rest about her, she often turned aside to wipe away a tear. Those were moments when she thought of her child; perhaps also of the man whom she had loved.

It is a mournful task to break the sombre attachments of the past.

It was ascertained that she wrote, at least twice a month, and always to the same address, and that she prepaid the postage. They succeeded in learning the address: *Monsieur, Monsieur Thénardier, inn-keeper, Montfermeil.* The public letter-writer, a simple old fellow, who could not fill his stomach with red wine without emptying his pocket of his secrets, was made to reveal this at a drinking-house. In short, it became known that Fantine had a child. 'She must be that sort of a woman.' And there was one old gossip who went to Montfermeil, talked with the Thénardiers, and said on her return: 'For my thirty-five francs, I have found out all about it. I have seen the child!'

The busybody who did this was a beldame, called Madame Victurnien, keeper and guardian of everybody's virtue. Madame Victurnien was fifty-six years old, and wore a mask of old age over her mask of ugliness. Her voice trembled, and she was capricious. It seemed strange, but this woman had been young. In her youth, in '93, she married a monk who had escaped from the cloister in a red cap, and passed from the Bernardines to the Jacobins. She was dry, rough, sour, sharp, crabbed, almost venomous; never forgetting her monk, whose widow she was, and who had ruled and curbed her harshly. She was a nettle bruised by a frock. At the restoration she became a bigot, and so energetically, that the priests had pardoned her monk episode. She had a little property, which she had bequeathed to a religious community with great flourish. She was in very good standing at the bishop's palace in Arras. This Madame Victurnien then went to Montfermeil, and returned saying: 'I have seen the child.'

All this took time; Fantine had been more than a year at the factory, when one morning the overseer of the workshop handed her, on behalf of the mayor, fifty francs, saying that she was no longer wanted in the shop, and enjoining her, on behalf of the mayor, to leave the city.

This was the very same month in which the Thénardiers, after having asked twelve francs instead of six, had demanded fifteen francs instead of twelve.

Fantine was thunderstruck. She could not leave the city; she was in debt for her lodging and her furniture. Fifty francs were not enough to clear off that debt. She faltered out some suppliant words. The overseer gave her to understand that she must leave the shop instantly. Fantine was moreover only a moderate worker. Overwhelmed with shame even more than with despair, she left the shop, and returned to her room. Her fault then was now known to all!

She felt no strength to say a word. She was advised to see the mayor; she dared not. The mayor gave her fifty francs, because he was kind, and sent her away, because he was just. She bowed to that decree.

9. *Success of Madame Victurnien*

THE MONK'S WIDOW was then good for something.

Monsieur Madeleine had known nothing of all this. These are combinations of events of which life is full. It was Monsieur Madeleine's habit scarcely ever to enter the women's workshop.

He had placed at the head of this shop an old spinster whom the curé had recommended to him, and he had entire confidence in this overseer, a very respectable person, firm, just, upright, full of that charity which consists in giving, but not having to the same extent that charity which consists in understanding and pardoning. Monsieur Madeleine left everything to her. The best men are often compelled to delegate their authority. It was in the exercise of this full power, and with the conviction that she was doing right, that the overseer had framed the indictment, tried, condemned and executed Fantine.

As to the fifty francs, she had given them from a fund that Monsieur Madeleine had entrusted her with for alms-giving and aid to the work-women, and of which she rendered no account.

Fantine offered herself as a servant in the neighbourhood; she went from one house to another. Nobody wanted her. She could not leave the city. The second-hand dealer to whom she was in debt for her furniture, and such furniture! had said to her: 'If you go away, I will have you arrested as a thief.' The landlord, whom she owed for rent, had said to her: 'You are young and pretty, you can pay.' She divided the fifty francs between the landlord and the dealer, returned to the latter three-quarters of his goods, kept only what was necessary, and found herself without work, without position, having nothing but her bed, and owing still about a hundred francs.

She began to make coarse shirts for the soldiers of the garrison, and earned twelve sous a day. Her daughter cost her ten. It was at this time that she began to get behindhand with the Thénardiers.

However, an old woman, who lit her candle for her when she came home at night, taught her the art of living in misery. Behind living on a little, lies the art of living on nothing. They are two rooms; the first is obscure, the second is utterly dark.

Fantine learned how to do entirely without fire in winter, how to give up a bird that eats a farthing's worth of millet every other day, how to make a coverlet of her petticoat, and a petticoat of her coverlet, how to save her candle in taking her meals by the light of an opposite window. Few know how much certain feeble beings, who have grown old in privation and honesty, can extract from a sou. This finally becomes a talent. Fantine acquired this sublime talent and took heart a little.

During these times, she said to a neighbour: 'Bah! I say to myself: by sleeping but five hours and working all the rest at my sewing, I shall always succeed in nearly earning bread. And then, when one is sad, one eats less. Well! what with sufferings, troubles, a little bread on the one hand, anxiety on the other, all that will keep me alive.'

In this distress, to have had her little daughter would have been a strange happiness. She thought of having her come. But what? to make her share her privation? and then, she owed the Thénardiers? How could she pay them? and the journey! how pay for that?

The old woman, who had given her what might be called lessons in indigent life, was a pious woman, Marguerite by name, a devotee of genuine devotion, poor, and charitable to the poor, and also to the rich, knowing how to write just enough to sign *Margeritte*, and believing in God, which is science.

There are many of these virtues in low places; someday they will be on high. This life has a morrow.

At first, Fantine was so much ashamed that she did not dare to go out.

When she was in the street, she imagined that people turned behind her and pointed at her; everybody looked at her and no one greeted her; the sharp and cold disdain of the passers-by penetrated her, body and soul, like a north wind.

In small cities an unfortunate woman seems to be laid bare to the sarcasm and the curiosity of all. In Paris, at least, nobody knows you, and that obscurity is a covering. Oh! how she longed to go to Paris! impossible.

She must indeed become accustomed to disrespect as she had to poverty. Little by little she learned her part. After two or three months she shook off her shame and went out as if there were nothing in the way. 'It is all one to me,' said she.

She went and came, holding her head up and wearing a bitter smile, and felt that she was becoming shameless.

Madame Victurnien sometimes saw her pass her window, noticed the distress of 'that creature', thanks to her 'put back to her place', and congratulated herself. The malicious have a dark happiness.

Excessive work fatigued Fantine, and the slight dry cough that she had increased. She sometimes said to her neighbour, Marguerite, 'just feel how hot my hands are.'

In the morning, however, when with an old broken comb she combed her fine hair which flowed down in silky waves, she enjoyed a moment of happiness.

10. *Results of the success*

SHE HAD BEEN discharged towards the end of winter; summer passed away, but winter returned. Short days, less work. In winter there is no heat, no light, no noon, evening touches morning, there is fog, and mist, the window is frosted, and you cannot see clearly. The sky is but the mouth of a cave. The whole day is the cave. The sun has the appearance of a pauper. Frightful season! Winter changes into stone the water of heaven and the heart of man. Her creditors harassed her.

Fantine earned too little. Her debts had increased. The Thénardiers being poorly paid, were constantly writing letters to her, the contents of which disheartened her, while the postage was ruining her. One day they wrote to her that her little Cosette was entirely destitute of clothing for the cold weather, that she needed a woollen skirt, and that her mother must send at least ten francs for that. She received the letter and crushed it in her hand for a whole day. In the evening she went into a barber's shop at the corner of the street, and pulled out her comb. Her beautiful fair hair fell below her waist.

'What beautiful hair!' exclaimed the barber.

'How much will you give me for it?' said she.

'Ten francs.'

'Cut it off.'

She bought a knit skirt and sent it to the Thénardiers.

This skirt made the Thénardiers furious. It was the money that they wanted. They gave the skirt to Eponine. The poor Lark still shivered.

Fantine thought: 'My child is no longer cold, I have clothed her with my hair.' She put on a little round cap which concealed her shorn head, and with that she was still pretty.

A gloomy work was going on in Fantine's heart.

When she saw that she could no longer dress her hair, she began to look with hatred on all around her. She had long shared in the universal veneration for Father Madeleine; nevertheless, by dint of repeating to herself that it was he who had turned her away, and that he was the cause of her misfortunes, she came to hate him also, and especially. When she passed the factory at the hours in which the labourers were at the door, she forced herself to laugh and sing.

An old working-woman who saw her once singing and laughing in this way, said: 'There is a girl who will come to a bad end.'

She took a lover, the first comer, a man whom she did not love, through bravado, and with rage in her heart. He was a wretch, a kind of mendicant musician, a lazy ragamuffin, who beat her, and who left her, as she had taken him, with disgust.

She worshipped her child.

The lower she sank, the more all became gloomy around her, the more the sweet little angel shone out in the bottom of her heart. She would say: 'When I am rich, I shall have my Cosette with me;' and she laughed. The cough did not leave her, and she had night sweats.

One day she received from the Thénardiers a letter in these words: 'Cosette is sick of an epidemic disease. A military fever they call it. The drugs necessary are dear. It is ruining us, and we can no longer pay for them. Unless you send us forty francs within a week the little one will die.'

She burst out laughing, and said to her old neighbour: 'Oh! they are nice! forty francs! think of that! that is two Napoleons! Where do they think I can get them? Are they fools, these boors?'

She went, however, to the staircase, near a dormer window, and read the letter again.

Then she went downstairs and out of doors, running and jumping, still laughing.

Somebody who met her said to her: 'What is the matter with you, that you are so gay?'

She answered: 'A stupid joke that some country people have just written me. They ask me for forty francs; the boors!'

As she passed through the square, she saw many people gathered about an odd-looking carriage on the top of which stood a man in red clothes, declaiming. He was a juggler and a travelling dentist, and was offering to the public complete sets of teeth, opiates, powders, and elixirs.

Fantine joined the crowd and began to laugh with the rest at this harangue, in which were mingled slang for the rabble and jargon for the better sort. The puller of teeth saw this beautiful girl laughing, and suddenly called out: 'You have pretty teeth, you girl who are laughing there. If you will sell me your two incisors, I will give you a gold Napoleon for each of them.'

'What is that? What are my incisors?' asked Fantine.

'The incisors,' resumed the professor of dentistry, 'are the front teeth, the two upper ones.'

'How horrible!' cried Fantine.

'Two Napoleons!' grumbled a toothless old hag who stood by. 'How lucky she is!'

Fantine fled away and stopped her ears not to hear the shrill voice of the man who called after her: 'Consider, my beauty! two Napoleons! how much good they will do you! If you have the courage for it, come this evening to the inn of the *Tillac d'Argent*; you will find me there.'

Fantine returned home; she was raving, and told the story to her good neighbour Marguerite: 'Do you understand that? isn't he an abominable man? Why do they let such people go about the country? Pull out my two front teeth!

why, I should be horrible! The hair is bad enough, but the teeth! Oh! what a monster of a man! I would rather throw myself from the fifth storey, head first, to the pavement! He told me that he would be this evening at the *Tillac d'Argent*.'

'And what was it he offered you?' asked Marguerite.

'Two Napoleons.'

'That is forty francs.'

'Yes,' said Fantine, 'that makes forty francs.'

She became thoughtful and went about her work. In a quarter of an hour she left her sewing and went to the stairs to read again the Thénardiers' letter.

On her return she said to Marguerite, who was at work near her:

'What does this mean, a military fever? Do you know?'

'Yes,' answered the old woman, 'it is a disease.'

'Then it needs a good many drugs?'

'Yes; terrible drugs.'

'How does it come upon you?'

'It is a disease that comes in a moment.'

'Does it attack children?'

'Children especially.'

'Do people die of it?'

'Very often,' said Marguerite.

Fantine withdrew and went once more to read over the letter on the stairs.

In the evening she went out, and took the direction of the Rue de Paris where the inns are.

The next morning, when Marguerite went into Fantine's chamber before daybreak, for they always worked together, and so made one candle do for the two, she found Fantine seated upon her couch, pale and icy. She had not been in bed. Her cap had fallen upon her knees. The candle had burned all night, and was almost consumed.

Marguerite stopped upon the threshold, petrified by this wild disorder, and exclaimed: 'Good Lord! the candle is all burned out. Something has happened.'

Then she looked at Fantine, who sadly turned her shorn head.

Fantine had grown ten years older since evening.

'Bless us!' said Marguerite, 'what is the matter with you, Fantine?'

'Nothing,' said Fantine. 'Quite the contrary. My child will not die with that frightful sickness for lack of aid. I am satisfied.'

So saying, she showed the old woman two Napoleons that glistened on the table.

'Oh! good God!' said Marguerite. 'Why there is a fortune! where did you get these louis d'or?'

'I got them,' answered Fantine.

At the same time she smiled. The candle lit up her face. It was a sickening smile, for the corners of her mouth were stained with blood, and a dark cavity revealed itself there.

The two teeth were gone.

She sent the forty francs to Montfermeil.

And this was a ruse of the Thénardiers to get money. Cosette was not sick.

Fantine threw her looking-glass out of the window. Long before she had left her little room on the second storey for an attic room with no other fastening than a latch; one of those garret rooms the ceiling of which makes an angle with the floor and hits your head at every moment. The poor cannot go to the end of their chamber or to the end of their destiny, but by bending continually more and more. She no longer had a bed, she retained a rag that she called her coverlet, a mattress on the floor, and a worn-out straw chair. Her little rose-bush was dried up in the corner, forgotten. In the other corner was a butter-pot for water, which froze in the winter, and the different levels at which the water had stood remained marked a long time by circles of ice. She had lost her modesty, she was losing her coquetry. The last sign. She would go out with a dirty cap. Either from want of time or from indifference she no longer washed her linen. As fast as the heels of her stockings wore out she drew them down into her shoes. This was shown by certain perpendicular wrinkles. She mended her old, worn-out corsets with bits of calico which were torn by the slightest motion. Her creditors quarrelled with her and gave her no rest. She met them in the street; she met them again on her stairs. She passed whole nights in weeping and thinking. She had a strange brilliancy in her eyes, and a constant pain in her shoulder near the top of her left shoulder-blade. She coughed a great deal. She hated Father Madeleine thoroughly, and never complained. She sewed seventeen hours a day; but a prison contractor, who was working prisoners at a loss, suddenly cut down the price, and this reduced the day's wages of free labourers to nine sous. Seventeen hours of work, and nine sous a day! Her creditors were more pitiless than ever. The second-hand dealer, who had taken back nearly all his furniture, was constantly saying to her: 'When will you pay me, wench?'

Good God! what did they want her to do? She felt herself hunted down, and something of the wild beast began to develop within her. About the same time, Thénardier wrote to her that really he had waited with too much generosity, and that he must have a hundred francs immediately, or else little Cosette, just convalescing after her severe sickness, would be turned out of doors into the cold and upon the highway, and that she would become what she could, and would perish if she must. 'A hundred francs,' thought Fantine. 'But where is there a place where one can earn a hundred sous a day?'

'Come!' said she, 'I will sell what is left.'

The unfortunate creature became a woman of the town.

11. Christus nos liberavit

WHAT IS THIS history of Fantine? It is society buying a slave.

From whom? From misery.

From hunger, from cold, from loneliness, from abandonment, from privation. Melancholy barter. A soul for a bit of bread. Misery makes the offer, society accepts.

The holy law of Jesus Christ governs our civilisation, but it does not yet permeate it; it is said that slavery has disappeared from European civilisation. This is a mistake. It still exists; but it weighs now only upon woman, and it is called prostitution.

It weighs upon woman, that is to say, upon grace, upon feebleness, upon beauty, upon maternity. This is not one of the least of man's shames.

At the stage of this mournful drama at which we have now arrived, Fantine has nothing left of what she had formerly been. She has become marble in becoming corrupted. Whoever touches her feels a chill. She goes her ways, she endures you and she knows you not; she wears a dishonoured and severe face. Life and social order have spoken their last word to her. All that can happen to her has happened. She has endured all, borne all, experienced all, suffered all, lost all, wept for all. She is resigned, with that resignation that resembles indifference as death resembles sleep. She shuns nothing now. She fears nothing now. Every cloud falls upon her, and all the ocean sweeps over her! What matters it to her! the sponge is already drenched.

She believed so at least, but it is a mistake to imagine that man can exhaust his destiny, or can reach the bottom of anything whatever.

Alas! what are all these destinies thus driven pell-mell? whither go they? why are they so?

He who knows that, sees all the shadow.

He is alone. His name is God.

12. *The idleness of Monsieur Bamatabois*

THERE IS IN ALL SMALL CITIES, and there was at M— sur M— in particular, a set of young men who nibble their fifteen hundred livres of income in the country with the same air with which their fellows devour two hundred thousand francs a year at Paris. They are beings of the great neuter species; geldings, parasites, nobodies, who have a little land, a little folly, and a little wit, who would be clowns in a drawing-room, and think themselves gentlemen in a bar-room, who talk about 'my fields, my woods, my peasants', hiss the actresses at the theatre to prove that they are persons of taste, quarrel with the officers of the garrison to show that they are gallant, hunt, smoke, gape, drink, take snuff, play billiards, stare at passengers getting out of the coach, live at the café, dine at the inn, have a dog who eats the bones under the table, and a mistress who sets the dishes upon it, hold fast to a sou, overdo the fashions, admire tragedy, despise women, wear out their old boots, copy London as reflected from Paris, and Paris as reflected from Pont-à-Mousson, grow stupid as they grow old, do no work, do no good, and not much harm.

Monsieur Félix Tholomyès, had he remained in his province and never seen Paris, would have been such a man.

If they were richer, we should say: they are dandies; if they were poorer, we should say: they are vagabonds. They are simply idlers. Among these idlers there are some that are bores, some that are bored, some dreamers, and some jokers.

In those days, a dandy was made up of a large collar, a large cravat, a watch loaded with chains, three waistcoats worn one over the other, of different colours, the red and the blue within, a short olive-coloured coat with a fish-tail skirt, a double row of silver buttons alternating with one another and running up to the shoulder, and pantaloons of a lighter olive, ornamented at the two seams with an indefinite, but always odd, number of ribs, varying from one to eleven, a limit which was never exceeded. Add to this, Blücher boots with little iron caps on the heel, a high-crowned and narrow-brimmed hat, hair bushed out, an enormous cane, and conversation spiced with the puns of Potier. Above all, spurs and moustaches. In those days, moustaches meant civilians, and spurs meant pedestrians.

The provincial dandy wore longer spurs and fiercer moustaches.

It was the time of the war of the South American Republics against the King of Spain, of Bolivar against Morillo. Hats with narrow brims were Royalist, and were called Morillos; the liberals wore hats with wide brims which were called Bolivars.

Eight or ten months after what has been related in the preceding pages, in the early part of January 1823, one evening when it had been snowing, one of these dandies, one of these idlers, a 'well-intentioned' man, for he wore a morillo, very warmly wrapped in one of those large cloaks which completed the fashionable costume in cold weather, was amusing himself with tormenting a creature who was walking back and forth before the window of the officers' café, in a ball-dress, with her neck and shoulders bare, and flowers upon her head. The dandy was smoking, for that was decidedly the fashion.

Every time that the woman passed before him, he threw out at her, with a puff of smoke from his cigar, some remark which he thought was witty and pleasant, as: 'How ugly you are!' 'Are you trying to hide?' 'You have lost your teeth!' etc., etc. This gentleman's name was Monsieur Bamatabois. The woman, a rueful, bedizened spectre, who was walking backwards and forwards upon the snow, did not answer him, did not even look at him, but continued her walk in silence and with a dismal regularity that brought her under his sarcasm every five minutes, like the condemned soldier who at stated periods returns under the rods. This failure to secure attention doubtless piqued the loafer, who, taking advantage of the moment when she turned, came up behind her with a stealthy step and stifling his laughter, stooped down, seized a handful of snow from the sidewalk, and threw it hastily into her back between her naked shoulders. The girl roared with rage, turned, bounded like a panther, and rushed upon the man, burying her nails in his face, and using the most frightful words that ever fell from the off-scouring of a guardhouse. These insults were thrown out in a voice roughened by brandy, from a hideous mouth which lacked the two front teeth. It was Fantine.

At the noise which this made, the officers came out of the café, a crowd gathered, and a large circle was formed, laughing, jeering, and applauding, around this centre of attraction composed of two beings who could hardly be recognised as a man and a woman, the man defending himself, his hat knocked off, the woman kicking and striking, her head bare, shrieking, toothless, and without hair, livid with wrath, and horrible.

Suddenly a tall man advanced quickly from the crowd, seized the woman by her muddy satin waist, and said: 'Follow me!'

The woman raised her head; her furious voice died out at once. Her eyes were glassy, from livid she had become pale, and she shuddered with a shudder of terror. She recognised Javert.

The dandy profited by this to steal away.

13. *Solution of some questions of municipal police*

JAVERT DISMISSED the bystanders, broke up the circle, and walked off rapidly towards the Bureau of Police, which is at the end of the square, dragging the poor creature after him. She made no resistance, but followed mechanically. Neither spoke a word. The flock of spectators, in a paroxysm of joy, followed with their jokes. The deepest misery, an opportunity for obscenity.

When they reached the Bureau of Police, which was a low hall warmed by a stove, and guarded by a sentinel, with a grated window looking on the street, Javert opened the door, entered with Fantine, and closed the door behind him, to the great disappointment of the curious crowd who stood upon tiptoe and stretched their necks before the dirty window of the guardhouse, in their endeavours to see. Curiosity is a kind of glutton. To see is to devour.

On entering Fantine crouched down in a corner motionless and silent, like a frightened dog.

The sergeant of the guard placed a lighted candle on the table. Javert sat down, drew from his pocket a sheet of stamped paper, and began to write.

These women are placed by our laws completely under the discretion of the police. They do what they will with them, punish them as they please, and confiscate at will those two sad things which they call their industry and their liberty. Javert was impassible; his grave face betrayed no emotion. He was, however, engaged in serious and earnest consideration. It was one of those moments in which he exercised without restraint, but with all the scruples of a strict conscience, his formidable discretionary power. At this moment he felt that his policeman's stool was a bench of justice. He was conducting a trial. He was trying and condemning. He called all the ideas of which his mind was capable around the grand thing that he was doing. The more he examined the conduct of this girl, the more he revolted at it. It was clear that he had seen a crime committed. He had seen, there in the street, society represented by a property holder and an elector,[23] insulted and attacked by a creature who was an outlaw and an outcast. A prostitute had assaulted a citizen. He, Javert, had seen that himself. He wrote in silence.

When he had finished, he signed his name, folded the paper, and handed it to the sergeant of the guard, saying: 'Take three men, and carry this girl to jail.' Then turning to Fantine: 'You are in for six months.'

The hapless woman shuddered.

'Six months! six months in prison!' cried she. 'Six months to earn seven sous a day! but what will become of Cosette! my daughter! my daughter! Why, I still owe more than a hundred francs to the Thénardiers, Monsieur Inspector, do you know that?'

She dragged herself along on the floor, dirted by the muddy boots of all these men, without rising, clasping her hands, and moving rapidly on her knees.

'Monsieur Javert,' said she, 'I beg your pity. I assure you that I was not in the wrong. If you had seen the beginning, you would have seen. I swear to you by the good God that I was not in the wrong. That gentleman, whom I do not know, threw snow in my back. Have they the right to throw snow into our backs when we are going along quietly like that without doing any harm to anybody? That made me wild. I am not very well, you see! and then he had already been saying things to me for some time. "You are homely!" "You have no teeth!" I know too well that I have lost my teeth. I did not do anything; I thought: "He is a gentleman who is amusing himself." I was not immodest with him, I did not speak to him. It was then that he threw the snow at me. Monsieur Javert, my good Monsieur Inspector! was there no one there who saw it and can tell you that this is true! I perhaps did wrong to get angry. You know, at the first moment, we cannot master ourselves. We are excitable. And then, to have something so cold thrown into your back when you are not expecting it. I did wrong to spoil the gentleman's hat. Why has he gone away? I would ask his pardon. Oh! I would beg his pardon. Have pity on me now this once, Monsieur Javert. Stop, you don't know how it is, in the prisons they only earn seven sous; that is not the fault of the government, but they earn seven sous, and just think that I have a hundred francs to pay, or else they will turn away my little one. O my God! I cannot have her with me. What I do is so vile! O my Cosette, O my little angel of the good, blessed Virgin, what will she become, poor famished child! I tell you the Thénardiers are inn-keepers, boors, they have no consideration. They must have money. Do not put me in prison! Do you see, she is a little one that they will put out on the highway, to do what she can, in the very heart of winter; you must feel pity for such a thing, good Monsieur Javert. If she were older, she could earn her living, but she cannot at such an age. I am not a bad woman at heart. It is not laziness and appetite that have brought me to this; I have drunk brandy, but it was from misery. I do not like it, but it stupefies. When I was happier, one would only have had to look into my wardrobe to see that I was not a disorderly woman. I had linen, much linen. Have pity on me, Monsieur Javert.'

She talked thus, bent double, shaken with sobs, blinded by tears, her neck bare, clenching her hands, coughing with a dry and short cough, stammering very feebly with an agonised voice. Great grief is a divine and terrible radiance which transfigures the wretched. At that moment Fantine had again become beautiful. At certain instants she stopped and tenderly kissed the policeman's coat. She would have softened a heart of granite; but you cannot soften a heart of wood.

'Come,' said Javert, 'I have heard you. Haven't you got through? March off at once! you have your six months! the Eternal Father in person could do nothing for you.'

At those solemn words, *The Eternal Father in person could do nothing for you*, she understood that her sentence was fixed. She sank down murmuring:

'Mercy!'

Javert turned his back.

The soldiers seized her by the arms.

A few minutes before a man had entered without being noticed. He had closed the door, and stood with his back against it, and heard the despairing supplication of Fantine.

When the soldiers put their hands upon the wretched being, who would not rise, he stepped forward out of the shadow and said:

'One moment, if you please!'

Javert raised his eyes and recognised Monsieur Madeleine. He took off his hat, and bowing with a sort of angry awkwardness:

'Pardon, Monsieur Mayor – '

This word, Monsieur Mayor, had a strange effect upon Fantine. She sprang to her feet at once like a spectre rising from the ground, pushed back the soldiers with her arms, walked straight to Monsieur Madeleine before they could stop her, and gazing at him fixedly, with a wild look, she exclaimed:

'Ah! it is you then who are Monsieur Mayor!'

Then she burst out laughing and spat in his face.

Monsieur Madeleine wiped his face and said:

'Inspector Javert, set this woman at liberty.'

Javert felt as though he were on the point of losing his senses. He experienced, at that moment, blow on blow, and almost simultaneously, the most violent emotions that he had known in his life. To see a woman of the town spit in the face of a mayor was a thing so monstrous that in his most daring suppositions he would have thought it sacrilege to believe it possible. On the other hand, deep down in his thought, he dimly brought into hideous association what this woman was and what this mayor might be, and then he perceived with horror something indescribably simple in this prodigious assault. But when he saw this mayor, this magistrate, wipe his face quietly and say: *set this woman at liberty*, he was stupefied with amazement; thought and speech alike failed him; the sum of possible astonishment had been overpassed. He remained speechless.

The mayor's words were not less strange a blow to Fantine. She raised her bare arm and clung to the damper of the stove as if she were staggered. Meanwhile she looked all around and began to talk in a low voice, as if speaking to herself:

'At liberty! they let me go! I am not to go to prison for six months! Who was it said that? It is not possible that anybody said that. I misunderstood. That cannot be this monster of a mayor! Was it you, my good Monsieur Javert, who told them to set me at liberty? Oh! look now! I will tell you and you will let me go. This monster of a mayor, this old whelp of a mayor, he is the cause of all this. Think of it, Monsieur Javert, he turned me away! on account of a parcel of beggars who told stories in the workshop. Was not that horrible! To turn away a poor girl who does her work honestly. Since that I could not earn enough, and all the wretchedness has come. To begin with, there is a change that you gentlemen of the police ought to make – that is, to stop prison contractors from wronging poor people. I will tell you how it is; listen. You earn twelve sous at shirt making, that falls to nine sous, not enough to live. Then we must do what we can. For me, I had my little Cosette, and I had to be a bad woman. You see now that it is this beggar of a mayor who has done all this, and then, I did stamp on the hat of this gentleman in front of the officers' café. But he, he had spoiled my whole dress with the snow. We women, we have only one silk dress, for evening. You see, I have never meant to do wrong, in truth, Monsieur Javert, and I see everywhere much worse women than I am who are much more fortunate. Oh, Monsieur Javert, it is you who said that they must let me go, is it not? Go and inquire, speak to my landlord; I pay my rent, and he will surely tell you that I am honest. Oh dear, I beg your pardon, I have touched – I did not know it – the damper of the stove, and it smokes.'

Monsieur Madeleine listened with profound attention. While she was talking, he had fumbled in his waistcoat, had taken out his purse and opened it. It was empty. He had put it back into his pocket. He said to Fantine:

'How much did you say that you owed?'

Fantine, who had only looked at Javert, turned towards him:

'Who said anything to you?'

Then addressing herself to the soldiers:

'Say now, did you see how I spat in his face? Oh! you old scoundrel of a mayor, you come here to frighten me, but I am not afraid of you. I am afraid of Monsieur Javert. I am afraid of my good Monsieur Javert!'

As she said this she turned again towards the inspector:

'Now, you see, Monsieur Inspector, you must be just. I know that you are just, Monsieur Inspector; in fact, it is very simple, a man who jocosely throws a little snow into a woman's back, that makes them laugh, the officers, they must divert themselves with something, and we poor things are only for their amusement. And then, you, you come, you are obliged to keep order, you arrest the woman who has done wrong, but on reflection, as you are good, you tell them to set me at liberty, that is for my little one, because six months in prison, that would prevent my supporting my child. Only never come back again, wretch! Oh! I will never come back again, Monsieur Javert! They may do anything they like with me now, I will not stir. Only, today, you see, I cried out because that hurt me. I did not in the least expect that snow from that gentleman, and then, I have told you, I am not very well, I cough, I have something in my chest like a ball which burns me, and the doctor tells me: "Be careful." Stop, feel, give me your hand, don't be afraid, here it is.'

She wept no more; her voice was caressing; she placed Javert's great coarse hand upon her white and delicate chest, and looked at him smiling.

Suddenly she hastily adjusted the disorder of her garments, smoothed down the folds of her dress, which, in dragging herself about, had been raised almost as high as her knees, and walked towards the door, saying in an undertone to the soldiers, with a friendly nod of the head:

'Boys, Monsieur the Inspector said that you must release me; I am going.'

She put her hand upon the latch. One more step and she would be in the street.

Javert until that moment had remained standing, motionless, his eyes fixed on the ground, looking, in the midst of the scene, like a statue which was waiting to be placed in position.

The sound of the latch roused him. He raised his head with an expression of sovereign authority, an expression always the more frightful in proportion as power is vested in beings of lower grade; ferocious in the wild beast, atrocious in the undeveloped man.

'Sergeant,' exclaimed he, 'don't you see that this vagabond is going off? Who told you to let her go?'

'I,' said Madeleine.

At the words of Javert, Fantine had trembled and dropped the latch, as a thief who is caught, drops what he has stolen. When Madeleine spoke, she turned, and from that moment, without saying a word, without even daring to breathe freely, she looked by turns from Madeleine to Javert and from Javert to Madeleine, as the one or the other was speaking.

It was clear that Javert must have been, as they say, 'thrown off his balance', or he would not have allowed himself to address the sergeant as he did, after the direction of the mayor to set Fantine at liberty. Had he forgotten the presence of the mayor? Had he finally decided within himself that it was impossible for 'an authority' to give such an order, and that very certainly the mayor must have said one thing when he meant another? Or, in view of the enormities which he had witnessed for the last two hours, did he say to himself that it was necessary to revert to extreme measures, that it was necessary for the little to make itself great, for the detective to transform himself into a magistrate, for the policeman to become a judge, and that in this fearful extremity, order, law, morality, government, society as a whole, were personified in him, Javert?

However this might be, when Monsieur Madeleine pronounced that *I* which we have just heard, the inspector of police, Javert, turned towards the mayor, pale, cold, with blue lips, a desperate look, his whole body agitated with an imperceptible tremor, and, an unheard-of thing, said to him, with a downcast look, but a firm voice:

'Monsieur Mayor, that cannot be done.'

'Why?' said Monsieur Madeleine.

'This wretched woman has insulted a citizen.'

'Inspector Javert,' replied Monsieur Madeleine, in a conciliating and calm tone, 'listen. You are an honest man, and I have no objection to explain myself to you. The truth is this. I was passing through the square when you arrested this woman; there was a crowd still there; I learned the circumstances; I know all about it; it is the citizen who was in the wrong, and who, by a faithful police, would have been arrested.'

Javert went on:

'This wretch has just insulted Monsieur the Mayor.'

'That concerns me,' said Monsieur Madeleine. 'The insult to me rests with myself, perhaps. I can do what I please about it.'

'I beg Monsieur the Mayor's pardon. The insult rests not with him, it rests with justice.'

'Inspector Javert,' replied Monsieur Madeleine, 'the highest justice is conscience. I have heard this woman. I know what I am doing.'

'And for my part, Monsieur Mayor, I do not know what I am seeing.'

'Then content yourself with obeying.'

'I obey my duty. My duty requires that this woman spend six months in prison.'

Monsieur Madeleine answered mildly:

'Listen to this. She shall not spend a day.'

At these decisive words, Javert had the boldness to look the mayor in the eye, and said, but still in a tone of profound respect:

'I am very sorry to resist Monsieur the Mayor; it is the first time in my life, but he will deign to permit me to observe that I am within the limits of my own authority. I will speak, since the mayor desires it, on the matter of the citizen. I was there. This girl fell upon Monsieur Bamatabois, who is an elector and the owner of that fine house with a balcony, that stands at the corner of the esplanade, three storeys high, and all of hewn stone. Indeed, there are some things in this world which must be considered. However that may be, Monsieur Mayor, this matter belongs to the police of the street; that concerns me, and I detain the woman Fantine.'

At this Monsieur Madeleine folded his arms and said in a severe tone which nobody in the city had ever yet heard:

'The matter of which you speak belongs to the municipal police. By the terms of articles nine, eleven, fifteen, and sixty-six of the code of criminal law, I am the judge of it. I order that this woman be set at liberty.'

Javert endeavoured to make a last attempt.

'But, Monsieur Mayor – '

'I refer you to article eighty-one of the law of December 13th, 1799, upon illegal imprisonment.'

'Monsieur Mayor, permit – '

'Not another word.'

'However – '

'Retire,' said Monsieur Madeleine.

Javert received the blow, standing in front, and with open breast like a Russian soldier. He bowed to the ground before the mayor, and went out.

Fantine stood by the door and looked at him with stupor as he passed before her.

Meanwhile she also was the subject of a strange revolution. She had seen herself somehow disputed about by two opposing powers. She had seen struggling before her very eyes two men who held in their hands her liberty, her life, her soul, her child; one of these men was drawing her to the side of darkness, the other was leading her towards the light. In this contest, seen with distortion through the magnifying power of fright, these two men had appeared to her like two giants; one spoke as her demon, the other as her good angel. The angel had vanquished the demon, and the thought of it made her shudder from head to foot; this angel, this deliverer, was precisely the man whom she abhorred, this mayor whom she had so long considered as the author of all her woes, this Madeleine! and at the very moment when she had insulted him in a hideous fashion, he had saved her! Had she then been deceived? Ought she then to change her whole heart? She did not know, she trembled. She listened with dismay, she looked around with alarm, and at each word that Monsieur Madeleine uttered, she felt the fearful darkness of her hatred melt within and flow away, while there was born in her heart an indescribable and unspeakable warmth of joy, of confidence, and of love.

When Javert was gone, Monsieur Madeleine turned towards her, and said to her, speaking slowly and with difficulty, like a man who is struggling that he may not weep:

'I have heard you. I knew nothing of what you have said. I believe that it is true. I did not even know that you had left my workshop. Why did you not apply to me? But now: I will pay your debts, I will have your child come to you, or you shall go to her. You shall live here, at Paris, or where you will. I take charge of your child and you. You shall do no more work, if you do not wish to. I will give you all the money that you need. You shall again become honest in again becoming happy. More than that, listen. I declare to you from this moment, if all is as you say, and I do not doubt it, that you have never ceased to be virtuous and holy before God. Oh, poor woman!'

This was more than poor Fantine could bear. To have Cosette! to leave this infamous life! to live free, rich, happy, honest, with Cosette! to see suddenly spring up in the midst of her misery all these realities of paradise! She looked as if she were stupefied at the man who was speaking to her, and could only pour out two or three sobs: 'Oh! oh! oh!' Her limbs gave way, she threw herself on her knees before Monsieur Madeleine, and, before he could prevent it, he felt that she had seized his hand and carried it to her lips.

Then she fainted.

BOOK 6: JAVERT

1. *The beginning of the rest*

MONSIEUR MADELEINE had Fantine taken to the infirmary, which was in his own house. He confided her to the sisters, who put her to bed. A violent fever came on, and she passed a part of the night in delirious ravings. Finally, she fell asleep.

Towards noon the following day, Fantine awoke. She heard a breathing near her bed, drew aside the curtain, and saw Monsieur Madeleine standing gazing at something above his head. His look was full of compassionate and supplicating agony. She followed its direction, and saw that it was fixed upon a crucifix nailed against the wall.

From that moment Monsieur Madeleine was transfigured in the eyes of Fantine; he seemed to her clothed upon with light. He was absorbed in a kind of prayer. She gazed at him for a long while without daring to interrupt him; at last she said timidly:

'What are you doing?'

Monsieur Madeleine had been in that place for an hour waiting for Fantine to awake. He took her hand, felt her pulse, and said:

'How do you feel?'

'Very well. I have slept,' she said. 'I think I am getting better – this will be nothing.'

Then he said, answering the question she had first asked him, as if she had just asked it:

'I was praying to the martyr who is on high.'

And in his thought he added: 'For the martyr who is here below.'

Monsieur Madeleine had passed the night and morning in informing himself about Fantine. He knew all now, he had learned, even in all its poignant details, the history of Fantine.

He went on:

'You have suffered greatly, poor mother. Oh! do not lament, you have now the portion of the elect. It is in this way that mortals become angels. It is not their fault; they do not know how to set about it otherwise. This hell from which you have come out is the first step towards Heaven. We must begin by that.'

He sighed deeply; but she smiled with this sublime smile from which two teeth were gone.

That same night, Javert wrote a letter. Next morning he carried this letter himself to the post-office of M— sur M—. It was directed to Paris and bore this address: 'To Monsieur Chabouillet, Secretary of Monsieur the Prefect of Police.'

As the affair of the Bureau of Police had been noised about, the postmistress and some others who saw the letter before it was sent, and who recognised Javert's handwriting in the address, thought he was sending in his resignation. Monsieur Madeleine wrote immediately to the Thénardiers. Fantine owed them a hundred and twenty francs. He sent them three hundred francs, telling them to pay themselves out of it, and bring the child at once to M— sur M— where her mother, who was sick, wanted her.

This astonished Thénardier.

'The Devil!' he said to his wife, 'we won't let go of the child. It may be that this Lark will become a milch cow. I guess some silly fellow had been smitten by the mother.'

He replied by a bill of five hundred and some odd francs carefully drawn up. In this bill figured two incontestable items for upwards of three hundred francs, one of a physician and the other of an apothecary who had attended and supplied Eponine and Azelma during two long illnesses. Cosette, as we have said, had not been ill. This was only a slight substitution of names. Thénardier wrote at the bottom of the bill: '*Received on account three hundred francs.*'

Monsieur Madeleine immediately sent three hundred francs more, and wrote: 'Make haste to bring Cosette.'

'Christy!' said Thénardier, 'we won't let go of the girl.'

Meanwhile Fantine had not recovered. She still remained in the infirmary.

It was not without some repugnance, at first, that the sisters received and cared for 'this girl'. He who has seen the bas-reliefs at Rheims will recall the distension of the lower lip of the wise virgins beholding the foolish virgins. This ancient contempt of vestals for less fortunate women is one of the deepest instincts of womanly dignity; the sisters had experienced it with the intensification of Religion. But in a few days Fantine had disarmed them. The motherly tenderness within her, with her soft and touching words, moved them. One day the sisters heard her say in her delirium: 'I have been a sinner, but when I shall have my child with me, that will mean that God has pardoned me. While I was bad I would not have had my Cosette with me; I could not have borne her sad and surprised looks. It was for her I sinned, and that is why God forgives me. I shall feel this benediction when Cosette comes. I shall gaze upon her; the sight of her innocence will do me good. She knows nothing of it all. She is an angel, you see, my sisters. At her age the wings have not yet fallen.'

Monsieur Madeleine came to see her twice a day, and at each visit she asked him:

'Shall I see my Cosette soon?'

He answered:

'Perhaps tomorrow. I expect her every moment.'

And the mother's pale face would brighten.

'Ah!' she would say, 'how happy I shall be.'

We have just said she did not recover: on the contrary, her condition seemed to become worse from week to week. That handful of snow applied to the naked skin between her shoulder-blades, had caused a sudden check of perspiration, in consequence of which the disease, which had been forming for some years, at last attacked her violently. They were just at that time beginning in the diagnosis and treatment of lung diseases to follow the fine theory of Laennec.[24] The doctor sounded her lungs and shook his head.

Monsieur Madeleine said to him:

'Well?'

'Has she not a child she is anxious to see?' said the doctor.

'Yes.'

'Well then, make haste to bring her.'

Monsieur Madeleine gave a shudder.

Fantine asked him: 'What did the doctor say?'

Monsieur Madeleine tried to smile.

'He told us to bring your child at once. That will restore your health.'

'Oh!' she cried, 'he is right. But what is the matter with these Thénardiers that they keep my Cosette from me? Oh! She is coming! Here at last I see happiness near me.'

The Thénardiers, however, did not 'let go of the child'; they gave a hundred bad reasons. Cosette was too delicate to travel in the wintertime, and then there were a number of little petty debts, of which they were collecting the bills, etc., etc.

'I will send somebody for Cosette,' said Monsieur Madeleine, 'if necessary, I will go myself.'

He wrote at Fantine's dictation this letter, which she signed.

> MONSIEUR THÉNARDIER:
> You will deliver Cosette to the bearer.
> He will settle all small debts.
> I have the honour to salute you with consideration.
>   FANTINE.

In the meanwhile a serious matter intervened. In vain we chisel, as best we can, the mysterious block of which our life is made, the black vein of destiny reappears continually.

2. *How Jean can become champ*

ONE MORNING Monsieur Madeleine was in his office arranging for some pressing business of the mayoralty, in case he should decide to go to Montfermeil himself, when he was informed that Javert, the inspector of police, wished to speak with him. On hearing this name spoken, Monsieur Madeleine could not repress a disagreeable impression. Since the affair of the Bureau of Police, Javert had more than ever avoided him, and Monsieur Madeleine had not seen him at all.

'Let him come in,' said he.

Javert entered.

Monsieur Madeleine remained seated near the fire, looking over a bundle of papers upon which he was making notes, and which contained the returns of the police patrol. He did not disturb himself at all for Javert: he could not but think of poor Fantine, and it was fitting that he should receive him very coldly.

Javert respectfully saluted the mayor, who had his back towards him. The mayor did not look up, but continued to make notes on the papers.

Javert advanced a few steps, and paused without breaking silence.

A physiognomist, had he been familiar with Javert's face, had he made a study for years of this savage in the service of civilisation, this odd mixture of the Roman, Spartan, monk, and corporal, this spy, incapable of a lie, this virgin detective – a physiognomist, had he known his secret and inveterate aversion for Monsieur Madeleine, his contest with the mayor on the subject of Fantine, and had he seen Javert at that moment, would have said: 'What has happened to him?'

It was evident to anyone who had known this conscientious, straight-forward, clear, sincere, upright, austere, fierce man, that Javert had suffered some great interior commotion. There was nothing in his mind that was not depicted on his face. He was, like all violent people, subject to sudden changes. Never had his face been stranger or more startling. On entering, he had bowed before Monsieur Madeleine with a look in which was neither rancour, anger, nor defiance; he paused some steps behind the mayor's chair, and was now standing in a soldierly attitude with the natural, cold rudeness of a man who was never kind, but has always been patient; he waited without speaking a word or making a motion, in genuine humility and tranquil resignation, until it should please Monsieur the Mayor to turn towards him, calm, serious, hat in hand, and eyes cast down with an expression between that of a soldier before his officer and a prisoner before his judge. All the feeling as well as all the remembrances which we should have expected him to have, disappeared. Nothing was left upon this face, simple and impenetrable as granite, except a gloomy sadness. His whole person expressed abasement and firmness, an indescribably coura-geous dejection.

At last the mayor laid down his pen and turned partly round:

'Well, what is it? What is the matter, Javert?'

Javert remained silent a moment as if collecting himself; then raised his voice with a sad solemnity which did not, however, exclude simplicity: 'There has been a criminal act committed, Monsieur Mayor.'

'What act?'

'An inferior agent of the government has been wanting in respect to a magistrate, in the gravest manner. I come, as is my duty, to bring the fact to your knowledge.'

'Who is this agent?' asked Monsieur Madeleine.

'I,' said Javert.

'You?'

'I.'

'And who is the magistrate who has to complain of this agent?'

'You, Monsieur Mayor.'

Monsieur Madeleine straightened himself in his chair. Javert continued, with serious looks and eyes still cast down.

'Monsieur Mayor, I come to ask you to be so kind as to make charges and procure my dismissal.'

Monsieur Madeleine, amazed, opened his mouth. Javert interrupted him:

'You will say that I might tender my resignation, but that is not enough. To resign is honourable; I have done wrong. I ought to be punished. I must be dismissed.'

And after a pause he added:

'Monsieur Mayor, you were severe to me the other day, unjustly. Be justly so today.'

'Ah, indeed! why? What is all this nonsense? What does it all mean? What is the criminal act committed by you against me? What have you done to me? How have you wronged me? You accuse yourself: do you wish to be relieved?'

'Dismissed,' said Javert.

'Dismissed it is then. It is very strange. I do not understand you.'

'You will understand, Monsieur Mayor,' Javert sighed deeply, and continued sadly and coldly:

'Monsieur Mayor, six weeks ago, after that scene about that girl, I was enraged and I denounced you.'

'Denounced me?'

'To the Prefecture of Police at Paris.'

Monsieur Madeleine, who did not laugh much oftener than Javert, began to laugh:

'As a mayor having encroached upon the police?'

'As a former convict.'

The mayor became livid.

Javert, who had not raised his eyes, continued:

'I believed it. For a long while I had had suspicions. A resemblance, information you obtained at Faverolles, your immense strength; the affair of old Fauchelevent; your skill as a marksman; your leg which drags a little – and in fact I don't know what other stupidities; but at last I took you for a man named Jean Valjean.'

'Named what? How did you call that name?'

'Jean Valjean. He was a convict I saw twenty years ago, when I was adjutant of the galley guard at Toulon. After leaving the galleys this Valjean, it appears, robbed a bishop's palace, then he committed another robbery with weapons in his hands, in a highway, on a little Savoyard. For eight years his whereabouts have been unknown, and search has been made for him. I fancied – in short, I have done this thing. Anger determined me, and I denounced you to the prefect.'

M. Madeleine, who had taken up the file of papers again, a few moments before, said with a tone of perfect indifference: 'And what answer did you get?'

'That I was crazy.'

'Well!'

'Well; they were right.'

'It is fortunate that you think so!'

'It must be so, for the real Jean Valjean has been found.'

The paper that M. Madeleine held fell from his hand; he raised his head, looked steadily at Javert, and said in an inexpressible tone:

'Ah!'

Javert continued:

'I will tell you how it is, Monsieur Mayor. There was, it appears, in the country, near Ailly-le-Haut Clocher, a simple sort of fellow who was called Father Champmathieu. He was very poor. Nobody paid any attention to him. Such folks live, one hardly knows how. Finally, this last autumn, Father Champmathieu was arrested for stealing cider apples from — , but that is of no consequence. There was a theft, a wall scaled, branches of trees broken. Our Champmathieu was arrested; he had even then a branch of an apple tree in his hand. The rogue was caged. So far, it was nothing more than a penitentiary matter. But here comes in the hand of Providence. The jail being in a bad condition, the police justice thought it best to take him to Arras, where the prison of the department is. In this prison at Arras there was a former convict named Brevet, who is there for some trifle, and who, for his good conduct, has been made turnkey. No sooner was Champmathieu set down, than Brevet cried out: "Ha, ha! I know that man. He is a *fagot*." *

' "Look up here, my good man. You are Jean Valjean." "Jean Valjean, who is Jean Valjean?" Champmathieu plays off the astonished. " Don't play ignorance," said Brevet. "You are Jean Valjean; you were in the galleys at Toulon. It is twenty years ago. We were there together." Champmathieu denied it all. Faith! you understand ; they fathomed it. The case was worked up and this was what they found. This Champmathieu thirty years ago was a pruner in divers places, particularly in Faverolles. There we lose trace of him. A long time afterwards we find him at Auvergne; then at Paris, where he is said to have been a wheelwright and to have had a daughter – a washerwoman, but that is not proven, and finally in this part of the country. Now before going to the galleys for burglary, what was Jean Valjean? A pruner. Where? At Faverolles. Another fact. This Valjean's baptismal name was Jean; his mother's family name, Mathieu. Nothing could be more natural, on leaving the galleys, than to take his mother's name to disguise himself; then he would be called Jean Mathieu. He goes to Auvergne, the pronunciation of that region would make *Chan* of *Jean* – they would call him Chan Mathieu. Our man adopts it, and now you have him transformed into Champmathieu. You follow me, do you not? Search has been made at Faverolles; the family of Jean Valjean are no longer there. Nobody knows where they are. You know in such classes these disappearances of families often occur. You search, but can find nothing. Such people, when they are not mud, are dust. And then as the commencement of this story dates back thirty years, there is nobody now at Faverolles who knew Jean Valjean. But search has been made at Toulon. Besides Brevet there are only two convicts who have seen Jean Valjean. They are convicts for life; their names are Cochepaille and Chenildieu. These men were brought from the galleys and confronted with the pretended Champmathieu. They did not hesitate. To them as well as to Brevet it was Jean Valjean. Same age; fifty-four years old; same height; same appearance, in fact the same man; it is he. At this time it was that I sent my denunciation to the Prefecture at Paris. They replied that I was out of my mind, and that Jean Valjean was at Arras in the hands of justice. You may imagine how that astonished me; I who believed that I had here the same Jean Valjean. I wrote to the justice; he sent for me and brought Champmathieu before me.'

'Well,' interrupted Monsieur Madeleine.

Javert replied, with an incorruptible and sad face:

'Monsieur Mayor, truth is truth. I am sorry for it, but that man is Jean Valjean. I recognised him also.'

Monsieur Madeleine said in a very low voice:

'Are you sure?'

Javert began to laugh with the suppressed laugh which indicates profound conviction.

'H'm, sure!'

He remained a moment in thought, mechanically taking up pinches of the powdered wood used to dry ink, from the box on the table, and then added:

'And now that I see the real Jean Valjean, I do not understand how I ever could have believed anything else. I beg your pardon, Monsieur Mayor.'

In uttering these serious and supplicating words to him, who six weeks before

* Former convict.

had humiliated him before the entire guard, and had said 'Retire!' Javert, this haughty man, was unconsciously full of simplicity and dignity. Monsieur Madeleine answered his request, by this abrupt question:

'And what did the man say?'

'Oh, bless me! Monsieur Mayor, the affair is a bad one. If it is Jean Valjean, it is a second offence. To climb a wall, break a branch, and take apples, for a child is only a trespass; for a man it is a misdemeanour; for a convict it is a crime. Scaling a wall and theft includes everything. It is not a case for a police court, but for the assizes. It is not a few days' imprisonment, but the galleys for life. And then there is the affair of the little Savoyard, who I hope will be found. The devil! There is something to struggle against, is there not? There would be for anybody but Jean Valjean. But Jean Valjean is a sly fellow. And that is just where I recognise him. Anybody else would know that he was in a hot place, and would rave and cry out, as the tea-kettle sings on the fire; he would say that he was not Jean Valjean, et cetera. But this man pretends not to understand, he says: "I am Champmathieu: I have no more to say." He puts on an appearance of astonishment; he plays the brute. Oh, the rascal is cunning! But it is all the same, there is the evidence. Four persons have recognised him, and the old villain will be condemned. It has been taken to the assizes at Arras. I am going to testify. I have been summoned.'

Monsieur Madeleine had turned again to his desk, and was quietly looking over his papers, reading and writing alternately, like a man pressed with business. He turned again towards Javert:

'That will do, Javert. Indeed all these details interest me very little. We are wasting time, and we have urgent business, Javert; go at once to the house of the good woman Buseaupied, who sells herbs at the corner of Rue Saint Saulve; tell her to make her complaint against the carman Pierre Chesnelong. He is a brutal fellow, he almost crushed this woman and her child. He must be punished. Then you will go to Monsieur Charcellay, Rue Montre-de-Champigny. He complains that the gutter of the next house when it rains throws water upon his house, and is undermining the foundation. Then you will inquire into the offences that have been reported to me, at the widow Doris's, Rue Guibourg, and Madame Renée le Bossé's, Rue du Garraud Blanc, and make out reports. But I am giving you too much to do. Did you not tell me you were going to Arras in eight or ten days on this matter?'

'Sooner than that, Monsieur Mayor.'

'What day then?'

'I think I told monsieur that the case would be tried tomorrow, and that I should leave by the diligence tonight.'

Monsieur Madeleine made an imperceptible motion.

'And how long will the matter last?'

'One day at longest. Sentence will be pronounced at latest tomorrow evening. But I shall not wait for the sentence which is certain; as soon as my testimony is given I shall return here.'

'Very well,' said Monsieur Madeleine.

And he dismissed him with a wave of his hand.

Javert did not go.

'Your pardon, monsieur,' said he.

'What more is there?' asked Monsieur Madeleine.

'Monsieur Mayor, there is one thing more to which I desire to call your attention.'

'What is it?'

'It is that I ought to be dismissed.'

Monsieur Madeleine arose.

'Javert, you are a man of honour and I esteem you. You exaggerate your fault. Besides, this is an offence which concerns me. You are worthy of promotion rather than disgrace. I desire you to keep your place.'

Javert looked at Monsieur Madeleine with his calm eyes, in whose depths it seemed that one beheld his conscience, unenlightened, but stern and pure, and said in a tranquil voice:

'Monsieur Mayor, I cannot agree to that.'

'I repeat,' said Monsieur Madeleine, 'that this matter concerns me.'

But Javert, with his one idea, continued:

'As to exaggerating, I do not exaggerate. This is the way I reason. I have unjustly suspected you. That is nothing. It is our province to suspect, although it may be an abuse of our right to suspect our superiors. But without proofs and in a fit of anger, with revenge as my aim, I denounced you as a convict – you, a respectable man, a mayor, and a magistrate. This is a serious matter, very serious. I have committed an offence against authority in your person, I who am the agent of authority. If one of my subordinates had done what I have, I would have pronounced him unworthy of the service, and sent him away. Well, listen a moment, Monsieur Mayor; I have often been severe in my life towards others. It was just. I did right. Now if I were not severe towards myself, all I have justly done would become injustice. Should I spare myself more than others? No. What! if I should be prompt only to punish others and not myself, I should be a wretch indeed! They who say: "That blackguard, Javert," would be right. Monsieur Mayor, I do not wish you to treat me with kindness. Your kindness, when it was for others, enraged me; I do not wish it for myself. That kindness which consists in defending a woman of the town against a citizen, a police agent against the mayor, the inferior against the superior, that is what I call ill-judged kindness. Such kindness disorganises society. Good God, it is easy to be kind, the difficulty is to be just. Had you been what I thought, I should not have been kind to you; not I. You would have seen, Monsieur Mayor. I ought to treat myself as I would treat anybody else. When I put down malefactors, when I rigorously brought up offenders, I often said to myself: "You, if you ever trip; if ever I catch you doing wrong, look out!" I have tripped, I have caught myself doing wrong. So much the worse! I must be sent away, broken, dismissed, that is right. I have hands: I can till the ground. It is all the same to me. Monsieur Mayor, the good of the service demands an example. I simply ask the dismissal of Inspector Javert.'

All this was said in a tone of proud humility, a desperate and resolute tone, which gave an indescribably whimsical grandeur to this oddly honest man.

'We will see,' said Monsieur Madeleine.

And he held out his hand to him.

Javert started back, and said fiercely:

'Pardon, Monsieur Mayor, that should not be. A mayor does not give his hand to a spy.'

He added between his teeth:

'Spy, yes; from the moment I abused the power of my position, I have been nothing better than a spy!'

Then he bowed profoundly, and went towards the door.

There he turned around: his eyes yet downcast.

'Monsieur Mayor, I will continue in the service until I am relieved.'

He went out. Monsieur Madeleine sat musing, listening to his firm and resolute step as it died away along the corridor.

BOOK 7: THE CHAMPMATHIEU AFFAIR

1. *Sister Simplice*

THE EVENTS which follow were never all known at M— sur M—. But the few which did leak out have left such memories in that city, that it would be a serious omission in this book if we did not relate them in their minutest details.

Among these details, the reader will meet with two or three improbable circumstances, which we preserve from respect for the truth.

In the afternoon following the visit of Javert, M. Madeleine went to see Fantine as usual.

Before going to Fantine's room, he sent for Sister Simplice.

The two nuns who attended the infirmary, Lazarists as all these Sisters of Charity are, were called Sister Perpétue and Sister Simplice.

Sister Perpétue was an ordinary village-girl, summarily become a Sister of Charity, who entered the service of God as she would have entered service anywhere. She was a nun as others are cooks. This type is not very rare. The monastic orders gladly accept this heavy peasant clay, easily shaped into a Capuchine or an Ursuline. Such rustics are useful for the coarser duties of devotion. There is no shock in the transition from a cowboy to a Carmelite; the one becomes the other without much labour; the common basis of ignorance of a village and a cloister is a ready-made preparation, and puts the rustic at once upon an even footing with the monk. Enlarge the smock a little and you have a frock. Sister Perpétue was a stout nun, from Marines, near Pontoise, given to patois, psalm-singing and muttering, sugaring a nostrum according to the bigotry or hypocrisy of the patient, treating invalids harshly, rough with the dying, almost throwing them into the face of God, belabouring the death agony with angry prayers, bold, honest, and florid.

Sister Simplice was white with a waxen clearness. In comparison with Sister Perpétue she was a sacramental taper by the side of a tallow candle. St Vincent de Paul has divinely drawn the figure of a Sister of Charity in these admirable words in which he unites so much liberty with so much servitude. 'Her only convent shall be the house of sickness; her only cell, a hired lodging; her chapel the parish church; her cloister the streets of the city, or the wards of the hospital; her only wall obedience; her grate the fear of God; her veil modesty.' This ideal was made alive in Sister Simplice. No one could have told Sister Simplice's age; she had never been young, and seemed as if she never should be old. She was a person – we dare not say a woman – gentle, austere, companionable, cold, and who had never told a lie. She was so gentle that she appeared fragile; but on the contrary she was more enduring than granite. She touched the unfortunate with charming fingers, delicate and pure. There was, so to say, silence in her speech; she said just what was necessary, and she had a tone of voice which would at the same time have edified a confessional, and enchanted a drawing-room. This delicacy accommodated itself to the serge dress, finding in its harsh touch a continual reminder of Heaven and of God. Let us dwell upon one circumstance. Never to have lied, never to have spoken, for any purpose whatever, even carelessly, a single word which was not the truth, the sacred truth, was the distinctive trait of Sister Simplice; it was the mark of her virtue. She was almost celebrated in the congregation for this imperturbable veracity. The Abbé Sicard speaks of Sister Simplice in a letter to the deaf mute, Massieu. Sincere and pure as we may be, we all have the mark of some little lie upon our truthfulness. She had none. A little lie, an innocent lie, can such a thing exist? To lie is the absolute of evil. To lie a little is not possible; he who lies, lies a whole lie; lying is the very face of the demon. Satan has two names; he is called Satan, and he is called the Liar. Such were her thoughts. And as she thought, she practised. From this resulted that whiteness of which we have spoken, a whiteness that covered with its radiance even her lips and her eyes. Her smile was white, her look was white. There was not a spider's web, not a speck of dust upon the glass of that conscience. When she took the vows of St Vincent de Paul, she had taken the name of Simplice by especial choice. Simplice of Sicily, it is well known, is that saint who preferred to have both her breasts torn out rather than answer, having been born at Syracuse, that she was born at Segesta, a lie which would have saved her. This patron saint was fitting for this soul.

Sister Simplice, on entering the order, had two faults of which she corrected herself gradually; she had had a taste for delicacies, and loved to receive letters. Now she read nothing but a prayer-book in large type and in Latin. She did not understand Latin, but she understood the book.

The pious woman had conceived an affection for Fantine, perceiving in her probably some latent virtue, and had devoted herself almost exclusively to her care.

Monsieur Madeleine took Sister Simplice aside and recommended Fantine to her with a singular emphasis, which the sister remembered at a later day.

On leaving the Sister, he approached Fantine.

Fantine awaited each day the appearance of Monsieur Madeleine as one awaits a ray of warmth and of joy. She would say to the sisters: 'I live only when the Mayor is here.'

That day she had more fever. As soon as she saw Monsieur Madeleine, she asked him:

'Cosette?'

He answered with a smile:

'Very soon.'

Monsieur Madeleine, while with Fantine, seemed the same as usual. Only he stayed an hour instead of half an hour, to the great satisfaction of Fantine. He made a thousand charges to everybody that the sick woman might want for nothing. It was noticed that at one moment his countenance became very sombre. But this was explained when it was known that the doctor had, bending close to his ear, said to him: 'She is sinking fast.'

Then he returned to the mayor's office, and the office boy saw him examine attentively a road-map of France which hung in his room. He made a few figures in pencil upon a piece of paper.

2. *Shrewdness of Master Scaufflaire*

FROM THE MAYOR'S OFFICE he went to the outskirts of the city, to a Fleming's, Master Scaufflaer, Frenchified into Scaufflaire, who kept horses to let and 'chaises if desired'.

In order to go to Scaufflaire's, the nearest way was by a rarely frequented street, on which was the parsonage of the parish in which Monsieur Madeleine lived. The curé was, it was said, a worthy and respectable man, and a good counsellor. At the moment when Monsieur Madeleine arrived in front of the parsonage, there was but one person passing in the street, and he remarked this: the mayor, after passing by the curé's house, stopped, stood still a moment, then turned back and retraced his steps as far as the door of the parsonage, which was a large door with an iron knocker. He seized the knocker quickly and raised it; then he stopped anew, stood a short time as if in thought, and after a few seconds, instead of letting the knocker fall smartly, he replaced it gently, and resumed his walk with a sort of haste that he had not shown before.

Monsieur Madeleine found Master Scaufflaire at home busy repairing a harness.

'Master Scaufflaire,' he asked, 'have you a good horse?'

'Monsieur Mayor,' said the Fleming, 'all my horses are good. What do you understand by a good horse?'

'I understand a horse that can go twenty leagues in a day.'

'The devil!' said the Fleming, 'twenty leagues!'

'Yes.'

'Before a chaise?'

'Yes.'

'And how long will he rest after the journey?'

'He must be able to start again the next day in case of need.'

'To do the same thing again?'

'Yes.'

'The devil! and it is twenty leagues?'

Monsieur Madeleine drew from his pocket the paper on which he had pencilled the figures. He showed them to the Fleming. They were the figures, 5, 6, $8^{1}/_{2}$.

'You see,' said he. 'Total, nineteen and a half, that is to say, twenty leagues.'

'Monsieur Mayor,' resumed the Fleming, 'I have just what you want. My little white horse, you must have seen him sometimes passing; he is a little beast from Bas-Boulonnais. He is full of fire. They tried at first to make a saddle horse of him. Bah! he kicked, he threw everybody off. They thought he was vicious, they didn't know what to do. I bought him. I put him before a chaise; Monsieur, that is what he wanted; he is as gentle as a girl, he goes like the wind. But, for example, it won't do to get on his back. It's not his idea to be a saddle horse. Everybody has his peculiar ambition. To draw, but not to carry: we must believe that he has said that to himself.'

'And he will make the trip?'

'Your twenty leagues, all the way at a full trot, and in less than eight hours. But there are some conditions.'

'Name them.'

'First, you must let him breathe an hour when you are half way; he will eat, and somebody must be by while he eats to prevent the tavern boy from stealing his oats; for I have noticed that at taverns, oats are oftener drunk by the stable boys than eaten by the horses.'

'Somebody shall be there.'

'Secondly – is the chaise for Monsieur the Mayor?'

'Yes.'

'Monsieur the Mayor knows how to drive?'

'Yes.'

'Well, Monsieur the Mayor will travel alone and without baggage, so as not to overload the horse.'

'Agreed.'

'But Monsieur the Mayor, having no one with him, will be obliged to take the trouble of seeing to the oats himself.'

'So said.'

'I must have thirty francs a day, the days he rests included. Not a penny less, and the fodder of the beast at the expense of Monsieur the Mayor.'

Monsieur Madeleine took three Napoleons from his purse and laid them on the table.

'There is two days, in advance.'

'Fourthly, for such a trip, a chaise would be too heavy; that would tire the horse. Monsieur the Mayor must consent to travel in a little tilbury that I have.'

'I consent to that.'

'It is light, but it is open.'

'It is all the same to me.'

'Has Monsieur the Mayor reflected that it is winter?'

Monsieur Madeleine did not answer; the Fleming went on:

'That it is very cold?'

Monsieur Madeleine kept silence.

Master Scaufflaire continued:

'That it may rain?'

Monsieur Madeleine raised his head and said:

'The horse and the tilbury will be before my door tomorrow at half-past four in the morning.'

'That is understood, Monsieur Major,' answered Scaufflaire, then scratching a stain on the top of the table with his thumb nail, he resumed with that careless air that Flemings so well know how to associate with their shrewdness:

'Why, I have just thought of it! Monsieur the Mayor has not told me where he is going. Where is Monsieur the Mayor going?'

He had thought of nothing else since the beginning of the conversation, but without knowing why, he had not dared to ask the question.

'Has your horse good forelegs?' said Monsieur Madeleine.

'Yes, Monsieur Mayor. You will hold him up a little going downhill. Is there much downhill between here and where you are going?'

'Don't forget to be at my door precisely at half-past four in the morning,' answered Monsieur Madeleine, and he went out.

The Fleming was left 'dumbfounded', as he said to himself sometime afterwards.

The mayor had been gone two or three minutes, when the door again opened; it was the mayor.

He had the same impassive and absent-minded air as ever.

'Monsieur Scaufflaire,' said he, 'at what sum do you value the horse and the tilbury that you furnish me, the one carrying the other?'

'The one drawing the other, Monsieur Mayor,' said the Fleming with a loud laugh.

'As you like. How much?'

'Does Monsieur the Mayor wish to buy them?'

'No, but at all events I wish to guarantee them to you. On my return you can give me back the amount. At how much do you value horse and chaise?'

'Five hundred francs, Monsieur Mayor!'

'Here it is.'

Monsieur Madeleine placed a banknote on the table, then went out, and this time did not return.

Master Scaufflaire regretted terribly that he had not said a thousand francs. In fact, the horse and tilbury, in the lump, were worth a hundred crowns.

The Fleming called his wife, and related the affair to her. Where the deuce could the mayor be going? They talked it over. 'He is going to Paris,' said the wife. 'I don't believe it,' said the husband. Monsieur Madeleine had forgotten the paper on which he had marked the figures, and left it on the mantel. The Fleming seized it and studied it. Five, six, eight and a half? this must mean the relays of the post. He turned to his wife: 'I have found it out.' 'How?' 'It is five leagues from here to Hesdin, six from Hesdin to Saint Pol, eight and a half from Saint Pol to Arras. He is going to Arras.'

Meanwhile Monsieur Madeleine had reached home. To return from Master Scaufflaire's he had taken a longer road, as if the door of the parsonage were a temptation to him, and he wished to avoid it. He went up to his room, and shut himself in, which was nothing remarkable, for he usually went to bed early. However, the janitress of the factory, who was at the same time Monsieur Madeleine's only servant, observed that his light was out at half-past eight, and she mentioned it to the cashier who came in, adding:

'Is Monsieur the Mayor sick? I thought that his manner was a little singular.'

The cashier occupied a room situated exactly beneath Monsieur Madeleine's. He paid no attention to the portress's words, went to bed, and went to sleep. Towards midnight he suddenly awoke; he had heard, in his sleep, a noise overhead. He listened. It was a step that went and came, as if someone were walking in the room above. He listened more attentively, and recognised Monsieur Madeleine's step. That appeared strange to him; ordinarily no noise was made in Monsieur Madeleine's room before his hour of rising. A moment afterwards, the cashier heard something that sounded like the opening and shutting of a wardrobe, then a piece of furniture was moved, there was another silence, and the step began again. The cashier rose up in bed, threw off his drowsiness, looked out, and through his window-panes, saw upon an opposite wall the ruddy reflection of a lighted window. From the direction of the rays, it could only be the window of Monsieur Madeleine's chamber. The reflection trembled as if it came rather from a bright fire than from a light. The shadow of the sash could not be seen, which indicated that the window was wide open. Cold as it was, this open window was surprising. The cashier fell asleep again. An hour or two afterwards he awoke again. The same step, slow and regular, was coming and going constantly over his head.

The reflection continued visible upon the wall, but it was now pale and steady like the light from a lamp or a candle. The window was still open.

Let us see what was passing in Monsieur Madeleine's room.

3. *A tempest in a brain*

THE READER has doubtless divined that Monsieur Madeleine is none other than Jean Valjean.

We have already looked into the depths of that conscience; the time has come to look into them again. We do so not without emotion, nor without trembling. There exists nothing more terrific than this kind of contemplation. The mind's eye can nowhere find anything more dazzling nor more dark than in man; it can fix itself upon nothing which is more awful, more complex, more mysterious, or more infinite. There is one spectacle grander than the sea, that is the sky; there is one spectacle grander than the sky, that is the interior of the soul.

To write the poem of the human conscience, were it only of a single man, were it only of the most infamous of men, would be to swallow up all epics in a superior and final epic. The conscience is the chaos of chimeras, of lusts and of temptations, the furnace of dreams, the cave of the ideas which are our shame; it is the pandemonium of sophisms, the battlefield of the passions. At certain hours, penetrate within the livid face of a human being who reflects, and look at what lies behind; look into that soul, look into that obscurity. There, beneath the external silence, there are combats of giants as in Homer, mêlées of dragons and hydras, and clouds of phantoms as in Milton, ghostly labyrinths as in Dante. What a gloom enwraps that infinite which each man bears within himself, and by which he measures in despair the desires of his will, and the actions of his life!

Alighieri arrived one day at an ill-omened door before which he hesitated. Here is one also before us, on the threshold of which we hesitate. Let us enter notwithstanding.

We have but little to add to what the reader already knows, concerning what had happened to Jean Valjean, since his adventure with Petit Gervais. From that moment, we have seen, he was another man. What the bishop had desired to do with him, that he had executed. It was more than a transformation – it was a transfiguration.

He succeeded in escaping from sight, sold the bishop's silver, keeping only the candlesticks as souvenirs, glided quietly from city to city across France, came to M— sur M—, conceived the idea that we have described, accomplished what we have related, gained the point of making himself unassailable and inaccessible, and thenceforward, established at M— sur M— , happy to feel his conscience saddened by his past, and the last half of his existence giving the lie to the first, he lived peaceable, reassured, and hopeful, having but two thoughts: to conceal his name, and to sanctify his life ; to escape from men and to return to God.

These two thoughts were associated so closely in his mind, that they formed but a single one; they were both equally absorbing and imperious, and ruled his slightest actions. Ordinarily they were in harmony in the regulation of the conduct of his life; they turned him towards the dark side of life; they made him benevolent and simple-hearted; they counselled him to the same things. Sometimes, however, there was a conflict between them. In such cases, it will be remembered, the man, whom all the country around M— sur M— called Monsieur Madeleine, did not waver in sacrificing the first to the second, his security to his virtue. Thus, in despite of all reserve and of all prudence, he had kept the bishop's candlesticks, worn mourning for him, called and questioned all the little Savoyards who passed by, gathered information concerning the families at Faverolles, and saved the life of old Fauchelevent, in spite of the disquieting insinuations of Javert. It would seem, we have already remarked, that he thought, following the example of all who have been wise, holy, and just, that his highest duty was not towards himself.

But of all these occasions, it must be said, none had ever been anything like that which was now presented.

Never had the two ideas that governed the unfortunate man whose sufferings we are relating, engaged in so serious a struggle. He comprehended this confusedly, but thoroughly, from the first words that Javert pronounced on entering his office. At the moment when that name which he had so deeply buried was so strangely uttered, he was seized with stupor, and as if intoxicated by the sinister grotesqueness of his destiny, and through that stupor he felt the shudder which precedes great shocks; he bent like an oak at the approach of a storm, like a soldier at the approach of an assault. He felt clouds full of thunderings and lightnings gathering upon his head. Even while listening to Javert, his first thought was to go, to run, to denounce himself, to drag this Champmathieu out of prison, and to put himself in his place; it was painful and sharp as an incision into the living flesh, but passed away, and he said to himself: 'Let us see! Let us see!' He repressed this first generous impulse and recoiled before such heroism.

Doubtless it would have been fine if, after the holy words of the bishop, after so many years of repentance and self-denial, in the midst of a penitence admirably commenced, even in the presence of so terrible a conjecture, he had not faltered an instant, and had continued to march on with even pace towards that yawning pit at the bottom of which was heaven; this would have been fine, but this was not the case. We must render an account of what took place in that soul, and we can relate only what was there. What first gained control was the instinct of self-preservation; he collected his ideas hastily, stifled his emotions, took into consideration the presence of Javert, the great danger, postponed any decision with the firmness of terror, banished from his mind all consideration of the course he should pursue, and resumed his calmness as a gladiator retakes his buckler.

For the rest of the day he was in this state, a tempest within, a perfect calm without; he took only what might be called precautionary measures. All was still confused and jostling in his brain; the agitation there was such that he did not see distinctly the form of any idea; and he could have told nothing of himself, unless it were that he had just received a terrible blow. He went according to his habit to the sick bed of Fantine, and prolonged his visit, by an instinct of kindness, saying to himself that he ought to do so, and recommend her earnestly to the sisters, in case it should happen that he would have to be absent. He felt vaguely that it would perhaps be necessary for him to go to Arras; and without having in the least decided upon this journey, he said to himself that, entirely free from suspicion as he was, there would be no difficulty in being a witness of what might pass, and he engaged Scaufflaire's tilbury, in order to be prepared for any emergency.

He dined with a good appetite.

Returning to his room he collected his thoughts.

He examined the situation and found it an unheard-of one; so unheard-of that in the midst of his reverie, by some strange impulse of almost inexplicable anxiety, he rose from his chair, and bolted his door. He feared lest something might yet enter. He barricaded himself against all possibilities.

A moment afterwards he blew out his light. It annoyed him.

It seemed to him that somebody could see him.

Who? Somebody?

Alas! what he wanted to keep out of doors had entered; what he wanted to render blind was looking upon him. His conscience.

His conscience, that is to say, God.

At the first moment, however, he deluded himself; he had a feeling of safety and solitude; the bolt drawn, he believed himself invisible. Then he took possession of himself; he placed his elbows on the table, rested his head on his hand, and set himself to meditating in the darkness.

'Where am I? Am I not in a dream? What have I heard? Is it really true that I saw this Javert, and that he talked to me so? Who can this Champmathieu be? He resembles me then? Is it possible? When I think that yesterday I was so calm, and so far from suspecting anything! What was I doing yesterday at this time? What is there in this matter? How will it turn out? What is to be done?'

Such was the torment he was in. His brain had lost the power of retaining its ideas; they passed away like waves, and he grasped his forehead with both hands to stop them.

Out of this tumult, which overwhelmed his will and his reason, and from which he sought to draw a certainty and a resolution, nothing came clearly forth but anguish.

His brain was burning. He went to the window and threw it wide open. Not a star was in the sky. He returned and sat down by the table.

The first hour thus rolled away.

Little by little, however, vague outlines began to take form and to fix themselves in his meditation; he could perceive, with the precision of reality, not the whole of the situation, but a few details.

He began by recognising that, however extraordinary and critical the situation was, he was completely master of it.

His stupor only became the deeper.

Independently of the severe and religious aim that his actions had in view, all that he had done up to this day was only a hole that he was digging in which to bury his name. What he had always most dreaded, in his hours of self-communion, in his sleepless nights, was the thought of ever hearing that name pronounced; he felt that would be for him the end of all; that the day on which that name should reappear would see vanish from around him his new life, and, who knows, even perhaps his new soul from within him. He shuddered at the bare thought that it was possible. Surely, if anyone had told him at such moments that an hour would come when that name would resound in his ear, when that hideous word, Jean Valjean, would start forth suddenly from the night and stand before him; when this fearful glare, destined to dissipate the mystery in which he had wrapped himself, would flash suddenly upon his head, and that this name would not menace him, and that this glare would only make his obscurity the deeper, that this rending of the veil would increase the mystery, that this earthquake would consolidate his edifice, that this prodigious event would have no other result, if it seemed good to him, to himself alone, than to render his existence at once more brilliant and more impenetrable, and that, from his encounter with the phantom of Jean Valjean, the good and worthy citizen, Monsieur Madeleine, would come forth more honoured, more peaceful, and more respected than ever – if anyone had said this to him, he would have shaken his head and looked upon the words as nonsense. Well! precisely that had happened; all this grouping of the impossible was now a fact, and God had permitted these absurdities to become real things!

His musings continued to grow clearer. He was getting a wider and wider view of his position.

It seemed to him that he had just awaked from some wondrous slumber, and that he found himself gliding over a precipice in the middle of the night, standing, shivering, recoiling in vain, upon the very edge of an abyss. He perceived distinctly in the gloom an unknown man, a stranger, whom fate had mistaken for him, and was pushing into the gulf in his place. It was necessary, in order that the gulf should be closed, that someone should fall in, he or the other.

He had only to let it alone.

The light became complete, and he recognised this: That his place at the galleys was empty, that do what he could it was always awaiting him, that the robbing of Petit Gervais sent him back there, that this empty place would await him and attract him until he should be there, that this was inevitable and fatal. And then he said to himself: That at this very moment he had a substitute, that it appeared that a man named Champmathieu had that unhappy lot, and that, as for himself, present in future at the galleys in the person of this Champmathieu, present in society under the name of Monsieur Madeleine, he had nothing more to fear, provided he did not prevent men from sealing upon the head of this Champmathieu that stone of infamy which, like the stone of the sepulchre, falls once never to rise again.

All this was so violent and so strange that he suddenly felt that kind of indescribable movement that no man experiences more than two or three times in his life, a sort of convulsion of the conscience that stirs up all that is dubious in the heart, which is composed of irony, of joy, and of despair, and which might be called a burst of interior laughter.

He hastily relighted his candle.

'Well, what!' said he, 'what am I afraid of? why do I ponder over these things? I am now safe? all is finished. There was but a single half-open door through which my past could make an irruption into my life; that door is now walled up! for ever! This Javert who has troubled me so long, that fearful instinct which seemed to have divined the truth, that had divined it, in fact! and which followed me everywhere, that terrible bloodhound always in pursuit of me, he is thrown off the track, engrossed elsewhere, absolutely baffled. He is satisfied henceforth, he will leave me in quiet, he holds his Jean Valjean fast! Who knows! it is even probable that he will want to leave the city! And all this is accomplished without my aid! And I have nothing to do with it! Ah, yes, but, what is there unfortunate in all this! People who should see me, upon my honour, would think that a catastrophe had befallen me! After all, if there is any harm done to anybody, it is in nowise my fault. Providence has done it all. This is what He wishes apparently. Have I the right to disarrange what He arranges? What is it that I ask for now? Why do I interfere? It does not concern me. How! I am not satisfied! But what would I have then? The aim to which I have aspired for so many years, my nightly dream, the object of my prayers to heaven, security, I have gained it. It is God's will. I must do nothing contrary to the will of God. And why is it God's will? That I may carry on what I have begun, that I may do good, that I may be one day a grand and encouraging example, that it may be said that there was finally some little happiness resulting from this suffering which I have undergone and this virtue to which I have returned! Really I do not understand why I was so much afraid to go to this honest curé and tell him the whole story as a confessor, and ask his advice; this is evidently what he would have said to me. It is decided, let the matter alone! let us not interfere with God.'

Thus he spoke in the depths of his conscience, hanging over what might be called his own abyss. He rose from his chair, and began to walk the room. 'Come,' said he, 'let us think of it no more. The resolution is formed!' But he felt no joy.

Quite the contrary.

One can no more prevent the mind from returning to an idea than the sea from returning to a shore. In the case of the sailor, this is called the tide; in the case of the guilty, it is called remorse. God upheaves the soul as well as the ocean.

After the lapse of a few moments, he could do no otherwise, he resumed this sombre dialogue, in which it was himself who spoke and himself who listened, saying what he wished to keep silent, listening to what he did not wish to hear, yielding to that mysterious power which said to him: 'think!' as it said two thousand years ago to another condemned: 'march!'

Before going further, and in order to be fully understood, it is necessary that we should make with some emphasis a single observation.

It is certain that we talk with ourselves; there is not a thinking being who has not experienced that. We may say even that the word is never a more magnificent mystery than when it goes, in the interior of a man, from his thoughts to his conscience, and returns from his conscience to his thought. It is in this sense only that the words must be understood, so often employed in this chapter, *he said, he exclaimed*; we say to ourselves, we speak to ourselves, we exclaim within ourselves, the external silence not being broken. There is a great tumult within; everything within us speaks, except the tongue. The realities of the soul, because they are not visible and palpable, are not the less realities.

He asked himself then where he was. He questioned himself upon this 'resolution formed.' He confessed to himself that all that he had been arranging in his mind was monstrous, that 'to let the matter alone, not to interfere with God,' was simply horrible, to let this mistake of destiny and of men be accomplished, not to prevent it, to lend himself to it by his silence, to do nothing, finally, was to do all! it was the last degree of hypocritical meanness! it was a base, cowardly, lying, abject, hideous crime!

For the first time within eight years, the unhappy man had just tasted the bitter flavour of a wicked thought and a wicked action.

He spat it out with disgust.

He continued to question himself. He sternly asked himself what he had understood by this: 'My object is attained.' He declared that his life, in truth, did have an object. But what object? to conceal his name? to deceive the police? was it for so petty a thing that he had done all that he had done? had he no other object, which was the great one, which was the true one? To save, not his body, but his soul. To become honest and good again. To be an upright man! was it not that above all, that alone, which he had always wished, and which the bishop had enjoined upon him? To close the door on his past? But he was not closing it, great God! he was re-opening it by committing an infamous act! for he became a robber again, and the most odious of robbers! he robbed another of his existence, his life, his peace, his place in the world, he became an assassin! he murdered, he murdered in a moral sense a wretched man, he inflicted upon him that frightful life in death, that living burial, which is called the galleys! on the contrary, to deliver himself up, to save this man stricken by so ghastly a mistake, to reassume his name, to become again from duty the convict Jean Valjean; that was really to achieve his resurrection, and to close for ever the hell from whence he had emerged! to fall back into it in appearance, was to emerge in reality! he must do that! all he had done was nothing, if he did not do that! all his life was useless, all his suffering was lost. He had only to ask the question: 'What is the use?' He felt that the bishop was there, that the bishop was present all the more that he was dead, that the bishop was looking fixedly at him, that henceforth Mayor Madeleine with all his virtues would be abominable to him, and the galley slave, Jean Valjean, would be admirable and pure in his sight. That men saw his mask, but the bishop saw his face. That men saw his life, but the bishop saw his conscience. He must then go to Arras, deliver the wrong Jean Valjean, denounce the right one. Alas! that was the greatest of sacrifices, the most poignant of victories, the final step to be taken, but he must do it. Mournful destiny! he could only enter into sanctity in the eyes of God, by returning into infamy in the eyes of men!

'Well,' said he, 'let us take this course! let us do our duty! Let us save this man!'

He pronounced these words in a loud voice, without perceiving that he was speaking aloud.

He took his books, verified them, and put them in order. He threw into the fire a package of notes which he held against needy small traders. He wrote a letter, which he sealed, and upon the envelope of which might have been read, if there had been anyone in the room at the time: *Monsieur Laffitte, banker, Rue d'Artois, Paris.*

He drew from a secretary a pocket-book containing some banknotes and the passport that he had used that same year in going to the elections.

Had anyone seen him while he was doing these various acts with such serious meditation, he would not have suspected what was passing within him. Still at intervals his lips quivered; at other times he raised his head and fixed his eye on some point of the wall, as if he saw just there something that he wished to clear up or to interrogate.

The letter to Monsieur Laffitte finished, he put it in his pocket as well as the pocket-book, and began his walk again.

The current of his thought had not changed. He still saw his duty clearly written in luminous letters which flared out before his eyes, and moved with his gaze: '*Go! avow thy name I denounce myself!*'

He saw also, and as if they were laid bare before him with sensible forms, the two ideas which had been hitherto the double rule of his life, to conceal his name, and to sanctify his soul. For the first time, they appeared to him absolutely distinct, and he saw the difference which separated them. He recognised that one of these ideas was necessarily good, while the other might become evil; that the former was devotion, and that the latter was selfishness; that the one said: '*the neighbour*', and that the other said: '*me*'; that the one came from the light, and the other from the night.

They were fighting with each other. He saw them fighting. While he was looking, they had expanded before his mind's eye; they were now colossal; and it seemed to him that he saw struggling within him, in that infinite of which we spoke just now, in the midst of darkness and gloom, a goddess and a giantess.

He was full of dismay, but it seemed to him that the good thought was gaining the victory.

He felt that he had reached the second decisive moment of his conscience, and his destiny; that the bishop had marked the first phase of his new life, and that this Champmathieu marked the second. After a great crisis, a great trial.

Meanwhile the fever, quieted for an instant, returned upon him little by little. A thousand thoughts flashed across him but they fortified him in his resolution.

One moment he had said: that perhaps he took the affair too much to heart, that after all this Champmathieu was not worthy of interest, that in fact he had committed theft.

He answered: If this man has in fact stolen a few apples, that is a month in prison. There is a wide distance between that and the galleys. And who knows even? has he committed theft? is it proven? the name of Jean Valjean overwhelms him, and seems to dispense with proofs. Are not prosecuting officers in the habit of acting thus? They think him a robber, because they know him to be a convict.

At another moment, the idea occurred to him that, if he should denounce himself, perhaps the heroism of his action, and his honest life for the past seven years, and what he had done for the country, would be considered, and he would be pardoned.

But this supposition quickly vanished, and he smiled bitterly at the thought, that the robbery of the forty sous from Petit Gervais made him a second offender, that that matter would certainly reappear, and by the precise terms of the law he would be condemned to hard labour for life.

He turned away from all illusion, disengaged himself more and more from the earth, and sought consolation and strength elsewhere. He said to himself that he must do his duty; that perhaps even he should not be more unhappy after having done his duty than after having evaded it; that if he let matters alone, if he remained at M— sur M—, his reputation, his good name, his good works, the deference, the veneration he commanded, his charity, his riches, his popularity, his virtue, would be tainted with a crime, and what pleasure would there be in all these holy things tied to that hideous thing? while, if he carried out the sacrifice, in the galleys, with his chain, with his iron collar, with his green cap, with his perpetual labour, with his pitiless shame, there would be associated a celestial idea.

Finally, he said to himself that it was a necessity, that his destiny was so fixed, that it was not for him to derange the arrangements of God, that at all events he must choose, either virtue without, and abomination within, or sanctity within, and infamy without.

In revolving so many gloomy ideas, his courage did not fail, but his brain was fatigued. He began in spite of himself to think of other things of indifferent things.

His blood rushed violently to his temples. He walked back and forth constantly. Midnight was struck first from the parish church, then from the city hall. He counted the twelve strokes of the two clocks, and he compared the sound of the two bells. It reminded him that, a few days before, he had seen at a junkshop an old bell for sale, upon which was this name: *Antoine Albin de Romainville.*

He was cold. He kindled a fire. He did not think to close the window.

Meanwhile he had fallen into his stupor again. It required not a little effort to recall his mind to what he was thinking of before the clocks struck. He succeeded at last.

'Ah! yes,' said he, 'I had formed the resolution to denounce myself.'

And then all at once he thought of Fantine.

'Stop!' said he, 'this poor woman!'

Here was a new crisis.

Fantine abruptly appearing in his reverie, was like a ray of unexpected light. It seemed to him that everything around him was changing its aspect; he exclaimed:

'Ah! yes, indeed! so far I have only thought of myself! have only looked to my own convenience! It is whether I shall keep silent or denounce myself, conceal my body or save my soul, be a despicable and respected magistrate, or an infamous and venerable galley slave; it is myself, always myself, only myself. But, good God! all this is egotism. Different forms of egotism, but still egotism! Suppose I should think a little of others? The highest duty is to think of others. Let us see, let us examine! I gone, I taken away, I forgotten; what will become of all this? I denounce myself? I am arrested, this Champmathieu is released, I am sent back to the galleys; very well, and what then? what takes place here? Ah! here, there is a country, a city, factories, a business, labourers, men, women, old grandfathers, children, poor people! I have created all this, I keep it all alive; wherever a chimney is smoking, I have put the brands in the fire and the meat in the pot; I have produced ease, circulation, credit; before me there was nothing; I have aroused, vivified, animated, quickened, stimulated, enriched, all the country; without me, the soul is gone. I take myself away; it all dies. And this woman who has suffered so much, who is so worthy in her fall, all whose misfortunes I have unconsciously caused! And that child which I was going for, which I have promised to the mother! Do I not also owe something to this woman, in reparation for the wrong that I have done her? If I should disappear, what happens? The mother dies. The child becomes what she may. This is what comes to pass, if I denounce myself; and if I do not denounce myself? Let us see, if I do not denounce myself?'

After putting this question, he stopped; for a moment he hesitated and trembled; but that moment was brief, and he answered with calmness:

'Well, this man goes to the galleys, it is true, but, what of that? He has stolen! It is useless for me to say he has not stolen, he has stolen! As for me, I remain here, I go on. In ten years I shall have made ten millions; I scatter it over the country, I keep nothing for myself; what is it to me? What I am doing is not for myself. The prosperity of all goes on increasing, industry is quickened and excited, manufactories and workshops are multiplied, families, a hundred families, a thousand families, are happy; the country becomes populous; villages spring up where there were only farms, farms spring up where there was nothing; poverty disappears, and with poverty disappear debauchery, prostitution, theft, murder, all vices, all crimes! And this poor mother brings up her child! and the whole country is rich and honest! Ah, yes! How foolish, how absurd I was! What was I speaking of in denouncing myself? This demands reflection, surely, and nothing must be precipitate. What! because it would have pleased me to do the grand and the generous! That is melodramatic, after all! Because I only thought of myself, of myself alone, what! to save from a punishment perhaps a little too severe, but in reality just, nobody knows who, a thief, a scoundrel at any rate. Must an entire country be let go to ruin! must a poor hapless woman perish in the hospital! must a poor little girl perish on the street! like dogs! Ah! that would be abominable! And the mother not even see her child again! and the child hardly have known her mother! And all that for this old whelp of an apple-thief, who, beyond all doubt, deserves the galleys for something else, if not for this. Fine scruples these, which save an old vagabond who has, after all, only a few years to live, and who will hardly be more unhappy in the galleys than in his hovel, and which sacrifice a whole population, mothers, wives, children! This poor little Cosette who has no one but me in the world, and who is doubtless at this moment all blue with cold, in the hut of these Thénardiers! They too are miserable rascals! And I should fail in my duty towards all these poor beings! And I should go away and denounce myself! And I should commit this silly blunder! Take it at the very worst. Suppose there were a misdeed for me in this, and that my conscience should someday reproach me; the acceptance for the good of others of these reproaches which weigh only upon me, of this misdeed which affects only my own soul, why, that is devotion, that is virtue.'

He arose and resumed his walk. This time it seemed to him that he was satisfied.

Diamonds are found only in the dark places of the earth; truths are found only in the depths of thought. It seemed to him that after having descended into these depths, after having groped long in the blackest of this darkness, he had at last found one of these diamonds, one of these truths, and that he held it in his hand; and it blinded him to look at it.

'Yes,' thought he, 'that is it! I am in the true road. I have the solution. I must end by holding fast to something. My choice is made. Let the matter alone! No more vacillation, no more shrinking. This is in the interest of all, not in my own. I am Madeleine, I remain Madeleine. Woe to him who is Jean Valjean! He and I are no longer the same. I do not recognise that man, I no longer know what he is; if it is found that anybody is Jean Valjean at this hour, let him take care of himself. That does not concern me. That is a fatal name which is floating about in the darkness; if it stops and settles upon any man, so much the worse for that man.'

He looked at himself in the little mirror that hung over his mantelpiece and said:

'Yes! To come to a resolution has solaced me! I am quite another man now!'

He took a few steps more, then he stopped short.

'Come!' said he, 'I must not hesitate before any of the consequences of the resolution I have formed. There are yet some threads which knit me to this Jean Valjean. They must be broken! There are, in this very room, objects which would accuse me, mute things which would be witnesses; it is done, all these must disappear.'

He felt in his pocket, drew out his purse, opened it, and took out a little key.

He put this key into a lock the hole of which was hardly visible, lost as it was in the darkest shading of the figures on the paper which covered the wall. A secret door opened; a kind of false press built between the corner of the wall and the casing of the chimney. There was nothing in this closet but a few refuse trifles, a blue smock-frock, an old pair of trousers, an old haversack, and a great thorn stick, iron-bound at both ends. Those who had seen Jean Valjean at the time he passed through D—, in October 1815, would have recognised easily all the fragments of this miserable outfit.

He had kept them, as he had kept the silver candlesticks, to remind him at all times of what he had been. But he concealed what came from the galleys, and left the candlesticks that came from the bishop in sight.

He cast a furtive look towards the door, as if he were afraid it would open in spite of the bolt that held it; then with a quick and hasty movement, and at a single armful, without even a glance at these things which he had kept so religiously and with so much danger during so many years, he took the whole, rags, stick, haversack, and threw them all into the fire.

He shut up the false press, and, increasing his precautions, henceforth useless, since it was empty, concealed the door behind a heavy piece of furniture which he pushed against it.

In a few seconds, the room and the wall opposite were lit up with a great, red, flickering glare. It was all burning; the thorn stick cracked and threw out sparks into the middle of the room.

The haversack, as it was consumed with the horrid rags which it contained, left something uncovered which glistened in the ashes. By bending towards it, one could have easily recognised a piece of silver. It was doubtless the forty sous piece stolen from the little Savoyard.

But he did not look at the fire; he continued his walk to and fro, always at the same pace.

Suddenly his eyes fell upon the two silver candlesticks on the mantel, which were glistening dimly in the reflection.

'Stop!' thought he, 'all Jean Valjean is contained in them too. They also must be destroyed.'

He took the two candlesticks.

There was fire enough to melt them quickly into an unrecognisable ingot.

He bent over the fire and warmed himself a moment. It felt really comfortable to him. 'The pleasant warmth!' said he.

He stirred the embers with one of the candlesticks.

A minute more, and they would have been in the fire.

At that moment, it seemed to him that he heard a voice crying within him: 'Jean Valjean!' 'Jean Valjean!'

His hair stood on end; he was like a man who hears some terrible thing.

'Yes! that is it, finish!' said the voice, 'complete what you are doing! destroy these candlesticks! annihilate this memorial! forget the bishop! forget all! ruin this Champmathieu, yes! very well. Applaud yourself! So it is arranged, it is determined, it is done. Behold a man, a greybeard who knows not what he is accused of, who has done nothing, it may be, an innocent man, whose only misfortune is caused by your name, upon whom your name weighs like a crime, who will be taken instead of you; will be condemned, will end his days in abjection and in horror! very well. Be an honoured man yourself. Remain, Monsieur Mayor, remain honourable and honoured, enrich the city feed the poor, bring up the orphans, live happy, virtuous, and admired, and all this time while you are here in joy and in the light, there shall be a man wearing your red blouse, bearing your name in ignominy, and dragging your chain in the galleys! Yes! this is a fine arrangement! Oh, wretch!'

The sweat rolled off his forehead. He looked upon the candlesticks with haggard eyes. Meanwhile the voice which spoke within him had not ended. It continued:

'Jean Valjean! there shall be about you many voices which will make great noise, which will speak very loud, and which will bless you; and one only which nobody shall hear, and which will curse you in the darkness. Well, listen, wretch! all these blessings shall fall before they reach Heaven; only the curse shall mount into the presence of God!'

This voice, at first quite feeble, and which was raised from the most obscure depths of his conscience, had become by degrees loud and formidable, and he heard it now at his ear. It seemed to him that it had emerged from himself, and that it was speaking now from without. He thought he heard the last words so distinctly that he looked about the room with a kind of terror.

'Is there anybody here?' asked he, aloud and in a startled voice.

Then he continued with a laugh, which was like the laugh of an idiot:

'What a fool I am! there cannot be anybody here.'

There was One; but He who was there was not of such as the human eye can see.

He put the candlesticks on the mantel.

Then he resumed this monotonous and dismal walk, which disturbed the man asleep beneath him in his dreams, and wakened him out of his sleep.

This walk soothed him and excited him at the same time. It sometimes seems that on the greatest occasions we put ourselves in motion in order to ask advice from whatever we may meet by change of place. After a few moments he no longer knew where he was.

He now recoiled with equal terror from each of the resolutions which he had formed in turn. Each of the two ideas which counselled him, appeared to him as fatal as the other. What a fatality! What a chance that this Champmathieu should be mistaken for him! To be hurled down headlong by the very means which Providence seemed at first to have employed to give him full security.

There was a moment during which he contemplated the future. Denounce himself, great God! Give himself up! He saw with infinite despair all that he must leave, all that he must resume. He must then bid farewell to this existence, so good, so pure, so radiant; to this respect of all, to honour, to liberty! No more would he go out to walk in the fields, never again would he hear the birds singing in the month of May, never more give alms to the little children! No longer would he feel the sweetness of looks of gratitude and of love! He would leave this house that he had built, this little room! Everything appeared charming to him now. He would read no more in these books, he would write no more on this little white wood table! His old portress, the only servant he had, would no longer bring him his coffee in the morning. Great God! instead of that, the galley-crew, the iron collar, the red blouse, the chain at his foot, fatigue, the dungeon, the plank-bed, all these horrors, which he knew so well! At his age, after having been what he was! If he were still young! But so old, to be insulted by the first comer, to be tumbled about by the prison guard, to be struck by the jailor's stick! To have his bare feet in ironbound shoes! To submit morning and evening his leg to the hammer of the roundsman who tests the fetters! To endure the curiosity of strangers who would be told: *This one is the famous Jean Valjean, who was Mayor of M— sur M—!*

At night, dripping with sweat, overwhelmed with weariness, the green cap over his eyes, to mount two by two, under the sergeant's whip, the step-ladder of the floating prison. Oh, what wretchedness! Can destiny then be malignant like an intelligent being, and become monstrous like the human heart?

And do what he might, he always fell back upon this sharp dilemma which was at the bottom of his thought. To remain in paradise and there become a demon! To re-enter into hell and there become an angel!

What shall be done, great God! what shall be done?

The torment from which he had emerged with so much difficulty, broke loose anew within him. His ideas again began to become confused. They took that indescribable, stupefied, and mechanical shape, which is peculiar to despair. The name of Romainville returned constantly to his mind, with two lines of a song he had formerly heard. He thought that Romainville is a little wood near Paris, where young lovers go to gather lilacs in the month of April.

He staggered without as well as within. He walked like a little child that is just allowed to go alone.

Now and then, struggling against his fatigue, he made an effort again to arouse his intellect. He endeavoured to state, finally and conclusively, the problem over which he had in some sort fallen exhausted. Must he denounce himself Must he be silent? He could see nothing distinctly. The vague forms of all the reasonings thrown out by his mind trembled, and were dissipated one after another in smoke. But this much he felt, that by whichever resolve he might abide, necessarily, and without possibility of escape, something of himself would surely die; that he was entering into a sepulchre on the right hand, as well as on the left; that he was suffering a death-agony, the death-agony of his happiness, or the death-agony of his virtue.

Alas! all his irresolutions were again upon him. He was no further advanced than when he began.

So struggled beneath its anguish this unhappy soul. Eighteen hundred years before this unfortunate man, the mysterious Being, in whom are aggregated all the sanctities and all the sufferings of humanity, He also, while the olive trees were shivering in the fierce breath of the Infinite, had long put away from his hand the fearful chalice that appeared before him, dripping with shadow and running over with darkness, in the star-filled depths.

4. *Forms assumed by suffering during sleep*

THE CLOCK STRUCK THREE. For five hours he had been walking thus, almost without interruption, when he dropped into his chair.

He fell asleep and dreamed.

This dream, like most dreams, had no further relation to the condition of affairs than its mournful and poignant character, but it made an impression upon him. This nightmare struck him so forcibly that he afterwards wrote it down. It is one of the papers in his own handwriting, which he has left behind him. We think it our duty to copy it here literally.

Whatever this dream may be, the story of that night would be incomplete if we should omit it. It is the gloomy adventure of a sick soul.

It is as follows. Upon the envelope we find this line written: '*The dream that I had that night.*'

I was in a field. A great sad field where there was no grass. It did not seem that it was day, nor that it was night.

I was walking with my brother, the brother of my childhood; this brother of whom I must say that I never think, and whom I scarcely remember.

We were talking, and we met others walking. We were speaking of a neighbour we had formerly, who, since she had lived in the street, always worked with her window open. Even while we talked, we felt cold on account of that open window.

There were no trees in the field.

We saw a man passing near us. He was entirely naked, ashen-coloured, mounted upon a horse which was of the colour of earth. The man had no hair; we saw his skull and the veins in his skull. In his hand he held a stick which was limber like a twig of grape vine, and heavy as iron. This horseman passed by and said nothing.

My brother said to me: 'Let us take the deserted road.'

There was a deserted road where we saw not a bush, nor even a sprig of moss. All was of the colour of earth, even the sky. A few steps further, and no one answered me when I spoke. I perceived that my brother was no longer with me.

I entered a village which I saw. I thought that it must be Romainville (why Romainville?) *

The first street by which I entered was deserted. I passed into a second street. At the corner of the two streets was a man standing against the wall, I said to this man: 'What place is this? Where am I?' The man made no answer. I saw the door of a house open, I went in.

The first room was deserted. I entered the second. Behind the door of this room was a man standing against the wall. I asked this man: 'Whose house is this? Where am I?' The man made no answer. The house had a garden.

---

* This parenthesis is in the hand of Jean Valjean.

I went out of the house and into the garden. The garden was deserted. Behind the first tree I found a man standing. I said to this man: 'What is this garden? Where am I?' The man made no answer.

I wandered about the village, and I perceived that it was a city. All the streets were deserted, all the doors were open. No living being was passing along the streets, or stirring in the rooms, or walking in the gardens. But behind every angle of a wall, behind every door, behind everything, there was a man standing who kept silence. But one could ever be seen at a time. These men looked at me as I passed by.

I went out of the city and began to walk in the fields.

After a little while, I turned and I saw a great multitude coming after me. I recognised all the men that I had seen in the city. Their heads were strange. They did not seem to hasten, and still they walked faster than I. They made no sound in walking. In an instant this multitude came up and surrounded me. The faces of these men were the colour of earth.

Then the first one whom I had seen and questioned on entering the city, said to me: 'Where are you going? Do you not know that you have been dead for a long time?'

I opened my mouth to answer, and I perceived that no one was near me.'

He awoke. He was chilly. A wind as cold as the morning wind made the sashes of the still open window swing on their hinges. The fire had gone out. The candle was low in the socket. The night was yet dark.

He arose and went to the window. There were still no stars in the sky.

From his window he could look into the courtyard and into the street. A harsh, rattling noise that suddenly resounded from the ground made him look down.

He saw below him two red stars, whose rays danced back and forth grotesquely in the shadow.

His mind was still half buried in the mist of his reverie: 'Yes!' thought he, 'there are none in the sky. They are on the earth now.'

This confusion, however, faded away; a second noise like the first awakened him completely; he looked, and he saw that these two stars were the lamps of a carriage. By the light which they emitted, he could distinguish the form of a carriage. It was a tilbury drawn by a small white horse. The noise which he had heard was the sound of the horse's hoofs upon the pavement.

'What carriage is that?' said he to himself. 'Who is it that comes so early?'

At that moment there was a low rap at the door of his room. He shuddered from head to foot and cried in a terrible voice:

'Who is there?'

Someone answered:

'I, Monsieur Mayor.'

He recognised the voice of the old woman, his portress.

'Well,' said he, 'what is it?'

'Monsieur Mayor, it is just five o'clock.'

'What is that to me?'

'Monsieur Mayor, it is the chaise.'

'What chaise?'

'The tilbury.'

'What tilbury?'

'Did not Monsieur the Mayor order a tilbury?'

'No,' said he.

'The driver says that he has come for Monsieur the Mayor.'

'What driver?'

'Monsieur Scaufflaire's driver.'

'Monsieur Scaufflaire?'

That name startled him as if a flash had passed before his face.

'Oh, yes!' he said, 'Monsieur Scaufflaire!'

Could the old woman have seen him at that moment she would have been frightened.

There was a long silence. He examined the flame of the candle with a stupid air, and took some of the melted wax from around the wick and rolled it in his fingers. The old woman was waiting. She ventured, however, to speak again:

'Monsieur Mayor, what shall I say?'

'Say that it is right, and I am coming down.'

5. *Clogs in the wheels*

THE POSTAL SERVICE from Arras to M— sur M— was still performed at this time by the little mail wagons of the date of the empire. These mail wagons were two-wheeled cabriolets, lined with buckskin, hung upon jointed springs, and having but two seats, one for the driver, the other for the traveller. The wheels were armed with those long threatening hubs which keep other vehicles at a distance, and which are still seen upon the roads of Germany. The letters were carried in a huge oblong box placed behind the cabriolet and making a part of it. This box was painted black and the cabriolet yellow.

These vehicles, which nothing now resembles, were indescribably misshapen and clumsy, and when they were seen from a distance crawling along some road in the horizon, they were like those insects called, I think, termites, which with a slender body draw a great train behind. They went, however, very fast. The mail that left Arras every night at one o'clock, after the passing of the courier from Paris, arrived at M— sur M— a little before five in the morning.

That night the mail that came down to M— sur M— by the road from Hesdin, at the turn of a street just as it was entering the city, ran against a little tilbury drawn by a white horse, which was going in the opposite direction, and in which there was only one person, a man wrapped in a cloak. The wheel of the tilbury received a very severe blow. The courier cried out to the man to stop, but the traveller did not listen and kept on his way at a rapid trot.

'There is a man in a devilish hurry!' said the courier.

The man who was in such a hurry was he whom we have seen struggling in such pitiable convulsions.

Where was he going? He could not have told. Why was he in haste? He did not know. He went forward at haphazard. Whither? To Arras, doubtless; but perhaps he was going elsewhere also. At moments he felt this, and he shuddered. He plunged into that darkness as into a yawning gulf. Something pushed him, something drew him on. What was passing within him, no one could describe, all will understand. What man has not entered, at least once in his life, into this dark cavern of the unknown?

But he had resolved upon nothing, decided nothing, determined nothing, done nothing. None of the acts of his conscience had been final. He was more than ever as at the first moment.

Why was he going to Arras?

He repeated what he had already said to himself when he engaged the cabriolet of Scaufflaire, that, whatever might be the result, there could be no objection to seeing with his own eyes, and judging of the circumstances for himself; that it was even prudent, that he ought to know what took place; that he could decide nothing without having observed and scrutinised; that in the distance every little thing seems a mountain; that after all, when he should have seen this Champmathieu, some wretch probably, his conscience would be very much reconciled to letting him go to the galleys in his place; that it was true that Javert would be there, and Brevet, Chenildieu, Cochepaille, old convicts who had known him; but surely they would not recognise him; bah! what an idea! that Javert was a hundred miles off the track; that all conjectures and all suppositions were fixed upon this Champmathieu, and that nothing is so stubborn as suppositions and conjectures; that there was, therefore, no danger.

That it was no doubt a dark hour, but that he should get through it; that after all he held his destiny, evil as it might be, in his own hand; that he was master of it. He clung to that thought.

In reality, to tell the truth, he would have preferred not to go to Arras.

Still he was on the way.

Although absorbed in thought, he whipped up his horse, which trotted away at that regular and sure full trot that gets over two leagues and a half an hour.

In proportion as the tilbury went forward, he felt something within him which shrank back.

At daybreak he was in the open country; the city of M— sur M— was a long way behind. He saw the horizon growing lighter; he beheld, without seeing them, all the frozen figures of a winter dawn pass before his eyes. Morning has its spectres as well as evening. He did not see them, but, without his consciousness, and by a kind of penetration which was almost physical, those black outlines of trees and hills added to the tumultuous state of his soul an indescribable gloom and apprehension.

Every time he passed one of the isolated houses that stood here and there by the side of the road, he said to himself: 'But yet, there are people there who are sleeping!'

The trotting of the horse, the rattling of the harness, the wheels upon the pavement, made a gentle, monotonous sound. These things are charming when one is joyful, and mournful when one is sad.

It was broad day when he arrived at Hesdin. He stopped before an inn to let his horse breathe and to have some oats given him.

This horse was, as Scaufflaire had said, of that small breed of the Boulonnais which has too much head, too much belly, and not enough neck, but which has an open chest, a large rump, fine and slender legs, and a firm foot; a homely race, but strong and sound. The excellent animal had made five leagues in two hours, and had not turned a hair.

He did not get out of the tilbury. The stable boy who brought the oats stooped down suddenly and examined the left wheel.

'Have you gone far so?' said the boy.

He answered, almost without breaking up his train of thought:

'Why?'

'Have you come far?' said the boy.

'Five leagues from here.'

'Ah!'

'Why do you say: ah?'

The boy stooped down again, was silent a moment, with his eye fixed on the wheel, then he rose up saying:

'To think that this wheel has just come five leagues, that is possible, but it is very sure that it won't go a quarter of a league now.'

He sprang down from the tilbury.

'What do you say, my friend?'

'I say that it is a miracle that you have come five leagues without tumbling, you and your horse, into some ditch on the way. Look for yourself.'

The wheel in fact was badly damaged. The collision with the mail wagon had broken two spokes and loosened the hub so that the nut no longer held.

'My friend,' said he to the stable-boy, 'is there a wheel-wright here?'

'Certainly, monsieur.'

'Do me the favour to go for him.'

'There he is, close by. Hallo, Master Bourgaillard!'

Master Bourgaillard the wheelwright was on his own doorstep. He came and examined the wheel, and made such a grimace as a surgeon makes at the sight of a broken leg.

'Can you mend that wheel on the spot?'

'Yes, monsieur.'

'When can I start again?'

'Tomorrow.'

'Tomorrow!'

'It is a good day's work. Is monsieur in a great hurry?'

'A very great hurry. I must leave in an hour at the latest.'

'Impossible, monsieur.'

'I will pay whatever you like.'

'Impossible.'

'Well! in two hours.'

'Impossible today. There are two spokes and a hub to be repaired. Monsieur cannot start again before tomorrow.'

'My business cannot wait till tomorrow. Instead of mending this wheel, cannot it be replaced?'

'How so?'

'You are a wheelwright?'

'Certainly, monsieur.'

'Have not you a wheel to sell me? I could start away at once.'

'A wheel to exchange?'

'Yes.'

'I have not a wheel made for your cabriolet. Two wheels make a pair. Two wheels don't go together haphazard.'

'In that case, sell me a pair of wheels.'

'Monsieur, every wheel doesn't go on to every axle.'

'But try.'

'It's of no use, monsieur. I have nothing but cart wheels to sell. We are a small place here.'

'Have you a cabriolet to let?'

The wheelwright, at the first glance, had seen that the tilbury was a hired vehicle. He shrugged his shoulders.

'You take good care of the cabriolets that you hire! I should have one a good while before I would let it to you.'

'Well, sell it to me.'

'I have not one.'

'What! not even a carriole? I am not hard to suit, as you see.'

'We are a little place. True, I have under the old shed there,' added the wheelwright, 'an old chaise that belongs to a citizen of the place, who has given it to me to keep, and who uses it every 29th of February. I would let it to you, of course it is nothing to me. The citizen must not see it go by, and then, it is clumsy; it would take two horses.'

'I will take two post-horses.'

'Where is monsieur going?'

'To Arras.'

'And monsieur would like to get there today?'

'I would.'

'By taking post-horses?'

'Why not?'

'Will monsieur be satisfied to arrive by four o'clock tomorrow morning?'

'No, indeed.'

'I mean, you see, that there is something to be said, in taking post-horses. Monsieur has his passport?'

'Yes.'

'Well, by taking post-horses, monsieur will not reach Arras before tomorrow. We are a crossroad. The relays are poorly served, the horses are in the fields. The ploughing season has just commenced; heavy teams are needed, and the horses are taken from everywhere, from the post as well as elsewhere. Monsieur will have to wait at least three or four hours at each relay, and then they go at a walk. There are a good many hills to climb.'

'Well, I will go on horseback. Unhitch the cabriolet. Somebody in the place can surely sell me a saddle.'

'Certainly, but will this horse go under the saddle?'

'It is true, I had forgotten it, he will not.'

'Then – '

'But I can surely find in the village a horse to let?'

'A horse to go to Arras at one trip?'

'Yes.'

'It would take a better horse than there is in our parts. You would have to buy him too, for nobody knows you. But neither to sell nor to let, neither for five hundred francs nor for a thousand, will you find such a one.'

'What shall I do?'

'The best thing to do, like a sensible man, is that I mend the wheel and you continue your journey tomorrow.'

'Tomorrow will be too late.'

'Confound it!'

'Is there no mail that goes to Arras? When does it pass?'

'Tonight. Both mails make the trip in the night, the up mail as well as the down.'

'How! must you take a whole day to mend this wheel?'

'A whole day, and a long one!'

'If you set two workmen at it?'

'If I should set ten.'

'If you should tie the spokes with cords?'

'The spokes I could, but not the hub. And then the tire is also in bad condition, too.'

'Is there no livery stables in the city?'

'No.'

'Is there another wheelwright?'

The stable boy and the wheelwright answered at the same time, with a shake of the head:

'No.'

He felt an immense joy.

It was evident that Providence was in the matter. It was Providence that had broken the wheel of the tilbury and stopped him on his way. He had not yielded to this sort of first summons; he had made all possible efforts to continue his journey; he had faithfully and scrupulously exhausted every means; he had shrunk neither before the season, nor from fatigue, nor from expense; he had nothing for which to reproach himself. If he went no further, it no longer concerned him. It was now not his fault; it was, not the act of his conscience, but the act of Providence.

He breathed. He breathed freely and with a full chest for the first time since Javert's visit. It seemed to him that the iron hand which had gripped his heart for twenty hours was relaxed.

It appeared to him that now God was for him, was manifestly for him.

He said to himself that he had done all that he could, and that now he had only to retrace his steps, tranquilly.

If his conversation with the wheelwright had taken place in a room of the inn, it would have had no witnesses, nobody would have heard it, the matter would have rested there, and it is probable that we should not have had to relate any of the events which follow, but that conversation occurred in the street. Every colloquy in the street inevitably gathers a circle. There are always people who ask nothing better than to be spectators. While he was questioning the wheelwright, some of the passers-by had stopped around them. After listening for a few minutes, a young boy whom no one had noticed, had separated from the group and ran away.

At the instant the traveller, after the internal deliberation which we have just indicated, was making up his mind to go back, this boy returned. He was accompanied by an old woman.

'Monsieur,' said the woman, 'my boy tells me that you are anxious to hire a cabriolet.'

This simple speech, uttered by an old woman who was brought there by a boy, made the sweat pour down his back. He thought he saw the hand he was but now freed from reappear in the shadow behind him, all ready to seize him again.

He answered:

'Yes, good woman, I am looking for a cabriolet to hire.'

And he hastened to add:

'But there is none in the place.'

'Yes, there is,' said the dame.

'Where is it then?' broke in the wheelwright.

'At my house,' replied the dame.

He shuddered. The fatal hand had closed upon him again.

The old woman had, in fact, under a shed, a sort of willow carriole. The blacksmith and the boy at the inn, angry that the traveller should escape them, intervened.

'It was a frightful go-cart, it had no springs, it was true the seat was hung inside with leather straps, it would not keep out the rain, the wheels were rusty and rotten, it couldn't go much further than the tilbury, a real jumper! This gentleman would do very wrong to set out in it,' etc., etc.

This was all true, but this go-cart, this jumper, this thing, whatever it might be, went upon two wheels and could go to Arras.

He paid what was asked, left the tilbury to be mended at the blacksmith's against his return, had the white horse harnessed to the carriole, got in, and resumed the route he had followed since morning.

The moment the carriole started, he acknowledged that he had felt an instant before a certain joy at the thought that he should not go where he was going. He examined that joy with a sort of anger, and thought it absurd. Why should he feel joy at going back? After all, he was making a journey of his own accord, nobody forced him to it.

And certainly, nothing could happen which he did not choose to have happen.

As he was leaving Hesdin, he heard a voice crying out: 'Stop! stop!' He stopped the carriole with a hasty movement, in which there was still something strangely feverish and convulsive which resembled hope.

It was the dame's little boy.

'Monsieur,' said he, 'it was I who got the carriole for you.'

'Well!'

'You have not given me anything.'

He, who gave to all, and so freely, felt this claim was exorbitant and almost odious.

'Oh! is it you, you beggar?' said he. 'You shall have nothing!'

He whipped up the horse and started away at a quick trot.

He had lost a good deal of time at Hesdin, he wished to make it up. The little horse was plucky, and pulled enough for two; but it was February, it had rained, the roads were bad. And then, it was no longer the tilbury. The carriole ran hard, and was very heavy. And besides there were many steep hills.

He was almost four hours going from Hesdin to Saint Pol. Four hours for five leagues.

At Saint Pol he drove to the nearest inn, and had the horse taken to the stable. As he had promised Scaufflaire, he stood near the manger while the horse was eating. He was thinking of things sad and confused.

The innkeeper's wife came into the stable.

'Does not monsieur wish breakfast?'

'Why, it is true,' said he, 'I have a good appetite.'

He followed the woman, who had a fresh and pleasant face. She led him into a low hall, where there were some tables covered with oilcloth.

'Be quick,' said he, 'I must start again. I am in a hurry.'

A big Flemish servant girl waited on him in all haste. He looked at the girl with a feeling of comfort.

'This is what ailed me,' thought he. 'I had not breakfasted.'

His breakfast was served. He seized the bread, bit a piece, then slowly put it back on the table, and did not touch anything more.

A teamster was eating at another table. He said to this man:

'Why is their bread so bitter?'

The teamster was a German, and did not understand him.

He returned to the stable to his horse.

An hour later he had left Saint Pol, and was driving towards Tinques, which is but five leagues from Arras.

What was he doing during the trip? What was he thinking about? As in the morning, he saw the trees pass by, the thatched roofs, the cultivated fields, and the dissolving views of the country which change at every turn of the road. Such scenes are sometimes sufficient for the soul, and almost do away with thought. To see a thousand objects for the first and for the last time, what can be deeper and more melancholy? To travel is to be born and to die at every instant. It may be that in the most shadowy portion of his mind, he was drawing a comparison between these changing horizons and human existence. All the facts of life are perpetually in flight before us. Darkness and light alternate with each other. After a flash, an eclipse; we look, we hasten, we stretch out our hands to seize what is passing; every event is a turn of the road; and all at once we are old. We feel a slight shock, all is black, we distinguish a dark door, this gloomy horse of life which was carrying us stops, and we see a veiled and unknown form that turns him out into the darkness.

Twilight was falling just as the children coming out of school beheld our traveller entering Tinques. It is true that the days were still short. He did not stop at Tinques. As he was driving out of the village, a countryman who was repairing the road, raised his head and said:

'Your horse is very tired.'

The poor beast, in fact, was not going faster than a walk.

'Are you going to Arras?' added the countryman.

'Yes.'

'If you go at this rate, you won't get there very early.'

He stopped his horse and asked the countryman:

'How far is it from here to Arras?'

'Near seven long leagues.'

'How is that? the post route only counts five and a quarter.'

'Ah!' replied the workman, 'then you don't know that the road is being repaired. You will find it cut off a quarter of an hour from here. There's no means of going further.'

'Indeed!'

'You will take the left, the road that leads to Carency, and cross the river; when you are at Camblin, you will turn to the right; that is the road from Mont Saint Éloy to Arras.'

'But it is night, I shall lose my way.'

'You are not of these parts?'

'No.'

'Besides, they are all crossroads.'

'Stop, monsieur,' the countryman continued, 'do you want I should give you some advice? Your horse is tired; go back to Tinques. There is a good house there. Sleep there. You can go on to Arras tomorrow.'

'I must be there tonight – this evening?'

'That is another thing. Then go back all the same to that inn, and take an extra horse. The boy that will go with the horse will guide you through the crossroads.'

He followed the countryman's advice, retraced his steps, and a half hour afterwards he again passed the same place, but at a full trot, with a good extra horse. A stable-boy, who called himself a postilion, was sitting upon the shaft of the carriole.

He felt, however, that he was losing time. It was now quite dark.

They were driving through a cross-path. The road became frightful. The carriole tumbled from one rut to the other. He said to the postilion:

'Keep up a trot, and double drink-money.'

In one of the jolts the whiffle-tree broke.

'Monsieur,' said the postilion, 'the whiffle-tree is broken; I do not know how to harness my horse now, this road is very bad at night, if you will come back and stop at Tinques, we can be at Arras early tomorrow morning.'

He answered: 'Have you a piece of string and a knife?'

'Yes, monsieur.'

He cut off the limb of a tree and made a whiffle-tree of it.

This was another loss of twenty minutes; but they started off at a gallop.

The plain was dark. A low fog, thick and black, was creeping over the hill-tops and floating away like smoke. There were glimmering flashes from the clouds. A strong wind, which came from the sea, made a sound all around the horizon like the moving of furniture. Everything that he caught a glimpse of had an attitude of terror. How all things shudder under the terrible breath of night.

The cold penetrated him. He had not eaten since the evening before. He recalled vaguely to mind his other night adventure in the great plain near D—, eight years before; and it seemed yesterday to him.

Some distant bell struck the hour. He asked the boy:

'What o'clock is that?'

'Seven o'clock, monsieur; we shall be in Arras at eight. We have only three leagues.'

At this moment he thought for the first time, and it seemed strange that it had not occurred to him sooner; that perhaps all the trouble he was taking might be useless; that he did not even know the hour of the trial; that he should at least have informed himself of that; that it was foolish to be going on at this rate, without knowing whether it would be of any use. Then he figured out some calculations in his mind: that ordinarily the sessions of the courts of assize began at nine o'clock in the morning; that this case would not occupy much time; this apple-stealing would be very short; that there would be nothing but a question of identity; four or five witnesses and some little to be said by the lawyers; that he would get there after it was all over!

The postilion whipped up the horses. They had crossed the river, and left Mont Saint-Eloy behind them.

The night grew darker and darker.

6. *Sister Simplice put to the proof*

MEANWHILE, at that very moment, Fantine was in ecstasies.

She had passed a very bad night. Cough frightful, fever redoubled; she had bad dreams. In the morning, when the doctor came, she was delirious. He appeared to be alarmed, and asked to be informed as soon as Monsieur Madeleine came.

All the morning she was low-spirited, spoke little and was making folds in the sheets, murmuring in a low voice over some calculations which appeared to be calculations of distances. Her eyes were hollow and fixed. The light seemed almost gone out, but then, at moments, they would be lighted up and sparkle like stars. It seems as though at the approach of a certain dark hour, the light of heaven infills those who are leaving the light of earth.

Whenever Sister Simplice asked her how she was, she answered invariably: 'Well. I would like to see Monsieur Madeleine.'

A few months earlier, when Fantine had lost the last of her modesty, her last shame and her last happiness, she was the shadow of herself; now she was the spectre of herself. Physical suffering had completed the work of moral suffering. This creature of twenty-five years had a wrinkled forehead, flabby cheeks, pinched nostrils, shrivelled gums, a leaden complexion, a bony neck, protruding collar-bones, skinny limbs, an earthy skin, and her fair hair was mixed with grey. Alas! how sickness extemporises old age.

At noon the doctor came again, left a few prescriptions, inquired if the mayor had been at the infirmary, and shook his head.

Monsieur Madeleine usually came at three o'clock to see the sick woman. As exactitude was kindness, he was exact.

About half-past two, Fantine began to be agitated. In the space of twenty minutes, she asked the nun more than ten times: 'My sister, what time is it?'

The clock struck three. At the third stroke, Fantine rose up in bed – ordinarily she could hardly turn herself – she joined her two shrunken and yellow hands in a sort of convulsive clasp, and the nun heard from her one of those deep sighs which seem to uplift a great weight. Then Fantine turned and looked towards the door.

Nobody came in; the door did not open.

She sat so for a quarter of an hour, her eyes fixed upon the door, motionless, and as if holding her breath. The sister dared not speak. The church clock struck the quarter. Fantine fell back upon her pillow.

She said nothing, and again began to make folds in the sheet.

A half-hour passed, then an hour, but no one came; every time the clock struck, Fantine rose and looked towards the door, then she fell back.

Her thought could be clearly seen, but she pronounced no name, she did not complain, she found no fault. She only coughed mournfully. One would have said that something dark was settling down upon her. She was livid, and her lips were blue. She smiled at times.

The clock struck five. Then the sister heard her speak very low and gently: 'But since I am going away tomorrow, he does wrong not to come today!'

Sister Simplice herself was surprised at Monsieur Madeleine's delay.

Meanwhile, Fantine was looking at the canopy of her bed. She seemed to be seeking to recall something to her mind. All at once she began to sing in a voice as feeble as a whisper. The nun listened. This is what Fantine sang:

> Nous achèterons de bien belles choses
> En nous promenant le long des faubourgs.
>
> Les bleuets sont bleus, les roses sont roses,
> Les bleuets sont bleus, j'aime mes amours.
>
> La vierge Marie auprès de mon poêle
> Est venue hier en manteau brodé;
> Et m'a dit – Voici, caché sous mon voile,
> Le petit qu'un jour tu m'as demandé.
> Courez à la ville, ayez de la toile,
> Achetez du fil, achetez un dé.
> > Nous achèterons de bien belles choses
> > En nous promenant le long des faubourgs.
>
> Bonne sainte Vierge, auprès de mon poêle
> J'ai mis un berceau de rubans orné;
> Dieu me donnerait sa plus belle étoile,
> J'aime mieux l'enfant que tu m'as donné.
> Madame, que faire avec cette toile?
> Faites en trousseau pour mon nouveau-né.
> > Les bleuets sont bleus, les roses sont roses,
> > Les bleuets sont bleus. j'aime mes amours.
>
> Lavez cette toile. – Où? – Dans la rivière.
> Faites-en, sans rien gâter ni salir,
> Une belle jupe avec sa brassière
> Que je veux broder et de fleurs emplir.
> > L'enfant n'est plus là, madame, qu'en faire?
> > Faites-en un drap pour m'ensevelir.
>
> Nous achèterons de bien belles choses
> En nous promenant le long de faubourgs.
> Les bleuets sont bleus, les roses sont roses,
> Les bleuets sont bleus j'aime mes amours.*

---

* We will buy very pretty things,
  A walking through the faubourgs.

Violets are blue, roses are red,
Violets are blue, I love my loves.

The Virgin Mary to my bed
Came yesterday in broidered cloak
And told me: 'Here hidden in my veil

Is the babe that once you asked of me.'
'Run to the town, get linen,
Buy thread, buy a thimble.'
  We will buy very pretty things,
  A walking through the faubourgs.

Good holy Virgin, by my bed
I have put a cradle draped with ribbons;
Were God to give me his fairest star,

This was an old nursery song with which she once used to sing her little Cosette to sleep, and which had not occurred to her mind for the five years since she had had her child with her. She sang it in a voice so sad, and to an air so sweet, that it could not but draw tears even from a nun. The sister, accustomed to austerity as she was, felt a drop upon her cheek.

The clock struck six. Fantine did not appear to hear. She seemed no longer to pay attention to anything around her.

Sister Simplice sent a girl to inquire of the portress of the factory if the mayor had come in, and if he would not very soon come to the infirmary. The girl returned in a few minutes.

Fantine was still motionless, and appeared to be absorbed in her own thoughts.

The servant related in a whisper to Sister Simplice that the mayor had gone away that morning before six o'clock in a little tilbury drawn by a white horse, cold as the weather was; that he went alone, without even a driver, that no one knew the road he had taken, that some said he had been seen to turn off by the road to Arras, that others were sure they had met him on the road to Paris. That when he went away he seemed, as usual, very kind, and that he simply said to the portress that he need not be expected that night.

While the two women were whispering, with their backs turned towards Fantine's bed, the sister questioning, the servant conjecturing, Fantine, with that feverish vivacity of certain organic diseases, which unites the free movement of health with the frightful exhaustion of death, had risen to her knees on the bed, her shrivelled hands resting on the bolster, and with her head passing through the opening of the curtains, she listened. All at once she exclaimed:

'You are talking there of Monsieur Madeleine! why do you talk so low? what has he done? why does he not come?'

Her voice was so harsh and rough that the two women thought they heard the voice of a man; they turned towards her affrighted.

'Why don't you answer?' cried Fantine.

The servant stammered out:

'The portress told me that he could not come today.'

'My child,' said the sister, 'be calm, lie down again.'

Fantine, without changing her attitude, resumed with a loud voice, and in a tone at once piercing and imperious:

'He cannot come. Why not? You know the reason. You were whispering it there between you. I want to know.'

I should love the babe thou hast given me more.
'Madame, what shall be done with this linen?'
'Make a trousseau for my newborn.'
    Violets are blue, roses are red,
    Violets are blue, I love my loves.

Wash this linen. 'Where?' In the river.
Make of it, without spoiling or soiling,

A pretty skirt, a very long skirt,
Which I will broider and fill with flowers.
'The child is gone, madame, what more?'
    'Make of it a shroud to bury me.'

We will buy very pretty things
A walking in the faubourgs.
Violets are blue, roses are red,
Violets are blue, I love my loves.

The servant whispered quickly in the nun's ear: 'Answer that he is busy with the City Council.'

Sister Simplice reddened slightly; it was a lie that the servant had proposed to her. On the other hand, it did seem to her that to tell the truth to the sick woman would doubtless be a terrible blow, and that it was dangerous in the state in which Fantine was. This blush did not last long. The sister turned her calm, sad eye upon Fantine, and said:

'The mayor has gone away.'

Fantine sprang up and sat upon her feet. Her eyes sparkled. A marvellous joy spread over that mournful face.

'Gone away!' she exclaimed. 'He has gone for Cosette!'

Then she stretched her hands towards heaven, and her whole countenance became ineffable. Her lips moved; she was praying in a whisper.

When her prayer was ended: 'My sister,' said she, 'I am quite willing to lie down again, I will do whatever you wish; I was naughty just now, pardon me for having talked so loud; it is very bad to talk loud; I know it, my good sister, but see how happy I am. God is kind, Monsieur Madeleine is good; just think of it, that he has gone to Montfermeil for my little Cosette.'

She lay down again, helped the nun to arrange the pillow, and kissed a little silver cross which she wore at her neck, and which Sister Simplice had given her.

'My child,' said the sister, 'try to rest now, and do not talk any more.'

Fantine took the sister's hand between hers; they were moist; the sister was pained to feel it.

'He started this morning for Paris. Indeed he need not even go through Paris. Montfermeil is a little to the left in coming. You remember what he said yesterday, when I spoke to him about Cosette: *Very soon, very soon!* This is a surprise he has for me. You know he had me sign a letter to take her away from the Thénardiers. They will have nothing to say, will they? They will give up Cosette. Because they have their pay. The authorities would not let them keep a child when they are paid. My sister, do not make signs to me that I must not talk. I am very happy, I am doing very well. I have no pain at all, I am going to see Cosette again, I am hungry even. For almost five years I have not seen her. You do not, you cannot imagine what a hold children have upon you! And then she will be so handsome, you will see! If you knew, she has such pretty little rosy fingers! First, she will have very beautiful hands. At a year old she had ridiculous hands, – so! She must be large now. She is seven years old. She is a little lady. I call her Cosette, but her name is Euphrasie. Now, this morning I was looking at the dust on the mantel, and I had an idea that I should see Cosette again very soon! Oh, dear! how wrong it is to be years without seeing one's children! We ought to remember that life is not eternal! Oh! how good it is in the mayor to go – true, it is very cold! He had his cloak, at least! He will be here tomorrow, will he not? That will make tomorrow a fête. Tomorrow morning, my sister, you will remind me to put on my little lace cap. Montfermeil is a country place. I made the trip on foot once. It was a long way for me. But the diligences go very fast. He will be here tomorrow with Cosette! How far is it from here to Montfermeil?'

The sister, who had no idea of the distance, answered: 'Oh! I feel sure that he will be here tomorrow.'

'Tomorrow! tomorrow!' said Fantine, 'I shall see Cosette tomorrow! See, good Sister of God, I am well now. I am wild; I would dance, if anybody wanted me to.'

One who had seen her a quarter of an hour before could not have understood this. Now she was all rosy; she talked in a lively, natural tone; her whole face was only a smile. At times she laughed while whispering to herself. A mother's joy is almost like a child's.

'Well,' resumed the nun, 'now you are happy, obey me – do not talk any more.'

Fantine laid her head upon the pillow, and said in a low voice: 'Yes, lie down again; be prudent now that you are going to have your child. Sister Simplice is right. All here are right.'

And then, without moving, or turning her head, she began to look all about with her eyes wide open and a joyous air, and she said nothing more.

The sister closed the curtains, hoping that she would sleep.

Between seven and eight o'clock the doctor came. Hearing no sound, he supposed that Fantine was asleep, went in softly, and approached the bed on tiptoe. He drew the curtains aside, and by the glimmer of the twilight he saw Fantine's large calm eyes looking at him.

She said to him: 'Monsieur, you will let her lie by my side in a little bed, won't you?'

The doctor thought she was delirious. She added:

'Look, there is just room.'

The doctor took Sister Simplice aside, who explained the matter to him, that Monsieur Madeleine was absent for a day or two, and that, not being certain, they had not thought it best to undeceive the sick woman, who believed the mayor had gone to Montfermeil; that it was possible, after all, that she had guessed aright. The doctor approved of this.

He returned to Fantine's bed again, and she continued:

'Then you see, in the morning, when she wakes, I can say good morning to the poor kitten; and at night, when I am awake, I can hear her sleep. Her little breathing is so sweet it will do me good.'

'Give me your hand,' said the doctor.

She reached out her hand, and exclaimed with a laugh:

'Oh, stop! Indeed, it is true you don't know! but I am cured. Cosette is coming tomorrow.'

The doctor was surprised. She was better. Her languor was less. Her pulse was stronger. A sort of new life was all at once reanimating this poor exhausted being.

'Doctor,' she continued, 'has the sister told you that Monsieur the Mayor has gone for the little thing?'

The doctor recommended silence, and that she should avoid all painful emotion. He prescribed an infusion of pure quinine, and, in case the fever should return in the night, a soothing potion. As he was going away he said to the sister: 'She is better. If by good fortune the mayor should really come back tomorrow with the child, who knows? there are such astonishing crises; we have seen great joy instantly cure diseases; I am well aware that this is an organic disease, and far advanced, but this is all such a mystery! We shall save her perhaps!'

7. *The traveller arrives and provides for his return*

IT WAS NEARLY eight o'clock in the evening when the carriole which we left on the road drove into the yard of the Hôtel de la Poste at Arras. The man whom we have followed thus far, got out, answered the hospitalities of the inn's people with an absent-minded air, sent back the extra horse, and took the little white one to the stable himself; then he opened the door of a billiard-room on the first floor, took a seat, and leaned his elbows on the table. He had spent fourteen hours in this trip, which he expected to make in six. He did himself the justice to feel that it was not his fault; but at bottom he was not sorry for it.

The landlady entered.

'Will monsieur have a bed? will monsieur have supper?'

He shook his head:

'The stable-boy says that monsieur's horse is very tired!'

Here he broke silence.

'Is not the horse able to start again tomorrow morning?'

'Oh! monsieur! he needs at least two days' rest.'

He asked:

'Is not the Bureau of the Post here?'

'Yes, sir.'

The hostess led him to the Bureau; he showed his passport and inquired if there were an opportunity to return that very night to M— sur M— by the mail coach; only one seat was vacant, that by the side of the driver; he retained it and paid for it. 'Monsieur,' said the booking clerk, 'don't fail to be here ready to start at precisely one o'clock in the morning.'

This done, he left the hôtel and began to walk in the city.

He was not acquainted in Arras, the streets were dark, and he went haphazard. Nevertheless he seemed to refrain obstinately from asking his way. He crossed the little river Crinchon, and found himself in a labyrinth of narrow streets, where he was soon lost. A citizen came along with a lantern. After some hesitation, he determined to speak to this man, but not until he had looked before and behind, as if he were afraid that somebody might overhear the question he was about to ask.

'Monsieur,' said he, 'the court house, if you please?'

'You are not a resident of the city, monsieur,' answered the citizen, who was an old man, 'well, follow me, I am going right by the court house, that is to say, the city hall. For they are repairing the court house just now, and the courts are holding their sessions at the city hall, temporarily.'

'Is it there,' asked he, 'that the assizes are held?'

'Certainly, monsieur; you see, what is the city hall today was the bishop's palace before the revolution. Monsieur de Conzié, who was bishop in 'eighty-two, had a large hall built. The court is held in that hall.'

As they walked along, the citizen said to him:

'If monsieur wishes to see a trial, he is rather late. Ordinarily the sessions close at six o'clock.'

However, when they reached the great square, the citizen showed him four long lighted windows on the front of a vast dark building.

'Faith, monsieur, you are in time, you are fortunate. Do you see those four windows? that is the court of assizes. There is a light there. Then they have not finished. The case must have been prolonged and they are having an evening session. Are you interested in this case? Is it a criminal trial? Are you a witness?'

He answered:

'I have no business; I only wish to speak to a lawyer.'

'That's another thing,' said the citizen. 'Stop, monsieur, here is the door. The doorkeeper is up there. You have only to go up the grand stairway.'

He followed the citizen's instructions, and in a few minutes found himself in a hall where there were many people, and scattered groups of lawyers in their robes whispering here and there.

It is always a chilling sight to see these gatherings of men clothed in black, talking among themselves in a low voice on the threshold of the chamber of justice.

It is rare that charity and pity can be found in their words. What are oftenest heard are sentences pronounced in advance. All these groups seem to the observer, who passes musingly by, like so many gloomy hives where buzzing spirits are building in common all sorts of dark structures.

This hall, which, though spacious, was lighted by a single lamp, was an ancient hall of the Episcopal palace, and served as a waiting-room. A double folding door, which was now closed, separated it from the large room in which the court of assizes was in session.

The obscurity was such that he felt no fear in addressing the first lawyer whom he met.

'Monsieur,' said he, 'how are they getting along?'

'It is finished,' said the lawyer.

'Finished!'

The word was repeated in such a tone that the lawyer turned around.

'Pardon me, monsieur, you are a relative, perhaps?'

'No. I know no one here. And was there a sentence?'

'Of course. It was hardly possible for it to be otherwise.'

'To hard labour?'

'For life.'

He continued in a voice so weak that it could hardly be heard:

'The identity was established, then?'

'What identity?' responded the lawyer. 'There was no identity to be established. It was a simple affair. This woman had killed her child, the infanticide was proven, the jury were not satisfied that there was any premeditation; she was sentenced for life.'

'It is a woman, then?' said he.

'Certainly. The Limosin girl. What else are you speaking of?'

'Nothing, but if it is finished, why is the hall still lighted up?'

'That is for the other case, which commenced nearly two hours ago.'

'What other case?'

'Oh! that is a clear one also. It is a sort of a thief, a second offender, a galley slave, a case of robbery. I forget his name. He looks like a bandit. Were it for nothing but having such a face, I would send him to the galleys.'

'Monsieur,' asked he, 'is there any means of getting into the hall?'

'I think not, really. There is a great crowd. However, they are taking a recess.

Some people have come out, and when the session is resumed, you can try.'

'How do you get in?'

'Through that large door.'

The lawyer left him. In a few moments, he had undergone, almost at the same time, almost together, all possible emotions. The words of this indifferent man had alternately pierced his heart like icicles and like flames of fire. When he learned that it was not concluded, he drew breath; but he could not have told whether what he felt was satisfaction or pain.

He approached several groups and listened to their talk. The calendar of the term being very heavy, the judge had set down two short, simple cases for that day. They had begun with the infanticide, and now were on the convict, the second offender, the 'old stager'. This man had stolen some apples, but that did not appear to be very well proven; what was proven, was that he had been in the galleys at Toulon. This was what ruined his case. The examination of the man had been finished, and the testimony of the witnesses had been taken; but there yet remained the argument of the counsel, and the summing up of his prosecuting attorney; it would hardly be finished before midnight. The man would probably be condemned; the prosecuting attorney was very good, and never *failed* with his prisoners; he was a fellow of talent, who wrote poetry.

An officer stood near the door which opened into the courtroom. He asked this officer:

'Monsieur, will the door be opened soon?'

'It will not be opened,' said the officer.

'How! it will not be opened when the session is resumed? is there not a recess?'

'The session has just been resumed,' answered the officer, 'but the door will not be opened again.'

'Why not?'

'Because the hall is full.'

'What! there are no more seats?'

'Not a single one. The door is closed. No one can enter.'

The officer added, after a silence: 'There are indeed two or three places still behind Monsieur the Judge, but Monsieur the Judge admits none but public functionaries to them.'

So saying, the officer turned his back.

He retired with his head bowed down, crossed the antechamber, and walked slowly down the staircase, seeming to hesitate at every step. It is probable that he was holding counsel with himself. The violent combat that had been going on within him since the previous evening was not finished; and, every moment, he fell upon some new turn. When he reached the turn of the stairway, he leaned against the railing and folded his arms. Suddenly he opened his coat, drew out his pocket-book, took out a pencil, tore out a sheet, and wrote rapidly upon that sheet, by the glimmering light, this line: *Monsieur Madeleine, Mayor of M— sur M—*; then he went up the stairs again rapidly, passed through the crowd, walked straight to the officer, handed him the paper, and said to him with authority: 'Carry that to Monsieur the Judge.'

The officer took the paper, cast his eye upon it, and obeyed.

8. *Admission by favour*

WITHOUT HIMSELF suspecting it, the Mayor of M— sur M— had a certain celebrity. For seven years the reputation of his virtue had been extending throughout Bas-Boulonnais; it had finally crossed the boundaries of the little county, and had spread into the two or three neighbouring departments. Besides the considerable service that he had rendered to the chief town by reviving the manufacture of jet-work, there was not one of the hundred and forty-one communes of the district of M— sur M— which was not indebted to him for some benefit. He had even in case of need aided and quickened the business of the other districts. Thus he had, in time of need, sustained with his credit and with his own funds the tulle factory at Boulogne, the flax-spinning factory at Frévent, and the linen factory at Boubers-sur-Canche. Everywhere the name of Monsieur Madeleine was spoken with veneration. Arras and Douai envied the lucky little city of M— sur M— its mayor.

The Judge of the Royal Court of Douai, who was holding this term of the assizes at Arras, was familiar, as well as everybody else, with this name so profoundly and so universally honoured. When the officer, quietly opening the door which led from the counsel chamber to the courtroom, bent behind the judge's chair and handed him the paper, on which was written the line we have just read, adding: '*This gentleman desires to witness the trial,*' the judge made a hasty movement of deference, seized a pen, wrote a few words at the bottom of the paper and handed it back to the officer, saying to him: 'Let him enter.'

The unhappy man, whose history we are relating, had remained near the door of the hall, in the same place and the same attitude as when the officer left him. He heard, through his thoughts, someone saying to him: 'Will monsieur do me the honour to follow me?' It was the same officer who had turned his back upon him the minute before, and who now bowed to the earth before him. The officer at the same time handed him the paper. He unfolded it, and, as he happened to be near the lamp, he could read:

'The Judge of the Court of Assizes presents his respects to Monsieur Madeleine.'

He crushed the paper in his hands, as if those few words had left some strange and bitter taste behind.

He followed the officer.

In a few minutes he found himself alone in a kind of panelled cabinet, of a severe appearance, lighted by two wax candles placed upon a table covered with green cloth. The last words of the officer who had left him still rang in his ear: 'Monsieur you are now in the counsel chamber; you have but to turn the brass knob of that door and you will find yourself in the courtroom, behind the judge's chair.' These words were associated in his thoughts with a vague remembrance of the narrow corridors and dark stairways through which he had just passed.

The officer had left him alone. The decisive moment had arrived. He endeavoured to collect his thoughts, but did not succeed. At those hours especially when we have sorest need of grasping the sharp realities of life do the threads of thought snap off in the brain. He was in the very place where the judges deliberate and decide. He beheld with a stupid tranquillity that silent and formidable room where so many existences had been terminated, where his own name would be heard so soon, and which his destiny was crossing at this moment. He looked at the walls, then he looked at himself, astonished that this could be this chamber, and that this could be he.

He had eaten nothing for more than twenty-four hours; he was bruised by the jolting of the carriole, but he did not feel it; it seemed to him that he felt nothing.

He examined a black frame which hung on the wall, and which contained under glass an old autograph letter of Jean Nicolas Pache, Mayor of Paris, and Minister, dated, doubtless by mistake, *June* 9th, year II, in which Pache sent to the Commune the list of the ministers and deputies held in arrest within their limits. A spectator, had he seen and watched him then, would have imagined, doubtless, that this letter appeared very remarkable to him, for he did not take his eyes off from it, and he read it two or three times. He was reading without paying any attention, and without knowing what he was doing. He was thinking of Fantine and Cosette.

Even while musing, he turned unconsciously, and his eyes encountered the brass knob of the door which separated him from the hall of the assizes. He had almost forgotten that door. His countenance, at first calm, now fell. His eyes were fixed on that brass knob, then became set and wild and little by little filled with dismay. Drops of sweat started out from his head, and rolled down over his temples.

At one moment he made, with a kind of authority united to rebellion, that indescribable gesture which means and which so well says: *Well! who is there to compel me?* Then he turned quickly, saw before him the door by which he had entered, went to it, opened it, and went out. He was no longer in that room; he was outside, in a corridor, a long, narrow corridor, cut up with steps and side-doors, making all sorts of angles, lighted here and there by lamps hung on the wall similar to nurse-lamps for the sick; it was the corridor by which he had come. He drew breath and listened; no sound behind him, no sound before him; he ran as if he were pursued.

When he had doubled several of the turns of this passage, he listened again. There was still the same silence and the same shadow about him. He was out of breath, he tottered, he leaned against the wall. The stone was cold; the sweat was icy upon his forehead; he roused himself with a shudder.

Then and there, alone, standing in that obscurity, trembling with cold and, perhaps, with something else, he reflected.

He had reflected all night, he had reflected all day; he now heard but one voice within him, which said: 'Alas!'

A quarter of an hour thus rolled away. Finally, he bowed his head, sighed with anguish, let his arms fall, and retraced his steps. He walked slowly and as if overwhelmed. It seemed as if he had been caught in his flight and brought back.

He entered the counsel chamber again. The first thing that he saw was the handle of the door. That handle, round and of polished brass, shone out before him like an ominous star. He looked at it as a lamb might look at the eye of a tiger.

His eyes could not move from it.

From time to time, he took another step towards the door.

Had he listened, he would have heard, as a kind of confused murmur, the noise of the neighbouring hall; but he did not listen and he did not hear.

Suddenly, without himself knowing how, he found himself near the door, he seized the knob convulsively; the door opened.

He was in the courtroom.

9. *A place for arriving at convictions*

HE TOOK A STEP, closed the door behind him, mechanically, and remained standing, noting what he saw.

It was a large hall, dimly lighted, and noisy and silent by turns, where all the machinery of a criminal trial was exhibited, with its petty, yet solemn gravity, before the multitude.

At one end of the hall, that at which he found himself, heedless judges, in threadbare robes, were biting their finger-nails, or closing their eyelids; at the other end was a ragged rabble; there were lawyers in all sorts of attitudes; soldiers with honest and hard faces; old, stained wainscoting, a dirty ceiling, tables covered with serge, which was more nearly yellow than green; doors blackened by finger-marks; tavern lamps, giving more smoke than light, on nails in the panelling; candles, in brass candlesticks, on the tables; everywhere obscurity, unsightliness, and gloom; and from all this there arose an austere and august impression; for men felt therein the presence of that great human thing which is called law, and that great divine thing which is called justice.

No man in this multitude paid any attention to him. All eyes converged on a single point, a wooden bench placed against a little door, along the wall at the left hand of the judge. Upon this bench, which was lighted by several candles, was a man between two gendarmes.

This was the man.

He did not look for him, he saw him. His eyes went towards him naturally, as if they had known in advance where he was.

He thought he saw himself, older, doubtless, not precisely the same in features, but alike in attitude and appearance, with that bristling hair, with those wild and restless eyeballs, with that blouse – just as he was on the day he entered D—, full of hatred, and concealing in his soul that hideous hoard of frightful thoughts which he had spent nineteen years in gathering upon the floor of the galleys.

He said to himself, with a shudder: 'Great God! shall I again come to this?'

This being appeared at least sixty years old. There was something indescribably rough, stupid, and terrified in his appearance.

At the sound of the door, people had stood aside to make room. The judge had turned his head, and supposing the person who entered to be the mayor of M— sur M—, greeted him with a bow. The prosecuting attorney, who had seen Madeleine at M— sur M—, whither he had been called more than once by the duties of his office, recognised him and bowed likewise. He scarcely perceived them. He gazed about him, a prey to a sort of hallucination.

Judges, clerk, gendarmes, a throng of heads, cruelly curious – he had seen all these once before, twenty-seven years ago. He had fallen again upon these fearful things; they were before him, they moved, they had being; it was no longer an effort of his memory, a mirage of his fancy, but real gendarmes and real judges, a real throng, and real men of flesh and bone. It was done; he saw reappearing and living again around him, with all the frightfulness of reality, the monstrous visions of the past.

All this was yawning before him.

Stricken with horror, he closed his eyes, and exclaimed from the depths of his soul: 'Never!'

And by a tragic sport of destiny, which was agitating all his ideas and rendering him almost insane, it was another self before him. This man on trial was called by all around him, Jean Valjean!

He had before his eyes an unheard-of vision, a sort of representation of the most horrible moment of his life, played by his shadow.

All, everything was there – the same paraphernalia, the same hour of the night – almost the same faces, judge and assistant judges, soldiers and spectators. But above the head of the judge was a crucifix, a thing which did not appear in courtrooms at the time of his sentence. When he was tried, God was not there.

A chair was behind him; he sank into it, terrified at the idea that he might be observed. When seated, he took advantage of a pile of papers on the judges' desk to hide his face from the whole room. He could now see without being seen. He entered fully into the spirit of the reality; by degrees he recovered his composure, and arrived at that degree of calmness at which it is possible to listen.

Monsieur Bamatabois was one of the jurors.

He looked for Javert, but did not see him. The witnesses' seat was hidden from him by the clerk's table. And then, as we have just said, the hall was very dimly lighted.

At the moment of his entrance, the counsel for the prisoner was finishing his plea. The attention of all was excited to the highest degree; the trial had been in progress for three hours. During these three hours, the spectators had seen a man, an unknown, wretched being, thoroughly stupid or thoroughly artful, gradually bending beneath the weight of a terrible probability. This man, as is already known, was a vagrant who had been found in a field, carrying off a branch, laden with ripe apples, which had been broken from a tree in a neighbouring close called the Pierron enclosure. Who was this man? An examination had been held, witnesses had been heard, they had been unanimous, light had been elicited from every portion of the trial. The prosecution said: 'We have here not merely a fruit thief, a marauder; we have here, in our hands, a bandit, an outlaw who has broken his ban, an old convict, a most dangerous wretch, a malefactor, called Jean Valjean, of whom justice has been long in pursuit, and who, eight years ago, on leaving the galleys at Toulon, committed a highway robbery, with force and arms, upon the person of a youth of Savoy, Petit Gervais by name, a crime which is specified in Article 383 of the Penal Code, and for which we reserve the right of further prosecution when his identity shall be judicially established. He has now committed a new theft. It is a case of second offence. Convict him for the new crime; he will be tried hereafter for the previous one.' Before this accusation, before the unanimity of the witnesses, the principal emotion evinced by the accused was astonishment. He made gestures and signs which signified denial, or he gazed at the ceiling. He spoke with difficulty, and answered with embarrassment, but from head to foot, his whole person denied the charge. He seemed like an idiot in the presence of all these intellects ranged in battle around him, and like a stranger in the midst of this society by whom he had been seized. Nevertheless, a most threatening future awaited him; probabilities increased every moment; and every spectator was looking with more anxiety than himself for the calamitous sentence which seemed to be hanging over his head with ever increasing surety. One contingency even gave a glimpse of the possibility, beyond the galleys, of a capital penalty should his identity be established, and the Petit Gervais affair result in his conviction. Who was this man? What was the nature of his apathy? Was it imbecility or artifice? Did he know too much or nothing at all? These were questions upon which the spectators took sides, and which seemed to affect the jury. There was something fearful and something mysterious in the trial; the drama was not merely gloomy, but it was obscure.

The counsel for the defence had made a very good plea in that provincial language which long constituted the eloquence of the bar, and which was formerly employed by all lawyers, at Paris as well as at Romorantin or Montbrison, but which, having now become classic, is used by few except the official orators of the bar, to whom it is suited by its solemn rotundity and majestic periods; a language in which husband and wife are called *spouses*, Paris, *the centre of arts and civilisation*, the king, *the monarch*, a bishop, a *holy pontiff*, the prosecuting attorney, *the eloquent interpreter of the vengeance of the law*, arguments, *the accents which we have just heard*, the time of Louis XIV, *the illustrious age*, a theatre, *the temple of Melpomene*, the reigning family, *the august blood of our kings*, a concert, *a musical solemnity*, the general in command, *the illustrious warrior who*, etc., students of theology, *those tender Levites*, mistakes imputed to newspapers, *the imposture which distils its venom into the columns of these organs*, etc., etc. The counsel for the defence had begun by expatiating on the theft of the apples, – a thing ill suited to a lofty style; but Benign Bossuet himself was once compelled to make allusion to a hen in the midst of a funeral oration, and acquitted himself with dignity. The counsel established that the theft of the apples was not in fact proved. His client, whom in his character of counsel he persisted in calling Champmathieu, had not been seen to scale the wall or break off the branch. He had been arrested in possession of this branch (which the counsel preferred to call *bough*); but he said that he had found it on the ground. Where was the proof to the contrary? Undoubtedly this branch had been broken and carried off after the scaling of the wall, then thrown away by the alarmed marauder; undoubtedly, there had been a thief. – But what evidence was there that this thief was Champmathieu? One single thing. That he was formerly a convict. The counsel would not deny that this fact unfortunately appeared to be fully proved; the defendant had resided at Faverolles; the defendant had been a pruner, the name of Champmathieu might well have had its origin in that of Jean Mathieu; all this was true, and finally, four witnesses had positively and without hesitation identified Champmathieu as the galley slave, Jean Valjean; to these circumstances and this testimony the counsel could oppose nothing but the denial of his client, an interested denial; but even supposing him to be the convict Jean Valjean, did this prove that he had stolen the apples? that was a presumption at most, not a proof. The accused, it was true, and the counsel 'in good faith' must admit it, had adopted 'a mistaken system of defence.' He had persisted in denying everything, both the theft and the fact that he had been a convict. An avowal on the latter point would have been better certainly, and would have secured to him the indulgence of the judges; the counsel had advised him to this course, but the defendant had obstinately refused, expecting probably to escape punishment entirely, by admitting nothing. It was a mistake, but must not the poverty of his intellect be taken into consideration? The man was evidently imbecile. Long suffering in the galleys, long suffering out of the galleys, had brutalised him, etc., etc.; if he made a bad defence, was this a reason for convicting him? As to the Petit Gervais affair, the counsel had nothing to say, it was not in the case. He concluded by entreating the jury and court, if the identity of Jean Valjean appeared evident to them, to apply to him the police penalties prescribed for the breaking of ban, and not the fearful punishment decreed to the convict found guilty of a second offence.

The prosecuting attorney replied to the counsel for the defence. He was violent and flowery, like most prosecuting attorneys.

He complimented the counsel for his 'frankness,' of which he shrewdly took advantage. He attacked the accused through all the concessions which his counsel had made. The counsel seemed to admit that the accused was Jean Valjean. He accepted the admission. This man then was Jean Valjean. This fact was conceded to the prosecution, and could be no longer contested. Here, by an adroit autonomasia, going back to the sources and causes of crime, the prosecuting attorney thundered against the immorality of the romantic school – then in its dawn, under the name of the *Satanic school*, conferred upon it by the critics of the *Quotidienne* and the *Oriflamme*;[25] and he attributed, not without plausibility, to the influence of this perverse literature, the crime of Champmathieu, or rather of Jean Valjean. These considerations exhausted, he passed to Jean Valjean himself. Who was Jean Valjean? Description of Jean Valjean: a monster vomited, etc. The model of all such descriptions may be found in the story of Théramène, which as tragedy is useless, but which does great service in judicial eloquence every day. The auditory and the jury 'shuddered.' This description finished, the prosecuting attorney resumed with an oratorical burst, designed to excite the enthusiasm of the *Journal de la Préfecture* to the highest pitch next morning. 'And it is such a man,' etc. etc. A vagabond, a mendicant, without means of existence, etc., etc. Accustomed through his existence to criminal acts, and profiting little by his past life in the galleys, as is proved by the crime committed upon Petit Gervais, etc., etc. It is such a man who, found on the highway in the very act of theft, a few paces from a wall that had been scaled, still holding in his hand the subject of his crime, denies the act in which he is caught, denies the theft, denies the escalade, denies everything, denies even his name, denies even his identity! Besides a hundred other proofs, to which we will not return, he is identified by four witnesses – Javert – the incorruptible inspector of police, Javert – and three of his former companions in disgrace, the convicts Brevet, Chenildieu, and Cochepaille. What has he to oppose to this overwhelming unanimity? His denial. What depravity! You will do justice, gentlemen of the jury, etc., etc. While the prosecuting attorney was speaking the accused listened open-mouthed, with a sort of astonishment, not unmingled with admiration. He was evidently surprised that a man could speak so well. From time to time, at the most 'forcible' parts of the argument, at those moments when eloquence, unable to contain itself, overflows in a stream of withering epithets, and surrounds the prisoner like a tempest, he slowly moved his head from right to left, and from left to right – a sort of sad, mute protest, with which he contented himself from the beginning of the argument. Two or three times the spectators nearest him heard him say in a low tone: 'This all comes from not asking for Monsieur Baloup!' The prosecuting attorney pointed out to the jury this air of stupidity, which was evidently put on, and which denoted, not imbecility, but address, artifice, and the habit of deceiving justice; and which showed in its full light the 'deep-rooted perversity' of the man. He concluded by reserving entirely the Petit Gervais affair, and demanding a sentence to the full extent of the law.

This was, for this offence, as will be remembered, hard labour for life.

The counsel for the prisoner rose, commenced by complimenting 'Monsieur, the prosecuting attorney, on his admirable argument,' then replied as best he could, but in a weaker tone; the ground was evidently giving way under him.

10. *The system of denegations*

THE TIME HAD COME for closing the case. The judge commanded the accused to rise, and put the usual question: 'Have you anything to add to your defence?'

The man, standing, and twirling in his hands a hideous cap which he had, seemed not to hear.

The judge repeated the question.

This time the man heard, and appeared to comprehend. He started like one awaking from sleep, cast his eyes around him, looked at the spectators, the gendarmes, his counsel, the jurors, and the court, placed his huge fist on the bar before him, looked around again, and suddenly fixing his eyes upon the prosecuting attorney, began to speak. It was like an eruption. It seemed from the manner in which the words escaped his lips, incoherent, impetuous, jostling each other pell-mell, as if they were all eager to find vent at the same time. He said:

'I have this to say: That I have been a wheelwright at Paris; that it was at M. Baloup's too. It is a hard life to be a wheelwright, you always work outdoors, in yards, under sheds when you have good bosses, never in shops, because you must have room, you see. In the winter, it is so cold that you thresh your arms to warm them; but the bosses won't allow that; they say it is a waste of time. It is tough work to handle iron when there is ice on the pavements. It wears a man out quick. You get old when you are young at this trade. A man is used up by forty. I was fifty-three; I was sick a good deal. And then the workmen are so bad! When a poor fellow isn't young, they always call you old bird, and old beast! I earned only thirty sous a day, they paid me as little as they could – the bosses took advantage of my age. Then I had my daughter, who was a washerwoman at the river. She earned a little for herself; between us two, we got on; she had hard work too. All day long up to the waist in a tub, in rain, in snow, with wind that cuts your face when it freezes, it is all the same, the washing must be done; there are folks who haven't much linen and are waiting for it; if you don't wash you lose your customers. The planks are not well matched, and the water falls on you everywhere. You get your clothes wet through and through; that strikes in. She washed too in the laundry of the Enfants-Rouges, where the water comes in through pipes. There you are not in the tub. You wash before you under the pipe, and rinse behind you in the trough. This is under cover, and you are not so cold. But there is a hot lye that is terrible and ruins your eyes. She would come home at seven o'clock at night, and go to bed right away, she was so tired. Her husband used to beat her. She is dead. We wasn't very happy. She was a good girl; she never went to balls, and was very quiet. I remember one Shrove Tuesday she went to bed at eight o'clock. Look here, I am telling the truth. You have only to ask if 'tisn't so. Ask! how stupid I am! Paris is a gulf. Who is there that knows Father Champmathieu? But there is M. Baloup. Go and see M. Baloup. I don't know what more you want of me.'

The man ceased speaking, but did not sit down. He had uttered these sentences in a loud, rapid, hoarse, harsh, and guttural tone, with a sort of angry and savage simplicity. Once, he stopped to bow to somebody in the crowd. The sort of affirmations which he seemed to fling out haphazard, came from him like hiccoughs, and he added to each the gesture of a man chopping wood. When he had finished, the auditory burst into laughter. He looked at them, and seeing them laughing and not knowing why, began to laugh himself.

That was an ill omen.

The judge, considerate and kindly man, raised his voice:

He reminded 'gentlemen of the jury' that M. Baloup, the former master wheelwright by whom the prisoner said he had been employed, had been summoned, but had not appeared. He had become bankrupt, and could not be found. Then, turning to the accused, he adjured him to listen to what he was about to say, and added: 'You are in a position which demands reflection. The gravest presumptions are weighing against you, and may lead to fatal results. Prisoner, on your own behalf, I question you a second time, explain yourself clearly on these two points. First, did you or did you not climb the wall of the Pierron close, break off the branch and steal the apples, that is to say, commit the crime of theft, with the addition of breaking into an enclosure? Secondly, are you or are you not the discharged convict, Jean Valjean?'

The prisoner shook his head with a knowing look, like a man who understands perfectly, and knows what he is going to say. He opened his mouth, turned towards the presiding judge, and said:

'In the first place – '

Then he looked at his cap, looked up at the ceiling, and was silent.

'Prisoner,' resumed the prosecuting attorney, in an austere tone, 'give attention. You have replied to nothing that has been asked you. Your agitation condemns you. It is evident that your name is not Champmathieu, but that you are the convict, Jean Valjean, disguised under the name at first, of Jean Mathieu, which was that of his mother; that you have lived in Auvergne; that you were born at Faverolles, where you were a pruner. It is evident that you have stolen ripe apples from the Pierron close, with the addition of breaking into the enclosure. The gentlemen of the jury will consider this.'

The accused had at last resumed his seat; he rose abruptly when the prosecuting attorney had ended, and exclaimed:

'You are a very bad man, you, I mean. This is what I wanted to say. I couldn't think of it first off. I never stole anything. I am a man who don't get something to eat every day. I was coming from Ailly, walking alone after a shower, which had made the ground all yellow with mud, so that the ponds were running over, and you only saw little sprigs of grass sticking out of the sand along the road, and I found a broken branch on the ground with apples on it; and I picked it up not knowing what trouble it would give me. It is three months that I have been in prison, being knocked about. More'n that, I can't tell. You talk against me and tell me "answer!" The gendarme, who is a good fellow, nudges my elbow, and whispers, "answer now." I can't explain myself; I never studied: I am a poor man. You are all wrong not to see that I didn't steal. I picked up off the ground things that was there. You talk about Jean Valjean, Jean Mathieu – I don't know any such people. They must be villagers. I have worked for Monsieur Baloup, Boulevard de l'Hopital. My name is Champmathieu. You must be very sharp to tell me where I was born. I don't know myself. Everybody can't have houses to be born in; that would be too handy. I think my father and mother were strollers, but I don't know. When I was a child they called me Little One; now, they call me Old Man. They're my Christian names. Take them as you like. I have been in Auvergne, I have been at Faverolles. Bless me! can't a man have been in Auvergne and Faverolles without having been at the galleys? I tell you I never stole, and that I am Father Champmathieu. I have been at Monsieur Baloup's; I lived in his house. I am tired of your everlasting nonsense. What is everybody after me for like a mad dog?'

The prosecuting attorney was still standing; he addressed the judge:

'Sir, in the presence of the confused but very adroit denegations of the accused, who endeavours to pass for an idiot, but who will not succeed in it – we will prevent him – we request that it may please you and the court to call again within the bar, the convicts, Brevet, Cochepaille, and Chenildieu, and police-inspector Javert, and to submit them to a final interrogation, concerning the identity of the accused with the convict Jean Valjean.'

'I must remind the prosecuting attorney,' said the presiding judge, 'that police-inspector Javert, recalled by his duties to the chief town of a neighbouring district, left the hall, and the city also, as soon as his testimony was taken. We granted him this permission, with the consent of the prosecuting attorney and the counsel of the accused.'

'True,' replied the prosecuting attorney; 'in the absence of Monsieur Javert, I think it a duty to recall to the gentlemen of the jury what he said here a few hours ago. Javert is an estimable man, who does honour to inferior but important functions, by his rigorous and strict probity. These are the terms in which he testified: "I do not need even moral presumptions and material proofs to contradict the denials of the accused. I recognise him perfectly. This man's name is not Champmathieu; he is a convict, Jean Valjean, very hard, and much feared. He was liberated at the expiration of his term, but with extreme regret. He served out nineteen years at hard labour for burglary; five or six times he attempted to escape. Besides the Petit Gervais and Pierron robberies, I suspect him also of a robbery committed on his highness, the late Bishop of D—. I often saw him when I was adjutant of the galley guard at Toulon. I repeat it; I recognise him perfectly." '

This declaration, in terms so precise, appeared to produce a strong impression upon the public and jury. The prosecuting attorney concluded by insisting that, in the absence of Javert, the three witnesses, Brevet, Chenildieu, and Cochepaille, should be heard anew and solemnly interrogated.

The judge gave an order to an officer, and a moment afterwards the door of the witness-room opened, and the officer, accompanied by a gendarme ready to lend assistance, led in the convict Brevet. The audience was in breathless suspense, and all hearts palpitated as if they contained but a single soul.

The old convict Brevet was clad in the black and grey jacket of the central prisons. Brevet was about sixty years old; he had the face of a man of business, and the air of a rogue. They sometimes go together. He had become something like a turnkey in the prison – to which he had been brought by new misdeeds. He was one of those men of whom their superiors are wont to say, 'He tries to make himself useful.' The chaplain bore good testimony to his religious habits. It must not be forgotten that this happened under the Restoration.

'Brevet,' said the judge, 'you have suffered infamous punishment, and cannot take an oath.'

Brevet cast down his eyes.

'Nevertheless,' continued the judge, 'even in the man whom the law has degraded there may remain, if divine justice permit, a sentiment of honour and equity. To that sentiment I appeal in this decisive hour. If it still exist in you, as I hope, reflect before you answer me; consider on the one hand this man, whom a word from you may destroy; on the other hand, justice, which a word from you may enlighten. The moment is a solemn one, and there is still time to retract if you think yourself mistaken. Prisoner, rise. Brevet, look well upon the prisoner; collect your remembrances, and say, on your soul and conscience, whether you still recognise this man as your former comrade in the galleys, Jean Valjean.'

Brevet looked at the prisoner, then turned again to the court.

'Yes, your honour, I was the first to recognise him, and still do so. This man is Jean Valjean, who came to Toulon in 1796, and left in 1815. I left a year after. He looks like a brute now, but he must have grown stupid with age; at the galleys he was sullen. I recognise him now, positively.'

'Sit down,' said the judge. 'Prisoner, remain standing.'

Chenildieu was brought in, a convict for life, as was shown by his red cloak and green cap. He was undergoing his punishment in the galleys of Toulon, whence he had been brought for this occasion. He was a little man, about fifty years old, active, wrinkled, lean, yellow, brazen, restless, with a sort of sickly feebleness in his limbs and whole person, and immense force in his eye. His companions in the galleys had nicknamed him Je-nie-Dieu.

The judge addressed nearly the same words to him as to Brevet. When he reminded him that his infamy had deprived him of the right to take an oath, Chenildieu raised his head and looked the spectators in the face. The judge requested him to collect his thoughts, and asked him, as he had Brevet, whether he still recognised the prisoner.

Chenildieu burst out laughing.

'Gad! do I recognise him! we were five years on the same chain. You're sulky with me, are you, old boy?'

'Sit down,' said the judge.

The officer brought in Cochepaille; this other convict for life, brought from the galleys and dressed in red like Chenildieu, was a peasant from Lourdes, and a semi-bear of the Pyrenees. He had tended flocks in the mountains, and from shepherd had glided into brigandage. Cochepaille was not less uncouth than the accused, and appeared still more stupid. He was one of those unfortunate men whom nature turns out as wild beasts, and society finishes up into galley slaves.

The judge attempted to move him by a few serious and pathetic words, and asked him, as he had the others, whether he still recognised without hesitation or difficulty the man standing before him.

'It is Jean Valjean,' said Cochepaille. 'The same they called Jean-the-Jack, he was so strong.'

Each of the affirmations of these three men, evidently sincere and in good faith, had excited in the audience a murmur of evil augury for the accused – a murmur which increased in force and continuance, every time a new declaration was added to the preceding one. The prisoner himself listened to them with that astonished countenance which, according to the prosecution, was his principal means of defence. At the first, the gendarmes by his side heard him mutter between his teeth: 'Ah, well! there is one of them!' After the second, he said in a louder tone, with an air almost of satisfaction, 'Good!' At the third, he exclaimed, 'Famous!'

The judge addressed him:

'Prisoner, you have listened. What have you to say?'

He replied:

'I say – famous!'

A buzz ran through the crowd and almost invaded the jury. It was evident that the man was lost.

'Officers,' said the judge, 'enforce order. I am about to sum up the case.'

At this moment there was a movement near the judge. A voice was heard exclaiming:

'Brevet, Chenildieu, Cochepaille, look this way!'

So lamentable and terrible was this voice that those who heard it felt their blood run cold. All eyes turned towards the spot whence it came. A man, who had been sitting among the privileged spectators behind the court, had risen, pushed open the low door which separated the tribunal from the bar, and was standing in the centre of the hall. The judge, the prosecuting attorney, Monsieur Bamatabois, twenty persons recognised him, and exclaimed at once:

'Monsieur Madeleine!'

11. *Champmathieu more and more astonished*

IT WAS HE, INDEED. The clerk's lamp lighted up his face. He held his hat in hand; there was no disorder in his dress; his overcoat was carefully buttoned. He was very pale, and trembled slightly. His hair, already grey when he came to Arras, was now perfectly white. It had become so during the hour that he had been there. All eyes were strained towards him.

The sensation was indescribable. There was a moment of hesitation in the auditory. The voice had been so thrilling, the man standing there appeared so calm, that at first nobody could comprehend it. They asked who had cried out. They could not believe that this tranquil man had uttered that fearful cry.

This indecision lasted but few seconds. Before even the judge and prosecuting attorney could say a word, before the gendarmes and officers could make a sign, the man, whom all up to this moment called Monsieur Madeleine, had advanced towards the witnesses, Cochepaille, Brevet, and Chenildieu.

'Do you not recognise me?' said he.

All three stood confounded, and indicated by a shake of the head that they did not know him. Cochepaille, intimidated, gave the military salute. Monsieur Madeleine turned towards the jurors and court, and said in a mild voice:

'Gentlemen of the jury, release the accused. Your honour, order my arrest. He is not the man whom you seek; it is I. I am Jean Valjean.'

Not a breath stirred. To the first commotion of astonishment had succeeded a sepulchral silence. That species of religious awe was felt in the hall which thrills the multitude at the accomplishment of a grand action.

Nevertheless, the face of the judge was marked with sympathy and sadness; he exchanged glances with the prosecuting attorney, and a few whispered words with the assistant judges. He turned to the spectators and asked in a tone which was understood by all:

'Is there a physician here?'

The prosecuting attorney continued:

'Gentlemen of the jury, the strange and unexpected incident which disturbs the audience, inspires us, as well as yourselves, with a feeling which we have no need to express. You all know, at least by reputation, the honourable Monsieur Madeleine, Mayor of M— sur M—. If there be a physician in the audience, we unite with his honour the judge in entreating him to be kind enough to lend his assistance to Monsieur Madeleine and conduct him to his residence.'

Monsieur Madeleine did not permit the prosecuting attorney to finish, but interrupted him with a tone full of gentleness and authority. These are the words he uttered; we give them literally, as they were written down immediately after the trial, by one of the witnesses of the scene – as they still ring in the ears of those who heard them, now nearly forty years ago.

'I thank you, Monsieur Prosecuting Attorney, but I am not mad. You shall see. You were on the point of committing a great mistake; release that man. I am accomplishing a duty; I am the unhappy convict. I am the only one who sees clearly here, and I tell you the truth. What I do at this moment, God beholds from on high, and that is sufficient. You can take me, since I am here. Nevertheless, I have done my best. I have disguised myself under another name, I have become rich, I have become a mayor, I have desired to enter again among honest men. It seems that this cannot be. In short, there are many things which I cannot tell. I shall not relate to you the story of my life: someday you will know it. I did rob Monseigneur the Bishop – that is true; I did rob Petit Gervais – that is true. They were right in telling you that Jean Valjean was a wicked wretch. But all the blame may not belong to him. Listen, your honours; a man so abased as I, has no remonstrance to make with Providence, nor advice to give to society; but, mark you, the infamy from which I have sought to rise is pernicious to men. The galleys make the galley-slave. Receive this in kindness, if you will. Before the galleys, I was a poor peasant, unintelligent, a species of idiot; the galleys changed me. I was stupid, I became wicked; I was a log, I became a firebrand. Later, I was saved by indulgence and kindness, as I had been lost by severity. But, pardon, you cannot comprehend what I say. You will find in my house, among the ashes of the fireplace, the forty-sous piece of which, seven years ago, I robbed Petit Gervais. I have nothing more to add. Take me. Great God! the prosecuting attorney shakes his head. You say, "Monsieur Madeleine has gone mad;" you do not believe me. This is hard to be borne. Do not condemn that man, at least. What! these men do not know me! Would that Javert were here. He would recognise me!'

Nothing could express the kindly yet terrible melancholy of the tone which accompanied these words.

He turned to the three convicts:

'Well! I recognise you, Brevet, do you remember – '

He paused, hesitated a moment, and said:

'Do you remember those checkered, knit suspenders that you had in the galleys?'

Brevet started as if struck with surprise, and gazed wildly at him from head to foot. He continued:

'Chenildieu, surnamed by yourself Je-nie-Dieu, the whole of your left shoulder has been burned deeply, from laying it one day on a chafing dish full of embers, to efface the three letters T. F. P., which yet are still to be seen there. Answer me, is this true?'

'It is true!' said Chenildieu.

He turned to Cochepaille:

'Cochepaille, you have on your left arm, near where you have been bled, a date put in blue letters with burnt powder. It is the date of the landing of the emperor at Cannes, *March 1st, 1815.* Lift up your sleeve.'

Cochepaille lifted up his sleeve: all eyes around him were turned to his naked arm. A gendarme brought a lamp; the date was there.

The unhappy man turned towards the audience and the court with a smile, the thought of which still rends the hearts of those who witnessed it. It was the smile of triumph; it was also the smile of despair.

'You see clearly,' said he, 'that I am Jean Valjean.'

There were no longer either judges, or accusers, or gendarmes in the hall; there were only fixed eyes and beating hearts. Nobody remembered longer the part which he had to play; the prosecuting attorney forgot that he was there to prosecute, the judge that he was there to preside, the counsel for the defence that he was there to defend. Strange to say no question was put, no authority intervened. It is the peculiarity of sublime spectacles that they take possession of every soul, and make of every witness a spectator. Nobody, perhaps, was positively conscious of what he experienced; and, undoubtedly, nobody said to himself that he there beheld the effulgence of a great light, yet all felt dazzled at heart.

It was evident that Jean Valjean was before their eyes. That fact shone forth. The appearance of this man had been enough fully to clear up the case, so obscure a moment before. Without need of any further explanation, the multitude, as by a sort of electric revelation, comprehended instantly, and at a single glance, this simple and magnificent story of a man giving himself up that another might not be condemned in his place. The details, the hesitation, the slight reluctance possible were lost in this immense, luminous fact.

It was an impression which quickly passed over, but for the moment it was irresistible.

'I will not disturb the proceeding further,' continued Jean Valjean. 'I am going, since I am not arrested. I have many things to do. Monsieur the prosecuting attorney knows where I am going, and will have me arrested when he chooses.'

He walked towards the outer door. Not a voice was raised, not an arm stretched out to prevent him. All stood aside. There was at this moment an indescribable divinity within him which makes the multitudes fall back and make way before a man. He passed through the throng with slow steps. It was never known who opened the door, but it is certain that the door was open when he came to it. On reaching it he turned and said:

'Monsieur the Prosecuting Attorney, I remain at your disposal.'

He then addressed himself to the auditory.

'You all, all who are here, think me worthy of pity, do you not? Great God! when I think of what I have been on the point of doing, I think myself worthy of envy. Still, would that all this had not happened!'

He went out, and the door closed as it had opened, for those who do deeds sovereignly great are always sure of being served by somebody in the multitude.

Less than an hour afterwards, the verdict of the jury discharged from all accusation the said Champmathieu; and Champmathieu, set at liberty forthwith, went his way stupefied, thinking all men mad, and understanding nothing of this vision.

BOOK 8: COUNTERSTROKE

1. *In what mirror M. Madeleine looks at his hair*

DAY BEGAN TO DAWN. Fantine had had a feverish and sleepless night, yet full of happy visions; she fell asleep at daybreak. Sister Simplice, who had watched with her, took advantage of this slumber to go and prepare a new potion of quinine. The good sister had been for a few moments in the laboratory of the infirmary, bending over her vials and drugs, looking at them very closely on account of the mist which the dawn casts over all objects, when suddenly she turned her head, and uttered a faint cry. M. Madeleine stood before her. He had just come in silently.

'You, Monsieur the Mayor!' she exclaimed.

'How is the poor woman?' he answered in a low voice.

'Better just now. But we have been very anxious indeed.'

She explained what had happened, that Fantine had been very ill the night before, but was now better, because she believed that the mayor had gone to Montfermeil for her child. The sister dared not question the mayor, but she saw clearly from his manner that he had not come from that place.

'That is well,' said he. 'You did right not to deceive her.'

'Yes,' returned the sister, 'but now, Monsieur the Mayor, when she sees you without her child, what shall we tell her?'

He reflected for a moment, then said:

'God will inspire us.'

'But, we cannot tell her a lie,' murmured the sister, in a smothered tone.

The broad daylight streamed into the room, and lighted up the face of M. Madeleine.

The sister happened to raise her eyes.

'O God, monsieur,' she exclaimed. 'What has befallen you? Your hair is all white!'

'White!' said he.

Sister Simplice had no mirror; she rummaged in a case of instruments, and found a little glass which the physician of the infirmary used to discover whether the breath had left the body of a patient. M. Madeleine took the glass, looked at his hair in it, and said, 'Indeed!'

He spoke the word with indifference, as if thinking of something else.

The sister felt chilled by an unknown something, of which she caught a glimpse in all this.

He asked: 'Can I see her?'

'Will not Monsieur the Mayor bring back her child?' asked the sister, scarcely daring to venture a question.

'Certainly, but two or three days are necessary.'

'If she does not see Monsieur the Mayor here,' continued the sister timidly, 'she will not know that he has returned; it will be easy for her to have patience, and when the child comes, she will think naturally that Monsieur the Mayor has just arrived with her. Then we will not have to tell her a falsehood.'

Monsieur Madeleine seemed to reflect for a few moments, then said with his calm gravity:

'No, my sister, I must see her. Perhaps I have not much time.'

The nun did not seem to notice this 'perhaps', which gave an obscure and singular significance to the words of Monsieur the Mayor. She answered, lowering her eyes and voice respectfully:

'In that case, she is asleep, but monsieur can go in.'

He made a few remarks about a door that shut with difficulty, the noise of which might awaken the sick woman; then entered the chamber of Fantine, approached her bed, and opened the curtains. She was sleeping. Her breath came from her chest with that tragic sound which is peculiar to these diseases, and which rends the heart of unhappy mothers, watching the slumbers of their fated children. But this laboured respiration scarcely disturbed an ineffable serenity, which overshadowed her countenance, and transfigured her in her sleep. Her pallor had become whiteness, and her cheeks were glowing. Her long, fair eyelashes, the only beauty left to her of her maidenhood and youth, quivered as they lay closed upon her cheek. Her whole person trembled as if with the fluttering of wings which were felt, but could not be seen, and which seemed about to unfold and bear her away. To see her thus, no one could have believed that her life was despaired of. She looked more as if about to soar away than to die.

The stem, when the hand is stretched out to pluck the flower, quivers, and seems at once to shrink back, and present itself. The human body has something of this trepidation at the moment when the mysterious fingers of death are about to gather the soul.

Monsieur Madeleine remained for some time motionless near the bed, looking by turns at the patient and the crucifix, as he had done two months before, on the day when he came for the first time to see her in this asylum. They were still there, both in the same attitude, she sleeping, he praying; only now, after these two months had rolled away, her hair was grey and his was white.

The sister had not entered with him. He stood by the bed, with his finger on his lips, as if there were someone in the room to silence. She opened her eyes, saw him, and said tranquilly, with a smile:

'And Cosette?'

2. *Fantine happy*

SHE DID NOT START with surprise or joy, she was joy itself. The simple question: 'And Cosette?' was asked with such deep faith, with so much certainty, with so complete an absence of disquiet or doubt, that he could find no word in reply. She continued:

'I knew that you were there; I was asleep, but I saw you. I have seen you for a long time; I have followed you with my eyes the whole night. You were in a halo of glory, and all manner of celestial forms were hovering around you!'

He raised his eyes towards the crucifix.

'But tell me, where is Cosette?' she resumed. 'Why not put her on my bed that I might see her the instant I woke?'

He answered something mechanically, which he could never afterwards recall.

Happily, the physician had come and had been apprised of this. He came to the aid of M. Madeleine.

'My child,' said he, 'be calm, your daughter is here.'

The eyes of Fantine beamed with joy, and lighted up her whole countenance. She clasped her hands with an expression full of the most violent and most gentle entreaty:

'Oh!' she exclaimed, 'bring her to me!'

Touching illusion of the mother; Cosette was still to her a little child to be carried in the arms.

'Not yet,' continued the physician, 'not at this moment. You have some fever still. The sight of your child will agitate you, and make you worse. We must cure you first.'

She interrupted him impetuously.

'But I am cured! I tell you I am cured! Is this physician a fool? I will see my child!'

'You see how you are carried away!' said the physician. 'So long as you are in this state, I cannot let you have your child. It is not enough to see her, you must live for her. When you are reasonable, I will bring her to you myself.'

The poor mother bowed her head.

'Sir, I ask your pardon. I sincerely ask your pardon. Once I would not have spoken as I have now, but so many misfortunes have befallen me that sometimes I do not know what I am saying. I understand, you fear excitement; I will wait as long as you wish, but I am sure that it will not harm me to see my daughter. I see her now, I have not taken my eyes from her since last night. Let them bring her to me now, and I will just speak to her very gently. That is all. Is it not very natural that I should wish to see my child, when they have been to Montfermeil on purpose to bring her to me? I am not angry. I know that I am going to be very happy. All night, I saw figures in white, smiling on me. As soon as the doctor pleases, he can bring Cosette. My fever is gone, for I am cured; I feel that there is scarcely anything the matter with me; but I will act as if I were ill, and do not stir so as to please the ladies here. When they see that I am calm, they will say: "You must give her the child." '

M. Madeleine was sitting in a chair by the side of the bed. She turned towards him, and made visible efforts to appear calm and 'very good', as she said, in that weakness of disease which resembles childhood, so that, seeing her so peaceful, there should be no objection to bringing her Cosette. Nevertheless, although restraining herself, she could not help addressing a thousand questions to M. Madeleine.

'Did you have a pleasant journey, Monsieur the Mayor? Oh! how good you have been to go for her! Tell me only how she is! Did she bear the journey well? Ah! she will not know me. In all this time, she has forgotten me, poor kitten! Children have no memory. They are like birds. Today they see one thing, and tomorrow another, and remember nothing. Tell me only, were her clothes clean? Did those Thénardiers keep her neat? How did they feed her? Oh, if you knew how I have suffered in asking myself all these things in the time of my wretchedness! Now, it is past. I am happy. Oh! how I want to see her! Monsieur the Mayor, did you think her pretty? Is not my daughter beautiful? You must have been very cold in the diligence? Could they not bring her here for one little moment? they might take her away immediately. Say! you are master here, are you willing?'

He took her hand. 'Cosette is beautiful,' said he. 'Cosette is well; you shall see her soon, but be quiet. You talk too fast; and then you throw your arms out of bed, which makes you cough.'

In fact, coughing fits interrupted Fantine at almost every word.

She did not murmur; she feared that by too eager entreaties she had weakened the confidence which she wished to inspire, and began to talk about indifferent subjects.

'Montfermeil is a pretty place, is it not? In summer people go there on pleasure parties. Do the Thénardiers do a good business? Not many great people pass through that country. Their inn is a kind of chop-house.'

Monsieur Madeleine still held her hand and looked at her with anxiety. It was evident that he had come to tell her things before which his mind now hesitated. The physician had made his visit and retired. Sister Simplice alone remained with them.

But in the midst of the silence, Fantine cried out:

'I hear her! Oh, darling! I hear her!'

There was a child playing in the court – the child of the portress or some workwoman. It was one of those chances which are always met with, and which seem to make part of the mysterious representation of tragic events. The child, which was a little girl, was running up and down to keep herself warm, singing and laughing in a loud voice. Alas! with what are not the plays of children mingled! Fantine had heard this little girl singing.

'Oh!' said she, 'it is my Cosette! I know her voice!'

The child departed as she had come, and the voice died away. Fantine listened for some time. A shadow came over her face, and Monsieur Madeleine heard her whisper, 'How wicked it is of that doctor not to let me see my child! That man has a bad face!'

But yet her happy train of thought returned. With her head on the pillow she continued to talk to herself. 'How happy we shall be! We will have a little garden in the first place; Monsieur Madeleine has promised it to me. My child will play in the garden. She must know her letters now. I will teach her to spell. She will chase the butterflies in the grass, and I will watch her. Then there will be her first communion. Ah! when will her first communion be?'

She began to count on her fingers.

'One, two, three, four. She is seven years old. In five years. She will have a white veil and open-worked stockings, and will look like a little lady. Oh, my good sister, you do not know how foolish I am; here I am thinking of my child's first communion!'

And she began to laugh.

He had let go the hand of Fantine. He listened to the words as one listens to the wind that blows, his eyes on the ground, and his mind plunged into unfathomable reflections. Suddenly she ceased speaking, and raised her head mechanically. Fantine had become appalling.

She did not speak; she did not breathe; she half-raised herself in the bed, the covering fell from her emaciated shoulders; her countenance, radiant a moment before, became livid, and her eyes, dilated with terror, seemed to fasten on something before her at the other end of the room.

'Good God!' exclaimed he. 'What is the matter, Fantine?'

She did not answer; she did not take her eyes from the object which she seemed to see, but touched his arm with one hand, and with the other made a sign to him to look behind him.

He turned, and saw Javert.

3. Javert satisfied

LET US SEE what had happened.

The half-hour after midnight was striking when M. Madeleine left the hall of the Arras Assizes. He had returned to his inn just in time to take the mail-coach, in which it will be remembered he had retained his seat. A little before six in the morning he had reached M— sur M—, where his first care had been to post his letter to M. Laffitte, then go to the infirmary and visit Fantine.

Meanwhile he had scarcely left the hall of the Court of Assizes when the prosecuting attorney, recovering from his first shock, addressed the court, deploring the insanity of the honourable Mayor of M— sur M—, declaring that his convictions were in no wise modified by this singular incident, which would be explained hereafter, and demanding the conviction of this Champmathieu, who was evidently the real Jean Valjean. The persistence of the prosecuting attorney was visibly in contradiction to the sentiment of all – the public, the court, and the jury. The counsel for the defence had little difficulty in answering this harangue, and establishing that, in consequence of the revelations of M. Madeleine – that is, of the real Jean Valjean – the aspect of the case was changed, entirely changed, from top to bottom, and that the jury now had before them an innocent man. The counsel drew from this a few passionate appeals, unfortunately not very new, in regard to judicial errors, etc., etc.; the judge, in his summing up, sided with the defence; and the jury, after a few moments' consultation, acquitted Champmathieu.

But yet the prosecuting attorney must have a Jean Valjean, and having lost Champmathieu he took Madeleine.

Immediately upon the discharge of Champmathieu the prosecuting attorney closeted himself with the judge. The subject of their conference was, 'Of the

necessity of the arrest of the person of Monsieur the Mayor of M— sur M—.'
This sentence, in which there is a great deal of *of*, is the prosecuting attorney's,
written by his own hand, on the minutes of his report to the Attorney-general.

The first sensation being over, the judge made few objections. Justice must
take its course. Then to confess the truth, although the judge was a kind man,
and really intelligent, he was at the same time a strong, almost a zealous royalist,
and had been shocked when the mayor of M— sur M—, in speaking of the
debarkation at Cannes, said the *Emperor*, instead of *Buonaparte*.

The order of arrest was therefore granted. The prosecuting attorney sent it to
M— sur M— by a courier, at full speed, to police inspector Javert.

It will be remembered that Javert had returned to M— sur M— immediately
after giving his testimony.

Javert was just rising when the courier brought him the warrant and order of
arrest.

The courier was himself a policeman, and an intelligent man; who, in three
words, acquainted Javert with what had happened at Arras.

The order of arrest, signed by the prosecuting attorney, was couched in these
terms:

'Inspector Javert will seize the body of Sieur Madeleine, Mayor of M— sur
M—, who has this day been identified in court as the discharged convict Jean
Valjean.'

One who did not know Javert, on seeing him as he entered the hall of the
infirmary, could have divined nothing of what was going on, and would have
thought his manner the most natural imaginable. He was cool, calm, grave; his
grey hair lay perfectly smooth over his temples, and he had ascended the
stairway with his customary deliberation. But one who knew him thoroughly
and examined him with attention, would have shuddered. The buckle of his
leather cravat, instead of being on the back of his neck, was under his left ear.
This denoted an unheard-of agitation.

Javert was a complete character, without a wrinkle in his duty or his uniform,
methodical with villains, rigid with the buttons of his coat.

For him to misplace the buckle of his cravat, he must have received one of
those shocks which may well be the earthquakes of the soul.

He came unostentatiously, had taken a corporal and four soldiers from a
station-house near-by, had left the soldiers in the court, and had been shown to
Fantine's chamber by the portress, without suspicion, accustomed as she was to
see armed men asking for the mayor.

On reaching the room of Fantine, Javert turned the key, pushed open the
door with the gentleness of a sick-nurse, or a police spy, and entered.

Properly speaking, he did not enter. He remained standing in the half-opened
door, his hat on his head, and his left hand in his overcoat, which was buttoned
to the chin. In the bend of his elbow might be seen the leaden head of his
enormous cane, which disappeared behind him.

He remained thus for nearly a minute, unperceived. Suddenly, Fantine raised
her eyes, saw him, and caused Monsieur Madeleine to turn round.

At the moment when the glance of Madeleine encountered that of Javert,
Javert, without stirring, without moving, without approaching, became terrible.
No human feeling can ever be so appalling as joy.

It was the face of a demon who had again found his victim.

The certainty that he had caught Jean Valjean at last brought forth upon his countenance all that was in his soul. The disturbed depths rose to the surface. The humiliation of having lost the scent for a little while, of having been mistaken for a few moments concerning Champmathieu, was lost in the pride of having divined so well at first, and having so long retained a true instinct. The satisfaction of Javert shone forth in his commanding attitude. The deformity of triumph spread over his narrow forehead. It was the fullest development of horror that a gratified face can show.

Javert was at this moment in heaven. Without clearly defining his own feelings, yet notwithstanding with a confused intuition of his necessity and his success, he, Javert, personified justice, light, and truth, in their celestial function as destroyers of evil. He was surrounded and supported by infinite depths of authority, reason, precedent, legal conscience, the vengeance of the law, all the stars in the firmament; he protected order, he hurled forth the thunder of the law, he avenged society, he lent aid to the absolute; he stood erect in a halo of glory; there was in his victory a reminder of defiance and of combat; standing haughty, resplendent, he displayed in full glory the superhuman beastliness of a ferocious archangel; the fearful shadow of the deed which he was accomplishing, made visible in his clenched fist, the uncertain flashes of the social sword; happy and indignant, he had set his heel on crime, vice, rebellion, perdition, and hell, he was radiant, exterminating, smiling; there was an incontestable grandeur in this monstrous St Michael.

Javert, though hideous, was not ignoble.

Probity, sincerity, candour, conviction, the idea of duty, are things which, mistaken, may become hideous, but which, even though hideous, remain great; their majesty, peculiar to the human conscience, continues in all their horror; they are virtues with a single vice – error. The pitiless, sincere joy of a fanatic in an act of atrocity preserves an indescribably mournful radiance which inspires us with veneration. Without suspecting it, Javert, in his fear-inspiring happiness, was pitiable, like every ignorant man who wins a triumph. Nothing could be more painful and terrible than this face, which revealed what we may call all the evil of good.

4. *Authority resumes its sway*

FANTINE had not seen Javert since the day the mayor had wrested her from him. Her sick brain accounted for nothing, only she was sure that he had come for her. She could not endure this hideous face, she felt as if she were dying, she hid her face with both hands, and shrieked in anguish:

'Monsieur Madeleine, save me!'

Jean Valjean, we shall call him by no other name henceforth, had risen. He said to Fantine in his gentlest and calmest tone:

'Be composed; it is not for you that he comes.'

He then turned to Javert and said:

'I know what you want.'

Javert answered:

'Hurry along.'

There was in the manner in which these two words were uttered, an inexpressible something which reminded you of a wild beast and of a madman. Javert did not say 'Hurry along!' he said: 'Hurr-'long!' No orthography can express the tone in which this was pronounced; it ceased to be human speech; it was a howl.

He did not go through the usual ceremony; he made no words; he showed no warrant. To him Jean Valjean was a sort of mysterious and intangible antagonist, a shadowy wrestler with whom he had been struggling for five years, without being able to throw him. This arrest was not a beginning, but an end. He only said: 'Hurry along!'

While speaking thus, he did not stir a step, but cast upon Jean Valjean a look like a noose, with which he was accustomed to draw the wretched to him by force.

It was the same look which Fantine had felt penetrate to the very marrow of her bones, two months before.

At the exclamation of Javert, Fantine had opened her eyes again. But the mayor was there, what could she fear?

Javert advanced to the middle of the chamber, exclaiming:

'Hey, there; are you coming?'

The unhappy woman looked around her. There was no one but the nun and the mayor. To whom could this contemptuous familiarity be addressed? To herself alone. She shuddered.

Then she saw a mysterious thing, so mysterious that its like had never appeared to her in the darkest delirium of fever.

She saw the spy Javert seize Monsieur the Mayor by the collar; she saw Monsieur the Mayor bow his head. The world seemed vanishing before her sight.

Javert, in fact, had taken Jean Valjean by the collar.

'Monsieur the Mayor!' cried Fantine.

Javert burst into a horrid laugh, displaying all his teeth.

'There is no Monsieur the Mayor here any longer!' said he.

Jean Valjean did not attempt to disturb the hand which grasped the collar of his coat. He said:

'Javert – '

Javert interrupted him: 'Call me Monsieur the Inspector!'

'Monsieur,' continued Jean Valjean, 'I would like to speak a word with you in private.'

'Aloud, speak aloud,' said Javert, 'people speak aloud to me.'

Jean Valjean went on, lowering his voice.

'It is a request that I have to make of you – '

'I tell you to speak aloud.'

'But this should not be heard by anyone but yourself.'

'What is that to me? I will not listen.'

Jean Valjean turned to him and said rapidly and in a very low tone;

'Give me three days! Three days to go for the child of this unhappy woman! I will pay whatever is necessary. You shall accompany me if you like.'

'Are you laughing at me!' cried Javert. 'Hey! I did not think you so stupid! You ask for three days to get away, and tell me that you are going for this girl's child! Ha, ha, that's good! That is good!'

Fantine shivered.

'My child!' she exclaimed, 'going for my child! Then she is not here! Sister, tell me, where is Cosette? I want my child! Monsieur Madeleine, Monsieur the Mayor!'

Javert stamped his foot.

'There is the other now! Hold your tongue, hussy! Miserable country, where galley slaves are magistrates and women of the town are nursed like countesses! Ha, but all this will be changed; it was time!'

He gazed steadily at Fantine, and added, grasping anew the cravat, shirt, and coat collar of Jean Valjean:

'I tell you that there is no Monsieur Madeleine, and that there is no Monsieur the Mayor. There is a robber, there is a brigand, there is a convict called Jean Valjean, and I have got him! That is what there is!'

Fantine started upright, supporting herself by her rigid arms and hands; she looked at Jean Valjean, then at Javert, and then at the nun; she opened her mouth as if to speak; a rattle came from her throat, her teeth stuck together, she stretched out her arms in anguish, convulsively opening her hands, and groping about her like one who is drowning; then sank suddenly back upon the pillow.

Her head struck the head of the bed and fell forward on her breast, the mouth gaping, the eyes open and glazed.

She was dead.

Jean Valjean put his hand on that of Javert which held him, and opened it as he would have opened the hand of a child; then he said:

'You have killed this woman.'

'Have done with this!' cried Javert, furious, 'I am not here to listen to sermons; save all that; the guard is below; come right along, or the handcuffs!'

There stood in a corner of the room an old iron bedstead in a dilapidated condition, which the sisters used as a camp-bed when they watched. Jean Valjean went to the bed, wrenched out the rickety head bar – a thing easy for muscles like his – in the twinkling of an eye, and with the bar in his clenched fist, looked at Javert. Javert recoiled towards the door.

Jean Valjean, his iron bar in hand, walked slowly towards the bed of Fantine. On reaching it, he turned and said to Javert in a voice that could scarcely be heard:

'I advise you not to disturb me now.'

Nothing is more certain than that Javert trembled.

He had an idea of calling the guard, but Jean Valjean might profit by his absence to escape. He remained therefore, grasped the bottom of his cane, and leaned against the framework of the door without taking his eyes from Jean Valjean.

Jean Valjean rested his elbow upon the post, and his head upon his hand, and gazed at Fantine, stretched motionless before him. He remained thus, mute and absorbed, evidently lost to everything of this life. His countenance and attitude bespoke nothing but inexpressible pity.

After a few moments' reverie, he bent down to Fantine, and addressed her in a whisper.

What did he say? What could this condemned man say to this dead woman? What were these words? They were heard by none on earth. Did the dead woman hear them? There are touching illusions which perhaps are sublime realities. One thing is beyond doubt; Sister Simplice, the only witness of what passed, has often related that, at the moment when Jean Valjean whispered in the ear of Fantine, she distinctly saw an ineffable smile beam on those pale lips and in those dim eyes, full of the wonder of the tomb.

Jean Valjean took Fantine's head in his hands and arranged it on the pillow, as a mother would have done for her child, then fastened the string of her night-dress, and replaced her hair beneath her cap. This done, he closed her eyes.

The face of Fantine, at this instant, seemed strangely illumined.

Death is the entrance into the great light.

Fantine's hand hung over the side of the bed. Jean Valjean knelt before this hand, raised it gently, and kissed it.

Then he rose, and, turning to Javert, said:

'Now, I am at your disposal.'

5. A fitting tomb

JAVERT put Jean Valjean in the city prison.

The arrest of Monsieur Madeleine produced a sensation, or rather an extraordinary commotion, at M— sur M—. We are sorry not to be able to disguise the fact that, on this single sentence, *he was a galley slave*, almost everybody abandoned him. In less than two hours, all the good he had done was forgotten, and he was 'nothing but a galley slave'. It is just to say that the details of the scene at Arras were not yet known. All day long, conversations like this were heard in every part of the town: 'Don't you know, he was a discharged convict!' 'He! Who?' 'The mayor.' 'Bah! Monsieur Madeleine.' 'Yes.' 'Indeed!' 'His name was not Madeleine; he has a horrid name, Béjean, Bojean, Bonjean!' 'Oh! bless me!' 'He has been arrested.' 'Arrested!' 'In prison, in the city prison to await his removal.' 'His removal! where will he be taken?' 'To the Court of Assizes for a highway robbery that he once committed.' 'Well! I always did suspect him. The man was too good, too perfect, too sweet. He refused fees, and gave sous to every little blackguard he met. I always thought that there must be something bad at the bottom of all this.'

'The drawing-rooms', above all, were entirely of this opinion.

An old lady, a subscriber to the *Drapeau Blanc*,[26] made this remark, the depth of which it is almost impossible to fathom:

'I am not sorry for it. That will teach the Bonapartists!'

In this manner the phantom which had been called Monsieur Madeleine was dissipated at M— sur M—. Three or four persons alone in the whole city remained faithful to his memory. The old portress who had been his servant was among the number.

On the evening of this same day, the worthy old woman was sitting in her lodge, still quite bewildered and sunk in sad reflections. The factory had been closed all day, the carriage doors were bolted, the street was deserted. There was no one in the house but the two nuns, Sister Perpétue and Sister Simplice, who were watching the corpse of Fantine.

Towards the time when Monsieur Madeleine had been accustomed to return, the honest portress rose mechanically, took the key of his room from a drawer, with the taper-stand that he used at night to light himself up the stairs, then hung the key on a nail from which he had been in the habit of taking it, and placed the taper-stand by its side, as if she were expecting him. She then seated herself again in her chair, and resumed her reflections. The poor old woman had done all this without being conscious of it.

More than two hours had elapsed when she started from her reverie and exclaimed, 'Why, bless me! I have hung his key on the nail!'

Just then, the window of her box opened, a hand passed through the opening, took the key and stand, and lighted the taper at the candle which was burning.

The portress raised her eyes; she was transfixed with astonishment; a cry rose to her lips, but she could not give it utterance.

She knew the hand, the arm, the coat-sleeve.

It was M. Madeleine.

She was speechless for some seconds, thunderstruck, as she said herself, afterwards, in giving her account of the affair.

'My God! Monsieur Mayor!' she exclaimed, 'I thought you were – '

She stopped; the end of her sentence would not have been respectful to the beginning. To her, Jean Valjean was still Monsieur the Mayor.

He completed her thought.

'In prison,' said he. 'I was there; I broke a bar from a window, let myself fall from the top of a roof, and here I am. I am going to my room; go for Sister Simplice. She is doubtless beside this poor woman.'

The old servant hastily obeyed.

He gave her no caution, very sure she would guard him better than he would guard himself.

It has never been known how he had succeeded in gaining entrance into the courtyard without opening the carriage-door. He had, and always carried about him, a pass-key which opened a little side door, but he must have been searched, and this taken from him. This point is not yet cleared up.

He ascended the staircase which led to his room. On reaching the top, he left his taper stand on the upper stair, opened his door with little noise, felt his way to the window and closed the shutter, then came back, took his taper, and went into the chamber.

The precaution was not useless; it will be remembered that his window could be seen from the street.

He cast a glance about him, over his table, his chair, his bed, which had not been slept in for three days. There remained no trace of the disorder of the night before the last. The portress had 'put the room to rights'. Only, she had picked up from the ashes, and laid in order on the table, the ends of the loaded club, and the forty-sous piece, blackened by the fire.

He took a sheet of paper and wrote: *These are the ends of my loaded club and the forty-sous piece stolen from Petit Gervais, of which I spoke at the Court of Assizes;* then placed the two bits of iron and the piece of silver on the sheet in such a way that it would be the first thing perceived on entering the room. He took from a wardrobe an old shirt which he tore into several pieces and in which he packed the two silver candlesticks. In all this there was neither haste nor agitation. And even while packing the bishop's candlesticks, he was eating a piece of black bread. It was probably prison-bread, which he had brought away in escaping.

This has been established by crumbs of bread found on the floor of the room, when the court afterwards ordered a search.

Two gentle taps were heard at the door.

'Come in,' said he.

It was Sister Simplice.

She was pale, her eyes were red, and the candle which she held trembled in her hand. The shocks of destiny have this peculiarity; however subdued or disciplined our feelings may be, they draw out the human nature from the depths of our souls, and compel us to exhibit it to others. In the agitation of this day the nun had again become a woman. She had wept, and she was trembling.

Jean Valjean had written a few lines on a piece of paper, which he handed to the nun, saying: 'Sister, you will give this to the curé.'

The paper was not folded. She cast her eyes on it.

'You may read it,' said he.

She read: 'I beg Monsieur the Curé to take charge of all that I leave here. He will please defray therefrom the expenses of my trial, and of the burial of the woman who died this morning. The remainder is for the poor.'

The sister attempted to speak, but could scarcely stammer out a few inarticulate sounds. She succeeded, however, in saying:

'Does not Monsieur the Mayor wish to see this poor unfortunate again for the last time?'

'No,' said he, 'I am pursued; I should only be arrested in her chamber; it would disturb her.'

He had scarcely finished when there was a loud noise on the staircase. They heard a tumult of steps ascending, and the old portress exclaiming in her loudest and most piercing tones:

'My good sir, I swear to you in the name of God, that nobody has come in here the whole day, and the whole evening; that I have not even once left my door!'

A man replied: 'But yet, there is a light in this room.'

They recognised the voice of Javert.

The chamber was so arranged that the door in opening covered the corner of the wall to the right. Jean Valjean blew out the taper, and placed himself in this corner.

Sister Simplice fell on her knees near the table.

The door opened.

Javert entered.

The whispering of several men, and the protestations of the portress were heard in the hall.

The nun did not raise her eyes. She was praying.

The candle was on the mantel, and gave but a dim light.

Javert perceived the sister, and stopped abashed.

It will be remembered that the very foundation of Javert, his element, the medium in which he breathed, was veneration for all authority. He was perfectly homogeneous, and admitted of no objection, or abridgement. To him, be it understood, ecclesiastical authority was the highest of all; he was devout, superficial, and correct, upon this point as upon all others. In his eyes, a priest was a spirit who was never mistaken, a nun was a being who never sinned. They were souls walled in from this world, with a single door which never opened but for the exit of truth.

On perceiving the sister, his first impulse was to retire.

But there was also another duty which held him, and which urged him imperiously in the opposite direction. His second impulse was to remain, and to venture at least one question.

This was the Sister Simplice, who had never lied in her life. Javert knew this, and venerated her especially on account of it.

'Sister,' said he, 'are you alone in this room?'

There was a fearful instant during which the poor portress felt her limbs falter beneath her. The sister raised her eyes, and replied:

'Yes.'

Then continued Javert – 'Excuse me if I persist, it is my duty – you have not seen this evening a person, a man – he has escaped, and we are in search of him – Jean Valjean – you have not seen him?'

The sister answered – 'No.'

She lied. Two lies in succession, one upon another, without hesitation, quickly, as if she were an adept in it.

'Your pardon!' said Javert, and he withdrew, bowing reverently.

Oh, holy maiden! for many years thou hast been no more in this world; thou hast joined the sisters, the virgins, and thy brethren, the angels, in glory; may this falsehood be remembered to thee in Paradise.

The affirmation of the sister was to Javert something so decisive that he did not even notice the singularity of this taper, just blown out, and smoking on the table.

An hour afterwards, a man was walking rapidly in the darkness beneath the trees from M— sur M— in the direction of Paris. This man was Jean Valjean. It has been established, by the testimony of two or three wagoners who met him, that he carried a bundle, and was dressed in a blouse. Where did he get this blouse? It was never known. Nevertheless, an old artisan had died in the infirmary of the factory a few days before, leaving nothing but his blouse. This might have been the one.

A last word in regard to Fantine.

We have all one mother – the earth. Fantine was restored to this mother.

The curé thought best, and did well perhaps, to reserve out of what Jean Valjean had left, the largest amount possible for the poor. After all, who were in question? – a convict and a woman of the town. This was why he simplified the burial of Fantine, and reduced it to that bare necessity called the Potter's Field.

And so Fantine was buried in the common grave of the cemetery, which is for everybody and for all, and in which the poor are lost. Happily, God knows where to find the soul. Fantine was laid away in the darkness with bodies which had no name; she suffered the promiscuity of dust. She was thrown into the public pit. Her tomb was like her bed.

PART TWO: COSETTE

1. *What you meet in coming from Nivelles*

ON A BEAUTIFUL MORNING in May, last year (1861), a traveller, he who tells this story, was journeying from Nivelles towards La Hulpe. He travelled a-foot. He was following, between two rows of trees, a broad road, undulating over hills, which, one after another, upheave it and let it fall again, like enormous waves. He had passed Lillois and Bois-Seigneur-Isaac. He saw to the west the slated steeple of Braine-l'Alleud, which has the form of an inverted vase. He had just passed a wood upon a hill, and at the corner of a crossroad, beside a sort of worm-eaten signpost, bearing the inscription – *Old Toll-Gate, No. 4* – a tavern with this sign – *The Four Winds. Echaleau, Private Café.*

Half a mile from this tavern, he reached the bottom of a little valley, where a stream flowed beneath an arch in the embankment of the road. The cluster of trees, thin-sown but very green, which fills the vale on one side of the road, on the other spreads out into meadows, and sweeps away in graceful disorder towards Braine l'Alleud.

At this point there was at the right, and immediately on the road, an inn, with a four-wheeled cart before the door, a great bundle of hop-poles, a plough, a pile of dry brush near a quickset hedge, some lime which was smoking in a square hole in the ground, and a ladder lying along an old shed with mangers for straw. A young girl was pulling weeds in a field, where a large green poster, probably of a travelling show at some annual fair, fluttered in the wind. At the corner of the inn, beside a pond, in which a flotilla of ducks was navigating, a difficult foot-path lost itself in the shrubbery. The traveller took this path.

At the end of a hundred paces, passing a wall of the fifteenth century, surmounted by a sharp gable of crossed bricks, he found himself opposite a great arched stone doorway, with rectilinear impost, in the solemn style of Louis XIV, and plain medallions on the sides. Over the entrance was a severe façade, and a wall perpendicular to the façade almost touched the doorway, flanking it at an abrupt right angle. On the meadow before the door lay three harrows, through which were blooming, as best they could, all the flowers of May. The doorway was closed. It was shut by two decrepit folding-doors, decorated with an old rusty knocker.

The sunshine was enchanting; the branches of the trees had that gentle tremulousness of the month of May which seems to come from the birds' nests rather than the wind. A spruce little bird, probably in love, was singing desperately in a tall tree.

The traveller paused and examined in the stone at the left of the door, near the ground, a large circular excavation like the hollow of a sphere. Just then the folding-doors opened, and a peasant woman came out.

She saw the traveller, and perceived what he was examining.

'It was a French ball which did that,' said she.

And she added:

'What you see there, higher up, in the door, near a nail, is the hole made by a

Biscay musket. The musket has not gone through the wood.'

'What is the name of this place?' asked the traveller.

'Hougomont,' the woman answered.

The traveller raised his head. He took a few steps and looked over the hedges. He saw in the horizon, through the trees, a sort of hillock, and on this hillock something which, in the distance, resembled a lion.

He was on the battlefield of Waterloo.

2. *Hougomont*

HOUGOMONT – this was the fatal spot, the beginning of the resistance, the first check encountered at Waterloo by this great butcher of Europe, called Napoleon; the first knot under the axe.

It was a château; it is now nothing more than a farm. Hougomont, to the antiquary, is *Hugomons*. This manor was built by Hugo, sire de Somerel, the same who endowed the sixth chaplainship of the abbey of Villiers.

The traveller pushed open the door, elbowed an old carriage under the porch, and entered the court.

The first thing that he noticed in this yard was a door of the sixteenth century, which seemed like an arch, everything having fallen down around it. The monumental aspect is often produced by ruin. Near the arch opens another door in the wall, with keystones of the time of Henry IV, which discloses the trees of an orchard. Beside this door were a dung-hill, mattocks and shovels, some carts, an old well with its flag-stone and iron pulley, a skipping colt, a strutting turkey, a chapel surmounted by a little steeple, a pear tree in bloom, trained in espalier on the wall of the chapel; this was the court, the conquest of which was the aspiration of Napoleon. This bit of earth, could he have taken it, would perhaps have given him the world. The hens are scattering the dust with their beaks. You hear a growling: it is a great dog, who shows his teeth, and takes the place of the English.

The English fought admirably there. The four companies of guards under Cooke held their ground for seven hours, against the fury of an assaulting army.

Hougomont, seen on the map, on a geometrical plan, comprising buildings and enclosure, presents a sort of irregular rectangle, one corner of which is cut off. At this corner is the southern entrance, guarded by this wall, which commands it at the shortest musket range. Hougomont has two entrances: the southern, that of the château, and the northern, that of the farm. Napoleon sent against Hougomont his brother Jerome. The divisions of Guilleminot, Foy, and Bachelu were hurled against it; nearly the whole corps of Reille was there employed and there defeated, and the bullets of Kellermann were exhausted against this heroic wall-front. It was too much for the brigade of Bauduin to force Hougomont on the north, and the brigade of Soye could only batter it on the south – it could not take it.

The buildings of the farm are on the southern side of the court. A small portion of the northern door, broken by the French, hangs dangling from the wall. It is composed of four planks, nailed to two cross-pieces, and in it may be seen the scars of the attack.

The northern door, forced by the French, and to which a piece has been added to replace the panel suspended from the wall, stands half open at the foot of the courtyard; it is cut squarely in a wall of stone below, and brick above, and closes the court on the north. It is a simple cart-door, such as are found on all small farms, composed of two large folding-doors, made of rustic planks; beyond this are the meadows. This entrance was furiously contested. For a long time there could be seen upon the door all sorts of prints of bloody hands. It was there that Bauduin was killed.

The storm of the combat is still in this court: the horror is visible there; the overturn of the conflict is there petrified; it lives, it dies; it was but yesterday. The walls are still in death agonies; the stones fall, the breaches cry out; the holes are wounds; the trees bend and shudder, as if making an effort to escape.

This court, in 1815, was in better condition than it is today. Structures which have since been pulled down formed redans, angles, and squares.

The English were barricaded there; the French effected an entrance, but could not maintain their position. At the side of the chapel, one wing of the château, the only remnant which exists of the manor of Hougomont, stands crumbling, one might almost say disembowelled. The château served as donjon; the chapel served as block-house. There was work of extermination. The French, shot down from all sides, from behind the walls, from the roofs of the barns, from the bottom of the cellars, through every window, through every air-hole, through every chink in the stones, brought fagots and fired the walls and the men: the storm of balls was answered by a tempest of flame.

A glimpse may be had in the ruined wing, through the iron-barred windows, of the dismantled chambers of a main building; the English guards lay in ambush in these chambers; the spiral staircase, broken from foundation to roof, appears like the interior of a broken shell. The staircase has two landings; the English, besieged in the staircase, and crowded upon the upper steps, had cut away the lower ones. These are large slabs of blue stone, now heaped together among the nettles. A dozen steps still cling to the wall; on the first is cut the image of a trident. These inaccessible steps are firm in their sockets; all the rest resembles a toothless jaw-bone. Two old trees are there; one is dead, the other is wounded at the root, and does not leaf out until April. Since 1850 it has begun to grow across the staircase.

There was a massacre in the chapel. The interior, again restored to quiet, is strange. No mass has been said there since the carnage. The altar remains, however – a clumsy wooden altar, backed by a wall of rough stone. Four whitewashed walls, a door opposite the altar, two little arched windows, over the door a large wooden crucifix, above the crucifix a square opening in which is stuffed a bundle of straw; in a corner on the ground, an old glazed sash all broken, such is this chapel. Near the altar hangs a wooden statue of St Anne of the fifteenth century; the head of the infant Jesus has been carried away by a musket-shot. The French, masters for a moment of the chapel, then dislodged, fired it. The flames filled this ruin; it was a furnace; the door was burned, the floor was burned, but the wooden Christ was not burned. The fire ate its way to his feet, the blackened stumps of which only are visible; then it stopped. A miracle, say the country people. The infant Jesus, decapitated, was not so fortunate as the Christ.

The walls are covered with inscriptions. Near the feet of the Christ we read this name: *Henquinez*. Then these others: *Conde de Rio Maior Marques y Marquesa de Almagre (Habana)*. There are French names with exclamation points, signs of anger. The wall was whitewashed in 1849. The nations were insulting each other on it.

At the door of this chapel a body was picked up holding an axe in its hand. This body was that of second-lieutenant Legros.

On coming out of the chapel, a well is seen at the left. There are two in this yard. You ask: why is there no bucket and no pulley to this one? Because no water is drawn from it now. Why is no more water drawn from it? Because it is full of skeletons.

The last man who drew water from that well was Guillaume Van Kylsom. He was a peasant, who lived in Hougomont, and was gardener there. On the 18th of June 1815, his family fled and hid in the woods.

The forest about the Abbey of Villiers concealed for several days and several nights all that scattered and distressed population. Even now certain vestiges may be distinguished, such as old trunks of scorched trees, which mark the place of these poor trembling bivouacs in the depths of the thickets.

Guillaume Van Kylsom remained at Hougomont 'to take care of the château', and hid in the cellar. The English discovered him there. He was torn from his hiding place, and, with blows of the flat of their swords, the soldiers compelled this frightened man to wait upon them. They were thirsty; this Guillaume brought them drink. It was from this well that he drew the water. Many drank their last quaff. This well, where drank so many of the dead, must die itself also.

After the action, there was haste to bury the corpses. Death has its own way of embittering victory, and it causes glory to be followed by pestilence. Typhus is the successor of triumph. This well was deep, it was made a sepulchre. Three hundred dead were thrown into it. Perhaps with too much haste. Were they all dead? Tradition says no. It appears that on the night after the burial, feeble voices were heard calling out from the well.

This well is isolated in the middle of the courtyard. Three walls, half brick and half stone, folded back like the leaves of a screen, and imitating a square turret, surround it on three sides. The fourth side is open. On that side the water was drawn. The back wall has a sort of shapeless bull's-eye, perhaps a hole made by a shell. This turret had a roof, of which only the beams remain. The iron that sustains the wall on the right is in the shape of a cross. You bend over the well, the eye is lost in a deep brick cylinder, which is filled with an accumulation of shadows. All around it, the bottom of the walls is covered by nettles.

This well has not in front the large blue flagging stone, which serves as kerb for all the wells of Belgium. The blue stone is replaced by a cross-bar on which rest five or six misshapen wooden stumps, knotty and hardened, that resemble huge bones. There is no longer either bucket, or chain, or pulley; but the stone basin is still there which served for the waste water. The rain water gathers there, and from time to time a bird from the neighbouring forest comes to drink and flies away.

One house among these ruins, the farm-house, is still inhabited. The door of this house opens upon the courtyard. By the side of a pretty Gothic keyhole plate there is upon the door a handful of iron in trefoil, slanting forward. At the moment that the Hanoverian lieutenant Wilda was seizing this to take refuge in the farm-house, a French sapper struck off his hand with the blow of an axe.

The family which occupies the house calls the former gardener Van Kylsom, long since dead, its grandfather. A grey-haired woman said to us: 'I was there. I was three years old. My sister, larger, was afraid, and cried. They carried us away into the woods; I was in my mother's arms. They laid their ears to the ground to listen. For my part, I mimicked the cannon, and I went *boom, boom.*'

One of the yard doors, on the left, we have said, opens into the orchard.

The orchard is terrible.

It is in three parts, one might almost say in three acts. The first part is a garden, the second is the orchard, the third is a wood. These three parts have a common enclosure; on the side of the entrance the buildings of the château and the farm, on the left a hedge, on the right a wall, at the back a wall. The wall on the right is of brick, the wall on the back is of stone. The garden is entered first. It is sloping, planted with currant bushes, covered with wild vegetation, and terminated by a terrace of cut stone, with balusters with a double swell. It is a seignorial garden, in this first French style, which preceded the modern; now ruins and briers. The pilasters are surmounted by globes which look like stone cannon-balls. We count forty-three balusters still in their places; the others are lying in the grass, nearly all show some scratches of musketry. A broken baluster remains upright like a broken leg.

It is in this garden, which is lower than the orchard, that six of the first Light Voltigeurs, having penetrated thither, and being unable to escape, caught and trapped like bears in a pit, engaged in a battle with two Hanoverian companies, one of which was armed with carbines. The Hanoverians were ranged along these balusters, and fired from above. These voltigeurs, answering from below, six against two hundred, intrepid, with the currant bushes only for a shelter, took a quarter of an hour to die.

You rise a few steps, and from the garden pass into the orchard proper. There, in these few square yards, fifteen hundred men fell in less than an hour. The wall seems ready to recommence the combat. The thirty-eight loopholes, pierced by the English at irregular heights, are there yet. In front of the sixteenth, lie two English tombs of granite. There are no loopholes except in the south-wall, the principal attack came from that side. This wall is concealed on the outside by a large quickset hedge; the French came up, thinking there was nothing in their way but the hedge, crossed it, and found the wall, an obstacle and an ambush, the English Guards behind, the thirty-eight loopholes pouring forth their fire at once, a storm of grape and of balls; and Soye's brigade broke there. Waterloo commenced thus.

The orchard, however, was taken. They had no scaling ladders, but the French climbed the wall with their hands. They fought hand to hand under the trees. All this grass was soaked with blood. A battalion from Nassau, seven hundred men, was annihilated there. On the outside, the wall, against which the two batteries of Kellermann were directed, is gnawed by grape.

This orchard is as responsive as any other to the month of May. It has its golden blossoms and its daisies; the grass is high; farm horses are grazing; lines on which clothes are drying cross the intervals between the trees, making travellers bend their heads; you walk over that sward, and your foot sinks in the path of the mole. In the midst of the grass you notice an uprooted trunk, lying on the ground, but still growing green. Major Blackmann leaned back against it to die. Under a large tree near by fell the German general, Duplat, of a French family which fled on the revocation of the edict of Nantes. Close beside it leans a diseased old apple tree swathed in a bandage of straw and loam. Nearly all the apple trees are falling from old age. There is not one which does not show its cannon ball or its musket shot. Skeletons of dead trees abound in this orchard. Crows fly in the branches; beyond it is a wood full of violets.

Bauduin killed, Foy wounded, fire, slaughter, carnage, a brook made of English blood, of German blood, and of French blood, mingled in fury; a well filled with corpses, the regiment of Nassau and the regiment of Brunswick destroyed, Duplat killed, Blackmann killed, the English Guards crippled, twenty French battalions, out of the forty of Reille's corps, decimated, three thousand men, in this one ruin of Hougomont, sabred, slashed, slaughtered, shot, burned; and all this in order that today a peasant may say to a traveller: *Monsieur, give me three francs; if you like, I will explain to you the affair of Waterloo.*

3. *The 18th of June 1815*

LET US GO BACK, for such is the story-teller's privilege, and place ourselves in the year 1815, a little before the date of the commencement of the action narrated in the first part of this book.

Had it not rained on the night of the 17th of June 1815, the future of Europe would have been changed. A few drops of water more or less prostrated Napoleon. That Waterloo should be the end of Austerlitz, Providence needed only a little rain, and an unseasonable cloud crossing the sky sufficed for the overthrow of a world.

The battle of Waterloo – and this gave Blücher time to come up – could not be commenced before half-past eleven. Why? Because the ground was soft. It was necessary to wait for it to acquire some little firmness so that the artillery could manoeuvre.

Napoleon was an artillery officer, and he never forgot it. The foundation of this prodigious captain was the man who, in his report to the Directory upon Aboukir, said: *Such of our balls killed six men.* All his plans of battle were made for projectiles. To converge the artillery upon a given point was his key of victory. He treated the strategy of the hostile general as a citadel, and battered it to a breach. He overwhelmed the weak point with grape; he joined and resolved battles with cannon. There was marksmanship in his genius. To destroy squares, to pulverise regiments, to break lines, to crush and disperse masses, all this was for him, to strike, strike, strike incessantly, and he entrusted this duty to the cannon ball. A formidable method, which, joined to genius, made this sombre athlete of the pugilism of war invincible for fifteen years.

On the 18th of June 1815, he counted on his artillery the more because he had the advantage in numbers. Wellington had only a hundred and fifty-nine guns; Napoleon had two hundred and forty.

Had the ground been dry, and the artillery able to move, the action would have been commenced at six o'clock in the morning. The battle would have been won and finished at two o'clock, three hours before the Prussians turned the scale of fortune.

How much fault is there on the part of Napoleon in the loss of this battle? Is the shipwreck to be imputed to the pilot?

Was the evident physical decline of Napoleon accompanied at this time by a corresponding mental decline? had his twenty years of war worn out the sword as well as the sheath, the soul as well as the body? was the veteran injuriously felt in the captain? in a word, was that genius, as many considerable historians have thought, under an eclipse? had he put on a frenzy to disguise his enfeeblement from himself? did he begin to waver, and be bewildered by a random blast? was he becoming, a grave fault in a general, careless of danger? in that class of material great men who may be called the giants of action, is there an age when their genius becomes shortsighted? Old age has no hold on the geniuses of the ideal; for the Dantes and the Michaelangelos, to grow old is to grow great; for the Hannibals and the Bonapartes is it to grow less? had Napoleon lost his clear sense of victory? could he no longer recognise the shoal, no longer divine the snare, no longer discern the crumbling edge of the abyss? had he lost the instinct of disaster? was he, who formerly knew all the paths of triumph, and who, from the height of his flashing car, pointed them out with sovereign finger, now under such dark hallucination as to drive his tumultuous train of legions over the precipices? was he seized, at forty-six years, with a supreme madness? was this titanic driver of Destiny now only a monstrous breakneck?

We think not.

His plan of battle was, all confess, a masterpiece. To march straight to the centre of the allied line, pierce the enemy, cut them in two, push the British half upon Hal and the Prussian half upon Tongres, make of Wellington and Blücher two fragments, carry Mont Saint Jean, seize Brussels, throw the German into the Rhine, and the Englishman into the sea. All this, for Napoleon, was in this battle. What would follow, anybody can see.

We do not, of course, profess to give here the history of Waterloo; one of the scenes that gave rise to the drama which we are describing hangs upon that battle; but the history of the battle is not our subject; that history moreover is told, and told in a masterly way, from one point of view by Napoleon, from the other point of view by Charras.[28] As for us, we leave the two historians to their contest; we are only a witness at a distance, a passer in the plain, a seeker bending over this ground kneaded with human flesh, taking perhaps appearances for realities; we have no right to cope in the name of science with a mass of facts in which there is doubtless some mirage; we have neither the military experience nor the strategic ability which authorises a system; in our opinion, a chain of accidents overruled both captains at Waterloo; and when destiny is called in, this mysterious accused, we judge like the people, that artless judge.

4. *A*

THOSE WHO WOULD get a clear idea of the battle of Waterloo have only to lay down upon the ground in their mind a capital A. The left stroke of the A is the road from Nivelles, the right stroke is the road from Genappe, the cross of the A is the sunken road from Ohain to Braine l'Alleud. The top of the A is Mont Saint Jean, Wellington is there; the left-hand lower point is Hougomont, Reille is there with Jerome Bonaparte; the right-hand lower point is La Belle Alliance, Napoleon is there. A little below the point where the cross of the A meets and cuts the right stroke, is La Haie Sainte. At the middle of this cross is the precise point where the final battle-word was spoken. There the lion is placed, the involuntary symbol of the supreme heroism of the Imperial Guard.

The triangle contained at the top of the A, between the two strokes and the cross, is the plateau of Mont Saint Jean. The struggle for this plateau was the whole of the battle.

The wings of the two armies extended to the right and left of the two roads from Genappe and from Nivelles; d'Erlon being opposite Picton, Reille opposite Hill.

Behind the point of the A, behind the plateau of Mont Saint Jean, is the forest of Soignes.

As to the plain itself, we must imagine a vast undulating country; each wave commanding the next, and these undulations rising towards Mont Saint Jean, are there bounded by the forest.

Two hostile armies upon a field of battle are two wrestlers. Their arms are locked; each seeks to throw the other. They grasp at every aid; a thicket is a point of support; a corner of a wall is a brace for the shoulder; for lack of a few sheds to lean upon a regiment loses its footing; a depression in the plain, a movement of the soil, a convenient cross path, a wood, a ravine, may catch the heel of this colossus which is called an army, and prevent him from falling. He who leaves the field is beaten. Hence, for the responsible chief, the necessity of examining the smallest tuft of trees and appreciating the slightest details of contour.

Both generals had carefully studied the plain of Mont Saint Jean, now called the plain of Waterloo. Already in the preceding year, Wellington, with the sagacity of prescience, had examined it as a possible site for a great battle. On this ground and for this contest Wellington had the favourable side, Napoleon the unfavourable. The English army was above, the French army below.

To sketch here the appearance of Napoleon, on horseback, glass in hand, upon the heights of Rossomme, at dawn on the 18th of June 1815, would be almost superfluous. Before we point him out, everybody has seen him. This calm profile under the little chapeau of the school of Brienne, this green uniform, the white facings concealing the stars on his breast, the overcoat concealing the epaulets, the bit of red sash under the waistcoat, the leather breeches, the white horse with his housings of purple velvet with crowned N's and eagles on the corners, the Hessian boots over silk stockings, the silver spurs, the Marengo sword, this whole form of the last Cæsar lives in all imaginations, applauded by half the world, reprobated by the rest.

That form has long been fully illuminated; it did have a certain traditional obscurity through which most heroes pass, and which always veils the truth for a longer or shorter time; but now the history is luminous and complete.

This light of history is pitiless; it has this strange and divine quality that, all luminous as it is, and precisely because it is luminous, it often casts a shadow just where we saw a radiance; of the same man it makes two different phantoms, and the one attacks and punishes the other, and the darkness of the despot struggles with the splendour of the captain. Hence results a truer measure in the final judgement of the nations. Babylon violated lessens Alexander; Rome enslaved lessens Cæsar; massacred Jerusalem lessens Titus. Tyranny follows the tyrant. It is woe to a man to leave behind him a shadow which has his form.

5. *The* quid obscurum *of battles*

EVERYBODY KNOWS the first phase of this battle; the difficult opening, uncertain, hesitating, threatening for both armies, but for the English still more than for the French.

It had rained all night; the ground was softened by the shower; water lay here and there in the hollows of the plain as in basins; at some points the wheels sank in to the axles; the horses' girths dripped with liquid mud; had not the wheat and rye spread down by that multitude of advancing carts filled the ruts and made a bed under the wheels, all movement, particularly in the valleys on the side of Papelotte, would have been impossible.

The affair opened late; Napoleon, as we have explained, had a habit of holding all his artillery in hand like a pistol, aiming now at one point, anon at another point of the battle, and he desired to wait until the field-batteries could wheel and gallop freely; for this the sun must come out and dry the ground. But the sun did not come out. He had not now the field of Austerlitz. When the first gun was fired, the English General Colville looked at his watch and noted that it was thirty-five minutes past eleven.

The battle was commenced with fury, more fury perhaps than the emperor would have wished, by the left wing of the French at Hougomont. At the same time Napoleon attacked the centre by hurling the brigade of Quiot upon La Haie Sainte, and Ney pushed the right wing of the French against the left wing of the English which rested upon Papelotte.

The attack upon Hougomont was partly a feint; to draw Wellington that way, to make him incline to the left; this was the plan. This plan would have succeeded, had not the four companies of the English Guards, and the brave Belgians of Perponcher's division, resolutely held the position, enabling Wellington, instead of massing his forces upon that point, to limit himself to reinforcing them only by four additional companies of guards, and a Brunswick battalion.

The attack of the French right wing upon Papelotte was intended to overwhelm the English left, cut the Brussels road, bar the passage of the Prussians, should they come, to carry Mont Saint Jean, drive back Wellington upon Hougomont, from thence upon Braine l'Alleud, from thence upon Hal; nothing is clearer. With the exception of a few incidents, this attack succeeded. Papelotte was taken; La Haie Sainte was carried.

Note a circumstance. There were in the English infantry, particularly in Kempt's brigade, many new recruits. These young soldiers, before our formidable infantry, were heroic; their inexperience bore itself boldly in the affair; they did especially good service as skirmishers; the soldier as a skirmisher, to some extent left to himself, becomes, so to speak, his own general; these recruits exhibited something of French invention and French fury. This raw infantry showed enthusiasm. That displeased Wellington.

After the capture of La Haie Sainte, the battle wavered.

There is in this day from noon to four o'clock, an obscure interval; the middle of this battle is almost indistinct, and partakes of the thickness of the conflict. Twilight was gathering. You could perceive vast fluctuations in this mist, a giddy mirage, implements of war now almost unknown, the flaming colbacks, the waving sabretaches, the crossed shoulder-belts, the grenade cartridge boxes, the dolmans of the hussars, the red boots with a thousand creases, the heavy shakos festooned with fringe, the almost black infantry of Brunswick united with the scarlet infantry of England, the English soldiers with great white circular pads on their sleeves for epaulets, the Hanoverian light horse, with their oblong leather cap with copper bands and flowing plumes of red horse-hair, the Scotch with bare knees and plaids, the large white gaiters of our grenadiers; tableaux, not strategic lines, the need of Salvator Rosa, not of Gribeauval.[29]

A certain amount of tempest always mingles with a battle. *Quid obscurum, quid divinum.* Each historian traces the particular lineament which pleases him in this hurly-burly. Whatever may be the combinations of the generals, the shock of armed masses has incalculable recoils in action, the two plans of the two leaders enter into each other, and are disarranged by each other. Such a point of the battlefield swallows up more combatants than such another, as the more or less spongy soil drinks up water thrown upon it faster or slower. You are obliged to pour out more soldiers there than you thought. An unforeseen expenditure. The line of battle waves and twists like a thread; streams of blood flow regardless of logic; the fronts of the armies undulate; regiments entering or retiring make capes and gulfs; all these shoals are continually swaying back and forth before each other; where infantry was, artillery comes; where artillery was, cavalry rushes up; battalions are smoke. There was something there; look for it; it is gone; the vistas are displaced; the sombre folds advance and recoil; a kind of sepulchral wind pushes forwards, crowds back, swells and disperses these tragic multitudes. What is a hand to hand fight? an oscillation. A rigid mathematical plan tells the story of a minute, and not a day. To paint a battle needs those mighty painters who have chaos in their touch. Rembrandt is better than Vandermeulen. Vandermeulen, exact at noon, lies at three o'clock. Geometry deceives; the hurricane alone is true. This is what gives Folard the right to contradict Polybius. We must add that there is always a certain moment when the battle degenerates into a combat, particularises itself, scatters into innumerable details, which, to borrow the expression of Napoleon himself, 'belong rather to the biography of the regiments than to the history of the army'. The historian, in this case, evidently has the right of abridgement. He can only seize upon the principal outlines of the struggle, and it is given to no narrator, however conscientious he may be, to fix absolutely the form of this horrible cloud which is called a battle.

This, which is true of all great armed encounters, is particularly applicable to Waterloo.

However, in the afternoon, at a certain moment, the battle assumed precision.

6. *Four o'clock in the afternoon*

TOWARDS FOUR O'CLOCK the situation of the English army was serious. The Prince of Orange commanded the centre, Hill the right wing, Picton the left wing. The Prince of Orange, desperate and intrepid, cried to the Hollando-Belgians: *Nassau! Brunswick! never retreat!* Hill, exhausted, had fallen back upon Wellington. Picton was dead. At the very moment that the English had taken from the French the colours of the 105th of the line, the French had killed General Picton by a ball through the head. For Wellington the battle had two points of support, Hougomont and La Haie Sainte; Hougomont still held out, but was burning; La Haie Sainte had been taken. Of the German battalion which defended it, forty-two men only survived; all the officers, except five, were dead or prisoners. Three thousand combatants were massacred in that grange. A sergeant of the English Guards, the best boxer in England, reputed invulnerable by his comrades, had been killed by a little French drummer. Baring had been dislodged, Alten put to the sword. Several colours had been lost, one belonging to Alten's division, and one to the Luneburg battalion, borne by a prince of the family of Deux-Ponts. The Scots Grays were no more; Ponsonby's heavy dragoons had been cut to pieces. That valiant cavalry had given way before the lancers of Bro and the cuirassiers of Travers; of their twelve hundred horses there remained six hundred; of three lieutenant-colonels, two lay on the ground, Hamilton wounded, Mather killed. Ponsonby had fallen, pierced with seven thrusts of a lance. Gordon was dead, Marsh was dead. Two divisions, the fifth and the sixth, were destroyed.

Hougomont yielding, La Haie Sainte taken, there was but one knot left, the centre. That still held; Wellington reinforced it. He called thither Hill who was at Merbe Braine, and Chassé who was at Braine l'Alleud.

The centre of the English army, slightly concave, very dense and very compact, held a strong position. It occupied the plateau of Mont Saint Jean, with the village behind it and in front the declivity, which at that time was steep. At the rear it rested on this strong stone-house, then an outlying property of Nivelles, which marks the intersection of the roads, a sixteenth century pile so solid that the balls ricocheted against it without injuring it. All about the plateau, the English had cut away the hedges here and there, made embrasures in the hawthorns, thrust the mouth of a cannon between two branches, made loopholes in the thickets. Their artillery was in ambush under the shrubbery. This punic labour, undoubtedly fair in war, which allows snares, was so well done that Haxo, sent by the emperor at nine o'clock in the morning to reconnoitre the enemy's batteries, saw nothing of it, and returned to tell Napoleon that there was no obstacle, except the two barricades across the Nivelles and Genappe roads. It was the season when grain is at its height; upon the verge of the plateau, a battalion of Kempt's brigade, the 95th, armed with carbines, was lying in the tall wheat.

Thus supported and protected, the centre of the Anglo-Dutch army was well situated.

The danger of this position was the forest of Soignes, then contiguous to the battlefield and separated by the ponds of Groenendael and Boitsfort. An army could not retreat there without being routed; regiments would have been dissolved immediately, and the artillery would have been lost in the swamps. A retreat, according to the opinion of many military men – contested by others, it is true – would have been an utter rout.

Wellington reinforced this centre by one of Chassé's brigades, taken from the right wing, and one of Wincke's from the left, in addition to Clinton's division. To his English, to Halkett's regiments, to Mitchell's brigade, to Maitland's guards, he gave as supports the infantry of Brunswick, the Nassau contingent, Kielmansegge's Hanoverians, and Ompteda's Germans. *The right wing*, as

Charras says, *was bent back behind the centre*. An enormous battery was faced with sandbags at the place where now stands what is called 'the Waterloo Museum.' Wellington had besides, in a little depression of the grounds, Somerset's Horse Guards, fourteen hundred. This was the other half of that English cavalry, so justly celebrated. Ponsonby destroyed, Somerset was left.

The battery, which, finished, would have been almost a redoubt, was disposed behind a very low garden wall, hastily covered with sandbags and a broad, sloping bank of earth. This work was not finished; they had not time to stockade it.

Wellington, anxious, but impassible, was on horseback, and remained there the whole day in the same attitude, a little in front of the old mill of Mont Saint Jean, which is still standing, under an elm which an Englishman, an enthusiastic vandal, has since bought for two hundred francs, cut down and carried away. Wellington was frigidly heroic. The balls rained down. His aide-de-camp, Gordon, had just fallen at his side. Lord Hill, showing him a bursting shell, said: My Lord, what are your instructions, and what orders do you leave us, if you allow yourself to be killed? – *To follow my example*, answered Wellington. To Clinton, he said laconically: *Hold this spot to the last man*. The day was clearly going badly. Wellington cried to his old companions of Talavera, Vittoria, and Salamanca: *Boys! We must not be beat: what would they say of us in England!*

About four o'clock, the English line staggered backwards. All at once only the artillery and the sharp-shooters were seen on the crest of the plateau, the rest disappeared; the regiments, driven by the shells and bullets of the French, fell back into the valley now crossed by the cow-path of the farm of Mont Saint Jean; a retrograde movement took place, the battle front of the English was slipping away, Wellington gave ground. Beginning retreat! cried Napoleon.

7. *Napoleon in good humour*

THE EMPEROR, although sick and hurt in his saddle by a local affliction, had never been in so good humour as on that day. Since morning, his impenetrable countenance had worn a smile. On the 18th of June 1815, that profound soul masked in marble, shone obscurely forth. The dark-browed man of Austerlitz was gay at Waterloo. The greatest, when foredoomed, present these contradictions. Our joys are shaded. The perfect smile belongs to God alone.

Ridet Cæsar, Pompeius flebit, said the legionaries of the Fulminatrix Legion. Pompey at this time was not to weep, but it is certain that Cæsar laughed.

From the previous evening, and in the night, at one o'clock, exploring on horseback, in the tempest and the rain, with Bertrand, the hills near Rossomme, and gratified to see the long line of the English fires illuminating all the horizon from Frischemont to Braine l'Alleud, it had seemed to him that destiny, for which he had made an appointment, for a certain day upon the field of Waterloo, was punctual; he stopped his horse, and remained some time motionless, watching the lightning and listening to the thunder; and this fatalist was heard to utter in the darkness these mysterious words: 'We are in accord.' Napoleon was deceived. They were no longer in accord.

He had not taken a moment's sleep; every instant of that night had brought him a new joy. He passed along the whole line of the advanced guards, stopping here and there to speak to the pickets. At half-past two, near the wood of Hougomont, he heard the tread of a column in march; he thought for a moment that Wellington was falling back. He said: *It is the English rear guard starting to get away. I shall take the six thousand Englishmen who have just arrived at Ostend prisoners.* He chatted freely; he had recovered that animation of the disembarkation of the first of March, when he showed to the Grand Marshal the enthusiastic peasant of Gulf Juan, crying: *Well, Bertrand, there is a reinforcement already!* On the night of the 17th of June, he made fun of Wellington: *This little Englishman must have his lesson,* said Napoleon. The rain redoubled; it thundered while the emperor was speaking.

At half-past three in the morning one illusion was gone; officers sent out on a reconnaissance announced to him that the enemy was making no movement. Nothing was stirring, not a bivouac fire was extinguished. The English army was asleep. Deep silence was upon the earth; there was no noise save in the sky. At four o'clock, a peasant was brought to him by the scouts; this peasant had acted as guide to a brigade of English cavalry, probably Vivian's brigade on its way to take position at the village of Ohain, at the extreme left. At five o'clock, two Belgian deserters reported to him that they had just left their regiment, and that the English army was expecting a battle. *So much the better!* exclaimed Napoleon, *I would much rather cut them to pieces than repulse them.*

In the morning, he alighted in the mud, upon the high bank at the corner of the road from Planchenoit, had a kitchen table and a peasant's chair brought from the farm of Rossomme, sat down, with a bunch of straw for a carpet, and spread out upon the table the plan of the battlefield, saying to Soult: '*Pretty chequer-board!*'

In consequence of the night's rain, the convoys of provisions, mired in the softened roads, had not arrived at dawn; the soldiers had not slept, and were wet and fasting; but for all this Napoleon cried out joyfully to Ney: *We have ninety chances in a hundred.* At eight o'clock the emperor's breakfast was brought. He had invited several generals. While breakfasting, it was related, that on the night but one before, Wellington was at a ball in Brussels, given by the Duchess of Somerset; and Soult, rude soldier that he was, with his archbishop's face, said: *The ball is today.* The emperor jested with Ney, who said: *Wellington will not be so simple as to wait for your majesty.* This was his manner usually. *He was fond of joking,* says Fleury de Chaboulon. *His character at bottom was a playful humour,* says Gourgaud. *He abounded in pleasantries, oftener grotesque than witty,* says Benjamin Constant. These gaieties of a giant are worthy of remembrance. He called his grenadiers 'the growlers'; he would pinch their ears and would pull their mustaches. *The emperor did nothing but play tricks on us;* so one of them said. During the mysterious voyage from the island of Elba to France, on the 27th of February, in the open sea, the French brig-of-war *Zephyr* having met the brig *Inconstant,* on which Napoleon was concealed, and having asked the *Inconstant* for news of Napoleon, the emperor, who still had on his hat the white and amaranth cockade, sprinkled with bees, adopted by him in the island of Elba, took the speaking-trumpet, with a laugh, and answered himself: *the emperor is getting on finely.* He who laughs in this way is on familiar terms with events; Napoleon had several of these bursts of laughter during his Waterloo breakfast. After breakfast, for a quarter of an hour, he collected his thoughts; then two generals were seated on the bundle of straw, pen in hand, and paper on knee, and the emperor dictated the order of battle.

At nine o'clock, at the instant when the French army, drawn up and set in motion in five columns, was deployed, the divisions upon two lines, the artillery between the brigades, music at the head, playing marches, with the rolling of drums and the sounding of trumpets – mighty, vast, joyous, – a sea of casques, sabres, and bayonets in the horizon, the emperor, excited, cried out, and repeated: 'Magnificent! magnificent!'

Between nine o'clock and half-past ten, the whole army, which seems incredible, had taken position, and was ranged in six lines, forming, to repeat the expression of the emperor, 'the figure of six V's'. A few moments after the formation of the line of battle, in the midst of this profound silence, like that at the commencement of a storm, which precedes the fight, seeing as they filed by the three batteries of twelve pounders, detached by his orders from the three corps of d'Erlon, Reille, and Lobau, to commence the action by attacking Mont Saint Jean at the intersection of the roads from Nivelles and Genappe, the emperor struck Haxo on the shoulder, saying: *There are twenty-four pretty girls, General.*

Sure of the event, he encouraged with a smile, as they passed before him, the company of sappers of the first corps, which he had designated to erect barricades in Mont Saint Jean, as soon as the village was carried. All this serenity was disturbed by but a word of haughty pity; on seeing, massed at his left, at a place where there is today a great tomb, those wonderful Scots Grays, with their superb horses, he said: '*It is a pity.*'

Then he mounted his horse, rode forward from Rossomme, and chose for his point of view a narrow grassy ridge, at the right of the road from Genappe to Brussels, which was his second station during the battle. The third station, that of seven o'clock, between La Belle Alliance and La Haie Sainte is terrible; it is a considerable hill which can still be seen, and behind which the guard was massed in a depression of the plain. About this hill the balls ricocheted over the paved road up to Napoleon. As at Brienne, he had over his head the whistling of balls and bullets. There have been gathered, almost upon the spot pressed by his horse's feet, crushed bullets, old sabre blades, and shapeless projectiles, eaten with rust. *Scabra rubigine.* Some years ago, a sixty-pound shell was dug up there, still loaded, the fuse having broken off even with the bomb. It was at this last station that the emperor said to his guide Lacoste, a hostile peasant, frightened, tied to a hussar's saddle, turning around at every volley of grape, and trying to hide behind Napoleon: *Dolt, this is shameful. You will get yourself shot in the back.* He who writes these lines has himself found in the loose slope of that hill, by turning up the earth, the remains of a bomb, disintegrated by the rust of forty-six years, and some old bits of iron which broke like alder twigs in his finger.

The undulations of the diversely inclined plains, which were the theatre of the encounter of Napoleon and Wellington, are, as everybody knows, no longer what they were on the 18th of June 1815. In taking from that fatal field wherewith to make its monument, its real form was destroyed: history, disconcerted, no longer recognises herself upon it. To glorify it, it has been disfigured. Wellington, two years afterwards, on seeing Waterloo, exclaimed: *They have changed my battlefield.* Where today is the great pyramid of earth surmounted by the lion, there was a ridge which sank away towards the Nivelles road in a practicable slope, but which, above the Genappe road, was almost an escarpment. The elevation of this escarpment may be measured today by the height of the two great burial mounds which embank the road from Genappe to Brussels; the English tomb at the left, the German tomb at the right. There is no French tomb. For France that whole plain is a sepulchre. Thanks to the thousands and thousands of loads of earth used in the mound of a hundred and fifty feet high and half a mile in circuit, the plateau of Mont St Jean is accessible by a gentle slope; on the day of the battle, especially on the side of La Haie Sainte, the declivity was steep and abrupt. The descent was there so precipitous that the English artillery did not see the farm below them at the bottom of the valley, the centre of the combat. On the 18th of June 1815, the rain had gullied out this steep descent still more; the mud made the ascent still more difficult; it was not merely laborious, but men actually stuck in the mire. Along the crest of the plateau ran a sort of ditch, which could not possibly have been suspected by a distant observer.

What was this ditch? we will tell. Braine l'Alleud is a village of Belgium, Ohain is another. These villages, both hidden by the curving of the ground, are connected by a road about four miles long which crosses an undulating plain, often burying itself in the hills like a furrow, so that at certain points it is a ravine. In 1815, as now, this road cut the crest of the plateau of Mont Saint Jean between the two roads from Genappe and Nivelles; only, today it is on a level with the plain; whereas then it was sunk between high banks. Its two slopes were taken away for the monumental mound. That road was and is still a trench for the greater part of its length; a trench in some parts a dozen feet deep, the slopes of which are so steep as to slide down here and there, especially in winter, after showers. Accidents happen there. The road was so narrow at the entrance of Braine l'Alleud that a traveller was once crushed by a wagon, as is attested by a stone cross standing near the cemetery, which gives the name of the dead, *Monsieur Bernard Debrye, merchant of Brussels,* and the date of the accident, February 1637.* It was so deep at the plateau of Mont Saint Jean, that a peasant, Matthew Nicaise, had been crushed there in 1783 by the falling of the bank, as another stone cross attested; the top of this has disappeared in the changes, but its overturned pedestal is still visible upon the sloping bank at the left of the road between La Haie Sainte and the farm of Mont Saint Jean.

On the day of the battle, this sunken road, of which nothing gave warning, along the crest of Mont Saint Jean, a ditch at the summit of the escarpement, a trench concealed by the ground, was invisible, that is to say terrible.

---

* The inscription is as follows:

DOM
CY A ETE ECRASE
PAR MALHEUR
SOUS UN CHARIOT
MONSIEUR BERNARD
DE BRYE MARCHAND
A BRUXELLES LE (ILLEGIBLE)
FEVRIER 1637

8. *The emperor puts a question to the guide Lacoste*

ON the morning of Waterloo then, Napoleon was satisfied.

He was right; the plan of battle which he had conceived, as we have shown, was indeed admirable.

After the battle was once commenced, its very diverse fortune, the resistance of Hougomont, the tenacity of La Haie Sainte, Bauduin killed, Foy put *hors de combat*, the unexpected wall against which Soye's brigade was broken, the fatal blunder of Guilleminot in having neither grenades nor powder, the miring of the batteries, the fifteen pieces without escort cut off by Uxbridge in a deep cut of a road, the slight effect of the bombs that fell within the English lines, burying themselves in the soil softened by the rain and only succeeding in making volcanoes of mud, so that the explosion was changed into a splash, the uselessness of Piré's demonstration upon Braine l'Alleud, all this cavalry, fifteen squadrons, almost destroyed, the English right wing hardly disturbed, the left wing hardly moved, the strange mistake of Ney in massing, instead of drawing out, the four divisions of the first corps, the depth of twenty-seven ranks and the front of two hundred men offered up in this manner to grape, the frightful gaps made by the balls in these masses, the lack of connection between the attacking columns, the slanting battery suddenly unmasked upon their flank, Bourgeois, Donzelot, and Durutte entangled, Quiot repulsed, Lieutenant Vieux, that Hercules sprung from the Polytechnic School, wounded at the moment when he was beating down with the blows of an axe the door of La Haie Sainte under the plunging fire of the English barricade barring the turn of the road from Genappe to Brussels, Marcognet's division, caught between infantry and cavalry, shot down at arm's length in the wheatfield by Best and Pack, sabred by Ponsonby, his battery of seven pieces spiked, the Prince of Saxe Weimar holding and keeping Frischemont and Smohain in spite of Count d'Erlon, the colours of the 105th taken, the colours of the 43rd taken, this Prussian Black Hussar, brought in by the scouts of the flying column of three hundred chasseurs scouring the country between Wavre and Planchenoit, the disquieting things that this prisoner had said, Grouchy's delay, the fifteen hundred men killed in less than an hour in the orchard of Hougomont, the eighteen hundred men fallen in still less time around La Haie Sainte – all these stormy events, passing like battle-clouds before Napoleon, had hardly disturbed his countenance, and had not darkened its imperial expression of certainty. Napoleon was accustomed to look upon war fixedly; he never made figure by figure the tedious addition of details; the figures mattered little to him, provided they gave this total: Victory; though beginnings went wrong he was not alarmed at it, he who believed himself master and possessor of the end; he knew how to wait, believing himself beyond contingency, and he treated destiny as an equal treats an equal. He appeared to say to Fate: thou would'st not dare.

Half light and half shadow, Napoleon felt himself protected in the right, and tolerated in the wrong. He had, or believed that he had, a connivance, one might almost say a complicity, with events, equivalent to the ancient invulnerability.

However, when one has Beresina, Leipsic, and Fontainebleau behind him, it seems as if he might distrust Waterloo. A mysterious frown is becoming visible in the depths of the sky.

At the moment when Wellington drew back, Napoleon started up. He saw the plateau of Mont Saint Jean suddenly laid bare, and the front of the English army disappear. It rallied, but kept concealed. The emperor half rose in his stirrups. The flash of victory passed into his eyes.

Wellington hurled back on the forest of Soignes and destroyed; that was the final overthrow of England by France; it was Cressy, Poitiers, Malplaquet, and Ramillies avenged. The man of Marengo was wiping out Agincourt.

The emperor then, contemplating this terrible turn of fortune, swept his glass for the last time over every point of the battlefield. His guard standing behind with grounded arms, looked up to him with a sort of religion. He was reflecting; he was examining the slopes, noting the ascents, scrutinising the tuft of trees, the square rye field, the footpath; he seemed to count every bush. He looked for some time at the English barricades on the two roads, two large abattis of trees, that on the Genappe road above La Haie Sainte, armed with two cannon, which alone, of all the English artillery, bore upon the bottom of the field of battle, and that of the Nivelles road where glistened the Dutch bayonets of Chassé's brigade. He noticed near that barricade the old chapel of Saint Nicholas, painted white, which is at the corner of the crossroad toward Braine l'Alleud. He bent over and spoke in an undertone to the guide Lacoste. The guide made a negative sign of the head, probably treacherous.

The emperor rose up and reflected. Wellington had fallen back. It remained only to complete this repulse by a crushing charge.

Napoleon, turning abruptly, sent off a courier at full speed to Paris to announce that the battle was won.

Napoleon was one of those geniuses who rule the thunder.

He had found his thunderbolt.

He ordered Milhaud's cuirassiers to carry the plateau of Mont Saint Jean.

9. *The unlooked for*

THEY WERE three thousand five hundred. They formed a line of half a mile. They were gigantic men on colossal horses. There were twenty-six squadrons, and they had behind them, as a support, the division of Lefebvre Desnouettes, the hundred and six gendarmes d'élite, the Chasseurs of the Guard, eleven hundred and ninety-seven men, and the Lancers of the Guard, eight hundred and eighty lances. They wore casques without plumes, and cuirasses of wrought iron, with horse pistols in their holsters, and long sabre-swords. In the morning, they had been the admiration of the whole army, when at nine o'clock, with trumpets sounding, and all the bands playing, *Veillons au salut de l'empire,*[30] they came, in heavy column, one of their batteries on their flank, the other at their centre, and deployed in two ranks between the Genappe road and Frischemont, and took their position of battle in this powerful second line, so wisely made up by Napoleon, which, having at its extreme left the cuirassiers of Kellermann, and at its extreme right the cuirassiers of Milhaud, had, so to speak, two wings of iron.

Aide-de-camp Bernard brought them the emperor's order. Ney drew his sword and placed himself at their head. The enormous squadrons began to move.

Then was seen a fearful sight.

All this cavalry, with sabres drawn, banners waving, and trumpets sounding, formed in column by division, descended with an even movement and as one man – with the precision of a bronze battering-ram opening a breach – the hill of La Belle Alliance, sank into that formidable depth where so many men had already fallen, disappeared in the smoke, then, rising from this valley of shadow reappeared on the other side, still compact and serried, mounting at full trot, through a cloud of grape emptying itself upon them, the frightful acclivity of mud of the plateau of Mont Saint Jean. They rose, serious, menacing, imperturbable; in the intervals of the musketry and artillery could be heard the sound of this colossal tramp. Being in two divisions, they formed two columns; Wathier's division had the right, Delord's the left. From a distance they would be taken for two immense serpents of steel stretching themselves towards the crest of the plateau. That ran through the battle like a prodigy.

Nothing like it had been seen since the taking of the grand redoubt at La Moscowa by the heavy cavalry; Murat was not there, but Ney was there. It seemed as if this mass had become a monster, and had but a single mind. Each squadron undulated and swelled like the ring of a polyp. They could be seen through the thick smoke, as it was broken here and there. It was one pell-mell of casques, cries, sabres; a furious bounding of horses among the cannon, and the flourish of trumpets, a terrible and disciplined tumult; over all, the cuirasses, like the scales of a hydra.

These recitals appear to belong to another age. Something like this vision appeared, doubtless, in the old Orphic epics which tell of centaurs, antique hippanthropes, those titans with human faces, and chests like horses, whose gallop scaled Olympus, horrible, invulnerable, sublime; at once gods and beasts.

An odd numerical coincidence, twenty-six battalions were to receive these twenty-six squadrons. Behind the crest of the plateau, under cover of the masked battery, the English infantry, formed in thirteen squares, two battalions to the square, and upon two lines – seven on the first, and six on the second – with musket to the shoulder, and eye upon their sights, waiting calm, silent, and immovable. They could not see the cuirassiers, and the cuirassiers could not see them. They listened to the rising of this tide of men. They heard the increasing sound of three thousand horses, the alternate and measured striking of their hoofs at full trot, the rattling of the cuirasses, the clicking of the sabres, and a sort of fierce roar of the coming host. There was a moment of fearful silence, then, suddenly, a long line of raised arms brandishing sabres appeared above the crest, with casques, trumpets, and standards, and three thousand faces with grey moustaches, crying, Vive l'empereur! All this cavalry debouched on the plateau, and it was like the beginning of an earthquake.

All at once, tragic to relate, at the left of the English, and on our right, the head of the column of cuirassiers reared with a frightful clamour. Arrived at the culminating point of the crest, unmanageable, full of fury, and bent upon the extermination of the squares and cannons, the cuirassiers saw between themselves and the English a ditch, a grave. It was the sunken road of Ohain.

It was a frightful moment. There was the ravine, unlooked for, yawning at the very feet of the horses, two fathoms deep between its double slope. The second rank pushed in the first, the third pushed in the second; the horses reared, threw themselves over, fell upon their backs, and struggled with their feet in the air, piling up and overturning their riders; no power to retreat; the whole column was nothing but a projectile. The force acquired to crush the English crushed the French. The inexorable ravine could not yield until it was filled; riders and horses rolled in together pell-mell, grinding each other, making common flesh in this dreadful gulf, and when this grave was full of living men, the rest marched over them and passed on. Almost a third of the Dubois' brigade sank into this abyss.

Here the loss of the battle began.

A local tradition, which evidently exaggerates, says that two thousand horses and fifteen hundred men were buried in the sunken road of Ohain. This undoubtedly comprises all the other bodies thrown into this ravine on the morrow after the battle.

Napoleon, before ordering this charge of Milhaud's cuirassiers, had examined the ground, but could not see this hollow road, which did not make even a wrinkle on the surface of the plateau. Warned, however, and put on his guard by the little white chapel which marks its junction with the Nivelles road, he had, probably on the contingency of an obstacle, put a question to the guide Lacoste. The guide had answered no. It may almost be said that from this shake of a peasant's head came the catastrophe of Napoleon.

Still other fatalities must arise.

Was it possible that Napoleon should win this battle? We answer no. Why? Because of Wellington? Because of Blücher? No. Because of God.

For Bonaparte to be conqueror at Waterloo was not in the law of the nineteenth century. Another series of facts were preparing in which Napoleon had no place. The ill-will of events had long been announced.

It was time that this vast man should fall.

The excessive weight of this man in human destiny disturbed the equilibrium. This individual counted, of himself alone, more than the universe besides. These plethoras of all human vitality concentrated in a single head, the world mounting to the brain of one man, would be fatal to civilisation if they should endure. The moment had come for incorruptible supreme equity to look to it. Probably the principles and elements upon which regular gravitations in the moral order as well as in the material depend, began to murmur. Reeking blood, overcrowded cemeteries, weeping mothers – these are formidable pleaders. When the earth is suffering from a surcharge, there are mysterious moanings from the deeps which the heavens hear.

Napoleon had been impeached before the Infinite, and his fall was decreed.

He vexed God.

Waterloo is not a battle; it is the change of front of the universe.

10. *The plateau of Mont Saint Jean*

AT THE SAME TIME with the ravine, the artillery was unmasked.

Sixty cannon and the thirteen squares thundered and flashed into the cuirassiers. The brave General Delord gave the military salute to the English battery.

All the English flying artillery took position in the squares at a gallop. The cuirassiers had not even time to breathe. The disaster of the sunken road had decimated, but not discouraged them. They were men who, diminished in number, grew greater in heart.

Wathier's column alone had suffered from the disaster; Delord's, which Ney had sent obliquely to the left, as if he had a presentiment of the snare, arrived entire.

The cuirassiers hurled themselves upon the English squares.

At full gallop, with free rein, their sabres in their teeth, and their pistols in their hands, the attack began.

There are moments in battle when the soul hardens a man even to changing the soldier into a statue, and all this flesh becomes granite. The English battalions, desperately assailed, did not yield an inch.

Then it was frightful.

All sides of the English squares were attacked at once. A whirlwind of frenzy enveloped them. This frigid infantry remained impassible. The first rank, with knee on the ground, received the cuirassiers on their bayonets, the second shot them down; behind the second rank, the cannoneers loaded their guns, the front of the square opened, made way for an eruption of grape, and closed again. The cuirassiers answered by rushing upon them with crushing force. Their great horses reared, trampled upon the ranks, leaped over the bayonets and fell, gigantic, in the midst of these four living walls. The balls made gaps in the ranks of the cuirassiers, the cuirassiers made breaches in the squares. Files of men disappeared, ground down beneath the horses' feet. Bayonets were buried in the bellies of these centaurs. Hence a monstrosity of wounds never perhaps seen elsewhere. The squares, consumed by this furious cavalry, closed up without wavering. Inexhaustible in grape, they kept up an explosion in the midst of their assailants. It was a monstrous sight. These squares were battalions no longer, they were craters; these cuirassiers were cavalry no longer, they were a tempest. Each square was a volcano attacked by a thundercloud; the lava fought with the lightning.

The square on the extreme right, the most exposed of all, being in the open field, was almost annihilated at the first shock. It was formed of the 75th regiment of Highlanders. The piper in the centre, while the work of extermination was going on, profoundly oblivious of all about him, casting down his melancholy eye full of the shadows of forests and lakes, seated upon a drum, his bagpipe under his arm, was playing his mountain airs. These Scotchmen died thinking of Ben Lothian, as the Greeks died remembering Argos. The sabre of a cuirassier, striking down the pibroch and the arm which bore it, caused the strain to cease by killing the player.

The cuirassiers, relatively few in number, lessened by the catastrophe of the ravine, had to contend with almost the whole of the English army, but they multiplied themselves, each man became equal to ten. Nevertheless some Hanoverian battalions fell back. Wellington saw it and remembered his cavalry. Had Napoleon, at that very moment, remembered his infantry, he would have won the battle. This forgetfulness was his great fatal blunder.

Suddenly the assailing cuirassiers perceived that they were assailed. The English cavalry was upon their back. Before them the squares, behind them Somerset; Somerset, with the fourteen hundred dragoon guards. Somerset had on his right Dornberg with his German light-horse, and on his left Trip, with the Belgian carbineers. The cuirassiers, attacked front, flank, and rear, by infantry and cavalry, were compelled to face in all directions. What was that to them? They were a whirlwind. Their valour became unspeakable.

Besides, they had behind them the ever thundering artillery. All that was necessary in order to wound such men in the back. One of their cuirasses, with a hole in the left shoulder-plate made by a musket ball, is in the collection of the Waterloo Museum.

With such Frenchmen only such Englishmen could cope.

It was no longer a conflict, it was a darkness, a fury, a giddy vortex of souls and courage, a hurricane of sword-flashes. In an instant the fourteen hundred horse guards were but eight hundred; Fuller, their lieutenant-colonel, fell dead. Ney rushed up with the lancers and chasseurs of Lefebvre-Desnouettes. The plateau of Mont Saint Jean was taken, retaken, taken again. The cuirassiers left the cavalry to return to the infantry, or more correctly, all this terrible multitude wrestled with each other without letting go their hold. The squares still held. There were twelve assaults. Ney had four horses killed under him. Half of the cuirassiers lay on the plateau. This struggle lasted two hours.

The English army was terribly shaken. There is no doubt, if they had not been crippled in their first shock by the disaster of the sunken road, the cuirassiers would have overwhelmed the centre, and decided the victory. This wonderful cavalry astounded Clinton, who had seen Talavera and Badajos. Wellington, though three-fourths conquered, was struck with heroic admiration. He said in a low voice: 'splendid!'

The cuirassiers annihilated seven squares out of thirteen, took or spiked sixty pieces of cannon, and took from the English regiments six colours, which three cuirassiers and three chasseurs of the guard carried to the emperor before the farm of La Belle Alliance.

The situation of Wellington was growing worse. This strange battle was like a duel between two wounded infuriates who, while yet fighting and resisting, lose all their blood. Which of the two shall fall first?

The struggle of the plateau continued.

How far did the cuirassiers penetrate? None can tell. One thing is certain: the day after the battle, a cuirassier and his horse were found dead under the frame of the hay-scales at Mont Saint Jean, at the point where the four roads from Nivelles, Genappe, La Hulpe, and Brussels meet. This horseman had pierced the English lines. One of the men who took away the body still lives at Mont Saint Jean. His name is Dehaze; he was then eighteen years old.

Wellington felt that he was giving way. The crisis was upon him.

The cuirassiers had not succeeded, in this sense, that the centre was not broken. All holding the plateau, nobody held it, and in fact it remained for the most part with the English. Wellington held the village and the crowning plain; Ney held only the crest and the slope. On both sides they seemed rooted in this funebrial soil.

But the enfeeblement of the English appeared irremediable. The hæmorrhage of this army was horrible. Kempt, on the left wing, called for reinforcements. '*Impossible,*' answered Wellington; '*we must die on the spot we now occupy.*' Almost at the same moment – singular coincidence which depicts the exhaustion of both armies – Ney sent to Napoleon for infantry, and Napoleon exclaimed: '*Infantry! where does he expect me to take them! Does he expect me to make them?*'

However, the English army was farthest gone. The furious onslaughts of these great squadrons with iron cuirasses and steel breastplates had ground up the infantry. A few men about a flag marked the place of a regiment; battalions were now commanded by captains or lieutenants. Alten's division, already so cut up at La Haie Sainte, was almost destroyed; the intrepid Belgians of Van Kluze's brigade strewed the rye field along the Nivelles road; there were hardly any left of those Dutch grenadiers who, in 1811, joined to our ranks in Spain, fought against Wellington, and who, in 1815, rallied on the English side, fought against Napoleon. The loss in officers was heavy. Lord Uxbridge, who buried his leg next day, had a knee fractured. If, on the side of the French, in this struggle of the cuirassiers, Delord, l'Heritier, Colbert, Dnop, Travers, and Blancard were *hors de combat*, on the side of the English, Alten was wounded, Barne was wounded, Delancey was killed, Van Meeren was killed, Ompteda was killed, the entire staff of Wellington was decimated, and England had the worst share in this balance of blood. The second regiment of foot guards had lost five lieutenant-colonels, four captains, and three ensigns; the first battalion of the thirtieth infantry had lost twenty-four officers and one hundred and twelve soldiers; the seventy-ninth Highlanders had twenty-four officers wounded, eighteen officers killed, and four hundred and fifty soldiers slain. Cumberland's Hanoverian hussars, an entire regiment, having at its head Colonel Hacke, who was afterwards courtmartialed and broken, had drawn rein before the fight, and were in flight in the Forest of Soignes, spreading the panic as far as Brussels. Carts, ammunition-wagons, baggage-wagons, ambulances full of wounded, seeing the French gain ground, and approach the forest, fled precipitately; the Dutch, sabred by the French cavalry, cried murder! From Vert-Coucou to Groenendael, for a distance of nearly six miles in the direction towards Brussels, the roads, according to the testimony of witnesses still alive, were choked with fugitives. This panic was such that it reached the Prince of Condé at Malines, and Louis XVIII at Ghent. With the exception of the small reserve drawn up in echelon behind the hospital established at the farm of Mont Saint Jean, and the brigades of Vivian and Vandeleur on the flank of the left wing, Wellington's cavalry was exhausted. A number of batteries lay dismounted. These facts are confessed by Siborne; and Pringle, exaggerating the disaster, says even that the Anglo-Dutch army was reduced to thirty-four thousand men. The Iron Duke remained calm, but his lips were pale. The Austrian Commissary, Vincent, the Spanish Commissary, Olava, present at the battle in the English staff, thought the duke was beyond hope. At five o'clock Wellington drew out his watch, and was heard to murmur these sombre words: *Blücher, or night!*

It was about this time that a distant line of bayonets glistened on the heights beyond Frischemont.

Here is the turning-point in this colossal drama.

11. *Sad guide for Napoleon; good guide for Bulow*

WE UNDERSTAND the bitter mistake of Napoleon; Grouchy hoped for, Blücher arriving; death instead of life.

Destiny has such turnings. Awaiting the world's throne, Saint Helena became visible.

If the little cowboy, who acted as guide to Bulow, Blücher's lieutenant, had advised him to debouch from the forest above Frischemont rather than below Planchenoit, the shaping of the nineteenth century would perhaps have been different. Napoleon would have won the battle of Waterloo. By any other road than below Planchenoit, the Prussian army would have brought up at a ravine impassable for artillery, and Bulow would not have arrived.

Now, an hour of delay, as the Prussian general Muffling declares, and Blücher would not have found Wellington in position; 'the battle was lost'.

It was time, we have seen, that Bulow should arrive. He had bivouacked at Dion le Mont, and started on at dawn. But the roads were impracticable, and his division stuck in the mire. The cannon sank to the hubs in the ruts. Furthermore, he had to cross the Dyle on the narrow bridge of Wavre; the street leading to the bridge had been fired by the French; the caissons and artillery wagons, being unable to pass between two rows of burning houses, had to wait till the fire was extinguished. It was noon before Bulow could reach Chapelle Saint Lambert.

Had the action commenced two hours earlier, it would have been finished at four o'clock, and Blücher would have fallen upon a field already won by Napoleon. Such are these immense chances, proportioned to an infinity, which we cannot grasp.

As early as mid-day, the emperor, first of all, with his field glass, perceived in the extreme horizon something which fixed his attention. He said: 'I see yonder a cloud which appears to me to be troops.' Then he asked the Duke of Dalmatia: 'Soult, what do you see towards Chapelle Saint Lambert?' The marshal, turning his glass that way, answered: 'Four or five thousand men, sire. Grouchy, of course.' Meanwhile it remained motionless in the haze. The glasses of the whole staff studied 'the cloud' pointed out by the emperor. Some said: 'They are columns halting.' The most said: 'It is trees.' The fact is, that the cloud did not stir. The emperor detached Domon's division of light cavalry to reconnoitre this obscure point.

Bulow, in fact, had not moved. His vanguard was very weak, and could do nothing. He had to wait for the bulk of his *corps d'armée*, and he was ordered to concentrate his force before entering into line; but at five o'clock, seeing Wellington's peril, Blücher ordered Bulow to attack, and uttered these remarkable words: 'We must give the English army a breathing spell.'

Soon after the divisions of Losthin, Hiller, Hacke, and Ryssel deployed in front of Lobau's corps, the cavalry of Prince William of Prussia debouched from the wood of Paris, Planchenoit was in flames, and the Prussian balls began to rain down even in the ranks of the guard in reserve behind Napoleon.

12. *The guard*

THE REST IS KNOWN; the irruption of a third army, the battle thrown out of joint, eighty-six pieces of artillery suddenly thundering forth, Pirch the First coming up with Bulow, Ziethen's cavalry led by Blücher in person, the French crowded back, Marcognet swept from the plateau of Ohain, Durutte dislodged from Papelotte, Donzelot and Quiot recoiling, Lobau taken en echarpe, a new battle falling at nightfall upon our dismantled regiments, the whole English line assuming the offensive and pushed forward, the gigantic gap made in the French army, the English grape and the Prussian grape lending mutual aid, extermination, disaster in front, disaster in flank, the guard entering into line amid this terrible crumbling.

Feeling that they were going to their death, they cried out: *Vive l'Empereur!* There is nothing more touching in history than this death-agony bursting forth in acclamations.

The sky had been overcast all day. All at once, at this very moment – it was eight o'clock at night – the clouds in the horizon broke, and through the elms on the Nivelles road streamed the sinister red light of the setting sun. The rising sun shone upon Austerlitz.

Each battalion of the guard, for this final effort, was commanded by a general. Friant, Michel, Roguet, Harlet, Mallet, Poret de Morvan, were there. When the tall caps of the grenadiers of the guard with their large eagle plates appeared, symmetrical, drawn up in line, calm, in the smoke of that conflict, the enemy felt respect for France; they thought they saw twenty victories entering upon the field of battle, with wings extended, and those who were conquerors, thinking themselves conquered, recoiled; but Wellington cried: '*Up, guards, and at them!*' The red regiment of English guards, lying behind the hedges, rose up, a shower of grape riddled the tricoloured flag fluttering about our eagles, all hurled themselves forward, and the final carnage began. The Imperial Guard felt the army slipping away around them in the gloom, and the vast overthrow of the rout; they heard the *sauve qui peut!* which had replaced the *vive l'Empereur!* and, with flight behind them, they held on their course, battered more and more and dying faster and faster at every step. There were no weak souls or cowards there. The privates of that band were as heroic as their generals. Not a man flinched from the suicide.

Ney, desperate, great in all the grandeur of accepted death, bared himself to every blow in this tempest. He had his horse killed under him. Reeking with sweat, fire in his eyes, froth upon his lips, his uniform unbuttoned, one of his epaulets half cut away by the sabre stroke of a horse-guard, his badge of the grand eagle pierced by a ball, bloody, covered with mud, magnificent, a broken sword in his hand, he said: '*Come and see how a marshal of France dies upon the field of battle!*' But in vain, he did not die. He was haggard and exasperated. He flung this question at Drouet d'Erlon. '*What! are you not going to die?*' He cried out in the midst of all this artillery which was mowing down a handful of men: '*Is there nothing, then, for me? Oh! would that all these English balls were buried in my body!*' Unhappy man! thou wast reserved for French bullets![31]

13. *The catastrophe*

THE ROUT behind the guard was dismal.

The army fell back rapidly from all sides at once, from Hougomont, from La Haie Sainte, from Papelotte, from Planchenoit. The cry: *Treachery!* was followed by the cry: *Sauve qui peut!* A disbanding army is a thaw. The whole bends, cracks, snaps, floats, rolls, falls, crashes, hurries, plunges. Mysterious disintegration. Ney borrows a horse, leaps upon him, and without hat, cravat, or sword, plants himself in the Brussels road, arresting at once the English and the French. He endeavours to hold the army, he calls them back, he reproaches them, he grapples with the rout. He is swept away. The soldiers flee from him, crying: *Vive Marshal Ney!* Durutte's two regiments come and go, frightened, and tossed between the sabres of the Uhlans and the fire of the brigades of Kempt, Best, Pack, and Rylandt; rout is the worst of all conflicts; friends slay each other in their flight; squadrons and battalions are crushed and dispersed against each other, enormous foam of the battle. Lobau at one extremity, like Reille, at the other, is rolled away in the flood. In vain does Napoleon make walls with the remains of the guard; in vain does he expend his reserve squadrons in a last effort. Quiot gives way before Vivian, Kellermann before Vandeleur, Lobau before Bulow, Moraud before Pirch, Domon and Lubervic before Prince William of Prussia. Guyot, who had led the emperor's squadrons to the charge, falls under the feet of the English horse. Napoleon gallops along the fugitives, harangues them, urges, threatens, entreats. The mouths, which in the morning were crying *vive l'Empereur*, are now agape; he is hardly recognised. The Prussian cavalry, just come up, spring forward, fling themselves upon the enemy, sabre, cut, hack, kill, exterminate. Teams rush off, the guns are left to the care of themselves; the soldiers of the train unhitch the caissons and take the horses to escape; wagons upset, with their four wheels in the air, block up the road, and are accessories of massacre. They crush and they crowd; they trample upon the living and the dead. Arms are broken. A multitude fills roads, paths, bridges, plains, hills, valleys, woods, choked up by this flight of forty thousand men. Cries, despair, knapsacks and muskets cast into the rye, passages forced at the point of the sword; no more comrades, no more officers, no more generals; inexpressible dismay. Ziethen sabring France at his ease. Lions become kids. Such was this flight.

At Genappe there was an effort to turn back, to form a line, to make a stand. Lobau rallied three hundred men. The entrance to the village was barricaded, but at the first volley of Prussian grape, all took to flight again, and Lobau was captured. The marks of that volley of grape are still to be seen upon the old gable of a brick ruin at the right of the road, a short distance before entering Genappe. The Prussians rushed into Genappe, furious, doubtless, at having conquered so little. The pursuit was monstrous. Blücher gave orders to kill all. Roguet had set this sad example by threatening with death every French grenadier who should bring him a Prussian prisoner. Blücher surpassed Roguet. The general of the Young Guard, Duhesme, caught at the door of a tavern in Genappe, gave up his sword to a Hussar of Death, who took the sword and killed the prisoner. The victory was completed by the assassination of the vanquished. Let us punish, since we are history: old Blücher disgraced himself. This ferocity filled the disaster to the brim. The desperate rout passed through Genappe, passed through Quatre Bras, passed through Sombreffe, passed through Frasnes, passed through Thuin, passed through Charleroi, and stopped only at the frontier. Alas! who now was flying in such wise? The Grand Army.

This madness, this terror, this falling to ruins of the highest bravery which ever astonished history, can that be without cause? No. The shadow of an enormous right hand rests on Waterloo. It is the day of Destiny. A power above man controlled that day. Hence, the loss of mind in dismay; hence, all these great souls yielding up their swords. Those who had conquered Europe fell to the ground, having nothing more to say or to do, feeling a terrible presence in the darkness. *Hoc erat in fatis.* That day, the perspective of the human race changed.

Waterloo is the hinge of the nineteenth century.[32] The disappearance of the great man was necessary for the advent of the great century. One, to whom there is no reply, took it in charge. The panic of heroes is explained. In the battle of Waterloo, there is more than a cloud, there is a meteor. God passed over it.

In the gathering night, on a field near Genappe, Bernard and Bertrand seized by a flap of his coat and stopped a haggard, thoughtful, gloomy man, who, dragged thus far by the current of the rout, had dismounted, passed the bridle of his horse under his arm, and, with bewildered eye, was returning alone towards Waterloo. It was Napoleon endeavouring to advance again, mighty somnambulist of a vanished dream.

14. The last square

A FEW SQUARES of the guard, immovable in the flow of the rout as rocks in running water, held out until night. Night approaching, and death also, they waited this double shadow, and yielded, unfaltering, to its embrace. Each regiment, isolated from the others, and having no further communication with the army, which was broken in all directions, was dying alone. They had taken position, for this last struggle, some upon the heights of Rossomme, others in the plain of Mont Saint Jean. There, abandoned, conquered, terrible, these sombre squares suffered formidable martyrdom. Ulm, Wagram, Jena, Friedland, were dying in them.

At dusk, towards nine o'clock in the evening, at the foot of the plateau of Mont Saint Jean, there remained but one. In this fatal valley, at the bottom of that slope which had been climbed by the cuirassiers, inundated now by the English masses, under the converging fire of the victorious artillery of the enemy, under a frightful storm of projectiles, this square fought on. It was commanded by an obscure officer whose name was Cambronne. At every discharge, the square grew less, but returned the fire. It replied to grape by bullets, narrowing in its four walls continually. Afar off the fugitives, stopping for a moment out of breath, heard in the darkness this dismal thunder decreasing.

When this legion was reduced to a handful, when their flag was reduced to a shred, when their muskets, exhausted of ammunition, were reduced to nothing but clubs, when the pile of corpses was larger than the group of the living, there spread among the conquerors a sort of sacred terror about these sublime martyrs, and the English artillery, stopping to take breath, was silent. It was a kind of respite. These combatants had about them, as it were, a swarm of spectres, the outlines of men on horseback, the black profile of the cannons, the white sky seen through the wheels and the gun-carriages; the colossal death's head which heroes always see in the smoke of the battle was advancing upon them, and glaring at them. They could hear in the gloom of the twilight the loading of the pieces, the lighted matches like tigers' eyes in the night made a circle about their heads; all the linstocks of the English batteries approached the guns, when, touched by their heroism, holding the death-moment suspended over these men, an English general, Colville, according to some, Maitland, according to others, cried to them: 'Brave Frenchmen, surrender!' Cambronne answered: '*Merde!*'[33]

15. *Cambronne*

OUT OF RESPECT to the French reader, the finest word, perhaps, that a Frenchman ever uttered cannot be repeated to him. We are prohibited from embalming a sublimity in history.

At our own risk and peril, we violate that prohibition.

Among these giants, then, there was one Titan – Cambronne.

To speak that word, and then to die, what could be more grand! for to accept death is to die, and it is not the fault of this man, if, in the storm of grape, he survived.

The man who won the battle of Waterloo is not Napoleon put to rout; nor Wellington giving way at four o'clock, desperate at five; not Blücher, who did not fight; the man who won the battle of Waterloo was Cambronne.

To fulminate such a word at the thunderbolt which kills you is victory.

To make this answer to disaster, to say this to destiny, to give this base for the future lion, to fling down this reply at the rain of the previous night, at the treacherous wall of Hougomont, at the sunken road of Ohain, at the delay of Grouchy, at the arrival of Blücher, to be ironical in the sepulchre, to act so as to remain upright after one shall have fallen, to drown in two syllables the European coalition, to offer to kings these privities already known to the Cæsars, to make the last of words the first, by associating it with the glory of France, to close Waterloo insolently by a Mardi Gras, to complete Leonidas by Rabelais, to sum up this victory in a supreme word which cannot be pronounced, to lose the field, and to preserve history, after this carnage to have the laugh on his side, is immense.

It is an insult to the thunderbolt. That attains the grandeur of Æschylus.

This word of Cambronne's gives the effect of a fracture. It is the breaking of a heart by scorn; it is an overplus of agony in explosion. Who conquered? Wellington? No. Without Blücher he would have been lost. Blücher? No. If Wellington had not commenced, Blücher could not have finished. This Cambronne, this passer at the last hour, this unknown soldier, this infinitesimal of war, feels that there is there a lie in a catastrophe, doubly bitter; and at the moment when it is bursting with rage, he is offered this mockery – life? How can he restrain himself? They are there, all the kings of Europe, the fortunate generals, the thundering Joves, they have a hundred thousand victorious soldiers, and behind the hundred thousand, a million; their guns, with matches lighted, are agape; they have the Imperial Guard and the Grand Army under their feet; they have crushed Napoleon, and Cambronne only remains; there is none but this worm of the earth to protest. He will protest. Then he seeks for a word as one seeks for a sword. He froths at the mouth, and this froth is the word. Before this mean and monstrous victory, before this victory without victors, this desperate man straightens himself up, he suffers its enormity, but he establishes its nothingness; and he does more than spit upon it; and overwhelmed in numbers and material strength he finds in the soul an expression – ordure. We repeat it, to say that, to do that, to find that, is to be the conqueror.

The soul of great days entered into this unknown man at that moment of death. Cambronne finds the word of Waterloo, as Rouget de l'Isle finds the

Marseillaise, through a superior inspiration. An effluence from the divine afflatus detaches itself, and passes over these men, and they tremble, and the one sings the supreme song, and the other utters the terrible cry. This word of titanic scorn Cambronne throws down not merely to Europe, in the name of the Empire, that would be but little; he throws it down to the past, in the name of the Revolution. It is heard, and men recognise in Cambronne the old soul of the giants. It seems as if it were a speech of Danton, or a roar of Kleber.

To this word of Cambronne, the English voice replied: 'Fire!' the batteries flamed, the hill trembled, from all those brazen throats went forth a final vomiting of grape, terrific; a vast smoke, dusky white in the light of the rising moon, rolled out, and when the smoke was dissipated, there was nothing left. That formidable remnant was annihilated; the guard was dead. The four walls of the living redoubt had fallen, hardly could a quivering be distinguished here and there among the corpses; and thus the French legions, grander than the Roman legions, expired at Mont Saint Jean on ground soaked in rain and blood, in the sombre wheatfields, at the spot where now, at four o'clock in the morning, whistling, and gaily whipping up his horse, Joseph passes, who drives the mail from Nivelles.

16. Quot libras in duce?

THE BATTLE OF WATERLOO is an enigma. It is as obscure to those who won it as to him who lost it. To Napoleon it is a panic;* Blücher sees in it only fire; Wellington comprehends nothing of it. Look at the reports. The bulletins are confused, the commentaries are foggy. The former stammer, the latter falter. Jomini separates the battle of Waterloo into four periods; Muffling divides it into three tides of fortune; Charras alone, though upon some points our appreciation differs from his, has seized with his keen glance the characteristic lineaments of that catastrophe of human genius struggling with divine destiny. All the other historians are blinded by the glare, and are groping about in that blindness. A day of lightnings, indeed, the downfall of the military monarchy, which, to the great amazement of kings, has dragged with it all kingdoms, the fall of force, the overthrow of war.

In this event, bearing the impress of superhuman necessity, man's part is nothing.

Does taking away Waterloo from Wellington and from Blücher, detract anything from England and Germany? No. Neither illustrious England nor august Germany is in question in the problem of Waterloo. Thank heaven, nations are great aside from the dismal chances of the sword. Neither Germany, nor England, nor France, is held in a scabbard. At this day when Waterloo is only a clicking of sabres, above Blücher, Germany has Goethe, and above Wellington, England has Byron.[34] A vast uprising of ideas is peculiar to our century, and in this aurora England and Germany have a magnificent share. They are majestic because they think. The higher plane which they bring to civilisation is intrinsic to them; it comes from themselves, and not from an

---

* 'A battle ended, a day finished, false measures repaired, greater successes assured for the morrow, all was lost by a moment of panic' – (Napoleon, *Dictations at St Helena*)

accident. The advancement which they have made in the nineteenth century does not spring from Waterloo. It is only barbarous nations who have a sudden growth after a victory. It is the fleeting vanity of the streamlet swelled by the storm. Civilised nations, especially in our times, are not exalted nor abased by the good or bad fortune of a captain. Their specific gravity in the human race results from something more than a combat. Their honour, thank God, their dignity, their light, their genius, are not numbers that heroes and conquerors, those gamblers, can cast into the lottery of battles. Oftentimes a battle lost is progress attained. Less glory, more liberty. The drum is silent, reason speaks. It is the game at which he who loses, gains. Let us speak, then, coolly of Waterloo on both sides. Let us render unto Fortune the things that are Fortune's, and unto God the things that are God's. What is Waterloo? A victory? No. A prize.

A prize won by Europe, paid by France.

It was not much to put a lion there.

Waterloo moreover is the strangest encounter in history. Napoleon and Wellington: they are not enemies, they are opposites. Never has God, who takes pleasure in antitheses, made a more striking contrast and a more extraordinary meeting. On one side, precision, foresight, geometry, prudence, retreat assured, reserves economised, obstinate composure, imperturbable method, strategy to profit by the ground, tactics to balance battalions, carnage drawn to the line, war directed watch in hand, nothing left voluntarily to chance, ancient classic courage, absolute correctness; on the other, intuition, inspiration, a military marvel, a superhuman instinct; a flashing glance, a mysterious something which gazes like the eagle and strikes like the thunder-bolt, prodigious art in disdainful impetuosity, all the mysteries of a deep soul, intimacy with Destiny; river, plain, forest, hill, commanded, and in some sort forced to obey, the despot going even so far as to tyrannise over the battlefield; faith in a star joined to strategic science, increasing it, but disturbing it. Wellington was the Barrême of war, Napoleon was its Michaelangelo, and this time genius was vanquished by calculation.

On both sides they were expecting somebody. It was the exact calculator who succeeded. Napoleon expected Grouchy; he did not come. Wellington expected Blücher; he came.

Wellington is classic war taking her revenge. Bonaparte, in his dawn, had met her in Italy, and defeated her superbly. The old owl fled before the young vulture. Ancient tactics had been not only thunderstruck, but had received mortal offence. What was this Corsican of twenty-six? What meant this brilliant novice who, having everything against him, nothing for him, with no provisions, no muni-tions, no cannon, no shoes, almost without an army, with a handful of men against multitudes, rushed upon allied Europe, and absurdly gained victories that were impossible? Whence came this thundering madman who, almost without taking breath, and with the same set of the combatants in hand, pulverised one after the other the five armies of the Emperor of Germany, overthrowing Beaulieu upon Alvinzi, Wurmser upon Beaulieu, Melas upon Wurmser, Mack upon Melas? Who was this newcomer in war with the confidence of destiny? The academic military school excommunicated him as it ran away. Thence an implacable hatred of the old system of war against the new, of the correct sabre against the flashing sword, and of the chequer-board against genius. On the 18th of June 1815, this hatred had the last word, and under Lodi, Montebello, Montenotte, Mantua,

Marengo, Arcola, it wrote: Waterloo. Triumph of the commonplace, grateful to majorities. Destiny consented to this irony. In his decline, Napoleon again found Wurmser before him, but young. Indeed, to produce Wurmser, it would have been enough to whiten Wellington's hair.

Waterloo is a battle of the first rank won by a captain of the second.

What is truly admirable in the battle of Waterloo is England, English firmness, English resolution, English blood; the superb thing which England had there – may it not displease her – is herself. It is not her captain, it is her army.

Wellington, strangely ungrateful, declared in a letter to Lord Bathurst that his army, the army that fought on the 18th of June 1815, was a 'detestable army'. What does this dark assemblage of bones, buried beneath the furrows of Waterloo, think of that?

England has been too modest in regard to Wellington. To make Wellington so great is to belittle England. Wellington is but a hero like the rest. These Scots Grays, these Horse Guards, these regiments of Maitland and of Mitchell, this infantry of Pack and Kempt, this cavalry of Ponsonby and of Somerset, these Highlanders playing the bagpipe under the storm of grape, these battalions of Rylandt, these raw recruits who hardly knew how to handle a musket, holding out against the veteran bands of Essling and Rivoli – all that is grand. Wellington was tenacious, that was his merit, and we do not undervalue it, but the least of his foot-soldiers or his horsemen was quite as firm as he. The iron soldier is as good as the Iron Duke. For our part, all our glorification goes to the English soldier, the English army, the English people. If trophy there be, to England the trophy is due. The Waterloo column would be more just if, instead of the figure of a man, it lifted to the clouds the statue of a nation.

But this great England will be offended at what we say here. She has still, after her 1688 and our 1789, the feudal illusion. She believes in hereditary right, and in the hierarchy. This people, surpassed by none in might and glory, esteems itself as a nation, not as a people. So much so that as a people they subordinate themselves willingly, and take a Lord for a head. Workmen, they submit to be despised; soldiers, they submit to be whipped. We remember that at the battle of Inkerman a sergeant who, as it appeared, had saved the army, could not be mentioned by Lord Raglan, the English military hierarchy not permitting any hero below the rank of officer to be spoken of in a report.

What we admire above all, in an encounter like that of Waterloo, is the prodigious skill of fortune. The night's rain, the wall of Hougomont, the sunken road of Ohain, Grouchy deaf to cannon, Napoleon's guide who deceives him, Bulow's guide who leads him right; all this cataclysm is wonderfully carried out.

Taken as a whole, let us say, Waterloo was more of a massacre than a battle.

Of all great battles, Waterloo is that which has the shortest line in proportion to the number engaged. Napoleon, two miles, Wellington, a mile and a half; seventy-two thousand men on each side. From this density came the carnage.

The calculation has been made and this proportion established: Loss of men: at Austerlitz, French, fourteen per cent.; Russians, thirty per cent.; Austrians, forty-four per cent. At Wagram, French, thirteen per cent.; Austrians, fourteen. At La Moscowa, French, thirty-seven per cent.; Russians, forty-four. At Bautzen, French, thirteen per cent.; Russians and Prussians, fourteen. At Waterloo, French, fifty-six per cent.; Allies, thirty-one. Average for Waterloo, forty-one per cent. A hundred and forty-four thousand men; sixty thousand dead.

The field of Waterloo today has that calm which belongs to the earth, impassive support of man; it resembles any other plain.

At night, however, a sort of visionary mist arises from it, and if some traveller be walking there, if he looks, if he listens, if he dreams like Virgil in the fatal plain of Philippi, he becomes possessed by the hallucination of the disaster. The terrible 18th of June is again before him; the artificial hill of the monument fades away, this lion, whatever it be, is dispelled; the field of battle resumes its reality; the lines of infantry undulate in the plain, furious gallops traverse the horizon; the bewildered dreamer sees the flash of sabres, the glistening of bayonets, the bursting of shells, the awful intermingling of the thunders; he hears, like a death-rattle from the depths of a tomb, the vague clamour of the phantom battle; these shadows are grenadiers; these gleams are cuirassiers; this skeleton is Napoleon; that skeleton is Wellington; all this is unreal, and yet it clashes and combats; and the ravines run red, and the trees shiver, and there is fury even in the clouds, and, in the darkness, all those savage heights, Mont Saint Jean, Hougomont, Frischemont, Papelotte, Planchenoit, appear confusedly crowned with whirlwinds of spectres exterminating each other.

17. Must we approve Waterloo?

THERE EXISTS a very respectable liberal school, which does not hate Waterloo. We are not of them. To us Waterloo is but the unconscious date of liberty. That such an eagle should come from such an egg, is certainly an unlooked-for thing

Waterloo, if we place ourselves at the culminating point of view of the question, is intentionally a counter-revolutionary victory. It is Europe against France; it is Petersburg, Berlin and Vienna against Paris; it is the *status quo* against the initiative; it is the 14th of June 1789, attacked by the 20th March 1815, it is the monarchies clearing the decks for action against indomitable French uprising. The final extinction of this vast people, for twenty-six years in eruption, such was the dream. It was the solidarity of the Brunswicks, the Nassaus, the Romanoffs, the Hohenzollerns, and the Hapsburgs, with the Bourbons. Divine right rides behind with Waterloo. It is true that the empire having been despotic, royalty, by the natural reaction of things, was forced to become liberal, and also that a constitutional order has indirectly sprung from Waterloo, to the great regret of the conquerors. The fact is, that revolution cannot be conquered, and that being providential and absolutely decreed, it reappears continually, before Waterloo in Bonaparte, throwing down the old thrones, after Waterloo in Louis XVIII granting and submitting to the charter. Bonaparte places a postilion on the throne of Naples and a sergeant on the throne of Sweden,[35] employing inequality to demonstrate equality; Louis XVIII at Saint Ouen countersigns the declaration of the rights of man. Would you realise what Revolution is, call it Progress; and would you realise what Progress is, call it Tomorrow. Tomorrow performs its work irresistibly, and it performs it from today. It always reaches its aim through unexpected means. It employs Wellington to make Foy, who was only a soldier, an orator. Foy falls at Hougomont and rises again at the rostrum. Thus progress goes on. No tool comes amiss to this workman. It adjusts to its divine work, without being disconcerted, the man who strode over the Alps, and the good old tottering invalid of the Père Elysée.[36] It makes use of the cripple as well as the conqueror, the conqueror without, the cripple within. Waterloo, by cutting short the demolition of European thrones by the sword, has had no other effect than to continue the revolutionary work in another way. The saberers have gone out, the time of the thinkers has come. The age which Waterloo would have checked has marched on and pursued its course. This inauspicious victory has been conquered by liberty.

In fine and incontestably, that which triumphed at Waterloo; that which smiled behind Wellington; that which brought him all the marshals' batons of Europe, among them, it is said, the baton of marshal of France; that which joyfully rolled barrows of earth full of bones to rear the mound of the lion; that which has written triumphantly on that pedestal this date: June 18th, 1815, that which encouraged Blücher sabering the fugitives; that which, from the height of the plateau of Mont Saint Jean, hung over France as over a prey, was Counter-revolution. It was Counter-revolution which murmured this infamous word – dismemberment. Arriving at Paris, it had a near view of the crater; it felt that these ashes were burning its feet, and took a second thought. It came back lisping of a charter.

Let us see in Waterloo only what there is in Waterloo. Of intentional liberty, nothing. The Counter-revolution was involuntarily liberal, as, by a corresponding phenomenon, Napoleon was involuntarily revolutionary. On the 18th June 1815, Robespierre on horseback was thrown from the saddle.

18. *Recrudescence of Divine Right*

END OF THE DICTATORSHIP. The whole European system fell.

The empire sank into a darkness which resembled that of the expiring Roman world. It rose again from the depths, as in the time of the Barbarians. Only, the barbarism of 1815, which should be called by its special name, the counter-revolution, was short-winded, soon out of breath, and soon stopped. The empire, we must acknowledge, was wept over, and wept over by heroic eyes. If there be glory in the sceptre-sword, the empire had been glory itself. It had spread over the earth all the light which tyranny can give – a sombre light. Let us say further – an obscure light. Compared to the real day, it is night. This disappearance of night had the effect of an eclipse.

Louis XVIII returned to Paris. The dancing in a ring of the 8th of July effaced the euthusiasm of the 20th of March.[37] The Corsican became the antithesis of the Bearnois. The flag of the dome of the Tuileries was white. The exile mounted the throne. The fir table of Hartwell took its place before the chair decorated with fleur-de-lis of Louis XIV. Men talked of Bouvines and Fontenoy as of yesterday, Austerlitz being out of date. The altar and the throne fraternised majestically. One of the most unquestionably safe forms of society in the nineteenth century was established in France and on the Continent. Europe put on the white cockade. Trestaillon became famous.[38] The device *non pluribus impar* reappeared in the radiations on the façade of the barracks of the quay of Orsay. Where there had been an imperial guard, there was a red house. The arc du Carrousel – covered with awkwardly gained victories – disowned by these new times, and a little ashamed, perhaps, of Marengo and Arcola, extricated itself from the affair by the statue of the Duke of Angoulême. The cemetery de la Madeleine, the terrible Potter's Field of '93, was covered with marble and jasper, the bones of Louis XVI and Marie-Antoinette being in this dust. In the ditch of Vincennes, a sepulchral column rose from the ground, recalling the fact that the Duke of Enghien died in the same month in which Napoleon was crowned. Pope Pius VII, who had performed this consecration very near the time of this death, tranquilly blessed the fall as he had blessed the elevation. At Schœnbrunn there was a little shadow four years old which it was seditious to call the King of Rome.[39] And these things were done, and these kings resumed their thrones, and the master of Europe was put in a cage, and the old *régime* became the new, and all the light and shade of the earth changed place, because, in the afternoon of a summer's day, a cowboy said to a Prussian in a wood: 'Pass this way and not that!'

This 1815 was a sort of gloomy April. The old unhealthy and poisonous realities took on new shapes. Falsehood espoused 1789, divine right masked itself under a charter, fictions became constitutional, prejudices, superstitions and mental reservations, with article 14[40] hugged to the heart, put on a varnish of liberalism. Serpents changing their skins.

Man had been at once made greater and made less by Napoleon. The ideal, under this splendid material reign, had received the strange name of ideology. Serious recklessness of a great man, to turn the future into derision. The people, however, that food for cannon so fond of the cannoneer, looked for him. Where is he? What is he doing? 'Napoleon is dead,' said a visitor to an invalid of Marengo and Waterloo. '*He dead!*' cried the soldier; '*are you sure of that?*' Imagination deified this prostrate man. The heart of Europe, after Waterloo, was gloomy. An enormous void remained long after the disappearance of Napoleon.

Kings threw themselves into this void. Old Europe profited by it to assume a new form. There was a Holy Alliance. Belle Alliance the fatal field of Waterloo had already said in advance.

In presence of and confronting this ancient Europe made over, the lineaments of a new France began to appear. The future, the jest of the emperor, made its appearance. It had on its brow this star, Liberty. The ardent eyes of rising generations turned towards it. Strange to tell, men became enamoured at the same time of this future, Liberty, and of this past, Napoleon. Defeat had magnified the vanquished. Bonaparte fallen seemed higher than Bonaparte in power. Those who had triumphed, were struck with fear. England guarded him through Hudson Lowe, and France watched him through Montchenu. His folded arms became the anxiety of thrones. Alexander called him, My Wakefulness. This terror arose from the amount of revolution he had in him. This is the explanation and excuse of Bonapartist liberalism. This phantom made the old world quake. Kings reigned ill at ease with the rock of Saint Helena in the horizon.

While Napoleon was dying at Longwood, the sixty thousand men fallen on the field of Waterloo tranquilly mouldered away, and something of their peace spread over the world. The congress of Vienna made from it the treaties of 1815, and Europe called that the Restoration.

Such is Waterloo.

But what is that to the Infinite? All this tempest, all this cloud, this war, then this peace, all this darkness, disturb not for a moment the light of that infinite Eye, before which the least of insects leaping from one blade of grass to another equals the eagle flying from spire to spire among the towers of Notre-Dame.

19. *The field of battle at night*

WE RETURN, for it is a requirement of this book, to the fatal field of battle.

On the 18th of June 1815, the moon was full. Its light favoured the ferocious pursuit of Blücher, disclosed the traces of the fugitives, delivered this helpless mass to the bloodthirsty Prussian cavalry, and aided in the massacre. Night sometimes lends such tragic assistance to catastrophe.

When the last gun had been fired the plain of Mont Saint Jean remained deserted.

The English occupied the camp of the French; it is the usual verification of victory to sleep in the bed of the vanquished. They established their bivouac around Rossomme. The Prussians, let loose upon the fugitives, pushed forward. Wellington went to the village of Waterloo to make up his report to Lord Bathurst.

If ever the *sic vos non vobis*[41] were applicable, it is surely to this village of Waterloo. Waterloo did nothing, and was two miles distant from the action. Mont Saint Jean was cannonaded, Hougomont was burned, Papelotte was burned, Planchenoit was burned, La Haie Sainte was taken by assault, La Belle Alliance witnessed the meeting of the two conquerors; these names are scarcely known, and Waterloo, which had nothing to do with the battle, has all the honour of it.

We are not of those who glorify war; when the opportunity presents itself we describe its realities. War has frightful beauties which we have not concealed; it has also, we must admit, some deformities. One of the most surprising is the eager spoliation of the dead after a victory. The day after a battle dawns upon naked corpses.

Who does this? Who thus sullies the triumph? Whose is this hideous furtive hand which glides into the pocket of victory? Who are these pickpockets following their trade in the wake of glory? Some philosophers, Voltaire among others, affirm that they are precisely those who have achieved the glory. They are the same, say they, there is no exchange; those who survive pillage those who succumb. The hero of the day is the vampire of the night. A man has a right, after all, to despoil in part a corpse which he has made.

For our part we do not believe this. To gather laurels and to steal the shoes from a dead man, seems to us impossible to the same hand.

One thing is certain, that, after the conquerors, come the robbers. But let us place the soldier, especially the soldier of today, beyond this charge.

Every army has a train, and there the accusation should lie. Bats, half brigand and half valet, all species of night bird engendered by this twilight which is called war, bearers of uniforms who never fight, sham invalids, formidable cripples, interloping sutlers, travelling, sometimes with their wives, on little carts and stealing what they sell, beggars offering themselves as guides to officers, army-servants, marauders; armies on the march formerly – we do not speak of the present time – were followed by all these, to such an extent that, in technical language, they are called 'camp-followers'. No army and no nation was responsible for these beings; they spoke Italian and followed the Germans; they spoke French and followed the English. It was by one of these wretches, a Spanish camp-follower who spoke French, that the Marquis of Fervacques, deceived by his

Picardy gibberish, and taking him for one of us, was treacherously killed and robbed on the very battlefield during the night which followed the victory of Cerisoles. From marauding came the marauder. The detestable maxim, *live on your enemy*, produced this leper, which rigid discipline alone can cure. There are reputations which are illusory; it is not always known why certain generals, though they have been great, have been so popular. Turenne was adored by his soldiers because he tolerated pillage; the permission to do wrong forms part of kindness; Turenne was so kind that he allowed the Palatinate to be burned and put to the sword. There were seen in the wake of armies more or less of marauders according as the commander was more or less severe. Hoche and Marceau had no camp-followers; Wellington – we gladly do him this justice – had few.

However, during the night of the 18th of June, the dead were despoiled. Wellington was rigid; he ordered whoever should be taken in the act to be put to death; but rapine is persevering. The marauders were robbing in one corner of the battlefield while they were shooting them in another.

The moon was an evil genius on this plain.

Towards midnight a man was prowling or rather crawling along the sunken road of Ohain. He was, to all appearance, one of those whom we have just described, neither English nor French, peasant nor soldier, less a man than a ghoul, attracted by the scent of the corpses, counting theft for victory, coming to rifle Waterloo. He was dressed in a blouse which was in part a capote, was restless and daring, looking behind and before as he went. Who was this man? Night, probably, knew more of his doings than day! He had no knapsack, but evidently large pockets under his capote. From time to time he stopped, examined the plain around him as if to see if he were observed, stooped down suddenly, stirred on the ground something silent and motionless, then rose up and skulked away. His gliding movement, his attitudes, his rapid and mysterious gestures, made him seem like those twilight spectres which haunt ruins and which the old Norman legends call the Goers.

Certain nocturnal water-birds make such motions in marshes.

An eye which had carefully penetrated all this haze, might have noticed at some distance, standing as it were concealed behind the ruin which is on the Nivelles road at the corner of the route from Mont Saint Jean to Braine l'Alleud, a sort of little sutler's wagon, covered with tarred osiers, harnessed to a famished jade browsing nettles through her bit, and in the wagon a sort of woman seated on some trunks and packages. Perhaps there was some connection between this wagon and the prowler.

The night was serene. Not a cloud was in the zenith. What mattered it that the earth was red the moon retained her whiteness. Such is the indifference of heaven. In the meadows, branches of trees broken by grape, but not fallen, and held by the bark, swung gently in the night wind. A breath, almost a respiration, moved the brushwood. There was a quivering in the grass which seemed like the departure of souls.

The tread of the patrols and groundsmen of the English camp could be heard dimly in the distance.

Hougomont and La Haie Sainte continued to burn, making, one in the east and the other in the west, two great flames, to which was attached, like a necklace of rubies with two carbuncles at its extremities, the cordon of bivouac fires of the English, extending in an immense semicircle over the hills of the horizon.

We have spoken of the catastrophe of the road to Ohain. The heart almost sinks with terror at the thought of such a death for so many brave men.

If anything is frightful, if there be a reality which surpasses dreams, it is this: to live, to see the sun, to be in full possession of manly vigour, to have health and joy, to laugh sturdily, to rush towards a glory which dazzlingly invites you on, to feel a very pleasure in respiration, to feel your heart beat, to feel yourself a reasoning being, to speak, to think, to hope, to love; to have mother, to have wife, to have children, to have sunlight, and suddenly, in a moment, in less than a minute, to feel yourself buried in an abyss, to fall, to roll, to crush, to be crushed, to see the grain, the flowers, the leaves, the branches, to be able to seize upon nothing, to feel your sword useless, men under you, horses over you, to strike about you in vain, your bones broken by some kick in the darkness, to feel a heel which makes your eyes leap from their sockets, to grind the horseshoes with rage in your teeth, to stifle, to howl, to twist, to be under all this, and to say: just now I was a living man!

There, where this terrible death-rattle had been, all was now silent. The cut of the sunken road was filled with horses and riders inextricably heaped together. Terrible entanglement. There were no longer slopes to the road; dead bodies filled it even with the plain, and came to the edge of the banks like a well-measured bushel of barley. A mass of dead above, a river of blood below – such was this road on the evening of the 18th of June 1815. The blood ran even to the Nivelles road, and oozed through in a large pool in front of the abattis of trees, which barred that road, at a spot which is still shown. It was, it will be remembered, at the opposite point, towards the road from Genappe, that the burying of the cuirassiers took place. The thickness of the mass of bodies was proportioned to the depth of the hollow road. Towards the middle, at a spot where it became shallower, over which Delord's division had passed, this bed of death became thinner.

The night prowler which we have just introduced to the reader went in this direction. He ferreted through this immense grave. He looked about. He passed an indescribably hideous review of the dead. He walked with his feet in blood.

Suddenly he stopped.

A few steps before him, in the sunken road, at a point where the mound of corpses ended, from under this mass of men and horses appeared an open hand, lighted by the moon.

This hand had something upon a finger which sparkled; it was a gold ring.

The man stooped down, remained a moment, and when he rose again there was no ring upon that hand.

He did not rise up precisely; he remained in a sinister and startled attitude, turning his back to the pile of dead, scrutinising the horizon, on his knees, all the front of his body being supported on his two forefingers, his head raised just enough to peep above the edge of the hollow road. The four paws of the jackal are adapted to certain actions.

Then, deciding upon his course, he arose.

At this moment he experienced a shock. He felt that he was held from behind.

He turned; it was the open hand, which had closed, seizing the lapel of his capote.

An honest man would have been frightened. This man began to laugh.

'Oh,' said he, 'it's only the dead man. I like a ghost better than a gendarme.'

However, the hand relaxed and let go its hold. Strength is soon exhausted in the tomb.

'Ah ha!' returned the prowler, 'is this dead man alive? Let us see.'

He bent over again, rummaged among the heap, removed whatever impeded him, seized the hand, laid hold of the arm, disengaged the head, drew out the body, and some moments after dragged into the shadow of the hollow road an inanimate man, at least one who was senseless. It was a cuirassier, an officer; an officer, also, of some rank; a great gold epaulet protruded from beneath his cuirass, but he had no casque. A furious sabre cut had disfigured his face, where nothing but blood was to be seen. It did not seem, however, that he had any limbs broken; and by some happy chance, if the word is possible here, the bodies were arched above him in such a way as to prevent his being crushed. His eyes were closed.

He had on his cuirass the silver cross of the Legion of Honour.

The prowler tore off this cross, which disappeared in one of the gulfs which he had under his capote.

After which he felt the officer's fob, found a watch there, and took it. Then he rummaged in his vest and found a purse, which he pocketed.

When he had reached this phase of the succour he was lending the dying man, the officer opened his eyes.

'Thanks,' said he feebly.

The rough movements of the man handling him, the coolness of the night, and breathing the fresh air freely, had roused him from his lethargy.

The prowler answered not. He raised his head. The sound of a footstep could be heard on the plain; probably it was some patrol who was approaching,.

The officer murmured, for there were still signs of suffering in his voice:

'Who has gained the battle?'

'The English,' answered the prowler.

The officer replied:

'Search my pockets. You will there find a purse and a watch. Take them.'

This had already been done.

The prowler made a pretence of executing the command, and said:

'There is nothing there.'

'I have been robbed,' replied the officer; 'I am sorry. They would have been yours.'

The step of the patrol became more and more distinct.

'Somebody is coming,' said the prowler, making a movement as if he would go.

The officer, raising himself up painfully upon one arm, held him back.

'You have saved my life. Who are you?'

The prowler answered quick and low:

'I belong, like yourself, to the French army. I must go. If I am taken I shall be shot. I have saved your life. Help yourself now.'

'What is your grade?'

'Sergeant.'

'What is your name?'

'Thénardier.'

'I shall not forget that name,' said the officer. 'And you, remember mine. My name is Pontmercy.'

BOOK 2: THE SHIP *ORION*

1. *Number 24601 becomes Number 9430*

JEAN VALJEAN has been retaken.

We shall be pardoned for passing rapidly over the painful details. We shall merely reproduce a couple of items published in the newspapers of that day, some few months after the remarkable events that occurred at M— sur M—.

The articles referred to are somewhat laconic. It will be remembered that the *Gazette des Tribunaux* [42] had not yet been established.

We copy the first from the *Drapeau Blanc*. It is dated the 25th of July 1823:

> A district of the Pas-de-Calais has just been the scene of an extraordinary occurrence. A stranger in that department, known as Monsieur Madeleine, had, within a few years past, restored, by means of certain new processes, the manufacture of jet and black glass ware – a former local branch of industry. He had made his own fortune by it, and, in fact, that of the entire district. In acknowledgement of his services he had been appointed mayor. The police has discovered that Monsieur Madeleine was none other than an escaped convict, condemned in 1796 for robbery, and named Jean Valjean. This Jean Valjean has been sent back to the galleys. It appears that previous to his arrest, he succeeded in withdrawing from Laffitte's a sum amounting to more than half a million which he had deposited there, and which it is said, by the way, he had very legitimately realised in his business. Since his return to the galleys at Toulon, it has been impossible to discover where Jean Valjean concealed this money.

The second article, which enters a little more into detail, is taken from the *Journal de Paris* of the same date:

> An old convict, named Jean Valjean, has recently been brought before the Var Assizes, under circumstances calculated to attract attention. This villain had succeeded in eluding the vigilance of the police; he had changed his name, and had even been adroit enough to procure the appointment of mayor in one of our small towns in the North. He had established in this town a very considerable business, but was, at length, unmasked and arrested, thanks to the indefatigable zeal of the public authorities. He kept, as his mistress, a prostitute, who died of the shock at the moment of his arrest. This wretch, who is endowed with herculean strength, managed to escape, but, three or four days afterwards, the police retook him, in Paris, just as he was getting into one of the small vehicles that ply between the capital and the village of Montfermeil (Seine-et-Oise). It is said that he had availed himself of the interval of these three or four days of freedom, to withdraw a considerable sum deposited by him with one of our principal bankers. The amount is estimated at six or seven hundred thousand francs. According to the minutes of the case, he has concealed it in some place known to himself alone, and it has been impossible to seize it; however that may be, the said Jean Valjean has

been brought before the assizes of the Department of the Var under indictment for an assault and robbery on the high road committed *vi et armis* some eight years ago on the person of one of those honest lads who, as the patriarch of Ferney has written in immortal verse,

> . . . De Savoie arrivent tous les ans,
> Et dont la main légèrement essuie
> Ces longs canaux engorgés par la suie.*[43]

This bandit attempted no defence. It was proven by the able and eloquent representative of the crown that the robbery was shared in by others, and that Jean Valjean formed one of a band of robbers in the South. Consequently, Jean Valjean, being found guilty, was condemned to death. The criminal refused to appeal to the higher courts, and the king, in his inexhaustible clemency, deigned to commute his sentence to that of hard labour in prison for life. Jean Valjean was immediately forwarded to the galleys at Toulon.

It will not be forgotten that Jean Valjean had at M— sur M— certain religious habits. Some of the newspapers and, among them, the *Constitutionnel*, held up this commutation as a triumph of the clerical party.

Jean Valjean changed his number at the galleys. He became 9430.

While we are about it, let us remark, in dismissing the subject, that with M. Madeleine, the prosperity of M— sur M— disappeared; all that he had foreseen, in that night of fever and irresolution, was realised; he gone, the *soul* was gone. After his downfall, there was at M— sur M— that egotistic distribution of what is left when great men have fallen – that fatal carving up of prosperous enterprises which is daily going on, out of sight, in human society, and which history has noted but once, and then, because it took place after the death of Alexander. Generals crown themselves kings; the foremen, in this case, assumed the position of manufacturers. Jealous rivalries arose. The spacious workshops of M. Madeleine were closed; the building fell into ruin, the workmen dispersed. Some left the country, others abandoned the business. From that time forth, everything was done on a small, instead of on the large scale, and for gain rather than for good. No longer any centre; competition on all sides, and on all sides venom. M. Madeleine had ruled and directed everything. He fallen, every man strove for himself; the spirit of strife succeeded to the spirit of organisation, bitterness to cordiality, hatred of each against each instead of the good will of the founder towards all; the threads knitted by M. Madeleine became entangled and were broken; the workmanship was debased, the manufacturers were degraded, confidence was killed; customers diminished, there were fewer orders, wages decreased, the shops became idle, bankruptcy followed. And, then, there was nothing left for the poor. All that was there disappeared.

Even the state noticed that someone had been crushed, in some direction. Less than four years after the decree of the court of assizes establishing the identity of M. Madeleine and Jean Valjean, for the benefit of the galleys, the expense of collecting the taxes was doubled in the district of M— sur M—; and M. de Villèle[44] remarked the fact, on the floor of the Assembly, in the month of February, 1827.

* . . . Who come from Savoy every year,
  And whose hand deftly wipes out
  Those long channels choked up with soot.

2. *In which a couple of lines will be read which came, perhaps, from The Evil One*

BEFORE PROCEEDING FURTHER, it will not be amiss to relate, in some detail, a singular incident which took place, about the same time, at Montfermeil, and which, perhaps, does not fall in badly with certain conjectures of the public authorities.

There exists, in the neighbourhood of Montfermeil, a very ancient superstition, all the more rare and precious from the fact that a popular superstition in the vicinity of Paris is like an aloe tree in Siberia. Now, we are of those who respect anything in the way of a rarity. Here, then, is the superstition of Montfermeil: they believe, there, that the Evil One has, from time immemorial, chosen the forest as the hiding-place for his treasure. The good wives of the vicinity affirm that it is no unusual thing to meet, at sundown, in the secluded portions of the woods, a black-looking man, resembling a wagoner or woodcutter, shod in wooden shoes, clad in breeches and sack of coarse linen, and recognisable from the circumstances that, instead of a cap or hat, he has two immense horns upon his head. That certainly ought to render him recognisable. This man is constantly occupied in digging holes. There are three ways of dealing when you meet him.

The first mode is to approach the man and speak to him. Then you perceive that the man is nothing but a peasant, that he looks black because it is twilight, that he is digging no hole whatever, but is merely cutting grass for his cows; and that what had been taken for horns are nothing but his pitchfork which he carries on his back, and the prongs of which, thanks to the night perspective, seemed to rise from his head. You go home and die within a week. The second method is to watch him, to wait until he has dug the hole, closed it up, and gone away; then, to run quickly to the spot, to open it and get the 'treasure' which the black-looking man has, of course, buried there. In this case, you die within a month. The third manner is not to speak to the dark man nor even to look at him, and to run away as fast as you can. You die within the year.

As all three of these methods have their drawbacks, the second, which, at least, offers some advantages, among others that of possessing a treasure, though it be but for a month, is the one generally adopted. Daring fellows, who never neglect a good chance, have, therefore, many times, it is asseverated, reopened the holes thus dug by the black-looking man, and tried to rob the Devil. It would appear, however, that it is not a very good business – at least, if we are to believe tradition, and, more especially, two enigmatic lines in barbarous Latin left us, on this subject, by a roguish Norman monk, named Tryphon, who dabbled in the black art. This Tryphon was buried in the abbey of St Georges de Bocherville, near Rouen, and toads are produced from his grave.

Well then, the treasure-seeker makes tremendous efforts, for the holes referred to are dug, generally, very deep; he sweats, he digs, he works away all night, for this is done in the night-time; he gets his clothes wet, he consumes his candle, he hacks and breaks his pickaxe, and when, at length, he has reached the bottom of the hole, when he has put his hand upon the 'treasure', what does he find? What is this treasure of the Evil One? A penny – sometimes a crown; a stone, a skeleton, a bleeding corpse, sometimes a spectre twice folded like a sheet of paper in a portfolio, sometimes nothing. This is what seems to be held forth to the indiscreet and prying by the lines of Tryphon:

> Fodit, et in fossa thesauros condit opaca,
> As, nummos, lapides, cadaver, simulacra, nihilque.[45]

It appears that, in our time, they find in addition sometimes a powder-horn with bullets, sometimes an old pack of brown and greasy cards which have evidently been used by the Devil. Tryphon makes no mention of these articles, as Tryphon lived in the twelfth century, and it does not appear that the Evil One had wit enough to invent powder in advance of Roger Bacon or cards before Charles VI.

Moreover, whoever plays with these cards is sure to lose all he has, and as to the powder in the flask, it has the peculiarity of bursting your gun in your face.

Now, very shortly after the time when the authorities took it into their heads that the liberated convict Jean Valjean had, during his escape of a few days' duration, been prowling about Montfermeil, it was remarked, in that village, that a certain old road-labourer named Boulatruelle had 'a fancy' for the woods. People in the neighbourhood claimed to know that Boulatruelle had been in the galleys; he was under police surveillance, and, as he could find no work anywhere, the government employed him at half wages as a mender on the crossroad from Gagny to Lagny.

This Boulatruelle was a man in bad odour with the people of the neighbourhood; he was too respectful, too humble, prompt to doff his cap to everybody; he always trembled and smiled in the presence of the gendarmes, was probably in secret connection with robber-bands, said the gossips, and suspected of lying in wait in the hedge corners, at nightfall. He had nothing in his favour except that he was a drunkard.

What had been observed was this:

For sometime past, Boulatruelle had left off his work at stone-breaking and keeping the road in order, very early, and had gone into the woods with his pick. He would be met towards evening in the remotest glades and the wildest thickets, having the appearance of a person looking for something and, sometimes, digging holes. The good wives who passed that way took him at first for Beelzebub, then they recognised Boulatruelle, and were by no means reassured. These chance meetings seemed greatly to disconcert Boulatruelle. It was clear that he was trying to conceal himself, and that there was something mysterious in his operations.

The village gossips said: 'It's plain that the Devil has been about, Boulatruelle has seen him and is looking for his treasure. The truth is, he is just the fellow to rob the Evil One.' The Voltairians added: 'Will Boulatruelle catch the Devil or the Devil catch Boulatruelle?' The old women crossed themselves very often.

However, the visits of Boulatruelle to the woods ceased and he recommenced his regular labour on the road. People began to talk about something else.

A few, however, retained their curiosity, thinking that there might be involved in the affair, not the fabulous treasures of the legend, but some goodly matter more substantial than the Devil's bank-bills, and that Boulatruelle had half spied out the secret. The worst puzzled of all were the schoolmaster and the tavern-keeper, Thénardier, who was everybody's friend, and who had not disdained to strike up an intimacy with even Boulatruelle.

'He has been in the galleys,' said Thénardier. 'Good Lord! nobody knows who is there or who may be there!'

One evening, the schoolmaster remarked that, in old times, the authorities would have inquired into what Boulatruelle was about in the woods, and that he would have been compelled to speak – even put to torture, if needs were – and that Boulatruelle would not have held out, had he been put to the question by water, for example.

'Let us put him to the wine question,' said Thénardier.

So they made up a party and plied the old roadsman with drink. Boulatruelle drank enormously, but said little. He combined with admirable art and in masterly proportions the thirst of a guzzler with the discretion of a judge. However, by dint of returning to the charge and by putting together and twisting the obscure expressions that he did let fall, Thénardier and the schoolmaster made out, as they thought, the following:

One morning about daybreak as he was going to his work, Boulatruelle had been surprised at seeing under a bush in a corner of the wood, a pickaxe and spade, *as one would say, hidden there.* However, he supposed that they were the pick and spade of old Six-Fours, the water-carrier, and thought no more about it. But, on the evening of the same day, he had seen, without being seen himself, for he was hidden behind a large tree, 'a person who did not belong at all to that region, and whom he, Boulatruelle, knew very well' – or, as Thénardier translated it, *'an old comrade at the galleys'* – turn off from the high road towards the thickest part of the wood. Boulatruelle obstinately refused to tell the stranger's name. This person carried a package, something square, like a large box or a small trunk. Boulatruelle was surprised. Seven or eight minutes, however, elapsed before it occurred to him to follow the 'person'. But he was too late. The person was already in the thick woods, night had come on, and Boulatruelle did not succeed in overtaking him. Thereupon he made up his mind to watch the outskirts of the wood. 'There was a moon.' Two or three hours later, Boulatruelle saw this person come forth again from the wood, this time carrying now not the little trunk but a pick and a spade. Boulatruelle let the person pass unmolested, because, as he thought to himself, the other was three times as strong as he, was armed with a pickaxe, and would probably murder him, on recognising his countenance and seeing that he, in turn, was recognised. Touching display of feeling in two old companions unexpectedly meeting! But the pick and the spade were a ray of light to Boulatruelle; he hastened to the bushes, in the morning, and found neither one nor the other. He thence concluded that this person, on entering the wood, had dug a hole with his pick, had buried the chest, and had, then, filled up the hole with his spade. Now, as the chest was too small to contain a corpse, it must contain money; hence his continued searches. Boulatruelle had explored, sounded, and ransacked the whole forest, and had rummaged every spot where the earth seemed to have been freshly disturbed. But all in vain.

He had turned up nothing. Nobody thought any more about it, at Montfermeil, excepting a few good gossips, who said: 'Be sure the road-labourer of Gagny didn't make all that fuss for nothing: the devil was certainly there.'

3. *Showing that the chain of the iron ring must needs have undergone a certain preparation to be thus broken by one blow of the hammer*

TOWARDS THE END OF OCTOBER, in that same year, 1823, the inhabitants of Toulon saw coming back into their port, in consequence of heavy weather, and in order to repair some damages, the ship *Orion*, which was at a later period employed at Brest as a vessel of instruction, and which then formed a part of the Mediterranean squadron. This ship, crippled as she was, for the sea had used her roughly, produced some sensation on entering the roadstead. She flew I forget what pennant, but it entitled her to a regular salute of eleven guns, which she returned shot for shot: in all twenty-two. It has been estimated that in salutes, royal and military compliments, exchanges of courteous hubbub, signals of etiquette, roadstead and citadel formalities, risings and settings of the sun saluted daily by all fortresses and all vessels of war, the opening and closing of gates, etc., etc., the civilised world, in every part of the globe, fires off, daily, one hundred and fifty thousand useless cannon shots. At six francs per shot, that would amount to nine hundred thousand francs per day, or three hundred millions per year, blown off in smoke. This is only an item. In the meanwhile, the poor are dying with hunger.

The year 1823 was what the Restoration has called the 'time of the Spanish War'.[46]

That war comprised many events in one, and no small number of singular things. It was a great family affair of the Bourbons; the French branch aiding and protecting the branch at Madrid, that is to say, performing the duties of seniority; an apparent return to our national traditions, mixed up with subserviency, and cringing to the cabinets of the North; the Duc d'Angoulême, dubbed by the liberal journals *the hero of Andujar*, repressing, with a triumphal attitude – rather contradicted by his peaceful mien – the old and very real terrorism of the Holy Office, in conflict with the chimerical terrorism of the Liberals; sansculottes revived, to the great alarm of all the old dowagers, under the name of *descamisados*; monarchists striving to impede progress, which they styled anarchy; the theories of '89 rudely interrupted in their undermining advances; a halt from all Europe, intimated to the French idea of revolution, making its tour of the globe; side by side with the son of France, general-in-chief, the Prince de Carignan, afterwards Charles Albert, enlisting in this crusade of the kings against the peoples, as a volunteer, with a grenadier's epaulets of red wool; the soldiers of the empire again betaking themselves to the field, but after eight years of rest, grown old, gloomy, and under the white cockade; the tricolour displayed abroad by a heroic handful of Frenchmen, as the white flag had been at Coblentz, thirty years before; monks mingling with our troopers; the spirit of liberty and of innovation reduced by bayonets; principles struck dumb by cannon-shot; France undoing by her arms what she had done with her mind; to cap the climax, the leaders on the other side sold, their troops irresolute; cities besieged by millions of money; no military dangers, and yet some explosions possible, as is the case in every mine entered and taken by surprise; but little blood shed, but little honour gained; shame for a few, glory for none. Such was this war, brought about by princes who descended from Louis XIV, and carried on by generals who sprang from Napoleon. It had this wretched fate, that it recalled neither the image of a great war nor of a great policy.

A few feats of arms were serious affairs; the taking of Trocadero, among others, was a handsome military exploit; but, taken all in all, we repeat, the trumpets of this war emit a cracked and feeble sound, the general appearance of it was suspicious, and history approves the unwillingness of France to father so false a triumph. It seemed clear that certain Spanish officers entrusted with the duty of resistance, yielded too easily, the idea of bribery was suggested by a contemplation of the victory; it appeared as if the generals rather than the battles had been won, and the victorious soldier returned humiliated. It was war grown petty indeed, where you could read *Bank of France* on the folds of the flag.

Soldiers of the war of 1808, under whose feet Saragossa had so terribly crumbled, knit their brows at this ready surrender of fastnesses and citadels, and regretted Palafox. It is the mood of France to prefer to have before her a Rostopchine rather than a Ballesteros.

In a still graver point of view, which it is well to urge, too, this war, which broke the military spirit of France, fired the democratic spirit with indignation. It was a scheme of subjugation. In this campaign, the object held out to the French soldier, son of democracy, was the conquest of a yoke for the neck of another. Hideous contradiction. France exists to arouse the soul of the peoples, not to stifle it. Since 1792, all the revolutions of Europe have been but the French Revolution: liberty radiates on every side from France. That is a fact as clear as noonday. Blind is he who does not see it! Bonaparte has said it.

The war of 1823, an outrage on the generous Spanish nation, was, at the same time, an outrage on the French Revolution. This monstrous deed of violence France committed, but by compulsion; for, aside from wars of liberation, all that armies do they do by compulsion. The words *passive obedience* tell the tale. An army is a wondrous masterpiece of combination, in which might is the result of an enormous sum-total of utter weakness. Thus only can we explain a war waged by humanity against humanity, in despite of humanity.

As to the Bourbons, the war of 1823 was fatal to them. They took it for a success. They did not see what danger there is in attempting to kill an idea by a military watchword. In their simplicity, they blundered to the extent of introducing into their establishment, as an element of strength, the immense enfeeblement of a crime. The spirit of ambuscade and lying in wait entered into their policy. The germ of 1830 was in 1823. The Spanish campaign became in their councils an argument on behalf of violent measures and intrigues in favour of divine right. France having restored *el rey neto* in Spain, could certainly restore the absolute monarchy at home. They fell into the tremendous error of mistaking the obedience of the soldier for the acquiescence of the nation. That fond delusion ruins thrones. It will not do to fall asleep either in the shade of a upas tree or in the shadow of an army.

But let us return to the ship *Orion*.

During the operations of the army of the Prince, commanding-in-chief, a squadron cruised in the Mediterranean. We have said that the *Orion* belonged to that squadron, and that she had been driven back by stress of weather to the port of Toulon.

The presence of a vessel of war in port has about it a certain influence which attracts and engages the multitude. It is because it is something grand, and the multitude like what is imposing.

A ship-of-the-line is one of the most magnificent struggles of human genius with the forces of nature.

A vessel of the line is composed of the heaviest, and at the same time the lightest materials, because she has to contend, at one and the same time, with the three forms of matter, the solid, the liquid, and the fluid. She has eleven claws of iron to grasp the rock at the bottom of the sea, and more wings and feelers than the butterfly to catch the breezes in the clouds. Her breath goes forth through her hundred and twenty guns as through enormous trumpets, and haughtily answers the thunderbolt. Ocean strives to lead her astray in the frightful sameness of his billows, but the ship has her compass, which is her soul, always counselling her and always pointing towards the north. In dark nights, her lanterns take the place of the stars. Thus, then, to oppose the wind, she has her ropes and canvas; against the water her timber; against the rock her iron, her copper, and her lead; against the darkness, light; against immensity, needle.

Whoever would form an idea of all these gigantic proportions, the aggregate of which constitutes a ship-of-the-line, has but to pass under one of the covered ship-houses, six storeys high, at Brest or Toulon. The vessels in process of construction are seen there under glass cases, so to speak. That colossal beam is a yard; that huge column of timber lying on the ground and reaching out of sight is the mainmast. Taking it from its root in the hold to its summit in the clouds, it is sixty fathoms long, and is three feet in diameter at its base. The English mainmast rises two hundred and seventeen feet above the water-line. The navy of our fathers used cables, ours uses chains. Now the mere coil of chains of a hundred-gun ship is four feet high, twenty feet broad, and eight feet thick. And for the construction of this vessel, how much timber is required? It is a floating forest.

And yet, be it remembered, that we are here speaking only of the war vessel of some forty years ago, the mere sailing craft; steam, then in its infancy, has, since that time, added new wonders to this prodigy called a man-of-war. At the present day, for example, the mixed vessel, the screw-propeller, is a surprising piece of mechanism moved by a spread of canvas measuring four thousand square yards of surface, and by a steam-engine of twenty-five hundred horse power.

Without referring to these fresher marvels, the old-fashioned ship of Christopher Columbus and of de Ruyter is one of the noblest works of man. It is exhaustless in force as the breath of infinitude; it gathers up the wind in its canvas, it is firmly fixed in the immense chaos of the waves, it floats and it reigns.

But a moment comes, when the white squall breaks that sixty-foot yard like a straw; and when the wind flow bends that four hundred foot mast like a reed; when that anchor, weighing its tons upon tons, is twisted in the maw of the wave like the angler's hook in the jaws of a pike; when those monster guns utter plaintive and futile roarings which the tempest whirls away into space and night, when all this might and all this majesty are engulfed in a superior might and majesty.

Whenever immense strength is put forth only to end in immense weakness, it makes men meditate. Hence it is that, in seaports, the curious, without themselves knowing exactly why, throng about these wonderful instruments of war and navigation.

Every day, then, from morning till night, the quays, the wharves, and the piers of the port of Toulon were covered with a throng of saunterers and idlers, whose occupation consisted in gazing at the *Orion*.

The *Orion* was a ship that had long been in bad condition. During her previous voyages, thick layers of shellfish had gathered on her bottom to such an extent as to seriously impede her progress; she had been put on the dry-dock the year before, to be scraped, and then she had gone to sea again. But this scraping had injured her fastening.

In the latitude of the Balearic Isles, her planking had loosened and opened, and as there was in those days no copper sheathing, the ship had leaked. A fierce equinoctial came on, which had stove in the larboard bows and a porthole, and damaged the fore-chain-wales. In consequence of these injuries, the *Orion* had put back to Toulon.

She was moored near the arsenal. She was in commission, and they were repairing her. The hull had not been injured on the starboard side, but a few planks had been taken off here and there, according to custom, to admit the air to the framework.

One morning, the throng which was gazing at her witnessed an accident.

The crew were engaged in furling sail. The topman, whose duty it was to take in the starboard upper corner of the main top-sail, lost his balance. He was seen tottering; the dense throng assembled on the wharf of the arsenal uttered a cry, the man's head overbalanced his body, and he whirled over the yard, his arms outstretched towards the deep; as he went over, he grasped the man-ropes, first with one hand, and then with the other, and hung suspended in that manner. The sea lay far below him at a giddy depth. The shock of his fall had given to the man-ropes a violent swinging motion, and the poor fellow hung dangling to and fro at the end of this line, like a stone in a sling.

To go to his aid was to run a frightful risk. None of the crew, who were all fishermen of the coast recently taken into service, dared attempt it. In the meantime, the poor topman was becoming exhausted; his agony could not be seen in his countenance, but his increasing weakness could be detected in the movements of all his limbs. His arms twisted about in horrible contortions. Every attempt he made to reascend only increased the oscillations of the man-ropes. He did not cry out, for fear of losing his strength. All were now looking forward to the moment when he should let go of the rope, and, at instants, all turned their heads away that they might not see him fall. There are moments when a rope's end, a pole, the branch of a tree, is life itself, and it is a frightful thing to see a living being lose his hold upon it, and fall like a ripe fruit.

Suddenly, a man was discovered clambering up the rigging with the agility of a wildcat. This man was clad in red – it was a convict; he wore a green cap – it was a convict for life. As he reached the round top, a gust of wind blew off his cap and revealed a head entirely white: it was not a young man.

In fact, one of the convicts employed on board in some prison task, had, at the first alarm, run to the officer of the watch, and, amid the confusion and hesitation of the crew, while all the sailors trembled and shrank back, had asked permission to save the topman's life at the risk of his own. A sign of assent being given, with one blow of a hammer he broke the chain riveted to the iron ring at his ankle, then took a rope in his hand, and flung himself into the shrouds. Nobody, at the moment, noticed with what ease the chain was broken. It was only sometime afterwards that anybody remembered it.

In a twinkling he was upon the yard. He paused a few seconds, and seemed to measure it with his glance. Those seconds, during which the wind swayed the sailor to and fro at the end of the rope, seemed ages to the lookers-on. At length, the convict raised his eyes to heaven, and took a step forward. The crowd drew a long breath. He was seen to run along the yard. On reaching its extreme tip, he fastened one end of the rope he had with him, and let the other hang at full length.

Thereupon, he began to let himself down by his hands along this rope, and then there was an inexpressible sensation of terror; instead of one man, two were seen dangling at that giddy height.

You would have said it was a spider seizing a fly; only, in this case, the spider was bringing life, and not death. Ten thousand eyes were fixed upon the group. Not a cry; not a word was uttered; the same emotion contracted every brow. Every man held his breath, as if afraid to add the least whisper to the wind which was swaying the two unfortunate men.

However, the convict had, at length, managed to make his way down to the seaman. It was time; one minute more, and the man, exhausted and despairing, would have fallen into the deep. The convict firmly secured him to the rope to which he clung with one hand while he worked with the other. Finally, he was seen reascending to the yard, and hauling the sailor after him; he supported him there, for an instant, to let him recover his strength, and then, lifting him in his arms, carried him, as he walked along the yard, to the cross-trees, and from there to the round-top, where he left him in the hands of his messmates.

Then the throng applauded; old galley sergeants wept, women hugged each other on the wharves, and, on all sides, voices were heard exclaiming, with a sort of tenderly subdued enthusiasm – 'This man must he pardoned!'

He, however, had made it a point of duty to descend again immediately, and go back to his work. In order to arrive more quickly, he slid down the rigging, and started to run along a lower yard. All eyes were following him. There was a certain moment when everyone felt alarmed; whether it was that he felt fatigued, or because his head swam, people thought they saw him hesitate and stagger. Suddenly, the throng uttered a thrilling outcry: the convict had fallen into the sea.

The fall was perilous. The frigate *Algesiras* was moored close to the *Orion*, and the poor convict had plunged between the two ships. It was feared that he would be drawn under one or the other. Four men sprang, at once, into a boat. The people cheered them on, and anxiety again took possession of all minds. The man had not again risen to the surface. He had disappeared in the sea, without making even a ripple, as though he had fallen into a cask of oil. They sounded and dragged the place. It was in vain. The search was continued until night, but not even the body was found.

The next morning, the *Toulon Journal* published the following lines:

November 17, 1823. Yesterday, a convict at work on board of the *Orion*, on his return from rescuing a sailor, fell into the sea, and was drowned. His body was not recovered. It is presumed that it has been caught under the piles at the pier-head of the arsenal. This man was registered by the number 9430, and his name was Jean Valjean.

BOOK 3: FULFILMENT OF THE PROMISE TO THE DEPARTED

1. *The water question at Montfermeil*

MONTFERMEIL is situated between Livry and Chelles, upon the southern slope of the high plateau which separates the Ourcq from the Marne. At present, it is a considerable town, adorned all the year round with stuccoed villas, and, on Sundays, with citizens in full blossom. In 1823, there were at Montfermeil neither so many white houses nor so many comfortable citizens; it was nothing but a village in the woods. You would find, indeed, here and there a few country seats of the last century, recognisable by their grand appearance, their balconies of twisted iron, and those long windows the little panes of which show all sorts of different greens upon the white of the closed shutters. But Montfermeil was none the less a village. Retired dry-goods merchants and amateur villagers had not yet discovered it. It was a peaceful and charming spot, and not upon the road to any place; the inhabitants cheaply enjoyed that rural life which is so luxuriant and so easy of enjoyment. But water was scarce there on account of the height of the plateau.

They had to go a considerable distance for it. The end of the village towards Gagny drew its water from the magnificent ponds in the forest on that side; the other end, which surrounds the church and which is towards Chelles, found drinking-water only at a little spring on the side of the hill, near the road to Chelles, about fifteen minutes' walk from Montfermeil.

It was therefore a serious matter for each household to obtain its supply of water. The great houses, the aristocracy, the Thénardier tavern included, paid a penny a bucketful to an old man who made it his business, and whose income from the Montfermeil waterworks was about eight sous per day; but this man worked only till seven o'clock in summer and five in the winter, and when night had come on, and the first-floor shutters were closed, whoever had no drinking-water went after it, or went without it.

This was the terror of the poor being whom the reader has not perhaps forgotten – little Cosette. It will be remembered that Cosette was useful to the Thénardiers in two ways, they got pay from the mother and work from the child. Thus when the mother ceased entirely to pay, we have seen why, in the preceding chapters, the Thénardiers kept Cosette. She saved them a servant. In that capacity she ran for water when it was wanted. So the child, always horrified at the idea of going to the spring at night, took good care that water should never be wanting at the house.

Christmas in the year 1823 was particularly brilliant at Montfermeil. The early part of the winter had been mild; so far there had been neither frost nor snow. Some jugglers from Paris had obtained permission from the mayor to set up their stalls in the main street of the village, and a company of pedlars had, under the same licence, put up their booths in the square before the church and even in the lane du Boulanger, upon which, as the reader perhaps remembers, the Thénardier chop-house was situated. This filled up the taverns and pot-houses, and gave to this little quiet place a noisy and joyous appearance. We ought also to say, to be a faithful historian, that, among the curiosities displayed in the square, there was a menagerie in which frightful clowns, clad in rags and come nobody knows whence, were exhibiting in 1823 to the peasants of Montfermeil one of those horrid Brazilian vultures, a specimen of which our Museum Royal did not obtain until 1845, and the eye of which is a tricoloured cockade. Naturalists call this bird, I believe, Caracara Polyborus, it belongs to the order of the Apicidæ and the family of the vultures. Some good old retired Bonapartist soldiers in the village went to see the bird as a matter of faith. The jugglers pronounced the tricoloured cockade a unique phenomenon, made expressly by God for their menagerie.

On that Christmas evening, several men, wagoners and pedlars, were seated at table and drinking around four or five candles in the low hall of the Thénardier tavern. This room resembled all bar-rooms; tables, pewter-mugs, bottles, drinkers, smokers; little light, and much noise. The date, 1823, was, however, indicated by the two things then in vogue with the middle classes, which were on the table, a kaleidoscope and a fluted tin lamp. Thénardier, the wife, was looking to the supper, which was cooking before a bright blazing fire; the husband, Thénardier, was drinking with his guests and talking politics.

Aside from the political discussions, the principal subjects of which were the Spanish war and the Duc d'Angoulême, local interludes were heard amid the hubbub, like these, for instance:

'Down around Nanterre and Suresnes wine is turning out well. Where they expected ten casks they are getting twelve. That is getting a good yield of juice out of the press.' 'But the grapes can't be ripe?' 'Oh, in these parts there is no need of harvesting ripe; the wine is fat enough by spring.' 'It is all light wine then?' 'There is a good deal lighter wines than they make hereabouts. You have to harvest green.'

Etc.

Or, indeed, a miller might be bawling:

'Are we responsible for what there is in the bags? We find a heap of little seeds there, that we can't amuse ourselves by picking out, and of course we have got to let 'em go through the stones; there's darnel, there's fennel, there's cockles, there's vetch, there's hemp, there's fox-tail, and a lot of other weeds, not counting the stones that there is in some wheat, especially Breton wheat. I don't like to grind Breton wheat, no more than carpenters like to saw boards with nails in 'em. Just think of the dirt that all that makes in the till. And then they complain of the flour. It's their own fault. We ain't to blame for the flour.'

Between two windows, a mower seated at a table with a farmer, who was making a bargain for a piece of work to be done the next season, was saying:

'There is no harm in the grass having the dew on. It cuts better. The dew is a good thing. It is all the same; that grass o' yours is young, and pretty hard to cut. You see it is so green; you see it bends under the scythe.'

Etc.

Cosette was at her usual place, seated on the cross-piece of the kitchen table, near the fireplace; she was clad in rags; her bare feet were in wooden shoes, and by the light of the fire she was knitting woollen stockings for the little Thénardiers. A young kitten was playing under the chairs. In a neighbouring room the fresh voices of two children were heard laughing and prattling; it was Eponine and Azelma.

In the chimney-corner, a cow-hide hung upon a nail.

At intervals, the cry of a very young child, which was somewhere in the house, was heard above the noise of the bar-room. This was a little boy which the woman had had some winters before – 'She didn't know why,' she said: 'it was the cold weather' – and which was a little more than three years old. The mother had nursed him, but did not love him. When the hungry clamour of the brat became too much to bear, 'Your boy is squalling,' said Thénardier, 'why don't you go and see what he wants?' 'Bah!' answered the mother; 'I am sick of him.' And the poor little fellow continued to cry in the darkness.

2. *Two portraits completed*

THE THÉNARDIERS have hitherto been seen in this book in profile only; the time has come to turn this couple about and look at them on all sides.

Thénardier has just passed his fiftieth year; Madame Thénardier had reached her fortieth, which is the fiftieth for woman; so that there was an equilibrium of age between the husband and wife.

The reader has perhaps, since her first appearance, preserved some remembrance of this huge Thénardiess – for such we shall call the female of this species – large, blonde, red, fat, brawny, square, enormous, and agile; she belonged, as we have said, to the race of those colossal wild women who posturise at fairs with paving-stones hung in their hair. She did everything about the house, the chamber-work, the washing, the cooking, anything she pleased, and played the deuce generally. Cosette was her only servant; a mouse in the service of an elephant. Everything trembled at the sound of her voice; windows and furniture as well as people. Her broad face, covered with freckles, had the appearance of a skimmer. She had a beard. She was the ideal of a butcher's boy dressed in petticoats. She swore splendidly; she prided herself on being able to crack a nut with her fist. Apart from the novels she had read, which at times gave you an odd glimpse of the affected lady under the ogress, the idea of calling her a woman never would have occurred to anybody. This Thénardiess seemed like a cross between a wench and a fishwoman. If you heard her speak, you would say it is a gendarme; if you saw her drink, you would say it is a cartman; if you saw her handle Cosette, you would say it is the hangman. When at rest, a tooth protruded from her mouth.

The other Thénardier was a little man, meagre, pale, angular, bony, and lean, who appeared to be sick, and whose health was excellent; here his knavery began. He smiled habitually as a matter of business, and tried to be polite to everybody, even to the beggar to whom he refused a penny. He had the look of a weazel, and the mien of a man of letters. He had a strong resemblance to the portraits of the Abbé Delille. He affected drinking with wagoners. Nobody ever saw him drunk. He smoked a large pipe. He wore a blouse, and under it an old black coat. He made pretensions to literature and materialism. There were names which he often pronounced in support of anything whatever that he might say. Voltaire, Raynal, Parny, and, oddly enough, St Augustine. He professed to have 'a system'. For the rest, a great swindler. A fellowsopher. There is such a variety. It will be remembered that he pretended to have been in the service; he related with some pomp that at Waterloo, being sergeant in a Sixth or Ninth Light something, he alone, against a squadron of Hussars of Death, had covered with his body, and saved amid a shower of grape, 'a general dangerously wounded'. Hence the flaming picture on his sign, and the name of his inn, which was spoken of in that region as the 'tavern of the sergeant of Waterloo'. He was liberal, classical, and a Bonapartist. He had subscribed for the Champ d'Asile.[47] It was said in the village that he had studied for the priesthood.

We believe that he had only studied in Holland to be an innkeeper. This whelp of the composite order was, according to all probability, some Fleming of Lille in Flanders, a Frenchman in Paris, a Belgian in Brussels, conveniently on the fence between the two frontiers. We understand his prowess at Waterloo. As we have seen, he exaggerated it a little. Ebb and flow, wandering, adventure, was his element; a violated conscience is followed by a loose life; and without doubt, at the stormy epoch of the 18th of June 1815, Thénardier belonged to that species of marauding sutlers of whom we have spoken, scouring the country, robbing here and selling there, and travelling in family style, man, woman, and children, in some rickety carry-all, in the wake of marching troops, with the instinct to attach himself always to the victorious army. This campaign over, having, as he said, some 'quibus', he had opened a 'chop-house' at Montfermeil.

This 'quibus', composed of purses and watches, gold rings and silver crosses, gathered at the harvest time in the furrows sown with corpses, did not form a great total, and had not lasted this sutler, now become a tavern-keeper, very long.

Thénardier had that indescribable stiffness of gesture which, with an oath, reminds you of the barracks, and, with a sign of the cross, of the seminary. He was a fine talker. He was fond of being thought learned. Nevertheless, the schoolmaster remarked that he made mistakes in pronunciation. He made out travellers' bills in a superior style, but practised eyes sometimes found them faulty in orthography. Thénardier was sly, greedy, lounging, and clever. He did not disdain servant girls, consequently his wife had no more of them. This giantess was jealous. It seemed to her that this little, lean, and yellow man must be the object of universal desire.

Thénardier, above all a man of astuteness and poise, was a rascal of the subdued order. This is the worst species; there is hypocrisy in it.

Not that Thénardier was not on occasion capable of anger, quite as much so as his wife; but that was very rare, and at such times, as if he were at war with the whole human race, as if he had in him a deep furnace of hatred, as if he were of those who are perpetually avenging themselves, who accuse everybody about them of the evils that befall them, and are always ready to throw on the first comer, as legitimate grievance, the sum-total of the deceptions, failures, and calamities of their life – as all this leaven worked in him, and boiled up into his mouth and eyes, he was frightful. Woe to him who came within reach of his fury, then!

Besides all his other qualities, Thénardier was attentive and penetrating, silent or talkative as occasion required, and always with great intelligence. He had somewhat the look of sailors accustomed to squinting the eye in looking through spy-glasses. Thénardier was a statesman.

Every newcomer who entered the chop-house said, on seeing the Thénardiess:

There is the master of the house. It was an error. She was not even *the mistress*. The husband was both master and mistress. She performed, he created. He directed everything by a sort of invisible and continuous magnetic action. A word sufficed, sometimes a sign; the mastodon obeyed. Thénardier was to her, without her being really aware of it, a sort of being apart and sovereign. She had the virtues of her order of creation; never would she have differed in any detail with 'Monsieur Thénardier' – nor – impossible supposition – would she have publicly quarrelled with her husband, on any matter whatever. Never had she committed 'before company' that fault of which women are so often guilty, and which is called in parliamentary language: discovering the crown. Although their accord had no other result than evil, there was food for contemplation in the submission of the Thénardiess to her husband. This bustling mountain of flesh moved under the little finger of this frail despot. It was, viewed from its dwarfed and grotesque side, this great universal fact: the homage of matter to spirit; for certain deformities have their origin in the depths even of eternal beauty. There was somewhat of the unknown in Thénardier; hence the absolute empire of this man over this woman. At times, she looked upon him as upon a lighted candle; at others, she felt him like a claw.

This woman was a formidable creation, who loved nothing but her children, and feared nothing but her husband. She was a mother because she was a mammal. Her maternal feelings stopped with her girls, and, as we shall see, did not extend to boys. The man had but one thought – to get rich.

He did not succeed. His great talents had no adequate opportunity. Thénardier at Montfermeil was ruining himself, if ruin is possible at zero. In Switzerland, or in the Pyrenees, this penniless rogue would have become a millionaire. But where fate places the innkeeper he must browse.

It is understood that the word *innkeeper* is employed here in a restricted sense, and does not extend to an entire class.

In this same year, 1823, Thénardier owed about fifteen hundred francs, of pressing debts, which rendered him moody.

However obstinately unjust destiny was to him, Thénardier was one of those men who best understood, to the greatest depth and in the most modern style, that which is a virtue among the barbarous, and a subject of merchandise among the civilised – hospitality. He was, besides, an admirable poacher, and was counted an excellent shot. He had a certain cool and quiet laugh, which was particularly dangerous.

His theories of innkeeping sometimes sprang from him by flashes. He had certain professional aphorisms which he inculcated in the mind of his wife. 'The duty of the innkeeper,' said he to her one day, emphatically, and in a low voice, 'is to sell to the first comer, food, rest, light, fire, dirty linen, servants, fleas, and smiles; to stop travellers, empty small purses, and honestly lighten large ones; to receive families who are travelling, with respect: scrape the man, pluck the woman, and pick the child; to charge for the open window, the closed window, the chimney corner, the sofa, the chair, the stool, the bench, the feather bed, the mattress, and the straw bed; to know how much the mirror is worn, and to tax that; and, by the five hundred thousand devils, to make the traveller pay for everything, even to the flies that his dog eats!'

This man and this woman were cunning and rage married – a hideous and terrible pair.

While the husband calculated and schemed, the Thénardiess thought not of absent creditors, took no care either for yesterday or the morrow, and lived passionately in the present moment.

Such were these two beings. Cosette was between them, undergoing their double pressure, like a creature who is at the same time being bruised by a millstone, and lacerated with pincers. The man and the woman had each a different way. Cosette was beaten unmercifully; that came from the woman. She went barefoot in winter; that came from the man.

Cosette ran upstairs and downstairs; washed, brushed, scrubbed, swept, ran, tired herself, got out of breath, lifted heavy things, and, puny as she was, did the rough work. No pity; a ferocious mistress, a malignant master. The Thénardier chop-house was like a snare, in which Cosette had been caught, and was trembling. The ideal of oppression was realised by this dismal servitude. It was something like a fly serving spiders.

The poor child was passive and silent.

When they find themselves in such condition at the dawn of existence, so young, so feeble, among men, what passes in these souls fresh from God!

3. *Men must have wine and horses water*

FOUR NEW GUESTS had just come in.

Cosette was musing sadly; for, though she was only eight years old, she had already suffered so much that she mused with the mournful air of an old woman.

She had a black eye from a blow of the Thénardiess's fist, which made the Thénardiess say from time to time, 'How ugly she is with her patch on her eye.'

Cosette was then thinking that it was evening, late in the evening, that the bowls and pitchers in the rooms of the travellers who had arrived must be filled immediately, and that there was no more water in the cistern.

One thing comforted her a little; they did not drink much water in the Thénardier tavern. There were plenty of people there who were thirsty; but it was that kind of thirst which reaches rather towards the jug than the pitcher. Had anybody asked for a glass of water among these glasses of wine, he would have seemed a savage to all those men. However, there was an instant when the child trembled; the Thénardiess raised the cover of a kettle which was boiling on the range, then took a glass and hastily approached the cistern. She turned the faucet; the child had raised her head and followed all her movements. A thin stream of water ran from the faucet, and filled the glass half full.

'Here,' said she, 'there is no more water!' Then she was silent for a moment. The child held her breath.

'Pshaw!' continued the Thénardiess, examining the half-filled glass, 'there is enough of it, such as it is.'

Cosette resumed her work, but for more than a quarter of an hour she felt her heart leaping into her throat like a great ball.

She counted the minutes as they thus rolled away, and eagerly wished it were morning.

From time to time, one of the drinkers would look out into the street and exclaim – 'It is as black as an oven!' or, 'It would take a cat to go along the street without a lantern tonight!' And Cosette shuddered.

All at once, one of the pedlars who lodged in the tavern came in, and said in a harsh voice:

'You have not watered my horse.'

'Yes, we have, sure,' said the Thénardiess.

'I tell you no, ma'am,' replied the pedlar.

Cosette came out from under the table.

'Oh, yes, monsieur!' said she, 'the horse did drink; he drank in the bucket, the bucket full, and 'twas me that carried it to him, and I talked to him.'

This was not true. Cosette lied.

'Here is a girl as big as my fist, who can tell a lie as big as a house,' exclaimed the pedlar. 'I tell you that he has not had any water, little wench! He has a way of blowing when he has not had any water, that I know well enough.'

Cosette persisted, and added in a voice stifled with anguish, and which could hardly be heard:

'But he did drink a good deal.'

'Come,' continued the pedlar, in a passion, 'that is enough; give my horse some water, and say no more about it.'

Cosette went back under the table.

'Well, of course that is right,' said the Thénardiess; 'if the beast has not had any water, he must have some.'

Then looking about her:

'Well, what has become of that girl?'

She stooped down and discovered Cosette crouched at the other end of the table, almost under the feet of the drinkers.

'Aren't you coming?' cried the Thénardiess.

Cosette came out of the kind of hole where she had hidden. The Thénardiess continued:

'Mademoiselle Dog-without-a-name, go and carry some drink to this horse.'

'But, ma'am,' said Cosette feebly, 'there is no water.'

The Thénardiess threw the street door wide open.

'Well, go after some!'

Cosette hung her head, and went for an empty bucket that was by the chimney corner.

The bucket was larger than she, and the child could have sat down in it comfortably.

The Thénardiess went back to her range, and tasted what was in the kettle with a wooden spoon, grumbling the while.

'There is some at the spring. She is the worst girl that ever was. I think 'twould have been better if I'd left out the onions.'

Then she fumbled in a drawer where there were some pennies, pepper, and garlic.

'Here, Mamselle Toad,' added she, 'get a big loaf at the baker's, as you come back. Here is fifteen sous.'

Cosette had a little pocket in the side of her apron; she took the piece without saying a word, and put it in that pocket.

Then she remained motionless, bucket in hand, the open door before her. She seemed to be waiting for somebody to come to her aid.

'Get along!' cried the Thénardiess.

Cosette went out. The door closed.

4. *A doll enters upon the scene*

THE ROW OF BOOTHS extended along the street from the church, the reader will remember, as far as the Thénardier tavern. These booths, on account of the approaching passage of the citizens on their way to the midnight mass, were all illuminated with candles, burning in paper lanterns, which, as the schoolmaster of Montfermeil, who was at that moment seated at one of Thénardier's tables, said, produced a magical effect. In retaliation, not a star was to be seen in the sky.

The last of these stalls, set up exactly opposite Thénardier's door, was a toy-shop, all glittering with trinkets, glass beads, and things magnificent in tin. In the first rank, and in front, the merchant had placed, upon a bed of white napkins, a great doll nearly two feet high dressed in a robe of pink-crape with golden wheat-ears on its head, and which had real hair and enamel eyes. The whole day, this marvel had been displayed to the bewilderment of the passers under ten years of age, but there had not been found in Montfermeil a mother rich enough, or prodigal enough to give it to her child. Eponine and Azelma had passed hours in contemplating it, and Cosette herself, furtively, it is true, had dared to look at it.

At the moment when Cosette went out, bucket in hand, all gloomy and overwhelmed as she was, she could not help raising her eyes towards this wonderful doll, towards *the lady*, as she called it. The poor child stopped petrified. She had not seen this doll so near before.

This whole booth seemed a palace to her; this doll was not a doll, it was a vision. It was joy, splendour, riches, happiness, and it appeared in a sort of chimerical radiance to this unfortunate little being, buried so deeply in a cold and dismal misery. Cosette was measuring with the sad and simple sagacity of childhood the abyss which separated her from that doll. She was saying to herself that one must be a queen, or at least a princess, to have a 'thing' like that. She gazed upon this beautiful pink dress, this beautiful smooth hair, and she was thinking, 'How happy must be that doll!' Her eye could not turn away from this fantastic booth. The longer she looked, the more she was dazzled. She thought she saw paradise. There were other dolls behind the large one that appeared to her to be fairies and genii. The merchant walking to and fro in the back part of his stall, suggested the Eternal Father.

In this adoration, she forgot everything, even the errand on which she had been sent. Suddenly, the harsh voice of the Thénardiess called her back to the reality: 'How, jade, haven't you gone yet? Hold on; I am coming for you! I'd like to know what she's doing there? Little monster, be off!'

The Thénardiess had glanced into the street, and perceived Cosette in ecstasy. Cosette fled with her bucket, running as fast as she could.

5. *The little girl all alone*

As THE THÉNARDIER TAVERN was in that part of the village which is near the church, Cosette had to go to the spring in the woods towards Chelles to draw water.

She looked no more at the displays in the booths, so long as she was in the lane Boulanger; and in the vicinity of the church, the illuminated stalls lighted the way, but soon the last gleam from the last stall disappeared. The poor child found herself in darkness. She became buried in it. Only, as she became the prey of a certain sensation, she shook the handle of the bucket as much as she could on her way. That made a noise, which kept her company.

The further she went, the thicker became the darkness. There was no longer anybody in the street. However, she met a woman who turned around on seeing her pass, and remained motionless, muttering between her teeth; 'Where in the world can that child be going? Is it a phantom child?' Then the woman recognised Cosette. 'Oh,' said she, 'it is the Lark!'

Cosette thus passed through the labyrinth of crooked and deserted streets, which terminates the village of Montfermeil towards Chelles. As long as she had houses, or even walls, on the sides of the road, she went on boldly enough. From time to time, she saw the light of a candle through the cracks of a shutter; it was light and life to her; there were people there; that kept up her courage. However, as she advanced, her speed slackened as if mechanically. When she had passed the corner of the last house, Cosette stopped. To go beyond the last booth had been difficult; to go further than the last house became impossible. She put the bucket on the ground, buried her hands in her hair, and began to scratch her head slowly, a motion peculiar to terrified and hesitating children. It was Montfermeil no longer, it was the open country; dark and deserted space was before her. She looked with despair into this darkness where nobody was, where there were beasts, where there were perhaps ghosts. She looked intensely, and she heard the animals walking in the grass, and she distinctly saw the ghosts moving in the trees. Then she seized her bucket again; fear gave her boldness: 'Pshaw,' said she, 'I will tell her there isn't any more water!' And she resolutely went back into Montfermeil.

She had scarcely gone a hundred steps when she stopped again, and began to scratch her head. Now, it was the Thénardiess that appeared to her; the hideous Thénardiess, with her hyena mouth, and wrath flashing from her eyes. The child cast a pitiful glance before her and behind her. What could she do? What would become of her? Where should she go? Before her, the spectre of the Thénardiess; behind her, all the phantoms of night and of the forest. It was at the Thénardiess that she recoiled. She took the road to the spring again, and began to run. She ran out of the village; she ran into the woods, seeing nothing, hearing nothing. She did not stop running until out of breath, and even then she staggered on. She went right on, desperate.

Even while running, she wanted to cry.

The nocturnal tremulousness of the forest wrapped her about completely.

She thought no more; she saw nothing more. The immensity of night confronted this little creature. On one side, the infinite shadow; on the other, an atom.

It was only seven or eight minutes' walk from the edge of the woods to the spring. Cosette knew the road, from travelling it several times a day. Strange thing, she did not lose her way. A remnant of instinct guided her blindly. But she neither turned her eyes to the right nor to the left, for fear of seeing things in the trees and in the bushes. Thus she arrived at the spring.

It was a small natural basin, made by the water in the loamy soil, about two feet deep, surrounded with moss, and with that long figured grass called Henry Fourth's collars, and paved with a few large stones. A brook escaped from it with a gentle, tranquil murmur.

Cosette did not take time to breathe. It was very dark, but she was accustomed to come to this fountain. She felt with her left hand in the darkness for a young oak which bent over the spring and usually served her as a support, found a branch, swung herself from it, bent down and plunged the bucket in the water. She was for a moment so excited that her strength was tripled. When she was thus bent over, she did not notice that the pocket of her apron emptied itself into the spring. The fifteen-sous piece fell into the water. Cosette neither saw it nor heard it fall. She drew out the bucket almost full and set it on the grass.

This done, she perceived that her strength was exhausted. She was anxious to start at once; but the effort of filling the bucket had been so great that it was impossible for her to take a step. She was compelled to sit down. She fell upon the grass and remained in a crouching posture.

She closed her eyes, then she opened them, without knowing why, without the power of doing otherwise. At her side, the water shaken in the bucket made circles that resembled serpents of white fire.

Above her head, the sky was covered with vast black clouds which were like sheets of smoke. The tragic mask of night seemed to bend vaguely over this child.

Jupiter was setting in the depths of the horizon.

The child looked with a startled eye upon that great star which she did not know and which made her afraid. The planet, in fact, was at that moment very near the horizon and was crossing a dense bed of mist which gave it a horrid redness. The mist, gloomily empurpled, magnified the star. One would have called it a luminous wound.

A cold wind blew from the plain. The woods were dark, without any rustling of leaves, without any of those vague and fresh coruscations of summer. Great branches drew themselves up fearfully. Mean and shapeless bushes whistled in the glades. The tall grass wriggled under the north wind like eels. The brambles twisted about like long arms seeking to seize their prey in their claws. Some dry weeds, driven by the wind, passed rapidly by, and appeared to flee with dismay before something that was following. The prospect was dismal.

Darkness makes the brain giddy. Man needs light. Whoever plunges into the opposite of day feels his heart chilled. When the eye sees blackness, the mind sees trouble. In an eclipse, in night, in the sooty darkness, there is anxiety even to the strongest. Nobody walks alone at night in the forest without trembling. Darkness and trees, two formidable depths – a reality of chimeras appears in the indistinct distance. The Inconceivable outlines itself a few steps from you with a spectral clearness. You see floating in space or in your brain something strangely vague and unseizable as the dreams of sleeping flowers. There are fierce phantoms in the horizon. You breathe in the odours of the great black void. You are afraid, and are tempted to look behind you. The hollowness of night, the haggardness of all things, the silent profiles that fade away as you advance, the obscure dishevelments, angry clumps, livid pools, the gloomy reflected in the funereal, the sepulchral immensity of silence, the possible unknown beings, the swaying of mysterious branches, the frightful twistings of the trees, long spires of shivering grass – against all this you have no defence. There is no bravery which does not shudder and feel the nearness of anguish. You feel something hideous, as if the soul were amalgamating with the shadow. This penetration of the darkness is inexpressibly dismal for a child.

Forests are apocalypses; and the beating of the wings of a little soul makes an agonising sound under their monstrous vault.

Without being conscious of what she was experiencing, Cosette felt that she was seized by this black enormity of nature. It was not merely terror that held her, but something more terrible even than terror. She shuddered. Words fail to express the peculiar strangeness of that shudder which chilled her through and through. Her eye had become wild. She felt that perhaps she would be compelled to return there at the same hour the next night.

Then, by a sort of instinct, to get out of this singular state, which she did not understand, but which terrified her, she began to count aloud one, two, three, four, up to ten, and when she had finished, she began again. This restored her to a real perception of things about her. Her hands, which she had wet in drawing the water, felt cold. She arose. Her fear had returned, a natural and insurmountable fear. She had only one thought, to fly; to fly with all her might, across woods, across fields, to houses, to windows, to lighted candles. Her eyes fell upon the bucket that was before her. Such was the dread with which the Thénardiess inspired her, that she did not dare to go without the bucket of water. She grasped the handle with both hands. She could hardly lift the bucket.

She went a dozen steps in this manner, but the bucket was full, it was heavy, she was compelled to rest it on the ground. She breathed an instant, then grasped the handle again, and walked on, this time a little longer. But she had to stop again. After resting a few seconds, she started on. She walked bending forward, her head down, like an old woman: the weight of the bucket strained and stiffened her thin arms. The iron handle was numbing and freezing her little wet hands; from time to time she had to stop, and every time she stopped, the cold water that splashed from the bucket fell upon her naked knees. This took place in the depth of a wood, at night, in the winter, far from all human sight; it was a child of eight years; there was none but God at that moment who saw this sad thing.

And undoubtedly her mother, alas!

For there are things which open the eyes of the dead in their grave.

She breathed with a kind of mournful rattle; sobs choked her, but she did not dare to weep, so fearful was she of the Thénardiess, even at a distance. She always imagined that the Thénardiess was near.

However she could not make much headway in this manner, and was getting along very slowly. She tried hard to shorten her resting spells, and to walk as far as possible between them. She remembered with anguish that it would take her more than an hour to return to Montfermeil thus, and that the Thénardiess would beat her. This anguish added to her dismay at being alone in the woods at night. She was worn out with fatigue, and was not yet out of the forest. Arriving near an old chestnut tree which she knew, she made a last halt, longer than the others, to get well rested; then she gathered all her strength, took up the bucket again, and began to walk on courageously. Meanwhile the poor little despairing thing could not help crying: 'Oh! my God! my God!'

At that moment she felt all at once that the weight of the bucket was gone. A hand, which seemed enormous to her, had just caught the handle, and was carrying it easily. She raised her head. A large dark form, straight and erect, was walking beside her in the gloom. It was a man who had come up behind her, and whom she had not heard. This man, without saying a word, had grasped the handle of the bucket she was carrying.

There are instincts for all the crises of life.

The child was not afraid.

6. *Which perhaps proves the intelligence of Boulatruelle*

IN the afternoon of that same Christmas Day, 1823, a man walked a long time in the most deserted portion of the Boulevard de l'Hôpital at Paris. This man had the appearance of someone who was looking for lodgings, and seemed to stop by preference before the most modest houses of this dilapidated part of the Faubourg Saint Marceau.

We shall see further on that this man did in fact hire a room in this isolated quarter.

This man, in his dress as in his whole person, realised the type of what might be called the mendicant of good society – extreme misery being combined with extreme neatness. It is a rare coincidence which inspires intelligent hearts with this double respect that we feel for him who is very poor and for him who is very worthy. He wore a round hat, very old and carefully brushed, a long coat, completely threadbare, of coarse yellow cloth, a colour which was in nowise extraordinary at that epoch, a large waistcoat with pockets of antique style, black trousers worn grey at the knees, black woollen stockings, and thick shoes with copper buckles. One would have called him an old preceptor of a good family, returned from the emigration. From his hair, which was entirely white, from his wrinkled brow, from his livid lips, from his face in which everything breathed exhaustion and weariness of life, one would have supposed him considerably over sixty. From his firm though slow step, and the singular vigour impressed upon all his motions, one would hardly have thought him fifty. The wrinkles on his forehead were well disposed, and would have prepossessed in his favour anyone who observed him with attention. His lip contracted with a strange expression, which seemed severe and yet which was humble. There was in the depths of his eye an indescribably mournful serenity. He carried in his left hand a small package tied in a handkerchief, with his right he leaned upon a sort of staff cut from a hedge. This staff had been finished with some care, and did not look very badly; the knots were smoothed down, and a coral head had been formed with red wax; it was a cudgel, and it seemed a cane.

There are few people on that boulevard, especially in winter. This man appeared to avoid them rather than seek them, but without affectation.

At that epoch the king, Louis XVIII, went almost every day to Choisy Le Roy. It was one of his favourite rides. About two o'clock, almost invariably, the carriage and the royal cavalcade were seen to pass at full speed through the Boulevard de l'Hôpital.

This supplied the place of watch and clock to the poor women of the quarter, who would say: 'It is two o'clock, there he is going back to the Tuileries.'

And some ran, and others fell into line; for when a king passes by, there is always a tumult. Moreover, the appearance and disappearance of Louis XVIII produced a certain sensation in the streets of Paris. It was rapid, but majestic. This impotent king had a taste for fast driving; not being able to walk, he wished to run; this cripple would have gladly been drawn by the lightning. He passed by, peaceful and severe, in the midst of naked sabres. His massive coach, all gilded, with great lily branches painted on the panels, rolled noisily along. One hardly had time to catch a glance of it. In the back corner on the right could be seen, upon cushions covered with white satin, a broad face, firm and red, a forehead freshly powdered à la bird of paradise, a proud eye, stern and keen, a well-read smile, two large epaulets of bullion waving over a citizen's dress, the Golden Fleece, the cross of Saint Louis, the cross of the Legion of Honour, the silver badge of the Holy Spirit, a big belly, and a large blue ribbon; that was the king. Outside of Paris, he held his hat with white feathers upon his knees, which were enclosed in high English gaiters; when he re-entered the city, he placed his hat upon his head, bowing but little. He looked coldly upon the people, who returned his look. When he appeared for the first time in the Quartier Saint Marceau, all he succeeded in eliciting was this saying of a resident to his comrade: 'It's that big fellow who is the government.'

This unfailing passage of the king at the same hour was then the daily event of the Boulevard de l'Hôpital.

The promenader in the yellow coat evidently did not belong to the quarter, and probably not to Paris, for he was ignorant of this circumstance. When at two o'clock the royal carriage, surrounded by a squadron of silver-laced bodyguard, turned into the boulevard, after passing La Salpêtrière, he appeared surprised, and almost frightened. There was no one else in the cross alley, and he retired hastily behind a corner of the side wall, but this did not prevent the Duke d'Havré seeing him. The Duke d'Havré, as captain of the guards in waiting that day, was seated in the carriage opposite the king. He said to his majesty: 'There is a man who has a bad look.' Some policemen, who were clearing the passage for the king, also noticed him; one of them was ordered to follow him. But the man plunged into the little solitary streets of the Faubourg, and as night was coming on the officer lost his track, as is established by a report addressed on the same evening to the Comte Anglès, Minister of State, Préfect of Police.

When the man in the yellow coat had thrown the officer off his track, he turned about, not without looking back many times to make sure that he was not followed. At a quarter past four, that is to say, after dark, he passed in front of the theatre of the Porte Saint Martin where the play that day was *The Two Convicts*. The poster, lit up by the reflection from the theatre, seemed to strike him, for, although he was walking rapidly, he stopped to read it. A moment after, he was in the Cul-de-sac de la Planchette, and entered the Pewter Platter, which was then the office of the Lagny stage. This stage started at half-past four. The horses were harnessed, and the travellers, who had been called by the driver hastily, were climbing the high iron steps of the vehicle.

The man asked:

'Have you a seat?'

'Only one, beside me, on the box,' said the driver.

'I will take it.'

'Get up then.'

Before starting, however, the driver cast a glance at the poor apparel of the traveller, and at the smallness of his bundle, and took his pay.

'Are you going through to Lagny?' asked the driver.

'Yes,' said the man.

The traveller paid through to Lagny.

They started off. When they had passed the barrière, the driver tried to start a conversation, but the traveller answered only in monosyllables. The driver concluded to whistle, and swear at his horses.

The driver wrapped himself up in his cloak. It was cold. The man did not appear to notice it. In this way they passed through Gournay and Neuilly sur Marne. About six o'clock in the evening they were at Chelles. The driver stopped to let his horses breathe, in front of the wagoners' tavern established in the old buildings of the royal abbey.

'I will get down here,' said the man.

He took his bundle and stick, and jumped down from the stage.

A moment afterwards he had disappeared.

He did not go into the tavern.

When, a few minutes afterwards, the stage started off for Lagny, it did not overtake him in the main street of Chelles.

The driver turned to the inside passengers:

'There,' said he, 'is a man who does not belong here, for I don't know him. He has an appearance of not having a sou; however, he don't stick about money; he pays to Lagny, and he only goes to Chelles. It is night, all the houses are shut, he don't go to the tavern, and we don't overtake him. He must, then, have sunk into the ground.'

The man had not sunk into the ground, but he had hurried rapidly in the darkness along the main street of Chelles; then he had turned to the left, before reaching the church, into the cross road leading to Montfermeil, like one who knew the country and had been that way before.

He followed this road rapidly. At the spot where it intersects the old road bordered with trees that goes from Gagny to Lagny, he heard footsteps approaching. He concealed himself hastily in a ditch, and waited there till the people who were passing were a good distance off. The precaution was indeed almost superfluous, for, as we have already said, it was a very dark December night. There were scarcely two or three stars to be seen in the sky.

It is at this point that the ascent of the hill begins. The man did not return to the Montfermeil road; he turned to the right, across the fields, and gained the woods with rapid strides.

When he reached the wood, he slackened his pace, and began to look carefully at all the trees, pausing at every step, as if he were seeking and following a mysterious route known only to himself. There was a moment when he appeared to lose himself, and when he stopped, undecided. Finally he arrived, by continual groping, at a glade where there was a heap of large whitish stones. He made his way quickly towards these stones, and examined them with attention in the dusk of the night, as if he were passing them in review. A large tree, covered with these excrescences which are the warts of vegetation, was a few steps from the heap of stones. He went to this tree, and passed his hand over the bark of the trunk, as if he were seeking to recognise and to count all the warts.

Opposite this tree, which was an ash, there was a chestnut tree wounded in the bark, which had been staunched with a bandage of zinc nailed on. He rose on tip-toe and touched that band of zinc.

Then he stamped for some time upon the ground in the space between the tree and the stones, like one who would be sure that the earth had not been freshly stirred.

This done, he took his course and resumed his walk through the woods.

This was the man who had fallen in with Cosette.

As he made his way through the copse in the direction of Montfermeil, he had perceived that little shadow, struggling along with a groan, setting her burden on the ground, then taking it up and going on again. He had approached her and seen that it was a very young child carrying an enormous bucket of water. Then he had gone to the child, and silently taken hold of the handle of the bucket.

7. *Cosette side by side with the unknown, in the darkness*

COSETTE, we have said, was not afraid.

The man spoke to her. His voice was serious, and was almost a whisper.

'My child, that is very heavy for you which you are carrying there.'

Cosette raised her head and answered:

'Yes, monsieur.'

'Give it to me,' the man continued, 'I will carry it for you.'

Cosette let go of the bucket. The man walked along with her.

'It is very heavy, indeed,' said he to himself. Then he added:

'Little girl, how old are you?'

'Eight years, monsieur.'

'And have you come far in this way?'

'From the spring in the woods.'

'And are you going far?'

'A good quarter of an hour from here.'

The man remained a moment without speaking, then he said abruptly:

'You have no mother then?'

'I don't know,' answered the child.

Before the man had had time to say a word, she added:

'I don't believe I have. All the rest have one. For my part, I have none.'

And after a silence, she added:

'I believe I never had any.'

The man stopped, put the bucket on the ground, stooped down and placed his hands upon the child's shoulders, making an effort to look at her and see her face in the darkness.

The thin and puny face of Cosette was vaguely outlined in the livid light of the sky.

'What is your name?' said the man.

'Cosette.'

It seemed as if the man had an electric shock. He looked at her again, then letting go of her shoulders, took up the bucket, and walked on.

A moment after, he asked:

'Little girl, where do you live?'

'At Montfermeil, if you know it.'

'It is there that we are going?'

'Yes, monsieur.'

He made another pause, then he began:

'Who is it that has sent you out into the woods after water at this time of night?'

'Madame Thénardier.'

The man resumed with a tone of voice which he tried to render indifferent, but in which there was nevertheless a singular tremor:

'What does she do, your Madame Thénardier?'

'She is my mistress,' said the child. 'She keeps the tavern.'

'The tavern,' said the man. 'Well, I am going there to lodge tonight. Show me the way.'

'We are going there,' said the child.

The man walked very fast. Cosette followed him without difficulty. She felt fatigue no more. From time to time, she raised her eyes towards this man with a sort of tranquillity and inexpressible confidence. She had never been taught to turn towards Providence and to pray. However, she felt in her bosom something that resembled hope and joy, and which rose towards heaven.

A few minutes passed. The man spoke:

'Is there no servant at Madame Thénardier's?'

'No, monsieur.'

'Are you alone?'

'Yes, monsieur.'

There was another interval of silence. Cosette raised her voice:

'That is, there are two little girls.'

'What little girls?'

'Ponine and Zelma.'

The child simplified in this way the romantic names dear to the mother.

'What are Ponine and Zelma?'

'They are Madame Thénardier's young ladies, you might say her daughters.'

'And what do they do?'

'Oh!' said the child, 'they have beautiful dolls, things which there's gold in; they are full of business. They play, they amuse themselves.'

'All day long?'

'Yes, monsieur.'

'And you?'

'Me! I work.'

'All day long?'

The child raised her large eyes in which there was a tear, which could not be seen in the darkness, and answered softly:

'Yes, monsieur.'

She continued after an interval of silence:

'Sometimes, when I have finished my work and they are willing, I amuse myself also.'

'How do you amuse yourself?'

'The best I can. They let me alone. But I have not many playthings. Ponine and Zelma are not willing for me to play with their dolls. I have only a little lead sword, not longer than that.'

The child showed her little finger.

'And which does not cut?'

'Yes, monsieur,' said the child, 'it cuts lettuce and flies' heads.'

They reached the village; Cosette guided the stranger through the streets. They passed by the bakery, but Cosette did not think of the bread she was to have brought back. The man questioned her no more, and now maintained a mournful silence. When they had passed the church, the man, seeing all these booths in the street, asked Cosette:

'Is it fair-time here?'

'No, monsieur, it is Christmas.'

As they drew near the tavern, Cosette timidly touched his arm:

'Monsieur?'

'What, my child?'

'Here we are close by the house.'

'Well?'

'Will you let me take the bucket now?'

'What for?'

'Because, if madame sees that anybody brought it for me, she will beat me.'

The man gave her the bucket. A moment after they were at the door of the chop-house.

8. *Inconvenience of entertaining a poor man who is perhaps rich*

COSETTE could not help casting one look towards the grand doll still displayed in the toy-shop, then she rapped. The door opened. The Thénardiess appeared with a candle in her hand.

'Oh! it is you, you little beggar! Lud-a-massy! you have taken your time! She has been playing, the wench!'

'Madame,' said Cosette, trembling, 'there is a gentleman who is coming to lodge.'

The Thénardiess very quickly replaced her fierce air by her amiable grimace, a change at sight peculiar to innkeepers, and looked for the newcomer with eager eyes.

'Is it monsieur?' said she.

'Yes, madame,' answered the man, touching his hat.

Rich travellers are not so polite. This gesture and the sight of the stranger's costume and baggage which the Thénardiess passed in review at a glance made the amiable grimace disappear and the fierce air reappear. She added drily:

'Enter, goodman.'

The 'goodman' entered. The Thénardiess cast a second glance at him, examined particularly his long coat which was absolutely threadbare, and his hat which was somewhat broken, and with a nod, a wink, and a turn of her nose, consulted her husband, who was still drinking with the wagoners. The husband answered by that imperceptible shake of the forefinger which, supported by a protrusion of the lips, signifies in such a case: 'complete destitution'. Upon this the Thénardiess exclaimed:

'Ah! my brave man, I am very sorry, but I have no room.'

'Put me where you will,' said the man, 'in the garret, in the stable. I will pay as if I had a room.'

'Forty sous.'

'Forty sous. Well.'

'In advance.'

'Forty sous,' whispered a wagoner to the Thénardiess, 'but it is only twenty sous.'

'It is forty sous for him,' replied the Thénardiess in the same tone. 'I don't lodge poor people for less.'

'That is true,' added her husband softly, 'it ruins a house to have this sort of people.'

Meanwhile the man, after leaving his stick and bundle on a bench, had seated himself at a table on which Cosette had been quick to place a bottle of wine and a glass. The pedlar, who had asked for the bucket of water, had gone himself to carry it to his horse. Cosette had resumed her place under the kitchen table and her knitting.

The man, who hardly touched his lips to the wine he had turned out, was contemplating the child with a strange attention.

Cosette was ugly. Happy, she might, perhaps, have been pretty. We have already sketched this little pitiful face. Cosette was thin and pale; she was nearly eight years old, but one would hardly have thought her six. Her large eyes, sunk in a sort of shadow, were almost put out by continual weeping. The corners of her mouth had that curve of habitual anguish, which is seen in the condemned and in the hopelessly sick. Her hands were, as her mother had guessed, 'covered with chilblains'. The light of the fire which was shining upon her, made her bones stand out and rendered her thinness fearfully visible. As she was always shivering, she had acquired the habit of drawing her knees together. Her whole dress was nothing but a rag, which would have excited pity in the summer, and which excited horror in the winter. She had on nothing but cotton, and that full of holes; not a rag of woollen. Her skin showed here and there, and black and blue spots could be distinguished, which indicated the places where the Thénardiess had touched her. Her naked legs were red and rough. The hollows under her collar bones would make one weep. The whole person of this child, her gait, her attitude, the sound of her voice, the intervals between one word and another, her looks, her silence, her least motion, expressed and uttered a single idea: fear.

Fear was spread all over her; she was, so to say, covered with it; fear drew back her elbows against her sides, drew her heels under her skirt, made her take the least possible room, prevented her from breathing more than was absolutely necessary, and had become what might be called her bodily habit, without possible variation, except of increase. There was in the depth of her eye an expression of astonishment mingled with terror.

This fear was such that on coming in, all wet as she was, Cosette had not dared go and dry herself by the fire, but had gone silently to her work.

The expression of the countenance of this child of eight years was habitually so sad and sometimes so tragical that it seemed, at certain moments, as if she were in the way of becoming an idiot or a demon.

Never, as we have said, had she known what it is to pray, never had she set foot within a church. 'How can I spare the time?' said the Thénardiess.

The man in the yellow coat did not take his eyes from Cosette.

Suddenly, the Thénardiess exclaimed out:

'Oh! I forgot! that bread!'

Cosette, according to her custom whenever the Thénardiess raised her voice, sprang out quickly from under the table.

She had entirely forgotten the bread. She had recourse to the expedient of children who are always terrified. She lied.

'Madame, the baker was shut.'

'You ought to have knocked.'

'I did knock, madame.'

'Well?'

'He didn't open.'

'I'll find out tomorrow if that is true,' said the Thénardiess, 'and if you are lying you will lead a pretty dance. Meantime, give me back the fifteen-sous piece.

Cosette plunged her hand into her apron pocket, and turned white. The fifteen-sous piece was not there.

'Come,' said the Thénardiess, 'didn't you hear me?'

Cosette turned her pocket inside out; there was nothing there. What could have become of that money? The little unfortunate could not utter a word. She was petrified.

'Have you lost it, the fifteen-sous piece?' screamed the Thénardiess, 'or do you want to steal it from me?'

At the same time she reached her arm towards the cowhide hanging in the chimney corner.

This menacing movement gave Cosette the strength to cry out:

'Forgive me! Madame! Madame! I won't do so any more!'

The Thénardiess took down the whip.

Meanwhile the man in the yellow coat had been fumbling in his waistcoat pocket, without being noticed. The other travellers were drinking or playing cards, and paid no attention to anything.

Cosette was writhing with anguish in the chimney-corner, trying to gather up and hide her poor half-naked limbs. The Thénardiess raised her arm.

'I beg your pardon, madame,' said the man, 'but I just now saw something fall out of the pocket of that little girl's apron and roll away. That may be it.'

At the same time he stooped down and appeared to search on the floor for an instant.

'Just so, here it is,' said he, rising.

And he handed a silver piece to the Thénardiess.

'Yes, that is it,' said she.

That was not it, for it was a twenty-sous piece, but the Thénardiess found her profit in it. She put the piece in her pocket, and contented herself with casting a ferocious look at the child and saying:

'Don't let that happen again, ever.'

Cosette went back to what the Thénardiess called 'her hole', and her large eye, fixed upon the unknown traveller, began to assume an expression that it had never known before. It was still only an artless astonishment, but a sort of blind confidence was associated with it.

'Oh! you want supper?' asked the Thénardiess of the traveller.

He did not answer. He seemed to be thinking deeply.

'What is that man?' said she between her teeth. 'It is some frightful pauper. He hasn't a penny for his supper. Is he going to pay me for his lodging only? It is very lucky, anyway, that he didn't think to steal the money that was on the floor.'

A door now opened, and Eponine and Azelma came in.

They were really two pretty little girls, rather city girls than peasants, very charming, one with her well-polished auburn tresses, the other with her long black braids falling down her back, and both so lively, neat, plump, fresh, and healthy, that it was a pleasure to see them. They were warmly clad, but with such maternal art, that the thickness of the stuff detracted nothing from the coquetry of the fit. Winter was provided against without effacing spring. These two little girls shed light around them. Moreover, they were regnant. In their toilet, in their gaiety, in the noise they made, there was sovereignty. When they entered, the Thénardiess said to them in a scolding tone, which was full of adoration: 'Ah! you are here then, you children!'

Then, taking them upon her knees one after the other, smoothing their hair, tying over their ribbons, and finally letting them go with that gentle sort of shake which is peculiar to mothers, she exclaimed:

'Are they dowdies!'

They went and sat down by the fire. They had a doll which they turned backwards and forwards upon their knees with many pretty prattlings. From time to time, Cosette raised her eyes from her knitting, and looked sadly at them as they were playing.

Eponine and Azelma did not notice Cosette. To them she was like the dog. These three little girls could not count twenty-four years among them all, and they already represented all human society; on one side envy, on the other disdain.

The doll of the Thénardier sisters was very much faded, and very old and broken; and it appeared none the less wonderful to Cosette, who had never in her life had a doll, *a real doll*, to use an expression that all children will understand.

All at once, the Thénardiess who was continually going and coming about the room, noticed that Cosette's attention was distracted, and that instead of working she was busied with the little girls who were playing.

'Ah! I've caught you!' cried she. 'That is the way you work! I'll make you work with a cowhide, I will.'

The stranger, without leaving his chair, turned towards the Thénardiess.

'Madame,' said he, smiling diffidently. 'Pshaw! let her play!'

On the part of any traveller who had eaten a slice of mutton, and drunk two bottles of wine at his supper, and who had not had the appearance of *a horrible pauper*, such a wish would have been a command. But that a man who wore that hat should allow himself to have a desire, and that a man who wore that coat should permit himself to have a wish, was what the Thénardiess thought ought not to be tolerated. She replied sharply:

'She must work, for she eats. I don't support her to do nothing.'

'What is it she is making?' said the stranger, in that gentle voice which contrasted so strangely with his beggar's clothes and his porter's shoulders.

The Thénardiess deigned to answer.

'Stockings, if you please. Stockings for my little girls who have none, worth speaking of, and will soon be going barefooted.'

The man looked at Cosette's poor red feet, and continued:

'When will she finish that pair of stockings?'

'It will take her at least three or four good days, the lazy thing.'

'And how much might this pair of stockings be worth, when it is finished?'

The Thénardiess cast a disdainful glance at him.

'At least thirty sous.'

'Would you take five francs for them?' said the man.

'Goodness!' exclaimed a wagoner who was listening, with a horse-laugh, 'Five francs? It's a humbug! five bullets!'

Thénardier now thought it time to speak.

'Yes, monsieur, if it is your fancy, you can have that pair of stockings for five francs. We can't refuse anything to travellers.'

'You must pay for them now,' said the Thénardiess, in her short and peremptory way.

'I will buy that pair of stockings,' answered the man, 'and,' added he, drawing a five-franc piece from his pocket and laying it on the table, 'I will pay for them.'

Then he turned towards Cosette.

'Now your work belongs to me. Play, my child.'

The wagoner was so affected by the five-franc piece, that he left his glass and went to look at it.

'It's so, that's a fact!' cried he, as he looked at it. 'A regular hindwheel! and no counterfeit!'

Thénardier approached, and silently put the piece in his pocket.

The Thénardiess had nothing to reply. She bit her lips, and her face assumed an expression of hatred.

Meanwhile Cosette trembled. She ventured to ask:

'Madame, is it true? can I play?'

'Play!' said the Thénardiess in a terrible voice.

'Thank you, madame,' said Cosette. And, while her mouth thanked the Thénardiess, all her little soul was thanking the traveller.

Thénardier returned to his drink. His wife whispered in his ear:

'What can that yellow man be?'

'I have seen,' answered Thénardier, in a commanding tone, 'millionaires with coats like that.'

Cosette had left her knitting, but she had not moved from her place. Cosette always stirred as little as was possible. She had taken from a little box behind her a few old rags, and her little lead sword.

Eponine and Azelma paid no attention to what was going on. They had just performed a very important operation; they had caught the kitten. They had thrown the doll on the floor, and Eponine, the elder, was dressing the kitten, in spite of her miaulings and contortions, with a lot of clothes and red and blue rags. While she was engaged in this serious and difficult labour, she was talking to her sister in that sweet and charming language of children, the grace of which, like the splendour of the butterfly's wings, escapes when we try to preserve it.

'Look! look, sister, this doll is more amusing than the other. She moves, she cries, she is warm. Come, sister, let us play with her. She shall be my little girl; I will be a lady. I'll come to see you, and you must look at her. By and by you must see her whiskers, and you must be surprised. And then you must see her ears, and then you must see her tail, and that will astonish you. And you must say to me: "Oh! my stars!" and I will say to you, "Yes, madame, it is a little girl that I have like that." Little girls are like that now.'

Azelma listened to Eponine with wonder.

Meanwhile, the drinkers were singing an obscene song, at which they laughed enough to shake the room. Thénardier encouraged and accompanied them.

As birds make a nest of anything, children make a doll of no matter what. While Eponine and Azelma were dressing up the cat, Cosette, for her part, had dressed up the sword. That done, she had laid it upon her arm, and was singing it softly to sleep.

The doll is one of the most imperious necessities, and at the same time one of the most charming instincts of female childhood. To care for, to clothe, to adorn, to dress, to undress, to dress over again, to teach, to scold a little, to rock, to cuddle, to put to sleep, to imagine that something is somebody – all the future of woman is there. Even while musing and prattling, while making little wardrobes and little baby-clothes, while sewing little dresses, little bodices, and little jackets, the child becomes a little girl, the little girl becomes a great girl, the great girl becomes a woman. The first baby takes the place of the last doll.

A little girl without a doll is almost as unfortunate and quite as impossible as a woman without children.

Cosette had therefore made a doll of her sword.

The Thénardiess, on her part, approached the *yellow man*. 'My husband is right,' thought she; 'it may be Monsieur Laffitte.[48] Some rich men are so odd.'

She came and rested her elbow on the table at which he was sitting.

'Monsieur,' said she –

At this word *monsieur*, the man turned. The Thénardiess had called him before only *brave man* or *goodman*.

'You see, monsieur,' she pursued, putting on her sweetest look, which was still more unendurable than her ferocious manner, 'I am very willing the child should play, I am not opposed to it; it is well for once, because you are generous. But, you see, she is poor; she must work.'

'The child is not yours, then?' asked the man.

'Oh dear! no, monsieur! It is a little pauper that we have taken in through charity. A sort of imbecile child. She must have water on her brain. Her head is big, as you see. We do all we can for her, but we are not rich. We write in vain to her country; for six months we have had no answer. We think that her mother must be dead.'

'Ah!' said the man, and he fell back into his reverie.

'This mother was no great shakes,' added the Thénardiess. 'She abandoned her child.'

During all this conversation, Cosette, as if an instinct had warned her that they were talking about her, had not taken her eyes from the Thénardiess. She listened. She heard a few words here and there.

Meanwhile the drinkers, all three-quarters drunk, were repeating their foul chorus with redoubled gaiety. It was highly spiced with jests, in which the names of the Virgin and the child Jesus were often heard. The Thénardiess had gone to take her part in the hilarity. Cosette, under the table, was looking into the fire, which was reflected from her fixed eye; she was again rocking the sort of rag baby that she had made, and as she rocked it, she sang in a low voice; 'My mother is dead! my mother is dead! my mother is dead!'

At the repeated entreaties of the hostess, the yellow man, 'the millionaire,' finally consented to sup.

'What will monsieur have?'

'Some bread and cheese,' said the man.

'Decidedly, it is a beggar,' thought the Thénardiess.

The revellers continued to sing their songs, and the child, under the table, also sang hers.

All at once, Cosette stopped. She had just turned and seen the little Thénardiers' doll, which they had forsaken for the cat and left on the floor, a few steps from the kitchen table.

Then she let the bundled-up sword, that only half satisfied her, fall, and ran her eyes slowly around the room. The Thénardiess was whispering to her husband and counting some money, Eponine and Azelma were playing with the cat, the travellers were eating or drinking or singing, nobody was looking at her. She had not a moment to lose. She crept out from under the table on her hands and knees, made sure once more that nobody was watching her, then darted quickly to the doll, and seized it. An instant afterwards she was at her place, seated, motionless, only turned in such a way as to keep the doll that she held in her arms in the shadow. The happiness of playing with a doll was so rare to her that it had all the violence of rapture.

Nobody had seen her, except the traveller, who was slowly eating his meagre supper.

This joy lasted for nearly a quarter of an hour.

But in spite of Cosette's precautions, she did not perceive that one of the doll's feet *stuck out*, and that the fire of the fireplace lighted it up very vividly. This rosy and luminous foot which protruded from the shadow suddenly caught Azelma's eye, and she said to Eponine: 'Oh! sister!'

The two little girls stopped, stupefied; Cosette had dared to take the doll.

Eponine got up, and without letting go of the cat, went to her mother and began to pull at her skirt.

'Let me alone,' said the mother; 'what do you want?'

'Mother,' said the child, 'look there.'

And she pointed at Cosette.

Cosette, wholly absorbed in the ecstasy of her possession, saw and heard nothing else.

The face of the Thénardiess assumed the peculiar expression which is composed of the terrible mingled with the commonplace, and which has given this class of women the name of furies.

This time wounded pride exasperated her anger still more. Cosette had leaped over all barriers. Cosette had laid her hands upon the doll of 'those young ladies'. A czarina who had seen a moujik trying on the grand *cordon* of her imperial son would have had the same expression.

She cried with a voice harsh with indignation:

'Cosette!'

Cosette shuddered as if the earth had quaked beneath her. She turned around.

'Cosette!' repeated the Thénardiess.

Cosette took the doll and placed it gently on the floor with a kind of veneration mingled with despair. Then, without taking away her eyes, she joined her hands, and, what is frightful to tell in a child of that age, she wrung them; then, what none of the emotions of the day had drawn from her, neither the run in the wood, nor the weight of the bucket of water, nor the loss of the money, nor the sight of the cowhide, nor even the stern words she had heard from the Thénardiess, she burst into tears. She sobbed.

Meanwhile the traveller arose.

'What is the matter?' said he to the Thénardiess.

'Don't you see?' said the Thénardiess, pointing with her finger to the *corpus delicti* lying at Cosette's feet.

'Well, what is that?' said the man.

'That beggar,' answered the Thénardiess, 'has dared to touch the children's doll.'

'All this noise about that?' said the man. 'Well, what if she did play with that doll?'

'She has touched it with her dirty hands!' continued the Thénardiess, 'with her horrid hands!'

Here Cosette redoubled her sobs.

'Be still!' cried the Thénardiess.

The man walked straight to the street door, opened it, and went out.

As soon as he had gone, the Thénardiess profited by his absence to give Cosette under the table a severe kick, which made the child shriek.

The door opened again, and the man reappeared, holding in his hands the fabulous doll of which we have spoken, and which had been the admiration of all the youngsters of the village since morning; he stood it up before Cosette, saying:

'Here, this is for you.'

It is probable that during the time he had been there – more than an hour – in the midst of his reverie, he had caught confused glimpses of this toy-shop, lighted up with lamps and candles so splendidly that it shone through the bar-room window like an illumination.

Cosette raised her eyes; she saw the man approach her with that doll as she would have seen the sun approach, she heard those astounding words: *This is for you.* She looked at him, she looked at the doll, then she drew back slowly, and went and hid as far as she could under the table in the corner of the room.

She wept no more, she cried no more, she had the appearance of no longer daring to breathe.

The Thénardiess, Eponine, and Azelma were so many statues. Even the drinkers stopped. There was a solemn silence in the whole bar-room.

The Thénardiess, petrified and mute, recommenced her conjectures anew: 'What is this old fellow? is he a pauper? is he a millionaire? Perhaps he's both, that is a robber.'

The face of the husband Thénardier presented that expressive wrinkle which marks the human countenance whenever the dominant instinct appears in it with all its brutal power. The innkeeper contemplated by turns the doll and the traveller; he seemed to be scenting this man as he would have scented a bag of money. This only lasted for a moment. He approached his wife and whispered to her:

'That machine cost at least thirty francs. No nonsense. Down on your knees before the man!'

Coarse natures have this in common with artless natures, that they have no transitions.

'Well, Cosette,' said the Thénardiess in a voice which was meant to be sweet, and which was entirely composed of the sour honey of vicious women, 'a'n't you going to take your doll?'

Cosette ventured to come out of her hole.

'My little Cosette,' said Thénardier with a caressing air, 'Monsieur gives you a doll. Take it. It is yours.'

Cosette looked upon the wonderful doll with a sort of terror. Her face was still flooded with tears, but her eyes began to fill, like the sky in the breaking of the dawn, with strange radiations of joy. What she experienced at that moment was almost like what she would have felt if someone had said to her suddenly: Little girl, you are queen of France.

It seemed to her that if she touched that doll, thunder would spring forth from it.

Which was true to some extent, for she thought that the Thénardiess would scold and beat her.

However, the attraction overcame her. She finally approached and timidly murmured, turning towards the Thénardiess:

'Can I, madame?'

No expression can describe her look, at once full of despair, dismay, and transport.

'Good Lord!' said the Thénardiess, 'it is yours. Since monsieur gives it to you.'

'Is it true, is it true, monsieur?' said Cosette; 'is the lady for me?'

The stranger appeared to have his eyes full of tears. He seemed to be at that stage of emotion in which one does not speak for fear of weeping. He nodded assent to Cosette, and put the hand of 'the lady' in her little hand.

Cosette withdrew her hand hastily, as if that of *the lady* burned her, and looked down at the floor. We are compelled to add, that at that instant she thrust out her tongue enormously. All at once she turned, and seized the doll eagerly.

'I will call her Catharine,' said she.

It was a strange moment when Cosette's rags met and pressed against the ribbons and the fresh pink muslins of the doll.

'Madame,' said she, 'may I put her in a chair?'

'Yes, my child,' answered the Thénardiess.

It was Éponine and Azelma now who looked upon Cosette with envy.

Cosette placed Catharine on a chair, then sat down on the floor before her, and remained motionless, without saying a word, in the attitude of contemplation.

'Why don't you play, Cosette?' said the stranger.

'Oh! I am playing,' answered the child.

This stranger, this unknown man, who seemed like a visit from Providence to Cosette, was at that moment the being which the Thénardiess hated more than aught else in the world. However, she was compelled to restrain herself. Her emotions were more than she could endure, accustomed as she was to dissimulation, by endeavouring to copy her husband in all her actions. She sent her daughters to bed immediately, then asked the yellow man's *permission* to send Cosette to bed – *who is very tired today*, added she, with a motherly air. Cosette went to bed, holding Catharine in her arms.

The Thénardiess went from time to time to the other end of the room, where her husband was, *to soothe her soul*, she said. She exchanged a few words with him, which were the more furious that she did not dare to speak them aloud:

'The old fool! what has he got into his head, to come here to disturb us! to want that little monster to play! to give her dolls! to give forty-franc dolls to a slut that I wouldn't give forty sous for. A little more, and he would say *Your Majesty* to her, as they do to the Duchess of Berry! Is he in his senses? he must be crazy, the strange old fellow!'

'Why? It is very simple,' replied Thénardier. 'If it amuses him! It amuses you for the girl to work; it amuses him for her to play. He has the right to do it. A traveller can do as he likes, if he pays for it. If this old fellow is a philanthropist, what is that to you? if he is crazy it don't concern you. What do you interfere for, as long as he has money?'

Language of a master and reasoning of an innkeeper, which neither in one case nor the other admits of reply.

The man had leaned his elbows on the table, and resumed his attitude of reverie. All the other travellers, pedlars, and wagoners, had drawn back a little, and sung no more. They looked upon him from a distance with a sort of respectful fear.

This solitary man, so poorly clad, who took five-franc pieces from his pocket with so much indifference, and who lavished gigantic dolls on little brats in wooden shoes, was certainly a magnificent and formidable goodman.

Several hours passed away. The midnight mass was said, the revel was finished, the drinkers had gone, the house was closed, the room was deserted, the fire had gone out, the stranger still remained in the same place and in the same posture. From time to time he changed the elbow on which he rested. That was all. But he had not spoken a word since Cosette was gone.

The Thénardiers alone, out of propriety and curiosity, had remained in the room.

'Is he going to spend the night like this?' grumbled the Thénardiess. When the clock struck two in the morning, she acknowledged herself beaten, and said to her husband: 'I am going to bed, you may do as you like.' The husband sat down at a table in a corner, lighted a candle, and began to read the *Courrier Français*.[49]

A good hour passed thus. The worthy innkeeper had read the *Courrier Français* at least three times, from the date of the number to the name of the printer. The stranger did not stir.

Thénardier moved, coughed, spat, blew his nose, and creaked his chair. The man did not stir. 'Is he asleep?' thought Thénardier. The man was not asleep, but nothing could arouse him.

Finally, Thénardier took off his cap, approached softly, and ventured to say:

'Is monsieur not going to repose?'

Not going to bed would have seemed to him too much and too familiar. *To repose* implied luxury, and there was respect in it. Such words have the mysterious and wonderful property of swelling the bill in the morning. A room in which *you go to bed* costs twenty sous; a room in which you *repose* costs twenty francs.

'Yes,' said the stranger, 'you are right. Where is your stable?'

'Monsieur,' said Thénardier, with a smile, 'I will conduct monsieur.'

He took the candle, the man took his bundle and his staff, and Thénardier led him into a room on the first floor, which was very showy, furnished all in mahogany, with a high-post bedstead and red calico curtains.

'What is this? 'said the traveller.

'It is properly our bridal chamber,' said the innkeeper. 'We occupy another like this, my spouse and I; this is not open more than three or four times in a year.'

'I should have liked the stable as well,' said the man, bluntly.

Thénardier did not appear to hear this not very civil answer.

He lighted two entirely new wax candles, which were displayed upon the mantel; a good fire was blazing in the fireplace. There was on the mantel, under a glass case, a woman's head-dress of silver thread and orange-flowers.

'What is this?' said the stranger.

'Monsieur,' said Thénardier, 'it is my wife's bridal cap.'

The traveller looked at the object with a look which seemed to say 'there was a moment, then, when this monster was a virgin'.

Thénardier lied, however. When he hired this shanty to turn it into a chop-house, he found the room thus furnished, and bought this furniture, and purchased at second-hand these orange-flowers, thinking that this would cast a gracious light over 'his spouse', and that the house would derive from them what the English call respectability.

When the traveller turned again the host had disappeared. Thénardier had discreetly taken himself out of the way without daring to say good-night, not desiring to treat with a disrespectful cordiality a man whom he proposed to skin royally in the morning.

The innkeeper retired to this room; his wife was in bed, but not asleep. When she heard her husband's step, she turned towards him, and said:

'You know that I am going to kick Cosette outdoors tomorrow!'

Thénardier coolly answered:

'You are, indeed!'

They exchanged no further words, and in a few moments their candle was blown out.

For his part, the traveller had put his staff and bundle in a corner. The host gone, he sat down in an armchair, and remained some time thinking. Then he drew off his shoes, took one of the two candles, blew out the other, pushed open the door, and went out of the room, looking about him as if he were searching for something. He passed through a hall, and came to the stairway. There he heard a very soft little sound, which resembled the breathing of a child. Guided by this sound he came to a sort of triangular nook built under the stairs, or, rather, formed by the staircase itself. This hole was nothing but the space beneath the stairs. There, among all sorts of old baskets and old rubbish, in the dust and among the cobwebs, there was a bed; if a mattress, so full of holes as to show the straw, and a covering so full of holes as to show the mattress, can be called a bed. There were no sheets. This was placed on the floor immediately on the tiles. In this bed Cosette was sleeping.

The man approached and looked at her.

Cosette was sleeping soundly; she was dressed. In the winter she did not undress on account of the cold. She held the doll clasped in her arms; its large open eyes shone in the obscurity. From time to time she heaved a deep sigh, as if she were about to wake, and she hugged the doll almost convulsively. There was only one of her wooden shoes at the side of her bed. An open door near Cosette's nook disclosed a large dark room. The stranger entered. At the further end, through a glass window, he perceived two little beds with very white spreads. They were those of Azelma and Eponine. Half hid behind these beds was a willow cradle without curtains, in which the little boy who had cried all the evening was sleeping.

The stranger conjectured that this room communicated with that of the Thénardiers. He was about to withdraw when his eye fell upon the fireplace, one of those huge tavern fireplaces where there is always so little fire, when there is a fire, and which are so cold to look upon. In this one there was no fire, there were not even any ashes. What there was, however, attracted the traveller's attention. It was two little children's shoes, of coquettish shape and of different sizes. The traveller remembered the graceful and immemorial custom of children putting their shoes in the fireplace on Christmas night, to wait there in the darkness in expectation of some shining gift from their good fairy. Eponine and Azelma had taken good care not to forget this, and each had put one of her shoes in the fireplace.

The traveller bent over them.

The fairy – that is to say, the mother – had already made her visit, and shining in each shoe was a beautiful new ten-sous piece.

The man rose up and was on the point of going away, when he perceived further along, by itself, in the darkest corner of the fireplace, another object. He looked, and recognised a shoe, a horrid wooden shoe of the clumsiest sort, half broken and covered with ashes and dried mud. It was Cosette's shoe. Cosette, with that touching confidence of childhood which can always be deceived without ever being discouraged, had also placed her shoe in the fireplace.

What a sublime and sweet thing is hope in a child who has never known anything but despair!

There was nothing in this wooden shoe.

The stranger fumbled in his waistcoat, bent over, and dropped into Cosette's shoe a gold Louis.

Then he went back to his room with stealthy tread.

9. *Thénardier manœuvring*

ON THE FOLLOWING MORNING, at least two hours before day, Thénardier, seated at a table in the bar-room a candle by his side, with pen in hand, was making out the bill of the traveller in the yellow coat.

His wife was standing, half bent over him, following him with her eyes. Not a word passed between them. It was, on one side, a profound meditation, on the other that religious admiration with which we observe a marvel of the human mind spring up and expand. A noise was heard in the house; it was the Lark, sweeping the stairs.

After a good quarter of an hour and some erasures, Thénardier produced this masterpiece.

Bill of Monsieur in No. 1.

Supper	3 frs
Room	10 ...
Candle	5 ...
Fire	4 ...
Service	1 ...
Total	23 frs

Service was written *servisse.*

'Twenty-three francs!' exclaimed the woman, with an enthusiasm which was mingled with some hesitation.

Like all great artists, Thénardier was not satisfied.

'Pooh!' said he.

It was the accent of Castlereagh drawing up for the Congress of Vienna the bill which France was to pay.

'Monsieur Thénardier, you are right, he deserves it,' murmured the woman, thinking of the doll given to Cosette in the presence of her daughters; 'it is right! but it's too much. He won't pay it.'

Thénardier put on his cold laugh, and said: 'He will pay it.'

This laugh was the highest sign of certainty and authority. What was thus said, must be. The woman did not insist. She began to arrange the tables; the husband walked back and forth in the room. A moment after he added:

'I owe, at least, fifteen hundred francs!'

He seated himself thoughtfully in the chimney corner, his feet in the warm ashes.

'Ah ha!' replied the woman, 'you don't forget that I kick Cosette out of the house today? The monster! it tears my vitals to see her with her doll! I would rather marry Louis XVIII than keep her in the house another day!'

Thénardier lighted his pipe, and answered between two puffs:

'You'll give the bill to the man.'

Then he went out.

He was scarcely out of the room when the traveller came in.

Thénardier reappeared immediately behind him, and remained motionless in the half-open door, visible only to his wife.

The yellow man carried his staff and bundle in his hand.

'Up so soon!' said the Thénardiess; 'is monsieur going to leave us already?'

While speaking, she turned the bill in her hands with an embarrassed look, and made creases in it with her nails. Her hard face exhibited a shade of timidity and doubt that was not habitual.

To present such a bill to a man who had so perfectly the appearance of 'a pauper' seemed too awkward to her.

The traveller appeared preoccupied and absent-minded.

He answered:

'Yes, madame, I am going away.'

'Monsieur, then, had no business at Montfermeil?' replied she.

'No, I am passing through; that is all. Madame,' added he, 'what do I owe?'

The Thénardiess, without answering, handed him the folded bill.

The man unfolded the paper and looked at it; but his thoughts were evidently elsewhere.

'Madame,' replied he, 'do you do a good business in Montfermeil?'

'So-so, monsieur,' answered the Thénardiess, stupefied at seeing no other explosion.

She continued in a mournful and lamenting strain:

'Oh! monsieur, the times are very hard, and then we have so few rich people around here! It is a very little place, you see. If we only had rich travellers now and then, like monsieur! We have so many expenses! Why, that little girl eats us out of house and home.'

'What little girl?'

'Why, the little girl you know! Cosette! the Lark, as they call her about here!'

'Ah!' said the man.

She continued:

'How stupid these peasants are with their nicknames! She looks more like a bat than a lark. You see, monsieur, we don't ask charity, but we are not able to give it. We make nothing, and have a great deal to pay. The licence, the excise, the doors and windows, the tax on everything! Monsieur knows that the government demands a deal of money. And then I have my own girls. I have nothing to spend on other people's children.

The man replied in a voice which he endeavoured to render indifferent, and in which there was a slight tremulousness.

'Suppose you were relieved of her?'

'Who? Cosette?'

'Yes.'

The red and violent face of the woman became illumined with a hideous expression.

'Ah, monsieur! my good monsieur! take her, keep her, take her away, carry her off, sugar her, stuff her, drink her, eat her, and be blessed by the holy Virgin and all the saints in Paradise!'

'Agreed.'

'Really! you will take her away?'

'I will.'

'Immediately?'

'Immediately. Call the child.'

'Cosette!' cried the Thénardiess.

'In the meantime,' continued the man, 'I will pay my bill. How much is it?'

He cast a glance at the bill, and could not repress a movement of surprise.

'Twenty-three francs?'

He looked at the hostess and repeated:

'Twenty-three francs?'

There was, in the pronunciation of these two sentences, thus repeated, the accent which lies between the point of exclamation and the point of interrogation.

The Thénardiess had had time to prepare herself for the shock. She replied with assurance:

'Yes, of course, monsieur! it is twenty-three francs.'

The stranger placed five five-franc pieces upon the table.

'Go for the little girl,' said he.

At this moment Thénardier advanced into the middle of the room and said:

'Monsieur owes twenty-six sous.'

'Twenty-six sous!' exclaimed the woman.

'Twenty sous for the room,' continued Thénardier coldly, 'and six for supper. As to the little girl, I must have some talk with monsieur about that. Leave us, wife.'

The Thénardiess was dazzled by one of those unexpected flashes which emanate from talent. She felt that the great actor had entered upon the scene, answered not a word, and went out.

As soon as they were alone, Thénardier offered the traveller a chair. The traveller sat down, but Thénardier remained standing, and his face assumed a singular expression of good-nature and simplicity.

'Monsieur,' said he, 'listen, I must say that I adore this child.'

The stranger looked at him steadily.

'What child?'

Thénardier continued:

'How strangely we become attached! What is all this silver? Take back your money. This child I adore.'

'Who is that?' asked the stranger.

'Oh, our little Cosette! And you wish to take her away from us? Indeed, I speak frankly, as true as you are an honourable man, I cannot consent to it. I should miss her. I have had her since she was very small. It is true, she costs us money; it is true she has her faults, it is true we are not rich, it is true I paid four hundred francs for medicines at one time when she was sick. But we must do something for God. She has neither father nor mother; I have brought her up. I have bread enough for her and for myself. In fact, I must keep this child. You understand, we have affections; I am a good beast; myself; I do not reason; I love this little girl; my wife is hasty, but she loves her also. You see, she is like our own child. I feel the need of her prattle in the house.'

The stranger was looking steadily at him all the while. He continued:

'Pardon me, excuse me, monsieur, but one does not give his child like that to a traveller. Isn't it true that I am right? After that, I don't say – you are rich and have the appearance of a very fine man – if it is for her advantage, – but I must know about it. You understand? On the supposition that I should let her go and sacrifice my own feelings, I should want to know where she is going. I would not want to lose sight of her, I should want to know who she was with, that I might come and see her now and then, and that she might know that her good foster-father was still watching over her. Finally, there are things which are not possible. I do not know even your name. If you should take her away, I should say, alas for the little Lark, where has she gone? I must, at least, see some poor rag of paper, a bit of a passport, something.'

The stranger, without removing from him this gaze which went, so to speak, to the bottom of his conscience, answered in a severe and firm tone:

'Monsieur Thénardier, people do not take a passport to come five leagues from Paris. If I take Cosette, I take her, that is all. You will not know my name, you will not know my abode, you will not know where she goes, and my intention is that she shall never see you again in her life. Do you agree to that? Yes or no?'

As demons and genii recognise by certain signs the presence of a superior God, Thénardier comprehended that he had to deal with one who was very powerful. It came like an intuition; he understood it with his clear and quick sagacity; although during the evening he had been drinking with the wagoners, smoking, and singing bawdy songs, still he was observing the stranger all the while, watching him like a cat, and studying him like a mathematician. He had been observing him on his own account, for pleasure and by instinct, and at the same time lying in wait as if he had been paid for it. Not a gesture, not a movement of the man in the yellow coat had escaped him. Before even the stranger had so clearly shown his interest in Cosette, Thénardier had divined it. He had surprised the searching glances of the old man constantly returning to the child. Why this interest? What was this man? Why, with so much money in his purse, this miserable dress? These were questions which he put to himself without being able to answer them, and they irritated him. He had been thinking it over all night. This could not be the Cosette's father. Was it a grandfather? Then why did he not make himself known at once? When a man has a right, he shows it. This man evidently had no right to Cosette. Then who was he? Thénardier was lost in conjectures. He caught glimpses of everything, but saw nothing. However it might be, when he commenced the conversation with this man, sure that there was a secret in all this, sure that the man had an interest in remaining unknown, he felt himself strong; at the stranger's clear and firm answer, when he saw that this mysterious personage was mysterious and nothing more, he felt weak. He was expecting nothing of the kind. His conjectures were put to flight. He rallied his ideas. He weighed all in a second. Thénardier was one of those men who comprehend a situation at a glance. He decided that this was the moment to advance straightforward and swiftly. He did what great captains do at that decisive instant which they alone can recognise; he unmasked his battery at once.

'Monsieur,' said he, 'I must have fifteen hundred francs.'

The stranger took from his side-pocket an old black leather pocket-book, opened it, and drew forth three bank bills which he placed upon the table. He then rested his large thumb on these bills, and said to the tavern-keeper:

'Bring Cosette.'

While this was going on what was Cosette doing?

Cosette, as soon as she awoke, had run to her wooden shoe. She had found the gold piece in it. It was not a Napoleon, but one of those new twenty-franc pieces of the Restoration, on the face of which the little Prussian queue had replaced the laurel crown. Cosette was dazzled. Her destiny began to intoxicate her. She did not know that it was a piece of gold; she had never seen one before; she hastily concealed it in her pocket as if she had stolen it. Nevertheless she felt it boded good to her. She divined whence the gift came, but she experienced a joy that was filled with awe. She was gratified; she was moreover stupefied. Such magnificent and beautiful things seemed unreal to her. The doll made her afraid, the gold piece made her afraid. She trembled with wonder before these magnificences. The stranger himself did not make her afraid. On the contrary, he reassured her. Since the previous evening, amid all her astonishment, and in her sleep, she was thinking in her little child's mind of this man who had such an old, and poor, and sad appearance, and who was so rich and so kind. Since she had met this goodman in the wood, it seemed as though all things were changed about her. Cosette, less happy than the smallest swallow of the sky, had never known what it is to take refuge under a mother's wing. For five years, that is to say, as far back as she could remember, the poor child had shivered and shuddered. She had always been naked under the biting north wind of misfortune, and now it seemed to her that she was clothed. Before her soul was cold, now it was warm. Cosette was no longer afraid of the Thénardiers; she was no longer alone; she had somebody to look to.

She hurriedly set herself to her morning task. This louis, which she had placed in the same pocket of her apron from which the fifteen-sous piece had fallen the night before, distracted her attention from her work. She did not dare to touch it, but she spent five minutes at a time contemplating it, and we must confess, with her tongue thrust out. While sweeping the stairs, she stopped and stood there, motionless, forgetting her broom, and the whole world besides, occupied in looking at this shining star at the bottom of her pocket.

It was in one of these reveries that the Thénardiess found her.

At the command of her husband, she had gone to look for her. Wonderful to tell, she did not give her a slap nor even call her a hard name.

'Cosette,' said she, almost gently, 'come quick.'

An instant after, Cosette entered the bar-room.

The stranger took the bundle he had brought and untied it. This bundle contained a little woollen frock, an apron, a coarse cotton under-garment, a petticoat, a scarf, woollen stockings, and shoes – a complete dress for a girl of seven years. It was all in black.

'My child,' said the man, 'take this and go and dress yourself quick.'

The day was breaking when those of the inhabitants of Montfermeil who were beginning to open their doors, saw pass on the road to Paris a poorly clad goodman leading a little girl dressed in mourning who had a pink doll in her arms. They were going towards Livry.

It was the stranger and Cosette.

No one recognised the man; as Cosette was not now in tatters, few recognised her.

Cosette was going away. With whom? She was ignorant. Where? She knew not. All she understood was, that she was leaving behind the Thénardier chophouse. Nobody had thought of bidding her goodbye, nor had she of bidding goodbye to anybody. She went out from that house, hated and hating.

Poor gentle being, whose heart had only been crushed hitherto.

Cosette walked seriously along, opening her large eyes, and looking at the sky. She had put her louis in the pocket of her new apron. From time to time she bent over and cast a glance at it, and then looked at the goodman. She felt somewhat as if she were near God.

10. *Who seeks the best may find the worst*

THE THÉNARDIESS, according to her custom, had left her husband alone. She was expecting great events. When the man and Cosette were gone, Thénardier, after a good quarter of an hour, took her aside, and showed her the fifteen hundred francs.

'What's that?' said she.

It was the first time, since the beginning of their housekeeping, that she had dared to criticise the act of her master.

He felt the blow.

'True, you are right,' said he; 'I am a fool. Give me my hat.'

He folded the three bank bills, thrust them into his pocket, and started in all haste, but he missed the direction and took the road to the right. Some neighbours of whom he inquired put him on the track; the lark and the man had been seen to go in the direction of Livry. He followed this indication, walking rapidly and talking to himself.

'This man is evidently a millionaire dressed in yellow, and as for me, I am a brute. He first gave twenty sous, then five francs, then fifty francs, then fifteen hundred francs, all so readily. He would have given fifteen thousand francs. But I shall catch him.'

And then this bundle of clothes, made ready beforehand for the little girl; all that was strange, there was a good deal of mystery under it. When one gets hold of a mystery, he does not let go of it. The secrets of the rich are sponges full of gold; a man ought to know how to squeeze them. All these thoughts were whirling in his brain. 'I am a brute,' said he.

On leaving Montfermeil and reaching the turn made by the road to Livry, the route may be seen for a long distance on the plateau. On reaching this point he counted on being able to see the man and the little girl. He looked as far as his eye could reach, but saw nothing. He inquired again. In the meanwhile he was losing time. The passers-by told him that the man and child whom he sought had travelled towards the wood in the direction of Gagny. He hastened in this direction.

They had the start of him, but a child walks slowly, and he went rapidly. And then the country was well known to him.

Suddenly he stopped and struck his forehead like a man who has forgotten the main thing, and who thinks of retracing his steps.

'I ought to have taken my gun!' said he.

Thénardier was one of those double natures who sometimes appear among us without our knowledge, and disappear without ever being known, because destiny has shown us but one side of them. It is the fate of many men to live thus half submerged. In a quiet ordinary situation, Thénardier had all that is necessary to make – we do not say to be – what passes for an honest tradesman, a good citizen. At the same time, under certain circumstances, under the operation of certain occurrences exciting his baser nature, he had in him all that was necessary to be a villain. He was a shopkeeper, in which lay hidden a monster. Satan ought for a moment to have squatted in some corner of the hole in which Thénardier lived and studied this hideous masterpiece.

After hesitating an instant:

'Bah!' thought he, 'they would have time to escape!'

And he continued on his way, going rapidly forward, and almost as if he were certain, with the sagacity of the fox scenting a flock of partridges.

In fact, when he had passed the ponds, and crossed obliquely the large meadow at the right of the Avenue de Bellevue, as he reached the grassy path which nearly encircles the hill, and which covers the arch of the old aqueduct of the abbey of Chelles, he perceived above a bush, the hat on which he had already built so many conjectures. It was the man's hat. The bushes were low. Thénardier perceived that the man and Cosette were seated there. The child could not be seen, she was so short, but he could see the head of the doll.

Thénardier was not deceived. The man had sat down there to give Cosette a little rest. The chop-house keeper turned aside the bushes, and suddenly appeared before the eyes of those whom he sought.

'Pardon me, excuse me, monsieur,' said he, all out of breath, 'but here are your fifteen hundred francs.'

So saying, he held out the three bank bills to the stranger.

The man raised his eyes:

'What does that mean?'

Thénardier answered respectfully:

'Monsieur, that means that I take back Cosette.'

Cosette shuddered, and hugged close to the goodman.

He answered, looking Thénardier straight in the eye, and spacing his syllables.

'You – take – back – Cosette?'

'Yes, monsieur, I take her back. I tell you I have reflected. Indeed, I haven't the right to give her to you. I am an honest man, you see. This little girl is not mine. She belongs to her mother. Her mother has confided her to me; I can only give her up to her mother. You will tell me: But her mother is dead. Well. In that case, I can only give up the child to a person who shall bring me a written order, signed by the mother, stating I should deliver the child to him. That is clear.'

The man, without answering, felt in his pocket, and Thénardier saw the pocket-book containing the bank bills reappear.

The tavern-keeper felt a thrill of joy.

'Good!' thought he; 'hold on. He is going to corrupt me!'

Before opening the pocket-book, the traveller cast a look about him. The place was entirely deserted. There was not a soul either in the wood, or in the valley. The man opened the pocket-book, and drew from it, not the handful of bank-bills which Thénardier expected, but a little piece of paper, which he unfolded and presented open to the innkeeper, saying:

'You are right. Read that!'

Thénardier took the paper and read.

M— sur M—, March 25, 1823.
MONSIEUR THÉNARDIER:
You will deliver Cosette to the bearer. He will settle all small debts.
I have the honour to salute you with consideration.
FANTINE

'You know that signature?' replied the man.

It was indeed the signature of Fantine. Thénardier recognised it.

There was nothing to say. He felt doubly enraged, enraged at being compelled to give up the bribe which he hoped for, and enraged at being beaten. The man added:

'You can keep this paper as your receipt.'

Thénardier retreated in good order.

'This signature is very well imitated,' he grumbled between his teeth. 'Well, so be it!'

Then he made a desperate effort.

'Monsieur,' said he, 'it is all right. Then you are the person. But you must settle "all small debts". There is a large amount due to me.'

The man rose to his feet, and said at the same time, snapping with his thumb and finger some dust from his threadbare sleeve:

'Monsieur Thénardier, in January the mother reckoned that she owed you a hundred and twenty francs; you sent her in February a memorandum of five hundred francs; you received three hundred francs at the end of February, and three hundred at the beginning of March. There has since elapsed nine months which, at fifteen francs per month, the price agreed upon, amounts to a hundred and thirty-five francs. You had received a hundred francs in advance. There remain thirty-five francs due you. I have just given you fifteen hundred francs.'

Thénardier felt what the wolf feels the moment when he finds himself seized and crushed by the steel jaws of the trap.

'What is this devil of a man?' thought he.

He did what the wolf does, he gave a spring. Audacity had succeeded with him once already.

'Monsieur-whatever-your-name- is,' said he resolutely, and putting aside this time all show of respect. 'I shall take back Cosette or you must give me a thousand crowns.'

The stranger said quietly:

'Come, Cosette.'

He took Cosette with his left hand, and with the right picked up his staff, which was on the ground.

Thénardier noted the enormous size of the cudgel, and the solitude of the place.

The man disappeared in the wood with the child, leaving the chop-house keeper motionless and nonplussed.

As they walked away, Thénardier observed his broad shoulders, a little rounded, and his big fists.

Then his eyes fell back upon his own puny arms and thin hands. 'I must have been a fool indeed,' thought he, 'not to have brought my gun, as I was going on a hunt.'

However, the innkeeper did not abandon the pursuit.

'I must know where he goes,' said he; and he began to follow them at a distance. There remained two things in his possession, one a bitter mockery, the piece of paper signed *Fantine*, and the other a consolation, the fifteen hundred francs.

The man was leading Cosette in the direction of Livry and Bondy. He was walking slowly, his head bent down, in an attitude of reflection and sadness. The winter had bereft the wood of foliage, so that Thénardier did not lose sight of them, though remaining at a considerable distance behind. From time to time the man turned, and looked to see if he were followed. Suddenly he perceived Thénardier. He at once entered a coppice with Cosette, and both disappeared from sight. 'The devil!' said Thénardier. And he redoubled his pace.

The density of the thicket compelled him to approach them. When the man reached the thickest part of the wood, he turned again. Thénardier had endeavoured to conceal himself in the branches in vain, he could not prevent the man from seeing him. The man cast an uneasy glance at him, then shook his head, and resumed his journey. The innkeeper again took up the pursuit They walked thus two or three hundred paces. Suddenly the man turned again. He perceived the innkeeper. This time he looked at him so forbiddingly that Thénardier judged it 'unprofitable' to go further. Thénardier went home.

11. *Number 9430 comes up again, and Cosette draws it*

JEAN VALJEAN was not dead.

When he fell into the sea, or rather when he threw himself into it, he was, as we have seen, free from his irons. He swam under water to a ship at anchor to which a boat was fastened.

He found means to conceal himself in this boat until evening. At night he betook himself again to the water, and reached the land a short distance from Cape Brun.

There, as he did not lack for money, he could procure clothes. A little public-house in the environs of Balaguier was then the place which supplied clothing for escaped convicts, a lucrative business. Then Jean Valjean, like all those joyless fugitives who are endeavouring to throw off the track the spy of the law and social fatality, followed an obscure and wandering path. He found an asylum first in Pradeaux, near Beausset. Then he went towards Grand Villard, near Briançon, in the Hautes Alpes. Groping and restless flight, threading the mazes of the mole whose windings are unknown. There were afterwards found some trace of his passage in Ain, on the territory of Civrieux, in the Pyrenees at Accons, at a place called the Grange-de-Domecq, near the hamlet of Chavailles, and in the environs of Périgneux, at Brunies, a canton of Chapelle Gonaguet. He finally reached Paris. We have seen him at Montfermeil.

His first care, on reaching Paris, had been to purchase a mourning dress for a little girl of seven years, then to procure lodgings. That done, he had gone to Montfermeil.

It will be remembered that, at the time of his former escape, or near that time, he had made a mysterious journey of which justice had had some glimpse.

Moreover, he was believed to be dead, and that thickened the obscurity which surrounded him. At Paris there fell into his hands a paper which chronicled the fact. He felt reassured, and almost as much at peace as if he really had been dead.

On the evening of the same day that Jean Valjean had rescued Cosette from the clutches of the Thénardiess, he entered Paris again. He entered the city at nightfall, with the child, by the barrière de Monceaux. There he took a cabriolet, which carried him as far as the esplanade of the Observatory. There he got out, paid the driver, took Cosette by the hand, and both in the darkness of the night, through the deserted streets in the vicinity of l'Ourcine and la Glacière, walked towards the boulevard de l'Hôpital.

The day had been strange and full of emotion for Cosette; they had eaten behind hedges bread and cheese bought at isolated chop-houses; they had often changed carriages, and had travelled short distances on foot. She did not complain; but she was tired, and Jean Valjean perceived it by her pulling more heavily at his hand while walking. He took her in his arms; Cosette, without letting go of Catharine, laid her head on Jean Valjean's shoulder, and went to sleep.

BOOK 4: THE OLD GORBEAU HOUSE

1. *Master Gorbeau*

FORTY YEARS AGO, the solitary pedestrian[50] who ventured into the unknown regions of La Salpêtrière and went up along the Boulevard as far as the Barrière d'Italie, reached certain points where it might be said that Paris disappeared. It was no longer a solitude, for there were people passing; it was not the country, for there were houses and streets; it was not a city, the streets had ruts in them, like the highways, and grass grew along their borders; it was not a village, the houses were too lofty. What was it then? It was an inhabited place where there was nobody, it was a desert place where there was somebody; it was a boulevard of the great city, a street of Paris, wilder, at night, than a forest, and gloomier, by day, than a graveyard.

It was the old quarter of the Horse Market.

Our pedestrian, if he trusted himself beyond the four tumbling walls of this Horse Market, if willing to go even further than the Rue du Petit Banquier, leaving on his right a courtyard shut in by lofty walls, then a meadow studded with stacks of tan-bark that looked like the gigantic beaver dams, then an enclosure half filled with lumber and piles of logs, sawdust and shavings, from the top of which a huge dog was baying, then a long, low, ruined wall with a small dark-coloured and decrepit gate in it, covered with moss, which was full of flowers in springtime, then, in the loneliest spot, a frightful broken-down structure on which could be read in large letters: POST NO BILLS; this bold promenader, we say, would reach the corner of the Rue des Vignes-Saint-Marcel, a latitude not much explored. There, near a manufactory and between two garden walls, could be seen at the time of which we speak an old ruined dwelling that, at first sight, seemed as small as a cottage, yet was, in reality, as vast as a cathedral. It stood with its gable end towards the highway, and hence its apparent diminutiveness. Nearly the whole house was hidden. Only the door and one window could be seen.

This old dwelling had but one storey.

On examining it, the peculiarity that first struck the beholder was that the door could never have been anything but the door of a hovel, while the window, had it been cut in freestone and not in rough material, might have been the casement of a lordly residence.

The door was merely a collection of worm-eaten boards rudely tacked together with cross-pieces that looked like pieces of firewood clumsily split out. It opened directly on a steep staircase with high steps covered with mud, plaster, and dust, and of the same breadth as the door, and which seemed from the street to rise perpendicularly like a ladder, and disappear in the shadow between two walls. The top of the shapeless opening which this door closed upon, was disguised by a narrow topscreen, in the middle of which had been sawed a three-cornered orifice that served both for skylight and ventilator when the door was shut. On the inside of the door a brush dipped in ink had, in a couple of strokes of the hand, traced the number 52, and above the screen, the same brush had daubed the number 50, so that a newcomer would hesitate, asking: Where am I?

The top of the entrance says, at number 50; the inside, however, replies, No! at number 52! The dust-coloured rags that hung in guise of curtains about the three-cornered ventilator, we will not attempt to describe.

The window was broad and of considerable height, with large panes in the sashes and provided with Venetian shutters; only the panes had received a variety of wounds which were at once concealed and made manifest by ingenious strips and bandages of paper, and the shutters were so broken and disjointed that they menaced the passers-by more than they shielded the occupants of the dwelling. The horizontal slats were lacking, here and there, and had been very simply replaced with boards nailed across, so that what had been a Venetian, in the first instance, ended as a regular close shutter. This door with its dirty look and this window with its decent though dilapidated appearance, seen thus in one and the same building, produced the effect of two ragged beggars bound in the same direction and walking side by side, with different mien under the same rags, one having always been a pauper while the other had been a gentleman.

The staircase led up to a very spacious interior, which looked like a barn converted into a house. This structure had for its main channel of communication a long hall, on which there opened, on either side, apartments of different dimensions scarcely habitable, rather resembling booths than rooms. These chambers looked out upon the shapeless grounds of the neighbourhood. Altogether, it was dark and dull and dreary, even melancholy and sepulchral, and it was penetrated, either by the dim, cold rays of the sun or by icy draughts, according to the situation of the cracks, in the roof, or in the door. One interesting and picturesque peculiarity of this kind of tenement is the monstrous size of the spiders.

To the left of the main door, on the boulevard, a small window that had been walled up formed a square niche some six feet from the ground, which was filled with stones that passing urchins had thrown into it.

A portion of this building has recently been pulled down, but what remains, at the present day, still conveys an idea of what it was. The structure, taken as a whole, is not more than a hundred years old. A hundred years is youth to a church, but old age to a private mansion. It would seem that the dwelling of Man partakes of his brief existence, and the dwelling of God, of His eternity.

The letter-carriers called the house No. 50–52; but it was known, in the quarter, as Gorbeau House.

Let us see how it came by that title.

The 'gatherers-up of unconsidered trifles' who collect anecdotes as the herbalist his samples, and prick the fleeting dates upon their memories with a pin, know that there lived in Paris, in the last century, about 1770, two attorneys of the Châtelet, one named Corbeau and the other Renard – two names, anticipated by La Fontaine. The chance for a joke was altogether too fine a one to be let slip by the goodly company of lawyers' clerks. So, very soon, the galleries of the courtrooms rang with the following parody, in rather gouty verse:

> Maître Corbeau, sur un dossier perché,
>> Tenait dans son bec une saisie executoire;
> Maître Renard, par l'odeur alléché,
>> Lui fit à peu près cette histoire:
> He! bonjour! etc.*

The two honest practitioners, annoyed by these shafts of wit, and rather disconcerted in their dignity by the roars of laughter that followed them, resolved to change their names, and, with that view, applied to the king. The petition was presented to Louis XV on the very day on which the Pope's Nuncio and the Cardinal de La Roche-Aymon in the presence of his Majesty, devoutly kneeling, one on each side of Madame du Barry, put her slippers on her naked feet, as she was getting out of bed. The king, who was laughing, continued his laugh; he passed gaily from the two bishops to the two advocates, and absolved these limbs of the law from their names almost. It was granted to Master Corbeau, by the king's good pleasure, to add a flourish to the first letter of his name, thus making it Gorbeau; Master Renard was less fortunate, as he only got permission to put a P. before the R. which made the word Prenard,† a name no less appropriate than the first one.

Now, according to tradition, this Master Gorbeau was the proprietor of the structure numbered 50–52, Boulevard de l'Hôpital. He was, likewise, the originator of the monumental window.

Hence, this building got its name of Gorbeau House.

Opposite No. 50–52 stands, among the shade-trees that line the Boulevard, a tall elm, three-quarters dead, and almost directly in front, opens the Rue de la Barrière des Gobelins – a street, at that time, without houses, unpaved, bordered with scrubby trees, grass-grown or muddy, according to the season, and running squarely up to the wall encircling Paris. An odour of vitriol ascended in puffs from the roofs of a neighbouring factory.

The Barrière was quite near. In 1823, the encircling wall yet existed.

This Barrière itself filled the mind with gloomy images. It was on the way to the Bicêtre. It was there that, under the Empire and the Restoration, condemned criminals re-entered Paris on the day of their execution. It was there that, about the year 1829, was committed the mysterious assassination, called 'the murder of the Barrière de Fontainebleau', the perpetrators of which the authorities have never discovered – a sombre problem which has not yet been solved, a terrible enigma not yet unravelled. Go a few steps further, and you find that fatal Rue Croulebarbe where Ulbach stabbed the goatherd girl of Ivry, in a thunderstorm, in the style of a melodrama.[51] Still a few steps, and you come to those destestable clipped elm trees of the Barrière Saint Jacques, that expedient of philanthropists to hide the scaffold, that pitiful and shameful Place de Grève of a cockney, shopkeeping society which recoils from capital punishment, yet dares neither to abolish it with lofty dignity, nor to maintain it with firm authority.

Thirty-seven years ago, excepting this place, Saint-Jacques, which seemed fore-doomed, and always was horrible, the gloomiest of all this gloomy Boulevard was the spot, still so unattractive, where stood the old building 50–52.

The city dwelling-houses did not begin to start up there until some twenty-five years later. The place was repulsive. In addition to the melancholy thought

---

* Master Crow, on a document perched,
    In his beak held a fat execution;
Master Fox, with his jaws well besmirched,
    Thus spoke up, to his neighbour's confusion.
'Good day! my fine fellow,' quoth he, etc.

† Prenard – a grasping fellow

that seized you there, you felt conscious of being between La Salpêtrière, the cupola of which was in sight, and Bicêtre, the barrier of which was close by – that is to say, between the wicked folly of woman and that of man. Far as the eye could reach, there was nothing to be seen but the public shambles, the city wall, and here and there the side of a factory, resembling a barrack or a monastery; on all sides, miserable hovels and heaps of rubbish, old walls as black as widows' weeds, and new walls as white as winding-sheets; on all sides, parallel rows of trees, buildings in straight lines, low, flat structures, long, cold perspectives, and the gloomy sameness of right angles. Not a variation of the surface of the ground, not a caprice of architecture, not a curve. Altogether, it was chilly, regular, and hideous. Nothing stifles one like this perpetual symmetry. Symmetry is ennui, and ennui is the very essence of grief and melancholy. Despair yawns. Something more terrible than a hell of suffering may be conceived; to wit, a hell of ennui. Were there such a hell in existence, this section of the Boulevard de l'Hôpital might well serve as the approach to it.

Then, at nightfall, at the moment when the day is dying out, especially in winter, at that hour when the evening breeze tears from the elms their faded and withered leaves, when the gloom is deep, without a single star, or when the moon and the wind make openings in the clouds, this boulevard became positively terrifying. The dark outlines shrank together, and even lost themselves in the obscurity like fragments of the infinite. The passer-by could not keep from thinking of the innumerable bloody traditions of the spot. The solitude of this neighbourhood in which so many crimes had been committed, had something fearful about it. One felt presentiments of snares in this obscurity; all the confused outlines visible through the gloom were eyed suspiciously, and the oblong cavities between the trees seemed like graves. In the day-time it was ugly; in the evening, it was dismal; at night, it was ominous of evil. In summer, in the twilight, some old woman might be seen seated, here and there, under the elms, on benches made mouldy by the rain. These good old dames were addicted to begging.

In conclusion, this quarter, which was rather superannuated than ancient, from that time began to undergo a transformation. Thenceforth, whoever would see it, must hasten. Each day, some of its details wholly passed away. Now, as has been the case for twenty years past, the terminus of the Orleans railroad lies just outside of the old suburb, and keeps it in movement. Wherever you may locate, in the outskirts of a capital, a railroad depôt, it is the death of a suburb and the birth of a city. It would seem as though around these great centres of the activity of nations, at the rumbling of these mighty engines, at the snorting of these giant draught-horses of civilisation, which devour coal and spout forth fire, the earth, teeming with germs of life, trembles and opens to swallow old dwellings of men and to bring forth new; old houses crumble, new houses spring up.

Since the depôt of the Orleans railway[52] invaded the grounds of La Salpêtrière, the old narrow streets that adjoin the Fossés Saint Victor and the Jardin des Plantes are giving way, violently traversed, as they are, three or four times a day, by those streams of diligences, hacks, and omnibuses, which, in course of time, push back the houses right and left; for there are things that sound strangely, and yet which are precisely correct; and, just as the remark is true that, in large cities, the sun causes the fronts of houses looking south to vegetate and grow, so is it undeniable that the frequent passage of vehicles widens the streets. The symptoms of a new life are evident. In that old provincial quarter, and in its wildest corners, pavement is beginning to appear, sidewalks are springing up and stretching to longer and longer distances, even in those parts where there are as yet no passers-by. One morning, a memorable morning in July, 1845, black kettles filled with bitumen were seen smoking there: on that day, one could exclaim that civilisation had reached the Rue de l'Ourcine, and that Paris had stepped across into the Faubourg Saint Marceau.

2. A nest for owl and wren

BEFORE this Gorbeau tenement Jean Valjean stopped. Like the birds of prey, he had chosen this lonely place to make his nest.

He fumbled in his waistcoat and took from it a sort of night-key, opened the door, entered, then carefully closed it again and ascended the stairway, still carrying Cosette.

At the top of the stairway he drew from his pocket another key, with which he opened another door. The chamber which he entered and closed again immediately was a sort of garret, rather spacious, furnished only with a mattress spread on the floor, a table, and a few chairs. A stove containing a fire, the coals of which were visible, stood in one corner. The street lamp of the boulevard shed a dim light through this poor interior. At the further extremity there was a little room containing a cot bed. On this Jean Valjean laid the child without waking her.

He struck a light with flint and steel and lit a candle, which, with his tinder-box, stood ready, beforehand, on the table; and, as he had done on the preceding evening, he began to gaze upon Cosette with a look of ecstasy, in which the expression of goodness and tenderness went almost to the verge of insanity. The little girl, with that tranquil confidence which belongs only to extreme strength or extreme weakness, had fallen asleep without knowing with whom she was, and continued to slumber without knowing where she was.

Jean Valjean bent down and kissed the child's hand.

Nine months before, he had kissed the hand of the mother, who also had just fallen asleep.

The same mournful, pious, agonising feeling now filled his heart.

He knelt down by the bedside of Cosette.

It was broad daylight, and yet the child slept on. A pale ray from the December sun struggled through the garret window and traced upon the ceiling long streaks of light and shade. Suddenly a carrier's wagon, heavily laden, trundled over the cobblestones of the boulevard, and shook the old building like the rumbling of a tempest, jarring it from cellar to roof-tree.

'Yes, madame!' cried Cosette, starting up out of sleep, 'here I am! here I am!'

And she threw herself from the bed, her eyelids still half closed with the weight of slumber, stretching out her hand towards the corner of the wall.

'Oh! what shall I do? Where is my broom?' said she.

By this time her eyes were fully open, and she saw the smiling face of Jean Valjean.

'Oh! yes – so it is!' said the child. 'Good morning, monsieur.'

Children at once accept joy and happiness with quick familiarity, being themselves naturally all happiness and joy.

Cosette noticed Catharine at the foot of the bed, laid hold of her at once, and, playing the while, asked Jean Valjean a thousand questions. – Where was she? Was Paris a big place? Was Madame Thénardier really very far away? Wouldn't she come back again, etc., etc. All at once she exclaimed, 'How pretty it is here!'

It was a frightful hovel, but she felt free.

'Must I sweep?' she continued at length.

'Play!' replied Jean Valjean.

And thus the day passed by. Cosette, without troubling herself with trying to understand anything about it, was inexpressibly happy with her doll and her good friend.

3. *Two misfortunes mingled make happiness*

THE DAWN of the next day found Jean Valjean again near the bed of Cosette. He waited there, motionless, to see her wake.

Something new was entering his soul.

Jean Valjean had never loved anything. For twenty-five years he had been alone in the world. He had never been a father, lover, husband or friend. At the galleys, he was cross, sullen, abstinent, ignorant and intractable. The heart of the old convict was full of freshness. His sister and her children had left in his memory only a vague and distant impression, which had finally almost entirely vanished. He had made every exertion to find them again, and, not succeeding, had forgotten them. Human nature is thus constituted. The other tender emotions of his youth, if any such he had, were lost in an abyss.

When he saw Cosette, when he had taken her, carried her away, and rescued her, he felt his heart moved. All that he had of feeling and affection was aroused and vehemently attracted towards this child. He would approach the bed where she slept, and would tremble there with delight; he felt inward yearnings, like a mother, and knew not what they were; for it is something very incomprehensible and very sweet, this grand and strange emotion of a heart in its first love.

Poor old heart, so young!

But, as he was fifty-five, and Cosette was but eight years old, all that he might have felt of love in his entire life melted into a sort of ineffable radiance.

This was the second white vision he had seen. The bishop had caused the dawn of virtue on his horizon, Cosette evoked the dawn of love.

The first few days rolled by amid this bewilderment.

On her part, Cosette, too, unconsciously underwent a change, poor little creature! She was so small when her mother left her, that she could not recollect her now. As all children do, like the young shoots of the vine that cling to everything, she had tried to love. She had not been able to succeed. Everybody had repelled her – the Thénardiers, their children, other children. She had loved the dog; it died, and after that no person and no thing would have aught to do with her. Mournful thing to tell, and one which we have already hinted, at the age of eight her heart was cold. This was not her fault; it was not the faculty of love that she lacked; alas! it was the possibility. And so, from the very first day, all that thought and felt in her began to love this kind old friend. She now felt sensations utterly unknown to her before – a sensation of budding and of growth.

Her kind friend no longer impressed as old and poor. In her eyes Jean Valjean was handsome, just as the garret had seemed pretty.

Such are the effects of the aurora-glow of childhood, youth, and joy. The newness of earth and of life has something to do with it. Nothing is so charming as the ruddy tints that happiness can shed around a garret room. We all, in the course of our lives, have had our rose-coloured sky-parlour.

Nature had placed a wide chasm – fifty years' interval of age – between Jean Valjean and Cosette. This chasm fate filled up. Fate abruptly brought together, and wedded with its resistless power, these two shattered lives, dissimilar in years, but similar in sorrow. The one, indeed, was the complement of the other. The instinct of Cosette sought for a father, as the instinct of Jean Valjean sought for a child. To meet, was to find one another. In that mysterious moment, when their hands touched, they were welded together. When their two souls saw each other, they recognised that they were mutually needed, and they closely embraced.

Taking the words in their most comprehensive and most absolute sense, it might be said that, separated from everything by the walls of the tomb, Jean Valjean was the husband bereaved, as Cosette was the orphan. This position made Jean Valjean become, in a celestial sense, the father of Cosette.

And, in truth, the mysterious impression produced upon Cosette, in the depths of the woods at Chelles, by the hand of Jean Valjean grasping her own in the darkness, was not an illusion but a reality. The coming of this man and his participation in the destiny of this child had been the advent of God.

In the meanwhile, Jean Valjean had well chosen his hiding-place. He was there in a state of security that seemed to be complete.

The apartment with the side chamber which he occupied with Cosette, was the one whose window looked out upon the boulevard. This window being the only one in the house, there was no neighbour's prying eye to fear either from that side or opposite.

The lower floor of No. 50–52 was a sort of dilapidated shed; it served as a sort of stable for market gardeners, and had no communication with the upper floor. It was separated from it by the flooring, which had neither stairway nor trap-door, and was, as it were, the diaphragm of the old building. The upper floor contained, as we have said, several rooms and a few lofts, only one of which was occupied – by an old woman, who was maid of all work to Jean Valjean. All the rest was uninhabited.

It was this old woman, honoured with the title of landlady, but, in reality, entrusted with the functions of portress, who had rented him these lodgings on Christmas Day. He had passed himself off to her as a gentleman of means, ruined by the Spanish Bonds, who was going to live there with his granddaughter. He had paid her for six months in advance, and engaged the old dame to furnish the chamber and the little bedroom, as we have described them. This old woman it was who had kindled the fire in the stove and made everything ready for them, on the evening of their arrival.

Weeks rolled by. These two beings led in that wretched shelter a happy life.

From the earliest dawn, Cosette laughed, prattled, and sang. Children have their morning song, like birds.

Sometimes it happened that Jean Valjean would take her little red hand, all chapped and frost-bitten as it was, and kiss it. The poor child, accustomed only to blows, had no idea what this meant, and would draw back ashamed.

At times, she grew serious and looked musingly at her little black dress. Cosette was no longer in rags; she was in mourning. She was issuing from utter poverty and was entering upon life.

Jean Valjean had begun to teach her to read. Sometimes, while teaching the child to spell, he would remember that it was with the intention of accomplishing evil that he had learned to read, in the galleys. This intention had now been changed into teaching a child to read. Then the old convict would smile with the pensive smile of angels.

He felt in this a pre-ordination from on high, a volition of someone more than man, and he would lose himself in reverie. Good thoughts as well as bad have their abysses.

To teach Cosette to read, and to watch her playing, was nearly all Jean Valjean's life. And then, he would talk to her about her mother, and teach her to pray.

She called him *Father*, and knew him by no other name.

He spent hours seeing her dress and undress her doll, and listening to her song and prattle. From that time on, life seemed full of interest to him, men seemed good and just; he no longer, in his thoughts, reproached anyone with any wrong; he saw no reason, now, why he should not live to grow very old, since his child loved him. He looked forward to a long future illuminated by Cosette with charming light. The very best of us are not altogether exempt from some tinge of egotism. At times, he thought with a sort of quiet satisfaction, that she would be by no means handsome.

This is but a personal opinion; but in order to express our idea thoroughly, at the point Jean Valjean had reached, when he began to love Cosette, it is not clear to us that he did not require this fresh supply of goodness to enable him to persevere in the right path. He had seen the wickedness of men and the misery of society under new aspects – aspects incomplete and, unfortunately, showing forth only one side of the truth – the lot of woman summed up in Fantine, public authority personified in Javert; he had been sent back to the galleys this time for doing good; new waves of bitterness had overwhelmed him; disgust and weariness had once more resumed their sway; the recollection of the bishop, even, was perhaps almost eclipsed, sure to reappear afterwards, luminous and triumphant; yet, in fact, this blessed remembrance was growing feebler. Who knows that Jean Valjean was not on the point of becoming discouraged and falling back to evil ways? Love came, and he again grew strong. Alas! he was no less feeble than Cosette. He protected her, and she gave strength to him. Thanks to him, she could walk upright in life; thanks to her, he could persist in virtuous deeds. He was the support of this child, and this child was his prop and staff. Oh, divine and unfathomable mystery of the compensations of Destiny!

4. *What the landlady discovered*

JEAN VALJEAN was prudent enough never to go out in the daytime. Every evening, however, about twilight, he would walk for an hour or two, sometimes alone, often with Cosette, selecting the most unfrequented side alleys of the boulevards and going into the churches at nightfall. He was fond of going to St

Médard, which is the nearest church. When he did not take Cosette, she remained with the old woman; but it was the child's delight to go out with her kind old friend. She preferred an hour with him even to her delicious *tête-à-têtes* with Catharine. He would walk along holding her by the hand, and telling her pleasant things.

It turned out that Cosette was very playful.

The old woman was housekeeper and cook, and did the marketing.

They lived frugally, always with a little fire in the stove, but like people in embarrassed circumstances. Jean Valjean made no change in the furniture described on the first day, excepting that he caused a solid door to be put up in place of the glass door of Cosette's little bed-chamber.

He still wore his yellow coat, his black pantaloons, and his old hat. On the street he was taken for a beggar. It sometimes happened that kind-hearted dames, in passing, would turn and hand him a penny. Jean Valjean accepted the penny and bowed humbly. It chanced, sometimes, also, that he would meet some wretched creature begging alms, and then, glancing about him to be sure that no one was looking, he would stealthily approach the beggar, slip a piece of money, often silver, into his hand, and walk rapidly away. This had its inconveniences. He began to be known in the quarter as *the beggar who gives alms*.

The old 'landlady', a crabbed creature, fully possessed with that keen observation as to all that concerned her neighbours, which is peculiar to the suburbs, watched Jean Valjean closely without exciting his suspicion. She was a little deaf, which made her talkative. She had but two teeth left, one in the upper and one in the lower jaw, and these she was continually rattling together. She had questioned Cosette, who, knowing nothing, could tell nothing, further than that she came from Montfermeil. One morning this old female spy saw Jean Valjean go, with an appearance which seemed peculiar to the old busybody, into one of the uninhabited apartments of the building. She followed him with the steps of an old cat, and could see him without herself being seen, through the chink of the door directly opposite. Jean Valjean had, doubtless for greater caution, turned his back towards the door in question. The old woman saw him fumble in his pocket, and take from it a needle-case, scissors, and thread, and then proceed to rip open the lining of one lapel of his coat and take from under it a piece of yellowish paper, which he unfolded. The beldame remarked with dismay, that it was a bank bill for a thousand francs. It was the second or third one only that she had ever seen. She ran away very much frightened.

A moment afterwards, Jean Valjean accosted her, and asked her to get this thousand-franc bill changed for him, adding that it was the half-yearly interest on his property which he had received on the previous day. 'Where?' thought the old woman. He did not go out until six o'clock, and the government treasury is certainly not open at that hour. The old woman got the note changed, all the while forming her conjectures. This bill of a thousand francs, commented upon and multiplied, gave rise to a host of breathless conferences among the gossips of the Rue des Vignes Saint Marcel.

Some days afterwards, it chanced that Jean Valjean, in his shirt-sleeves, was sawing wood in the entry. The old woman was in his room doing the chamberwork. She was alone. Cosette was intent upon the wood he was sawing. The old woman saw the coat hanging on a nail, and examined it. The lining had been sewed over. She felt it carefully and thought she could detect in the lapels and in the padding, thicknesses of paper. Other thousand-franc bills beyond a doubt!

She noticed, besides, that there were all sorts of things in the pockets. Not only were there the needles, scissors, and thread, which she had already seen, but a large pocket-book, a very big knife, and, worst symptom of all, several wigs of different colours. Every pocket of this coat had the appearance of containing something to be provided with against sudden emergencies.

Thus, the occupants of the old building reached the closing days of winter.

5. A five-franc piece falling on the floor makes a noise

THERE WAS, in the neighbourhood of Saint Médard, a mendicant who sat crouching over the edge of a condemned public well near by, and to whom Jean Valjean often gave alms. He never passed this man without giving him a few pennies. Sometimes he spoke to him. Those who were envious of this poor creature said he was in the pay of the police. He was an old church beadle of seventy-five, who was always mumbling prayers.

One evening, as Jean Valjean was passing that way, unaccompanied by Cosette, he noticed the beggar sitting in his usual place, under the street lamp which had just been lighted. The man, according to custom, seemed to be praying and was bent over. Jean Valjean walked up to him, and put a piece of money in his hand, as usual. The beggar suddenly raised his eyes, gazed intently at Jean Valjean, and then quickly dropped his head. This movement was like a flash; Jean Valjean shuddered; it seemed to him that he had just seen, by the light of the street-lamp, not the calm, sanctimonious face of the aged beadle, but a terrible and well-known countenance. He experienced the sensation one would feel on finding himself suddenly face to face, in the gloom, with a tiger. He recoiled, horror-stricken and petrified, daring neither to breathe nor to speak, to stay nor to fly, but gazing upon the beggar who had once more bent down his head, with its tattered covering, and seemed to be no longer conscious of his presence. At this singular moment, an instinct, perhaps the mysterious instinct of self-preservation, prevented Jean Valjean from uttering a word. The beggar had the same form, the same rags, the same general appearance as on every other day. 'Pshaw!' said Jean Valjean to himself, 'I am mad! I am dreaming! It cannot be!' And he went home, anxious and ill at ease.

He scarcely dared to admit, even to himself, that the countenance he thought he had seen was the face of Javert.

That night, upon reflection, he regretted that he had not questioned the man so as to compel him to raise his head a second time. On the morrow, at nightfall, he went thither, again. The beggar was in his place. 'Good day! Good day!' said Jean Valjean, with firmness, as he gave him the accustomed alms. The beggar raised his head and answered in a whining voice: 'Thanks, kind sir, thanks!' It was, indeed, only the old beadle.

Jean Valjean now felt fully reassured. He even began to laugh. 'What the deuce was I about to fancy that I saw Javert,' thought he; 'is my sight growing poor already?' And he thought no more about it.

Some days after, it might be eight o'clock in the evening, he was in his room, giving Cosette her spelling lesson, which the child was repeating in a loud voice, when he heard the door of the building open and close again. That seemed odd to him. The old woman, the only occupant of the house besides himself and Cosette, always went to bed at dark to save candles. Jean Valjean made a sign to Cosette to be silent. He heard someone coming upstairs. Possibly, it might be the old woman who had felt unwell and had been to the druggist's. Jean Valjean listened. The footstep was heavy, and sounded like a man's; but the old woman wore heavy shoes, and there is nothing so much like the step of a man as the step of an old woman. However, Jean Valjean blew out his candle.

He sent Cosette to bed, telling her in a suppressed voice to lie down very quietly – and, as he kissed her forehead, the footsteps stopped. Jean Valjean remained silent and motionless, his back turned towards the door, still seated on his chair from which he had not moved, and holding his breath in the darkness. After a considerable interval, not hearing anything more, he turned round without making any noise, and as he raised his eyes towards the door of his room, he saw a light through the keyhole. This ray of light was an evil star in the black background of the door and the wall. There was, evidently, somebody outside with a candle who was listening.

A few minutes elapsed, and the light disappeared. But he heard no sound of footsteps, which seemed to indicate that whoever was listening at the door had taken off his shoes.

Jean Valjean threw himself on his bed without undressing, but could not shut his eyes that night.

At daybreak, as he was sinking into slumber from fatigue, he was aroused, again, by the creaking of the door of some room at the end of the hall, and then he heard the same footstep which had ascended the stairs, on the preceding night. The step approached. He started from his bed and placed his eye to the keyhole, which was quite a large one, hoping to get a glimpse of the person, whoever it might be, who had made his way into the building in the night-time and had listened at his door. It was a man, indeed, who passed by Jean Valjean's room, this time without stopping. The hall was still too dark for him to make out his features; but, when the man reached the stairs, a ray of light from without made his figure stand out like a profile, and Jean Valjean had a full view of his back. The man was tall, wore a long frock-coat, and had a cudgel under his arm. It was the redoubtable form of Javert.

Jean Valjean might have tried to get another look at him through his window that opened on the boulevard, but he would have had to raise the sash, and that he dared not do.

It was evident that the man had entered by means of a key, as if at home. 'Who, then, had given him the key? – and what was the meaning of this?'

At seven in the morning, when the old lady came to clear up the rooms, Jean Valjean eyed her sharply, but asked her no questions. The good dame appeared as usual.

While she was doing her sweeping, she said:

'Perhaps monsieur heard someone come in, last night?'

At her age and on that boulevard, eight in the evening is the very darkest of the night.

'Ah! yes, by the way, I did,' he answered in the most natural tone. 'Who was it?'

'It's a new lodger,' said the old woman, 'who has come into the house.'

'And his name is?'

'Well, I hardly recollect now. Dumont or Daumont. – Some such name as that.'

'And what is he – this M. Daumont?'

The old woman studied him, a moment, through her little foxy eyes, and answered:

'He's a gentleman living on his income like you.'

She may have intended nothing by this, but Jean Valjean thought he could make out that she did.

When the old woman was gone, he made a roll of a hundred francs he had in a drawer and put it into his pocket. Do what he would to manage this so that the clinking of the silver should not be heard, a five-franc piece escaped his grasp and rolled jingling away over the floor.

At dusk, he went to the street-door and looked carefully up and down the boulevard. No one was to be seen. The boulevard seemed to be utterly deserted. It is true that there might have been someone hidden behind a tree.

He went upstairs again.

'Come,' said he to Cosette.

He took her by the hand and they both went out.

BOOK 5: A DARK CHASE NEEDS A SILENT HOUND

1. *The zigzags of strategy*

IN ORDER TO UNDERSTAND the pages immediately following, and others also which will be found further on, an observation is here necessary.

Many years have already passed away since the author of this book, who is compelled, reluctantly, to speak of himself, was in Paris.[53] Since then, Paris has been transformed. A new city has arisen, which to him is in some sense unknown. He need not say that he loves Paris; Paris is the native city of his heart. Through demolition and reconstruction, the Paris of his youth, that Paris which he religiously treasures in his memory, has become a Paris of former times. Let him be permitted to speak of that Paris as if it still existed. It is possible that where the author is about to conduct his readers, saying: 'In such a street there is such a house,' there is now no longer either house or street. The reader will verify it, if he chooses to take the trouble. As to himself, the author knows not the new Paris, and writes with the old Paris before his eyes in an illusion which is precious to him. It is a sweet thing for him to imagine that there still remains something of what he saw when he was in his own country, and that all is not vanished. While we are living in our native land, we fancy that these streets are indifferent to us, that these windows, these roofs, and these doors are nothing to us, that these walls are strangers to us, that these trees are no more than other trees, that these houses which we never enter are useless to us, that this pavement on which we walk is nothing but stone. In after times, when we are there no longer, we find that those streets are very dear, that we miss those roofs, those windows, and those doors; that those walls are necessary to us, that those trees are our well-beloved, that those houses which we never entered we entered every day, and that we have left something of our affections, our life, and our heart in those streets. All those places which we see no more, which perhaps we shall never see again, but the image of which we have preserved, assume a mournful charm, return to us with the sadness of a spectre, make the holy land visible to us, and are, so to speak, the very form of France; and we love them and call them up such as they are, such as they were, and hold to them, unwilling to change anything, for one clings to the form of his fatherland as to the face of his mother.

Permit us, then, to speak of the past in the present. Saying which, we beg the reader to take note of it, and we proceed.

Jean Valjean had immediately left the boulevard and began to thread the streets, making as many turns as he could, returning sometimes upon his track to make sure that he was not followed.

This manoeuvre is peculiar to the hunted stag. On ground where the foot leaves a mark, it has, among other advantages, that of deceiving the hunters and the dogs by the counter-step. It is what is called in venery *false reimbushment*.

The moon was full. Jean Valjean was not sorry for that. The moon, still near the horizon, cut large prisms of light and shade in the streets. Jean Valjean could glide along the houses and the walls on the dark side and observe the light side. He did not, perhaps, sufficiently realise that the obscure side escaped him. However, in all the deserted little streets in the neighbourhood of the Rue de Poliveau, he felt sure that no one was behind him.

Cosette walked without asking any questions. The sufferings of the first six years of her life had introduced something of the passive into her nature. Besides – and this is a remark to which we shall have more than one occasion to return – she had become familiar, without being fully conscious of them, with the peculiarities of her good friend and the eccentricities of destiny. And then, she felt safe, being with him.

Jean Valjean knew, no more than Cosette, where he was going. He trusted in God, as she trusted in him. It seemed to him that he also held someone greater than himself by the hand; he believed he felt a being leading him, invisible. Finally, he had no definite idea, no plan, no project. He was not even absolutely sure that this was Javert, and then it might be Javert, and Javert not know that he was Jean Valjean. Was he not disguised? was he not supposed to be dead? Nevertheless, singular things had happened within the last few days. He wanted no more of them. He was determined not to enter Gorbeau House again. Like the animal hunted from his den, he was looking for a hole to hide in until he could find one to remain in.

Jean Valjean described many and varied labyrinths in the Quartier Mouffetard, which was asleep already as if it were still under the discipline of the middle age and the yoke of the curfew; he produced different combinations, in wise strategy, with the Rue Censier and the Rue Copeau, the Rue du Battoir Saint Victor and the Rue du Puits l'Ermite. There are lodgings in that region, but he did not even enter them, not finding what suited him. He had no doubt whatever that if, perchance, they had sought his track, they had lost it.

As eleven o'clock struck in the tower of Saint Etienne du Mont, he crossed the Rue de Pontoise in front of the bureau of the Commissary of Police, which is at No. 14. Some moments afterwards, the instinct of which we have already spoken made him turn his head. At this moment he saw distinctly – thanks to the commissary's lamp which revealed them – three men following him quite near, pass one after another under this lamp on the dark side of the street. One of these men entered the passage leading to the commissary's house. The one in advance appeared to him decidedly suspicious.

'Come, child!' said he to Cosette, and he made haste to get out of the Rue de Pontoise.

He made a circuit, went round the Arcade des Patriarches, which was closed on account of the lateness of the hour, walked rapidly through the Rue de l'Epée-de-Bois and the Rue de l'Arbalète, and plunged into the Rue des Postes.

There was a square there, where the Collège Rollin now is, and from which branches off the Rue Neuve-Sainte-Geneviève.

(We need not say that the Rue Neuve-Sainte-Geneviève is an old street, and that there a postchaise did not pass once in ten years through the Rue des Postes. This Rue des Postes was in the thirteenth century inhabited by potters, and its true name is Rue des Pots.)

The moon lighted up this square brightly. Jean Valjean concealed himself in a doorway, calculating that if these men were still following him, he could not fail to get a good view of them when they crossed this lighted space.

In fact, three minutes had not elapsed when the men appeared. There were now four of them; all were tall, dressed in long brown coats, with round hats, and great clubs in their hands. They were not less fearfully forbidding by their size and their large fists than by their stealthy tread in the darkness. One would have taken them for four spectres in citizen's dress.

They stopped in the centre of the square and formed a group like people consulting. They appeared undecided. The man who seemed to be the leader turned and energetically pointed in the direction in which Jean Valjean was; one of the others seemed to insist with some obstinacy on the contrary direction. At the instant when the leader turned, the moon shone full in his face. Jean Valjean recognised Javert perfectly.

2. *It is fortunate that vehicles can cross the bridge of Austerlitz*

UNCERTAINTY WAS AT AN END for Jean Valjean; happily, it still continued with these men. He took advantage of their hesitation; it was time lost for them, gained for him. He came out from the doorway in which he was concealed, and made his way into the Rue des Postes towards the region of the Jardin des Plantes. Cosette began to be tired; he took her in his arms, and carried her. There was nobody in the streets, and the lamps had not been lighted on account of the moon.

He doubled his pace.

In a few steps, he reached the Goblet pottery, on the façade of which the old inscription stood out distinctly legible in the light of the moon:

> De Goblet fils c'est ici la fabrique;
> Venez choisir des cruches et des brocs,
> Des pots à fleurs, des tugaux, de la brique.
> A tout venant le Cœur vend des Carreaux.[54]

He passed through the Rue de la Clef, then by the Fontaine de Saint Victor along the Jardin des Plantes by the lower streets, and reached the quay. There he looked around. The quay was deserted. The streets were deserted. Nobody behind him. He took breath.

He arrived at the bridge of Austerlitz.

It was still a toll-bridge at this period.

He presented himself at the toll-house and gave a sous.

'It is two sous,' said the toll-keeper. 'You are carrying a child who can walk. Pay for two.'

He paid, annoyed that his passage should have attracted observation. All flight should be a gliding.

A large cart was passing the Seine at the same time, and like him was going towards the right bank. This could be made of use. He could go the whole length of the bridge in the shade of this cart.

Towards the middle of the bridge, Cosette, her feet becoming numb, desired to walk. He put her down and took her by the hand.

The bridge passed, he perceived some wood-yards a little to the right and walked in that direction. To get there, he must venture into a large clear open space. He did not hesitate. Those who followed him were evidently thrown off his track, and Jean Valjean believed himself out of danger. Sought for, he might be, but followed he was not.

A little street, the Rue du Chemin Vert Saint Antoine, opened between two wood-yards enclosed by walls. This street was narrow, obscure, and seemed made expressly for him. Before entering it, he looked back.

From the point where he was, he could see the whole length of the bridge of Austerlitz.

Four shadows, at that moment, entered upon the bridge.

These shadows were coming from the Jardin des Plantes towards the right bank.

These four shadows were the four men.

Jean Valjean felt a shudder like that of the deer when he sees the hounds again upon his track.

One hope was left him; it was that these men had not entered upon the bridge, and had not perceived him when he crossed the large square clear space leading Cosette by the hand.

In that case, by plunging into the little street before him, if he could succeed in reaching the wood-yards, the marshes, the fields, the open grounds, he could escape.

It seemed to him that he might trust himself to this silent little street. He entered it.

3. See the plan of Paris of 1727

SOME THREE HUNDRED paces on, he reached a point where the street forked. It divided into two streets, the one turning off obliquely to the left, the other to the right. Jean Valjean had before him the two branches of a Y. Which should he choose?

He did not hesitate, but took the right.

Why?

Because the left branch led towards the faubourg – that is to say, towards the inhabited region, and the right branch towards the country – that is, towards the uninhabited region.

But now, they no longer walked very fast. Cosette's step slackened Jean Valjean's pace.

He took her up and carried her again. Cosette rested her head upon the goodman's shoulder, and did not say a word.

He turned, from time to time, and looked back. He took care to keep always on the dark side of the street. The street was straight behind him. The two or three first times he turned, he saw nothing; the silence was complete, and he kept on his way somewhat reassured. Suddenly, on turning again, he thought he saw in the portion of the street through which he had just passed, far in the obscurity, something which stirred.

He plunged forward rather than walked, hoping to find some side street by which to escape, and once more to elude his pursuers.

He came to a wall.

This wall, however, did not prevent him from going further; it was a wall forming the side of a cross alley, in which the street Jean Valjean was then in came to an end.

Here again he must decide; should he take the right or the left?

He looked to the right. The alley ran out to a space between some buildings that were mere sheds or barns, then terminated abruptly. The end of this blind alley was plain to be seen – a great white wall.

He looked to the left. The alley on this side was open, and, about two hundred paces further on, ran into a street of which it was an affluent. In this direction lay safety.

The instant Jean Valjean decided to turn to the left, to try to reach the street which he saw at the end of the alley, he perceived, at the corner of the alley and the street towards which he was just about going, a sort of black, motionless statue.

It was a man, who had just been posted there, evidently, and who was waiting for him, guarding the passage.

Jean Valjean was startled.

This part of Paris where Jean Valjean was, situated between the Faubourg Saint Antoine and the La Râpée, is one of those which have been entirely transformed by the recent works – a change for the worse, in the opinion of some, a transfiguration, according to others. The vegetable gardens, the wood-yards, and the old buildings are gone. There are now broad new streets, amphitheatres, circuses, hippodromes, railroad depôts, a prison, Mazas; progress, as we see, with its corrective.

Half a century ago, in the common popular language, full of tradition, which obstinately calls l'Institut *Les Quatre Nations*, and l'Opera Comique *Feydeau*, the precise spot which Jean Valjean had reached was called the *Petit Picpus*. The Porte Saint Jacques, the Porte Paris, the Barrière des Sergents, the Porcherons, the Galiote, the Célestins, the Capuchins, the Mail, the Bourbe, the Arbre de Cracovie, the Petite Pologne, the Petit Picpus, these are names of the old Paris floating over into the new. The memory of the people buoys over these waifs of the past.

The Petit Picpus, which in fact hardly had a real existence, and was never more than a mere outline of a quarter, had almost the monkish aspect of a

Spanish city. The roads were poorly paved, the streets were thinly built up. Beyond the two or three streets of which we are about to speak, there was nothing there but wall and solitude. Not a shop, not a vehicle, hardly a light here and there in the windows; all the lights put out after ten o'clock. Gardens, convents, wood-yards, market gardens, a few scattered low houses, and great walls as high as the houses.

Such was the quarter in the last century. The Revolution had already very much altered it. The republican authorities had pulled down buildings and run streets into and through it. Depositories of rubbish had been established there. Thirty years ago, this quarter was being gradually erased by the construction of new buildings. It is now completely blotted out. The Petit Picpus, of which no present plan retains a trace, is clearly enough indicated in the plan of 1727, published at Paris by Denis Thierry, Rue Saint Jacques, opposite the Rue du Plâtre, and at Lyons by Jean Girin, Rue Mercière, à la Prudence. The Petit Picpus had what we have just called a Y of streets, formed by the Rue du Chemin Vert Saint Antoine dividing into two branches and taking on the left the name Petite Rue Picpus and on the right the name of the Rue Polonceau. The two branches of the Y were joined at the top as by a bar. This bar was called the Rue Droit Mur. The Rue Polonceau ended there; the Petite Rue Picpus passed beyond, rising towards the Marché Lenoir. He who, coming from the Seine, reached the extremity of the Rue Polonceau, had on his left the Rue Droit Mur turning sharply at a right angle, before him the side wall of that street, and on his right a truncated prolongation of the Rue Droit Mur, without thoroughfare, called the Cul-de-sac Genrot.

Jean Valjean was in this place.

As we have said, on perceiving the black form standing sentry at the corner of the Rue Droit Mur and the Petite Rue Picpus, he was startled. There was no doubt. He was watched by this shadow.

What should he do?

There was now no time to turn back. What he had seen moving in the obscurity some distance behind him, the moment before, was undoubtedly Javert and his squad. Javert probably had already reached the commencement of the street of which Jean Valjean was at the end. Javert, to all appearance, was acquainted with this little trap, and had taken his precautions by sending one of his men to guard the exit. These conjectures, so like certainties, whirled about wildly in Jean Valjean's troubled brain, as a handful of dust flies before a sudden blast. He scrutinised the Cul-de-sac Genrot; there were high walls. He scrutinised the Petite Rue Picpus; there was a sentinel. He saw that dark form repeated in black upon the white pavement flooded with the moonlight. To advance, was to fall upon that man. To go back, was to throw himself into Javert's hands. Jean Valjean felt as if caught by a chain that was slowly winding up. He looked up into the sky in despair.

4. *Groping for escape*

IN ORDER TO UNDERSTAND what follows, it is necessary to form an exact idea of the little Rue Droit Mur, and particularly the corner which it makes at the left as you leave the Rue Polonceau to enter this alley. The little Rue Droit Mur was almost entirely lined on the right, as far as the Petite Rue Picpus, by houses of poor appearance; on the left by a single building of severe outline, composed of several structures which rose gradually a storey or two, one above another, as they approached the Petite Rue Picpus, so that the building, very high on the side of the Petite Rue Picpus, was quite low on the side of the Rue Polonceau. There, at the corner of which we have spoken, it became so low as to be nothing more than a wall. This wall did not abut squarely on the corner, which was cut off diagonally, leaving a considerable space that was shielded by the two angles thus formed from observers at a distance in either the Rue Polonceau, or the Rue Droit Mur.

From these two angles of the truncated corner, the wall extended along the Rue Polonceau as far as a house numbered 49, and along the Rue Droit Mur, where its height was much less, to the sombre-looking building of which we have spoken, cutting its gable, and thus making a new re-entering angle in the street. This gable had a gloomy aspect; there was but one window to be seen, or rather two shutters covered with a sheet of zinc, and always closed.

The situation of the places which we describe here is rigorously exact, and will certainly awaken a very precise remembrance in the minds of the old inhabitants of the locality.

This truncated corner was entirely filled by a thing which seemed like a colossal and miserable door. It was a vast shapeless assemblage of perpendicular planks, broader above than below, bound together by long transverse iron bands. At the side there was a *porte-cochère* of the ordinary dimensions, which had evidently been cut in within the last fifty years.

A lime tree lifted its branches above this corner, and the wall was covered with ivy towards the Rue Polonceau.

In the imminent peril of Jean Valjean, this sombre building had a solitary and uninhabited appearance which attracted him. He glanced over it rapidly. He thought if he could only succeed in getting into it, he would perhaps be safe. Hope came to him with the idea.

Midway of the front of this building on the Rue Droit Mur, there were at all the windows of the different storeys old leaden waste-pipes. The varied branchings of the tubing which was continued from a central conduit to each of these waste-pipes, outlined on the façade a sort of tree. These ramifications of the pipes with their hundred elbows seemed like those old closely-pruned grape-vines which twist about over the front of ancient farm-houses.

This grotesque espalier, with its sheet-iron branches, was the first object which Jean Valjean saw. He seated Cosette with her back against a post, and, telling her to be quiet, ran to the spot where the conduit came to the pavement. Perhaps there was some means of scaling the wall by that and entering the house. But the conduit was dilapidated and out of use, and scarcely held by its fastening. Besides, all the windows of this silent house were protected by thick bars of iron, even the dormer windows. And then the moon shone full upon this façade, and the man who was watching from the end of the street would have seen Jean Valjean making the escalade. And then what should he do with Cosette? How could he raise her to the top of a three-storey house?

He gave up climbing by the conduit, and crept along the wall to the Rue Polonceau.

When he reached this flattened corner where he had left Cosette, he noticed that there no one could see him. He escaped, as we have just explained, all observation from every side. Besides, he was in the shade. Then there were two doors. Perhaps they might be forced. The wall, above which he saw the lime and the ivy, evidently surrounded a garden, where he could at least conceal himself, although there were no leaves on the trees yet, and pass the rest of the night.

Time was passing. He must act quickly.

He tried the carriage door, and found at once that it was fastened within and without.

He approached the other large door with more hope. It was frightfully decrepit, its immense size even rendering it less solid; the planks were rotten, the iron fastenings, of which there were three, were rusted. It seemed possible to pierce this worm-eaten structure.

On examining it, he saw that this door was not a door. It had neither hinges, braces, lock, nor crack in the middle. The iron bands crossed from one side to the other without a break. Through the crevices of the planks he saw the rubble-work and stones, roughly cemented, which passers-by could have seen within the last ten years. He was compelled to admit with consternation that this appearance of a door was simply an ornamentation in wood of a wall, upon which it was placed. It was easy to tear off a board, but then he would find himself face to face with a wall.

5. *Which would be impossible were the streets lighted with gas*

AT THIS MOMENT a muffled and regular sound began to make itself heard at some distance. Jean Valjean ventured to thrust his head a little way around the corner of the street. Seven or eight soldiers, formed in platoon, had just turned into the Rue Polonceau. He saw the gleam of their bayonets. They were coming towards him.

These soldiers, at whose head he distinguished the tall form of Javert, advanced slowly and with precaution. They stopped frequently. It was plain they were exploring all the recesses of the walls and all the entrances of doors and alleys.

It was – and here conjecture could not be deceived – some patrol which Javert had met and which he had put in requisition.

Javert's two assistants marched in the ranks.

At the rate at which they were marching, and with the stops they were making, it would take them about a quarter of an hour to arrive at the spot where Jean Valjean was. It was a frightful moment. A few minutes separated Jean Valjean from that awful precipice which was opening before him for the third time. And the galleys now were no longer simply the galleys, they were Cosette lost for ever; that is to say, a life in death.

There was now only one thing possible.

Jean Valjean had this peculiarity, that he might be said to carry two knapsacks; in one he had the thoughts of a saint, in the other the formidable talents of a convict. He helped himself from one or the other as occasion required.

Among other resources, thanks to his numerous escapes from the galleys at Toulon, he had, it will be remembered, become master of that incredible art of raising himself, in the right angle of a wall, if need be to the height of a sixth storey; an art without ladders or props, by mere muscular strength, supporting himself by the back of his neck, his shoulders, his hips, and his knees, hardly making use of the few projections of the stone, which rendered so terrible and so celebrated the corner of the yard of the Conciergerie of Paris by which, some twenty years ago, the convict Battemolle made his escape.

Jean Valjean measured with his eyes the wall above which he saw the lime tree. It was about eighteen feet high. The angle that it made with the gable of the great building was filled in its lower part with a pile of masonry of triangular shape, probably intended to preserve this too convenient recess from a too public use. This preventive filling-up of the corners of a wall is very common in Paris.

This pile was about five feet high. From its top the space to climb to get upon the wall was hardly more than fourteen feet.

The wall was capped by a flat stone without any projection.

The difficulty was Cosette. Cosette did not know how to scale a wall. Abandon her? Jean Valjean did not think of it. To carry her was impossible. The whole strength of a man is necessary to accomplish these strange ascents. The least burden would make him lose his centre of gravity and he would fall.

He needed a cord. Jean Valjean had none. Where could he find a cord, at midnight, in the Rue Polonceau? Truly at that instant, if Jean Valjean had had a kingdom, he would have given it for a rope.

All extreme situations have their flashes which sometimes make us blind, sometimes illuminate us.

The despairing gaze of Jean Valjean encountered the lamp-post in the Cul-de-sac Genrot.

At this epoch there were no gas-lights in the streets of Paris. At nightfall they lighted the street lamps, which were placed at intervals, and were raised and lowered by means of a rope traversing the street from end to end, running through the grooves of posts. The reel on which this rope was wound was enclosed below the lantern in a little iron box, the key of which was kept by the lamp-lighter, and the rope itself was protected by a casing of metal.

Jean Valjean, with the energy of a final struggle, crossed the street at a bound, entered the cul-de-sac, sprang the bolt of the little box with the point of his knife, and an instant after was back at the side of Cosette. He had a rope. These desperate inventors of expedients, in their struggles with fatality, move electrically in case of need.

We have explained that the street lamps had not been lighted that night. The lamp in the Cul-de-sac Genrot was then, as a matter of course, extinguished like the rest, and one might pass by without even noticing that it was not in its place.

Meanwhile the hour, the place, the darkness, the preoccupation of Jean Valjean, his singular actions, his going to and fro, all this began to disturb Cosette. Any other child would have uttered loud cries long before. She contented herself with pulling Jean Valjean by the skirt of his coat. The sound of the approaching patrol was constantly becoming more and more distinct.

'Father,' said she, in a whisper, 'I am afraid. Who is that is coming?'

'Hush!' answered the unhappy man, 'it is the Thénardiess.'

Cosette shuddered. He added:

'Don't say a word; I'll take care of her. If you cry, if you make any noise, the Thénardiess will hear you. She is coming to catch you.'

Then, without any haste, but without doing anything a second time, with a firm and rapid decision, so much the more remarkable at such a moment when the patrol and Javert might come upon him at any instant, he took off his cravat, passed it around Cosette's body under the arms, taking care that it should not hurt the child, attached this cravat to an end of the rope by means of the knot which seamen call a swallow-knot, took the other end of the rope in his teeth, took off his shoes and stockings and threw them over the wall, climbed upon the pile of masonry and began to raise himself in the angle of the wall and the gable with as much solidity and certainty as if he had the rounds of a ladder under his heels and his elbows. Half a minute had not passed before he was on his knees on the wall.

Cosette watched him, stupefied, without saying a word. Jean Valjean's charge and the name of the Thénardiess had made her dumb.

All at once, she heard Jean Valjean's voice calling to her in a low whisper:

'Put your back against the wall.'

She obeyed.

'Don't speak, and don't be afraid,' added Jean Valjean.

And she felt herself lifted from the ground.

Before she had time to think where she was she was at the top of the wall.

Jean Valjean seized her, put her on his back, took her two little hands in his left hand, lay down flat and crawled along the top of the wall as far as the cut-off corner. As he had supposed, there was a building there, the roof of which sloped from the top of the wooden casing we have mentioned very nearly to the ground, with a gentle inclination, and just reaching to the lime tree.

A fortunate circumstance, for the wall was much higher on this side than on the street. Jean Valjean saw the ground beneath him at a great depth.

He had just reached the inclined plane of the roof, and had not yet left the crest of the wall, when a violent uproar proclaimed the arrival of the patrol. He heard the thundering voice of Javert:

'Search the cul-de-sac! The Rue Droit Mur is guarded, the Petite Rue Picpus also. I'll answer for it he is in the cul-de-sac.'

The soldiers rushed into the Cul-de-sac Genrot.

Jean Valjean slid down the roof, keeping hold of Cosette, reached the lime tree, and jumped to the ground. Whether from terror, or from courage, Cosette had not uttered a whisper. Her hands were a little scraped.

6. *Commencement of an enigma*

JEAN VALJEAN found himself in a sort of garden, very large and of a singular appearance; one of those gloomy gardens which seem made to be seen in the winter and at night. This garden was oblong, with a row of large poplars at the further end, some tall forest trees in the corners, and a clear space in the centre, where stood a very large isolated tree, then a few fruit trees, contorted and shaggy, like big bushes, some vegetable beds, a melon patch the glass covers of which shone in the moonlight, and an old well. There were here and there stone benches which seemed black with moss. The walks were bordered with sorry little shrubs perfectly straight. The grass covered half of them, and a green moss covered the rest.

Jean Valjean had on one side the building, down the roof of which he had come, a wood-pile, and behind the wood, against the wall, a stone statue, the mutilated face of which was now nothing but a shapeless mask which was seen dimly through the obscurity.

The building was in ruins, but some dismantled rooms could be distinguished in it, one of which was well filled, and appeared to serve as a shed.

The large building of the Rue Droit Mur which ran back on the Petite Rue Picpus, presented upon this garden two square façades. These inside façades were still more gloomy than those on the outside. All the windows were grated. No light was to be seen. On the upper storeys there were shutters as in prisons. The shadow of one of these façades was projected upon the other, and fell on the garden like an immense black pall.

No other house could be seen. The further end of the garden was lost in mist and in darkness. Still, he could make out walls intersecting, as if there were other cultivated grounds beyond, as well as the low roofs of the Rue Polonceau.

Nothing can be imagined more wild and more solitary than this garden. There was no one there, which was very natural on account of the hour; but it did not seem as if the place were made for anybody to walk in, even in broad noon.

Jean Valjean's first care had been to find his shoes, and put them on; then he entered the shed with Cosette. A man trying to escape never thinks himself sufficiently concealed. The child, thinking constantly of the Thénardiess, shared his instinct, and cowered down as closely as she could.

Cosette trembled, and pressed closely to his side. They heard the tumultuous clamour of the patrol ransacking the cul-de-sac and the street, the clatter of their muskets against the stones, the calls of Javert to the watchmen he had stationed, and his imprecations mingled with words which they could not distinguish.

At the end of a quarter of an hour it seemed as though this stormy rumbling began to recede. Jean Valjean did not breathe.

He had placed his hand gently upon Cosette's mouth.

But the solitude about him was so strangely calm that that frightful din, so furious and so near, did not even cast over it a shadow of disturbance. It seemed as if these walls were built of the deaf stones spoken of in Scripture.

Suddenly, in the midst of this deep calm, a new sound arose; a celestial, divine, ineffable sound, as ravishing as the other was horrible. It was a hymn which came forth from the darkness, a bewildering mingling of prayer and harmony in the obscure and fearful silence of the night; voices of women, but voices with the pure accents of virgins, and artless accents of children; those voices which are not of earth, and which resemble those that the newborn still hear, and the dying hear already. This song came from the gloomy building which overlooked the garden. At the moment when the uproar of the demons receded, one would have said, it was a choir of angels approaching in the darkness.

Cosette and Jean Valjean fell on their knees.

They knew not what it was; they knew not where they were; but they both felt, the man and the child, the penitent and the innocent, that they ought to be on their knees.

These voices had this strange effect; they did not prevent the building from appearing deserted. It was like a supernatural song in an uninhabited dwelling.

While these voices were singing Jean Valjean was entirely absorbed in them. He no longer saw the night, he saw a blue sky. He seemed to feel the spreading of these wings which we all have within us.

The chant ceased. Perhaps it had lasted a long time. Jean Valjean could not have told. Hours of ecstasy are never more than a moment.

All had again relapsed into silence. There was nothing more in the street, nothing more in the garden. That which threatened, that which reassured, all had vanished. The wind rattled the dry grass on the top of the wall, which made a low, soft, and mournful noise.

7. *The enigma continued*

THE NIGHT WIND had risen, which indicated that it must be between one and two o'clock in the morning. Poor Cosette did not speak. As she had sat down at his side and leaned her head on him, Jean Valjean thought that she was asleep. He bent over and looked at her. Her eyes were wide open, and she had a look that gave Jean Valjean pain.

She was still trembling.

'Are you sleepy?' said Jean Valjean.

'I am very cold,' she answered.

A moment after she added:

'Is she there yet?'

'Who?' said Jean Valjean.

'Madame Thénardier.'

Jean Valjean had already forgotten the means he had employed to secure Cosette's silence.

'Oh!' said he. 'She has gone. Don't be afraid any longer.' The child sighed as if a weight were lifted from her breast.

The ground was damp, the shed open on all sides, the wind freshened every moment. The goodman took off his coat and wrapped Cosette in it.

'Are you warmer, so?'

'Oh! yes, father!'

'Well, wait here a moment for me. I shall soon be back.'

He went out of the ruin, and along by the large building, in search of some better shelter. He found doors, but they were all closed. All the windows of the ground-floor were barred.

As he passed the interior angle of the building, he noticed several arched windows before him, where he perceived some light. He rose on tiptoe and looked in at one of these windows. They all opened into a large hall, paved with broad slabs, and intersected by arches and pillars, he could distinguish nothing but a slight glimmer in the deep obscurity. This glimmer came from a night-lamp burning in a corner. The hall was deserted; everything was motionless. However, by dint of looking, he thought he saw something, stretched out on the pavement, which appeared to be covered with a shroud, and which resembled a human form. It was lying with the face downwards, the arms crossed, in the immobility of death. One would have said, from a sort of serpent which trailed along the pavement, that this ill-omened figure had a rope about its neck.

The whole hall was enveloped in that mist peculiar to dimly-lighted places, which always increases horror.

Jean Valjean has often said since that, although in the course of his life he had seen many funereal sights, never had he seen anything more freezing and more terrible than this enigmatical figure fulfilling some strange mystery, he knew not what, in that gloomy place, and thus dimly seen in the night. It was terrifying to suppose that it was perhaps dead, and still more terrifying to think that it might be alive.

He had the courage to press his forehead against the glass, and watch to see if the thing would move. He remained what seemed to him a long time in vain; the prostrate form made no movement. Suddenly he was seized with an inexpressible dismay, and he fled. He ran towards the shed without daring to look behind him. It seemed to him that if he should turn his head he would see the figure walking behind him with rapid strides and shaking its arms.

He reached the ruin breathless. His knees gave way; a cold sweat oozed out from every pore.

Where was he? who would ever have imagined anything equal to this species of sepulchre in the midst of Paris? what was this strange house? A building full of nocturnal mystery, calling to souls in the shade with the voice of angels, and, when they came, abruptly presenting to them this frightful vision – promising to open the radiant gate of Heaven and opening the horrible door of the tomb. And that was in fact a building, a house which had its number in a street? It was not a dream? He had to touch the walls to believe it.

The cold, the anxiety, the agitation, the anguish of the night, were giving him a veritable fever, and all his ideas were jostling in his brain.

He went to Cosette. She was sleeping.

8. *The enigma redoubles*

THE CHILD had laid her head upon a stone and gone to sleep.

He sat down near her and looked at her. Little by little, as he beheld her, he grew calm, and regained possession of his clearness of mind.

He plainly perceived this truth, the basis of his life henceforth, that so long as she should be alive, so long as he should have her with him, he should need nothing except for her, and fear nothing save on her account. He did not even realise that he was very cold, having taken off his coat to cover her.

Meanwhile, through the reverie into which he had fallen, he had heard for some time a singular noise. It sounded like a little bell that someone was shaking. This noise was in the garden. It was heard distinctly, though feebly. It resembled the dimly heard tinkling of cow-bells in the pastures at night.

This noise made Jean Valjean turn.

He looked, and saw that there was someone in the garden.

Something which resembled a man was walking among the glass cases of the melon patch, rising up, stooping down, stopping, with a regular motion, as if he were drawing or stretching something upon the ground. This being appeared to limp.

Jean Valjean shuddered with the continual tremor of the outcast. To them everything is hostile and suspicious. They distrust the day because it helps to discover them, and the night because it helps to surprise them. Just now he was shuddering because the garden was empty, now he shuddered because there was someone in it.

He fell again from chimerical terrors into real terrors. He said to himself that perhaps Javert and his spies had not gone away, that they had doubtless left somebody on the watch in the street; that, if this man should discover him in the garden, he would cry thief, and would deliver him up. He took the sleeping Cosette gently in his arms and carried her into the furthest corner of the shed behind a heap of old furniture that was out of use. Cosette did not stir.

From there he watched the strange motions of the man in the melon patch. It seemed very singular, but the sound of the bell followed every movement of the man. When the man approached, the sound approached; when he moved away, the sound moved away; if he made some sudden motion, a trill accompanied the motion; when he stopped, the noise ceased. It seemed evident that the bell was fastened to this man; but then what could that mean? what was this man to whom a bell was hung as to a ram or a cow?

While he was revolving these questions, he touched Cosette's hands. They were icy.

'Oh! God!' said he.

He called to her in a low voice:

'Cosette!'

She did not open her eyes.

He shook her smartly.

She did not wake.

'Could she be dead?' said he, and he sprang up, shuddering from head to foot.

The most frightful thoughts rushed through his mind in confusion. There are moments when hideous suppositions besiege us like a throng of furies and violently force the portals of our brain. When those whom we love are in danger, our solicitude invents all sorts of follies. He remembered that sleep may be fatal in the open air in a cold night.

Cosette was pallid; she had fallen prostrate on the ground at his feet, making no sign.

He listened for her breathing; she was breathing; but with a respiration that appeared feeble and about to stop.

How should he get her warm again? how rouse her? All else was banished from his thoughts. He rushed desperately out of the ruin.

It was absolutely necessary that in less than a quarter of an hour Cosette should be in bed and before a fire.

9. *The man with the bell*

HE WALKED STRAIGHT to the man whom he saw in the garden. He had taken in his hand the roll of money which was in his vest-pocket.

This man had his head down, and did not see him coming. A few strides, Jean Valjean was at his side.

Jean Valjean approached him, exclaiming:

'A hundred francs!'

The man started and raised his eyes.

'A hundred francs for you,' continued Jean Valjean, 'if you will give me refuge tonight.'

The moon shone full in Jean Valjean's bewildered face.

'What, it is you, Father Madeleine!' said the man.

This name, thus pronounced, at this dark hour, in this unknown place, by this unknown man, made Jean Valjean start back.

He was ready for anything but that. The speaker was an old man, bent and lame, dressed much like a peasant, who had on his left knee a leather knee-cap from which hung a bell. His face was in the shade, and could not be distinguished.

Meanwhile the goodman had taken off his cap, and was exclaiming, tremulously:

'Ah! my God! how did you come here, Father Madeleine? How did you get in, O Lord? Did you fall from the sky? There is no doubt, if you ever do fall, you will fall from there. And what has happened to you? You have no cravat, you have no hat, you have no coat? Do you know that you would have frightened anybody who did not know you? No coat? Merciful heavens! are the saints all crazy now? But how did you get in?'

One word did not wait for another. The old man spoke with a rustic volubility in which there was nothing disquieting. All this was said with a mixture of astonishment, and frank good nature.

'Who are you? and what is this house!' asked Jean Valjean.

'Oh! indeed, that is good now,' exclaimed the old man, 'I am the one you got the place for here, and this house is the one you got me the place in. What! you don't remember me?'

'No,' said Jean Valjean. 'And how does it happen that you know me?'

'You saved my life,' said the man.

He turned, a ray of the moon lighted up his side face, and Jean Valjean recognised old Fauchelevent.

'Ah!' said Jean Valjean, 'it is you? yes, I remember you.'

'That is very fortunate!' said the old man, in a reproachful tone.

'And what are you doing here?' added Jean Valjean.

'Oh! I am covering my melons.'

Old Fauchelevent had in his hand, indeed, at the moment when Jean Valjean accosted him, the end of a piece of awning which he was stretching out over the melon patch. He had already spread out several in this way during the hour he had been in the garden. It was this work which made him go through the peculiar motions observed by Jean Valjean from the shed.

He continued:

'I said to myself: the moon is bright, there's going to be a frost. Suppose I put their jackets on my melons? And,' added he, looking at Jean Valjean, with a loud laugh, 'you would have done well to do as much for yourself! but how did you come here?'

Jean Valjean, finding that he was known by this man, at least under his name of Madeleine, went no further with his precautions. He multiplied questions. Oddly enough their parts seemed reversed. It was he, the intruder, who put questions.

'And what is this bell you have on your knee?'

'That!' answered Fauchelevent, 'that is so that they may keep away from me.'

'How! keep away from you?'

Old Fauchelevent winked in an indescribable manner.

'Ah! Bless me! there's nothing but women in this house; plenty of young girls. It seems that I am dangerous to meet. The bell warns them. When I come they go away.'

'What is this house?'

'Why, you know very well.'

'No, I don't.'

'Why, you got me this place here as gardener.'

'Answer me as if I didn't know.'

'Well, it is the Convent of the Petit Picpus, then.'

Jean Valjean remembered. Chance, that is to say, Providence, had thrown him precisely into this convent of the Quartier Saint Antoine, to which old Fauchelevent, crippled by his fall from his cart, had been admitted, upon his recommendation, two years before. He repeated as if he were talking to himself:

'The Convent of the Petit Picpus!'

'But now, really,' resumed Fauchelevent, 'how the deuce did you manage to get in, you, Father Madeleine? It is no use for you to be a saint, you are a man; and no men come in here.'

'But you are here.'

'There is none but me.'

'But,' resumed Jean Valjean, 'I must stay here.'

'Oh! my God,' exclaimed Fauchelevent.

Jean Valjean approached the old man, and said to him in a grave voice:

'Father Fauchelevent, I saved your life.'

'I was first to remember it,' answered Fauchelevent.

'Well, you can now do for me what I once did for you.'

Fauchelevent grasped in his old wrinkled and trembling hands the robust hands of Jean Valjean, and it was some seconds before he could speak; at last he exclaimed:

'Oh! that would be a blessing of God if I could do something for you, in return for that! I save your life! Monsieur Mayor, the old man is at your disposal.'

A wonderful joy had, as it were, transfigured the old gardener. A radiance seemed to shine forth from his face.

'What do you want me to do?' he added.

'I will explain. You have a room?'

'I have a solitary shanty, over there, behind the ruins of the old convent, in a corner that nobody ever sees. There are three rooms.'

The shanty was in fact so well concealed behind the ruins, and so well arranged, that no one should see it – that Jean Valjean had not seen it.

'Good,' said Jean Valjean. 'Now I ask of you two things.'

'What are they, Monsieur Madeleine?'

'First, that you will not tell anybody what you know about me. Second, that you will not attempt to learn anything more.'

'As you please. I know that you can do nothing dishonourable, and that you have always been a man of God. And then, besides, it was you that put me here. It is your place, I am yours.'

'Very well. But now come with me. We will go for the child.'

'Ah!' said Fauchelevent, 'there is a child!'

He said not a word more, but followed Jean Valjean as a dog follows his master.

In half an hour Cosette, again become rosy before a good fire, was asleep in the old gardener's bed. Jean Valjean had put on his cravat and coat; his hat, which he had thrown over the wall, had been found and brought in. While Jean Valjean was putting on his coat, Fauchelevent had taken off his knee-cap with the bell attached, which now, hanging on a nail near a shutter, decorated the wall. The two men were warming themselves, with their elbows on a table, on which Fauchelevent had set a piece of cheese, some brown bread, a bottle of wine, and two glasses, and the old man said to Jean Valjean, putting his hand on his knee:

'Ah! Father Madeleine! you didn't know me at first? You save people's lives and then you forget them? Oh! that's bad; they remember you. You are ungrateful!'

10. *In which is explained how Javert lost the game*

THE EVENTS, the reverse of which, so to speak, we have just seen, had been brought about under the simplest conditions.

When Jean Valjean, on the night of the very day that Javert arrested him at the death-bed of Fantine, escaped from the municipal prison of M— sur M—, the police supposed that the escaped convict would start for Paris. Paris is a maelstrom in which everything is lost; and everything disappears in this whirlpool of the world as in the whirlpool of the sea. No forest conceals a man like this multitude. Fugitives of all kinds know this. They go to Paris to be swallowed up; there are swallowings-up which save. The police know it also, and it is in Paris that they search for what they have lost elsewhere. They searched there for the ex-mayor of M— sur M—. Javert was summoned to Paris to aid in the investigation. Javert, in fact, was of great aid in the recapture of Jean Valjean. The zeal and intelligence of Javert on this occasion were remarked by M. Chabouillet, Secretary of the Prefecture, under Count Angles. M. Chabouillet, who had already interested himself in Javert, secured the transfer of the inspector of M— sur M— to the police of Paris. There Javert rendered himself in various ways, and, let us say, although the word seems unusual for such service, honourably, useful.

He thought no more of Jean Valjean – with these hounds always upon the scent, the wolf of today banishes the memory of the wolf of yesterday – when, in

December 1823, he read a newspaper, he who never read the newspapers; but Javert, as a monarchist, made a point of knowing the details of the triumphal entry of the 'Prince generalissimo' into Bayonne. Just as he finished the article which interested him, a name – the name of Jean Valjean – at the bottom of the page attracted his attention. The newspaper announced that the convict Jean Valjean was dead, and published the fact in terms so explicit, that Javert had no doubt of it. He merely said: '*That settles it.*' Then he threw aside the paper, and thought no more of it.

Sometime afterwards it happened that a police notice was transmitted by the Prefecture of Seine-et-Oise to the Prefecture of Police of Paris in relation to the kidnapping of a child, which had taken place, it was said, under peculiar circumstances, in the commune of Montfermeil. A little girl, seven or eight years old, the notice said, who had been confided by her mother to an innkeeper of the country, had been stolen by an unknown man; this little girl answered to the name of Cosette, and was the child of a young woman named Fantine, who had died at the Hospital, nobody knew when or where. This notice came under the eyes of Javert, and set him to thinking.

The name of Fantine was well known to him. He remembered that Jean Valjean had actually made him – Javert – laugh aloud by asking of him a respite of three days, in order to go for the child of this creature. He recalled the fact that Jean Valjean had been arrested at Paris, at the moment he was getting into the Montfermeil diligence. Some indications had even led him to think then that it was the second time that he was entering this diligence, and that he had already, the night previous, made another excursion to the environs of this village, for he had not been seen in the village itself. What was he doing in this region of Montfermeil? Nobody could divine. Javert understood it. The daughter of Fantine was there. Jean Valjean was going after her. Now this child had been stolen by an unknown man! Who could this man be? Could it be Jean Valjean? But Jean Valjean was dead. Javert, without saying a word to anyone, took the diligence at the Plat d'Etain, Cul-de-sac de Planchette, and took a trip to Montfermeil.

He expected to find great developments there; he found great obscurity.

For the first few days, the Thénardiers, in their spite, had blabbed the story about. The disappearance of the Lark had made some noise in the village. There were soon several versions of the story, which ended by becoming a case of kidnapping. Hence the police notice. However, when the first ebullition was over, Thénardier, with admirable instinct, very soon arrived at the conclusion that it is never useful to set in motion the Procureur du Roi; that the first result of his complaints in regard to the *kidnapping* of Cosette would be to fix upon himself, and on many business troubles which he had, the keen eye of justice. The last thing that owls wish is a candle. And first of all, how should he explain the fifteen hundred francs he had received? He stopped short, and enjoined secrecy upon his wife, and professed to be astonished when anybody spoke to him of the *stolen child*. He knew nothing about it; undoubtedly he had made some complaint at the time that the dear little girl should be 'taken away' so suddenly; he would have liked, for affection's sake, to keep her two or three days; but it was her 'grandfather' who had come for her, the most natural thing in the world. He had added the grandfather, which sounded well. It was upon this story that Javert fell on reaching Montfermeil. The grandfather put Jean Valjean out of the question.

Javert, however, dropped a few questions like plummets into Thénardier's story. Who was this grandfather, and what was his name? Thénardier answered with simplicity: 'He is a rich farmer, I saw his passport. I believe his name is M. Guillaume Lambert.'

Lambert is a very respectable reassuring name. Javert returned to Paris.

'Jean Valjean is really dead,' said he, 'and I am a fool.'

He had begun to forget all this story, when, in the month of March 1824, he heard an odd person spoken of who lived in the parish of Saint Médard, and who was called 'the beggar who gives alms'. This person was, it was said, a man living on his income, whose name nobody knew exactly, and who lived alone with a little girl eight years old, who knew nothing of herself except that she came from Montfermeil. Montfermeil! This name constantly recurring, excited Javert's attention anew. An old begging police spy, formerly a beadle, to whom this person had extended his charity, added some other details. 'This man was very unsociable, never going out except at night, speaking to nobody, except to the poor sometimes, and allowing nobody to get acquainted with him. He wore a horrible old yellow coat which was worth millions, being lined all over with bank bills.' This decidedly piqued Javert's curiosity. That he might get a near view of this fantastic rich man without frightening him away, he borrowed one day of the beadle his old frock, and the place where the old spy squatted every night droning out his orisons and playing the spy as he prayed.

'The suspicious individual' did indeed come to Javert thus disguised, and gave him alms; at that moment Javert raised his head, and the shock which Jean Valjean received, thinking that he recognised Javert, Javert received, thinking that he recognised Jean Valjean.

However, the obscurity might have deceived him, the death of Jean Valjean was officially certified; Javert had still serious doubts; and in case of doubt, Javert, scrupulous as he was, never seized any man by the collar.

He followed the old man to Gorbeau House, and set 'the old woman' talking, which was not at all difficult. The old woman confirmed the story of the coat lined with millions, and related to him the episode of the thousand-franc note. She had seen it! she had touched it! Javert hired a room. That very night he installed himself in it. He listened at the door of the mysterious lodger, hoping to hear the sound of his voice, but Jean Valjean perceived his candle through the keyhole and baulked the spy by keeping silence.

The next day Jean Valjean decamped. But the noise of the five-franc piece which he dropped was noticed by the old woman, who hearing money moving, suspected that he was going to move, and hastened to forewarn Javert. At night, when Jean Valjean went out, Javert was waiting for him behind the trees of the boulevard with two men.

Javert had called for assistance from the Prefecture, but he had not given the name of the person he hoped to seize. That was his secret; and he kept it for three reasons; first, because the least indiscretion might give the alarm to Jean Valjean; next, because the arrest of an old escaped convict who was reputed dead, a criminal whom the records of justice had already classed for ever *among malefactors of the most dangerous kind*, would be a magnificent success which the old members of the Parisian police certainly would never leave to a newcomer like Javert, and he feared they would take his galley-slave away from him; finally, because Javert, being an artist, had a liking for surprises. He hated these boasted successes which are deflowered by talking of them long in advance. He liked to elaborate his masterpieces in the shade, and then to unveil them suddenly afterwards.

Javert had followed Jean Valjean from tree to tree, then from street corner to street corner, and had not lost sight of him a single instant; even in the moments when Jean Valjean felt himself most secure, the eye of Javert was upon him. Why did not Javert arrest Jean Valjean? Because he was still in doubt.

It must be remembered that at that time the police was not exactly at its ease; it was cramped by a free press. Some arbitrary arrests, denounced by the newspapers, had been re-echoed even in the Chambers, and rendered the Prefecture timid. To attack individual liberty was a serious thing. The officers were afraid of making mistakes; the Prefect held them responsible; an error was the loss of their place. Imagine the effect which this brief paragraph, repeated in twenty papers, would have produced in Paris. 'Yesterday, an old white-haired grandsire, a respectable person living on his income, who was taking a walk with his grand-daughter, eight years old, was arrested and taken to the Station of the Prefecture as an escaped convict!'

Let us say, in addition, that Javert had his own personal scruples; the injunctions of his conscience were added to the injunctions of the Prefect. He was really in doubt.

Jean Valjean turned his back, and walked away in the darkness.

Sadness, trouble, anxiety, weight of cares, this new sorrow of being obliged to fly by night, and to seek a chance asylum in Paris for Cosette and himself, the necessity of adapting his pace to the pace of a child, all this, without his knowing it even, had changed Jean Valjean's gait, and impressed upon his carriage such an appearance of old age that the police itself, incarnated in Javert, could be deceived. The impossibility of approaching too near, his dress of an old preceptor of the emigration, the declaration of Thénardier, who made him a grandfather; finally, the belief in his death at the galleys, added yet more to the uncertainty which was increasing in Javert's mind.

For a moment he had an idea of asking him abruptly for his papers. But if the man were not Jean Valjean, and if the man were not a good old honest man of means, he was probably some sharper profoundly and skilfully adept in the obscure web of Parisian crime, some dangerous chief of bandits, giving alms to conceal his other talents, an old trick. He had comrades, accomplices, retreats on all hands, in which he would take refuge without doubt. All these windings which he was making in the streets seemed to indicate that he was not a simple honest man. To arrest him too soon would be 'to kill the goose that laid the golden eggs.' What inconvenience was there in waiting? Javert was very sure that he would not escape.

He walked on, therefore, in some perplexity, questioning himself continually in regard to this mysterious personage.

It was not until quite late, in the Rue de Pontoise, that, thanks to the bright light which streamed from a bar-room, he decidedly recognised Jean Valjean.

There are in this world two beings who can be deeply thrilled: the mother, who finds her child, and the tiger, who finds his prey. Javert felt this profound thrill.

As soon as he had positively recognised Jean Valjean, the formidable convict, he perceived that there were only three of them, and sent to the commissary of police, of the Rue de Pontoise, for additional aid. Before grasping a thorny stick, men put on gloves.

This delay and stopping at the Rollin square to arrange with his men made him lose the scent. However, he had very soon guessed that Jean Valjean's first wish would be to put the river between his pursuers and himself. He bowed his head and reflected, like a hound who put his nose to the ground to be sure of the way. Javert, with his straightforward power of instinct, went directly to the bridge of Austerlitz. A word to the toll-keeper set him right. 'Have you seen a man with a little girl?' 'I made him pay two sous,' answered the tollman. Javert reached the bridge in time to see Jean Valjean on the other side of the river leading Cosette across the space lighted by the moon. He saw him enter the Rue de Chemin Vert Saint Antoine, he thought of the Cul-de-sac Genrot placed there like a trap, and of the only outlet from the Rue Droit Mur into the Petite Rue Picpus. He *put out beaters*, as hunters say; he sent one of his men hastily by a detour to guard that outlet. A patrol passing, on its return to the station at the arsenal, he put it in requisition, and took it along with him. In such games soldiers are trumps. Moreover, it is a maxim that, to take the boar requires the science of the hunter, and the strength of the dogs. These combinations being effected, feeling that Jean Valjean was caught between the Cul-de-sac Genrot on the right, his officer on the left, and himself, Javert, in the rear, he took a pinch of snuff.

Then he began to play. He enjoyed a ravishing and infernal moment; he let his man go before him, knowing that he had him, but desiring to put off as long as possible the moment of arresting him, delighting to feel that he was caught, and to see him free, fondly gazing upon him with the rapture of the spider which lets the fly buzz, or the cat which lets the mouse run. The paw and the talon find a monstrous pleasure in the quivering of the animal imprisoned in their grasp. What delight there is in this suffocation!

Javert was rejoicing. The links of his chain were solidly welded. He was sure of success; he had now only to close his hand.

Accompanied as he was, the very idea of resistance was impossible, however energetic, however vigorous, and however desperate Jean Valjean might be.

Javert advanced slowly, sounding and ransacking on his way all the recesses in the street as he would the pockets of a thief.

When he reached the centre of the web, the fly was no longer there.

Imagine his exasperation.

He questioned his sentinel at the corner of the Rue Droit Mur and Rue Picpus; this officer, who had remained motionless at his post, had not seen the man pass.

It happens sometimes that a stag breaks with the head covered, that is to say escapes, although the hound is upon him; then the oldest hunters know not what to say. Duvivier, Ligniville and Desprez are at fault. On the occasion of a mishap of this sort, Artonge exclaimed: *It is not a stag, it is a sorcerer.*

Javert would fain have uttered the same cry.

His disappointment had a moment of despair and fury.

It is certain that Napoleon blundered in the campaign in Russia, that Alexander blundered in the war in India, that Cæsar blundered in the African war, that Cyrus blundered in the war in Scythia, and that Javert blundered in this campaign against Jean Valjean. He did wrong perhaps in hesitating to recognise the old galley slave. The first glance should have been enough for him. He did wrong in not seizing him without ceremony in the old building. He did wrong in not arresting him when he positively recognised him in the Rue de

Pontoise. He did wrong to hold a council with his aids, in full moonlight, in the Rollin square. Certainly advice is useful, and it is well to know and to question those of the dogs which are worthy of credit; but the hunter cannot take too many precautions when he is chasing restless animals, like the wolf and the convict. Javert, by too much forethought in setting his bloodhounds on the track, alarmed his prey by giving him wind of the pursuit, and allowed him the start. He did wrong, above all, when he had regained the scent at the bridge of Austerlitz, to play the formidable and puerile game of holding such a man at the end of a thread. He thought himself stronger than he was and believed he could play mouse with a lion. At the same time, he esteemed himself too weak when he deemed it necessary to obtain a reinforcement. Fatal precaution, loss of precious time. Javert made all these blunders, and yet he was none the less one of the wisest and most correct detectives that ever existed. He was, in the full force of the term, what in venery is called a *gentle dog*. But who is perfect?

Great strategists have their eclipses.

Great blunders are often made, like large ropes, of a multitude of fibres. Take the cable thread by thread, take separately all the little determining motives, you break them one after another, and you say: that is all. Wind them and twist them together they become an enormity; Attila hesitating between Marcian in the East and Valentinian in the West; Hannibal delaying at Capua; Danton falling to sleep at Arcis sur Aube.

However this may be, even at the moment when he perceived that Jean Valjean had escaped him, Javert did not lose his presence of mind. Sure that the convict who had broken his ban could not be far away, he set watches, arranged traps and ambushes, and beat the quarter the night through. The first thing that he saw was the displacement of the lamp, the rope of which was cut. Precious indication, which led him astray, however, by directing all his researches towards the Cul-de-sac Genrot. There are in that cul-de-sac some rather low walls which face upon gardens the limits of which extend to some very large uncultivated grounds. Jean Valjean evidently must have fled that way. The fact is that, if he had penetrated into the Cul-de-sac Genrot a little further, he would have done so, and would have been lost. Javert explored these gardens and these grounds, as if he were searching for a needle.

At daybreak, he left two intelligent men on the watch, and returned to the Prefecture of Police, crestfallen as a spy who has been caught by a thief.

BOOK 6: PETIT PICPUS[55]

1. *Petite Rue Picpus, No. 62*

NOTHING RESEMBLED more closely, half a century ago, the commonest *porte-cochère* of the time than the *porte-cochère* of No. 62 Petite Rue Picpus. This door was usually half open in the most attractive manner, disclosing two things which have nothing very funereal about them – a court surrounded with walls bedecked with vines, and the face of a lounging porter. Above the rear wall large trees could be seen. When a beam of sunshine enlivened the court, when a glass of wine enlivened the porter, it was difficult to pass by No. 62 Petite Rue Picpus, without carrying away a pleasant idea. It was, however, a gloomy place of which you had had a glimpse.

The door smiled; the house prayed and wept.

If you succeeded, which was not easy, in passing the porter – which for almost everybody was even impossible, for there was an *open sesame* which you must know; – if, having passed the porter, you entered on the right a little vestibule which led to a stairway shut in between two walls, and so narrow that but one person could pass at a time; if you did not allow yourself to be frightened by the yellow wall paper with the chocolate surbase that extended along the stairs, if you ventured to go up, you passed by a first broad stair, then a second, and reached the second storey in a hall where the yellow hue and the chocolate plinth followed you with a peaceful persistency. Staircase and hall were lighted by two handsome windows. The hall made a sudden turn and became dark. If you doubled that cape, you came, in a few steps, to a door, all the more mysterious that it was not quite closed. You pushed it open, and found yourself in a little room about six feet square, the floor tiled, scoured, neat and cold, and the walls hung with fifteen-cent paper, nankeen-coloured paper with green flowers. A dull white light came from a large window with small panes which was at the left, and which took up the whole width of the room. You looked, you saw no one; you listened, you heard no step and no human sound. The wall was bare; the room had no furniture, not even a chair.

You looked again, and you saw in the wall opposite the door a quadrangular opening about a foot square, covered with a grate of iron bars crossing one another, black, knotted, solid, which formed squares, I had almost said meshes, less than an inch across. The little green flowers on the nankeen paper came calmly and in order to these iron bars, without being frightened or scattered by the dismal contact. In case any living being had been so marvellously slender as to attempt to get in or out by the square hole, this grate would have prevented it. It did not let the body pass, but it did let the eyes pass, that is to say, the mind. This seemed to have been cared for, for it had been doubled by a sheet of tin inserted in the wall a little behind it, and pierced with a thousand holes more microscopic than those of a skimmer. At the bottom of this plate there was an opening cut exactly like the mouth of a letter-box. A piece of broad tape attached to a bell hung at the right of the grated opening.

If you pulled this tape, a bell tinkled and a voice was heard, very near you, which startled you.

'Who is there?' asked the voice.

It was a woman's voice, a gentle voice, so gentle that it was mournful.

Here again there was a magic word which you must know. If you did not know it, the voice was heard no more, and the wall again became silent as if the wild obscurity of the sepulchre had been on the other side.

If you knew the word, the voice added:

'Enter at the right.'

You then noticed at your right, opposite the window, a glazed door surmounted by a glazed sash and painted grey. You lifted the latch, you passed through the door, and you felt exactly the same impression as when you enter a grated box at the theatre before the grate is lowered and the lights are lit. You were in fact in a sort of theatre box, hardly made visible by the dim light of the glass door, narrow, furnished with two old chairs and a piece of tattered straw matting – a genuine box with its front to lean upon, upon which was a tablet of black wood. This box was grated, but it was not a grate of gilded wood as at the Opera; it was a monstrous trellis of iron bars frightfully tangled together, and bolted to the wall by enormous bolts which resembled clenched fists.

After a few minutes, when your eyes began to get accustomed to this cavernous light, you tried to look through the grate, but could not see more than six inches beyond. There you saw a barrier of black shutters, secured and strengthened by wooden cross-bars painted gingerbread colour. These shutters were jointed, divided into long slender strips, and covered the whole length of the grate. They were always closed.

In a few moments, you heard a voice calling to you from behind these shutters and saying:

'I am here. What do you want of me?'

It was a loved voice, perhaps sometimes an adored one. You saw nobody. You hardly heard a breath. It seemed as if it were a ghostly voice speaking to you across the portal of the tomb.

If you appeared under certain necessary conditions, very rare, the narrow strip of one of these shutters opened in front of you, and the ghostly voice became an apparition. Behind the grate, behind the shutter, you perceived, as well as the grate permitted, a head, of which you saw only the mouth and chin; the rest was covered with a black veil. You caught a glimpse of a black guimp and an ill-defined form covered with a black shroud. This head spoke to you, but did not look at you and never smiled at you.

The light which came from behind you was disposed in such wise that you saw her in the light, and she saw you in the shade. This light was symbolic.

Meantime your eyes gazed eagerly, through this aperture thus opened, into this place closed against all observation.

A deep obscurity enveloped this form thus clad in mourning. Your eyes strained into this obscurity, and sought to distinguish what was about the apparition. In a little while you perceived that you saw nothing. What you saw was night, void, darkness, a wintry mist mingled with a sepulchral vapour, a sort of terrifying quiet, a silence from which you distinguished nothing, not even sighs – a shade in which you discerned nothing, not even phantoms.

What you saw was the interior of a cloister.

It was the interior of that stern and gloomy house that was called the convent of the Bernardines of the Perpetual Adoration. This box where you were was the parlour. This voice, the first that spoke to you, was the voice of the portress, who was always seated, motionless and silent, on the other side of the wall, near the square aperture, defended by the iron grate and the plate with the thousand holes, as by a double visor.

The obscurity in which the grated box was sunk arose from this, that the locutory, which had a window on the side towards the outside world, had none on the convent side. Profane eyes must see nothing of this sacred place.

There was something, however, beyond this shade, there was a light; there was a life within this death. Although this convent was more inaccessible than any other, we shall endeavour to penetrate it, and to take the reader with us, and to relate, as fully as we may, something which story-tellers have never seen, and consequently have never related.

2. *The obedience of Martin Verga* [56]

THIS CONVENT, which in 1824 had existed for long years in the Petite Rue Picpus, was a community of Bernardines of the Obedience of Martin Verga.

These Bernardines, consequently, were attached, not to Clairvaux, like other Bernardines, but to Cîteaux, like the Benedictines. In other words, they were subjects, not of Saint Bernard, but of Saint Benedict.

Whoever is at all familiar with old folios, knows that Martin Verga founded in 1425 a congregation of Bernardine-Benedictines, having their chief convent at Salamanca and an affiliation at Alcalá.

This congregation had put out branches in all the Catholic countries of Europe.

These grafts of one order upon another are not unusual in the Latin church. To speak only of the single order of St Benedict, which is here in question – to this order are attached, without counting the Obedience of Martin Verga, four congregations; two in Italy, Monte Cassino and Santa Giustina of Padua, two in France, Cluny and Saint Maur; and nine orders, Vallombrosa, Grammont, the Cœlestines, the Camaldules, the Carthusians, the Humiliati, the Olivetans, the Sylvestrines, and finally Cîteaux; for Cîteaux itself, the trunk of other orders, is only an off-shoot from Saint Benedict. Cîteaux dates from St Robert, Abbé of Molesme, in the diocese of Langres in 1098. Now it was in 529 that the devil, who had retired to the desert of Subiaco (he was old; had he become a hermit?), was driven from the ancient temple of Apollo where he was living with St Benedict, then seventeen years old.

Next to the rules of the Carmelites, who go bare-footed, wear a withe about their throat, and never sit down, the most severe rules are those of the Bernardine-Benedictines of Martin Verga. They are clothed with a black guimp, which, according to the express command of Saint Benedict, comes up to the chin. A serge dress with wide sleeves, a large woollen veil, the guimp which rises to the chin, cut square across the breast, and the fillet which comes down to the eyes, constitute their dress. It is all black, except the fillet, which is white. The novices wear the same dress, all in white. The professed nuns have in addition a rosary by their side.

The Bernardine-Benedictines of Martin Verga perform the devotion of the Perpetual Adoration, as do the Benedictines called Ladies of the Holy Sacrament, who, at the commencement of this century, had at Paris two houses, one at the Temple, the other in the Rue Neuve Sainte Geneviève. In other respects, the Bernardine-Benedictines of the Petit Picpus, of whom we are speaking, were an entirely separate order from the Ladies of the Holy Sacrament, whose cloisters were in the Rue Neuve Sainte Geneviève and at the Temple. There were many differences in their rules, there were some in their costume. The Bernardine-Benedictines of the Petit Picpus wore a black guimp, and the Benedictines of the Holy Sacrament and of the Rue Neuve Sainte Geneviève wore a white one, and had moreover upon their breast a crucifix about three inches long in silver or copper gilt. The nuns of the Petit Picpus did not wear this crucifix. The devotion of the Perpetual Adoration, common to the house of the Petit Picpus and to the house of the Temple, left the two orders perfectly distinct. There is a similarity only in this respect between the Ladies of the Holy Sacrament and the Bernardines of Martin Verga, even as there is a similitude, in the study and the glorification of all the mysteries relative to the infancy, the life and the death of Jesus Christ, and to the Virgin, between two orders widely separated and occasionally inimical; the Oratory of Italy, established at Florence by Philip di Neri, and the Oratory of France, established at Paris by Pierre de Bérulle. The Oratory of Paris claims the precedence, Philip di Neri being only a saint, and Bérulle being a cardinal.

Let us return to the severe Spanish rules of Martin Verga.

The Bernardine-Benedictines of this Obedience abstain from meat all the year round, fast during Lent and many other days peculiar to them, rise out of their first sleep at one o'clock in the morning to read their breviary and chant matins until three, sleep in coarse woollen sheets at all seasons and upon straw, use no baths, never light any fire, scourge themselves every Friday, observe the rule of silence, speak to one another only at recreations, which are very short, and wear haircloth chemises for six months, from the fourteenth of September, the Exaltation of the Holy Cross, until Easter. These six months are a moderation – the rules say all the year; but this haircloth chemise, insupportable in the heat of summer, produced fevers and nervous spasms. It became necessary to limit its use. Even with this mitigation, after the fourteenth of September, when the nuns put on this chemise, they have three or four days of fever. Obedience, poverty, chastity, continuance in cloister; such are their vows, rendered much more difficult of fulfilment by the rules.

The prioress is elected for three years by the mothers, who are called *vocal mothers*, because they have a voice in the chapter. A prioress can be re-elected but twice, which fixes the longest possible reign of a prioress at nine years.

They never see the officiating priest, who is always concealed from them by a woollen curtain nine feet high. During sermon, when the preacher is in the chapel, they drop their veil over their face; they must always speak low, walk with their eyes on the ground and their head bowed down. But one man can enter the convent, the archbishop of the diocese.

There is indeed one other, the gardener; but he is always an old man, and in order that he may be perpetually alone in the garden and that the nuns may be warned to avoid him, a bell is attached to his knee.

They are subject to the prioress with an absolute and passive submission. It is canonical subjection in all its abnegation. As at the voice of Christ, *ut voci Christi*, at a nod, at the first signal, *ad nutum, ad primum signum*, promptly, with pleasure, with perseverance, with a certain blind obedience, *promptè, hilariter, perseveranter, et cœcâ quâdam obedientiâ*, like the file in the workman's hands, *quasi limam in manibus, fabri*, forbidden to read or write without express permission, *legere vel scribere non addiscerit sine expressâ superioris licentiâ*.

Each one of them in turn performed what they call *the reparation*. The Reparation is prayer for all sins, for all faults, for all disorders, for all violations, for all iniquities, for all the crimes which are committed upon the earth. During twelve consecutive hours, from four o'clock in the afternoon till four o'clock in the morning, or from four o'clock in the morning till four o'clock in the afternoon, the sister who performs *the reparation* remains on her knees upon the stone before the holy sacrament, her hands clasped and a rope around her neck. When fatigue becomes insupportable, she prostrates herself, her face against the marble and her arms crossed; this is all her relief. In this attitude, she prays for all the guilty in the universe. This is grand even to sublimity.

As this act is performed before a post on the top of which a taper is burning, they say indiscriminately, *to perform the reparation* or *to be at the post*. The nuns even prefer, from humility, this latter expression, which involves an idea of punishment and of abasement.

The performance of the reparation is a process in which the whole soul is absorbed. The sister at the post would not turn were a thunderbolt to fall behind her.

Moreover, there is always a nun on her knees before the holy sacrament. They remain for an hour. They are relieved like soldiers standing sentry. That is the Perpetual Adoration.

The prioresses and the mothers almost always have names of peculiar solemnity, recalling not the saints and the martyrs, but moments in the life of Christ, like Mother Nativity, Mother Conception, Mother Presentation, Mother Passion. The names of saints, however, are not prohibited.

When you see them, you see only their mouth.

They all have yellow teeth. Never did a toothbrush enter the convent. To brush the teeth is the top round of a ladder, the bottom round of which is – to lose the soul.

They never say *my* or *mine*. They have nothing of their own, and must cherish nothing. They say our of everything; thus: our veil, our chaplet; if they speak of their chemise, they say *our chemise*. Sometimes they become attached to some little object, to a prayer-book, a relic, or a sacred medal. As soon as they perceive that they are beginning to cherish this object, they must give it up. They remember the reply of Saint Theresa, to whom a great lady, at the moment of entering her order, said: permit me, mother, to send for a holy Bible which I cherish very much. '*Ah! you cherish something! In that case, do not enter our house.*'

None are allowed to shut themselves up, and to have a *home*, a *room*. They live in open cells. When they meet one another, one says: *Praise and adoration to the most holy sacrament of the altar!* The other responds: *Forever*. The same ceremony when one knocks at another's door. Hardly is the door touched when a gentle voice is heard from the other side hastily saying, Forever. Like all rituals, this becomes mechanical from habit; and one sometimes says *forever* before the other has had time to say, what is indeed rather lengthy, *Praise and adoration to the most holy sacrament of the altar!*

Among the Visitandines, the one who comes in says: *Ave Maria*, and the one to whose cell she comes says: *Gratiâ plena*. This is their good day, which is, in fact, 'graceful'.

At each hour of the day, three supplementary strokes sound from the bell of the convent church. At this signal, prioress, mothers, professed nuns, sister servants, novices, postulants, all break off from what they are saying, doing, or thinking, and say at once, if it is five o'clock, for example: *At five o'clock and at all times praise and adoration to the most holy sacrament of the altar!* If it is eight o'clock: *At eight and at all times*, etc., and so on, according to whatever hour it may be.

This custom, which is intended to interrupt the thoughts, and to lead them back constantly to God, exists in many communities; the formula only varies. Thus, at the Infant Jesus, they say: *At the present hour and at all hours may the love of Jesus enkindle my heart!*

The Benedictine-Bernardines of Martin Verga, cloistered fifty years ago in the Petit Picpus, chant the offices in a grave psalmody, pure plain-chant, and always in a loud voice for the whole duration of the office. Wherever there is an asterisk in the missal, they make a pause and say in a low tone: *Jesus-Mary-Joseph*. For the office for the dead, they take so low a pitch that it is difficult for female voices to reach it. The effect is thrilling and tragical.

Those of the Petit Picpus had had a vault made under their high altar for the burial of their community. The *government*, as they call it, does not permit corpses to be deposited in this vault. They therefore were taken from the convent when they died. This was an affliction to them, and horrified them as if it were a violation.

They had obtained – small consolation – the privilege of being buried at a special hour and in a special place in the old Vaugirard Cemetery, which was located in ground formerly belonging to the community.

On Thursday these nuns heard high mass, vespers, and all the offices the same as on Sunday. They moreover scrupulously observed all the little feast days, unknown to the people of the world, of which the church was formerly lavish in France, and is still lavish in Spain and Italy. Their attendance at chapel is interminable. As to the number and duration of their prayers, we cannot give a better idea than by quoting the frank words of one of themselves: *The prayers of the postulants are frightful, the prayers of the novices worse, and the prayers of the professed nuns still worse.*

Once a week the chapter assembles; the prioress presides, the mothers attend. Each sister comes in her turn, kneels upon the stone, and confesses aloud, before all, the faults and sins which she has committed during the week. The mothers consult together after each confession, and announce the penalty aloud.

In addition to open confession, for which they reserve all serious faults, they have for venial faults what they call the *coulpe*. To perform the coulpe is to prostrate yourself on your face during the office, before the prioress until she, who is never spoken of except as *our mother*, indicates to the sufferer, by a gentle rap upon the side of her stall, that she may rise. The coulpe is performed for very petty things; a glass broken, a veil torn, an involuntary delay of a few seconds at an office, a false note in church, etc., – these are enough for the coulpe. The coulpe is entirely spontaneous; it is the *culpable* herself (this word is here etymologically in its place) who judges herself and who inflicts it upon herself. On feast-days and Sundays there are four chorister mothers who sing the offices before a large desk with four music stands. One day a mother chorister intoned a psalm which commenced by *Ecce*, and, instead of *Ecce*, she pronounced in a loud voice these three notes: *ut; si, sol;* for this absence of mind she underwent a coulpe which lasted through the whole office. What rendered the fault peculiarly enormous was, that the chapter laughed.

When a nun is called to the locutory, be it even the prioress, she drops her veil, it will be remembered, in such a way as to show nothing but her mouth.

The prioress alone can communicate with strangers. The others can see only their immediate family, and that very rarely. If by chance persons from without present themselves to see a nun whom they have known or loved in the world, a formal negotiation is necessary. If it be a woman, permission may be sometimes accorded; the nun comes and is spoken to through the shutters, which are never opened except for a mother or sister. It is unnecessary to say that permission is always refused to men.

Such are the rules of St Benedict, rendered more severe by Martin Verga.

These nuns are not joyous, rosy, and cheerful, as are often the daughters of other orders. They are pale and serious. Between 825 and 1830 three became insane.

3. *Severities*

A POSTULANCY of at least two years is required, often four; a novitiate of four years. It is rare that the final vows can be pronounced under twenty-three or twenty-four years. The Bernardine-Benedictines of Martin Verga admit no widows into their order.

They subject themselves in their cells to many unknown self-mortifications of which they must never speak.

The day on which a novice makes her profession she is dressed in her finest attire, with her head decked with white roses, and her hair glossy and curled; then she prostrates herself; a great black veil is spread over her, and the office for the dead is chanted. The nuns then divide into two files, one file passes near her, saying in plaintive accents: *Our sister is dead*, and the other file responds in ringing tones: *living in Jesus Christ!*

At the period to which this history relates, a boarding-school was attached to the convent. A school of noble young girls, for the most part rich, among whom were noticeable Mesdemoiselles de Sainte Aulaire and de Bélissen, and an English girl bearing the illustrious Catholic name of Talbot. These young girls, reared by these nuns between four walls, grew up in horror of the world and of the age. One of them said to us one day: *To see the pavement of the street made me shiver from head to foot.* They were dressed in blue with a white cap, and a Holy Spirit, in silver or copper gilt, upon their breast. On certain grand feastdays, particularly on St Martha's day, they were allowed, as a high favour and a supreme pleasure, to dress as nuns and perform the offices and the ritual of St Benedict for a whole day. At first the professed nuns lent them their black garments. That appeared profane, and the prioress forbade it. This loan was permitted only to novices. It is remarkable that these representations, undoubtedly tolerated and encouraged in the convent by a secret spirit of proselytism, and to give these children some foretaste of the holy dress, were a real pleasure and a genuine recreation for the scholars. They simply amused themselves. *It was new; it was a change.* Candid reasons of childhood, which do not succeed, however, in making us, mundane people, comprehend the felicity of holding a holy sprinkler in the hand, and remaining standing entire hours singing in quartet before a desk.

The pupils, austerities excepted, conformed to all the ritual of the convent. There are young women who, returned to the world, and after several years of marriage, have not yet succeeded in breaking off the habit of saying hastily, whenever there is a knock at the door: *Forever!* Like the nuns, the boarders saw their relatives only in the locutory. Even their mothers were not permitted to embrace them. Strictness upon this point was carried to the following extent: One day a young girl was visited by her mother accompanied by a little sister three years old. The young girl wept, for she wished very much to kiss her sister. Impossible. She begged that the child should at least be permitted to pass her little hand through the bars that she might kiss it. This was refused almost with indignation.

4. *Gaities*

THESE YOUNG GIRLS have none the less filled this solemn house with charming reminiscences.

At certain hours, childhood sparkled in this cloister. The hour of recreation struck. A door turned upon its hinges. The birds said good! here are the children! An irruption of youth inundated this garden, which was cut by walks in the form of a cross, like a shroud. Radiant faces, white foreheads, frank eyes full of cheerful light, auroras of all sorts scattered through this darkness. After the chants, the bell-ringing, the knells, and the offices, all at once this hum of little girls burst forth sweeter than the hum of bees. The hive of joy opened, and each one brought her honey. They played, they called to one another, they formed groups, they ran; pretty little white teeth chattered in the corners; veils from a distance watched over the laughter, shadows spying the sunshine; but what matter! They sparkled and they laughed. These four dismal walls had their moments of bewilderment. They too shared, dimly lighted up by the reflection of so much joy, in this sweet and swarming whirl. It was like a shower of roses upon this mourning. The young girls frolicked under the eyes of the nuns; the gaze of sinlessness does not disturb innocence. Thanks to these children, among so many hours of austerity, there was one hour of artlessness. The little girls skipped, the larger ones danced. In this cloister, play was mingled with heaven. Nothing was so transporting and superb, as all these fresh, blooming souls. Homer might have laughed there with Perrault, and there were, in this dark garden, enough of youth, health, murmurs, cries, uproar, pleasure and happiness, to smooth the wrinkles from off all grandames, those of the epic as well as the tale, those of the throne as well as the hut, from Hecuba to Mother Goose.

In this house, more than anywhere else, perhaps, have been heard these *children's sayings*, which have so much grace, and which make one laugh with a laugh full of thought. It was within these four forbidding walls that a child of five years exclaimed one day: *'Mother, a great girl has just told me that I have only nine years and ten months more to stay here. How glad I am!'*

Here, also, that this memorable dialogue occurred:

A MOTHER – 'What are you crying for, my child?'

THE CHILD (six years old), sobbing. – 'I told Alice I knew my French history. She says I don't know it, and I do know it.'

ALICE, larger (nine years). – 'No, she doesn't know it.'

THE MOTHER – 'How is that, my child?'

ALICE – 'She told me to open the book anywhere and ask her any question there was in the book, and she could answer it.'

'Well?'

'She didn't answer it.'

'Let us see. What did you ask her?

'I opened the book anywhere, just as she said, and I asked her the first question I found.'

'And what was the question?'

'It was: *What happened next?*'

Here this profound observation was made about a rather dainty parrot, which belonged to a lady boarder:

'*Isn't she genteel! she picks off the top of her tart, like a lady.*'

From one of the tiles of the cloister, the following confession was picked up, written beforehand, so as not to be forgotten, by a little sinner seven years old.

'Father, I accuse myself of having been avaricious.

'Father, I accuse myself of having been adulterous.

'Father, I accuse myself of having raised my eyes towards the gentlemen.'

Upon one of the grassy banks of this garden, the following story was improvised by a rosy mouth six years old, and listened to by blue eyes four and five years old: 'There were three little chickens who lived in a country where there were a good many flowers. They picked the flowers, and they put them in their pockets. After that, they picked the leaves, and they put them in their playthings. There was a wolf in the country, and there was a good many woods; and the wolf was in the woods; and he ate up the little chickens.'

And again, this other poem:

> 'There was a blow with a stick.
> It was Punchinello who struck the cat.
> That didn't do him any good; it did her harm.
> Then a lady put Punchinello in prison.'

There, also, these sweet and heart-rending words were said by a little foundling that the convent was rearing through charity. She heard the others talking about their mothers, and she murmured in her little place:

'*For my part, my mother was not there when I was born.*'

There was a fat portress, who was always to be seen hurrying about the corridors with her bunch of keys, and whose name was Sister Agatha. The *great big* girls – over ten – called her *Agathocles*.

The refectory, a large oblong room, which received light only from a cloister window with a fluted arch opening on a level with the garden, was dark and damp, and, as the children said – full of beasts. All the surrounding places furnished it their contingents of insects. Each of its four corners had received, in the language of the pupils, a peculiar and expressive name. There was the Spiders' corner, the Caterpillars' corner, the Woodlice's corner, and the Crickets' corner. The crickets' corner was near the kitchen, and was highly esteemed. It was not so cold as the others. From the refectory the names had passed to the schoolroom, and served to distinguish there, as at the old Mazarin College, four nations. Each pupil belonged to one of these four nations according to the corner of the refectory in which she sat at meals. One day, the archbishop, making his pastoral visit, saw enter the class which he was passing, a pretty little blushing girl with beautiful fair hair; and he asked another scholar, a charming fresh-cheeked brunette, who was near him:

'What is this little girl?'

'She is a spider, monseigneur.'

'Pshaw! – and this other one?'

'She is a cricket.'

'And that one?'

'She is a caterpillar.'

'Indeed! And what are you?'

'I am a woodlouse, monseigneur.'

Every house of this kind has its peculiarities. At the commencement of this century, Ecouen was one of those serene and graceful places where, in a shade which was almost august, the childhood of young girls was passed. At Ecouen, by way of rank in the procession of the Holy Sacrament, they made a distinction between the virgins and the florists. There were also 'the canopies', and the 'censers', the former carrying the cords of the canopy, the latter swinging censers before the Holy Sacrament. The flowers returned of right to the florists. Four 'virgins' walked at the head of the procession. On the morning of the great day, it was not uncommon to hear the question in the dormitory.

'Who is a virgin?'

Madame Campan relates this saying of a 'little girl' seven years old to a 'great girl' of sixteen who took the head of the procession, while she, the little one, remained in the rear. 'You're a virgin, you are; but I am not.'

5. *Distractions*

ABOVE the door of the refectory was written in large black letters this prayer, which was called *the white Paternoster*, and which possessed the virtue of leading people straight in to Paradise:

'Little white paternoster, which God made, which God said, which God laid in Paradise. At night, on going to bed, I finded *(sic)* three angels lying on my bed, one at the foot, two at the head, the good Virgin Mary in the middle, who to me said that I should went to bed, and nothing suspected. The good God is my father, the Holy Virgin is my mother, the three apostles are my brothers, the three virgins are my sisters. The chemise in which God was born, my body is enveloped in; the cross of Saint Marguerite on my breast is writ; Madame the Virgin goes away through the fields, weeping for God, meeted Monsieur Saint John. Monsieur Saint John, where do you come from? I come from *Ave Salus*. You have not seen the good God, have you? He is on the tree of the cross, his feet hanging, his hands nailing, a little hat of white thorns upon his head. Whoever shall say this three times at night, three times in the morning, will win Paradise in the end.'

In 1827, this characteristic orison had disappeared from the wall under a triple layer of paper. It is fading away to this hour in the memory of some young girls of that day, old ladies now.

A large crucifix hanging upon the wall completed the decoration of this refectory, the only door of which, as we believe we have said, opened upon the garden. Two narrow tables, at the sides of each of which were two wooden benches, extended along the refectory in parallel lines from one end to the other. The walls were white, and the tables black; these two mourning colours are the only variety in convents. The meals were coarse, and the diet of even the children strict. A single plate, meat and vegetables together, or salt fish, constituted the fare. This brief bill of fare was, however, an exception, reserved for the scholars alone. The children ate in silence, under the watchful eyes of the mother for the week, who, from time to time, if a fly ventured to hum or to buzz contrary to rule, noisily opened and shut a wooden book. This silence was seasoned with the Lives of the Saints, read in a loud voice from a little reading desk placed at the foot of a crucifix. The reader was a large pupil, selected for the week. There were placed at intervals along the bare table, glazed earthen bowls, in which each pupil washed her cup and dish herself, and sometimes threw refuse bits, tough meat or tainted fish, this was punished. These bowls were called *water basins*.

A child who broke the silence made a 'cross with her tongue'. Where? On the floor. She licked the tiles. Dust, that end of all joys, was made to chastise these poor little rosebuds, when guilty of prattling.

There was a book in the convent, which is the *only copy* ever printed, and which it is forbidden to read. It is the Rules of St Benedict; arcana into which no profane eye must penetrate. *Nemo regulas, seu constitutiones nostras, externis communicabit.*[57]

The scholars succeeded one day in purloining this book, and began to read it eagerly, a reading often interrupted by fears of being caught, which made them close the volume very suddenly. But from this great risk they derived small pleasure. A few unintelligible pages about the sins of young boys, were what they thought 'most interesting'.

They played in one walk of the garden, along which were a few puny fruit trees. In spite of the close watch and the severity of the punishments, when the wind had shaken the trees, they sometimes succeeded in furtively picking up a green apple, a half-rotten apricot, or a worm-eaten pear. But I will let a letter speak, which I have at hand; a letter written twenty-five years ago by a former pupil, now Madame the Duchess of, one of the most elegant women of Paris.[58] I quote verbatim – 'We hide our pear or our apple as we can. When we go up to spread the covers on our beds before supper, we put them under our pillows, and at night eat them in bed, and when we cannot do that, we eat them in the closets.' This was one of their most vivid pleasures.

At another time, also on the occasion of a visit of the archbishop to the convent, one of the young girls, Mademoiselle Bouchard, a descendant of the Montmorencys, wagered that she would ask leave of absence for a day, a dreadful thing in a community so austere. The wager was accepted, but no one of those who took it believed she would dare do it. When the opportunity came, as the archbishop was passing before the scholars, Mademoiselle Bouchard, to the indescribable dismay of her companions, left the ranks, and said: 'Monseigneur, leave of absence for a day.' Mademoiselle Bouchard was tall and fresh-looking, with the prettiest little rosy face in the world. M. de Quélen smiled and said. '*How now, my dear child, leave of absence for a day! Three days, if you like. I grant you three days.*' The prioress could do nothing; the archbishop had spoken. A scandal to the convent, but a joyful thing for the school. Imagine the effect.

This rigid cloister was not, however, so well walled in, that the life of the passions of the outside world, that drama, that romance even, did not penetrate it. To prove this, we will merely state briefly an actual, incontestable fact, which, however, has in itself no relation to our story, not being attached to it even by a thread. We mention this merely to complete the picture of the convent in the mind of the reader.

There was about that time, then, in the convent, a mysterious person, not a nun, who was treated with great respect, and who was called *Madame Albertine*. Nothing was known of her, except that she was insane, and that in the world she was supposed to be dead. There were, it was said, involved in her story, some pecuniary arrangements necessary for a great marriage.

This woman, hardly thirty years old, a beautiful brunette, stared wildly with her large black eyes. Was she looking at anything? It was doubtful. She glided along rather than walked; she never spoke; it was not quite certain that she breathed. Her nostrils were as thin and livid as if she had heaved her last sigh. To touch her hand was like touching snow. She had a strange spectral grace. Wherever she came, all were cold. One day, a sister seeing her pass, said to another, 'She passes for dead.' 'Perhaps she is,' answered the other.

Many stories were told about Madame Albertine. She was the eternal subject of curiosity of the boarders. There was in the chapel a gallery, which was called l'Œil-de-Bœuf. In this gallery, which had only a circular opening, an œil-de-bœuf, Madame Albertine attended the offices. She was usually alone there, because from this gallery, which was elevated, the preacher or the officiating priest could be seen, which was forbidden to the nuns. One day, the pulpit was occupied by a young priest of high rank, the Duke de Rohan, peer of France, who was an officer of the Mousquetaires Rouges in 1815, when he was Prince de Léon, and who died afterwards in 1830, a cardinal, and Archbishop of Besançon. This was the first time that M. de Rohan had preached in the convent of the Petit Picpus. Madame Albertine ordinarily attended the sermons and the offices with perfect calmness and complete silence. On that day, as soon as she saw M. de Rohan, she half rose, and, in all the stillness of the chapel, exclaimed: 'What? Auguste?' The whole community were astounded, and turned their heads; the preacher raised his eyes, but Madame Albertine had fallen back into her motionless silence. A breath from the world without, a glimmer of life, had passed for a moment over that dead and icy form, then all had vanished, and the lunatic had again become a corpse.

These two words, however, set everybody in the convent who could speak to chattering. How many things there were in that What? Auguste? How many revelations! M. de Rohan's name was, in fact, Auguste. It was clear that Madame Albertine came from the highest society, since she knew M. de Rohan; that she had occupied a high position herself, since she spoke of so great a noble so familiarly; and that she had some connection with him, of relationship perhaps, but beyond all doubt very intimate, since she knew his 'pet name'.

Two very severe duchesses, Mesdames de Choiseul and de Sérent, often visited the community, to which they doubtless were admitted by virtue of the privilege of Magnates mulieres, greatly to the terror of the school. When the two old ladies passed, all the poor young girls trembled and lowered their eyes.

M. de Rohan was, moreover, without knowing it, the object of the attention of the schoolgirls. He had just at that time been made, while waiting for the episcopacy, grand-vicar of the Archbishop of Paris. He was in the habit of coming rather frequently to chant the offices in the chapel of the nuns of the Petit Picpus. None of the young recluses could see him, on account of the serge curtain, but he had a gentle, penetrating voice, which they came to recognise and distinguish. He had been a mousquetaire; and then he was said to be very agreeable, with beautiful chestnut hair, which he wore in curls, and a large girdle of magnificent moire, while his black cassock was of the most elegant cut in the world. All these girlish imaginations were very much occupied with him.

No sound from without penetrated the convent. There was, however, one year when the sound of a flute was heard. This was an event, and the pupils of the time remember it yet.

It was a flute on which somebody in the neighbourhood was playing. This flute always played the same air, an air long since forgotten: *My Zétulba, come reign o'er my soul*, and they heard it two or three times a nday. The young girls passed hours in listening, the mothers were distracted, heads grew giddy, punishments were exhausted. This lasted for several months. The pupils were all more or less in love with the unknown musician. Each one imagined herself Zétulba. The sound of the flute came from the direction of the Rue Droit Mur; they would have given everything, sacrificed everything, dared everything to see, were it only for a second, to catch a glimpse of the 'young man' who played so deliciously on that flute, and who, without suspecting it, was playing at the same time upon all their hearts. There were some who escaped by a back door, and climbed up to the third storey on the Rue Droit Mur, incurring days of suffering in the endeavour to see him. Impossible. One went so far as to reach her arm above her head through the grate and wave her white handkerchief. Two were bolder still. They found means to climb to the top of a roof, and risking themselves there, they finally succeeded in seeing the 'young man'. He was an old gentleman of the emigration, ruined and blind, who was playing upon the flute in his garret to while away the time.

6. *The little convent*

THERE were in this enclosure of the Petit Picpus three perfectly distinct buildings, the Great Convent, in which the nuns lived, the school building, in which the pupils lodged, and finally what was called the Little Convent. This was a detached building with a garden, in which dwelt in common many old nuns of various orders, remnants of cloisters destroyed by the revolution; a gathering of all shades, black, grey, and white, from all the communities and of all the varieties possible; what might be called, if such a coupling of names were not disrespectful, a sort of motley convent.

From the time of the empire, all these poor scattered and desolate maidens had been permitted to take shelter under the wings of the Benedictine-Bernardines. The government made them a small allowance; the ladies of the Petit Picpus had received them with eagerness. It was a grotesque mixture. Each followed her own rules. The schoolgirls were sometimes permitted, as a great recreation, to make them a visit; so that these young memories have retained among others a reminiscence of holy Mother Bazile, of holy Mother Scholastique, and of Mother Jacob.

One of these refugees found herself again almost in her own home. She was a nun of Sainte Aure, the only one of her order who survived. The ancient convent of the Ladies of Sainte Aure occupied at the beginning of the eighteenth century this same house of the Petit Picpus which afterwards belonged to the Benedictines of Martin Verga. This holy maiden, too poor to wear the magnificent dress of her order, which was a white robe with a scarlet scapular, had piously clothed a little image with it, which she showed complacently, and which at her death she bequeathed to the house. In 1824, there remained of this order only one nun; today there remains only a doll.

In addition to these worthy mothers, a few old women of fashion had obtained permission of the prioress, as had Madame Albertine, to retire into the Little

Convent. Among the number were Madame de Beaufort, d'Hautpoul, and Madame la Marquise Dufresne. Another was known in the convent only by the horrible noise she made in blowing her nose. The pupils called her Racketini.

About 1820 or 1821, Madame de Genlis, who at that time was editing a little magazine called the *Intrépide*, asked permission to occupy a room at the convent of the Petit Picpus. Monsieur the Duke of Orleans recommended her. A buzzing in the hive; the mothers were all in a tremor; Madame de Genlis had written romances; but she declared that she was the first to detest them, and then she had arrived at her phase of fierce devotion. God aiding, and the prince also, she entered.

She went away at the end of six or eight months, giving as a reason that the garden had no shade. The nuns were in raptures. Although very old, she still played on the harp, and that very well.

On going away, she left her mark on her cell. Madame de Genlis was superstitious and fond of Latin. These two terms give a very good outline of her. There could still be seen a few years ago, pasted up in a little closet in her cell, in which she locked up her money and jewellery, these five Latin lines written in her hand with red ink upon yellow paper, and which, in her opinion, possessed the virtue of frightening away thieves:

> Imparibus meritis pendent tria corpora ramis:
> Dismas et Gesmas, media est divina potestas;
> Alta petit Dismas, infelix, infima, Gesmas;
> Nos et res nostras conservet summa potestas,
> Hos versus dicas, ne tu furto tua perdas.[59]

These lines in Latin of the Sixth Century, raise the question as to whether the names of the two thieves of Calvary were, as is commonly believed, Dimas and Gestas, or Dismas and Gesmas. The latter orthography would make against the pretensions which the Vicomte de Gestas put forth, in the last century, to be a descendant of the unrepentant thief. The convenient virtue attributed to these lines was, moreover, an article of faith in the order of the Hospitallers.

The church of the convent, which was built in such a manner as to separate as much as possible the Great Convent from the school, was, of course, common to the school, the Great Convent and the Little Convent. The public even were admitted there by a beggarly entrance opening from the street. But everything was arranged in such a way that none of the inmates of the cloister could see a face from without. Imagine a church, the choir of which should be seized by a gigantic hand, and bent round in such a way as to form, not, as in ordinary churches, a prolongation behind the altar, but a sort of room or obscure cavern at the right of the priest; imagine this room closed by the curtain seven feet high of which we have already spoken; heap together in the shade of this curtain, on wooden stalls, the nuns of the choir at the left, the pupils at the right, the sister servants and the novices in the rear, and you will have some idea of the nuns of the Petit Picpus, attending divine service. This cavern, which was called the choir, communicated with the cloister by a narrow passage. The church received light from the garden. When the nuns were attending offices in which their rules commanded silence, the public was advised of their presence only by the sound of the rising and falling stall-seats.

7. A few outlines in this shade

DURING THE SIX YEARS which separate 1819 from 1825, the prioress of the Petit Picpus was Mademoiselle de Blemeur, whose religious name was Mother Innocent. She was of the family of Marguerite de Blemeur, author of the *Lives of the Saints of the Order of St Benedict.* She had been re-elected. A woman of about sixty, short, fat, 'chanting like a cracked kettle', says the letter from which we have already quoted; but an excellent woman, the only one who was cheerful in the whole convent, and on that account adored.

Mother Innocent resembled her ancestor Marguerite, the Dacier of the Order. She was well-read, erudite, learned, skilful, curious in history, stuffed with Latin, crammed with Greek, full of Hebrew, and rather a monk than a nun.

The sub-prioress was an old Spanish nun almost blind, Mother Cineres.

The most esteemed among the mothers were Mother Sainte Honorine, the treasurer, Mother Sainte Gertrude, first mistress of the novices, Mother Sainte Ange, second mistress, Mother Annunciation, sacristan, Mother Sainte Augustin, nurse, the only nun in the convent who was ill-natured; then Mother Sainte Mechthilde (Mlle Gauvain), quite young and having a wonderful voice; Mother des Anges (Mlle Drouet), who had been in the convent of the Filles-Dieu and in the convent of the Trésor, between Gisors and Magny; Mother Sainte Joseph (Mlle de Cogolludo), Mother Sainte Adelaide (Mlle d'Auverney), Mother Mercy (Mlle de Cifuentes), who could not endure the austerities, Mother Compassion (Mlle de la Miltière, received at sixty in spite of the rules, very rich); Mother Providence (Mlle de Laudinière), Mother Presentation (Mlle de Siguenza), who was prioress in 1847; finally, Mother Sainte Céligne (sister of the sculptor Ceracchi), since insane, Mother Sainte Chantal (Mlle de Suzon), since insane.

There was still among the prettiest a charming girl of twenty-three, from the Isle of Bourbon, a descendant of the Chevalier Roze, who was called in the world Mademoiselle Roze, and who called herself Mother Assumption.

Mother Sainte Mechthilde, who had charge of the singing and the choir, gladly availed herself of the pupils. She usually took a complete gamut of them, that is to say, seven, from ten years old to sixteen inclusive, of graduated voice and stature, and had them sing, standing in a row, ranged according to their age from the smallest to the largest. This presented to the sight something like a harp of young girls, a sort of living pipe of Pan made of angels.

Those of the servant sisters whom the pupils liked best were Sister Sainte Euphrasie, Sister Sainte Marguerite, Sister Sainte Marthe, who was in her dotage, and Sister Sainte Michael, whose long nose made them laugh.

All these women were gentle to all these children. The nuns were severe only to themselves. The only fires were in the school building, and the fare, compared with that of the convent, was choice. Besides that, they received a thousand little attentions. Only when a child passed near a nun and spoke to her, the nun never answered.

This rule of silence had had this effect that, in the whole convent, speech was withdrawn from human creatures and given to inanimate objects. Sometimes it was the church-bell that spoke, sometimes the gardener's. A very sonorous bell, placed beside the portress and which was heard all over the house, indicated by its variations, which were a kind of acoustic telegraph, all the acts of material life to be performed, and called to the locutory, if need were, this or that inhabitant of the house. Each person and each thing had its special ring. The prioress had one and one; the sub-prioress one and two. Six-five announced the recitation, so that the pupils never said going to recitation, but going to six-five. Four-four was Madame de Genlis' signal. It was heard very often. *It is the four deuce*, said the uncharitable. Nineteen strokes announced a great event. It was the opening of the *close door*, a fearful iron plate bristling with bolts which turned upon its hinges only before the archbishop.

He and the gardener excepted, as we have said, no man entered the convent. The pupils saw two others; one, the almoner, the Abbé Banès, old and ugly, whom they had the privilege of contemplating through a grate in the choir; the other, the drawing-master, M. Ansiaux, whom the letter from which we have already quoted a few lines, calls *M. Anciot*, and describes as a *horrid old hunchback*.

We see that all the men were select.

Such was this rare house.

8. Post corda lapides [60]

AFTER SKETCHING its moral features, it may not be useless to point out in a few words its material configuration. The reader has already some idea of it.

The convent of the Petit Picpus Saint Antoine almost entirely filled the large trapezium which was formed by the intersection of the Rue Polonceau, the Rue Droit Mur, the Petite Rue Picpus, and the built-up alley called in the old plans Rue Aumarais. These four streets surrounded this trapezium like a ditch. The convent was composed of several buildings and a garden. The principal building, taken as a whole, was an aggregation of hybrid constructions which, in a bird's-eye view, presented with considerable accuracy the form of a gibbet laid down on the ground.

The long arm of the gibbet extended along the whole portion of the Rue Droit Mur comprised between the Petite Rue Picpus and the Rue Polonceau; the short arm was a high, grey, severe, grated façade which overlooked the Petite Rue Picpus; the *porte cochère*, No. 62, marked the end of it. Towards the middle of this façade, the dust and ashes had whitened an old low arched door where the spiders made their webs and which was opened only for an hour or two on Sunday and on the rare occasions when the corpse of a nun was taken out of the convent. It was the public entrance of the church. The elbow of the gibbet was a square hall which served as pantry, and which the nuns called *the expense*. In the long arm were the cells of the mothers, sisters and novices. In the short arm were the kitchens, the refectory, lined with cells, and the church. Between the door, No. 62, and the corner of the closed alley Aumarais, was the school, which could not be seen from the outside. The rest of the trapezium formed the garden, which was much lower than the level of the Rue Polonceau, so that the walls were considerably higher on the inside than on the outside. The garden, which was slightly convex, had in the centre, on the top of a knoll, a beautiful fir, pointed and conical, from which parted, as from the centre of a buckler, four broad walks, and, arranged two by two between the broad walks, eight narrow ones, so that, if the enclosure had been circular, the geometrical plan of the walks would have resembled a cross placed over a wheel. The walks, all extending to the very irregular walls of the garden, were of unequal length. They were bordered with gooseberry bushes. At the further end of the garden a row of large poplars extended from the ruins of the old convent, which was at the corner of the Rue Droit Mur, to the house of the Little Convent, which was at the corner of the alley Aumarais. Before the Little Convent, was what was called the Little Garden. Add to this outline a courtyard, all manner of angles made by detached buildings, prison walls, no prospect and no neighbourhood, but the long black line of roofs which ran along the other side of the Rue Polonceau, and you can form a complete image of what was, forty-five years ago, the houses of the Bernardines of the Petit Picpus. This holy house had been built on the exact site of a famous tennis-court, which existed from the fourteenth to the sixteenth century, and which was called the *court of the eleven thousand devils*.

All these streets, moreover, were among the most ancient in Paris. These names, Droit Mur and Aumarais, are very old; the streets which bear them are much older still. The alley Aumarais was called the alley Maugout; the Rue Droit Mur was called the Rue des Eglantiers, for God opened the flowers before man cut stone.

9. *A century under a* guimpe

SINCE WE ARE DEALING with the details of what was formerly the convent of the Petit Picpus, and have dared to open a window upon that secluded asylum, the reader will pardon us another little digression, foreign to the object of this book, but characteristic and useful, as it teaches us that the cloister itself has its original characters.

There was in the Little Convent a centenarian who came from the Abbey of Fontevrault. Before the revolution she had even been in society. She talked much of M. de Miromesnil, keeper of the seals under Louis XVI, and of the lady of a President Duplat whom she had known very well. It was her pleasure and her vanity to bring forward these names on all occasions. She told wonders of the Abbey of Fontevrault, that it was like a city, and that there were streets within the convent.

She spoke with a Picardy accent which delighted the pupils. Every year she solemnly renewed her vows, and, at the moment of taking the oath, she would say to the priest: Monseigneur St Francis gave it to Monseigneur St Julian, Monseigneur St Julian gave it to Monseigneur St Eusebius, Monseigneur St Eusebius gave it to Monseigneur St Procopius, etc., etc.; so I give it to you, my father. And the pupils would laugh, not in their sleeves, but in their veils, joyous little stifled laughs which made the mothers frown.

At one time, the centenarian was telling stories. She said that *in her youth the Bernardines did not yield the precedence to the Mousquetaires.* It was a century which was speaking, but it was the eighteenth century. She told of the custom in Champagne and Burgundy before the revolution, of the four wines. When a great personage, a marshal of France, a prince, a duke or peer, passed through a city of Burgundy or Champagne, the corporation of the city waited on him, delivered an address, and presented him with four silver goblets in which were four different wines. Upon the first goblet he read this inscription: *Monkey wine,* upon the second: *lion wine*, upon the third: *sheep wine*, upon the fourth: *swine wine*. These four inscriptions expressed the four descending degrees of drunkenness: the first, that which enlivens; the second, that which irritates; the third, that which stupefies; finally the last, that which brutalises.

She had in a closet, under key, a mysterious object, which she cherished very highly. The rules of Fontevrault did not prohibit it. She would not show this object to anybody. She shut herself up, which her rules permitted, and hid herself whenever she wished to look at it. If she heard a step in the hall, she shut the closet as quick as she could with her old hands. As soon as anybody spoke to her about this, she was silent, although she was so fond of talking. The most curious were foiled by her silence, and the most persevering by her obstinacy. This also was a subject of comment for all who were idle or listless in the convent. What then could this thing be, so secret and so precious, which was the treasure of the centenarian? Doubtless, some sacred book, or some unique chaplet? or some proven relic? They lost themselves in conjecture. On the death of the poor old woman they ran to the closet sooner, perhaps, than was seemly, and opened it. The object of their curiosity was found under triple cloths, like a blessed patine. It was a Faenza plate, representing Loves in flight, pursued by apothecaries' boys, armed with enormous syringes. The pursuit is full of grimaces and comic postures. One of the charming little Loves is already spitted. He struggles, shakes his little wings, and still tries to fly away, but the lad capering about, laughs with a Satanic laughter. Moral – love conquered by cholic. This plate, very curious, moreover, and which had the honour, perhaps, of giving an idea to Molière, was still in existence in September 1845; it was for sale in a second-hand store in the Boulevard Beaumarchais.

This good old woman would receive no visit from the outside world, *because*, said she, *the locutory is too gloomy*.

10. *Origin of the Perpetual Adoration*

THAT ALMOST SEPULCHRAL locutory, of which we have endeavoured to give an idea, is an entirely local feature, which is not reproduced with the same severity in other convents. At the convent of the Rue du Temple in particular, which, indeed, was of another order, the black shutters were replaced by brown curtains, and the locutory itself was a nicely floored parlour, the windows of which were draped with white muslin, while the walls admitted a variety of pictures, a portrait of a Benedictine nun, with uncovered face, flower-pieces, and even a Turk's head.

It was in the garden of the convent of the Rue du Temple, that that horse-chestnut tree stood, which passed for the most beautiful and the largest in France, and which, among the good people of the eighteenth century, had the name of being *the father of all the horse-chestnuts in the kingdom*.

As we have said, this convent of the Temple was occupied by the Benedictines of the Perpetual Adoration, Benedictines quite distinct from those who spring from Citeaux. This order of the Perpetual Adoration is not very ancient, and does not date back more than two hundred years. In 1649, the Holy Sacrament was profaned twice, within a few days, in two churches in Paris, at Saint Sulpice, and at Saint Jean en Grève – a rare and terrible sacrilege, which shocked the whole city. The Prior Grand-vicar of Saint Germain des Prés ordained a solemn procession of all his clergy, in which the Papal Nuncio officiated. But this expiation was not sufficient for two noble women, Madame Courtin, Marquise de Boucs, and the Countess of Châteauvieux. This outrage, committed before the 'most august sacrament of the altar', although transient, did not pass away from these two holy souls, and it seemed to them that it could be atoned for only by a 'Perpetual Adoration' in some convent. They both, one in 1652, the other in 1653, made donations of considerable sums to Mother Catharine de Bar, surnamed of the Holy Sacrament, a Benedictine nun, to enable her to found, with that pious object, a monastery of the order of Saint Benedict; the first permission for this foundation was given to Mother Catharine de Bar, by M. de Metz, Abbé of Saint Germain, 'with the stipulation that no maiden shall be received unless she brings three hundred livres of income, which is six thousand livres of principal'. After the Abbé of Saint Germain, the king granted letters patent, and the whole, abbatial charter and letters royal, was confirmed in 1654, by the Chamber of Accounts and by the Parliament.

Such is the origin and the legal consecration of the establishment of Benedictines of the Perpetual Adoration of the Holy Sacrament at Paris. Their first convent was 'built new' in Rue Cassette with the money of Mesdames de Boucs and de Châteauvieux.

This order, as we see, is not to be confounded with the Benedictines called Cistercians. It sprang from the Abbé of Saint Germain des Prés, in the same manner as the Ladies of the Sacred Heart spring from the General of the Jesuits and the Sisters of Charity from the General of the Lazarists.

It is also entirely different from the Bernardines of the Petit Picpus, whose interior life we have been exhibiting. In 1657, Pope Alexander VII, by special bull, authorised the Bernardines of the Petit Picpus to practise the Perpetual Adoration like the Benedictines of the Holy Sacrament. But the two orders, none the less, remained distinct.

11. *End of the Petit Picpus*

FROM THE TIME of the restoration, the convent of the Petit Picpus had been dwindling away; this was a portion of the general death of the order, which, since the eighteenth century, has been going the way of all religious orders. Meditation is, as well as prayer, a necessity of humanity; but, like everything which the revolution has touched, it will transform itself, and, from being hostile to social progress, will become favourable to it.

The house of the Petit Picpus dwindled rapidly. In 1840, the little convent had disappeared; the school had disappeared. There were no longer either the old women, or the young girls; the former were dead, the latter had gone away. *Volaverunt.*

The rules of the Perpetual Adoration are so rigid that they inspire dismay; inclinations recoil, the order gets no recruits. In 1845, it still gathered here and there a few sister servants; but no nuns of the choir. Forty years ago there were nearly a hundred nuns, fifteen years ago there were only twenty-eight. How many are there today? In 1847 the prioress was young, a sign that the opportunity for choice was limited. She was not forty. As the number diminishes the fatigue increases; the service of each becomes more difficult, thenceforth they saw the moment approaching when there should be only a dozen sorrowful and bowed shoulders to bear the hard rules of Saint Benedict. The burden is inflexible, and remains the same for the few as for the many. It weighs down, it crushes. Thus they died. Since the author of this book lived in Paris, two have died. One was twenty-five, the other twenty-three. The latter might say with Julia Alpinula: *Hic jaceo, Vixi annos viginti et tres.*[61] It was on account of this decay that the convent abandoned the education of girls.

We could not pass by this extraordinary, unknown, obscure house without entering and leading in those who accompany us, and who listen as we relate, for the benefit of some, perhaps, the melancholy history of Jean Valjean. We have penetrated into that community full of its old practices which seem so novel today. It is the closed garden. *Hortus conclusus.* We have spoken of this singular place with minuteness, but with respect, as much at least as respect and minuteness are reconcilable.

We do not comprehend everything, but we insult nothing. We are equally distant from the hosannahs of Joseph de Maistre,[62] who goes so far as to sanctify the executioner, and the mockery of Voltaire, who goes so far as to rail at the crucifix.

Illogicality of Voltaire, be it said by the way; for Voltaire would have defended Jesus as he defended Calas, and, for those even who deny the superhuman incarnation, what does the crucifix represent? The assassinated sage.

In the nineteenth century the religious idea is undergoing a crisis. We are unlearning certain things, and we do well, provided that while unlearning one thing we are learning another. No vacuum in the human heart! Certain forms are torn down, and it is well that they should be, but on condition that they are followed by reconstructions.

In the meantime let us study the things which are no more. It is necessary to understand them, were it only to avoid them. The counterfeits of the past take assumed names, and are fond of calling themselves the future. That spectre, the past, not unfrequently falsifies its passport. Let us be ready for the snare. Let us beware. The past has a face, superstition, and a mask, hypocrisy. Let us denounce the face and tear off the mask.

As to convents, they present a complex question. A question of civilisation, which condemns them; a question of liberty, which protects them.

BOOK 7: A PARENTHESIS

1. *The convent as an abstract idea*

THIS BOOK is a drama the first character of which is the Infinite.

Man is the second.

This being the case, when a convent was found on our path, we were compelled to penetrate it. Why so? Because the convent, which is common to the East as well as to the West, to ancient as well as to modern times, to Paganism as well as to Buddhism, to Mahometanism as well as to Christianity, is one of the optical appliances turned by man upon the Infinite.

This is not the place for the development at length of certain ideas; however, while rigidly maintaining our reservations, our limits of expression, and even our impulses of indignation; whenever we meet with the Infinite in man, whether well or ill understood, we are seized with an involuntary feeling of respect. There in the synagogue, in the mosque, a hideous side that we detest, and in the pagoda and in the wigwam, a sublime aspect that we adore. What a subject of meditation for the mind, and what a limitless source of reverie is this reflection of God upon the human wall!

2. *The convent as a historical fact*

In the light of history, reason and truth, monastic life stands condemned.

Monasteries, when they are numerous in a country, are knots in the circulation; encumbrances, centres of indolence, where there should be centres of industry. Monastic communities are to the great social community what the ivy is to the oak, what the wart is to the human body. There prosperity and fatness are the impoverishment of the country. The monastic system, useful as it is in the dawn of civilisation, in effecting the abatement of brutality by the development of the spiritual, is injurious in the manhood of nations. Especially when it relaxes and enters upon its period of disorganisation, the period in which we now see it, does it become baneful, for every reason that made it salutary, in its period of purity.

These withdrawals into convents and monasteries have had their day. Cloisters, although beneficial in the first training of modern civilisation, cramped its growth, and are injurious to its development. Regarded as an institution, and as a method of culture for man, monasteries, good in the tenth century, were open to discussion in the fifteenth, and are detestable in the nineteenth. The leprosy of monasticism has gnawed, almost to a skeleton, two admirable nations, Italy and Spain, one the light, and the other the glory of Europe, for centuries; and, in our time, the cure of these two illustrious peoples is beginning, thanks only to the sound and vigorous hygiene of 1789.

The convent, the old style convent especially, such as it appeared on the threshold of this century, in Italy, Austria, and Spain, is one of the gloomiest concretions of the Middle Ages. The cloister, the cloister as there beheld, was the intersecting point of multiplied horrors. The Catholic cloister, properly so-called, is filled with the black effulgence of death.

The Spanish convent is dismal above all the rest. There, rise in the obscurity, beneath vaults filled with mist, beneath domes dim with thick shadow, massive Babel-like altars, lofty as cathedrals; there, hang by chains in the deep gloom, immense white emblems of the crucifixion; there, are extended, naked on the ebon wood, huge ivory images of Christ – more than bloody, bleeding – hideous and magnificent, their bones protruding from the elbows, their knee-pans disclosing the strained integuments, their wounds revealing the raw flesh – crowned with thorns of silver, nailed with nails of gold, with drops of blood in rubies on their brows, and tears of diamonds in their eyes. The diamonds and the rubies seem real moisture; and down below there, in the shadow, make veiled ones weep, whose loins are scratched and torn with haircloth, and scourges set thick with iron points, whose breasts are bruised with wicker pads, and whose knees are lacerated by the continual attitude of prayer; women who deem themselves wives; spectres that fancy themselves seraphim. Do these women think? No. Have they a will? No. Do they love? No. Do they live? No. Their nerves have become bone; their bones have become rock. Their veil is the enwoven night. Their breath, beneath that veil, is like some indescribable, tragic respiration of death itself. The abbess, a phantom, sanctifies and terrifies them. The immaculate is there, austere to behold. Such are the old convents of Spain – dens of terrible devotion, lairs inhabited by virgins, wild and savage places.

Catholic Spain was more Roman than Rome herself. The Spanish convent was the model of the Catholic convent. The air was redolent of the East. The archbishop, as officiating *kislaraga*[63] of heaven, locked in, and zealously watched this seraglio of souls set apart for God. The nun was the odalisque, the priest was the eunuch. The fervently devout were, in their dreams, the chosen ones, and were possessed of Christ. At night, the lovely naked youth descended from the cross, and became the rapture of the cell. Lofty walls guarded from all the distractions of real life the mystic Sultana, who had the Crucified for Sultan. A single glance without was an act of perfidy. The *in pace* took the place of the leather sack. What they threw into the sea in the East, they threw into the earth in the West. On either side, poor women wrung their hands; the waves to those – to these the pit; there the drowned and here the buried alive. Monstrous parallelism!

In our day, the champions of the Past, unable to deny these things, have adopted the alternative of smiling at them. It has become the fashion, a convenient and a strange one, to suppress the revelations of history, to invalidate the comments of philosophy, and to draw the pen across all unpleasant facts and all gloomy inquiries. '*Topics for declamation*,' throw in the skilful. '*Declamation*,' echo the silly. Jean Jacques, a declaimer; Diderot, a declaimer; Voltaire on Calas, Labarre, and Sirven, a declaimer! I forget who it is who has lately made out Tacitus, too, a declaimer, Nero a victim, and 'that poor Holophernes' a man really to be pitied.

Facts, however, are stubborn, and hard to baffle. The author of this book has seen, with his own eyes, about twenty miles from Brussels, a specimen of the Middle Ages, within everybody's reach, at the Abbey of Villars – the orifices of the secret dungeons in the middle of the meadow which was once the courtyard of the cloister, and, on the banks of the Dyle, four stone cells, half underground and half under water. These were *in pace*. Each of these dungeons has a remnant of an iron wicket, a closet, and a barred skylight, which, on the outside, is two feet above the surface of the river, and from the inside is six feet above the ground. Four feet in depth, the river flows along the outer face of the wall; the ground nearby is constantly wet.

This saturated soil was the only bed of the *in pace* occupant. In one of these dungeons there remains the stump of an iron collar fixed in the wall; in another may be seen a kind of square box, formed of four slabs of granite, too short for a human being to lie down in, too low to stand in erect. Now, in this was placed a creature like ourselves, and then a lid of stone was closed above her head. There it is. You can see it; you can touch it. These *in pace*; these dungeons; these iron hinges; these metal collars; this lofty skylight, on a level with which the river runs; this box of stone, covered by its lid of granite, like a sepulchre, with this difference, that it shut in the living and not the dead; this soil of mud, this cesspool; these oozing walls. Oh! what declaimers!

3. *Upon what conditions we can respect the past*

MONASTICISM such as it was in Spain, and such as it is in Tibet, is for civilisation a kind of consumption. It stops life short. It, in one word, depopulates. Monastic incarceration is castration. In Europe, it has been a scourge. Add to that, the violence so often done to conscience; the ecclesiastical calling so frequently compulsory; the feudal system leaning on the cloister; primogeniture emptying into the monastery the surplus of the family; the ferocious cruelties which we have just described; the *in pace*; mouths closed, brains walled-up, so many hapless intellects incarcerated in the dungeons of eternal vows; the assumption of the gown, the burial of souls alive. Add these individual torments to the national degradation, and, whoever you may be, you will find yourself shuddering at the sight of the frock and the veil, those two winding sheets of human invention.

However, on certain points and in certain places, in spite of philosophy, and in spite of progress, the monastic spirit perseveres in the full blaze of the nineteenth century, and a singular revival of asceticism, at this very moment, amazes the civilised world. The persistance of superannuated institutions in striving to perpetuate themselves is like the obstinacy of a rancid odour clinging to the hair; the pretension of spoiled fish that insists on being eaten, the tenacious folly of a child's garment trying to clothe a man, or the tenderness of a corpse returning to embrace the living.

'Ingrates!' exclaims the garment. 'I shielded you in weakness. Why do you reject me now?' 'I come from the depths of the sea,' says the fish; 'I was once a rose,' cries the odour; 'I loved you,' murmurs the corpse; 'I civilised you,' says the convent.

To this there is but one reply; 'In the past.'[64]

To dream of the indefinite prolongation of things dead and the government of mankind by embalming; to restore dilapidated dogmas, regild the shrines, replaster the cloisters, reconsecrate the reliquaries, revamp old superstitions, replenish fading fanaticism, put new handles in worn-out sprinkling brushes, reconstitute monasticism; to believe in the salvation of society by the multiplication of parasites; to foist the past upon the present, all this seems strange. There are, however, advocates for such theories as these. These theorists, men of mind too, in other things, have a very simple process; they apply to the past a coating of what they term divine right, respect for our forefathers, time-honoured authority, sacred tradition, legitimacy; and they go about, shouting, 'Here! take this, good people!' This kind of logic was familiar to the ancients; their soothsayers practised it. Rubbing over a black heifer with chalk, they would exclaim 'She is white.' *Bos cretatus.*

As for ourselves, we distribute our respect, here and there, and spare the past entirely, provided it will but consent to be dead. But, if it insist upon being alive, we attack it and endeavour to kill it.

Superstitions, bigotries, hypocrisies, prejudices, these phantoms, phantoms though they be, are tenacious of life; they have teeth and nails in their shadowy substance, and we must grapple with them, body to body, and make war upon them and that, too, without cessation; for it is one of the fatalities of humanity to be condemned to eternal struggle with phantoms. A shadow is hard to seize by the throat and dash upon the ground.

A convent in France, in the high noon of the nineteenth century, is a college of owls confronting the day. A cloister in the open act of asceticism in the full face of the city, of '89, of 1830 and of 1848, Rome blooming forth in Paris, is an anachronism. In ordinary times, to disperse an anachronism and cause it to vanish, one has only to make it spell the year of our Lord. But, we do not live in ordinary times.

Let us attack, then.

Let us attack, but let us distinguish. The characteristic of truth is never to run into excess. What need has she of exaggeration? Some things must be destroyed, and some things must be merely cleared up and investigated. What power there is in a courteous and serious examination! Let us not therefore carry flame where light alone will suffice.

Well, then assuming that we are in the nineteenth century, we are opposed, as a general proposition, and in every nation, in Asia as well as in Europe, in Judea as well as in Turkey, to ascetic seclusion in monasteries. He who says 'convent' says 'marsh'. Their putrescence is apparent, their stagnation is baleful, their fermentation fevers and infects the nations, and their increase becomes an Egyptian plague. We cannot, without a shudder, think of those countries where Fakirs, Bonzes, Santons, Caloyers, Marabouts and Talapoins multiply in swarms, like vermin.

Having said this much, the religious question still remains. This question has some mysterious aspects, and we must ask leave to look it steadily in the face.

4. The convent viewed in the light of principle

MEN COME TOGETHER and live in common. By what right? By virtue of the right of association.

They shut themselves up. By what right? By virtue of the right every man has to open or to shut his door.

They do not go out. By what right? By virtue of the right to go and come which implies the right to stay at home.

And what are they doing there, at home?

They speak in low tones; they keep their eyes fixed on the ground; they work. They give up the world, cities, sensual enjoyments, pleasures, vanities, pride, interest. They go clad in coarse woollen or coarse linen. Not one of them possesses any property whatever. Upon entering, he who was rich becomes poor. What he had, he gives to all. He who was what is called a nobleman, a man of rank, a lord, is the equal of him who was a peasant. The cell is the same for all. All undergo the same tonsure, wear the same frock, eat the same black bread, sleep on the same straw, and die on the same ashes. The same sack-cloth is on every back, the same rope about every waist. If it be the rule to go bare-footed, all go with naked feet. There may be a prince among them; the prince is a shadow like all the rest. Titles there are none. Family names even have disappeared. They answer only to Christian names. All are bowed beneath the equality of their baptismal names. They have dissolved the family of the flesh, and have formed, in their community, the family of the spirit. They have no other relatives than all mankind. They succour the poor, they tend the sick. They choose out those whom they are to obey, and they address one another by the title: 'Brother!'

You stop me, exclaiming: 'But, that is the ideal monastery!'

It is enough that it is a possible monastery, for me to take it into consideration.

Hence it is that, in the preceding book, I spoke of a convent with respect. The Middle Ages aside, Asia aside, and the historical and political question reserved, in the purely philosophical point of view, beyond the necessities of militant polemics, on condition that the monastery be absolutely voluntary and contain none but willing devotees, I should always look upon the monastic community with a certain serious, and, in some respects, deferential attention. Where community exists, there likewise exists the true body politic, and where the latter is, there too is justice. The monastery is the product of the formula: 'Equality, Fraternity.' Oh! how great is liberty! And how glorious the transfiguration! Liberty suffices to transform the monastery into a republic!

Let us proceed.

These men or women who live within those four walls, and dress in haircloth, are equal in condition and call each other brother and sister. It is well, but do they do aught else?

Yes.

What?

They gaze into the gloom, they kneel, and they join their hands.

What does that mean?

5. *Prayer*

THEY PRAY.

To whom?

To God.

Pray to God, what is meant by that?

Is there an infinite outside of us? Is this infinite, one, inherent, permanent; necessarily substantial, because it is infinite, and because, if matter were wanting to it, it would in that respect be limited; necessarily intelligent, because it is infinite, and because, if it lacked intelligence, it would be to that extent, finite? Does this infinite awaken in us the idea of essence, while we are able to attribute to ourselves the idea of existence only? In other words, is it not the absolute of which we are the relative?

At the same time, while there is an infinite outside of us, is there not an infinite within us? These two infinites (fearful plural!) do they not rest superposed on one another? Does not the second infinite underlie the first, so to speak? Is it not the mirror, the reflection, the echo of the first, an abyss concentric with another abyss? Is this second infinite, intelligent also? Does it think? Does it love? Does it will? If the two infinites be intelligent, each one of them has a will principle, and there is a 'me' in the infinite above, as there is a 'me' in the infinite below. The 'me' below is the soul; the 'me' above is God.

To place, by process of thought, the infinite below in contact with the infinite above, is called 'prayer'.

Let us not take anything away from the human mind; suppression is evil. We must reform and transform. Certain faculties of man are directed towards the Unknown; thought, meditation, prayer. The Unknown is an ocean. What is conscience? It is the compass of the Unknown. Thought, meditation, prayer, these are the great, mysterious pointings of the needle. Let us respect them. Whither tend these majestic irradiations of the soul? into the shadow, that is, towards the light.

The grandeur of democracy is that it denies nothing and renounces nothing of humanity. Close by the rights of Man, side by side with them, at least, are the rights of the Soul.

To crush out fanaticisms and revere the Infinite, such is the law. Let us not confine ourselves to falling prostrate beneath the tree of Creation and contemplating its vast ramifications full of stars. We have a duty to perform, to cultivate the human soul, to defend mystery against miracle, to adore the incomprehensible and reject the absurd; to admit nothing that is inexplicable excepting what is necessary, to purify faith and obliterate superstition from the face of religion, to remove the vermin from the garden of God.

6. *Absolute excellence of prayer*

As to methods of prayer, all are good, if they be but sincere. Turn your book over and be in the infinite.

There is, we are aware, a philosophy that denies the infinite. There is also a philosophy, classed pathologically, which denies the sun; this philosophy is called blindness.

To set up a sense we lack as a source of truth, is a fine piece of blind man's assurance.

And the rarity of it consists in the haughty air of superiority and compassion which is assumed towards the philosophy that sees God, by this philosophy that has to grope its way. It makes one think of a mole exclaiming: 'How they excite my pity with their prate about a sun!'

There are, we know, illustrious and mighty atheists. These men, in fact, led round again towards truth by their very power, are not absolutely sure of being atheists, with them, the matter is nothing but a question of definitions, and, at all events, if they do not believe in God, being great minds, they prove God.

We hail, in them, philosophers, while, at the same time, inexorably disputing their philosophy.

But, let us proceed.

An admirable thing, too, is the facility of settling everything to one's satisfaction with words. A metaphysical school at the North,[65] slightly impregnated with the fogs, has imagined that it effected a revolution in the human understanding by substituting for the word 'Force' the word 'Will'.

To say, 'the plant wills', instead of 'the plant grows', would be indeed pregnant with meaning if you were to add, 'the universe wills'. Why? Because this would flow from it: the plant wills, then it has a 'me', the universe wills, then it has a God.

To us, however, who, in direct opposition to this school, reject nothing *a priori*, a will in the plant, which is accepted by this school, appears more difficult to admit, than a will in the universe, which it denies.

To deny the will of the infinite, that is to say God, can be done only on condition of denying the infinite itself. We have demonstrated that.

Denial of the infinite leads directly to nihilism. Everything becomes 'a conception of the mind'.

With nihilism no discussion is possible. For the logical nihilist doubts the existence of his interlocutor, and is not quite sure that he exists himself.

From his point of view it is possible that he may be to himself only a 'conception of his mind'.

However, he does not perceive that all he has denied he admits in a mass by merely pronouncing the word 'mind.'

To sum up, no path is left open for thought by a philosophy that makes everything come to but one conclusion, the monosyllable 'No.'

To 'No,' there is but one reply: 'Yes'.

Nihilism has no scope. There is no nothing. Zero does not exist. Everything is something. Nothing is nothing.

Man lives by affirmation even more than he does by bread.

To behold and to show forth, even these will not suffice. Philosophy should be an energy; it should find its aim and its effect in the amelioration of mankind. Socrates should enter into Adam and produce Marcus Aurelius – in other words, bring forth from the man of enjoyment, the man of wisdom – and change Eden into the Lyceum. Science should be a cordial. Enjoyment! What wretched aim, and what pitiful ambition! The brute enjoys. Thought, this is the true triumph of the soul. To proffer thought to the thirst of men, to give to all, as an elixir, the idea of God, to cause conscience and science to fraternise in them, and to make them good men by this mysterious confrontation – such is the province of true philosophy. Morality is truth in full bloom. Contemplation leads to action. The absolute should be practical. The ideal must be made air and food and drink to the human mind. It is the ideal which has the right to say: *Take of it, this is my flesh, this is my blood.* Wisdom is a sacred communion. It is upon that condition that it ceases to be a sterile love of science, and becomes the one and supreme method by which to rally humanity; from philosophy it is promoted to religion.

Philosophy should not be a mere watch-tower, built upon mystery, from which to gaze at ease upon it, with no other result than to be a convenience for the curious.

For ourselves, postponing the development of our thought to some other occasion, we will only say that we do not comprehend either man as a starting-point, or progress as the goal, without those two forces which are the two great motors, faith and love.

Progress is the aim, the ideal is the model.

What is the ideal? It is God.

Ideal, absolute, perfection, the infinite – these are identical words.

7. *Precautions to be taken in censure*

HISTORY AND PHILOSOPHY have eternal duties, which are, at the same time, simple duties – to oppose Caiaphas as bishop, Draco as judge, Trimalcion as legislator, and Tiberius as emperor. This is clear, direct, and limpid, and presents no obscurity. But the right to live apart, even with its inconveniences and abuses, must be verified and dealt with carefully. The life of the cenobite is a human problem.

When we speak of convents, those seats of error but of innocence, of mistaken views but of good intentions, of ignorance but of devotion, of torment but of martyrdom, we must nearly always have 'Yes' and 'No' upon our lips.

A convent is a contradiction, – its object salvation, its means self-sacrifice. The convent is supreme egotism resulting in supreme self-denial.

'Abdicate that you may reign' seems to be the device of monasticism.

In the cloister they suffer that they may enjoy – they draw a bill of exchange on death – they discount the celestial splendour in terrestrial night. In the cloister, hell is accepted as the charge made in advance on the future inheritance of heaven.

The assumption of the veil or the frock is a suicide reimbursed by an eternity.

It seems to us that, in treating such a subject, raillery would be quite out of place. Everything relating to it is serious, the good as well as the evil.

The good man knits his brows, but never smiles with the bad man's smile. We can understand anger but not malignity.

8. *Faith – Law*

A FEW WORDS more.

We blame the Church when it is saturated with intrigues; we despise the spiritual when it is harshly austere to the temporal; but we honour everywhere, the thoughtful man.

We bow to the man who kneels.

A faith is a necessity to man. Woe to him who believes nothing.

A man is not idle, because he is absorbed in thought. There is a visible labour and there is an invisible labour.

To meditate is to labour; to think is to act.

Folded arms work, closed hands perform, a gaze fixed on heaven is a toil.

Thales remained motionless for four years. He founded philosophy.

In our eyes, cenobites are not idlers, nor is the recluse a sluggard.

To think of the Gloom is a serious thing.

Without at all invalidating what we have just said, we believe that a perpetual remembrance of the tomb is proper for the living. On this point, the priest and the philosopher agree: *We must die.* The Abbé of La Trappe answers Horace.

To mingle with one's life a certain presence of the sepulchre is the law of the wise man, and it is the law of the ascetic. In this relation, the ascetic and the sage tend towards a common centre.

There is a material advancement; we desire it. There is, also, a moral grandeur; we hold fast to it.

Unreflecting, headlong minds say:

'Of what use are those motionless figures by the side of mystery? What purpose do they serve? What do they effect?'

Alas! in the presence of that obscurity which surrounds us and awaits us, not knowing what the vast dispersion of all things will do with us, we answer: There is, perhaps, no work more sublime than that which is accomplished by these souls; and we add, There is no labour, perhaps, more useful.

Those who pray always are necessary to those who never pray.

In our view, the whole question is in the amount of thought that is mingled with prayer.

Leibnitz, praying, is something grand; Voltaire, worshipping, is something beautiful. *Deo erexit Voltaire.*[66]

We are for religion against the religions.

We are of those who believe in the pitifulness of orisons, and in the sublimity of prayer.

Besides, in this moment through which we are passing, a moment which happily will not leave its stamp upon the nineteenth century; in this hour which finds so many with their brows abased so low and their souls so little uplifted, among so many of the living whose motto is happiness, and who are occupied with the brief, mis-shapen things of matter, whoever is self-exiled seems venerable to us.[67] The monastery is a renunciation. Self-sacrifice, even when misdirected, is still self-sacrifice. To assume as duty an uninviting error has its peculiar grandeur.

Considered in itself, ideally, and holding it up to truth, until it is impartially and exhaustively examined in all its aspects, the monastery, and particularly the convent – for woman suffers most under our system of society, and in this exile of the cloister there is an element of protest – the convent, we repeat, has, unquestionably, a certain majesty.

This monastic existence, austere and gloomy as it is, of which we have delineated a few characteristics, is not life, is not liberty: for it is not the grave, for it is not completion: it is that singular place, from which, as from the summit of a lofty mountain, we perceive, on one side, the abyss in which we are, and, on the other, the abyss wherein we are to be: it is a narrow and misty boundary, that separates two worlds, at once illuminated and obscured by both, where the enfeebled ray of life commingles with the uncertain ray of death; it is the twilight of the tomb.

For ourselves, we, who do not believe what these women believe, but live, like them, by faith, never could look without a species of tender and religious awe, a kind of pity full of envy, upon those devoted beings, trembling yet confident – those humble yet august souls, who dare to live upon the very confines of the great mystery, waiting between the world closed to them and heaven not yet opened; turned towards the daylight not yet seen, with only the happiness of thinking that they know where it is; their aspirations directed towards the abyss and the unknown, their gaze fixed on the motionless gloom, kneeling, dismayed, stupefied, shuddering, and half borne away at certain times by the deep pulsations of Eternity.

BOOK 8: CEMETRIES TAKE WHAT IS GIVEN THEM

1. *Which treats of the manner of entering the convent*

INTO THIS HOUSE it was that Jean Valjean had, as Fauchelevent said, 'fallen from heaven.'

He had crossed the garden wall at the corner of the Rue Polonceau. That angels' hymn which he had heard in the middle of the night, was the nuns chanting matins; that hall of which he had caught a glimpse in the obscurity, was the chapel; that phantom which he had seen extended on the floor was the sister performing the reparation; that bell the sound of which had so strangely surprised him was the gardener's bell fastened to old Fauchelevent's knee.

When Cosette had been put to bed, Jean Valjean and Fauchelevent had, as we have seen, taken a glass of wine and a piece of cheese before a blazing fire; then, the only bed in the shanty being occupied by Cosette, they had thrown themselves each upon a bundle of straw. Before closing his eyes, Jean Valjean had said: 'Henceforth I must remain here.' These words were chasing one another through Fauchelevent's head the whole night.

To tell the truth, neither of them had slept.

Jean Valjean, feeling that he was discovered and Javert was upon his track, knew full well that he and Cosette were lost should they return into the city. Since the new blast which had burst upon him, had thrown him into this cloister, Jean Valjean had but one thought, to remain there. Now, for one in his unfortunate position, this convent was at once the safest and the most dangerous place; the most dangerous, for, no man being allowed to enter, if he should be discovered, it was a flagrant crime, and Jean Valjean would take but one step from the convent to prison; the safest, for if he succeeded in getting permission to remain, who would come there to look for him? To live in an impossible place; that would be safety.

For his part, Fauchelevent was racking his brains. He began by deciding that he was utterly bewildered. How did Monsieur Madeleine come there, with such walls! The walls of a cloister are not so easily crossed. How did he happen to be with a child? A man does not scale a steep wall with a child in his arms. Who was this child? Where did they both come from? Since Fauchelevent had been in the convent, he had not heard a word from M— sur M—, and he knew nothing of what had taken place. Father Madeleine wore that air which discourages questions; and moreover Fauchelevent said to himself: 'One does not question a saint.' To him Monsieur Madeleine had preserved all his prestige. From some words that escaped from Jean Valjean, however, the gardener thought he might conclude that Monsieur Madeleine had probably failed on account of the hard times, and that he was pursued by his creditors; or it might be that he was compromised in some political affair and was concealing himself; which did not at all displease Fauchelevent, who, like many of our peasants of the north, had an old Bonapartist heart. Being in concealment, Monsieur Madeleine had taken the convent for an asylum, and it was natural that he should wish to remain there. But the mystery to which Fauchelevent constantly returned and over which he was racking his brains was, that Monsieur Madeleine should be there, and that this little girl should be with him. Fauchelevent saw them, touched them, spoke to them, and yet did not believe it. An incomprehensibility had made its way into Fauchelevent's hut. Fauchelevent was groping amid conjectures, but saw nothing clearly except this: Monsieur Madeleine has saved my life. This single certainty was sufficient, and determined him. He said aside to himself: It is my turn now. He added in his conscience: Monsieur Madeleine did not deliberate so long when the question was about squeezing himself under the wagon to draw me out. He decided that he would save Monsieur Madeleine.

He however put several questions to himself and made several answers: 'After what he has done for me, if he were a thief, would I save him? just the same. If he were an assassin, would I save him? just the same. Since he is a saint, shall I save him? just the same.'

But to have him remain in the convent, what a problem was that! Before that almost chimerical attempt, Fauchelevent did not recoil; this poor Picardy peasant, with no other ladder than his devotion, his goodwill, a little of that old country cunning, engaged for once in the service of a generous intention, undertook to scale the impossibilities of the cloister and the craggy escarpments of the rules of St Benedict. Fauchelevent was an old man who had been selfish throughout his life, and who, near the end of his days, crippled, infirm, having no interest longer in the world, found it sweet to be grateful, and seeing a virtuous action to be done, threw himself into it like a man who, at the moment of death, finding at hand a glass of some good wine which he had never tasted, should drink it greedily. We might add that the air which he had been breathing now for several years in this convent had destroyed his personality, and had at last rendered some good action necessary to him.

He formed his resolution then: to devote himself to Monsieur Madeleine.

We have just described him as a *poor Picardy peasant*. The description is true, but incomplete. At the point of this story at which we now are, a closer acquaintance with Fauchelevent becomes necessary. He was a peasant, but he had been a notary, which added craft to his cunning, and penetration to his simplicity. Having, from various causes, failed in his business, from a notary he had fallen to a cartman and labourer. But, in spite of the oaths and blows which seem necessary with horses, he had retained something of the notary. He had some natural wit; he said neither I is nor I has; he could carry on a conversation, a rare thing in a village; and the other peasants said of him: he talks almost like a gentleman. Fauchelevent belonged in fact to that class which the flippant and impertinent vocabulary of the last century termed: *half-yeoman, half-clown;* and which the metaphors falling from the castle to the hovel, label in the distribution of the commonalty: *half-rustic, half-citizen, pepper-and-salt*. Fauchelevent, although sorely tried and sorely used by Fortune; a sort of poor old soul worn threadbare, was nevertheless an impulsive man, and had a very willing heart; a precious quality, which prevents one from ever being wicked. His faults and his vices, for such he had, were superficial; and finally, his physiognomy was one of those which attract the observer. That old face had none of those ugly wrinkles in the upper part of the forehead which indicate wickedness or stupidity.

At daybreak, having dreamed enormously, old Fauchelevent opened his eyes, and saw Monsieur Madeleine, who, seated upon his bunch of straw, was looking at Cosette as she slept. Fauchelevent half arose, and said:

'Now that you are here, how are you going to manage to come in?'

This question summed up the situation, and wakened Jean Valjean from his reverie.

The two men took counsel.

'To begin with,' said Fauchelevent, 'you will not set foot outside of this room, neither the little girl nor you. One step in the garden, we are ruined.'

'That is true.'

'Monsieur Madeleine,' resumed Fauchelevent, 'you have arrived at a very good time; I mean to say very bad; there is one of these ladies dangerously sick. On that account they do not look this way much. She must be dying. They are saying the forty-hour prayers. The whole community is in derangement. That takes up their attention. She who is about departing is a saint. In fact, we are all saints here; all the difference between them and me is, that they say: our cell, and I say: my shanty. They are going to have the orison for the dying, and then the orison for the dead. For today we shall be quiet here; and I do not answer for tomorrow.'

'However,' observed Jean Valjean, 'this shanty is under the corner of the wall; it is hidden by a sort of ruin; there are trees; they cannot see it from the convent.'

'And I add, that the nuns never come near it.'

'Well?' said Jean Valjean.

The interrogation point which followed that well, meant: it seems to me that we can remain here concealed. This interrogation point Fauchelevent answered:

'There are the little girls.'

'What little girls?' asked Jean Valjean.

As Fauchelevent opened his mouth to explain the words he had just uttered, a single stroke of a bell was heard.

'The nun is dead,' said he. 'There is the knell.'

And he motioned to Jean Valjean to listen.

The bell sounded a second time.

'It is the knell, Monsieur Madeleine. The bell will strike every minute, for twenty-four hours, until the body goes out of the church. You see they play. In their recreations, if a ball roll here, that is enough for them to come after it, in spite of the rules, and rummage all about here. Those cherubs are little devils.'

'Who?' asked Jean Valjean.

'The little girls. You would be found out very soon. They would cry, "What! a man!" But there is no danger today. There will be no recreation. The day will be all prayers. You hear the bell. As I told you, a stroke every minute. It is the knell.'

'I understand, Father Fauchelevent. There are boarding scholars.'

And Jean Valjean thought within himself:

'Here, then, Cosette can be educated, too.'

Fauchelevent exclaimed:

'Zounds! they are the little girls for you! And how they would scream at sight of you! and how they would run! Here, to be a man, is to have the plague. You see how they fasten a bell to my leg, as they would to a wild beast.'

Jean Valjean was studying more and more deeply. 'The convent would save us,' murmured he. Then he raised his voice:

'Yes, the difficulty is in remaining.'

'No,' said Fauchelevent, 'it is to get out.'

Jean Valjean felt his blood run cold.

'To get out?'

'Yes, Monsieur Madeleine, in order to come in, it is necessary that you should get out.'

And, after waiting for a sound from the tolling bell to die away, Fauchelevent pursued:

'It would not do to have you found here like this. Whence do you come? for me you have fallen from heaven, because I know you; but for the nuns, you must come in at the door.'

Suddenly they heard a complicated ringing upon another bell.

'Oh!' said Fauchelevent, 'that is the ring for the mothers. They are going to the chapter. They always hold a chapter when anybody dies. She died at daybreak. It is usually at daybreak that people die. But cannot you go out the way you came in? Let us see; this is not to question you, but where did you come in?'

Jean Valjean became pale; the bare idea of climbing down again into that formidable street, made him shudder. Make your way out of a forest full of tigers, and when out, fancy yourself advised by a friend to return. Jean Valjean imagined all the police still swarming in the quarter, officers on the watch, sentries everywhere, frightful fists stretched out towards his collar, Javert, perhaps, at the corner of the square.

'Impossible,' said he. 'Father Fauchelevent, let it go that I fell from on high.'

'Ah! I believe it, I believe it,' replied Fauchelevent. 'You have no need to tell me so. God must have taken you into his hand, to have a close look at you, and then put you down. Only he meant to put you into a monastery; he made a mistake. Hark! another ring; that is to warn the porter to go and notify the municipality, so that they may go and notify the death-physician, so that he may come and see that there is really a dead woman. All that is the ceremony of dying. These good ladies do not like this visit very much. A physician believes in nothing. He lifts the veil. He even lifts something else, sometimes. How soon they have notified the inspector, this time! What can be the matter? Your little one is asleep yet. What is her name?'

'Cosette.'

'She is your girl? that is to say: you should be her grandfather?'

'Yes.'

'For her, to get out will be easy. I have my door, which opens into the court. I knock; the porter opens. I have my basket on my back; the little girl is inside; I go out. Father Fauchelevent goes out with his basket – that is all simple. You will tell the little girl to keep very still. She will be under cover. I will leave her as soon as I can, with a good old friend of mine, a fruiteress, in the Rue du Chemin Vert, who is deaf, and who has a little bed. I will scream into the fruiteress's ear that she is my niece, and she must keep her for me till tomorrow. Then the little girl will come back with you; for I shall bring you back. It must be done. But how are you going to manage to get out?'

Jean Valjean shook his head.

'Let nobody see me, that is all, Father Fauchelevent. Find some means to get me out, like Cosette, in a basket, and under cover.'

Fauchelevent scratched the tip of his ear with the middle finger of his left hand – a sign of serious embarrassment.

A third ring made a diversion.

'That is the death-physician going away,' said Fauchelevent. 'He has looked, and said she is dead; it is right. When the inspector has viséd the passport for paradise, the undertaker sends a coffin. If it is a mother, the mothers lay her out; if it is a sister, the sisters lay her out. After which, I nail it up. That's a part of my gardening. A gardener is something of a gravedigger. They put her in a low room in the church which communicates with the street, and where no man can enter except the death-physician. I do not count the bearers and myself for men. In that room I nail the coffin. The bearers come and take her, and whip-up, driver: that is the way they go to heaven. They bring in a box with nothing in it, they carry it away with something inside. That is what an interment is. *De profundis.*'

A ray of the rising sun beamed upon the face of the sleeping Cosette, who half-opened her mouth dreamily, seeming like an angel drinking in the light. Jean Valjean was looking at her. He no longer heard Fauchelevent.

Not being heard is no reason for silence. The brave old gardener quietly continued his garrulous rehearsal.

'The grave is at the Vaugirard cemetery. They pretend that this Vaugirard cemetery is going to be suppressed. It is an ancient cemetery, which is not according to the regulations, which does not wear the uniform, and which is going to be retired. I am sorry for it, for it is convenient. I have a friend there – Father Mestienne, the gravedigger. The nuns here have the privilege of being carried to that cemetery at nightfall. There is an order of the Préfecture, expressly for them. But what events since yesterday? Mother Crucifixion is dead, and Father Madeleine – '

'Is buried,' said Jean Valjean, sadly smiling.

Fauchelevent echoed the word.

'Really, if you were here for good, it would be a genuine burial.'

A fourth time the bell rang out. Fauchelevent quickly took down the knee-piece and bell from the nail, and buckled it on his knee.

'This time, it is for me. The mother prioress wants me. Well! I am pricking myself with the tongue of my buckle. Monsieur Madeleine, do not stir, but wait for me. There is something new. If you are hungry, there is the wine, and bread and cheese.'

And he went out of the hut, saying: 'I am coming, I am coming.'

Jean Valjean saw him hasten across the garden, as fast as his crooked leg would let him, with side glances at his melons the while.

In less than ten minutes, Father Fauchelevent, whose bell put the nuns to flight as he went along, rapped softly at a door, and a gentle voice answered – *Forever, Forever!* that is to say, *Come in.*

This door was that of the parlour allotted to the gardener, for use when it was necessary to communicate with him. This parlour was near the hall of the chapter. The prioress, seated in the only chair in the parlour, was waiting for Fauchelevent.

2. *Fauchelevent facing the difficulty*

A SERIOUS and troubled bearing is peculiar, on critical occasions, to certain characters and certain professions, especially priests and monastics. At the moment when Fauchelevent entered, this double sign of preoccupation marked the countenance of the prioress, the charming and learned Mademoiselle de Blemeur, Mother Innocent, who was ordinarily cheerful.

The gardener made a timid bow, and stopped at the threshold of the cell. The prioress, who was saying her rosary, raised her eyes and said:

'Ah! it is you, Father Fauvent.'

This abbreviation had been adopted in the convent.

Fauchelevent again began his bow.

'Father Fauvent, I have called you.'

'I am here, reverend mother.'

'I wish to speak to you.'

'And I, for my part,' said Fauchelevent, with a boldness at which he was alarmed himself, 'I have something to say to the most reverend mother.'

The prioress looked at him.

'Ah, you have a communication to make to me.'

'A petition!'

'Well, what is it?'

Goodman Fauchelevent, ex-notary, belonged to that class of peasants who are never disconcerted. A certain combination of ignorance and skill is very effective; you do not suspect it, and you accede to it. Within little more than two years that he had lived in the convent, Fauchelevent had achieved a success in the community. Always alone, and even while attending to his garden, he had hardly anything to do but to be curious. Being, as he was, at a distance from all these veiled women, going to and fro, he saw before him hardly more than a fluttering of shadows. By dint of attention and penetration, he had succeeded in clothing all these phantoms with flesh, and these dead were alive to him. He was like a deaf man whose sight is extended, and like a blind man whose hearing is sharpened. He had applied himself to unravelling the meaning of the various rings, and had made them out; so that in this enigmatic and taciturn cloister, nothing was hidden from him; this sphynx blabbed all her secrets in his ear. Fauchelevent, knowing everything, concealed everything. That was his art. The whole convent thought him stupid – a great merit in religion. The mothers prized Fauchelevent. He was a rare mute. He inspired confidence. Moreover, he was regular in his habits, and never went out except when it was clearly necessary on account of the orchard and the garden. This discretion in his conduct was counted to his credit. He had, nevertheless, learned the secrets of two men; the porter of the convent, who knew the peculiarities of the parlour, and the gravedigger of the cemetery, who knew the singularities of burial: in this manner, he had a double-light in regard to these nuns – one upon their life, the other upon their death. But he did not abuse it. The congregation thought much of him, old, lame, seeing nothing, probably a little deaf – how many good qualities! It would have been difficult to replace him.

The goodman, with the assurance of one who feels that he is appreciated, began before the reverend prioress a rustic harangue, quite diffuse and very profound. He spoke at length of his age, his infirmities, of the weight of years henceforth doubly heavy upon him, of the growing demands of his work, of the size of the garden, of the nights to be spent, like last night for example, when he had to put awnings over the melons on account of the moon; and he finally ended with this: 'that he had a brother – (the prioress gave a start) – a brother not young – (second start of the prioress, but a reassured start) – that if it was desired, this brother could come and live with him and help him; that he was an excellent gardener; that the community would get good services from him, better than his own; that, otherwise, if his brother were not admitted, as he, the oldest, felt that he was broken down, and unequal to the labour, he would be obliged to leave, though with much regret; and that his brother had a little girl that he would bring with him, who would be reared under God in the house, and who, perhaps, – who knows? – would someday become a nun.

When he had finished, the prioress stopped the sliding of her rosary through her fingers, and said:

'Can you, between now and night, procure a strong iron bar?'

'For what work?'

'To be used as a lever?'

'Yes, reverend mother,' answered Fauchelevent.

The prioress, without adding a word, arose, and went into the next room, which was the hall of the chapter, where the vocal mothers were probably assembled: Fauchelevent remained alone.

3. *Mother Innocent*

ABOUT A quarter of an hour elapsed. The prioress returned and resumed her seat. Both seemed preoccupied. We report as well as we can the dialogue that followed.

'Father Fauvent?'

'Reverend mother?'

'You are familiar with the chapel?'

'I have a little box there to go to mass, and the offices.'

'And you have been in the choir about your work?'

'Two or three times.'

'A stone is to be raised.'

'Heavy?'

'The slab of the pavement at the side of the altar.'

'The stone that covers the vault?'

'Yes.'

'That is a piece of work where it would be well to have two men.'

'Mother Ascension, who is as strong as a man, will help you.'

'A woman is never a man.'

'We have only a woman to help you. Everybody does what he can. Because Dom Mabillon gives four hundred and seventeen epistles of St Bernard, and Merlonus Horstius gives only three hundred and sixty-seven, I do not despise Merlonus Horstius.'

'Nor I either.'

'Merit consists in work according to our strength. A cloister is not a shipyard.'

'And a woman is not a man. My brother is very strong.'

'And then you will have a lever.'

'That is the only kind of key that fits that kind of door.'

'There is a ring in the stone.'

'I will pass the lever through it.'

'And the stone is arranged to turn on a pivot.'

'Very well, reverend mother, I will open the vault.'

'And the four mother choristers will assist you.'

'And when the vault is opened?'

'It must be shut again.'

'Is that all?'

'No.'

'Give me your orders, most reverend mother.'

'Fauvent, we have confidence in you.'

'I am here to do everything.'

'And to keep silent about everything.'

'Yes, reverend mother.'

'When the vault is opened – '

'I will shut it again.'

'But before – '

'What, reverend mother?'

'Something must be let down.'

There was silence. The prioress, after a quivering of the under-lip which resembled hesitation, spoke:

'Father Fauvent – '

'Reverend mother?'

'You know that a mother died this morning?'

'No.'

'You have not heard the bell then?'

'Nothing is heard at the further end of the garden.'

'Really?'

'I can hardly distinguish my ring.'

'She died at daybreak.'

'And then, this morning, the wind didn't blow my way.'

'It is Mother Crucifixion. One of the blest.'

The prioress was silent, moved her lips a moment as in a mental orison, and resumed:

'Three years ago, merely from having seen Mother Crucifixion at prayer, a Jansenist, Madame de Béthune, became orthodox.'

'Ah! yes, I hear the knell now, reverend mother.'

'The mothers have carried her into the room of the dead, which opens into the church.'

'I know.'

'No other man than you can or must enter that room. Be watchful. It would look well for a man to enter the room of the dead!'

'Oftener.'

'Eh?'

'Oftener.'

'What do you say?'

'I say oftener.'

'Oftener than what?'

'Reverend mother, I don't say oftener than what; I say oftener.'

'I do not understand you. Why do you say oftener?'

'To say as you do, reverend mother.'

'But I did not say oftener.'

'You did not say it; but I said it to say as you did.'

The clock struck nine.

'At nine o'clock in the morning, and at all hours, praise and adoration to the most holy sacrament of the altar,' said the prioress.

'Amen!' said Fauchelevent.

The clock struck in good time. It cut short that Oftener. It is probable, that without it the prioress and Fauchelevent would never have got out of that snarl.

Fauchelevent wiped his forehead.

The prioress again made a little low murmur, probably sacred, then raised her voice.

'During her life, Mother Crucifixion worked conversions; after her death, she will work miracles.'

'She will!' answered Fauchelevent, correcting his step, and making an effort not to blunder again.

'Father Fauvent, the community has been blessed in Mother Crucifixion. Doubtless, it is not given to everybody to die like Cardinal de Bérulle, saying the holy mass, and to breathe out his soul to God, pronouncing these words: *Hanc igitur oblationem*. But without attaining to so great happiness, Mother Crucifixion had a very precious death. She had her consciousness to the last. She spoke to us, then she spoke to the angels. She gave us her last commands. If you had a little more faith, and if you could have been in her cell, she would have cured your leg by touching it. She smiled. We felt that she was returning to life in God. There was something of Paradise in that death.'

Fauchelevent thought that he had been listening to a prayer.

'Amen!' said he.

'Father Fauvent, we must do what the dead wish.'

The prioress counted a few beads on her chaplet. Fauchelevent was silent. She continued:

'I have consulted upon this question several ecclesiastics labouring in Our Lord, who are engaged in the exercise of clerical functions, and with admirable results.'

'Reverend mother, we hear the knell much better here than in the garden.'

'Furthermore, she is more than a departed one; she is a saint.'

'Like you, reverend mother.'

'She slept in her coffin for twenty years, by the express permission of our Holy Father, Pius VII.'

'He who crowned the Emp – Buonaparte.'

For a shrewd man like Fauchelevent, the reminiscence was untoward. Luckily the prioress, absorbed in her thoughts, did not hear him. She continued:

'Father Fauvent?'

'Reverend mother?'

'St Diodorus, Archbishop of Cappadocia, desired that this single word might be written upon his tomb: *Acarus*, which signifies a worm of the dust; that was done. Is it true?'

'Yes, reverend mother.'

'The blessed Mezzocane, Abbé of Aquila, desired to be buried under the gibbet; that was done.'

'It is true.'

'St Terence, Bishop of Ostia, at the mouth of the Tiber, requested to have engraved upon his tomb the mark which was put upon the graves of parricides, in the hope that travellers would spit upon his grave. That was done. We must obey the dead.'

'So be it.'

'The body of Bernard Guidonis, who was born in France near Roche Abeille, was, as he has ordered, and in spite of the king of Castile, brought to the church of the Dominicans at Limoges, although Bernard Guidonis was Bishop of Tuy, in Spain. Can this be denied?'

The fact is attested by Plantavit de la Fosse.

'No, indeed, reverend mother.'

A few beads of her chaplet were told over silently. The prioress went on:

'Father Fauvent, Mother Crucifixion will be buried in the coffin in which she has slept for twenty years.'

'That is right.'

'It is a continuation of sleep.'

'I shall have to nail her up then in that coffin.'

'Yes.'

'And we will put aside the undertaker's coffin?'

'Precisely.'

'I am at the disposal of the most reverend community.'

'The four mother choristers will help you.'

'To nail up the coffin I don't need them.'

'No. To let it down.'

'Where?'

'Into the vault.'

'What vault?'

'Under the altar.'

Fauchelevent gave a start.

'The vault under the altar!'

'Under the altar.'

'But – '

'You will have an iron bar.'

'Yes, but – '

'You will lift the stone with the bar by means of the ring.'

'But – '

'We must obey the dead. To be buried in the vault under the altar of the chapel, not to go into profane ground, to remain in death where she prayed in life; this was the last request of Mother Crucifixion. She has asked it, that is to say, commanded it.'

'But it is forbidden.'

'Forbidden by men, enjoined by God.'

'If it should come to be known?'

'We have confidence in you.'

'Oh! as for me, I am like a stone in your wall.'

'The chapter has assembled. The vocal mothers, whom I have just consulted again and who are now deliberating, have decided that Mother Crucifixion should be, according to her desire, buried in her coffin under our altar. Think, Father Fauvent, if there should be miracles performed here! what glory under God for the community! Miracles spring from tombs.'

'But, reverend Mother, if the agent of the Health Commission – '

'St Benedict II, in the matter of burial, resisted Constantine Pogonatus.'

'However, the Commissary of Police – '

'Chonodemaire, one of the seven German kings who entered Gaul in the reign of Constantius, expressly recognised the right of conventuals to be inhumed in religion, that is to say, under the altar.'

'But the Inspector of the Prefecture – '

'The world is nothing before the cross. Martin, eleventh general of the Carthusians, gave to his order this device: *Stat crux dum volvitur orbis.*'[68]

'Amen,' said Fauchelevent, imperturbable in this method of extricating himself whenever he heard any Latin.

Any audience whatever is sufficient for one who has been too long silent. On the day that the rhetorician Gymnastoras came out of prison, full of suppressed dilemmas and syllogisms, he stopped before the first tree he met with, harangued it, and put forth very great efforts to convince it. The prioress, habitually subject to the constraint of silence, and having a surplus in her reservoir, rose, and exclaimed with the loquacity of an opened mill-sluice:[69]

'I have on my right Benedict, and on my left Bernard. What is Bernard? he is the first Abbot of Clairvaux. Fontaines in Burgundy is blessed for having been his birthplace. His father's name was Tecelin, and his mother's Alethe. He began at Citeaux, and ended at Clairvaux; he was ordained abbot by the Bishop of Chalons-sur-Saône, Guillaume de Champeaux; he had seven hundred novices, and founded a hundred and sixty monasteries; he overthrew Abeilard at the Council of Sens in 1140, and Peter de Bruys and Henry his disciple, and another heterodox set called the Apostolicals; he confounded Arnold of Brescia, struck monk Ralph dumb, the slayer of the Jews, presided in 1148 over the Council of Rheims, caused Gilbert de la Porée, Bishop of Poitiers, to be condemned, caused Eon de l'Etoile to be condemned, arranged the differences of princes, advised the King, Louis the Young, counselled Pope Eugenius III, regulated the Temple, preached the Crusade, performed two hundred and fifty miracles in his lifetime, and as many as thirty-nine in one day. What is Benedict? he is the patriarch of Monte Cassino; he is the second founder of the Claustral Holiness, he is the Basil of the West. His order has produced forty popes, two hundred cardinals, fifty patriarchs, sixteen hundred archbishops, four thousand six hundred bishops, four emperors, twelve empresses, forty-six kings, forty-one queens, three thousand six hundred canonised saints, and has existed for fourteen hundred years. On one side, St Bernard; on the other the agent of the Health Commission! On one side, St Benedict; on the other the sanitary inspector! The state, Health Department, funeral regulations, rules, the administration, do we recognise these things? Anybody would be indignant to see how we are treated. We have not even the right to give our dust to Jesus Christ! Your sanitary commission is an invention of the revolution. God subordinated to the commissary of police; such is this age. Silence, Fauvent!'

Fauchelevent, beneath this douche, was not quite at ease. The prioress continued:

'The right of the convent to burial cannot be doubted by anybody There are none to deny it save fanatics and those who have gone astray. We live in times of terrible confusion. People are ignorant of what they ought to know, and know those things of which they ought to be ignorant. They are gross and impious. There are people in these days who do not distinguish between the great St Bernard and the Bernard entitled des Pauvres Catholiques, a certain good ecclesiastic who lived in the thirteenth century. Others blaspheme so far as to couple the scaffold of Louis XVI with the cross of Jesus Christ. Louis XVI was only a king. Let us then take heed for God! There are no longer either just or unjust. Voltaire's name is known, and the name of Cæsar de Bus is not known. Nevertheless Cæsar de Bus is in bliss and Voltaire is in torment. The last archbishop, the Cardinal of Perigord, did not even know that Charles de Gondren succeeded Bérulle, and Francis Bourgoin, Gondren, and Jean François Senault, Bourgoin, and Father de Sainte-Marthe, Jean François Senault. The name of Father Cotton is known, not because he was one of the three who laboured in the foundation of the Oratory, but because he was the subject of an oath for the Huguenot King Henry IV. St Francois de Sales is popular with the world, because he cheated at play. And then religion is attacked. Why? Because there have been wicked priests, because Sagittaire, Bishop of Gap, was a brother of Salone, Bishop of Embrun, and both were followers of Mammon. What does that amount to? Does that prevent Martin de Tours from being a saint and having given half his cloak to a poor man? The saints are persecuted. Men shut their eyes to the truth. Darkness becomes habitual. The most savage beasts are blind beasts. Nobody thinks of hell in earnest. Oh! the wicked people! By the king, now means, by the revolution. Men no longer know what is due to the living or the dead. Holy death is forbidden. The sepulchre is a civil affair. This is horrible. St Leo II wrote two letters expressly, one to Peter Notaire, the other to the King of the Visigoths, to combat and overthrow, upon questions touching the dead, the authority of the ex-arch and the supremacy of the emperor. Walter, Bishop of Châlons, in this matter made opposition to Otho, Duke of Burgundy. The ancient magistracy acceded to it. Formerly we had votes in the chapter concerning secular affairs. The Abbot of Cîteaux, general of the order, was hereditary counsellor of the Parliament of Burgundy. We do with our dead as we please. Is not the body of St Benedict himself in France in the Abbey of Fleury, called St Benedict sur Loire, though he died in Italy, at Monte Cassino, on a Saturday, the 21st of the month of March in the year 543! All this is incontestable. I abhor the Psallants, I hate the Prayers, I execrate heretics, but I should detest still more whoever might sustain the contrary of what I have said. You have only to read Arnold Wion, Gabriel Bucelin, Trithemius, Maurolicus, and Dom Luke d'Achery.'

The prioress drew breath, then turning towards Fauchelevent: 'Father Fauvent, is it settled?'

'It is settled, reverend mother.'

'Can we count upon you?'

'I shall obey.'

'It is well.'

'I am entirely devoted to the convent.'

'It is understood, you will close the coffin. The sisters will carry it into the chapel. The office for the dead will be said. Then they will return to the cloister. Between eleven o'clock and midnight, you will come with your iron bar. All will be done with the greatest secrecy. There will be in the chapel only the four mother choristers, Mother Ascension, and you.'

'And the sister who will be at the post.'

'She will not turn.'

'But she will hear.'

'She will not listen; moreover, what the cloister knows, the world does not know.'

There was a pause again. The prioress continued:

'You will take off your bell. It is needless that the sister at the post should perceive that you are there.'

'Reverend mother?'

'What, Father Fauvent?'

'Has the death-physician made his visit?'

'He is going to make it at four o'clock today. The bell has been sounded which summons the death-physician. But you do not hear any ring then?'

'I only pay attention to my own.'

'That is right, Father Fauvent.'

'Reverend mother, I shall need a lever at least six feet long.'

'Where will you get it?'

'Where there are gratings there are always iron bars. I have my heap of old iron at the back of the garden.'

'About three-quarters of an hour before midnight; do not forget.'

'Reverend mother?'

'What?'

'If you should ever have any other work like this, my brother is very strong. A Turk.'

'You will do it as quickly as possible.'

'I cannot go very fast. I am infirm; it is on that account I need help. I limp.'

'To limp is not a crime, and it may be a blessing. The Emperor Henry II, who fought the Antipope Gregory, and re-established Benedict VIII, has two surnames: the Saint and the Lame.'

'Two surtouts are very good,' murmured Fauchelevent, who, in reality, was a little hard of hearing.

'Father Fauvent, now I think of it, we will take a whole hour. It is not too much. Be at the high altar with the iron bar at eleven o'clock. The office commences at midnight. It must all be finished a good quarter of an hour before.'

'I will do everything to prove my zeal for the community. This is the arrangement. I shall nail up the coffin. At eleven o'clock precisely I will be in the chapel. The mother choristers will be there. Mother Ascension will be there. Two men would be better. But no matter! I shall have my lever. We shall open the vault, let down the coffin, and close the vault again. After which, there will be no trace of anything. The government will suspect nothing. Reverend mother, is this all so?'

'No.'

'What more is there, then?'

'There is still the empty coffin.'

This brought them to a stand. Fauchelevent pondered. The prioress pondered.

'Father Fauvent, what shall be done with the coffin?'

'It will be put in the ground.'

'Empty?'

Another silence. Fauchelevent made with his left hand that peculiar gesture, which dismisses an unpleasant question.

'Reverend mother, I nail up the coffin in the lower room in the church, and nobody can come in there except me, and I will cover the coffin with the pall.'

'Yes, but the bearers, in putting it into the hearse and in letting it down into the grave, will surely perceive that there is nothing inside.'

'Ah! the de – !' exclaimed Fauchelevent.

The prioress began to cross herself, and looked fixedly at the gardener. *Vil* stuck in his throat.

He made haste to think of an expedient to make her forget the oath.

'Reverend mother, I will put some earth into the coffin. That will have the effect of a body.'

'You are right. Earth is the same thing as man. So you will prepare the empty coffin?'

'I will attend to that.'

The face of the prioress, till then dark and anxious, became again serene. She made him the sign of a superior dismissing an inferior. Fauchelevent moved towards the door. As he was going out, the prioress gently raised her voice.

'Father Fauvent, I am satisfied with you; tomorrow after the burial, bring your brother to me, and tell him to bring his daughter.'

4. *In which Jean Valjean has quite the appearance of having read Austin Castillejo*

THE STRIDES OF THE LAME are like the glances of the one-eyed; they do not speedily reach their aim. Furthermore, Fauchelevent was perplexed. It took him nearly a quarter of an hour to get back to the shanty in the garden. Cosette was awake. Jean Valjean had seated her near the fire. At the moment when Fauchelevent entered, Jean Valjean was showing her the gardener's basket hanging on the wall and saying to her:

'Listen attentively to me, my little Cosette. We must go away from this house, but we shall come back, and we shall be very well off here. The good man here will carry you out on his back inside there. You will wait for me at a lady's. I shall come and find you. Above all, if you do not want the Thénardiess to take you back, obey and say nothing.'

Cosette nodded her head with a serious look.

At the sound of Fauchelevent opening the door, Jean Valjean turned.

'Well?'

'All is arranged, and nothing is,' said Fauchelevent. 'I have permission to bring you in; but before bringing you in, it is necessary to get you out. That is where the cart is blocked! For the little girl, it is easy enough.'

'You will carry her out?'

'And she will keep quiet?'

'I will answer for it.'

'But you, Father Madeleine?'

And, after an anxious silence, Fauchelevent exclaimed:

'But why not go out the way you came in?'

Jean Valjean, as before, merely answered: 'Impossible.'

Fauchelevent, talking more to himself than to Jean Valjean, grumbled:

'There is another thing that torments me. I said I would put in some earth. But I think that earth inside, instead of a body, will not be like it; that will not do, it will shake about; it will move. The men will feel it. You understand, Father Madeleine, the government will find it out.'

Jean Valjean stared at him, and thought that he was raving.

Fauchelevent resumed:

'How the d—ickens are you going to get out? For all this must be done tomorrow. Tomorrow I am to bring you in. The prioress expects you.'

Then he explained to Jean Valjean that this was a reward for a service that he, Fauchelevent, was rendering to the community. That it was a part of his duties to assist in burials, that he nailed up the coffins, and attended the gravedigger at the cemetery. That the nun who died that morning had requested to be buried in the coffin which she had used as a bed, and interred in the vault under the altar of the chapel. That this was forbidden by the regulations of the police, but that she was one of those departed ones to whom nothing is refused. That the prioress and the vocal mothers intended to carry out the will of the deceased. So much the worse for the government. That he, Fauchelevent, would nail up the coffin in the cell, raise the stone in the chapel, and let down the body into the vault. And that, in return for this, the prioress would admit his brother into the house as gardener and his niece as boarder. That his brother was M. Madeleine, and that his niece was Cosette. That the prioress had told him to bring his brother the next evening, after the fictitious burial at the cemetery. But that he could not bring M. Madeleine from the outside, if M. Madeleine were not outside. That that was the first difficulty. And then that he had another difficulty; the empty coffin.'

'What is the empty coffin?' asked Jean Valjean.

Fauchelevent responded:

'The coffin from the administration.'

'What coffin? and what administration?'

'A nun dies. The municipality physician comes and says: there is a nun dead. The government sends a coffin. The next day it sends a hearse and some bearers to take the coffin and carry it to the cemetery. The bearers will come and take up the coffin; there will be nothing in it.'

'Put somebody in it.'

'A dead body? I have none.'

'No.'

'What then?'

'A living body.'

'What living body?'

'Me,' said Jean Valjean.

Fauchelevent, who had taken a seat, sprang up as if a cracker had burst under his chair.

'You!'

'Why not?'

Jean Valjean had one of those rare smiles which came over him like the aurora in a winter sky.

'You know, Fauchelevent, that you said: Mother Crucifixion is dead, and that I added: and Father Madeleine is buried. It will be so.'

'Ah! good, you are laughing, you are not talking seriously.'

'Very seriously. I must get out!'

'Undoubtedly.'

'And I told you to find a basket and a cover for me also.'

'Well!'

'The basket will be of pine, and the cover will be a black cloth.'

'In the first place, a white cloth. The nuns are buried in white.'

'Well, a white cloth.'

'You are not like other men, Father Madeleine.'

To see such devices, which are nothing more than the savage and foolhardy inventions of the galleys, appear in the midst of the peaceful things that surrounded him and mingled with what he called the 'little jog-jog of the convent', was to Fauchelevent an astonishment comparable to that of a person who should see a seamew fishing in the brook in the Rue St Denis.

Jean Valjean continued:

'The question is, how to get out without being seen. This is the means. But in the first place tell me, how is it done? where is this coffin?'

'The empty one?'

'Yes.'

'Down in what is called the dead-room. It is on two trestles and under the pall.'

'What is the length of the coffin?'

'Six feet.'

'What is the dead-room?'

'It is a room on the ground floor, with a grated window towards the garden, closed on the outside with a shutter, and two doors; one leading to the convent, the other to the church.'

'What church?'

'The church on the street, the church for everybody.'

'Have you the keys of those two doors?'

'No. I have the key of the door that opens into the convent; the porter has the key of the door that opens into the church.'

'When does the porter open that door?'

'Only to let in the bearers, who come after the coffin; as soon as the coffin goes out, the door is closed again.'

'Who nails up the coffin?'

'I do.'

'Who puts the cloth on it?'

'I do.'

'Are you alone?'

'No other man, except the police physician, can enter the dead-room. That is even written upon the wall.'

'Could you, tonight, when all are asleep in the convent, hide me in that room?'

'No. But I can hide you in a little dark closet which opens into the dead-room, where I keep my burial tools, and of which I have the care and the key.'

'At what hour will the hearse come after the coffin tomorrow?'

'About three o'clock in the afternoon. The burial takes place at the Vaugirard cemetery, a little before night. It is not very near.'

'I shall remain hidden in your tool-closet all night and all the morning. And about eating? I shall be hungry.'

'I will bring you something.'

'You can come and nail me up in the coffin at two o'clock.'

Fauchelevent started back, and began to snap his fingers.

'But it is impossible!'

'Pshaw! to take a hammer and drive some nails into a board?'

What seemed unheard-of to Fauchelevent was, we repeat, simple to Jean Valjean. Jean Valjean had been in worse straits. He who has been a prisoner knows the art of making himself small according to the dimensions of the place for escape. The prisoner is subject to flight as the sick man is to the crisis which cures or kills him. An escape is a cure. What does not one undergo to be cured? To be nailed up and carried out in a chest like a bundle, to live a long time in a box, to find air where there is none, to economise the breath for entire hours, to know how to be stifled without dying – that was one of the gloomy talents of Jean Valjean.

Moreover, a coffin in which there is a living being, that convict's expedient, is also an emperor's expedient. If we can believe the monk Austin Castillejo,[70] this was the means which Charles V, desiring after his abdication to see La Plombes again a last time, employed to bring her into the monastery of St Juste and to take her out again.

Fauchelevent, recovering a little, exclaimed:

'But how will you manage to breathe?'

'I shall breathe.'

'In that box? Only to think of it suffocates me.'

'You surely have a gimlet, you can make a few little holes about the mouth here and there, and you can nail it without drawing the upper board tight.'

'Good! But if you happen to cough or sneeze?'

'He who is escaping never coughs and never sneezes.'

And Jean Valjean added:

'Father Fauchelevent, I must decide: either to be taken here, or to be willing to go out in the hearse.'

Everybody has noticed the taste which cats have for stopping and loitering in a half-open door. Who has not said to a cat: Why don't you come in? There are men who, with an opportunity half-open before them, have a similar tendency to remain undecided between two resolutions, at the risk of being crushed by destiny abruptly closing the opportunity. The over prudent, cats as they are, and because they are cats, sometimes run more danger than the bold. Fauchelevent was of this hesitating nature. However, Jean Valjean's coolness won him over in spite of himself. He grumbled:

'It is true, there is no other way.'

Jean Valjean resumed:

'The only thing that I am anxious about, is what will be done at the cemetery.'

'That is just what does not embarrass me,' exclaimed Fauchelevent. 'If you are sure of getting yourself out of the coffin, I am sure of getting you out of the grave. The gravedigger is a drunkard and a friend of mine. He is Father Mestienne. An old son of the old vine. The gravedigger puts the dead in the grave, and I put the gravedigger in my pocket. I will tell you what will take place. We shall arrive a little before dusk, three-quarters of an hour before the cemetery gates are closed. The hearse will go to the grave. I shall follow; that is my business. I will have a hammer, a chisel, and some pincers in my pocket. The hearse stops, the bearers tie a rope around your coffin and let you down. The priest says the prayers, makes the sign of the cross, sprinkles the holy water, and is off. I remain alone with Father Mestienne. He is my friend, I tell you. One of two things; either he will be drunk, or he will not be drunk. If he is not drunk, I say to him: come and take a drink before the Good Quince is shut. I get him away, I fuddle him; Father Mestienne is not long in getting fuddled, he is always half way. I lay him under the table, I take his card from him to return to the cemetery with, and I come back without him. You will have only me to deal with. If he is drunk, I say to him: be off. I'll do your work. He goes away, and I pull you out of the hole.'

Jean Valjean extended his hand, upon which Fauchelevent threw himself with a rustic outburst of touching devotion.

'It is settled, Father Fauchelevent. All will go well.'

'Provided nothing goes amiss,' thought Fauchelevent. 'How terrible that would be!'

5. *It is not enough to be a drunkard to be immortal*

NEXT DAY, as the sun was declining, the scattered passers on the Boulevard du Maine took off their hats at the passage of an old-fashioned hearse, adorned with death's-heads, crossbones, and tear-drops. In this hearse there was a coffin covered with a white cloth, upon which was displayed a large black cross like a great dummy with hanging arms. A draped carriage, in which might be seen a priest in a surplice, and a choirboy in a red calotte, followed. Two bearers in grey uniform with black trimmings walked on the right and left of the hearse. In the rear came an old man dressed like a labourer, who limped. The procession moved towards the Vaugirard cemetery.

Sticking out of the man's pocket were the handle of a hammer, the blade of a cold chisel, and the double handles of a pair of pincers.

The Vaugirard cemetery was an exception among the cemeteries of Paris. It had its peculiar usages, so far that it had its *porte-cochère*, and its small door which, in the quarter, old people, tenacious of old words, called the cavalier door, and the pedestrian door. The Bernardine-Benedictines of the Petit Picpus had obtained the right, as we have said, to be buried in a corner apart and at night, this ground having formerly belonged to their community. The gravediggers, having thus to work in the cemetery in the evening in summer, and at night in winter, were subject to a peculiar discipline. The gates of the cemeteries of Paris closed at that epoch at sunset, and, this being a measure of municipal order, the Vaugirard cemetery was subject to it like the rest. The cavalier door and the pedestrian door were two contiguous gratings; near which was a pavilion built by the architect Perronet, in which the door-keeper of the cemetery lived. These gratings therefore inexorably turned upon their hinges the instant the sun disappeared behind the dome of the Invalides. If any gravedigger, at that moment, was belated in the cemetery, his only resource for getting out was his gravedigger's card, given him by the administration of funeral ceremonies. A sort of letterbox was arranged in the shutter of the gate-keeper's window. The gravedigger dropped his card into this box, the gate-keeper heard it fall, pulled the string, and the pedestrian door opened. If the gravedigger did not have his card, he gave his name; the gate-keeper, sometimes in bed and asleep, got up, went to identify the gravedigger, and open the door with the key; the gravedigger went out, but paid fifteen francs fine.

This cemetery, with its peculiarities breaking over the rules, disturbed the symmetry of the administration. It was suppressed shortly after 1830. The Mont Parnasse Cemetery called the Cemetery of the East, has succeeded it, and has inherited this famous drinking house let into the Vaugirard cemetery, which was surmounted by a quince painted on a board, which looked on one side upon the tables of the drinkers, and on the other upon graves, with this inscription: The Good Quince.

The Vaugirard cemetery was what might be called a decayed cemetery. It was falling into disuse. Mould was invading it, flowers were leaving it. The well-to-do citizens little cared to be buried at Vaugirard; it sounded poor. Père Lachaise is very fine! to be buried in Père Lachaise is like having mahogany furniture. Elegance is understood by that. The Vaugirard cemetery was a venerable enclosure, laid out like an old French garden. Straight walks, box, evergreens, hollies, old tombs under old yews, very high grass. Night there was terrible. There were some very dismal outlines there.

The sun had not yet set when the hearse with the white pall and the black cross entered the avenue of the Vaugirard cemetery. The lame man who followed it was no other than Fauchelevent.

The burial of Mother Crucifixion in the vault under the altar, the departure of Cosette, the introduction of Jean Valjean into the dead-room, all had been carried out without obstruction, and nothing had gone wrong.

We will say, by the way, the inhumation of Mother Crucifixion under the convent altar is, to us, a perfectly venial thing. It is one of those faults which resemble a duty. The nuns had accomplished it, not only without discomposure, but with an approving conscience. In the cloister, what is called the 'government' is only an interference with authority, an interference which is always questionable. First the rules; as to the code, we will see. Men, make as many laws as you please, but keep them for yourselves. The tribute to Cæsar is never more than the remnant of the tribute to God. A prince is nothing in presence of a principle.

Fauchelevent limped behind the hearse, very well satisfied. His two twin plots, one with the nuns, the other with M. Madeleine, one for the convent, the other against it, had succeeded equally well. Jean Valjean's calmness had that powerful tranquillity which is contagious. Fauchelevent had now no doubt of success. What remained to be done was nothing. Within two years he had fuddled the gravedigger ten times, good Father Mestienne, a rubicund old fellow. Father Mestienne was play for him. He did what he liked with him. He got him drunk at will and at his fancy. Mestienne saw through Fauchelevent's eyes. Fauchelevent's security was complete.

At the moment the convoy entered the avenue leading to the cemetery, Fauchelevent, happy, looked at the hearse and rubbed his big hands together, saying in an undertone:

'Here's a farce!'

Suddenly the hearse stopped; they were at the gate. It was necessary to exhibit the burial permit. The undertaker whispered with the porter of the cemetery. During this colloquy, which always causes a delay of a minute or two, somebody, an unknown man, came and placed himself behind the hearse at Fauchelevent's side. He was a working-man, who wore a vest with large pockets, and had a pick under his arm.

Fauchelevent looked at this unknown man.

'Who are you?' he asked.

The man answered: 'The gravedigger.'

Should a man survive a cannon-shot through his breast, he would present the appearance that Fauchelevent did.

'The gravedigger?'

'Yes.'

'You!'

'Me.'

'The gravedigger is Father Mestienne.'

'He was.'

'How! he was?'

'He is dead.'

Fauchelevent was ready for anything but this, that a gravedigger could die. It is, however, true; gravediggers themselves die. By dint of digging graves for others, they open their own.

Fauchelevent remained speechless. He had hardly the strength to stammer out:

'But it's not possible !'

'It is so.'

'But,' repeated he, feebly, 'the gravedigger is Father Mestienne.'

'After Napoleon, Louis XVIII. After Mestienne, Gribier. Peasant, my name is Gribier.'

Fauchelevent grew pale; he stared at Gribier.

He was a long, thin, livid man, perfectly funereal. He had the appearance of a broken-down doctor turned gravedigger.

Fauchelevent burst out laughing.

'Ah! what droll things happen! Father Mestienne is dead. Little Father Mestienne is dead, but hurrah for little Father Lenoir! You know what little Father Lenoir is? It is the mug of red for a six spot. It is the mug of Surêne. Zounds! real Paris Surêne. So he is dead, old Mestienne! I am sorry for it; he was a jolly fellow. But you too, you are a jolly fellow. Isn't that so, comrade? we will go and take a drink together, right away.'

The man answered: 'I have studied, I have graduated. I never drink.'

The hearse had started, and was rolling along the main avenue of the cemetery.

Fauchelevent had slackened his pace. He limped still more from anxiety than from infirmity.

The gravedigger walked before him.

Fauchelevent again scrutinised the unexpected Gribier.

He was one of those men who, though young, have an old appearance, and who, though thin, are very strong.

'Comrade!' cried Fauchelevent.

The man turned.

'I am the gravedigger of the convent.'

'My colleague,' said the man.

Fauchelevent, illiterate, but very keen, understood that he had to do with a very formidable species, a good talker.

He mumbled out:

'Is it so, Father Mestienne is dead?'

The man answered:

'Perfectly. The good God consulted his list of bills payable. It was Father Mestienne's turn. Father Mestienne is dead.'

Fauchelevent repeated mechanically.

'The good God.'

'The good God,' said the man authoritatively. 'What the philosophies call the Eternal Father; the Jacobins, the Supreme Being.'

'Are we not going to make each other's acquaintance?' stammered Fauchelevent.

'It is made. You are a peasant, I am a Parisian.'

'We are not acquainted as long as we have not drunk together. He who empties his glass empties his heart. Come and drink with me. You can't refuse.'

'Business first.'

Fauchelevent said to himself: I am lost.

They were now only a few rods from the path that led to the nuns' corner.

The gravedigger continued:

'Peasant, I have seven youngsters that I must feed. As they must eat, I must not drink.'

And he added with the satisfaction of a serious being who is making a sententious phrase:

'Their hunger is the enemy of my thirst.'

The hearse turned a huge cypress, left the main path, took a little one, entered upon the grounds, and was lost in a thicket. This indicated the immediate proximity of the grave. Fauchelevent slackened his pace, but could not slacken that of the hearse. Luckily the mellow soil, wet by the winter rains, stuck to the wheels, and made the track heavy.

He approached the gravedigger.

'They have such a good little Argenteuil wine,' suggested Fauchelevent.

'Villager,' continued the man, 'I ought not to be a gravedigger. My father was porter at the Prytanée. He intended me for literature. But he was unfortunate. He met with losses at the Bourse, I was obliged to renounce the condition of an author. However, I am still a public scribe.'

'But then you are not the gravedigger?' replied Fauchelevent, catching at a straw, feeble as it was.

'One does not prevent the other. I cumulate.'

Fauchelevent did not understand this last word.

'Let us go and drink,' said he.

Here an observation is necessary. Fauchelevent, whatever was his anguish, proposed to drink, but did not explain himself on one point; who should pay? Ordinarily Fauchelevent proposed, and Father Mestienne paid. A proposal to drink resulted evidently from the new situation produced by the fact of the new gravedigger, and this proposal he must make; but the old gardener left, not unintentionally, the proverbial quarter of an hour of Rabelais in the shade. As for him, Fauchelevent, however excited he was, he did not care about paying.

The gravedigger went on, with a smile of superiority:

'We must live. I accepted the succession of Father Mestienne. When one has almost finished his classes, he is a philosopher. To the labour of my hand, I have added the labour of my arm. I have my little writer's shop at the Market in the Rue de Sèvres. You know? the market of the Parapluies. All the cooks of the Croix Rouge come to me; I patch up their declarations to their true loves. In the morning I write love letters; in the evening I dig graves. Such is life, countryman.'

The hearse advanced; Fauchelevent, full of anxiety, looked about him on all sides. Great drops of sweat were falling from his forehead.

'However,' continued the gravedigger, 'one cannot serve two mistresses; I must choose between the pen and the pick. The pick hurts my hand.'

The hearse stopped.

The choirboy got out of the mourning carriage, then the priest.

One of the forward wheels of the hearse mounted on a little heap of earth, beyond which was seen an open grave.

'Here is a farce!' repeated Fauchelevent in consternation.

6. *In the narrow house*

WHO WAS in the coffin? We know. Jean Valjean.

Jean Valjean had arranged it so that he could live in it, and could breathe a very little.

It is a strange thing to what extent an easy conscience gives calmness in other respects. The entire combination prearranged by Jean Valjean had been executed, and executed well, since the night before. He counted, as did Fauchelevent, upon Father Mestienne. He had no doubt of the result. Never was a situation more critical, never calmness more complete.

The four boards of the coffin exhaled a kind of terrible peace. It seemed as if something of the repose of the dead had entered into the tranquillity of Jean Valjean.

From within that coffin he had been able to follow, and he had followed, all the phases of the fearful drama which he was playing with Death.

Soon after Fauchelevent had finished nailing down the upper board, Jean Valjean had felt himself carried out, then wheeled along. By the diminished jolting, he had felt that he was passing from the pavement to the hard ground; that is to say, that he was leaving the streets and entering upon the boulevards. By a dull sound, he had divined that they were crossing the bridge of Austerlitz. At the first stop he had comprehended that they were entering the cemetery; at the second stop he had said: here is the grave.

He felt that hands hastily seized the coffin, then a harsh scraping upon the boards; he concluded that that was a rope which they were tying around the coffin to let it down into the excavation.

Then he felt a kind of dizziness.

Probably the bearer and the gravedigger had tipped the coffin and let the head down before the feet. He returned fully to himself on feeling that he was horizontal and motionless. He had touched the bottom.

He felt a certain chill.

A voice arose above him, icy and solemn. He heard pass away, some Latin words which he did not understand, pronounced so slowly that he could catch them one after another:

'*Qui dormiunt in terræ pulvere, evigilabunt; alii in vitam æternam, et alii in opprobrium, ut videant semper.*'[71]

A child's voice said:

'*De profundis.*'

The deep voice recommenced:

'*Requiem æternam dona ei, Domine.*'

The child's voice responded:

'*Et lux perpetua luceat ei.*'

He heard upon the board which covered him something like the gentle patter of a few drops of rain. It was probably the holy water.

He thought: 'This will soon be finished. A little more patience. The priest is going away. Fauchelevent will take Mestienne away to drink. They will leave me. Then Fauchelevent will come back alone, and I shall get out. That will take a good hour.'

The deep voice resumed.

'*Requiescat in pace.*'

And the child's voice said:

'*Amen.*'

Jean Valjean, intently listening, perceived something like receding steps. 'Now there they go,' thought he. 'I am alone.' All at once he heard a sound above his head which seemed to him like a clap of thunder. It was a spadeful of earth falling upon the coffin. A second spadeful of earth fell. One of the holes by which he breathed was stopped up. A third spadeful of earth fell. Then a fourth. There are things stronger than the strongest man. Jean Valjean lost consciousness.

7. *In which will be found the origin of the saying: Don't lose your card*

LET US SEE what occurred over the coffin in which Jean Valjean lay.

When the hearse had departed and the priest and the choirboy had got into the carriage, and were gone, Fauchelevent, who had never taken his eyes off the gravedigger, saw him stoop, and grasp his spade, which was standing upright in the heap of earth.

Hereupon, Fauchelevent formed a supreme resolve.

Placing himself between the grave and the gravedigger, and folding his arms, he said:

'I'll pay for it!'

The gravedigger eyed him with amazement, and replied: 'What, peasant?'

Fauchelevent repeated:

'I'll pay for it.'

'For what?'

'For the wine.'

'What wine?'

'The Argenteuil.'

'Where's the Argenteuil?'

'At the Good Quince.'

'Go to the devil!' said the gravedigger.

And he threw a spadeful of earth upon the coffin.

The coffin gave back a hollow sound. Fauchelevent felt himself stagger, and nearly fell into the grave. In a voice in which the strangling sound of the death-rattle began to be heard, he cried:

'Come, comrade, before the Good Quince closes!'

The gravedigger took up another spadeful of earth. Fauchelevent continued:

'I'll pay,' and he seized the gravedigger by the arm.

'Hark ye, comrade,' he said, 'I am the gravedigger of the convent, and have come to help you. It's a job we can do at night. Let us take a drink first.'

And as he spoke, even while clinging desperately to this urgent effort, he asked himself, with some misgiving: 'And even should he drink – will he get tipsy?'

'Good rustic,' said the gravedigger, 'if you insist, I consent. We'll have a drink, but after my work, never before it.'

And he tossed his spade again. Fauchelevent held him.

'It is Argenteuil at six sous the pint!'

'Ah, bah!' said the gravedigger, 'you're a bore. Ding-dong, ding-dong, the same thing over and over again; that's all you can say. Be off, about your business.'

And he threw in the second spadeful.

Fauchelevent had reached that point where a man knows no longer what he is saying.

'Oh! come on, and take a glass, since I'm the one to pay,' he again repeated.

'When we've put the child to bed,' said the gravedigger.

He tossed in the third spadeful: then, plunging his spade into the earth, he added:

'You see, now, it's going to be cold tonight, and the dead one would cry out after us, if we were to plant her there without good covering.'

At this moment, in the act of filling his spade, the gravedigger stooped low, and the pocket of his vest gaped open.

The bewildered eye of Fauchelevent rested mechanically on this pocket, and remained fixed.

The sun was not yet hidden behind the horizon, and there was still light enough to distinguish something white in the gaping pocket.

All the lightning which the eye of a Picardy peasant can contain flashed into the pupils of Fauchelevent. A new idea had struck him.

Without the gravedigger, who was occupied with his spadeful of earth, perceiving him, he slipped his hand from behind into the pocket, and took from him the white object it contained.

The gravedigger flung into the grave the fourth spadeful.

Just as he was turning to take the fifth, Fauchelevent, looking at him with imperturbable calmness, asked:

'By the way, my new friend, have you your card?'

The gravedigger stopped.

'What card?'

'The sun is setting.'

'Well, let him put on his night-cap.'

'The cemetery-gate will be closed.'

'Well, what then?'

'Have you your card?'

'Oh! my card!' said the gravedigger, and he felt in his pocket.

Having rummaged one pocket, he tried another. From these, he proceeded to try his watch-fobs, exploring the first, and turning the second inside out.

'No!' said he, 'no! I haven't got my card. I must have forgotten it.'

'Fifteen francs fine!' said Fauchelevent

The gravedigger turned green. Green is the paleness of people naturally livid.

'Oh, good-gracious God, what a fool I am!' he exclaimed. 'Fifteen francs fine!'

'Three hundred-sou pieces,' said Fauchelevent.

The gravedigger dropped his spade.

Fauchelevent's turn had come.

'Come! come, recruit,' said Fauchelevent, 'never despair; there's nothing to kill oneself about, and feed the worms. Fifteen francs are fifteen francs, and besides, you may not have them to pay. I am an old hand, and you a new one. I know all the tricks and traps and turns and twists of the business. I'll give you a friend's advice. One thing is clear – the sun is setting – and the graveyard will be closed in five minutes.'

'That's true,' replied the gravedigger.

'Five minutes is not time enough for you to fill the grave – it's as deep as the very devil – and get out of this before the gate is shut.'

'You're right.'

'In that case, there is fifteen francs fine.'

'Fifteen francs!'

'But you have time . . . Where do you live?'

'Just by the barrière. Fifteen minutes' walk. Number 87 Rue de Vaugirard.'

'You have time, if you will hang your toggery about your neck, to get out at once.'

'That's true.'

'Once outside of the gate, you scamper home, get your card, come back, and the gatekeeper will let you in again. Having your card, there's nothing to pay. Then you can bury your dead man. I'll stay here, and watch him while you're gone, to see that he doesn't run away.'

'I owe you my life, peasant!'

'Be off, then, quick!' said Fauchelevent.

The gravedigger, overcome with gratitude, shook his hands, and started at a run.

When the gravedigger had disappeared through the bushes, Fauchelevent listened until his footsteps died away, and then, bending over the grave, called out in a low voice:

'Father Madeleine!'

No answer.

Fauchelevent shuddered. He dropped rather than clambered down into the grave, threw himself upon the head of the coffin, and cried out:

'Are you there?'

Silence in the coffin.

Fauchelevent, no longer able to breathe for the shiver that was on him, took his cold chisel and hammer, and wrenched off the top board. The face of Jean Valjean could be seen in the twilight, his eyes closed and his cheeks colourless.

Fauchelevent's hair stood erect with alarm; he rose to his feet, and then tottered with his back against the side of the grave, ready to sink down upon the coffin. He looked upon Jean Valjean.

Jean Valjean lay there pallid and motionless.

Fauchelevent murmured in a voice low as a whisper:

'He is dead!'

Then straightening himself, and crossing his arms so violently that his clenched fists sounded against his shoulders, he exclaimed:

'This is the way I have saved him!'

Then the poor old man began to sob, talking aloud to himself the while, for it is a mistake to think that talking to oneself is not natural. Powerful emotions often speak aloud.

'It's Father Mestienne's fault. What did he die for, the fool? What was the use of going off in that way, just when no one expected it? It was he who killed poor M. Madeleine. Father Madeleine! He is in the coffin. He's settled. There's an end of it. Now, what's the sense of such things? Good God! he's dead! Yes, and his little girl – what am I to do with her? What will the fruit-woman say? That such a man could die in that way. Good Heaven, is it possible! When I think that he put himself under my cart! . . . Father Madeleine! Father Madeleine! Mercy, he's suffocated, I said so but, he wouldn't believe me. Now, here's a pretty piece of business! He's dead – one of the very best men God ever made; aye, the best, the very best! And his little girl! I'm not going back there again. I'm going to stay here. To have done such a thing as this! It's well worth while to be two old greybeards, in order to be two old fools. But, to begin with, how did he manage to get into the convent – that's where it started. Such things shouldn't be done. Father Madeleine! Father Madeleine! Father Madeleine! Madeleine! Monsieur Madeleine! Monsieur Mayor! He doesn't hear me. Get yourself out of this now, if you please.'

And he tore his hair.

At a distance, through the trees, a harsh grating sound was heard. It was the gate of the cemetery closing.

Fauchelevent again bent over Jean Valjean, but suddenly started back with all the recoil that was possible in a grave. Jean Valjean's eyes were open, and gazing at him.

To behold death is terrifying, and to see a sudden restoration is nearly as much so. Fauchelevent became cold and white as a stone, haggard and utterly disconcerted by all these powerful emotions, and not knowing whether he had the dead or the living to deal with, stared at Jean Valjean, who in turn stared at him.

'I was falling asleep,' said Jean Valjean.

And he rose to a sitting posture.

Fauchelevent dropped on his knees.

'Oh, blessed Virgin! How you frightened me!'

Then, springing again to his feet, he cried:

'Thank you, Father Madeleine!'

Jean Valjean had merely swooned. The open air had revived him.

Joy is the reflex of terror. Fauchelevent had nearly as much difficulty as Jean Valjean in coming to himself.

'Then you're not dead! Oh, what good sense you have! I called you so loudly that you got over it. When I saw you with your eyes shut, I said, "Well, there now! he's suffocated!" I should have gone raving mad – mad enough for a straitjacket. They'd have put me in the Bicêtre. What would you have had me do, if you had been dead? And your little girl! the fruit-woman would have understood nothing about it! A child plumped into her lap, and its grandfather dead! What a story to tell! By all the saints in heaven, what a story! Ah! but you're alive – that's the best of it.'

'I am cold,' said Jean Valjean.

These words recalled Fauchelevent completely to the real state of affairs, which were urgent. These two men, even when restored, felt, without knowing it, a peculiar agitation and a strange inward trouble, which was but the sinister bewilderment of the place.

'Let us get away from here at once,' said Fauchelevent.

He thrust his hand into his pocket, and drew from it a flask with which he was provided.

'But a drop of this first!' said he.

The flask completed what the open air had begun. Jean Valjean took a swallow of brandy, and felt thoroughly restored.

He got out of the coffin, and assisted Fauchelevent to nail down the lid again. Three minutes afterwards, they were out of the grave.

After this, Fauchelevent was calm enough. He took his time. The cemetery was closed. There was no fear of the return of Gribier the gravedigger. That recruit was at home, hunting up his 'card', and rather unlikely to find it, as it was in Fauchelevent's pocket. Without his card, he could not get back into the cemetery.

Fauchelevent took the spade and Jean Valjean the pick, and together they buried the empty coffin.

When the grave was filled, Fauchelevent said to Jean Valjean:

'Come, let us go; I'll keep the spade, you take the pick.'

Night was coming on rapidly.

Jean Valjean found it hard to move and walk. In the coffin he had stiffened considerably, somewhat in reality like a corpse. The anchylosis of death had seized him in that narrow wooden box. He had, in some sort, to thaw himself out of the sepulchre.

'You are benumbed,' said Fauchelevent; 'and what a pity that I'm bandy-legged or we'd run a bit.'

'No matter!' replied Jean Valjean, 'a few steps will put my legs into walking order.'

They went out by the avenues the hearse had followed. When they reached the closed gate and the porter's lodge, Fauchelevent, who had the gravedigger's card in his hand, dropped it into the box, the porter drew the cord, the gate opened, and they went through.

'How well everything goes!' said Fauchelevent; 'what a good plan that was of yours, Father Madeleine!'

They passed the Barrière Vaugirard in the easiest way in the world. In the neighbourhood of a graveyard, a pick and spade are two passports.

The Rue de Vaugirard was deserted.

'Father Madeleine,' said Fauchelevent, as he went along, looking up at the houses, 'you have better eyes than mine – which is number 87?'

'Here it is, now,' said Jean Valjean.

'There's no one in the street,' resumed Fauchelevent. 'Give me the pick, and wait for me a couple of minutes.'

Fauchelevent went in at number 87, ascended to the topmost flight, guided by the instinct which always leads the poor to the garret, and knocked, in the dark, at the door of a little attic room. A voice called:

'Come in!'

It was Gribier's voice.

Fauchelevent pushed open the door. The lodging of the gravedigger was, like all these shelters of the needy, an unfurnished but much littered loft. A packing-case of some kind – a coffin, perhaps – supplied the place of a bureau, a straw pallet the place of a bed, a butter-pot the place of water-cooler, and the floor served alike for chairs and table. In one corner, on a ragged old scrap of carpet, was a haggard woman, and a number of children were huddled together. The whole of this wretched interior bore the traces of recent overturn. One would have said that there had been an earthquake served up there 'for one'. The coverlets were displaced, the ragged garments scattered about, the pitcher broken, the mother had been weeping, and the children probably beaten; all traces of a headlong and violent search. It was plain that the gravedigger had been looking, wildly, for his card, and had made everything in the attic, from his pitcher to his wife, responsible for the loss. He had a desperate appearance.

But Fauchelevent was in too great a hurry for the end of his adventure, to notice this gloomy side of his triumph.

As he came in, he said:

'I've brought your spade and pick.'

Gribier looked at him with stupefaction.

'What, is it you, peasant?'

'And, tomorrow morning, you will find your card with the gatekeeper of the cemetery.'

And he set down the pick and the spade on the floor.

'What does all this mean?' asked Gribier.

'Why, it means that you let your card drop out of your pocket; that I found it on the ground when you had gone; that I buried the corpse; that I filled in the grave; that I finished your job; that the porter will give you your card, and that you will not have to pay the fifteen francs. That's what it means, recruit!'

'Thanks, villager!' exclaimed Gribier, in amazement. 'The next time I will treat.'

8. *Successful examination*

AN HOUR LATER, in the depth of night, two men and a child stood in front of No. 62, Petite Rue Picpus. The elder of the men lifted the knocker and rapped.

It was Fauchelevent, Jean Valjean, and Cosette.

The two men had gone to look for Cosette at the shop of the fruiteress of the Rue de Chemin Vert, where Fauchelevent had left her on the preceding evening. Cosette had passed the twenty-four hours wondering what it all meant and trembling in silence. She trembled so much that she had not wept, nor had she tasted food nor slept. The worthy fruit-woman had asked her a thousand questions without obtaining any other answer than a sad look that never varied. Cosette did not let a word of all she had heard and seen, in the last two days, escape her. She divined that a crisis had come. She felt, in her very heart, that she must be 'good'. Who has not experienced the supreme effect of these two words pronounced in a certain tone in the ear of some little frightened creature, 'Don't speak!' Fear is mute. Besides, no one ever keeps a secret so well as a child.

But when, after those mournful four-and-twenty hours, she again saw Jean Valjean, she uttered such a cry of joy that any thoughtful person hearing her would have divined in it an escape from some yawning gulf.

Fauchelevent belonged to the convent and knew all the pass-words. Every door opened before him.

Thus was that doubly fearful problem solved of getting out and getting in again.

The porter, who had his instructions, opened the little side door which served to communicate between the court and the garden, and which, twenty years ago, could still be seen from the street, in the wall at the extremity of the court, facing the *porte-cochère*. The porter admitted all three by this door, and from that point they went to this private inner parlour, where Fauchelevent had, on the previous evening, received the orders of the prioress.

The prioress, rosary in hand, was awaiting them. A mother, with her veil down, stood near her. A modest taper lighted, or one might almost say, pretended to light up the parlour.

The prioress scrutinised Jean Valjean. Nothing scans so carefully as a downcast eye.

Then she proceeded to question: 'You are the brother?'

'Yes, reverend mother,' replied Fauchelevent.

'What is your name?'

Fauchelevent replied: 'Ultimus Fauchelevent!'

He had, in reality, had a brother named Ultimus, who was dead.

'From what part of the country are you?'

Fauchelevent answered: 'From Picquigny, near Amiens.'

'What is your age?'

Fauchelevent answered: 'Fifty.'

'What is your business?'

Fauchelevent answered: 'Gardener.'

'Are you a true Christian?'

Fauchelevent answered: 'All of our family are such.'

'Is this your little girl?'

Fauchelevent answered: 'Yes, reverend mother.'

'You are her father?'

Fauchelevent answered: 'Her grandfather.'

The mother said to the prioress in an undertone: 'He answers well.'

Jean Valjean had not spoken a word.

The prioress looked at Cosette attentively, and then said, aside to the mother: 'She will be homely.'

The two mothers talked together very low for a few minutes in a corner of the parlour, and then the prioress turned and said:

'Father Fauvent, you will have another knee-cap and bell. We need two, now.'

So, next morning, two little bells were heard tinkling in the garden, and the nuns could not keep from lifting a corner of their veils. They saw two men digging side by side, in the lower part of the garden under the trees – Fauvent and another. Immense event! The silence was broken, so far as to say:

'It's an assistant-gardener!'

The mothers added:

'He is Father Fauvent's brother.'

In fact, Jean Valjean was regularly installed; he had the leather knee-cap and the bell; henceforth he had his commission. His name was Ultimus Fauchelevent.

The strongest recommendation for Cosette's admission had been the remark of the prioress: *She will be homely*.

The prioress having uttered this prediction, immediately took Cosette into her friendship and gave her a place in the school building as a charity pupil.

There is nothing not entirely logical in this.

It is all in vain to have no mirrors in convents; women are conscious of their own appearance; young girls who know that they are pretty do not readily become nuns; the inclination to the calling being in inverse proportion to good looks, more is expected from the homely than from the handsome ones. Hence a marked preference for the homely.

This whole affair elevated good old Fauchelevent greatly; he had achieved a triple success; – in the eyes of Jean Valjean whom he had rescued and sheltered; with the gravedigger, Gribier, who said he had saved him from a fine; and, at the convent, which, thanks to him, in retaining the coffin of Mother Crucifixion under the altar, eluded Cæsar and satisfied God. There was a coffin with a body in it at the Petit Picpus, and a coffin without a body in the Vaugirard cemetery. Public order was greatly disturbed thereby, undoubtedly, but nobody perceived it. As for the convent, its gratitude to Fauchelevent was deep. Fauchelevent became the best of servants and the most precious of gardeners.

At the next visit of the archbishop the prioress related the affair to his grace, half by way of a confession and half as a boast.

The archbishop, on returning from the convent, spoke of it with commendation and very quietly to M. de Latil, the confessor of Monsieur, and, subsequently, Archbishop of Rheims and a cardinal. This praise and admiration for

Fauchelevent travelled far, for it went to Rome. We have seen a note addressed by the then reigning pope, Leo XII, to one of his relatives, Monsignore of the Papal Embassy at Paris, who bore the same name as his own, Della Genga. It contained these lines: 'It seems that there is in a convent in Paris, an excellent gardener who is a holy man, named Fauvent.' Not a whisper of all this fame reached Fauchelevent in his shanty; he continued to weed and graft and cover his melon-beds without being, in the least, aware of his excellence and holiness. He had no more suspicion of his splendid reputation than any Durham or Surrey ox whose picture is published in the *London Illustrated News* with this inscription: '*The ox which won the premium at the cattle show.*'

9. *The Close*

COSETTE, AT THE CONVENT, still kept silent. She very naturally thought herself Jean Valjean's daughter. Moreover, knowing nothing, there was nothing she could tell, and then, in any case, she would not have told anything. As we have remarked, nothing habituates children to silence like misfortune. Cosette had suffered so much that she was afraid of everything, even to speak, even to breathe. A single word had so often brought down an avalanche on her head! She had hardly begun to feel reassured since she had been with Jean Valjean. She soon became accustomed to the convent. Still, she longed for Catharine, but dared not say so. One day, however, she said to Jean Valjean, 'If I had known it, father, I would have brought her with me.'

Cosette, in becoming a pupil at the convent, had to assume the dress of the school girls. Jean Valjean succeeded in having the garments which she laid aside, given to him. It was the same mourning suit he had carried for her to put on when she left the Thénardiers. It was not much worn. Jean Valjean rolled up these garments, as well as the woollen stockings and shoes, with much camphor and other aromatic substances of which there is such an abundance in convents, and packed them in a small valise which he managed to procure. He put this valise in a chair near his bed, and always kept the key of it in his pocket.

'Father,' Cosette one day asked him, 'what is that box there that smells so good?'

Father Fauchelevent, besides the 'glory' we have just described, and of which he was unconscious, was recompensed for his good deed; in the first place it made him happy, and then he had less work to do, as it was divided. Finally, as he was very fond of tobacco, he found the presence of M. Madeleine advantageous in another point of view; he took three times as much tobacco as before, and that too in a manner infinitely more voluptuous, since M. Madeline paid for it. The nuns did not adopt the name of *Ultimus;* they called Jean Valjean *the other Fauvent*.

If those holy women had possessed aught of the discrimination of Javert, they might have remarked, in course of time, that when there was any little errand to run outside for on account of the garden, it was always the elder Fauchelevent, old, infirm, and lame as he was, who went, and never the other; but, whether it be that eyes continually fixed upon God cannot play the spy, or whether they were too constantly employed in watching one another, they noticed nothing.

However, Jean Valjean was well satisfied to keep quiet and still. Javert watched the quarter for a good long month.

The convent was to Jean Valjean like an island surrounded by wide waters. These four walls were, henceforth, the world to him. Within them he could see enough of the sky to be calm, and enough of Cosette to be happy.

A very pleasant life began again for him.

He lived with Fauchelevent in the out-building at the foot of the garden. This petty structure, built of rubbish, which was still standing in 1845, consisted, as we have already stated, of three rooms, all of which were bare to the very walls. The principal one had been forcibly pressed upon M. Madeleine by Fauchelevent, for Jean Valjean had resisted in vain. The wall of this room, besides the two nails used for hanging up the knee-leather and the hoe, was decorated with a royalist specimen of paper-money of '93, pasted above the fireplace, of which the following is a counterpart:

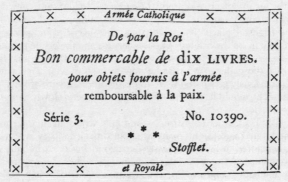

This Vendean assignat had been tacked to the wall by the preceding gardener, a former member of the Chouan party,[72] who had died at the convent, and whom Fauchelevent had succeeded.

Jean Valjean worked every day in the garden, and was very useful there. He had formerly been a pruner, and now found it quite in his way to be a gardener. It may be remembered that he knew all kinds of receipts and secrets of field-work. These he turned to account. Nearly all the orchard trees were wild stock; he grafted them and made them bear excellent fruit.

Cosette was allowed to come every day, and pass an hour with him. As the sisters were melancholy, and he was kind, the child compared him with them, and worshipped him. Every day, at the hour appointed, she would hurry to the little building. When she entered the old place, she filled it with Paradise. Jean Valjean basked in her presence and felt his own happiness increase by reason of the happiness he conferred on Cosette. The delight we inspire in others has this enchanting peculiarity that, far from being diminished like every other reflection, it returns to us more radiant than ever. At the hours of recreation, Jean Valjean from a distance watched her playing and romping, and he could distinguish her laughter from the laughter of the rest.

For, now, Cosette laughed.

Even Cosette's countenance had, in a measure, changed. The gloomy cast had disappeared. Laughter is sunshine; it chases winter from the human face.

When the recreation was over and Cosette went in, Jean Valjean watched the windows of her schoolroom, and, at night, would rise from his bed to take a look at the windows of the room in which she slept.

God has his own ways. The convent contributed, like Cosette, to confirm and complete, in Jean Valjean, the work of the bishop. It cannot be denied that one of virtue's phases ends in pride. Therein is a bridge built by the Evil One. Jean Valjean was, perhaps, without knowing it, near that very phase of virtue, and that very bridge, when Providence flung him into the convent of the Petit Picpus. So long as he compared himself only with the bishop, he found himself unworthy and remained humble; but, for sometime past, he had been comparing himself with the rest of men, and pride was springing up in him. Who knows? He might have finished by going gradually back to hate.

The convent stopped him on this descent.

It was the second place of captivity he had seen. In his youth, in what had been for him the commencement of life, and, later, quite recently too, he had seen another, a frightful place, a terrible place, the severities of which had always seemed to him to be the iniquity of public justice and the crime of the law. Now, after having seen the galleys, he saw the cloister, and reflecting that he had been an inmate of the galleys, and that he now was, so to speak, a spectator of the cloister, he anxiously compared them in his meditations with anxiety.

Sometimes he would lean upon his spade and descend slowly along the endless rounds of reverie.

He recalled his former companions, and how wretched they were. They rose at dawn and toiled until night. Scarcely allowed to sleep, they lay on camp-beds, and were permitted to have mattresses but two inches thick in halls which were warmed only during the most inclement months. They were attired in hideous red sacks, and had given to them, as a favour, a pair of canvas pantaloons in the heats of midsummer, and a square of woollen stuff to throw over their shoulders, during the bitterest frosts of winter. They had no wine to drink, no meat for food excepting when sent upon 'extra hard work'. They lived without names, distinguished solely by numbers, and reduced, as it were, to ciphers, lowering their eyes, lowering their voices, with their hair cropped close, under the rod, and plunged in shame.

Then, his thoughts reverted to the beings before his eyes.

These beings, also, lived with their hair cut close, their eyes bent down, their voices hushed, not in shame indeed, but amid the scoffs of the world; not with their backs bruised by the gaoler's staff, but with their shoulders lacerated by self-inflicted penance. Their names, too, had perished from among men, and they now existed under austere designations alone. They never ate meat and never drank wine; they often remained until evening without food. They were attired not in red sacks, but in black habits of woollen, heavy in summer, light in winter, unable to increase or diminish them, without even the privilege, according to the season, of substituting a linen dress or a woollen cloak, and then, for six months in the year, they wore underclothing of serge which fevered them. They dwelt not in dormitories warmed only in the bitterest frosts of winter, but in cells where fire was never kindled. They slept not on mattresses two inches thick, but upon straw. Moreover, they were not even allowed to sleep, for, every night, after a day of labour, they were, when whelmed beneath the weight of the first sleep, at the moment when they were just beginning to slumber, and, with difficulty, to collect a little warmth, required to waken, rise and assemble for prayers in an icy-cold and gloomy chapel, with their knees on the stone pavement.

On certain days, each one of these beings, in her turn, had to remain twelve hours in succession kneeling upon the flags, or prostrate on her face, with her arms crossed.

The others were men, these were women. What had these men done? They had robbed, ravished, plundered, killed, assassinated. They were highwaymen, forgers, poisoners, incendiaries, murderers, parricides. What had these women done? They had done nothing.

On one side, robbery, fraud, imposition, violence, lust, homicide, every species of sacrilege, every description of offence; on the other, one thing only, – innocence.

A perfect innocence almost borne upwards in a mysterious Assumption, clinging still to Earth through virtue, already touching Heaven through holiness.

On the one hand, the mutual avowal of crimes detailed with bated breath; on the other, faults confessed aloud. And oh! what crimes! and oh! what faults!

On one side foul miasma, on the other, ineffable perfume. On the one side, a moral pestilence, watched day and night, held in subjection at the cannon's mouth, and slowly consuming its infected victims; on the other, a chaste kindling of every soul together on the same hearthstone. There, utter gloom; here, the shadow, but a shadow full of light, and the light full of glowing radiations.

Two seats of slavery; but, in the former, rescue possible, a legal limit always in view, and, then, escape. In the second, perpetuity, the only hope at the most distant boundary of the future, that gleam of liberty which men call death.

In the former, the captives were enchained by chains only; in the other, they were enchained by faith alone.

What resulted from the first? One vast curse, the gnashing of teeth, hatred, desperate depravity, a cry of rage against human society, a sarcasm against heaven.

What issued from the second? Benediction and love.

And, in these two places, so alike and yet so different, these two species of beings so dissimilar were performing the same work of expiation.

Jean Valjean thoroughly comprehended the expiation of the first; personal expiation, expiation for oneself. But, he did not understand that of the others, of these blameless, spotless creatures, and he asked himself with a tremor: 'Expiation of what? What expiation?'

A voice responded in his conscience: the most divine of all human generosity, expiation for others.

Here we withhold all theories of our own: we are but the narrator; at Jean Valjean's point of view we place ourselves and we merely reproduce his impressions.

He had before his eyes the sublime summit of self-denial, the loftiest possible height of virtue; innocence forgiving men their sins and expiating them in their stead; servitude endured, torture accepted, chastisement and misery invoked by souls that had not sinned in order that these might not fall upon souls which had; the love of humanity losing itself in the love of God, but remaining there, distinct and suppliant; sweet, feeble beings supporting all the torments of those who are punished, yet retaining the smile of those who are rewarded. And then he remembered that he had dared to complain.

Often, in the middle of the night, he would rise from his bed to listen to the grateful anthem of these innocent beings thus overwhelmed with austerities, and he felt the blood run cold in his veins as he reflected that they who were justly punished never raised their voices towards Heaven excepting to blaspheme, and that he, wretch that he was, had uplifted his clenched fist against God.

Another strange thing which made him muse and meditate profoundly seemed like an intimation whispered in his ear by Providence itself: the scaling of walls, the climbing over enclosures, the risk taken in defiance of danger or death, the difficult and painful ascent – all those very efforts that he had made to escape from the other place of expiation, he had made to enter this one. Was this an emblem of his destiny?

This house, also, was a prison, and bore dismal resemblance to the other from which he had fled, and yet he had never conceived anything like it.

He once more saw gratings, bolts and bars of iron – to shut in whom? Angels.

Those lofty walls which he had seen surrounding tigers, he now saw encircling lambs.

It was a place of expiation, not of punishment; and yet it was still more austere, more sombre and more pitiless than the other. These virgins were more harshly bent down than the convicts. A harsh, cold blast, the blast that had frozen his youth, careered across that grated moat and manacled the vultures; but a wind still more biting and more cruel beat upon the dove cage.

And why?

When he thought of these things, all that was in him gave way before this mystery of sublimity. In these meditations, pride vanished. He reverted, again and again, to himself; he felt his own pitiful unworthiness, and often wept. All that had occurred in his existence, for the last six months, led him back towards the holy injunctions of the bishop; Cosette through love, the convent through humility.

Sometimes, in the evening, about dusk, at the hour when the garden was solitary, he was seen kneeling, in the middle of the walk that ran along the chapel, before the window through which he had looked, on the night of his first arrival, turned towards the spot where he knew that the sister who was performing the reparation was prostrate in prayer. Thus he prayed kneeling before this sister.

It seemed as though he dared not kneel directly before God.

Everything around him, this quiet garden, these balmy flowers, these children, shouting with joy, these meek and simple women, this silent cloister, gradually entered into all his being, and, little by little, his soul subsided into silence like this cloister, into fragrance like these flowers, into peace like this garden, into simplicity like these women, into joy, like these children. And then he reflected that two houses of God had received him in succession at the two critical moments of his life, the first when every door was closed and human society repelled him; the second, when human society again howled upon his track, and the galleys once more gaped for him; and that, had it not been for the first, he should have fallen back into crime, and, had it not been for the second, into punishment.

His whole heart melted in gratitude, and he loved more and more.

Several years passed thus. Cosette was growing.

PART THREE: MARIUS

1. Parvulus[73]

PARIS HAS A CHILD, and the forest has a bird; the bird is called the sparrow; the child is called the *gamin.*

Couple these two ideas, the one containing all the heat of the furnace, the other all the light of the dawn; strike together these two sparks, Paris and infancy; and there leaps forth from them a little creature. *Homuncio,* Plautus would say.

This little creature is full of joy. He has not food to eat every day, yet he goes to the show every evening, if he sees fit. He has no shirt to his back, no shoes to his feet, no roof over his head; he is like the flies in the air who have none of all these things. He is from seven to thirteen years of age, lives in troops, ranges the streets, sleeps in the open air, wears an old pair of his father's pantaloons down about his heels, an old hat of some other father, which covers his ears, and a single suspender of yellow listing, runs about, is always on the watch and on the search, kills time, colours pipes, swears like an imp, hangs about the wine-shop, knows thieves and robbers, is hand in glove with the street-girls, rattles off slang, sings smutty songs, and, withal, has nothing bad in his heart. This is because he has a pearl in his soul, innocence; and pearls do not dissolve in mire. So long as man is a child, God wills that he be innocent.

If one could ask of this vast city: what is that creature? She would answer: 'it is my bantling.'

2. *Some of his private marks*

THE GAMIN OF PARIS[74] is the dwarf of the giantess.

We will not exaggerate. This cherub of the gutter sometimes has a shirt, but then he has only one; sometimes he has shoes, but then they have no soles; sometimes he has a shelter, and he loves it, for there he finds his mother; but he prefers the street for there he finds his liberty. He has sports of his own, roguish tricks of his own, of which a hearty hatred of the bourgeois is the basis; he has his own metaphors; to be dead he calls *eating dandelions by the root;* he has his own occupations, such as running for hacks, letting down carriage-steps, sweeping the crossings in rainy weather, which he styles making *ponts des arts,* crying the speeches often made by the authorities on behalf of the French people, and digging out the streaks between the flags of the pavement; he has his own kind of money, consisting of all the little bits of wrought copper that can be found on the public thoroughfares. This curious coin, which takes the name of *scraps,* has an unvarying and well regulated circulation throughout this little gypsy-land of children.

He has a fauna of his own, which he studies carefully in the corners; the good God's bug, the death's head grub, the mower, the devil, a black insect that threatens you by twisting about its tail which is armed with two horns. He has

his fabulous monster which has scales on its belly, and yet is not a lizard, has
warts on its back, and yet is not a toad, which lives in the crevices of old lime-
kilns and dry-cisterns, a black, velvety, slimy, crawling creature, sometimes swift
and sometimes slow of motion, emitting no cry, but which stares at you, and is
so terrible that nobody has ever seen it; this monster he calls the 'deaf thing'.
Hunting for deaf things among the stones is a pleasure which is thrillingly
dangerous. Another enjoyment is to raise a flag of the pavement suddenly and
see the woodlice. Every region of Paris is famous for the discoveries which can
be made in it. There are earwigs in the wood-yards of the Ursulines, there are
woodlice at the Pantheon, and tadpoles in the ditches of the Champ-de-Mars.

In repartee, this youngster is as famous as Talleyrand. He is equally cynical,
but he is more sincere. He is gifted with an odd kind of unpremeditated jollity;
he stuns the shopkeeper with his wild laughter. His gamut slides merrily from
high comedy to farce.

A funeral is passing. There is a doctor in the procession. 'Hullo!' shouts a
gamin, 'how long is it since the doctors began to take home their work?'

Another happens to be in a crowd. A grave-looking man, who wears spectacles
and trinkets, turns upon him indignantly: 'You scamp, you've been seizing my
wife's waist!'

'I, sir! search me!'

3. *He is agreeable*

IN THE EVENING, by means of a few pennies which he always manages to scrape
together, the *homuncio* goes to some theatre. By the act of passing that magic
threshold, he becomes transfigured; he was a *gamin*, he becomes a *titi*. Theatres
are a sort of vessel turned upside down with the hold at the top; in this hold the
titi gather in crowds. The *titi* is to the *gamin* what the butterfly is to the grub; the
same creature on wings and sailing through the air. It is enough for him to be
there with his radiance of delight, his fulness of enthusiasm and joy, and his
clapping of hands like the clapping of wings, to make that hold, close, dark,
foetid, filthy, unwholesome, hideous, and detestable, as it is, a very Paradise.

Give to a being the useless, and deprive him of the needful, and you have the
gamin.

The *gamin* is not without a certain inclination towards literature. His
tendency, however – we say it with the befitting quantum of regret – would not
be considered as towards the classic. He is, in his nature, but slightly academic.
For instance, the popularity of Mademoiselle Mars among this little public of
children was spiced with a touch of irony. The *gamin* called her Mademoiselle
Muche.

This being jeers, wrangles, sneers, jangles, has frippery like a baby and rags
like a philosopher, fishes in the sewer, hunts in the drain, extracts gaiety from
filth, lashes the street corners with his wit, fleers and bites, hisses and sings,
applauds and hoots, tempers Hallelujah with turalural, psalmodises all sorts of
rhythms from De Profundis to the *Chie-en-lit*, finds without searching, knows
what he does not know, is Spartan even to roguery, is witless even to wisdom, is
lyric even to impurity, would squat upon Olympus, wallows in the dung-heap
and comes out of it covered with stars. The *gamin* of Paris is an urchin Rabelais.

He is never satisfied with his pantaloons unless they have a watch-fob.

He is seldom astonished, is frightened still less frequently, turns superstitions into doggerel verses and sings them, collapses exaggerations, makes light of mysteries, sticks out his tongue at ghosts, dismounts everything that is on stilts, and introduces caricature into all epic pomposities. This is not because he is prosaic, far from it; but he substitutes the phantasmagoria of fun for solemn dreams. Were Adamaster[75] to appear to him, he would shout out: 'Hallo, there, old Bug-a-boo!'

4. *He may be useful*

PARIS BEGINS with the cockney and ends with the *gamin*, two beings of which no other city is capable; passive acceptation satisfied with merely looking on, and exhaustless enterprise; Prudhomme and Fouillou. Paris alone comprises this in its natural history. All monarchy is comprised in the cockney; all anarchy in the *gamin*.

This pale child of the Paris suburbs lives, develops, and gets into and out of 'scrapes', amid suffering, a thoughtful witness of our social realities and our human problems. He thinks himself careless, but he is not. He looks on, ready to laugh; ready, also, for something else. Whoever ye are who call yourselves Prejudice, Abuse, Ignominy, Oppression, Iniquity, Despotism, Injustice, Fanaticism, Tyranny, beware of the gaping *gamin*.

This little fellow will grow.

Of what clay is he made? Of the first mud of the street. A handful of common soil, a breath and, behold, Adam! It is enough that a God but pass. A God always has passed where the *gamin* is. Chance works in the formation of this little creature. By this word chance we mean, in some degree, hazard. Now, will this pigmy, thoroughly kneaded with the coarse common earth, ignorant, illiterate, wild, vulgar, mobbish, as he is, become an Ionian, or a Bœotian? Wait, *currit rota*, the life of Paris, that demon which creates the children of chance and the men of destiny, reversing the work of the Latin potter, makes of the jug a costly vase.

5. *His frontiers*

THE GAMIN LOVES THE CITY, he loves solitude also, having something of the sage in him. *Urbis amator*, like Fuscus; *ruris amator*, like Flaccus.

To rove about, musing, that is to say loitering, is, for a philosopher, a good way of spending time; especially in that kind of mock rurality, ugly but odd, and partaking of two natures, which surrounds certain large cities, particularly Paris. To study the banlieue is to study the amphibious. End of trees, beginning of houses, end of grass, beginning of pavement, end of furrows, beginning of shops, end of ruts, beginning of passions, end of the divine murmur, beginning of the human hubbub; hence, the interest is extraordinary.

Hence, it is that in these by no means inviting spots which are always termed *gloomy*, the dreamer selects his apparently aimless walks.

He who writes these lines has long been a loiterer about the Barrière of Paris, and to him it is a source of deepest remembrances. That close-clipped grass, those stony walks, that chalk, that clay, that rubbish, those harsh monotones of open lots and fallow land, those early plants of the market gardeners suddenly descried in some hollow of the ground, that mixture of wild nature with the urban landscape, those wide unoccupied patches where the drummers of the garrison hold their noisy school and imitate, as it were, the lighter din of battle, those solitudes by day and ambuscades by night, the tottering old mill turning with every breeze, the hoisting-wheels of the stone-quarries, the drinking shops at the corners of the cemeteries, the mysterious charm of those dark high walls, which divide into squares immense grounds, dimly seen in the distance, but bathed in sunshine and alive with butterflies – all these attracted him.

There is hardly anybody but knows those singular places, [76] the Glacière, the Cunette, the hideous wall of Grenelle spotted with balls, the Mont-Parnasse, the Fosse-aux-Loups, the white hazel trees on the high banks of the Marne, Mont-Souris, the Tombe-Issoire, the Pierre Plate de Chatillon where there is an old exhausted quarry which is of no further use but as a place for the growth of mushrooms, and is closed on a level with the ground by a trap-door of rotten boards. The Campagna of Rome is one idea; the banlieue of Paris is another; to see in whatever forms our horizon, nothing but fields, houses, or trees, is to be but superficial; all the aspects of things are thoughts of God. The place where an open plain adjoins a city always bears the impress of some indescribable, penetrating melancholy. There, nature and humanity address you at one and the same moment. There, the originalities of place appear.

He who, like ourselves, has rambled through these solitudes contiguous to our suburbs, which one might term the limbo of Paris, has noticed dotted about, here and there, always in the most deserted spot and at the most unexpected moment, beside some straggling hedge or in the corner of some dismal wall, little helter-skelter groups of children, filthy, muddy, dusty, uncombed, dishevelled, playing mumble-peg crowned with violets. These are all the runaway children of poor families. The outer boulevard is their breathing medium, and the banlieue belongs to them. There, they play truant, continually. There they sing, innocently, their collection of low songs. They are, or rather, they live there, far from every eye, in the soft radiance of May or June, kneeling around a hole in the ground, playing marbles, squabbling for pennies, irresponsible, birds flown, let loose and happy; and, the moment they see you, remembering that they have a trade and must make their living, they offer to sell you an old woollen stocking full of May-bugs, or a bunch of lilacs. These meetings with strange children are among the seductive but at the same time saddening charms of the environs of Paris.

Sometimes among this crowd of boys, there are a few little girls – are they their sisters? – almost young women, thin, feverish, freckled, gloved with sunburn, with head-dresses of rye-straw and poppies, gay, wild, barefooted. Some of them are seen eating cherries among the growing grain. In the evening, they are heard laughing. These groups, warmly lighted up by the full blaze of noon-day, or seen dimly in the twilight, long occupy the attention of the dreamer, and these visions mingle with his reveries.

Paris, the centre; the banlieue, the circumference; to these children, this is the whole world. They never venture beyond it. They can no more live out of the atmosphere of Paris than fish can live out of water. To them, beyond two leagues from the barrières there is nothing more. Ivry, Gentilly, Arcueil, Belleville, Aubervilliers, Menilmontant, Choisy-le-Roi, Billancourt, Meudon, Issy, Vanvre, Sèvres, Puteaux, Neuilly, Gennevilliers, Colombes, Romainville, Chatou, Asnières, Bougival, Nanterre, Enghien, Noisy-le-Sec, Nogent, Gournay, Drancy, Gonesse; these are the end of the world.

6. *A scrap of history*

AT THE PERIOD, although it is almost contemporaneous, in which the action of this story is laid, there was not, as there now is, a police officer at every street-corner (an advantage we have no time to enlarge upon); truant children abounded in Paris. The statistics gave an average of two hundred and sixty homeless children, picked up annually by the police on their rounds, in open lots, in houses in process of building, and under the arches of bridges. One of these nests, which continues famous, produced 'the swallows of the bridge of Arcola'. This, moreover, is the most disastrous of our social symptoms. All the crimes of man begin with the vagrancy of childhood.

We must except Paris, however. To a considerable degree, and notwithstanding the reminiscence we have just recalled, the exception is just. While in every other city, the truant boy is the lost man; while, almost everywhere, the boy given up to himself is, in some sort, devoted and abandoned to a species of fatal immersion in public vices which eat out of him all that is respectable, even conscience itself, the *gamin* of Paris, we must insist, chipped and spotted as he is on the surface, is almost intact within. A thing magnificent to think of, and one that shines forth resplendently in the glorious probity of our popular revolutions; a certain incorruptibility results from the mental fluid which is to the air of Paris what salt is to the water of the ocean. To breathe the air of Paris preserves the soul.

What we here say alleviates, in no respect, that pang of the heart which we feel whenever we meet one of these children, around whom we seem to see floating the broken ties of the disrupted family. In our present civilisation, which is still so incomplete, it is not a very abnormal thing to find these disruptions of families, separating in the darkness, scarcely knowing what has become of their children – dropping fragments of their life, as it were, upon the public highway. Hence arise dark destinies. This is called, for the sad chance has coined its own expression, 'being cast upon the pavement of Paris'.

These abandonments of children, be it said, in passing, were not discouraged by the old monarchy. A little of Egypt and of Bohemia in the lower strata, accommodated the higher spheres, and answered the purpose of the powerful. Hatred to the instruction of the children of the people was a dogma. What was the use of 'a little learning?' Such was the password. Now the truant child is the corollary of the ignorant child. Moreover, the monarchy sometimes had need of children, and then it skimmed the street.

Under Louis XIV, not to go any further back, the king, very wisely, desired to build up a navy. The idea was a good one. But let us look at the means. No navy could there be, if, side by side with the sailing vessel, the sport of the wind, to tow it along, in case of need, there were not another vessel capable of going where it pleased, either by the oar or by steam; the galleys were to the navy, then, what steamers now are. Hence, there must be galleys; but galleys could be moved only by galley-slaves, and therefore there must be galley-slaves. Colbert, through the provincial intendants and the parliaments, made as many galley-slaves as possible. The magistracy set about the work with good heart. A man kept his hat on before a procession, a Huguenot attitude; he was sent to the galleys. A boy was found in the street; if he had no place to sleep in, and was fifteen years old, he was sent to the galleys. Great reign, great age.

Under Louis XV children disappeared in Paris; the police carried them off – nobody knows for what mysterious use. People whispered with affright horrible conjectures about the purple baths of the king. Barbier speaks ingenuously of these things. It sometimes happened that the officers, running short of children, took some who had fathers. The fathers, in despair, rushed upon the officers. In such cases, the parliament interfered and hung – whom? The officers? No; the fathers.

7. *The* gamin *will have his place among the classifications of India*

THE PARISIAN ORDER of *gamins* is almost a caste. One might say: nobody wants to have anything to do with them.

This word *gamin* was printed for the first time, and passed from the popular language into that of literature, in 1834. It was in a little work entitled *Claude Gueux*[77] that the word first appeared. It created a great uproar. The word was adopted.

The elements that go to make up respectability among the *gamins* are very varied. We knew and had to do with one who was greatly respected and admired, because he had seen a man fall from the towers of Notre Dame; another, because he had succeeded in making his way into the rear enclosure where the statues intended for the dome of the Invalides were deposited, and had scraped off some of the lead; a third, because he had seen a diligence upset; and still another, because he knew a soldier who had almost knocked out the eye of a bourgeois.

This explains that odd exclamation of a Parisian *gamin*, a depth of lamentation which the multitude laugh at without comprehending. '*Oh, Lordy, lordy! a'nt I unlucky! only think I never even saw anybody fall from a fifth storey;*' the words pronounced with an inexpressible twang of his own.

What a rich saying for a peasant was this! 'Father so-and-so, your wife's illness has killed her; why didn't you send for a doctor?' 'What are you thinking about, friend?' says the other. 'Why, we poor people *we haves to die ourselves.*' But, if all the passiveness of the peasant is found in this saying, all the rollicking anarchy of the urchin of the suburbs is contained in the following – A poor wretch on his way to the gallows was listening to his confessor, who sat beside him in the cart. A Paris boy shouted out: '*He's talking to his long-gown. Oh, the sniveller!*'

A certain audacity in religious matters sets off the *gamin*. It is a great thing to be strong-minded.

To be present at executions is a positive duty. These imps point at the guillotine and laugh. They give it all kinds of nicknames: 'End of the Soup' – 'Old Growler' – 'Sky-Mother' – 'The Last Mouthful', etc., etc. That they may lose nothing of the sight, they scale walls, hang on to balconies, climb trees, swing to gratings, crouch into chimneys. The *gamin* is a born slater as he is a born sailor. A roof inspires him with no more fear than a mast. No festival is equal to the execution-ground – La Grève, Samson[78] and the Abbé Montes are the really popular names. They shout to the victim to encourage him. Sometimes, they admire him. The *gamin* Lacenaire, seeing the horrible Dautun die bravely, used an expression which was full of future: '*I was jealous of him!*' In the order of *gamins* Voltaire is unknown, but they are acquainted with Papavoine. They mingle in the same recital, 'the politicals' with murderers. They have traditions of the last clothes worn by them all. They know that Tolleron had on a forgeman's cap, and that Avril wore one of otter skin; that Louvel had on a round hat, that old Delaporte was bald and bareheaded, that Castaing was ruddy and good-looking, that Bories had a sweet little beard, that Jean Martin kept on his suspenders, and that Lecouffé and his mother quarrelled. *Don't be finding fault now with your basket*, shouted a *gamin* to the latter couple. Another, to see Debacker pass, being too short in the crowd, began to climb a lamp-post on the quay. A gendarme on that beat scowled at him. 'Let me get up, Mister Gendarme,' said the *gamin*. And then, to soften the official, he added: 'I won't fall.' 'Little do I care about your falling,' replied the gendarme.

In the order of *gamins*, a memorable accident is greatly prized. One of their number reaches the very pinnacle of distinction, if he happen to cut himself badly, 'into the bone', as they say.

The fist is by no means an inferior element of respect. One of the things the *gamin* is fondest of saying is, 'I'm jolly strong, I am!' To be left-handed makes you an object of envy. Squinting is highly esteemed.

8. *In which will be found a charming pleasantry of the late king*

IN SUMMER, he transforms himself into a frog; and in the evening, at nightfall, opposite the bridges of Austerlitz and Jena, from the coal rafts and washerwomen's boats, he plunges head-foremost into the Seine, and into all sorts of infractions of the laws of modesty and the police. However, the policemen are on the look-out, and there results from this circumstance a highly dramatic situation which, upon one occasion, gave rise to a fraternal and memorable cry. This cry, which was quite famous about 1830, is a strategic signal from *gamin* to *gamin;* it is scanned like a verse of Homer, with a style of notation almost as inexplicable as the Eleusinian melody of the Panathenæans, recalling once more the ancient 'Evohe!' It is as follows: '*Ohé! Titi, ohé! lookee yonder! they're comin' to ketch ye! Grab yer clothes and cut through the drain!*'

Sometimes this gnat – it is thus that he styles himself – can read; sometimes he can write; he always knows how to scrawl. He gets by some unknown and mysterious mutual instruction, all talents which may be useful in public affairs; from 1815 to 1830, he imitated the call of the turkey; from 1830 to 1848, he scratched a pear on the walls. One summer evening, Louis Philippe returning to the palace on foot, saw one of them, a little fellow, so high, sweating and stretching upon tiptoe, to make a charcoal sketch of a gigantic pear,[79] on one of the pillars of the Neuilly gateway; the king, with that good nature which he inherited from Henry IV, helped the boy, completed the pear, and gave the youngster a gold Louis, saying: '*The pear's on that, too!*' The *gamin* loves uproar. Violence and noise please him. He execrates 'the curés'. One day, in the Rue de l'Université, one of these young scamps was making faces at the *porte-cochère* of No. 69. 'Why are you doing that at this door?' asked a passer-by. The boy replied: 'There's a curé there.' It was, in fact, the residence of the Papal Nuncio. Nevertheless, whatever may be the Voltairean tendencies of the *gamin*, should an occasion present itself to become a choirboy, he would, very likely, accept, and in such case would serve the mass properly. There are two things of which he is the Tantalus, which he is always wishing for, but never attains – to overthrow the government, and to get his trousers mended.

The *gamin*, in his perfect state, possesses all the policemen of Paris, and, always, upon meeting one, can put a name to the countenance. He counts them off on his fingers. He studies their ways, and has special notes of his own upon each one of them. He reads their souls as an open book. He will tell you off-hand and without hesitating – Such a one is a *traitor;* such a one is *very cross;* such a one is *great,* such a one is *ridiculous;* (all these expressions, traitor, cross, great and ridiculous, have in his mouth a peculiar signification) – 'That chap thinks the Pont Neuf belongs to him, and hinders *people* from walking on the cornice outside of the parapets; that other one has a mania for pulling *persons'* ears;' etc. etc.

9. *The ancient soul of Gaul*

THERE WAS SOMETHING of this urchin in Poquelin,[80] the son of the market-place; there was something of him in Beaumarchais. The *gamin* style of life is a shade of the Gallic mind. Mingled with good sense, it sometimes gives it additional strength, as alcohol does to wine. Sometimes, it is a defect; Homer nods; one might say Voltaire plays *gamin*. Camille Desmoulins was a suburban. Championnet, who brutalised miracles, was a child of the Paris streets; he had when a little boy *besprinkled the porticoes* of St Jean de Beauvais and St Etienne du Mont; he had chatted with the shrine of St Genevieve enough to throw into convulsions the sacred vial of St Januarius.

The Paris *gamin* is respectful, ironical, and insolent. He has bad teeth, because he is poorly fed, and his stomach suffers, and fine eyes because he has genius. In the very presence of Jehovah, he would go hopping and jumping up the steps of Paradise. He is very good at boxing with both hands and feet. Every description of growth is possible to him. He plays in the gutter and rises from it by revolt; his effrontery is not cured by grape; he was a blackguard, lo! he is a hero! like the little Theban, he shakes the lion's skin; Barra the drummer was a Paris *gamin;* he shouts 'Forward!' as the charger of Holy Writ says 'Ha! ha!' and in a moment, he passes from the urchin to the giant.

This child of the gutter is, also, the child of the ideal. Measure this sweep of wing which reaches from Molière to Barra.

As sum total, and to embrace all in a word, the *gamin* is a being who amuses himself because he is unfortunate.

10. Ecce Paris, ecce homo

To SUM UP ALL once more, the *gamin* of Paris of the present day is, as the *græculus* of Rome was in ancient times, the people as a child, with the wrinkles of the old world on its brow.

The *gamin* is a beauty and, at the same time, a disease of the nation – a disease that must be cured. How? By light.

Light makes whole.

Light enlightens.

All the generous irradiations of society spring from science, letters, the arts, and instruction. Make men, make men. Give them light, that they may give you warmth. Soon or late, the splendid question of universal instruction will take its position with the irresistible authority of absolute truth; and then those who govern under the superintendence of the French idea will have to make this choice: the children of France or the *gamins* of Paris; flames in the light or will o' the wisps in the gloom.

The *gamin* is the expression of Paris, and Paris is the expression of the world.[81]

For Paris is a sum total. Paris is the ceiling of the human race. All this prodigious city is an epitome of dead and living manners and customs. He who sees Paris, seems to see all history through with sky and constellations in the intervals. Paris has a Capitol, the Hôtel de Ville; a Parthenon, Notre Dame; a Mount Aventine, the Faubourg St Antoine; an Asinarium, the Sorbonne; a Pantheon, the Pantheon; a Viâ Sacra, the Boulevard des Italiens; a tower of the Winds; public opinion – and supplies the place of the Gemoniæ by ridicule. Its *majo* is the 'faraud', its *Trasteverino* is the suburban; its *hammal* is the strong man of the market-place; its *lazzarone* is the *pègre*; its cockney is the *gandin*. All that can be found anywhere can be found in Paris. The fish-woman of Dumarsais can hold her own with the herb-woman of Euripides, the discobolus Vejanus lives again in Forioso the rope-dancer, Therapontigonus Miles might go arm in arm with the grenadier Vadebonccœur, Damasippus the curiosity broker would be happy among the old curiosity shops, Vincennes would lay hold of Socrates just as the whole Agora would clap Diderot into a strong box; Grimod de la Reyniere discovered roast-beef cooked with its own fat as Curtillus had invented roast hedgehog; we see, again, under the balloon of the Arc de l'Etoile the trapezium mentioned in Plautus; the sword-eater of the Poecilium met with by Apuleius is the swallower of sabres on the Pont Neuf; the nephew of Rameau and Curculion the parasite form a pair; Ergasilus would get himself presented to Cambacérès by d'Aigrefeuille; the four dandies of Rome, Alcesimarchus, Phoedromus, Diabolus, and Argyrippe, may be seen going down la Courtille in the Labutat post-coach; Aulus Gellius did not stop longer in front of Congrio than Charles Nodier before Punch and Judy; Marton is not a tigress, but Pardalisca was not a dragon; Pantolabus the buffoon chaffs Nomentanus the fast-liver at the Café Anglais; Hermogenus is a tenor in the Champs Elysées, and, around him, Thrasius the beggar in the costume of Bobèche plies his trade; the bore who buttonholes you in the Tuileries makes you repeat, after the lapse of two thousand years, the apostrophe of Thesprion: *quis properantem me prehendit pallio?* [82]The wine of Surène parodies the wine of Alba; the red rim of

Desaugiers balances the huge goblet of Balatron, Père Lachaise exhales, under the nocturnal rains, the same lurid emanations that were seen in the Esquilies, and the grave of the poor purchased for five years, is about the equivalent of the hired coffin of the slave.

Ransack your memory for something which Paris has not. The vat of Trophonius contains nothing that is not in the wash-tub of Mesmer; Ergaphilas is resuscitated in Cagliostro; the Brahmin Vasaphantâ is in the flesh again in the Count Saint Germain; the cemetery of St Médard turns out quite as good miracles as the Oumoumié mosque at Damascus.

Paris has an Æsop in Mayeux, and a Canidia in Mademoiselle Lenormand. It stands aghast like Delphos at the blinding realities of visions; it tips tables as Dodona did tripods. It enthrones the grisette as Rome did the courtesan; and, in fine, if Louis XV is worse than Claudius, Madame Dubarry is better than Messalina. Paris combines in one wonderful type which has had real existence, and actually elbowed us, the Greek nudity, the Hebrew ulcer, and the Gascon jest. It mingles Diogenes, Job, and Paillasse, dresses up a ghost in old numbers of the *Constitutionnel*, and produces Shadrac Duclos.

Although Plutarch may say: the *tyrant never grows old*, Rome, under Sylla as well as under Domitian, resigned herself and of her own accord put water in her wine. The Tiber was a Lethe, if we may believe the somewhat doctrinal eulogy pronounced upon it by Varus Vibiscus: *Contra Gracchos Tiberim habemus. Bibere Tiberim, id est seditionem oblivisci.*[83] Paris drinks a quarter of a million of gallons of water per day, but that does not prevent it upon occasion from beating the alarm and sounding the tocsin.

With all that, Paris is a good soul. It accepts everything right royally; it is not difficult in the realms of Venus; its Callipyge is of the Hottentot stamp; if it but laughs, it pardons, ugliness makes it merry; deformity puts it in good humour, vice diverts its attention; be droll and you may venture to be a scamp; even hypocrisy, that sublimity of cynicism, it does not revolt at; it is so literary that it does not hold its nose over Basilius, and is no more shocked at the prayer of Tartuffe than Horace was at the hiccough of Priapus. No feature of the universal countenance is wanting in the profile of Paris. The Mabile dancing garden is not the polyhymnian dance of the Janiculum, but the costume-hirer devours the lorette there with her eyes exactly as the procuress Staphyla watched the virgin Planesium. The Barrière du Combat is not a Coliseum, but there is as much ferocity exhibited as though Cæsar were a spectator. The Syrian hostess has more grace than Mother Saguet, but, if Virgil haunted the Roman wine-shop, David d'Angers, Balzac, and Charlet have sat down in the drinking-places of Paris. Paris is regnant. Geniuses blaze on all sides, and red perukes[84] flourish. Adonaïs passes by in his twelve-wheeled car of thunder and lightning; Silenus makes his entry upon his tun. For Silenus read Ramponneau.

Paris is a synonym of Cosmos. Paris is Athens, Rome, Sybaris, Jerusalem, Pantin. All the eras of civilisation are there in abridged edition, all the epochs of barbarism also. Paris would be greatly vexed, had she no guillotine.

A small admixture of the Place de Grève is good. What would all this continual merrymaking be without that seasoning? Our laws have wisely provided for this, and, thanks to them, this relish turns its edge upon the general carnival.

11. *Ridicule and reign*

OF BOUNDS AND LIMITS, Paris has none. No other city ever enjoyed that supreme control which sometimes derides those whom it reduces to submission. *To please you, O Athenians!* exclaimed Alexander. Paris does more than lay down the law; it lays down the fashion; Paris does more than lay down the fashion; it lays down the routine. Paris may be stupid if it please; sometimes it allows itself this luxury; then, the whole universe is stupid with it. Upon this, Paris awakes, rubs its eyes, and says: 'Am I stupid!' and bursts out laughing in the face of mankind. What a marvel is such a city! how strange a thing that all this mass of what is grand and what is ludicrous should be so harmonious, that all this majesty is not disturbed by all this parody, and that the same month can today blow the trump of the last judgement and tomorrow a penny whistle; Paris possesses an all-commanding joviality. Its gaiety is of the thunderbolt, and its frolicking holds a sceptre. Its hurricanes spring sometimes from a wry face. Its outbursts, its great days, its masterpieces, its prodigies, its epics fly to the ends of the universe, and so do its cock and bull stories also. Its laughter is the mouth of a volcano that bespatters the whole earth. Its jokes are sparks that kindle. It forces upon the nations its caricatures as well as its ideal; the loftiest monuments of human civilisation accept its sarcasms and lend their eternity to its waggeries. It is superb; it has a marvellous Fourteenth of July that delivers the globe; it makes all the nations take the oath of the tennis-court; its night of the Fourth of August disperses in three hours a thousand years of feudalism; it makes of its logic the muscle of the unanimous will; it multiplies itself under all the forms of the sublime; it fills with its radiance Washington, Kosciusko, Bolivar, Botzaris, Riego, Bem, Manin, Lopez, John Brown, Garibaldi; it is everywhere, where the future is being enkindled, at Boston in 1779, at the Isle de St Leon in 1820, at Pesth in 1848, at Palermo in 1860; it whispers the mighty watchword *Liberty* in the ears of the American Abolitionists grouped together in the boat at Harper's Ferry, and also in the ears of the patriots of Ancona assembled in the gloom at the Archi, in front of the Gozzi tavern, on the seaside; it creates Canaris; it creates Quiroga; it creates Pisicane; it radiates greatness over the earth; it is in going whither its breath impels, that Byron dies at Missolonghi, and Mazet at Barcelona; it is a rostrum beneath the feet of Mirabeau, and a crater beneath the feet of Robespierre; its books, its stage, its art, its science, its literature, its philosophy are the manuals of the human race; to it belong Pascal, Regnier, Corneille, Descartes, Jean Jacques; Voltaire for every moment, Molière for every century; it makes the universal mouth speak its language, and that language becomes the Word; it builds up in every mind the idea of progress; the liberating dogmas which it forges are swords by the pillows of the generations, and with the soul of its thinkers and poets have all the heroes of all nations since 1789 been made; but that does not prevent it from playing the *gamin;* and this enormous genius called Paris, even while transfiguring the world with its radiance, draws the nose of Bouginier in charcoal on the wall of the Temple of Theseus, and writes *Crédeville the robber* on the Pyramids.[85]

Paris is always showing its teeth; when it is not scolding, it is laughing.

Such is Paris. The smoke of its roofs is the ideas of the universe. A heap of mud and stone, if you will, but above all, a moral being. It is more than great, it is immense. Why? Because it dares.

To dare; progress is at this price.

All sublime conquests are, more or less, the rewards of daring. That the revolution should come, it was not enough that Montesquieu should foresee it, that Diderot should preach it, that Beaumarchais should announce it, that Condorcet should calculate it, that Arouet should prepare it, that Rousseau should premeditate it; Danton must dare it.

That cry, *'Audace'*, is a *Fiat Lux!* The onward march of the human race requires that the heights around it should be ablaze with noble and enduring lessons of courage. Deeds of daring dazzle history, and form one of the guiding lights of man. The dawn dares when it rises. To strive, to brave all risks, to persist, to persevere, to be faithful to yourself, to grapple hand to hand with destiny, to surprise defeat by the little terror it inspires, at one time to confront unrighteous power, at another to defy intoxicated triumph, to hold fast, to hold hard – such is the example which the nations need, and the light that electrifies them. The same puissant lightning darts from the torch of Prometheus and the clay-pipe of Cambronne.

12. *The future latent in the people*

AS TO THE PEOPLE OF PARIS, even when grown to manhood, it is, always, the *gamin;* to depict the child is to depict the city, and therefore it is that we have studied this eagle in this open-hearted sparrow.

It is in the suburbs especially, we insist, that the Parisian race is found; there is the pure blood ; there is the true physiognomy; there this people works and suffers, and suffering and toil are the two forms of men. There are vast numbers of unknown beings teeming with the strangest types of humanity, from the stevedore of the Rapée to the horsekiller of Montfaucon. *Fex urbis,*[86] exclaims Cicero; *mob,* adds the indignant Burke; the herd, the multitude, the populace. Those words are quickly said. But if it be so, what matters it? What is it to me that they go barefoot? They cannot read. So much the worse. Will you abandon them for that? Would you make their misfortune their curse? Cannot the light penetrate these masses? Let us return to that cry: Light! and let us persist in it! Light! light! Who knows but that these opacities will become transparent? are not revolutions transfigurations? Proceed, philosophers, teach, enlighten, enkindle, think aloud, speak aloud, run joyously towards the broad daylight, fraternise in the public squares, announce the glad tidings, scatter plenteously your alphabets, proclaim human rights, sing your Marseillaises, sow enthusiasms broadcast, tear off green branches from the oak trees. Make thought a whirlwind. This multitude can be sublimated. Let us learn to avail ourselves of this vast combustion of principles and virtues, which sparkles, crackles, and thrills at certain periods. These bare feet, these naked arms, these rags, these shades of ignorance, these depths of abjectness, these abysses of gloom may be employed in the conquest of the ideal. Look through the medium of the people, and you shall discern the truth. This lowly sand which you trample beneath your feet, if you cast it into the furnace, and let it melt and seethe, shall become resplendent crystal, and by means of such as it a Galileo and a Newton shall discover stars.

13. *Little Gavroche*[87]

ABOUT EIGHT OR NINE YEARS after the events narrated in the second part of this story, there was seen, on the Boulevard du Temple, and in the neighbourhood of the Chateau d'Eau, a little boy of eleven or twelve years of age, who would have realised with considerable accuracy the ideal of the *gamin* previously sketched, if, with the laughter of his youth upon his lips, his heart had not been absolutely dark and empty. This child was well muffled up in a man's pair of pantaloons, but he had not got them from his father, and in a woman's chemise, which was not an inheritance from his mother. Strangers had clothed him in these rags out of charity. Still, he had a father and a mother. But his father never thought of him, and his mother did not love him. He was one of those children so deserving of pity from all, who have fathers and mothers, and yet are orphans.

This little boy never felt so happy as when in the street. The pavement was not so hard to him as the heart of his mother.

His parents had thrown him out into life with a kick.

He had quite ingenuously spread his wings, and taken flight.

He was a boisterous, pallid, nimble, wide-awake, roguish urchin, with an air at once vivacious and sickly. He went, came, sang, played pitch and toss, scraped the gutters, stole a little, but he did it gaily, like the cats and the sparrows, laughed when people called him an errand-boy, and got angry when they called him a ragamuffin. He had no shelter, no food, no fire, no love, but he was light-hearted because he was free.

When these poor creatures are men, the millstone of our social system almost always comes in contact with them, and grinds them, but while they are children they escape because they are little. The smallest hole saves them.

However, deserted as this lad was, it happened sometimes, every two or three months, that he would say to himself: 'Come, I'll go and see my mother!' Then he would leave the Boulevard, the Cirque, the Porte Saint Martin, go down along the quays, cross the bridges, reach the suburbs, walk as far as the Salpêtrière, and arrive – where? Precisely at that double number, 50–52, which is known to the reader, the Gorbeau building.

At the period referred to, the tenement No. 50–52, usually empty, and permanently decorated with the placard 'Rooms to let', was, for a wonder, tenanted by several persons who, in all other respects, as is always the case at Paris, had no relation to or connection with each other. They all belonged to that indigent class which begins with the small bourgeois in embarrassed circumstances, and descends, from grade to grade of wretchedness, through the lower strata of society, until it reaches those two beings in whom all the material things of civilisation terminate, the scavenger and the rag-picker.

The 'landlady' of the time of Jean Valjean was dead, and had been replaced by another exactly like her. I do not remember what philosopher it was who said: 'There is never any lack of old women.'

The new old woman was called Madame Burgon, and her life had been remarkable for nothing except a dynasty of three paroquets, which had in succession wielded the sceptre of her affections.

Among those who lived in the building, the wretchedest of all were a family of four persons, father, mother, and two daughters nearly grown, all four lodging in the same garret room, one of those cells of which we have already spoken.

This family at first sight presented nothing very peculiar but its extreme destitution; the father, in renting the room, had given his name as Jondrette. Sometime after his moving in, which had singularly resembled, to borrow the memorable expression of the landlady, the entrance of *nothing at all*, this Jondrette said to the old woman, who, like her predecessor, was, at the same time, portress and swept the stairs: 'Mother So and So, if anybody should come and ask for a Pole or an Italian or, perhaps, a Spaniard, that is for me.'

Now, this family was the family of our sprightly little barefooted urchin. When he came there, he found distress and, what is sadder still, no smile; a cold hearthstone and cold hearts. When he came in, they would ask: 'Where have you come from?' He would answer: 'From the street.' When he was going away they would ask him: 'Where are you going to?' He would answer: 'Into the street.' His mother would say to him: 'What have you come here for?'

The child lived, in this absence of affection, like those pale plants that spring up in cellars. He felt no suffering from this mode of existence, and bore no ill-will to anybody. He did not know how a father and mother ought to be.

But yet his mother loved his sisters.

We had forgotten to say that on the Boulevard du Temple this boy went by the name of little Gavroche. Why was his name Gavroche? Probably because his father's name was Jondrette.

To break all links seems to be the instinct of some wretched families.

The room occupied by the Jondrettes in the Gorbeau tenement was the last at the end of the hall. The adjoining cell was tenanted by a very poor young man who was called Monsieur Marius.

Let us see who and what Monsieur Marius was.

BOOK 2: THE GRAND BOURGEOIS

1. *Ninety years old and thirty-two teeth*

IN THE RUE BOUCHERAT, Rue de Normandie, and Rue de Saintonge, there still remain a few old inhabitants who preserve a memory of a fine old man named M. Gillenormand, and who like to talk about him. This man was old when they were young. This figure, to those who look sadly upon that vague swarm of shadows which they call the past, has not yet entirely disappeared from the labyrinth of streets in the neighbourhood of the Temple, to which, under Louis XIV, were given the names of all the provinces of France, precisely as in our days the names of all the capitals of Europe have been given to the streets in the new Quartier Tivoli; an advance, be it said by the way, in which progress is visible.

M. Gillenormand, who was as much alive as any man can be, in 1831, was one of those men who have become curiosities, simply because they have lived a long time; and who are strange, because formerly they were like everybody else, and now they are no longer like anybody else. He was a peculiar old man, and very truly a man of another age – the genuine bourgeois of the eighteenth century, a very perfect specimen, a little haughty, wearing his good old bourgeoisie as marquises wear their marquisates. He had passed his ninetieth year, walked erect, spoke in a loud voice, saw clearly, drank hard, ate, slept, and snored. He had every one of his thirty-two teeth. He wore glasses only when reading. He was of an amorous humour, but said that for ten years past he had decidedly and entirely renounced women. He was no longer pleasing, he said; he did not add: 'I am too old,' but, 'I am too poor.' He would say: 'If I were not ruined, he! he!' His remaining income in fact was only about fifteen thousand livres. His dream was of receiving a windfall, and having an income of a hundred thousand francs, in order to keep mistresses. He did not belong, as we see, to that sickly variety of octogenarians who, like M. de Voltaire, are dying all their life; it was not a milk and water longevity; this jovial old man was always in good health. He was superficial, hasty, easily angered. He got into a rage on all occasions, most frequently when most unseasonable. When anybody contradicted him he raised his cane; he beat his servants as in the time of Louis XIV. He had an unmarried daughter over fifty years old, whom he belaboured severely when he was angry, and whom he would gladly have horsewhipped. She seemed to him about eight years old. He cuffed his domestics vigorously and would say: Ah! slut! One of his oaths was: *By the big slippers of big slipperdom!* In some respects he was of a singular tranquillity: he was shaved every day by a barber who had been crazy and who hated him, being jealous of M. Gillenormand on account of his wife, a pretty coquettish woman. M. Gillenormand admired his own discernment in everything, and pronounced himself very sagacious; this is one of his sayings: 'I have indeed some penetration; I can tell when a flea bites me, from what woman it comes.' The terms which he oftenest used were: *sensible men*, and *nature*. He did not give to this last word the broad acceptation which our epoch has assigned to it. But he twisted it into his own use in his little chimney-corner satires: 'Nature,' he would say, 'in order that civilisation may have a little of everything, gives it even some specimens of amusing barbarism. Europe has samples of Asia and Africa, in miniature. The cat is a drawing-room tiger, the lizard is a pocket crocodile. The danseuses of the opera are rosy savagesses. They do not eat men, they feed upon them. Or rather, the little magicians change them into oysters, and swallow them. The Caribs leave nothing but the bones, they leave nothing but the shells. Such are our customs. We do not devour, we gnaw; we do not exterminate, we clutch.'

2. *Like master, like dwelling*

HE LIVED IN THE MARAIS, Rue des Filles de Calvaire, No. 6. The house was his own. This house has been torn down, and rebuilt since, and its number has probably been changed in the revolutions of numbering to which the streets of Paris are subject. He occupied an ancient and ample apartment on the first storey, between the street and the gardens, covered to the ceiling with fine Gobelin and Beauvais tapestry representing pastoral scenes; the subjects of the ceiling and the panels were repeated in miniature upon the armchairs. He surrounded his bed with a large screen with nine leaves varnished with Coromandel lac. Long, full curtains hung at the windows, and made great, magnificent broken folds. The garden, which was immediately beneath his windows, was connected with the angle between them by means of a staircase of twelve or fifteen steps, which the old man ascended and descended very blithely. In addition to a library adjoining his room, he had a boudoir which he thought very much of, a gay retreat, hung with magnificent straw-colour tapestry, covered with fleur-de-lis and with figures from the galleries of Louis XIV, and ordered by M. de Vivonne from his convicts for his mistress. M. Gillenormand had inherited this from a severe maternal great-aunt, who died at the age of a hundred. He had had two wives. His manners held a medium between the courtier which he had never been, and the counsellor which he might have been. He was gay, and kind when he wished to be. In his youth, he had been one of those men who are always deceived by their wives and never by their mistresses, because they are at the same time the most disagreeable husbands and the most charming lovers in the world. He was a connoisseur in painting. He had in his room a wonderful portrait of nobody knows who, painted by Jordaens, done in great dabs with the brush, with millions of details, in a confused manner and as if by chance. M. Gillenormand's dress was not in the fashion of Louis XV, nor even in the fashion of Louis XVI; he wore the costume of the *incroyables* of the Directory. He had thought himself quite young until then, and had kept up with the fashions. His coat was of light cloth, with broad facings, a long swallow tail, and large steel buttons. Add to this short breeches and shoe buckles. He always carried his hands in his pockets. He said authoritatively: *The French Revolution is a mess of scamps.*

3. *Luke Esprit*

WHEN SIXTEEN YEARS OLD, one evening, at the opera, he had had the honour of being stared at, at the same time, by two beauties then mature and celebrated and besung by Voltaire, La Camargo and La Sallé. Caught between two fires, he had made a heroic retreat towards a little danseuse, a girl named Nahenry, who was sixteen years old, like him obscure as a cat, and with whom he fell in love. He was full of reminiscences. He would exclaim: 'How pretty she was, that Guimard Guimardin Guimardinette, the last time I saw her at Longchamps, frizzled in lofty sentiments, with her curious trinkets in turquoise, her dress the colour of a newborn child, and her muff in agitation!' He had worn in his youth a vest of London short, of which he talked frequently and fluently 'I was dressed like a Turk of the Levantine Levant,' said he. Madame de Boufflers, having accidentally seen him when he was twenty years old, described him as a 'charming fool.' He ridiculed all the names which he saw in politics or in power, finding them low and vulgar. He read the journals, *the newspapers, the gazettes,* as he said, stifling with bursts of laughter. 'Oh!' said he, 'what are these people! Corbière! Humann! Casimir Perier! those are ministers for you. I imagine I see this in a journal: M. Gillenormand, Minister; that would be a joke. Well! they are so stupid that it would go!' He called everything freely by its name, proper or improper, and was never restrained by the presence of women. He would say coarse, obscene, and indecent things with an inexpressible tranquillity and coolness which was elegant. It was the off-hand way of his time. It is worthy of remark, that the age of periphrases in verse was the age of crudities in prose. His godfather had predicted that he would be a man of genius, and gave him these two significant names: Luke Esprit.

4. *An inspiring centenarian*

HE HAD TAKEN several prizes in his youth at the college at Moulins, where he was born, and had been crowned by the hands of the Duke de Nivernais, whom he called the Duke de Nevers. Neither the Convention, nor the death of Louis XVI, nor Napoleon, nor the return of the Bourbons, had been able to efface the memory of this coronation. *The Duke de Nevers* was to him the great figure of the century. 'What a noble, great lord,' said he, 'and what a fine air he had with his blue ribbon!' In Monsieur Gillenormand's eyes, Catharine II had atoned for the crime of the partition of Poland by buying the secret of the elixir of gold from Bestuchef, for three thousand roubles. Over this, he grew animated, 'The elixir of gold,' exclaimed he, 'Bestuchef's yellow dye, General Lamotte's drops, these were in the eighteenth century, at a louis for a half ounce flask, the great remedy for the catastrophes of love, the panacea against Venus. Louis XV sent two hundred flasks to the Pope.' He would have been greatly exasperated and thrown off his balance if anybody had told him that the elixir of gold was nothing but the perchloride of iron. Monsieur Gillenormand worshipped the Bourbons and held 1789 in horror, he was constantly relating how he saved himself during the Reign of Terror, and how, if he had not had a good deal of gaiety and a good deal of wit, his head would have been cut off. If any young man ventured to eulogise the republic in his presence, he turned black in the face, and was angry enough to faint. Sometimes he would allude to his ninety years of age, and say, *I really hope that I shall not see ninety-three twice*. At other times he intimated to his people that he intended to live a hundred years.

5. *Basque and Nicolette*

HE HAD HIS THEORIES. Here is one of them: 'When a man passionately loves women, and has a wife of his own for whom he cares but little, ugly, cross, legitimate, fond of asserting her rights, roosting on the code and jealous on occasion, he has but one way to get out of it and keep the peace, that is to let his wife have the purse-strings. This abdication makes him free. The wife keeps herself busy then, devotes herself to handling specie, verdigrises her fingers, takes charge of the breeding of the tenants, the bringing up of the farmers, convokes lawyers, presides over notaries, harangues justices, visits pettifoggers, follows up lawsuits, writes out leases, dictates contracts, feels herself sovereign, sells, buys, regulates, promises and compromises, binds and cancels, cedes, concedes, and retrocedes, arranges, deranges, economises, wastes; she does foolish things, a magisterial and personal pleasure, and this consoles her. While her husband disdains her, she has the satisfaction of ruining her husband.' This theory, Monsieur Gillenormand had applied to himself, and it had become his history. His wife, the second one, had administered his fortune in such wise that there remained to Monsieur Gillenormand, when one fine day he found himself a widower, just enough to obtain, by turning almost everything into an annuity, an income of fifteen thousand francs, three-quarters of which would expire with himself. He had no hesitation, little troubled with the care of leaving an inheritance. Moreover, he had seen that patrimonies met with adventures, and, for example, became *national property;* he had been present at the avatars of the consolidated thirds, and he had little faith in the ledger. '*Rue Quincampoix*[88] *for all that!*' said he. His house in Rue des Filles du Calvaire, we have said, belonged to him. He had two domestics, 'a male and a female'. When a domestic entered his service, Monsieur Gillenormand rebaptised him. He gave to the men the name of their province: Nîmois, Comtois, Poitevin, Picard. His last valet was a big, pursy, wheezy man of fifty-five, incapable of running twenty steps, but as he was born at Bayonne, Monsieur Gillenormand called him Basque. As for female servants, they were all called Nicolette in his house (even Magnon, who will reappear as we proceed). One day a proud cook, with a blue sash, of the lofty race of porters, presented herself. 'How much do you want a month?' asked Monsieur Gillenormand. 'Thirty francs.' 'What is your name?' 'Olympie.' 'You shall have fifty francs, and your name shall be Nicolette.'

6. *In which we see La Magnon and her two little ones*

AT MONSIEUR GILLENORMAND's grief was translated into anger; he was furious at being in despair. He had every prejudice, and took every licence. One of the things of which he made up his external relief and his internal satisfaction was, we have just indicated, that he was still a youthful gallant, and that he passed for such energetically. He called this having 'royal renown'. His royal renown sometimes attracted singular presents. One day there was brought to his house in a basket, something like an oyster basket, a big boy, newborn, crying like the deuce, and duly wrapped in swaddling clothes, which a servant girl turned away six months before attributed to him. Monsieur Gillenormand was at that time fully eighty-four years old. Indignation and clamour on the part of the bystanders. And who did this bold wench think would believe this? What effrontery! What an abominable calumny! Monsieur Gillenormand, however, manifested no anger. He looked upon the bundle with the amiable smile of a man who is flattered by a calumny, and said aside: 'Well, what? what is it? what is the matter there? what have we here? you are in a pretty state of amazement, and indeed seem like any ignorant people. The Duke d'Angoulême, natural son of his majesty Charles IX, married at eighty-five a little hussy of fifteen; Monsieur Virginal, Marquis d'Alhuye, brother of Cardinal de Sourdis, Archbishop of Bordeaux, at eighty-three, had, by a chambermaid of the wife of President Jacquin, a son, a true love son, who was a Knight of Malta, and knighted Councillor of State; one of the great men of this century, Abbé Tabarand, was the son of a man eighty-seven years old. These things are anything but uncommon. And then the Bible! Upon that, I declare that this little gentleman is not mine. But take care of him. It is not his fault.' This process was too easy. The creature, she whose name was Magnon, made him a second present the year after. It was a boy again. This time Monsieur Gillenormand capitulated. He sent the two brats back to the mother, engaging to pay eighty francs a month for their support, upon condition that the said mother should not begin again. He added, 'I wish the mother to treat them well. I will come to see them from time to time.' Which he did. He had had a brother, a priest, who had been for thirty-three years rector of the Academy of Poitiers, and who died at seventy-nine. '*I lost him young,*' said he. This brother, of whom hardly a memory is left, was a quiet miser, who, being a priest, felt obliged to give alms to the poor whom he met, but never gave them anything more than coppers or worn-out sous, finding thus the means of going to Hell by the road to Paradise. As to Monsieur Gillenormand, the elder, he made no trade of almsgiving, but gave willingly and nobly. He was benevolent, abrupt, charitable, and had he been rich, his inclination would have been to be magnificent. He wished that all that concerned him should be done in a large way, even rascalities. One day, having been swindled in an inheritance by a business man, in a gross and palpable manner, he uttered this solemn exclamation: 'Fie! this is not decent! I am really ashamed of these petty cheats. Everything is degenerate in this century, even the rascals. 'Sdeath! this is not the way to rob a man like me. I am robbed as if in a wood, but meanly robbed. *Silvæ sint consule dignæ!*' He had had, we have said, two wives; by the first a daughter, who had remained unmarried, and by the second another daughter, who died when about thirty years old, and who had married for love, or luck, or otherwise, a soldier of fortune, who had served in the armies of the republic and the empire, had won the cross at Austerlitz, and been made colonel at Waterloo. '*This is the disgrace of my family,*' said the old bourgeois. He took a great deal of snuff, and had a peculiar skill in ruffling his lace frill with the back of his hand. He had very little belief in God.

7. *Rule: Never receive anybody except in the evening*

SUCH WAS M. Luke Esprit Gillenormand, who had not lost his hair, which was rather grey than white, and always combed in dog's-ears. To sum up, and with all this, a venerable man.

He was of the eighteenth century, frivolous and great.

In 1814, and in the early years of the Restoration, Monsieur Gillenormand, who was still young – he was only seventy-four – had lived in the Faubourg Saint Germain, Rue Servandoni, near Saint Sulpice. He had retired to the Marais only upon retiring from society, after his eighty years were fully accomplished.

And in retiring from society, he had walled himself up in his habits; the principal one, in which he was invariable, was to keep his door absolutely closed by day, and never to receive anybody whatever, on any business whatever, except in the evening. He dined at five o'clock, then his door was open. This was the custom of his century, and he would not swerve from it. 'The day is vulgar,' said he, 'and only deserves closed shutters. People who are anybody light up their wit when the zenith lights up its stars.' And he barricaded himself against everybody, were it even the king. The old elegance of his time.

8. *Two do not make a pair*

AS TO THE TWO DAUGHTERS of Monsieur Gillenormand, we have just spoken of them. They were born ten years apart. In their youth they resembled each other very little; and in character as well as in countenance, were as far from being sisters as possible. The younger was a cheerful soul, attracted towards everything that is bright, busy with flowers, poetry, and music, carried away into the glories of space, enthusiastic, ethereal, affianced from childhood in the ideal to a dim heroic figure. The elder had also her chimera; in the azure depth she saw a contractor, some good, coarse commissary, very rich, a husband splendidly stupid, a million-made man, or even a prefect; receptions at the prefecture, an usher of the antechamber, with the chain on his neck, official balls, harangues at the mayor's, to be '*Madame la Préfète*', this whirled in her imagination. The two sisters wandered thus, each in her own fancy, when they were young girls. Both had wings, one like an angel, the other like a goose.

No ambition is fully realised, here below at least. No paradise becomes terrestrial at the period in which we live. The younger had married the man of her dreams, but she was dead. The elder was not married.

At the moment she makes her entry into the story which we are relating, she was an old piece of virtue, an incombustible prude, one of the sharpest noses and one of the most obtuse minds which could be discovered. A characteristic incident. Outside of the immediate family nobody had ever known her first name. She was called *Mademoiselle Gillenormand the elder*.

In cant, Mademoiselle Gillenormand the elder could have given odds to an English miss. She was immodestly modest. She had one frightful reminiscence in her life: one day a man had seen her garter.

Age had only increased this pitiless modesty. Her dress front was never thick enough, and never rose high enough. She multiplied hooks and pins where nobody thought of looking. The peculiarity of prudery is to multiply sentinels, in proportion as the fortress is less threatened.

However, explain who can these ancient mysteries of innocence, she allowed herself to be kissed without displeasure, by an officer of lancers who was her grand-nephew and whose name was Théodule.

Spite of this favoured lancer, the title *Prude*, under which we have classed her, fitted her absolutely. Mademoiselle Gillenormand was a kind of twilight soul. Prudery is half a virtue and half a vice.

To prudery she added bigotry, a suitable lining. She was of the fraternity of the Virgin, wore a white veil on certain feast-days, muttered special prayers, revered 'the holy blood!' venerated 'the sacred heart', remained for hours in contemplation before an old-fashioned Jesuit altar in a chapel closed to the vulgar faithful, and let her soul fly away among the little marble clouds and along the grand rays of gilded wood.

She had a chapel friend, an old maid like herself, called Mademoiselle Vaubois, who was perfectly stupid, and in comparison with whom Mademoiselle Gillenormand had the happiness of being an eagle. Beyond her Agnus Deis and her Ave Marias, Mademoiselle Vaubois had no light except upon the different modes of making sweetmeats. Mademoiselle Vaubois, perfect in her kind, was the ermine of stupidity without a single stain of intelligence.

We must say that in growing old, Mademoiselle Gillenormand had rather gained than lost. This is the case with passive natures. She had never been peevish, which is a relative goodness; and then, years wear off angles, and the softening of time had come upon her. She was sad with an obscure sadness of which she had not the secret herself. There was in her whole person the stupor of a life ended but never commenced.

She kept her father's house. Monsieur Gillenormand had his daughter with him as we have seen Monseigneur Bienvenu have his sister with him. These households of an old man and an old maid are not rare, and always have the touching aspect of two feeblenesses leaning upon each other.

There was besides in the house, between this old maid and this old man, a child, a little boy, always trembling and mute before M. Gillenormand. M. Gillenormand never spoke to this child but with stern voice, and sometimes with uplifted cane: '*Here! Monsieur – rascal, black-guard, come here! Answer me, rogue! Let me see you, scapegrace!*' etc. etc. He idolised him.

It was his grandson. We shall see this child again.

BOOK 3: THE GRANDFATHER AND THE GRANDSON

1. *An old salon*[89]

WHEN M. GILLENORMAND lived in the Rue Servandoni, he frequented several very fine and very noble salons. Although a bourgeois, M. Gillenormand was welcome. As he was twice witty, first with his own wit, then with the wit which was attributed to him, he was even sought after and lionised. He went nowhere save on condition of ruling there. There are men who at any price desire influence and to attract the attention of others; where they cannot be oracles, they make themselves laughing-stocks. Monsieur Gillenormand was not of this nature; his dominance in the royalist salons which he frequented cost him none of his self-respect. He was an oracle everywhere. It was his fortune to have as an antagonist, Monsieur de Bonald, and even Monsieur Bengy-Puy-Vallée.

About 1817, he always spent two afternoons a week at a house in his neighbourhood, in the Rue Férou, that of the Baroness of T—, a worthy and venerable lady, whose husband had been, under Louis XVI, French Ambassador at Berlin. The Baron of T., who, during his life, had devoted himself passionately to ecstasies and magnetic visions, died in the emigration, ruined, leaving no fortune but ten manuscript volumes bound in red morocco with gilt edges, of very curious memoirs upon Mesmer and his trough. Madame de T. had not published the memoirs from motives of dignity, and supported herself on a small income, which had survived the flood nobody knows how. Madame de T. lived far from the court – *a very mixed society* said she, – in a noble, proud, and poor isolation. A few friends gathered about her widow's hearth twice a week, and this constituted a pure royalist salon. They took tea, and uttered, as the wind set towards elegy or dithyrambic, groans or cries of horror over the century, over the charter, over the Buonapartists, over the prostitution of the blue ribbon to bourgeois, over the Jacobinism of Louis XVIII; and they amused themselves in whispers with hopes which rested upon Monsieur, since Charles X.

They hailed the vulgar songs in which Napoleon was called *Nicolas* with transports of joy. Duchesses, the most delicate and the most charming women in the world, went into ecstasies over couplets like this addressed 'to the federals':

> Refoncez dans vos culottes
> Le bout d'chems' qui vous pend.
> Qu'on n' dis pas qu' les patriotes
> Ont arboré l'drapeau blanc![90]

They amused themselves with puns which they thought terrible, with innocent plays upon words which they supposed to be venomous, with quatrains and even distiches; thus upon the Dessolles ministry, a moderate cabinet of which MM. Decazes and Deserre were members:

> Pour raffermir le trone ébranlé sur sa base,
> Il faut changer de sol, et de serre et de case.

Or sometimes they drew up the list of the Chamber of Peers, 'Chamber abominably Jacobin', and in this list they arranged the names, so as to make, for example, phrases like this: *Damas. Sabran. Gouvion Saint Cyr.* All this gaily.

In this little world they parodied the revolution. They had some inclinations or other which sharpened the same anger in the inverse sense. They sang their little *ça ira*:

> Ah! ça ira! ça ira! ça ira!
> Les Buonapartists' à la lanterne!

Songs are like the guillotine; they cut indifferently, today this head, tomorrow that. It is only a variation.

In the Fualdès affair, which belongs to this time, 1816, they took sides with Bastide and Jausion, because Fualdès was a 'Buonapartist'. They called the liberals, *the brothers and friends;* this was the highest degree of insult.

Like certain menageries, the Baroness de T—'s salon had two lions. One was M. Gillenormand, the other was Count de Lamothe Valois, of whom it was whispered, with a sort of consideration: '*Do you know? He is the Lamothe of the necklace affair.*' Partisans have such singular amnesties as these.

We will add also: Among the bourgeois, positions of honour are lowered by too easy intercourse; you must take care whom you receive; just as there is a loss of caloric in the neighbourhood of those who are cold, there is a diminution of consideration in the approach of people who are despised. The old highest society held itself above this law as it did above all others. Marigny, la Pompadour's brother, is a visitor of the Prince de Soubise. Although? no, because, du Barry, godfather of la Vaubernier, is very welcome at the Marshal de Richelieu's. This society is Olympus. Mercury and the Prince de Guéménée are at home there. A thief is admitted, provided he be a lord.

The Count de Lamothe, who, in 1815, was a man of seventy-five, was remarkable for nothing save his silent and sententious air, his cold, angular face, his perfectly polished manners, his coat buttoned up to his cravat, and his long legs, always crossed in long, loose pantaloons, of the colour of burnt sienna. His face was of the colour of his pantaloons.

This M. de Lamothe was 'esteemed' in this salon, on account of his 'celebrity', and, strange to say, but true, on account of the name of Valois.

As to M. Gillenormand, his consideration was absolutely for himself alone. He made authority. He had, sprightly as he was, and without detriment to his gaiety, a certain fashion of being, which was imposing, worthy, honourable, and genteelly lofty; and his great age added to it. A man is not a century for nothing. Years place at last a venerable crown upon a head.

He gave, moreover, some of those repartees which certainly have in them the genuine sparkle. Thus when the King of Prussia, after having restored Louis XVIII, came to make him a visit under the name of Count de Ruppin, he was received by the descendant of Louis XIV somewhat like a Marquis of Brandenburg, and with the most delicate impertinence. Monsieur Gillenormand approved this. *'All kings who are not the King of France,'* said he, *'are kings of a province.'* The following question and answer were uttered one day in his presence: 'What is the sentence of the editor of the *Courier Français?'* 'To be hung up for awhile.' *'Up* is superfluous,' observed Monsieur Gillenormand. Sayings of this kind make position for a man.

At an anniversary *Te Deum* for the return of the Bourbons, seeing Monsieur de Talleyrand pass, he said: *There goes His Excellency the Bad.*

M. Gillenormand was usually accompanied by his daughter, this long mademoiselle, then past forty, and seeming fifty, and by a beautiful little boy of seven, white, rosy, fresh-looking, with happy and trustful eyes, who never appeared in this salon without hearing a buzz about him: 'How pretty he is! What a pity! poor child!' This child was the boy to whom we have but just alluded. They called him 'poor child', because his father was 'a brigand of the Loire'.[91]

This brigand of the Loire was M. Gillenormand's son-in-law, already mentioned, and whom M. Gillenormand called *the disgrace of his family.*

2. *One of the Red Spectres of that time*

WHOEVER, AT THAT DAY, had passed through the little city of Vernon, and walked over that beautiful monumental bridge which will be very soon replaced, let us hope, by some horrid wire bridge, would have noticed, as his glance fell from the top of the parapet, a man of about fifty, with a leather casque on his head, dressed in pantaloons and waistcoat of coarse grey cloth, to which something yellow was stitched which had been a red ribbon, shod in wooden shoes, browned by the sun, his face almost black and his hair almost white, a large scar upon his forehead extending down his cheek, bent, bowed down, older than his years, walking nearly every day with a spade and a pruning knife in his hand, in one of those walled compartments, in the vicinity of the bridge, which, like a chain of terraces border the left bank of the Seine – charming enclosures full of flowers of which one would say, if they were much larger, they are gardens, and if they were a little smaller, they are bouquets. All these enclosures are bounded by the river on one side and by a house on the other. The man in the waistcoat and wooden shoes of whom we have just spoken lived, about the year 1817, in the smallest of these enclosures and the humblest of these houses. He lived there solitary and alone, in silence and in poverty, with a woman who was neither young nor old, neither beautiful nor ugly, neither peasant nor bourgeois, who waited upon him. The square of earth which he called his garden was celebrated in the town for the beauty of the flowers which he cultivated in it. Flowers were his occupation.

By dint of labour, perseverance, attention, and pails of water, he had succeeded in creating after the Creator, and had invented certain tulips and dahlias which seemed to have been forgotten by Nature. He was ingenious; he anticipated Soulange Bodin in the formation of little clumps of heather earth for the culture of rare and precious shrubs from America and China. By break of day, in summer, he was in his walks, digging, pruning, weeding, watering, walking in the midst of his flowers with an air of kindness, sadness, and gentleness, sometimes dreamy and motionless for whole hours, listening to the song of a bird in a tree, the prattling of a child in a house, or oftener with his eyes fixed on some drop of dew at the end of a spear of grass, of which the sun was making a carbuncle. His table was very frugal, and he drank more milk than wine. An urchin would make him yield, his servant scolded him. He was timid, so much so as to seem unsociable, he rarely went out, and saw nobody but the poor who rapped at his window, and his cure, Abbé Mabeuf, a good old man. Still, if any of the inhabitants of the city or strangers, whoever they might be, curious to see his tulips and roses, knocked at his little house, he opened his door with a smile. This was the brigand of the Loire.

Whoever, at the same time, had read the military memoirs, the biographies, the *Moniteur*, and the bulletins of the Grand Army, would have been struck by a name which appears rather often, the name of George Pontmercy. When quite young, this George Pontmercy was a soldier in the regiment of Saintonge. The revolution broke out. The regiment of Saintonge was in the Army of the Rhine. For the old regiments of the monarchy kept their province names even after the fall of the monarchy, and were not brigaded until 1794. Pontmercy fought at Spires, at Worms, at Neustadt, at Turkheim, at Alzey, at Mayence where he was one of the two hundred who formed Houchard's rear-guard. He with eleven others held their ground against the Prince of Hesse's corps behind the old rampart of Andernach, and only fell back upon the bulk of the army when the hostile cannon had effected a breach from the top of the parapet to the slope of the glacis. He was under Kleber at Marchiennes, and at the battle of Mont Palissel, where he had his arm broken by a musket-ball. Then he passed to the Italian frontier, and he was one of the thirty grenadiers who defended the Col di Tende with Joubert. Joubert was made Adjutant-General, and Pontmercy Second-lieutenant. Pontmercy was by the side of Berthier in the midst of the storm of balls on that day of Lodi of which Bonaparte said: *Berthier was cannoneer, cavalier, and grenadier*. He saw his old general Joubert, fall at Novi, at the moment when, with uplifted sword he was crying: Forward! Being embarked with his company through the necessities of the campaign, in a pinnace, which was on the way from Genoa to some little port on the coast, he fell into a wasp's-nest of seven or eight English vessels. The Genoese captain wanted to throw the guns into the sea, hide the soldiers in the hold, and slip through in the dark like a merchantman. Pontmercy had the colours seized to the halyards of the ensign-staff, and passed proudly under the guns of the British frigates. Fifty miles further on, his boldness increasing, he attacked with his pinnace and captured a large English transport carrying troops to Sicily, so loaded with men and horses that the vessel was full to the hatches. In 1805, he was in that division of Malher which captured Günzburg from the Archduke Ferdinand. At Weltingen he received in his arms under a shower of balls Colonel Maupetit, who was mortally wounded at the head of the 9th Dragoons. He distinguished himself at Austerlitz in that wonderful march in echelon under the enemy's fire. When the cavalry of the Russian Imperial Guard crushed a battalion of the 4th of the Line, Pontmercy was one of those who revenged the repulse, and overthrew the Guard. The emperor gave him the cross. Pontmercy successively saw Wurmser made prisoner in Mantua, Melas in Alexandria, and Mack in Ulm. He was in the eighth corps, of the Grand Army, which Mortier commanded, and which took Hamburg. Then he passed into the 55th of the Line, which was the old Flanders regiment. At Eylau, he was in the churchyard where the heroic captain Louis Hugo, uncle of the author of this book, sustained alone with his company of eighty-three men, for two hours, the whole effort of the enemy's army. Pontmercy was one of the three who came out of that churchyard alive. He was at Friedland. Then he saw Moscow, then the Beresina, then Lutzen, Bautzen, Dresden, Wachau, Leipsic, and the defiles of Glenhausen, then Montmirail, Chateau-Thierry, Craon, the banks of the Marne, the banks of the Aisne, and the formidable position at Laon. At Arnay le Duc, a captain, he sabred ten cossacks, and saved, not his general, but his corporal. He was wounded on that occasion, and twenty-seven splinters were extracted from his left arm alone. Eight days before the capitulation of Paris, he exchanged with a comrade, and entered the cavalry. He had what was called under the old régime *the double-hand*, that is to say equal skill in managing, as a soldier, the sabre or the musket, as an officer, a squadron or a battalion. It is this skill, perfected by military education, which gives rise to certain special arms, the dragoons, for instance, who are both cavalry and infantry. He accompanied Napoleon to the island of Elba. At Waterloo he led a squadron of cuirassiers in Dubois' brigade. He it was who took the colours from the Lunenburg battalion. He carried the colours to the emperor's feet. He was covered with blood. He had received, in seizing the colours, a sabre stroke across his face. The emperor, well pleased, cried to him: *You are a Colonel, you are a Baron, you are an Officer of the Legion of Honour!* Pontmercy answered: *Sire, I thank you for my widow.* An hour afterwards, he fell in the ravine of Ohain. Now who was this George Pontmercy? He was that very brigand of the Loire.

We have already seen something of his history. After Waterloo, Pontmercy, drawn out, as will be remembered, from the sunken road of Ohain, succeeded in regaining the army, and was passed along from ambulance to ambulance to the cantonments of the Loire.

The Restoration put him on half-pay, then sent him to a residence, that is to say under surveillance at Vernon. The king, Louis XVIII, ignoring all that had been done in the Hundred Days, recognised neither his position of officer of the Legion of Honour, nor his rank of colonel, nor his title of baron. He, on his part, neglected no opportunity to sign himself *Colonel Baron Pontmercy*. He had only one old blue coat, and he never went out without putting on the rosette of an officer of the Legion of Honour. The *procureur du roi* notified him that he would be prosecuted for 'illegally' wearing this decoration. When this notice was given to him by a friendly intermediary, Pontmercy answered with a bitter smile: 'I do not know whether it is that I no longer understand French, or you no longer speak it; but the fact is I do not understand you.' Then he went out every day for a week with his rosette. Nobody dared to disturb him. Two or three times the minister of war or the general commanding the department wrote to him with this address: *Monsieur Commandant Pontmercy.* He returned the letters unopened. At the same time, Napoleon at St Helena was treating Sir Hudson Lowe's missives addressed *to General Bonaparte* in the same way. Pontmercy at last, excuse the word, came to have in his mouth the same saliva as his emperor.

So too, there were in Rome a few Carthaginian soldiers, taken prisoners, who refused to bow to Flaminius, and who had a little of Hannibal's soul.

One morning, he met the *procureur du roi* in one of the streets of Vernon, went up to him and said: 'Monsieur *procureur du roi*, am I allowed to wear my scar?'

He had nothing but his very scanty half-pay as chief of squadron. He hired the smallest house he could find in Vernon. He lived there alone; how we have just seen. Under the empire, between two wars, he had found time to marry Mademoiselle Gillenormand. The old bourgeois, who really felt outraged, consented with a sigh, saying: '*The greatest families are forced to it.*' In 1815, Madame Pontmercy, an admirable woman in every respect, noble and rare, and worthy of her husband, died, leaving a child. This child would have been the colonel's joy in his solitude; but the grandfather had imperiously demanded his grandson, declaring that, unless he were given up to him, he would disinherit him. The father yielded for the sake of the little boy, and not being able to have his child he set about loving flowers.

He had moreover given up everything, making no movement nor conspiring with others. He divided his thoughts between the innocent things he was doing, and the grand things he had done. He passed his time hoping for a pink or remembering Austerlitz.

M. Gillenormand had no intercourse with his son-in-law. The colonel was to him 'a bandit', and he was to the colonel 'a blockhead'. M. Gillenormand never spoke of the colonel, unless sometimes to make mocking allusions to 'his barony'. It was expressly understood that Pontmercy should never endeavour to see his son or speak to him, under pain of the boy being turned away, and disinherited. To the Gillenormands, Pontmercy was pestiferous. They intended to bring up the child to their liking. The colonel did wrong perhaps to accept these conditions, but he submitted to them, thinking that he was doing right, and sacrificing himself alone.

The inheritance from the grandfather Gillenormand was a small affair, but the inheritance from Mlle Gillenormand the elder was considerable. This aunt, who had remained single, was very rich from the maternal side, and the son of her sister was her natural heir. The child, whose name was Marius, knew that he had a father, but nothing more. Nobody spoke a word to him about him. However, in the society into which his grandfather took him, the whisperings, the hints, the winks, enlightened the little boy's mind at length; he finally comprehended something of it, and as he naturally imbibed, by a sort of infiltration and slow penetration, the ideas and opinion which formed, so to say, the air he breathed, he came little by little to think of his father only with shame and with a closed heart.

While he was thus growing up, every two or three months the colonel would escape, come furtively to Paris like a fugitive from justice breaking his ban, and go to Saint Sulpice, at the hour when Aunt Gillenormand took Marius to mass. There, trembling lest the aunt should turn round, concealed behind a pillar, motionless, not daring to breathe, he saw his child. The scarred veteran was afraid of the old maid.

From this, in fact, came his connection with the curé of Vernon, Abbé Mabeuf.

This worthy priest was the brother of a warden of Saint Sulpice, who had several times noticed this man gazing upon his child, and the scar on his cheek, and the big tears in his eyes. This man, who had so really the appearance of a man, and who wept like a woman, had attracted the warden's attention. This face remained in his memory. One day, having gone to Vernon to see his brother, he met Colonel Pontmercy on the bridge, and recognised the man of Saint Sulpice. The warden spoke of it to the curé, and the two, under some pretext, made the colonel a visit. This visit led to others. The colonel, who at first was very reserved, finally unbosomed himself, and the curé and the warden came to know the whole story, and how Pontmercy was sacrificing his own happiness to the future of his child. The result was that the curé felt a veneration and tenderness for him, and the colonel, on his part, felt an affection for the curé. And, moreover, when it happens that both are sincere and good, nothing will mix and amalgamate more easily than an old priest and an old soldier. In reality, they are the same kind of man. One has devoted himself to his country upon earth, the other to his country in heaven; there is no other difference.

Twice a year, on the first of January and on St George's Day, Marius wrote filial letters to his father, which his aunt dictated, and which, one would have said, were copied from some Complete Letter Writer; this was all that M. Gillenormand allowed; and the father answered with very tender letters, which the grandfather thrust into his pocket without reading.

3. Requiescant [92]

THE SALON OF MADAME DE T. was all that Marius Pontmercy knew of the world. It was the only opening by which he could look out into life. This opening was sombre, and through this porthole there came more cold than warmth, more night than day. The child, who was nothing but joy and light on entering this strange world, in a little while became sad, and, what is still more unusual at his age, grave. Surrounded by all these imposing and singular persons, he looked about him with a serious astonishment. Everything united to increase his amazement. There were in Madame de T.'s salon some very venerable noble old ladies, whose names were Mathan, Noah, Lévis which was pronounced Lévi, Cambis which was pronounced Cambyse. These antique faces and these biblical names mingled in the child's mind with his Old Testament, which he was learning by heart, and when they were all present, seated in a circle about a dying fire, dimly lighted by a green-shaded lamp, with their stern profiles, their grey or white hair, their long dresses of another age, in which mournful colours only could be distinguished, at rare intervals dropping a few words which were at once majestic and austere, the little Marius looked upon them with startled eyes, thinking that he saw, not women, but patriarchs and magi, not real beings, but phantoms.

Among these phantoms were scattered several priests, who frequented this old salon, and a few gentlemen; the Marquis de Sass—, secretary of commands to Madame de Berry, the Viscount de Val—, who published some monorhymed odes under the pseudonym of *Charles Antoine*, the Prince de Beauff—, who, quite young, was turning grey, and had a pretty and witty wife whose dress of scarlet velvet with gold trimmings, worn very low in the neck, startled this darkness, the Marquis de C— d'E—, the man in all France who best understood 'proportioned politeness', the Count d'Am—, the goodman with the benevolent chin, and the Chevalier de Port de Guy, a frequenter of the library of the Louvre, called the king's cabinet. M. de Port de Guy, bald and rather old than aged, related that in 1793, when sixteen years of age, he was sent to the galleys as 'refractory', and chained with an octogenarian, the Bishop of Mirepoix, refractory also, but as a priest, while he was so as a soldier. This was at Toulon. Their business was to go to the scaffold at night, and gather up the heads and bodies of those that had been guillotined during the day; they carried these dripping trunks upon their backs, and their red galley caps were encrusted behind with blood, dry in the morning, wet at night. These tragic anecdotes abounded in Madame de T.'s salon; and by dint of cursing Marat, they came to applaud Trestaillon. A few deputies of the undiscoverable kind played their whist there, M. Thibord du Chalard, M. Lemarchant de Gomicourt, and the celebrated jester of the Right, M. Cornet Dincourt. The Bailli de Ferrette, with his short breeches and his thin legs, sometimes passed through this salon on the way to M. de Talleyrand's. He had been the pleasure companion of the Count d'Artois, and reversing Aristotle cowering before Campaspe, he had made La Guimard walk on all fours, and in this manner shown to the centuries a philosopher avenged by a bailli.

As for the priests, there was Abbé Halma, the same to whom M. Larose, his assistant on *La Foudre*, said: *Pshaw! who is there that is not fifty years old? a few greenhorns perhaps?* Abbé Letourneur, the king's preacher, Abbé Frayssinous, was not yet either count, or bishop, or minister, or peer, and who wore an old cassock short of buttons, and Abbé Keravenant, curé de Saint Germain des Prés; besides these the Pope's Nuncio, at that time Monsignor Macchi, Archbishop of Nisibi, afterwards cardinal, remarkable for his long pensive nose, and another monsignor with the following titles: Abbate Palmieri, Domestic Prelate, one of the seven participating prothonotaries of the Holy See, canon of the Insignia of the Liberian Basilicate, advocate of the Saints, *postulatore di santi*, which relates to the business of canonisation and signifies very nearly: master of requests for the section of paradise. Finally, two cardinals, M. de la Luzerne and Monsieur de Cl— T—. The Cardinal de la Luzerne was a writer, and was to have, some years later, the honour of signing articles in the *Conservateur* side by side with Chateaubriand; Monsieur de Cl— T— was Archbishop of Toul—, and often came to rusticate at Paris with his nephew the Marquis of T—, who has been Minister of Marine and of War. The Cardinal de Cl— T— was a little, lively old man, showing his red stockings under his turned-up cassock; his peculiarities were hate of the Encyclopedia and desperate play at billiards, and people who, at that time, on summer evenings passed along the Rue M—, where the Hôtel de Cl— T— was at that time, stopped to hear the clicking of the balls and the sharp voice of the cardinal crying to his fellow conclavist, Monseigneur Cottret, Bishop *in partibus* of Carysta: *Mark, Abbé, I have caromed.* The Cardinal de Cl— T— had been brought to Madame de T.'s by his most intimate friend, M. de Roquelaure, formerly Bishop of Senlis and one of the Forty. M. de Roquelaure was noteworthy for his tall stature and his assiduity at the Academy; through the glass door of the hall near the Library in which the French Academy then held its sessions, the curious could every Friday gaze upon the old Bishop of Senlis, usually standing, freshly powdered, with violet stockings, and turning his back to the door, apparently to show his little collar to better advantage. All these ecclesiastics, though for the most part courtiers as well as churchmen, added to the importance of the T. salon, the lordly aspect of which was emphasised by five peers of France, the Marquis de Vib—, the Marquis de Tal—, the Marquis d'Herb—, the Viscount Damo—, and the Duke de Val—. This Duke de Val—, although Prince de Mon—, that is to say, a foreign sovereign prince, had so high an idea of France and the peerage that he saw everything through their medium. He it was who said: *The cardinals are the French peers of Rome; the lords are the French peers of England.* Finally, since, in this century, the revolution must make itself felt everywhere, this feudal salon was, as we have said, ruled by a bourgeois. Monsieur Gillenormand reigned there.

There was the essence and the quintessence of Parisian Legitimatist society. People of renown, even though royalists, were held in quarantine. There is always anarchy in renown. Chateaubriand, had he entered there, would have had the same effect as Père Duchêne. Some repentant backsliders, however, penetrated, by sufferance, into this orthodox world. Count Beug— was received there by favour.

The 'noble' salons of the present day bear no resemblance to those salons. The Faubourg Saint Germain of the present smells of heresy. The royalists of this age are demagogues, we must say it to their praise.

At Madame de T.'s, the society being superior, there was exquisite and haughty taste under a full bloom of politeness. Their manners comported with all sorts of involuntary refinements which were the ancient régime itself, buried, but living. Some of these peculiarities, in language especially, seemed grotesque. Superficial observers would have taken for provincial what was only ancient. They called a woman *madame la générale*. *Madame la colonelle* was not entirely out of use. The charming Madame de Léon, in memory doubtless of the Duchesses de Longueville and de Chevreuse, preferred this appellation to her title of Princess. The Marchioness of Créquy also called herself *madame la colonelle*.

It was this little lofty world which invented at the Tuileries the refinement of always saying, when speaking to the king in person, *the king*, in the third person, and never, *your majesty*, the title *your majesty* having been 'sullied by the usurper'.

Facts and men were judged there. They ridiculed the century, which dispensed with comprehending it. They assisted one another in astonishment. Each communicated to the rest the quantity of light he had. Methuselah instructed Epimenides. The deaf kept the blind informed. They declared, that the time since Coblentz had not elapsed. Just as Louis XVIII was, by the grace of God, in the twenty-fifth year of his reign, the *emigrées* were, in reality, in the twenty-fifth year of their youth.

All was harmonious; nothing was too much alive; speech was hardly a breath; the journal, suiting the salon, seemed a papyrus. There were young people there, but they were slightly dead. In the ante-chamber, the liveries were old. These personages, completely out of date, were served by domestics of the same kind. Altogether they had the appearance of having lived a long time ago, and of being obstinate with the sepulchre. Conserve, Conservatism, Conservative, was nearly all the dictionary; *to be in good odour*, was the point. There was in fact something aromatic in the opinions of these venerable groups, and their ideas smelt of Indian herbs. It was a mummy world. The masters were embalmed, the valets were stuffed.

A worthy old marchioness, a ruined *emigrée*, having now but one servant, continued to say: *My people*.

What was done in Madame de T.'s parlour? They were ultra.

To be ultra; this word, although what it represents has not perhaps disappeared, – this word has now lost its meaning. Let us explain it.

To be ultra is to go beyond. It is to attack the sceptre in the name of the throne, and the mitre in the name of the altar; it is to maltreat the thing you support; it is to kick in the traces; it is to cavil at the stake for undercooking heretics; it is to reproach the idol with a lack of idolatry; it is to insult by excess of respect; it is to find in the pope too little papistry, in the king too little royalty, and too much light in the night; it is to be dissatisfied with the albatross, with snow, with the swan, and the lily in the name of whiteness; it is to be the partisan of things to the point of becoming their enemy; it is to be so very pro, that you are con.

The ultra spirit is a peculiar characteristic of the first place of the Restoration.

There was never anything in history like this little while, beginning in 1814, and ending about 1820, on the advent of Monsieur de Villèle, the practical man of the Right. These six years were an extraordinary moment; at once brilliant and gloomy, smiling and sombre, lighted as by the radiance of dawn, and at the same time enveloped in the darkness of the great catastrophes which still filled the horizon, though they were slowly burying themselves in the past. There was there, in that light and that shade, a little world by itself, new and old, merry and sad, juvenile and senile, rubbing its eyes; nothing resembles an awaking so much as a return; a group which looked upon France whimsically, and upon which France looked with irony; streets full of good old owl marquises returned and returning, 'ci-devants', astounded at everything, brave and noble gentlemen smiling at being in France, and weeping over it also; delighted to see their country again, in despair at finding their monarchy no more; the nobility of the crusades spitting upon the nobility of the empire, that is to say the nobility of the sword; historic races losing the meaning of history; sons of the companions of Charlemagne disdaining the companions of Napoleon. Swords, as we have said, insulted each other; the sword of Fontenoy was ridiculous, and nothing but rust; the sword of Marengo was hateful, and nothing but a sabre. Formerly disowned Yesterday. The sense of the grand was lost, as well as the sense of the ridiculous. There was somebody who called Bonaparte Scapin. That world is no more. Nothing, we repeat, now remains of it. When we happen to draw some form from it, and endeavour to make it live again in our thought, it seems as strange to us as an antediluvian world. It also, in fact, has been swallowed up by a deluge. It has disappeared under two revolutions. What floods are ideas! How quickly they cover all that they are commissioned to destroy and to bury, and how rapidly they create frightful abysses!

Such was the character of the salons in those far-off and simple ages when M. Martainville was wittier than Voltaire.

These salons had a literature and politics of their own. They believed in Fiévée. M. Agier gave laws to them. They criticised M. Colnet, the publicist of the bookstall of the Quai Malaquais. Napoleon was nothing but the Corsican Ogre. At a later day, the introduction into history of M. the Marquis de Buonaparte, Lieutenant-General of the armies of the king, was a concession to the spirit of the century.

These salons did not long maintain their purity. As early as 1818, doctrinaires began to bud out in them, a troublesome species. Their style was to be royalists, and to apologise for it. Just where the ultras were proudest, the doctrinaries were a little ashamed. They were witty; they were silent; their political dogmas were suitably starched with pride; they ought to have been successful. They indulged in what was moreover convenient, an excess of white cravat and close-buttoned coat. The fault, or the misfortune of the doctrinaire-party was the creation of an old youth. They assumed the postures of sages. Their dream was to engraft upon an absolute and excessive principle a limited power. They opposed, and sometimes with a rare intelligence, destructive liberalism by conservative liberalism. We heard them say: 'Be considerate towards royalism; it has done much real service. It has brought us back tradition, worship, religion, respect. It is faithful, brave, chivalric, loving, devoted. It comes to associate, although with regret, to the new grandeur of the nation the old grandeur of the monarchy. It is wrong in not comprehending the revolution, the empire, glory, liberty, new ideas, new generations, the century. But this wrong which it does us, have we not sometimes done it the same? The revolution, whose heirs we are, ought to comprehend all. To attack royalism is a misconception of liberalism. What a blunder, and what blindness? Revolutionary France is wanting in respect for historic France, that is to say for her mother, that is to say for herself. After the 5th of September, the nobility of the monarchy is treated as the nobility of the empire was treated after the 8th of July.[93] They were unjust towards the eagle, we are unjust towards the fleur-de-lis. Must we then always have something to proscribe? Of what use is it to deface the crown of Louis XIV, or to scratch off the escutcheon of Henry IV? We rail at Monsieur de Vaublanc who effaced the Ns. from the Bridge of Jena? But what did he do? What we are doing. Bouvines belongs to us as well as Marengo. The fleurs-de-lis are ours as well as the Ns. They are our patrimony. What is gained by diminishing it? We must not disown our country in the past more than in the present. Why not desire our whole history? Why not love all of France?'

This is the way in which the doctrinaires criticised and patronised royalism, which was displeased at being criticised and furious at being patronised.

The ultras marked the first period of royalism; the assemblage characterised the second. To fervency succeeded skill. Let us not prolong this sketch.

In the course of this narrative, the author of this book found in his path this strange moment of contemporary history; he was obliged to glance at it in passing, and to trace some of the singular lineaments of that society now unknown. But he does it rapidly and without any bitter or derisive intention. Reminiscences, affectionate and respectful, for they relate to his mother, attach him to this period. Besides, we must say, that same little world had its greatness. We may smile at it, but we can neither despise it nor hate it. It was the France of former times.

Marius Pontmercy went, like all children, through various studies. When he left the hands of Aunt Gillenormand, his grandfather entrusted him to a worthy professor, of the purest classic innocence. This young, unfolding soul passed from a prude to a pedant. Marius had his years at college, then he entered the law-school. He was royalist, fanatical, and austere. He had little love for his grandfather, whose gaiety and cynicism wounded him, and the place of his father was a dark void.

For the rest, he was an ardent but cool lad, noble, generous, proud, religious, lofty; honourable even to harshness, pure even to unsociableness.

4. *End of the brigand*

THE COMPLETION of Marius' classical studies was coincident with M. Gillenormand's retirement from the world. The old man bade farewell to the Faubourg Saint Germain, and to Madame de T.'s salon, and established himself in the Marais, at his house in the Rue des Filles du Calvaire. His servants there were, in addition to the porter, this chambermaid Nicolette who had succeeded Magnon, and this short-winded and pursy Basque whom we have already mentioned.

In 1827, Marius had just attained his eighteenth year. On coming in one evening, he saw his grandfather with a letter in his hand.

'Marius,' said M. Gillenormand, 'you will set out tomorrow for Vernon.'

'What for?' said Marius.

'To see your father.'

Marius shuddered. He had thought of everything but this, that a day might come, when he would have to see his father. Nothing could have been more unlooked for, more surprising, and, we must say, more disagreeable. It was aversion compelled to intimacy. It was not chagrin; no, it was pure drudgery.

Marius, besides his feelings of political antipathy, was convinced that his father, the sabrer, as M. Gillenormand called him in his gentler moments, did not love him; that was clear, since he had abandoned him and left him to others. Feeling that he was not loved at all, he had no love. Nothing more natural, said he to himself.

He was so astounded that he did not question M. Gillenormand. The grandfather continued:

'It appears that he is sick. He asks for you.'

And after a moment of silence he added:

'Start tomorrow morning. I think there is at the Cour des Fontaines a conveyance which starts at six o'clock and arrives at night. Take it. He says the case is urgent.'

Then he crumpled up the letter and put it in his pocket. Marius could have started that evening and been with his father the next morning. A diligence then made the trip to Rouen from the Rue du Bouloi by night passing through Vernon. Neither M. Gillenormand nor Marius thought of inquiring.

The next day at dusk, Marius arrived at Vernon. Candles were just beginning to be lighted. He asked the first person he met for the 'house of Monsieur Pontmercy'. For in his feelings he agreed with the Restoration, and he, too, recognised his father neither as baron nor as colonel.

The house was pointed out to him. He rang; a woman came and opened the door with a small lamp in her hand.

'Monsieur Pontmercy?' said Marius.

The woman remained motionless.

'Is it here?' asked Marius.

The woman gave an affirmative nod of the head.

'Can I speak with him?'

The woman gave a negative sign.

'But I am his son!' resumed Marius. 'He expects me.'

'He expects you no longer,' said the woman.

Then he perceived that she was in tears.

She pointed to the door of a low room; he entered.

In this room, which was lighted by a tallow candle on the mantel, there were three men, one of them standing, one on his knees, and one stripped to his shirt and lying at full length upon the floor. The one upon the floor was the colonel.

The two others were a physician and a priest who was praying.

The colonel had been three days before attacked with a brain fever. At the beginning of the sickness, having a presentiment of ill, he had written to Monsieur Gillenormand to ask for his son. He had grown worse. On the very evening of Marius' arrival at Vernon, the colonel had had a fit of delirium; he sprang out of his bed in spite of the servant, crying: 'My son has not come! I am going to meet him!' Then he had gone out of his room and fallen upon the floor of the hall. He had but just died.

The doctor and the curé had been sent for. The doctor had come too late, the curé had come too late. The son also had come too late.

By the dim light of the candle, they could distinguish upon the cheek of the pale and prostrate colonel a big tear which had fallen from his death-stricken eye. The eye was glazed, but the tear was not dry. This tear was for his son's delay.

Marius looked upon this man, whom he saw for the first time, and for the last – this venerable and manly face, these open eyes which saw not, this white hair, these robust limbs upon which he distinguished here and there brown lines which were sabre-cuts, and a species of red stars which were bullet-holes. He looked upon that gigantic scar which imprinted heroism upon this face on which God had impressed goodness. He thought that this man was his father and that this man was dead, and he remained unmoved.

The sorrow which he experienced was the sorrow which he would have felt before any other man whom he might have seen stretched out in death.

Mourning, bitter mourning was in that room. The servant was lamenting by herself in a corner, the curé was praying, and his sobs were heard; the doctor was wiping his eyes; the corpse itself wept.

This doctor, this priest, and this woman, looked at Marius through their affliction without saying a word; it was he who was the stranger. Marius, too little moved, felt ashamed and embarrassed at his attitude; he had his hat in his hand, he let it fall to the floor, to make them believe that grief deprived him of strength to hold it.

At the same time he felt something like remorse, and he despised himself for acting thus. But was it his fault? He did not love his father, indeed!

The colonel left nothing. The sale of his furniture hardly paid for his burial. The servant found a scrap of paper which she handed to Marius. It contained this, in the handwriting of the colonel:

'*For my Son* – The emperor made me a baron upon the battlefield of Waterloo. Since the Restoration contests this title which I have bought with my blood, my son will take it and bear it. I need not say that he will be worthy of it.' On the back, the colonel had added: 'At this same battle of Waterloo, a sergeant saved my life. This man's name is Thénardier. Not long ago, I believe he was keeping a little tavern in a village in the suburbs of Paris, at Chelles or at Montfermeil. If my son meets him, he will do Thénardier all the service he can.'

Not from duty towards his father, but on account of that vague respect for death which is always so imperious in the heart of man, Marius took this paper and pressed it.

No trace remained of the colonel. Monsieur Gillenormand had his sword and uniform sold to a second-hand dealer. The neighbours stripped the garden and carried off the rare flowers. The other plants became briery and scraggy, and died.

Marius remained only forty-eight hours at Vernon. After the burial, he returned to Paris and went back to his law, thinking no more of his father than if he had never lived. In two days the colonel had been buried, and in three days forgotten.

Marius wore crape on his hat. That was all.

5. The utility of going to mass, to become revolutionary

MARIUS HAD PRESERVED the religious habits of his childhood.

One Sunday he had gone to hear mass at Saint Sulpice, at this same chapel of the Virgin to which his aunt took him when he was a little boy, and being that day more absent-minded and dreamy than usual, he took his place behind a pillar and knelt down, without noticing it, before a Utrecht velvet chair, on the back of which this name was written: *Monsieur Mabeuf, churchwarden.* The mass had hardly commenced when an old man presented himself and said to Marius:

'Monsieur, this is my place.'

Marius moved away readily, and the old man took his chair.

After mass, Marius remained absorbed in thought a few steps distant; the old man approached him again and said: 'I beg your pardon, monsieur, for having disturbed you a little while ago, and for disturbing you again now; but you must have thought me impertinent, and I must explain myself.'

'Monsieur,' said Marius, 'it is unnecessary.'

'Yes!' resumed the old man; 'I do not wish you to have a bad opinion of me. You see I think a great deal of that place. It seems to me that the mass is better there. Why? I will tell you. To that place I have seen for ten years, regularly, every two or three months, a poor, brave father come, who had no other opportunity and no other way of seeing his child, being prevented through some family arrangements. He came at the hour when he knew his son was brought to mass. The little one never suspected that his father was here. He did not even know, perhaps, that he had a father, the innocent boy! The father, for his part, kept behind a pillar, so that nobody should see him. He looked at his child, and wept. This poor man worshipped this little boy. I saw that. This place has become sanctified, as it were, for me, and I have acquired the habit of coming here to hear mass. I prefer it to the bench, where I have a right to be as a warden. I was even acquainted slightly with this unfortunate gentleman. He had a father-in-law, a rich aunt, relatives, I do not remember exactly, who threatened to disinherit the child if he, the father, should see him. He had sacrificed himself that his son might someday be rich and happy. They were separated by political opinions. Certainly I approve of political opinions, but there are people who do not know where to stop. Bless me! because a man was at Waterloo he is not a monster; a father is not separated from his child for that. He was one of

Buonaparte's colonels. He is dead, I believe. He lived at Vernon, where my brother is curé, and his name is something like Pontmarie, or Montpercy. He had a handsome sabre cut.'

'Pontmercy,' said Marius, turning pale.

'Exactly; Pontmercy. Did you know him?'

'Monsieur,' said Marius, 'he was my father.'

The old churchwarden clasped his hands, and exclaimed:

'Ah! you are the child! Yes, that is it; he ought to be a man now. Well! poor child, you can say that you had a father who loved you well.'

Marius offered his arm to the old man, and walked with him to his house. Next day he said to Monsieur Gillenormand:

'We have arranged a hunting party with a few friends. Will you permit me to be absent for three days?'

'Four,' answered the grandfather; 'go; amuse yourself.'

And, with a wink he whispered to his daughter:

'Some love affair!'

6. *What it is to have met a churchwarden*

WHERE MARIUS WENT we shall see a little further on.

Marius was absent three days, then he returned to Paris, went straight to the library of the law-school, and asked for the file of the *Moniteur*.

He read the *Moniteur*; he read all the histories of the republic and the empire; the *Memorial de Sainte-Hélène*; all the memoirs, journals, bulletins, proclamations; he devoured everything. The first time he met his father's name in the bulletins of the grand army he had a fever for a whole week. He went to see the generals under whom George Pontmercy had served – among others, Count H.[94] The churchwarden, Mabeuf, whom he had gone to see again, gave him an account of the life at Vernon, the colonel's retreat, his flowers and his solitude. Marius came to understand fully this rare, sublime, and gentle man, this sort of lion-lamb who was his father.

In the meantime, engrossed in this study, which took up all his time, as well as all his thoughts, he hardly saw the Gillenormands more. At the hours of meals he appeared; then when they looked for him, he was gone. The aunt grumbled. The grandfather smiled. 'Poh, poh! it is the age for the lasses!' Sometimes the old man added: 'The devil! I thought that it was some gallantry. It seems to be a passion.'

It was a passion, indeed. Marius was on the way to adoration for his father.

At the same time an extraordinary change took place in his ideas. The phases of this change were numerous and gradual. As this is the history of many minds of our time, we deem it useful to follow these phases step by step, and to indicate them all.

This history on which he had now cast his eyes, startled him. The first effect was bewilderment.

The republic, the empire, had been to him, till then, nothing but monstrous words. The republic, a guillotine in a twilight; the empire, a sabre in the night. He had looked into them, and there, where he expected to find only a chaos of darkness, he had seen, with a sort of astounding surprise, mingled with fear and joy, stars shining, Mirabeau, Vergniaud, Saint-Just, Robespierre, Camille Desmoulins, Danton, and a sun rising, Napoleon. He knew not where he was. He recoiled blinded by the splendours. Little by little, the astonishment passed away, he accustomed himself to this radiance; he looked upon acts without dizziness, he examined personages without error; the revolution and the empire set themselves in luminous perspective before his straining eyes; he saw each of these two groups of events and men arrange themselves into two enormous facts: the republic into the sovereignty of the civic right restored to the masses, the empire into the sovereignty of the French idea imposed upon Europe; he saw spring out of the revolution the grand figure of the people, and out of the empire the grand figure of France. He declared to himself that all that had been good.

What his bewilderment neglected in this first far too synthetic appreciation, we do not think it necessary to indicate here. We are describing the state of a mind upon the march. Progress is not accomplished at a bound. Saying this, once for all, for what precedes as well as for what is to follow, we continue.

He perceived then that up to that time he had comprehended his country no more than he had his father. He had known neither one nor the other, and he had had a sort of voluntary night over his eyes. He now saw, and on the one hand he admired, on the other he worshipped.

He was full of regret and remorse, and he thought with despair that all he had in his soul he could say now only to a tomb. Oh! if his father were living, if he had had him still, if God in his mercy and in his goodness had permitted that his father might be still alive, how he would have run, how he would have plunged headlong, how he would have cried to his father: 'Father! I am here! it is I! my heart is the same as yours! I am your son!' How he would have embraced his white head, wet his hair with tears, gazed upon his scar, pressed his hands, worshipped his garments, kissed his feet! oh! why had this father died so soon, before the adolescence, before the justice, before the love of his son! Marius had a continual sob in his heart which said at every moment: 'Alas!' At the same time he became more truly serious, more truly grave, surer of his faith and his thought. Gleams of the true came at every instant to complete his reasoning. It was like an interior growth. He felt a sort of natural aggrandisement which these two new things, his father and his country, brought to him.

As when one has a key, everything opened; he explained to himself what he had hated, he penetrated what he had abhorred; he saw clearly henceforth the providential, divine, and human meaning of the great things which he had been taught to detest, and the great men whom he had been instructed to curse. When he thought of his former opinions, which were only of yesterday, but which seemed so ancient to him already, he became indignant at himself, and he smiled. From the rehabilitation of his father he had naturally passed to the rehabilitation of Napoleon.

This, however, we must say, was not accomplished without labour.

From childhood he had been imbued with the judgement of the party of 1814 in regard to Bonaparte. Now, all the prejudices of the Restoration, all its interests, all its instincts, tended to the disfigurement of Napoleon. It execrated him still more than it did Robespierre. It made skilful use of the fatigue of the nation and the hatred of mothers. Bonaparte had become a sort of monster almost fabulous, and to depict him to the imagination of the people, which, as we have already said, resembles the imagination of children, the party of 1814 present in succession every terrifying mask, from that which is terrible, while yet it is grand, to that which is terrible in the grotesque, from Tiberius to Bugaboo. Thus, in speaking of Bonaparte, you might either weep, or burst with laughter, provided hatred was the basis. Marius had never had – about that man, as he was called – any other ideas in his mind. They had grown together with the tenacity of his nature. There was in him a complete little man who was devoted to hatred of Napoleon.

On reading his history, especially in studying it in documents and materials, the veil which covered Napoleon from Marius' eyes gradually fell away. He perceived something immense, and suspected that he had been deceiving himself up to that moment about Bonaparte as well as about everything else; each day he saw more clearly; and he began to mount slowly, step by step, in the beginning almost with regret, afterwards with rapture, and as if drawn by an irresistible fascination, at first the sombre stages, then the dimly lighted stages, finally the luminous and splendid stages of enthusiasm.

One night he was alone in his little room next the roof. His candle was lighted; he was reading, leaning on his table by the open window. All manner of reveries came over him from the expanse of space and mingled with his thought. What a spectacle is night! We hear dull sounds, not knowing whence they come; we see Jupiter, twelve hundred times larger than the earth, glistening like an ember, the welkin is black, the stars sparkle, it is terror-inspiring.

He was reading the bulletins of the Grand Army, those heroic strophes written on the battlefield; he saw there at intervals his father's name, the emperor's name everywhere; the whole of the grand empire appeared before him; he felt as if a tide were swelling and rising within him; it seemed to him at moments that his father was passing by him like a breath, and whispering in his ear; gradually he grew wandering; he thought he heard the drums, the cannon, the trumpets, the measured tread of the battalions, the dull and distant gallop of the cavalry; from time to time he lifted his eyes to the sky and saw the colossal constellations shining in the limitless abysses, then they fell back upon the book, and saw there other colossal things moving about confusedly. His heart was full. He was transported, trembling, breathless; suddenly, without himself knowing what moved him, or what he was obeying, he arose, stretched his arms out of the window, gazed fixedly into the gloom, the silence, the darkling infinite, the eternal immensity, and cried: Vive l'empereur!

From that moment it was all over; the Corsican Ogre – the usurper – the tyrant – the monster who was the lover of his sisters – the actor who took lessons from Talma – the poisoner of Jaffa – the tiger – Buonaparté – all this vanished, and gave place in his mind to a suffused and brilliant radiance in which shone out from an inaccessible height the pale marble phantom of Cæsar. The emperor had been to his father only the beloved captain, whom one admires, and for whom one devotes himself; to Marius he was something more. He was the predestined constructor of the French group, succeeding the Roman group in the mastery of the world. He was the stupendous architect of a downfall, the successor of Charlemagne, of Louis XI, of Henry IV, of Richelieu, of Louis XIV, and of the Committee of Public Safety, having doubtless his blemishes, his faults, and even his crimes, that is to say being man; but august in his faults, brilliant in his blemishes, mighty in his crimes.

He was the man foreordained to force all nations to say: the Grand Nation.

He was better still; he was the very incarnation of France, conquering Europe by the sword which he held, and the world by the light which he shed. Marius saw in Bonaparte the flashing spectre which will always rise upon the frontier, and which will guard the future. Despot, but dictator; despot resulting from a republic and summing up a revolution. Napoleon became to him the people-man as Jesus is the God-man.

We see, like all new converts to a religion, his conversion intoxicated him, he plunged headlong into adhesion, and he went too far. His nature was such; once upon a descent it was almost impossible for him to hold back. Fanaticism for the sword took possession of him, and became complicated in his mind with enthusiasm for the idea. He did not perceive that along with genius, and indiscriminately, he was admiring force, that is to say that he was installing in the two compartments of his idolatry, on one side what is divine, and on the other what is brutal. In several respects he began to deceive himself in other matters. He admitted everything. There is a way of meeting error while on the road of truth. He had a sort of wilful implicit faith which swallowed everything in mass. On the new path upon which he had entered, in judging the crimes of the ancient régime as well as in measuring the glory of Napoleon, he neglected the attenuating circumstances.

However this might be, a great step had been taken. Where he had formerly seen the fall of the monarchy, he now saw the advent of France. His pole-star was changed. What had been the setting, was now the rising of the sun. He had turned around.

All these revolutions were accomplished in him without a suspicion of it in his family.

When, in this mysterious labour, he had entirely cast off his old Bourbon and ultra skin, when he had shed the aristocrat, the jacobite, and the royalist, when he was fully revolutionary, thoroughly democratic, and almost republican, he went to an engraver on the Quai des Orfèvres, and ordered a hundred cards bearing this name: *Baron Marius Pontmercy.*

This was but a very logical consequence of the change which had taken place in him, a change in which everything gravitated about his father.

However, as he knew nobody, and could not leave his cards at anybody's door, he put them in his pocket.

By another natural consequence, in proportion as he drew nearer to his father, his memory, and the things for which the colonel had fought for twenty-five years, he drew off from his grandfather. As we have mentioned, for a long time M. Gillenormand's capriciousness had been disagreeable to him. There was already between them all the distaste of a serious young man for a frivolous old man. Geront's gaiety shocks and exasperates Werther's melancholy. So long as the same political opinions and the same ideas had been common to them, Marius had met M. Gillenormand by means of them as if upon a bridge. When this bridge fell, the abyss appeared. And then, above all, Marius felt inexpressibly revolted when he thought that M. Gillenormand, from stupid motives, had pitilessly torn him from the colonel, thus depriving the father of the child, and the child of the father.

Through affection and veneration for his father, Marius had almost reached aversion for his grandfather.

Nothing of this, however, as we have said, was betrayed externally. Only he was more and more frigid; laconic at meals, and scarcely ever in the house. When his aunt scolded him for it, he was very mild, and gave as an excuse his studies, courts, examinations, dissertations, etc. The grandfather did not change his infallible diagnosis: 'In love? I understand it.'

Marius was absent for a while from time to time.

'Where can he go to?' asked the aunt.

On one of these journeys, which were always very short, he went to Montfermeil in obedience to the injunction which his father had left him, and sought for the former sergeant of Waterloo, the innkeeper Thénardier. Thénardier had failed, the inn was closed, and nobody knew what had become of him. While making these researches, Marius was away from the house four days.

'Decidedly,' said the grandfather, 'he is going astray.'

They thought they noticed that he wore something, upon his breast and under his shirt, hung from his neck by a black ribbon.

7. Some petticoat

WE HAVE SPOKEN of a lancer.

He was a grand-nephew of M. Gillenormand's on the paternal side, who passed his life away from his family, and far from all domestic hearths in garrison. Lieutenant Théodule Gillenormand fulfilled all the conditions required for what is called a handsome officer. He had 'the waist of a girl', a way of trailing the victorious sabre, and a curling mustache. He came to Paris very rarely, so rarely that Marius had never seen him. The two cousins knew each other only by name. Théodule was, we think we have mentioned, the favourite of Aunt Gillenormand, who preferred him because she did not see him. Not seeing people permits us to imagine in them every perfection.

One morning, Mlle Gillenormand the elder had retired to her room as much excited as her placidity allowed. Marius had asked his grandfather again for permission to make a short journey, adding that he intended to set out that evening. 'Go!' the grandfather had answered, and M. Gillenormand had added aside, lifting his eyebrows to the top of his forehead: 'He is getting to be an old offender.' Mlle Gillenormand had returned to her room very much perplexed, dropping this exclamation point on the stairs: 'That is pretty!' and this interrogation point: 'But where can he be going?' She imagined some more or less illicit affair of the heart, a woman in the shadow, a rendezvous, a mystery, and she would not have been sorry to thrust her spectacles into it. The taste of a mystery resembles the first freshness of a slander; holy souls never despise that. There is in the secret compartments of bigotry some curiosity for scandal.

She was therefore a prey to a blind desire for learning a story.

As a diversion from this curiosity which was giving her a little more agitation than she allowed herself, she took refuge in her talents, and began to festoon cotton upon cotton, in one of those embroideries of the time of the empire and the restoration in which a great many cab wheels appear. Clumsy work, crabbed worker. She had been sitting in her chair for some hours when the door opened. Mlle Gillenormand raised her eyes; Lieutenant Théodule was before her making the regulation bow. She uttered a cry of pleasure. You may be old, you may be prude, you may be a bigot, you may be his aunt, but it is always pleasant to see a lancer enter your room.

'You here, Théodule!' exclaimed she.

'On my way, aunt.'

'Embrace me then.'

'Here goes!' said Théodule.

And he embraced her. Aunt Gillenormand went to her secretary, and opened it.

'You stay with us at least all the week?'

'Aunt, I leave this evening.'

'Impossible!'

'Mathematically.'

'Stay, my dear Théodule, I beg you.'

'The heart says yes, but my orders say no. The story is simple. Our station is changed; we were at Melun, we are sent to Gaillon. To go from the old station to the new, we must pass through Paris. I said: I am going to go and see my aunt.'

'Take this for your pains.'

She put ten louis into his hand.

'You mean for my pleasure, dear aunt.'

Théodule embraced her a second time, and she had the happiness of having her neck a little chafed by the braid of his uniform.

'Do you make the journey on horseback with your regiment?' she asked.

'No, aunt. I wanted to see you. I have a special permit. My servant takes my horse; I go by the diligence. And, speaking of that, I have a question to ask you.'

'What?'

'My cousin, Marius Pontmercy, is travelling also, is he?'

'How do you know that?' exclaimed the aunt, her curiosity suddenly excited to the quick.

'On my arrival, I went to the diligence to secure my place in the coupé.'

'Well?'

'A traveller had already secured a place on the impériale, I saw his name on the book.'

'What name?'

'Marius Pontmercy.'

'The wicked fellow!' exclaimed the aunt. 'Ah! your cousin is not a steady boy like you. To think that he is going to spend the night in a diligence.'

'Like me.'

'But for you, it is from duty; for him, it is from dissipation.'

'What is the odds?' said Théodule.

Here, an event occurred in the life of Mademoiselle Gillenormand the elder; she had an idea. If she had been a man, she would have slapped her forehead. She apostrophised Théodule:

'Are you sure that your cousin does not know you?'

'Yes. I have seen him; but he has never deigned to notice me.'

'And you are going to travel together so?'

'He on the impériale, I in the coupé.'

'Where does this diligence go?'

'To Les Andelys.'

'Is there where Marius is going?'

'Unless, like me, he stops on the road. I get off at Vernon to take the branch for Gaillon. I know nothing of Marius's route.'

'Marius! what an ugly name! What an idea it was to name him Marius! But you at least – your name is Théodule!'

'I would rather it were Alfred,' said the officer.

'Listen, Théodule.'

'I am listening, aunt.'

'Pay attention.'

'I am paying attention.'

'Are you ready?'

'Yes.'

'Well, Marius is often away.'

'Eh! eh!'

'He travels.'

'Ah! ah!'

'He sleeps away.'

'Oh! oh!'

'We want to know what is at the bottom of it.'

Théodule answered with the calmness of a man of bronze:

'Some petticoat.'

And with that stifled chuckle which reveals certainty, he added:

'A lass.'

'That is clear,' exclaimed the aunt, who thought she heard Monsieur Gillenormand speak, and who felt her conviction spring irresistibly from this word *lass*, uttered almost in the same tone by the grand-uncle and the grand-nephew. She resumed:

'Do us a kindness. Follow Marius a little way. He does not know you, it will be easy for you. Since there is a lass, try to see the lass. You can write us the account. It will amuse grandfather.'

Théodule had no excessive taste for this sort of watching; but he was much affected by the ten louis, and he thought he saw a possible succession of them. He accepted the commission and said: 'As you please, aunt.' And he added aside: 'There I am, a duenna.'

Mademoiselle Gillenormand embraced him.

'You would not play such pranks, Théodule. You are obedient to discipline, you are the slave of your orders, you are a scrupulous and dutiful man, and you would not leave your family to go to see such a creature.'

The lancer put on the satisfied grimace of Cartouche praised for his honesty.

Marius, on the evening which followed this dialogue, mounted the diligence without suspecting that he was watched. As to the watchman, the first thing that he did, was to fall asleep. His slumber was sound and indicated a clear conscience. Argus snored all night.

At daybreak, the driver of the diligence shouted: 'Vernon! Vernon relay! passengers for Vernon?' And Lieutenant Théodule awoke.

'Good,' growled he, half asleep, 'here I get off.'

Then, his memory clearing up by degrees, an effect of awakening, he remembered his aunt, the ten louis, and the account he was to render of Marius's acts and deeds. It made him laugh.

'Perhaps he has left the coach,' thought he, while he buttoned up his undress waistcoat. 'He may have stopped at Poissy; he may have stopped at Triel; if he did not get off at Meulan, he may have got off at Mantes, unless he got off at Rolleboise, or unless he only came to Pacy, with the choice of turning to the left towards Evreux, or to the right towards Laroche Guyon. Run after him, aunt. What the devil shall I write to her, the good old woman?'

At this moment a pair of black pantaloons getting down from the impériale, appeared before the window of the coupé.

'Can that be Marius?' said the lieutenant.

It was Marius.

A little peasant girl, beside the coach, among the horses and postilions, was offering flowers to the passengers. 'Flowers for your ladies,' cried she.

Marius approached her and bought the most beautiful flowers in her basket.

'Now,' said Théodule leaping down from the coach, 'there is something that interests me. Who the deuce is he going to carry those flowers to? It ought to be a mighty pretty woman for so fine a bouquet. I would like to see her.'

And, no longer now by command, but from personal curiosity, like those dogs who hunt on their own account, he began to follow Marius.

Marius paid no attention to Théodule. Some elegant women got out of the diligence; he did not look at them. He seemed to see nothing about him.

'Is he in love?' thought Théodule.

Marius walked towards the church.

'All right,' said Théodule to himself. 'The church! that is it. These rendezvous which are spiced with a bit of mass are the best of all. Nothing is so exquisite as an ogle which passes across the good God.'

Arriving at the church, Marius did not go in, but went behind the building. He disappeared at the corner of one of the buttresses of the apsis.

'The rendezvous is outside,' said Théodule. 'Let us see the lass.'

And he advanced on tiptoe towards the corner which Marius had turned.

On reaching it, he stopped, astounded.

Marius, his face hid in his hands, was kneeling in the grass, upon a grave. He had scattered his bouquet. At the end of the grave, at an elevation which marked the head, there was a black wooden cross, with this name in white letters: COLONEL BARON PONTMERCY. He heard Marius sobbing.

The lass was a tomb.

8. *Marble against granite*

IT WAS HERE that Marius had come the first time that he absented himself from Paris. It was here that he returned every time that M. Gillenormand said: he sleeps out.

Lieutenant Théodule was absolutely disconcerted by this unexpected encounter with a sepulchre; he experienced a disagreeable and singular sensation which he was incapable of analysing, and which was made up of respect for a tomb mingled with respect for a colonel. He retreated, leaving Marius alone in the churchyard, and there was something of discipline in this retreat. Death appeared to him with huge epaulets, and he gave him almost a military salute. Not knowing what to write to his aunt, he decided to write nothing at all; and probably nothing would have resulted from the discovery made by Théodule in regard to Marius' amours, had not, by one of those mysterious arrangements so frequently accidental, the scene at Vernon been almost immediately followed by a sort of counter-blow at Paris.

Marius returned from Vernon early in the morning of the third day, was set down at his grandfather's, and, fatigued by the two nights passed in the diligence, feeling the need of making up for his lack of sleep by an hour at the swimming school, ran quickly up to his room, took only time enough to lay off his travelling coat and the black ribbon which he wore about his neck, and went away to the bath.

M. Gillenormand, who had risen early like all old persons who are in good health, had heard him come in, and hastened as fast as he could with his old legs, to climb to the top of the stairs where Marius' room was, that he might embrace him, question him while embracing him, and find out something about where he came from.

But the youth had taken less time to go down than the octogenarian to go up, and when Grandfather Gillenormand entered the garret room, Marius was no longer there.

The bed was not disturbed, and upon the bed were displayed without distrust the coat and the black ribbon.

'I like that better,' said M. Gillenormand.

And a moment afterwards he entered the parlour where Mademoiselle Gillenormand the elder was already seated, embroidering her cab wheels.

The entrance was triumphal.

M. Gillenormand held in one hand the coat and in the other the neck ribbon, and cried:

'Victory! We are going to penetrate the mystery! we shall know the end of the end, we shall feel of the libertinism of our trickster! here we are with the romance even. I have the portrait!'

In fact, a black shagreen box, much like to a medallion, was fastened to the ribbon.

The old man took this box and looked at it some time without opening it, with that air of desire, ravishment, and anger, with which a poor, hungry devil sees an excellent dinner pass under his nose, when it is not for him.

'For it is evidently a portrait. I know all about that. This is worn tenderly upon the heart. What fools they are! Some abominable quean, enough to make one shudder probably! Young folks have such bad taste in these days!'

'Let us see, father,' said the old maid.

The box opened by pressing a spring. They found nothing in it but a piece of paper carefully folded.

'*From the same to the same,*' said M. Gillenormand, bursting with laughter. 'I know what that is. A love-letter!'

'Ah! then let us read it!' said the aunt.

And she put on her spectacles. They unfolded the paper and read this:

'*For my son* – The emperor made me a baron upon the battlefield of Waterloo. Since the restoration contests this title which I have bought with my blood, my son will take it and bear it. I need not say that he will be worthy of it.'

The feelings of the father and daughter cannot be described. They felt chilled as by the breath of a death's head. They did not exchange a word. M. Gillenormand, however, said in a low voice, and as if talking to himself:

'It is the handwriting of that sabrer.'

The aunt examined the paper, turned it on all sides, then put it back in the box.

Just at that moment, a little oblong package, wrapped in blue paper, fell from a pocket of the coat. Mademoiselle Gillenormand picked it up and unfolded the blue paper. It was Marius' hundred cards. She passed one of them to M. Gillenormand, who read: *Baron Marius Pontmercy.*

The old man rang. Nicolette came. M. Gillenormand took the ribbon, the box, and the coat, threw them all on the floor in the middle of the parlour, and said:

'Take away those things.'

A full hour passed in complete silence. The old man and the old maid sat with their backs turned to one another, and were probably, each on their side, thinking over the same things. At the end of that hour, aunt Gillenormand said:

'Pretty!'

A few minutes afterwards, Marius made his appearance. He came in. Even before crossing the threshold of the parlour he perceived his grandfather holding one of his cards in his hand, who, on seeing him, exclaimed with his crushing air of sneering, bourgeois superiority:

'Stop! stop! stop! stop! stop! you are a baron now. I present you my compliments. What does this mean?'

Marius coloured slightly, and answered:

'It means that I am my father's son.'

M. Gillenormand checked his laugh, and said harshly:

'Your father; I am your father.'

'My father,' resumed Marius with downcast eyes and stern manner, 'was a humble and heroic man, who served the republic and France gloriously, who was great in the greatest history that men have ever made, who lived a quarter of a century in the camp, by day under grape and under balls, by night in the snow, in the mud, and in the rain, who captured colours, who received twenty wounds, who died forgotten and abandoned, and who had but one fault; that was in loving too dearly two ingrates, his country and me.'

This was more than M. Gillenormand could listen to. At the word, *Republic,* he rose, or rather, sprang to his feet. Every one of the words which Marius had pronounced, had produced the effect upon the old royalist's face, of a blast from a bellows upon a burning coal. From dark he had become red, from red purple, and from purple glowing.

'Marius!' exclaimed he, 'abominable child! I don't know what your father was! I don't want to know! I know nothing about him and I don't know him! but what I do know is, that there was never anything but miserable wretches among all that rabble! that they were all beggars, assassins, red caps, thieves! I say all! I say all! I know nobody! I say all! do you hear, Marius? Look you, indeed, you are as much a baron as my slipper! they were all bandits who served Robespierre! all brigands who served B-u-o-naparte! all traitors who betrayed, betrayed, betrayed! their legitimate king! all cowards who ran from the Prussians and English at Waterloo! That is what I know. If your father is among them I don't know him, I am sorry for it, so much the worse, your servant!'

In his turn, Marius now became the coal, and M. Gillenormand the bellows. Marius shuddered in every limb, he knew not what to do, his head burned. He was the priest who sees all his wafers thrown to the winds, the fakir who sees a passer-by spit upon his idol. He could not allow such things to be said before him unanswered. But what could he do? His father had been trodden under foot and stamped upon in his presence, but by whom? by his grandfather. How should he avenge the one without outraging the other? It was impossible for him to insult his grandfather, and it was equally impossible for him not to avenge his father. On one hand a sacred tomb, on the other white hairs. He was for a few moments dizzy and staggering with all this whirlwind in his head; then he raised his eyes, looked straight at his grandfather, and cried in a thundering voice:

'Down with the Bourbons, and that great hog Louis XVIII!'

Louis XVIII had been dead for four years; but it was all the same to him.

The old man, scarlet as he was, suddenly became whiter than his hair. He turned towards a bust of the Duke de Berry which stood upon the mantle, and bowed to it profoundly with a sort of peculiar majesty. Then he walked twice, slowly and in silence, from the fireplace to the window and from the window to the fireplace, traversing the whole length of the room and making the floor crack as if an image of stone were walking over it. The second time, he bent towards his daughter, who was enduring the shock with the stupor of an aged sheep, and said to her with a smile that was almost calm:

'A baron like Monsieur and a bourgeois like me cannot remain under the same roof.'

And all at once straightening up, pallid, trembling, terrible, his forehead swelling with the fearful radiance of anger, he stretched his arm towards Marius and cried to him:

'Be off.'

Marius left the house.

The next day, M. Gillenormand said to his daughter:

'You will send sixty pistoles every six months to this blood-drinker, and never speak of him to me again.'

Having an immense residuum of fury to expend, and not knowing what to do with it, he spoke to his daughter with coldness for more than three months.

Marius, for his part, departed in indignation. A circumstance, which we must mention, had aggravated his exasperation still more. There are always such little fatalities complicating domestic dramas. Feelings are embittered by them, although in reality the faults are none the greater. In hurriedly carrying away, at the old man's command, Marius' 'things' to his room, Nicolette had, without perceiving it, dropped, probably on the garret stairs, which were dark, the black shagreen medallion which contained the paper written by the colonel. Neither the paper nor the medallion could be found. Marius was convinced that 'Monsieur Gillenormand' – from that day forth he never named him otherwise – had thrown 'his father's will' into the fire. He knew by heart the few lines written by the colonel, and consequently nothing was lost. But the paper, the writing, that sacred relic, all that was his heart itself. What had been done with it?

Marius went away without saying where he was going, and without knowing where he was going, with thirty francs, his watch, and a few clothes in a carpet bag. He hired a cabriolet by the hour, jumped in, and drove at random towards the Latin quarter.

What was Marius to do?

BOOK 4: THE FRIENDS OF THE ABC[95]

1. *A group which almost became historic*

AT THAT PERIOD, apparently indifferent, something of a revolutionary thrill was vaguely felt. Whispers coming from the depths of '89 and of '92 were in the air. Young Paris was, excuse the expression, in the process of moulting. People were transformed almost without suspecting it, by the very movement of the time. The hand which moves over the dial moves also among souls. Each one took the step forward which was before him. Royalists became liberals, liberals became democrats.

It was like a rising tide, complicated by a thousand ebbs; the peculiarity of the ebb is to make mixtures; thence very singular combinations of ideas; men worshipped at the same time Napoleon and liberty. We are now writing history. These were the mirages of that day. Opinions pass through phases. Voltairian royalism, a grotesque variety, had a fellow not less strange, Bonapartist liberalism.

Other groups of minds were more serious. They fathomed principle; they attached themselves to right. They longed for the absolute, they caught glimpses of the infinite realisations; the absolute, by its very rigidity, pushes the mind towards the boundless, and makes it float in the illimitable. There is nothing like dream to create the future. Utopia today, flesh and blood tomorrow.

Advanced opinions had double foundations. The appearance of mystery threatened 'the established order of things', which was sullen and suspicious – a sign in the highest degree revolutionary. The reservations of power meet the reservations of the people in the sap. The incubation of insurrections replies to the plotting of *coups d'état*.

At that time there were not yet in France any of those underlying organisations like the German Tugendbund[96] and the Italian Carbonari; but here and there obscure excavations were branching out. La Cougourde was assuming form at Aix; there was in Paris, among other affiliations of this kind, the Society of the Friends of the ABC.

Who were the Friends of the ABC? A society having as its aim, in appearance, the education of children; in reality, the elevation of men.

They declared themselves the Friends of the ABC.* The *abaissé* [the abased] were the people. They wished to raise them up. A pun at which you should not laugh. Puns are sometimes weighty in politics, witness the *Castratus ad castra*, which made Narses a general of an army; witness, *Barbari et Barbarini*; witness, *Fueros y Fuegos*; witness, *Tu es Petrus et super hanc Petram*, etc., etc.

The Friends of the ABC were not numerous, it was a secret society in the embryonic state; we should almost say a coterie, if coteries produced heroes. They met in Paris, at two places, near the Halles, in a wine shop called *Corinthe*, which will be referred to hereafter, and near the Pantheon, in a little coffee-house on the Place Saint Michel, called *Le Café Musain*, now torn down; the first of these two places of rendezvous was near the working-men, the second near the students.

---

* ABC in French, is pronounced ah-bay-say, exactly like the French word; *abaissé*.

The ordinary conventicles of the Friends of the ABC were held in a back room of the Café Musain.

This room, quite distant from the café, with which it communicated by a very long passage, had two windows, and an exit by a private stairway upon the little Rue des Grès. They smoked, drank, played, and laughed there. They talked very loud about everything, and in whispers about something else. On the wall was nailed, an indication sufficient to awaken the suspicion of a police officer, an old map of France under the republic.

Most of the Friends of the ABC were students, in thorough understanding with a few working-men. The names of the principal are as follows. They belong to a certain extent to history: Enjolras, Combeferre, Jean Prouvaire, Feuilly, Courfeyrac, Bahorel, Lesgle or Laigle, Joly, Grataire.

These young men constituted a sort of family among themselves, by force of friendship. All except Laigle were from the South.

This was a remarkable group. It has vanished into the invisible depths which are behind us. At the point of this drama which we have now reached, it may not be useless to throw a ray of light upon these young heads before the reader sees them sink into the shadow of a tragic fate.

Enjolras, whom we have named first, the reason why will be seen by and by, was an only son and was rich.

Enjolras was a charming young man, who was capable of being terrible. He was angelically beautiful. He was Antinoüs wild. You would have said, to see the thoughtful reflection of his eye, that he had already, in some preceding existence, passed through the revolutionary apocalypse. He had the tradition of it like an eye-witness. He knew all the little details of the grand thing, a pontifical and warrior nature, strange in a youth. He was officiating and militant; from the immediate point of view, a soldier of democracy; above the movement of the time, a priest of the ideal. He had a deep eye, lids a little red, thick under lip, easily becoming disdainful, and a high forehead. Much forehead in a face is like much sky in a horizon. Like certain young men of the beginning of this century and the end of the last century, who became illustrious in early life, he had an exceedingly youthful look, as fresh as a young girl's, although he had hours of pallor. He was now a man, but he seemed a child still. His twenty-two years of age appeared seventeen; he was serious, he did not seem to know that there was on the earth a being called woman. He had but one passion, the right; but one thought, to remove all obstacles. Upon Mount Aventine, he would have been Gracchus, in the Convention, he would have been Saint Just. He hardly saw the roses, he ignored the spring, he did not hear the birds sing; Evadne's bare bosom would have moved him no more than Aristogeiton; to him, as to Harmodius, flowers were good only to hide the sword. He was severe in his pleasures. Before everything but the republic, he chastely dropped his eyes. He was the marble lover of liberty. His speech was roughly inspired and had the tremor of a hymn. He astonished you by his soaring. Woe to the love affair that should venture to intrude upon him! Had any grisette of the Place Cambrai or the Rue Saint Jean de Beauvais, seeing this college boy's face, this form of a page, those long fair lashes, those blue eyes, that hair flying in the wind, those rosy cheeks, those pure lips, those exquisite teeth, felt a desire to taste all this dawn, and tried her beauty upon Enjolras, a surprising and terrible look would have suddenly shown her the great gulf, and taught her not to confound with the gallant cherubim of Beaumarchais the fearful cherubim of Ezekiel.

Beside Enjolras who represented the logic of the revolution, Combeferre represented its philosophy. Between the logic of the revolution and its philosophy, there is this difference – that its logic could conclude with war, while its philosophy could only end in peace. Combeferre completed and corrected Enjolras. He was lower and broader. His desire was to instil into all minds the broad principles of general ideas; he said: 'Revolution, but civilisation;' and about the steep mountain he spread the vast blue horizon. Hence, in all Combeferre's views, there was something attainable and practicable. Revolution with Combeferre was more respirable than with Enjolras. Enjolras expressed its divine right, and Combeferre its natural right. The first went as far as Robespierre; the second stopped at Condorcet. Combeferre more than Enjolras lived the life of the world generally. Had it been given to these two young men to take a place in history, one would have been the upright man, the other would have been the wise man. Enjolras was more manly, Combeferre was more humane. *Homo* and *Vir* indeed express the exact shade of difference. Combeferre was gentle, as Enjolras was severe, from natural purity. He loved the word citizen, but he preferred the word man. He would have gladly said: *Hombre*, like the Spaniards. He read everything, went to the theatres, attended the public courts, learned the polarisation of light from Arago, was enraptured with a lecture in which Geoffroy Saint-Hilaire had explained the double function of the exterior carotid artery and the interior carotid artery, one of which supplies the face, the other the brain; he kept pace with the times, followed science step by step, confronted Saint Simon with Fourier, deciphered hieroglyphics, broke the pebbles which he found and talked about geology, drew a moth-butterfly from memory, pointed out the mistakes in French in the dictionary of the Academy, studied Puységur and Deleuze, affirmed nothing, not even miracles; denied nothing, not even ghosts; looked over the files of the *Moniteur*, reflected. He declared the future was in the hands of the schoolmaster, and busied himself with questions of education. He desired that society should work without ceasing at the elevation of the intellectual and moral level; at the coining of knowledge, at bringing ideas into circulation, at the growth of the mind in youth; and he feared that the poverty of the methods then in vogue, the meanness of a literary world which was circumscribed by two or three centuries, called classical, the tyrannical dogmatism of official pedants, scholastic prejudices and routine, would result in making artificial oyster-beds of our colleges. He was learned, purist, precise, universal, a hard student, and at the same time given to musing, 'even chimerical', said his friends. He believed in all the dreams: railroads, the suppression of suffering in surgical operations, the fixing of the image in the camera obscura, the electric telegraph, the steering of balloons. Little dismayed, moreover, by the citadels built upon all sides against the human race by superstitions, despotisms, and prejudices, he was one of those who think that science will at last turn the position. Enjolras was a chief; Combeferre was a guide. You would have preferred to fight with the one and march with the other. Not that Combeferre was not capable of fighting; he did not refuse to close with an obstacle, and to attack it by main strength and by explosion, but to put, gradually, by the teaching of axioms and the promulgation of positive laws, the human race in harmony with its destinies, pleased him better; and of the two lights, his inclination was rather for illumination than for conflagration. A fire would cause a dawn, undoubtedly, but why not wait for the break of day? A volcano enlightens, but the morning enlightens still better.

Combeferre, perhaps, preferred the pure radiance of the beautiful to the glory of the sublime. A light disturbed by smoke, an advance purchased by violence, but half satisfied this tender and serious mind. A headlong plunge of a people into the truth, a '93, startled him; still stagnation repelled him yet more, in it he felt putrefaction and death; on the whole, he liked foam better than miasma, and he preferred the torrent to the cesspool, and the Falls of Niagara to the Lake of Montfaucon. In short, he desired neither halt nor haste. While his tumultuous friends, chivalrously devoted to the absolute, adored and asked for splendid revolutionary adventures, Combeferre inclined to let progress do her work – the good progress; cold, perhaps, but pure; methodical, but irreproachable! phlegmatic, but imperturbable. Combeferre would have knelt down and clasped his hands, asking that the future might come in all its radiant purity and that nothing might disturb the unlimited virtuous development of the people. 'The good must be innocent,' he repeated incessantly. And in fact, if it is the grandeur of the revolution to gaze steadily upon the dazzling ideal, and to fly to it through the lightnings, with blood and fire in its talons, it is the beauty of progress to be without a stain; and there is between Washington, who represents the one, and Danton, who incarnates the other, the difference which separates the angel with the wings of a swan, from the angel with the wings of an eagle.

Jean Prouvaire was yet a shade more subdued than Combeferre. He called himself Jehan, from that little momentary fancifulness which mingled with the deep and powerful movement from which arose the study of the Middle Ages, then so necessary. Jean Prouvaire was addicted to love; he cultivated a pot of flowers, played on the flute, made verses, loved the people, mourned over woman, wept over childhood, confounded the future and God in the same faith, and blamed the revolution for having cut off a royal head, that of André Chénier. His voice was usually delicate, but at times suddenly became masculine. He was well read, even to erudition, and almost an orientalist. Above all, he was good, and, a very natural thing to one who knows how near goodness borders upon grandeur, in poetry he preferred the grand. He understood Italian, Latin, Greek, and Hebrew; and that served him only to read four poets: Dante, Juvenal, Æschylus, and Isaiah. In French, he preferred Corneille to Racine, and Agrippa d'Aubigné to Corneille. He was fond of strolling in fields of wild oats and bluebells, and paid almost as much attention to the clouds as to passing events. His mind had two attitudes – one towards man, the other towards God; he studied, or he contemplated. All day he pondered over social questions: wages, capital, credit, marriage, religion, liberty of thought, liberty of love, education, punishment, misery, association, property, production and distribution, the lower enigma which covers the human ant-hill with a shadow; and at night he gazed upon the stars, those enormous beings. Like Enjolras, he was rich, and an only son. He spoke gently, bent his head, cast down his eyes, smiled with embarrassment, dressed badly, had an awkward air, blushed at nothing, was very timid, still intrepid.

Feuilly was a fan-maker, an orphan, who with difficulty earned three francs a day, and who had but one thought, to deliver the world. He had still another desire – to instruct himself; which he also called deliverance. He had taught himself to read and write; all that he knew, he had learned alone. Feuilly was a generous heart. He had an immense embrace. This orphan had adopted the people. Being without a mother, he had meditated upon his mother country. He was not willing that there should be any man upon the earth without a country. He nurtured within himself, with the deep divination of the man of the people, what we now call *the idea of nationality*. He had learned history expressly that he might base his indignation upon a knowledge of its cause. In this new upper room of utopists particularly interested in France, he represented the foreign nations. His specialty was Greece, Poland, Hungary, the Danubian Provinces, and Italy. He uttered these names incessantly, in season and out of season, with the tenacity of the right. Turkey upon Greece and Thessaly, Russia upon Warsaw, Austria upon Venice, these violations exasperated him. The grand highway robbery of 1772[97] excited him above all. There is no more sovereign eloquence than the truth in indignation; he was eloquent with this eloquence. He was never done with that infamous date, 1772, that noble and valiant people blotted out by treachery, that threefold crime, that monstrous ambuscade, prototype and pattern of all those terrible suppressions of states which, since, have stricken several noble nations, and have, so to say, erased the record of their birth. All the contemporary assaults upon society date from the partition of Poland. The partition of Poland is a theorem of which all the present political crimes are corollaries. Not a despot, not a traitor, for a century past, who has not viséd, confirmed, countersigned, and set his initials to, *ne varietur*, the partition of Poland. When you examine the list of modern treasons, that appears first of all. The Congress of Vienna took advice of this crime before consummating its own. The halloo was sounded by 1772, 1815 is the quarry. Such was the usual text of Feuilly. This poor working man had made himself a teacher of justice, and she rewarded him by making him grand. For there is in fact eternity in the right. Warsaw can no more be Tartar than Venice can be Teutonic. The kings lose their labour at this, and their honour. Sooner or later, the submerged country floats to the surface and reappears. Greece again becomes Greece, Italy again becomes Italy. The protest of the right against the fact, persists for ever. The robbery of a people never becomes prescriptive. These lofty swindles have no future. You cannot pick the mark out of a nation as you can out of a handkerchief.

Courfeyrac had a father whose name was M. de Courfeyrac. One of the false ideas of the restoration in point of aristocracy and nobility was its faith in the particle. The particle, we know, has no significance. But the bourgeois of the time of *La Minerve* considered this poor *de* so highly that men thought themselves obliged to renounce it. M. de Chauvelin called himself M. Chauvelin, M. de Caumartin, M. Caumartin, M. de Constant de Rebecque, Benjamin Constant,[98] M. de Lafayette, M. Lafayette. Courfeyrac did not wish to be behind, and called himself briefly Courfeyrac.

We might almost, in what concerns Courfeyrac, stop here, and content ourselves with saying as to the remainder: Courfeyrac, see Tholomyès.

Courfeyrac had in fact that youthful animation which we might call the diabolic beauty of the mind. In later life, this dies out, like the playfulness of the kitten, and all that grace ends, on two feet in the bourgeois, and on four paws in the mouser.

This style of mind is transmitted from generation to generation of students, passed from hand to hand by the successive growths of youth, *quasi cursores*, nearly always the same: so that, as we have just indicated, any person who had listened to Courfeyrac in 1828, would have thought he was hearing Tholomyès in 1817. Courfeyrac only was a brave fellow. Beneath the apparent similarities of the exterior mind, there was great dissimilarity between Tholomyès and him. The latent man which existed in each, was in the first altogether different from what it was in the second. There was in Tholomyès an attorney, and in Courfeyrac a paladin.

Enjolras was the chief, Combeferre was the guide, Courfeyrac was the centre. The others gave more light, he gave more heat; the truth is, that he had all the qualities of a centre, roundness and radiance.

Bahorel had figured in the bloody tumult of June 1822,[99] on the occasion of the burial of young Lallemand.

Bahorel was a creature of good humour and bad company, brave, a spend-thrift, prodigal almost to generosity, talkative almost to eloquence, bold almost to effrontery; the best possible devil's-pie; with fool-hardy waistcoats and scarlet opinions; a wholesale blusterer, that is to say, liking nothing so well as a quarrel unless it were an *émeute*, and nothing so well as an *émeute* unless it were a revolution; always ready to break a paving-stone, then to tear up a street, then to demolish a government, to see the effect of it; a student of the eleventh year. He had adopted for his motto: *never a lawyer*, and for his coat of arms a bedroom table on which you might discern a square cap. Whenever he passed by the law-school, which rarely happened, he buttoned up his overcoat, the paletot was not yet invented, and he took hygenic precautions. He said of the portal of the school: what a fine old man! and of the dean, M. Delvincourt: what a monument! He saw in his studies subjects for ditties, and in his professors opportunities for caricatures. He ate up in doing nothing a considerable allowance, something like three thousand francs. His parents were peasants, in whom he had succeeded in inculcating a respect for their son.

He said of them: 'They are peasants and not bourgeois; which explains their intelligence.'

Bahorel, a capricious man, was scattered over several cafés; the others had habits, he had none. He loafed. To err is human. To loaf is Parisian. At bottom, a penetrating mind and more of a thinker than he seemed.

He served as a bond between the Friends of the ABC and some other groups which were without definite shape, but which were to take form afterwards.

In this conclave of young heads there was one bald member.

The Marquis d'Avaray, whom Louis XVIII made a duke for having helped him into a cab the day that he emigrated, related that in 1814, on his return to France, as the king landed at Calais, a man presented a petition to him.

'What do you want?' said the king.

'Sire, a post-office.'

'What is your name?'

'L'Aigle.' *[The eagle].*

The king scowled, looked at the signature of the petition and saw the name written thus: LESGLE. This orthography, anything but Bonapartist, pleased the king, and he began to smile. 'Sire,' resumed the man with the petition, 'my ancestor was a dog-trainer surnamed Lesgueules [The Chaps]. This surname has become my name. My name is Lesgueulès, by contraction Lesgle, and by corruption L'Aigle.' This made the king finish his smile. He afterwards gave the man the post-office at Meaux, either intentionally or inadvertently.

The bald member of the club was son of this Lesgle, or Lègle, and signed his name Lègle (de Meaux). His comrades, for the sake of brevity, called him Bossuet.

Bossuet was a cheery fellow who was unlucky. His specialty was to succeed in nothing. On the other hand, he laughed at everything. At twenty-five he was bald. His father had died owning a house and some land; but he, the son, had found nothing more urgent than to lose this house and land in a bad speculation. He had nothing left. He had considerable knowledge and wit, but he always miscarried. Everything failed him, everything deceived him; whatever he built up fell upon him. If he split wood, he cut his finger. If he had a mistress, he very soon discovered that he had also a friend. Every moment some misfortune happened to him; hence his joviality. He said; *I live under the roof of the falling tiles.* Rarely astonished, since he was always expecting some accident, he took ill luck with serenity and smiled at the vexations of destiny like one who hears a jest. He was poor, but his fund of good-humour was inexhaustible. He soon reached his last sou, never his last burst of laughter. When met by adversity, he saluted that acquaintance cordially, he patted catastrophes on the back; he was so familiar with fatality as to call it by its nick-name. 'Good morning, old Genius,' he would say.

These persecutions of fortune had made him inventive. He was full of resources. He had no money, but he found means, when it seemed good to him, to go to 'reckless expenses'. One night, he even spent a hundred francs on a supper with a quean, which inspired him in the midst of the orgy with this memorable saying: *'Daughter of five Louis, pull off my boots.'*

Bossuet was slowly making his way towards the legal profession; he was doing his law, in the manner of Bahorel. Bossuet had never much domicile, sometimes none at all. He lodged sometimes with one, sometimes with another, oftenest with Joly. Joly was studying medicine. He was two years younger than Bossuet.

Joly was a young Malade Imaginaire. What he had learned in medicine was rather to be a patient than a physician. At twenty-three, he thought himself a valetudinarian, and passed his time in looking at his tongue in a mirror. He declared that man is a magnet, like the needle, and in his room he placed his bed with the head to the south and the foot to the north, so that at night the circulation of the blood should not be interfered with by the grand magnetic current of the globe. In stormy weather, he felt his pulse. Nevertheless, the gayest of all. All these incoherences, young, notional, sickly, joyous, got along very well together, and the result was an eccentric and agreeable person whom his comrades, prodigal of consonants, called Jolllly. 'You can fly upon four L's' [*ailes*, wings], said Jean Prouvaire.

Joly had the habit of rubbing his nose with the end of his cane, which is an indication of a sagacious mind.

All these young men, diverse as they were, and of whom, as a whole, we ought only to speak seriously, had the same religion: Progress.

All were legitimate sons of the French Revolution. The lightest became solemn when pronouncing this date: '89. Their fathers according to the flesh, were, or had been Feuillants, Royalists, Doctrinaires; it mattered little; this hurly-burly which antedated them, had nothing to do with them; they were young; the pure blood of principles flowed in their veins. They attached themselves without an intermediate shade to incorruptible right and to absolute duty.

Affiliated and initiated, they secretly sketched out their ideas.

Among all these passionate hearts and all these undoubting minds there was one sceptic. How did he happen to be there? from juxtaposition. The name of this sceptic was Grantaire, and he usually signed with this rebus: R [*grand R*, great R]. Grantaire was a man who took good care not to believe anything. He was, moreover, one of the students who had learned most during their course in Paris; he knew that the best coffee was at the Café Lemblin, and the best billiard table at the Café Voltaire; that you could find good rolls and good girls at the hermitage on the Boulevard du Maine, broiled chickens at Mother Saguet's, excellent chowders at the Barrière de la Cunette, and a peculiar light white wine at the Barrière du Combat. He knew the good places for everything; further-more, boxing, tennis, a few dances, and he was a profound cudgel-player. A great drinker to boot. He was frightfully ugly; the prettiest shoe-binder of that period, Irma Boissy, revolting at his ugliness, had uttered this sentence: '*Grantaire is impossible,*' but Grantaire's self-conceit was not disconcerted. He looked tenderly and fixedly upon every woman, appearing to say of them all: *if I only would;* and trying to make his comrades believe that he was in general demand.

All these words: rights of the people, rights of man, social contract, French Revolution, republic, democracy, humanity, civilisation, religion, progress, were, to Grantaire, very nearly meaningless. He smiled at them. Scepticism, that caries of the intellect, had not left one entire idea in his mind. He lived in irony. This was his axiom: There is only one certainty, my full glass. He ridiculed all devotion, under all circumstances, in the brother as well as the father, in Robespierre the younger as well as Loizerolles. 'They were very forward to be dead,' he exclaimed. He said of the cross: 'There is a gibbet which has made a success.' A rover, a gambler, a libertine, and often drunk, he displeased these young thinkers by singing incessantly: '*I loves the girls and I loves good wine.*' Air: Vive Henri IV.

Still, this sceptic had a fanaticism. This fanaticism was neither an idea, nor a dogma, nor an art, nor a science; it was a man: Enjolras. Grantaire admired, loved, and venerated Enjolras. To whom did this anarchical doubter ally himself in this phalanx of absolute minds? To the most absolute. In what way did Enjolras subjugate him? By ideas? No. By character. A phenomenon often seen. A sceptic adhering to a believer; that is as simple as the law of the complemen-tary colours. What we lack attracts us. Nobody loves the light like the blind man. The dwarf adores the drum-major. The toad is always looking up at the sky; why? To see the bird fly. Grantaire, in whom doubt was creeping, loved to see faith soaring in Enjolras. He had need of Enjolras. Without understanding it himself clearly, and without trying to explain it, that chaste, healthy, firm, direct, hard, candid nature charmed him. He admired, by instinct, his opposite. His soft, wavering, disjointed, diseased, deformed ideas, attached themselves to Enjolras as to a backbone. His moral spine leaned upon that firmness. Grantaire, by the side of Enjolras, became somebody again. He was himself, moreover, composed of two apparently incompatible elements. He was ironical and cordial. His indifference was loving. His mind dispensed with belief, yet his heart could not dispense with friendship. A thorough contradiction; for an affection is a conviction. His nature was so. There are men who seem born to be the opposite, the reverse, the counterpart. They are Pollux, Patroclus, Nisus, Eudamidas, Hephæstion, Pechméja. They live only upon condition of leaning on another; their names are continuations, and are only written preceded by the conjunction *and*; their existence is not their own; it is the other side of a destiny which is not theirs. Grantaire was one of these men. He was the reverse of Enjolras.

We might almost say that affinities commence with the letters of the alphabet. In the series, O and P are inseparable. You can, as you choose, pronounce O and P, or Orestes and Pylades.

Grantaire, a true satellite of Enjolras, lived in this circle of young people; he dwelt in it; he took pleasure only in it; he followed them everywhere. His delight was to see these forms coming and going in the fumes of the wine. He was tolerated for his good-humour.

Enjolras, being a believer, disdained this sceptic, and being sober, scorned this drunkard. He granted him a little haughty pity. Grantaire was an unaccepted Pylades. Always rudely treated by Enjolras, harshly repelled, rejected, yet returning, he said of Enjolras: 'What a fine statue!'

2. *Funeral oration upon Blondeau, by Bossuet*

ON A CERTAIN AFTERNOON, which had, as we shall see, some coincidence with events before related, Laigle de Meaux was leaning lazily back against the doorway of the Café Musain. He had the appearance of a caryatid in vacation; he was supporting nothing but his reverie. He was looking at the Place Saint Michel. Leaning back is a way of lying down standing which is not disliked by dreamers. Laigle de Meaux was thinking, without melancholy, of a little mishap which had befallen him the day before at the law school, and which modified his personal plans for the future – plans which were, moreover, rather indefinite.

Reverie does not hinder a cabriolet from going by, nor the dreamer from noticing the cabriolet. Laigle de Meaux, whose eyes were wandering in a sort of general stroll, perceived, through all his somnambulism, a two-wheeled vehicle turning into the square, which was moving at a walk, as if undecided. What did this cabriolet want? why was it moving at a walk? Laigle looked at it. There was inside, beside the driver, a young man, and before the young man, a large carpet-bag. The bag exhibited to the passers this name, written in big black letters upon a card sewed to the cloth: MARIUS PONTMERCY.

This name changed Laigle's attitude. He straightened up and addressed this apostrophe to the young man in the cabriolet:

'Monsieur Marius Pontmercy?'

The cabriolet, thus called upon, stopped.

The young man, who also seemed to be profoundly musing, raised his eyes.

'Well?' said he.

'You are Monsieur Marius Pontmercy?'

'Certainly.'

'I was looking for you,' said Laigle de Meaux.

'How is that?' inquired Marius, for he it was, in fact; he had just left his grandfather's, and he had before him a face which he saw for the first time. 'I do not know you.'

'Nor I either. I do not know you,' answered Laigle.

Marius thought he had met a buffoon, and that this was the beginning of a mystification in the middle of the street. He was not in a pleasant humour just at that moment. He knit his brows; Laigle de Meaux, imperturbable, continued:

'You were not at school yesterday.'

'It is possible.'

'It is certain.'

'You are a student?' inquired Marius.

'Yes, Monsieur. Like you. The day before yesterday I happened to go into the school. You know, one sometimes has such notions. The professor was about to call the roll. You know that they are very ridiculous just at that time. If you miss the third call, they erase your name. Sixty francs gone.'

Marius began to listen. Laigle continued:

'It was Blondeau who was calling the roll. You know Blondeau; he has a very sharp and very malicious nose, and delights in smelling out the absent. He slyly commenced with the letter P. I was not listening, not being concerned in that letter. The roll went on well, no erasure, the universe was present, Blondeau was sad. I said to myself, Blondeau, my love, you won't do the slightest execution today. Suddenly, Blondeau calls *Marius Pontmercy;* nobody answers. Blondeau, full of hope, repeats louder: *Marius Pontmercy?* And he seizes his pen. Monsieur, I have bowels. I said to myself rapidly: Here is a brave fellow who is going to be erased. Attention. This is a real live fellow who is not punctual. He is not a good boy. He is not a book-worm, a student who studies, a white-billed pedant, strong on science, letters, theology, and wisdom, one of those numskulls drawn out with four pins; a pin for each faculty. He is an honourable idler who loafs, who likes to rusticate, who cultivates the grisette, who pays his court to beauty, who is perhaps, at this very moment, with my mistress. Let us save him. Death to Blondeau! At that moment Blondeau dipped his pen, black with erasures, into the ink, cast his tawny eye over the room, and repeated for the third time: *Marius Pontmercy!* I answered: *Present!* In that way you were not erased.'

'Monsieur! – ' said Marius.

'And I was,' added Laigle de Meaux.

'I do not understand you,' said Marius.

Laigle resumed:

'Nothing more simple. I was near the chair to answer, and near the door to escape. The professor was looking at me with a certain fixedness. Suddenly, Blondeau, who must be the malignant nose of which Boileau speaks, leaps to the letter L. L is my letter; I am of Meaux, and my name is Lesgle.'

'L'Aigle!' interrupted Marius, 'what a fine name.'

'Monsieur, the Blondeau re-echoes this fine name and cries: "*Laigle!*" I answer: *Present!* Then Blondeau looks at me with the gentleness of a tiger, smiles, and says: If you are Pontmercy, you are not Laigle. A phrase which is uncomplimentary to you, but which brought me only to grief. So saying, he erases me.'

Marius exclaimed:

'Monsieur, I am mortified – '

'First of all,' interrupted Laigle, 'I beg leave to embalm Blondeau in a few words of feeling eulogy. I suppose him dead. There wouldn't be much to change in his thinness, his paleness, his coldness, his stiffness, and his odour. And I say: *Erudimini qui judicatis terram.* Here lies Blondeau, Blondeau the Nose, Blondeau Nasica, the ox of discipline, *bos disciplinæ*, the Molossus of his orders, the angel of the roll, who was straight, square, exact, rigid, honest, and hideous. God has erased him as he erased me.'

Marius resumed:

'I am very sorry – '

'Young man,' said Laigle of Meaux, 'let this be a lesson to you. In future, be punctual.'

'I really must give a thousand excuses.'

'Never expose yourself again to having your neighbour erased.'

'I am very sorry.'

Laigle burst out laughing.

'And I, in raptures; I was on the brink of being a lawyer. This rupture saves me. I renounce the triumphs of the bar. I shall not defend the widow, and I shall not attack the orphan. No more toga, no more probation. Here is my erasure obtained. It is to you that I owe it, Monsieur Pontmercy. I intend to pay you a solemn visit of thanks. Where do you live?'

'In this cabriolet,' said Marius.

'A sign of opulence,' replied Laigle calmly. 'I congratulate you. You have here rent of nine thousand francs a year.'

Just then Courfeyrac came out of the café.

Marius smiled sadly.

'I have been paying this rent for two hours, and I hope to get out of it; but, it is the usual story, I do not know where to go.'

'Monsieur,' said Courfeyrac, 'come home with me.'

'I should have priority,' observed Laigle, 'but I have no home.'

'Silence, Bossuet,' replied Courfeyrac.

'Bossuet,' said Marius, 'but I thought you called yourself Laigle.'

'Of Meaux,' answered Laigle; 'metaphorically, Bossuet.'

Courfeyrac got into the cabriolet.

'Driver,' said he, 'Hôtel de la Porte Saint Jacques.'

And that same evening, Marius was installed in a room at the Hôtel de la Porte Saint Jacques, side by side with Courfeyrac.

3. *The astonishment of Marius*

IN A FEW DAYS, Marius was the friend of Courfeyrac. Youth is the season of prompt weldings and rapid cicatrisations. Marius, in Courfeyrac's presence, breathed freely, a new thing for him. Courfeyrac asked him no questions. He did not even think of it. At that age, the countenance tells all at once. Speech is useless. There are some young men of whom we might say their physiognomies are talkative. They look at one another, they know one another.

One morning, however, Courfeyrac abruptly put this question to him.

'By the way, have you any political opinions?'

'What do you mean?' said Marius, almost offended at the question.

'What are you?'

'Bonapartist democrat.'

'Grey shade of quiet mouse colour,' said Courfeyrac.

The next day, Courfeyrac introduced Marius to the Café Musain. Then he whispered in his ear with a smile: 'I must give you your admission into the revolution.' And he took him into the room of the Friends of the ABC. He presented him to the other members, saying in an undertone this simple word which Marius did not understand: 'A pupil.'

Marius had fallen into a mental wasps' nest. Still, although silent and serious, he was not the less winged, nor the less armed.

Marius, up to this time solitary and inclined to soliloquy and privacy by habit and by taste, was a little bewildered at this flock of young men about him. All these different progressives attacked him at once, and perplexed him. The tumultuous sweep and sway of all these minds at liberty and at work set his ideas in a whirl. Sometimes, in the confusion, they went so far from him that he had some difficulty in finding them again. He heard talk of philosophy, of literature, of art, of history, of religion, in a style he had not looked for. He caught glimpses of strange appearances; and, as he did not bring them into perspective, he was not sure that it was not a chaos that he saw. On abandoning his grandfather's opinions for his father's, he had thought himself settled; he now suspected, with anxiety, and without daring to confess it to himself, that he was not. The angle under which he saw all things was beginning to change anew. A certain oscillation shook the whole horizon of his brain. A strange internal moving-day. He almost suffered from it.

It seemed that there were to these young men no 'sacred things'. Marius heard, upon every subject, a singular language annoying to his still timid mind.

A theatre poster presented itself, decorated with the title of a tragedy of the old repertory, called classic: 'Down with tragedy dear to the bourgeois!' cried Bahorel. And Marius heard Combeferre reply.

'You are wrong, Bahorel. The bourgeoisie love tragedy, and upon that point we must let the bourgeoisie alone. Tragedy in a wig has its reason for being, and I am not one of those who, in the name of Æschylus, deny it the right of existence. There are rough drafts in nature; there are, in creation, ready-made parodies; a bill which is not a bill, wings which are not wings, fins which are not fins, claws which are not claws, a mournful cry which inspires us with the desire to laugh, there is the duck. Now, since the fowl exists along with the bird, I do not see why classic tragedy should not exist in the face of antique tragedy.'

At another time Marius happened to be passing through the Rue Jean Jacques Rousseau between Enjolras and Courfeyrac.

Courfeyrac took his arm:

'Give attention. This is the Rue Plâtrière, now called Rue Jean Jacques Rousseau, on account of a singular household which lived on it sixty years ago. It consisted of Jean Jacques and Thérèse. From time to time, little creatures were born in it. Thérèse brought them forth. Jean Jacques turned them forth.'[100]

And Enjolras replied with severity:

'Silence before Jean Jacques! I admire that man. He disowned his children; very well; but he adopted the people.'

None of these young men uttered this word: the emperor. Jean Prouvaire alone sometimes said Napoleon; all the rest said Bonaparte. Enjolras pronounced *Buonaparte*.

Marius became confusedly astonished. *Initium sapientiæ.*[101]

4. The back room of the Café Musain

OF THE CONVERSATIONS among these young men which Marius frequented and in which he sometimes took part, one shocked him severely.

This was held in the back room of the Café Musain. Nearly all the Friends of the ABC were together that evening. The large lamp was ceremoniously lighted. They talked of one thing and another, without passion and with noise. Save Enjolras and Marius, who were silent, each one harangued a little at random. The talk of comrades does sometimes amount to these harmless tumults. It was a play and a fracas as much as a conversation. One threw out words which another caught up. They were talking in each of the four corners.

No woman was admitted into this back room, except Louison, the dish-washer of the café, who passed through it from time to time to go from the washroom to the 'laboratory'.

Grantaire, perfectly boozy, was deafening the corner of which he had taken possession, he was talking sense and nonsense with all his might; he cried:

'I am thirsty. Mortals, I have a dream: that the tun of Heidelberg[102] has an attack of apoplexy, and that I am the dozen leeches which is to be applied to it. I would like a drink. I desire to forget life. Life is a hideous invention of somebody I don't know who. It doesn't last, and it is good for nothing. You break your neck to live. Life is a stage scene in which there is little that is practical. Happiness is an old sash painted on one side. The ecclesiast says: all is vanity; I agree with that goodman who perhaps never existed. Zero, not wishing to go entirely naked, has clothed himself in vanity. O vanity! the patching up of everything with big words! a kitchen is a laboratory, a dancer is a professor, a mountebank is a gymnast, a boxer is a pugilist, an apothecary is a chemist, a hod-carrier is an architect, a jockey is a sportsman, a woodlouse is a pterygobranchiate. Vanity has a right side and a wrong side; the right side is stupid, it is the negro with his beads; the wrong side is silly, it is the philosopher with his rags. I weep over one and I laugh over the other. That which is called honours and dignities, and even honour and dignity, is generally pinchbeck. Kings make a plaything of human pride. Caligula made a horse consul; Charles II made a sirloin a knight. Now parade yourselves then between the consul Incitatus[103] and the baronet Roastbeef. As to the intrinsic value of people, it is hardly respectable any longer. Listen to the panegyric which neighbours pass upon each other. White is ferocious upon white; should the lily speak, how it would fix out the dove? a bigot gossiping about a devotee is more venomous than the asp and the blue viper. It is a pity that I am ignorant, for I would quote you a crowd of things, but I don't know anything. For instance, I always was bright; when I was a pupil with Gros, instead of daubing pictures, I spent my time in pilfering apples. So much for myself; as for the rest of you, you are just as good as I am. I make fun of your perfections, excellences, and good qualities. Every good quality runs into a defect; economy borders on avarice, the generous are not far from the prodigal, the brave man is close to the bully; he who says very pious says slightly sanctimonious; there are just as many vices in virtue as there are holes in the mantle of Diogenes. Which do you admire, the slain or the slayer, Cæsar or Brutus? People generally are for the slayer. Hurrah for Brutus! he slew. That is virtue. Virtue, if it may be, but folly also. There are some queer stains on these great men. The Brutus who slew Cæsar was in love with a statue of a little boy. This statue was by the Greek sculptor Strongylion, who also designed that statue of an amazon called the Beautiful-limbed, Euknemos, which Nero carried with him on his journeys. This Strongylion left nothing but two statues which put Brutus and Nero in harmony. Brutus was in love with one and Nero with the other. All history is only a long repetition. One century plagiarises another. The battle of Marengo copies the battle of Pydna; the Tolbach of Clovis and the Austerlitz of Napoleon are as like as two drops of blood. I make little account of victory. Nothing is so stupid as to vanquish; the real glory is to convince. But try now to prove something! you are satisfied with succeeding, what mediocrity! and with conquering, what misery! Alas, vanity and cowardice everywhere. Everything obeys success, even grammar. *Si volet usus*, says Horace. I despise therefore the human race. Shall we descend from the whole to a part? Will you have me set about admiring the peoples? what people, if you please? Greece? The Athenians, those Parisians of old times, killed Phocion, as if we should say Coligny, and fawned upon the tyrants to such a degree that Anacephoras said of Pisistratus: His water attracts the bees. The most considerable man in Greece for fifty years was that grammarian Philetas, who was so small and so thin that he was obliged to put lead on his shoes so as not to be blown away by the wind. There was in the grand square of Corinth a statue by the sculptor Silanion, catalogued by Pliny; this statue represented Episthates. What did Episthates do? He invented the trip in wrestling. This sums up Greece and glory. Let us pass to others. Shall I admire England? Shall I admire France? France? what for? on account of Paris. I have just told you my opinion of Athens. England? for what? on account of London? I hate Carthage. And then, London, the metropolis of luxury, is the capital of misery. In the single parish of Charing Cross, there are a hundred deaths a year from starvation. Such is Albion. I add, as a completion, that I have seen an English girl dance with a crown of roses and blue spectacles. A groan then for England. If I do not admire John Bull, shall I admire Brother Jonathan then? I have little taste for this brother with his slaves. Take away *time is money*, and what is left of England? take away *cotton is king*, and what is left of America? Germany is the lymph; Italy is the bile. Shall we go into ecstasies over Russia? Voltaire admired her. He admired China also. I confess that Russia has her beauties, among others a strong despotism; but I am sorry for the despots. They have very delicate health. An Alexis decapitated, a Peter stabbed, a Paul strangled, another Paul trampled down by blows from the heel of a boot, divers Ivans butchered, several Nicholases and Basils poisoned, all that indicates that the palace of the Emperors of Russia is in an alarming condition of insalubrity. All civilised nations offer to the admiration of the thinker this circumstance: war; but war, civilised war, exhausts and sums up every form of banditism, from the brigandage of the Trabucaires of the gorges of Mount Jaxa to the marauding of the Camanche Indians in the Doubtful Pass. Pshaw! will you tell me Europe is better than Asia for all that? I admit that Asia is ridiculous; but I do not quite see what right you have to laugh at the Grand Lama, you people of the Occident who have incorporated into your fashions and your elegancies all the multifarious ordures of majesty, from Queen Isabella's dirty chemise to the chamber-chair of the dauphin. Messieurs humans, I tell you, not a bit of it! It is at Brussels that they consume the most brandy, at Madrid the most chocolate, at Amsterdam the most gin, at London the most wine, at Constantinople the most coffee, at Paris the most absinthe; those are all the useful notions. Paris takes the palm on the whole. In Paris, the rag-pickers even are Sybarites; Diogenes would have much rather been a rag-picker in the Place Maubert than a philosopher in the Piræus. Learn this also: the wine-shops of the rag-pickers are called *bibines;* the most celebrated are the Saucepan and the Slaughter-house. Therefore, O drinking-shops, eating shops, tavern signs, bar-rooms, tea parties, meat markets, dance houses, brothels, rag-pickers' tippling shops, caravanserai of the caliphs, I swear to you, I am a voluptuary, I eat at Richard's at forty sous a head, I must have Persian carpets on which to roll Cleopatra naked! Where is Cleopatra? Ah! it is you, Louison. Good morning.'

Thus Grantaire, more than drunk, spread himself out in words, catching up the dishwasher on her way, in his corner of the Musain back room.

Bossuet, extending his hand, endeavoured to impose silence upon him, and Grantaire started again still more beautifully:

'Eagle of Meaux, down with your claws. You have no effect upon me with your gesture of Hippocrates refusing his drugs to Artaxerxes. I dispense you from quieting me. Moreover, I am sad. What would you have me tell you? Man is wicked, man is deformed; the butterfly has succeeded, man has missed fire. God failed on this animal. A crowd gives you nothing but choice of ugliness. The first man you meet will be a wretch. *Femme* [woman] rhymes with *infâme* [infamous]. Yes, I have the spleen, in addition to melancholy, with nostalgia, besides hypochondria, and I sneer, and I rage, and I yawn, and I am tired, and I am knocked in the head, and I am tormented! Let God go to the Devil!'

'Silence, capital R!' broke in Bossuet, who was discussing a point of law aside, and who was more than half buried in a string of judicial argot, of which here is the conclusion:

' – And as for me, although I am hardly a legist, and at best an amateur attorney, I maintain this: that by the terms of the common law of Normandy, at St Michael's, and for every year, an equivalent must be paid for the benefit of the seigneur, saving the rights of others, by each and every of them, as well proprietaries as those seized by inheritance, and this for all terms of years, leases, freeholds, contracts domainiary and domainial, of mortgagees and mortgagors – '

'Echo, plaintive nymph,' muttered Grantaire.

Close beside Grantaire, at a table which was almost silent, a sheet of paper, an inkstand and a pen between two wine glasses, announced that a farce was being sketched out. This important business was carried on in a whisper, and the two heads at work touched each other.

'We must begin by finding the names. When we have found the names, we will find a subject.'

'That is true. Dictate: I will write.'

'Monsieur Dorimon.'

'Wealthy?'

'Of course.'

'His daughter Celestine.'

' – tine. What next?'

'Colonel Sainval.'

'Sainval is old. I would say Valsin.'

Besides these dramatic aspirants, another group, who also were taking advantage of the confusion to talk privately, were discussing a duel. An old man, of thirty, was advising a young one, of eighteen, and explaining to him what sort of an adversary he had to deal with.

'The devil! Look out for yourself. He is a beautiful sword. His play is neat. He comes to the attack, no lost feints, a pliant wrist, sparkling play, a flash, step exact, and ripostes mathematical. Zounds! and he is left-handed, too.'

In the corner opposite to Grantaire, Joly and Bahorel were playing dominoes and talking of love.

'You are lucky,' said Joly; 'you have a mistress who is always laughing.'

'That is a fault of hers,' answered Bahorel. 'Your mistress does wrong to laugh. It encourages you to deceive her. Seeing her gay, takes away your remorse; if you see her sad, your conscience troubles you.'

'Ingrate! A laughing woman is so good a thing! And you never quarrel!'

'That is a part of the treaty we have made. When we made our little Holy Alliance, we assigned to each our own boundary which we should never pass. What is situated towards the north belongs to Vaud, towards the south to Gex. Hence our peace.'

'Peace is happiness digesting.'

'And you, Jolllly, how do you come on in your falling out with Mamselle – you know who I mean?'

'She sulks with cruel patience.'

'So you are a lover pining away.'

'Alas!'

'If I were in your place, I would get rid of her.'

'That is easily said.'

'And done. Isn't it Musichetta that she calls herself?'

'Yes. Ah! my poor Bahorel, she is a superb girl, very literary, with small feet, small hands, dresses well, white, plump, and has eyes like a fortune-teller. I am crazy about her.'

'My dear fellow, then you must please her, be fashionable, and show off your legs. Buy a pair of doeskin pantaloons at Staub's.[104] They yield.'

'At what rate?' cried Grantaire.

The third corner had fallen a prey to a poetical discussion. The Pagan mythology was wrestling with the Christian mythology. The subject was Olympus, for which Jean Prouvaire, by very romanticism, took sides. Jean Prouvaire was timid only in repose. Once excited, he burst forth, a sort of gaiety characterised his enthusiasm, and he was at once laughing and lyric.

'Let us not insult the gods,' said he. 'The gods, perhaps, have not left us. Jupiter does not strike me as dead. The gods are dreams, say you. Well, even in nature, such as it now is, we find all the grand old pagan myths again. Such a mountain, with the profile of a citadel, like the Vignemarle, for instance, is still to me the head-dress of Cybele; it is not proved that Pan does not come at night to blow into the hollow trunks of the willows, while he stops the holes with his fingers one after another; and I have always believed that Io had something to do with the cascade of Pissevache.'

In the last corner, politics was the subject. They were abusing the Charter of Louis XVIII. Combeferre defended it mildly, Courfeyrac was energetically battering it to a breach. There was on the table an unlucky copy of the famous Touquet Charter.[105] Courfeyrac caught it up and shook it, mingling with his arguments the rustling of that sheet of paper.

'First, I desire no kings; were it only from the economical point of view, I desire none; a king is a parasite. We do not have kings gratis. Listen to this: cost of kings. At the death of Francis I, the public debt of France was thirty thousand livres de rente; at the death of Louis XIV, it was two thousand six hundred millions at twenty-eight livres the mark, which was equivalent in 1760, according to Desmarest, to four thousand five hundred millions, and which is equivalent today to twelve thousand millions. Secondly, no offence to Combeferre, a charter granted is a vicious expedient of civilisation. To avoid the transition, to smoothe the passage, to deaden the shock, to make the nation pass insensibly from monarchy to democracy by the practice of constitutional fictions, these are all detestable arguments! No! no! never give the people a false light. Principles wither and grow pale in your constitutional cave. No half measures, no compromises, no grant from the king, to the people. In all these grants, there is an Article 14.[106] Along with the hand which gives there is the claw which takes back. I wholly refuse your charter. A charter is a mask; the lie is beneath it. A people who accept a charter, abdicate. Right is right only when entire. No! no charter!'

It was winter; two logs were crackling in the fireplace. It was tempting, and Courfeyrac could not resist. He crushed the poor Touquet Charter in his hand, and threw it into the fire. The paper blazed up. Combeferre looked philosophically upon the burning of Louis XVIII's masterpiece, and contented himself with saying:

'The charter metamorphosed in flames.'

And the sarcasms, the sallies, the jests, that French thing which is called high spirits, that English thing which is called humour, good taste and bad taste, good reasons and bad reasons, all the commingled follies of dialogue, rising at once and crossing from all points of the room, made above their heads a sort of joyous bombardment.

5. *Enlargement of the horizon*

THE JOSTLINGS of young minds against each other have this wonderful attribute, that one can never foresee the spark, nor predict the flash. What may spring up in a moment? Nobody knows. A burst of laughter follows a scene of tenderness. In a moment of buffoonery, the serious makes its entrance. Impulses depend upon a chance word. The spirit of each is sovereign. A jest suffices to open the door to the unlooked for. Theirs are conferences with sharp turns, where the perspective suddenly changes. Chance is the director of these conversations.

A stern thought, oddly brought out of a clatter of words, suddenly crossed the tumult of speech in which Grantaire, Bahorel, Prouvaire, Bossuet, Combeferre, and Courfeyrac were confusedly fencing.

How does a phrase make its way into a dialogue? whence comes it that it makes its mark all at once upon the attention of those who hear it? We have just said, nobody knows. In the midst of the uproar Bossuet suddenly ended some apostrophe to Combeferre with this date:

'The 18th of June 1815: Waterloo.'

At this name, Waterloo, Marius, who was leaning on a table with a glass of water by him, took his hand away from under his chin, and began to look earnestly about the room.

'Pardieu,' exclaimed Courfeyrac (*Parbleu*, at that period, was falling into disuse), 'that number 18 is strange, and striking to me. It is the fatal number of Bonaparte. Put Louis before and Brumaire behind, you have the whole destiny of the man, with this expressive peculiarity, that the beginning is hard pressed by the end.'

Enjolras, till now dumb, broke the silence, and thus addressed Courfeyrac:

'You mean the crime by the expiation.'

This word, *crime*, exceeded the limits of the endurance of Marius, already much excited by the abrupt evocation of Waterloo.

He rose, he walked slowly towards the map of France spread out upon the wall, at the bottom of which could be seen an island in a separate compartment; he laid his finger upon this compartment and said:

'Corsica. A little island which has made France truly great.'

This was a breath of freezing air. All was silent. They felt that now something was to be said.

Bahorel, replying to Bossuet, was just assuming a pet attitude. He gave it up to listen.

Enjolras, whose blue eye was not fixed upon anybody, and seemed staring into space, answered without looking at Marius:

'France needs no Corsica to be great. France is great because she is France. *Quia nominor leo.*'[107]

Marius felt no desire to retreat; he turned towards Enjolras, and his voice rang with a vibration which came from the quivering of his nerves:

'God forbid that I should lessen France! but it is not lessening her to join her with Napoleon. Come, let us talk then. I am a newcomer among you, but I confess that you astound me. Where are we? who are we? who are you? who am I? Let us explain ourselves about the emperor. I hear you say Buonaparte, accenting the *u* like the royalists. I can tell you that my grandfather does better yet; he says Buonaparté. I thought you were young men. Where is your enthusiasm then? and what do you do with it? whom do you admire, if you do not admire the emperor? and what more must you have? If you do not like that great man, what great men would you have? He was everything. He was complete. He had in his brain the cube of human faculties. He made codes like Justinian, he dictated like Cæsar, his conversation joined the lightning of Pascal to the thunderbolt of Tacitus, he made history and he wrote it, his bulletins are Iliads, he combined the figures of Newton with the metaphors of Mahomet, he left behind him in the Orient words as grand as the pyramids, at Tilsit he taught majesty to emperors, at the Academy of Sciences he replied to Laplace, in the Council of State he held his ground with Merlin, he gave a soul to the geometry of those and to the trickery of these, he was legal with the attorneys and sidereal with the astronomers; like Cromwell blowing out one candle when two were lighted, he went to the Temple to cheapen a curtain tassel; he saw everything; he knew everything; which did not prevent him from laughing a goodman's laugh by the cradle of his little child; and all at once, startled Europe listened, armies set themselves in march, parks of artillery rolled along, bridges of boats stretched over the rivers, clouds of cavalry galloped in the hurricane, cries, trumpets, a trembling of thrones everywhere, the frontiers of the kingdoms oscillated upon the map, the sound of a superhuman blade was heard leaping from its sheath, men saw him, him, standing erect in the horizon with a flame in his hands and a resplendence in his eyes, unfolding in the thunder his two wings, the Grand Army and the Old Guard, and he was the archangel of war!'

All were silent, and Enjolras bowed his head. Silence always has something of the effect of an acquiescence or of a sort of pushing to the wall. Marius, almost without taking breath, continued with a burst of enthusiasm:

'Be just, my friends! to be the empire of such an emperor, what a splendid destiny for a people, when that people is France, and when it adds its genius to the genius of such a man! To appear and to reign, to march and to triumph, to have every capital for a magazine, to take his grenadiers and make kings of them, to decree the downfall of dynasties, to transfigure Europe at a double quickstep, so that men feel, when you threaten, that you lay your hand on the hilt of the sword of God, to follow, in a single man, Hannibal, Cæsar, and Charlemagne, to be the people of one who mingles with your every dawn the glorious announce- ment of a battle gained, to be wakened in the morning by the cannon of the Invalides, to hurl into the vault of day mighty words which blaze for ever, Marengo, Arcola, Austerlitz, Jena, Wagram! to call forth at every moment constellations of victories in the zenith of the centuries, to make the French Empire, the successor of the Roman Empire, to be the grand nation and to bring forth the grand army, to send your legions flying over the whole earth as a mountain sends its eagles upon all sides, to vanquish, to rule, to thunderstrike, to be in Europe a kind of gilded people through much glory, to sound through history a Titan trumpet call, to conquer the world twice, by conquest and by resplendence, this is sublime, and what can be more grand?'

'To be free,' said Combeferre.

Marius in his turn bowed his head: these cold and simple words had pierced his epic effusion like a blade of steel, and he felt it vanish within him. When he raised his eyes, Combeferre was there no longer. Satisfied probably with his reply to the apotheosis, he had gone out, and all, except Enjolras, had followed him. The room was empty. Enjolras, remaining alone with Marius, was looking at him seriously. Marius, meanwhile, having rallied his ideas a little, did not consider himself beaten; there was still something left of the ebullition within him, which doubtless was about to find expression in syllogisms arrayed against Enjolras, when suddenly they heard somebody singing as he was going down- stairs. It was Combeferre, and what he was singing is this:

> Si César m'avait donné
>   La gloire et la guerre,
> Et qu'il me fallût quitter
>   L'amour de ma mère,
> Je dirais au grand César:
> Reprends ton sceptre et ton char,
>   J'aime mieux ma mère, ô gué!
>   J'aime mieux ma mère.*

---

* If Cæsar had given me / Glory and war, / And if I must abandon / The love of my mother, / I would say to great Cæsar: / Take thy sceptre and car, / I prefer my mother,ah me! / I prefer my mother.

The wild and tender accent with which Combeferre sang, gave to this stanza a strange grandeur. Marius, thoughtful and with his eyes directed to the ceiling, repeated almost mechanically: 'my mother – '

At this moment, he felt Enjolras' hand on his shoulder.

'Citizen,' said Enjolras to him, 'my mother is the republic.'

6. Res Angusta [108]

THAT EVENING left Marius in a profound agitation, with a sorrowful darkness in his soul. He was experiencing what perhaps the earth experiences at the moment when it is furrowed with the share that the grains of wheat may be sown; it feels the wound alone; the thrill of the germ and the joy of the fruit do not come until later.

Marius was gloomy. He had but just attained a faith; could he so soon reject it? He decided within himself that he could not. He declared to himself that he would not doubt, and he began to doubt in spite of himself. To be between two religions, one which you have not yet abandoned, and another which you have not yet adopted, is insupportable; and twilight is pleasant only to bat-like souls. Marius was an open eye, and he needed the true light. To him the dusk of doubt was harmful. Whatever might be his desire to stop where he was, and to hold fast there, he was irresistibly compelled to continue, to advance, to examine, to think, to go forward. Where was that going to lead him ? he feared, after having taken so many steps which had brought him nearer to his father, to take now any steps which should separate them. His dejection increased with every reflection which occurred to him. Steep cliffs rose about him. He was on good terms neither with his grandfather nor with his friends; rash towards the former, backward towards the others; and he felt doubly isolated, from old age, and also from youth. He went no more to the Café Musain.

In this trouble in which his mind was plunged he scarcely gave a thought to certain serious phases of existence. The realities of life do not allow themselves to be forgotten. They came and jogged his memory sharply.

One morning, the keeper of the house entered Marius' room, and said to him: 'Monsieur Courfeyrac is responsible for you.'

'Yes.'

'But I am in need of money.'

'Ask Courfeyrac to come and speak with me,' said Marius.

Courfeyrac came; the host left them. Marius related to him what he had not thought of telling him before, that he was, so to speak, alone in the world, without any relatives.

'What are you going to become?' said Courfeyrac.

'I have no idea,' answered Marius.

'What are you going to do?'

'I have no idea.'

'Have you any money?'

'Fifteen francs.'

'Do you wish me to lend you some?'

'Never.'

'Have you any clothes?'

'What you see.'

'Have you any jewellery?'

'A watch.'

'A silver one?'

'Gold, here it is.'

'I know a dealer in clothing who will take your overcoat and one pair of trousers.'

'That is good.'

'You will then have but one pair of trousers, one waistcoat, one hat, and one coat.'

'And my boots.'

'What? you will not go barefoot? what opulence!'

'That will be enough.'

'I know a watchmaker who will buy your watch.'

'That is good.'

'No, it is not good. What will you do afterwards?'

'What I must. Anything honourable at least.'

'Do you know English?'

'No.'

'Do you know German?'

'No.'

'That is bad.'

'Why?'

'Because a friend of mine, a bookseller, is making a sort of encyclopædia, for which you could have translated German or English articles. It is poor pay, but it gives a living.'

'I will learn English and German.'

'And in the meantime?'

'In the meantime I will eat my coats and my watch.'

The clothes dealer was sent for. He gave twenty francs for the clothes. They went to the watchmaker. He gave forty-five francs for the watch.

'That is not bad,' said Marius to Courfeyrac, on returning to the house; 'with my fifteen francs, this makes eighty francs.'

'The hôtel bill?' observed Courfeyrac.

'Ah! I forgot,' said Marius.

The host presented his bill, which must be paid on the spot. It amounted to seventy francs.

'I have ten francs left,' said Marius.

'The devil,' said Courfeyrac, 'you will have five francs to eat while you are learning English, and five francs while you are learning German. That will be swallowing a language very rapidly or a hundred-sous piece very slowly.'

Meanwhile Aunt Gillenormand, who was really a kind person on sad occasions, had finally unearthed Marius' lodgings.

One morning when Marius came home from the school, he found a letter from his aunt, and the *sixty pistoles*, that is to say, six hundred francs in gold, in a sealed box.

Marius sent the thirty louis back to his aunt, with a respectful letter, in which he told her that he had the means of living, and that he could provide henceforth for all his necessities. At that time he had three francs left.

The aunt did not inform the grandfather of this refusal, lest she should exasperate him. Indeed, had he not said: 'Let nobody ever speak to me of this blood-drinker?'

Marius left the Porte Sainte Jacques Hôtel, unwilling to contract debt.

BOOK 5: THE EXCELLENCE OF MISFORTUNE

1. Marius needy [109]

LIFE BECAME STERN to Marius. To eat his coats and his watch was nothing. He chewed that inexpressible thing which is called the 'cud of bitterness'. A horrible thing, which includes days without bread, nights without sleep, evenings without a candle, a hearth without a fire, weeks without labour, a future without hope, a coat out at the elbows, an old hat which makes young girls laugh, the door found shut against you at night because you have not paid your rent, the insolence of the porter and the landlord, the jibes of neighbours, humiliations, self-respect outraged, any drudgery acceptable, disgust, bitterness, prostration – Marius learned how one swallows down all these things, and how they are often the only things that one has to swallow. At that period of existence, when man has need of pride, because he has need of love, he felt that he was mocked at because he was badly dressed, and ridiculed because he was poor. At the age when youth swells the heart with an imperial pride, he more than once dropped his eyes upon his worn-out boots, and experienced the undeserved shame and the poignant blushes of misery. Wonderful and terrible trial, from which the feeble come out infamous, from which the strong come out sublime. Crucible into which destiny casts a man whenever she desires a scoundrel or a demi-god.

For there are many great deeds done in the small struggles of life. There is a determined though unseen bravery, which defends itself foot to foot in the darkness against the fatal invasions of necessity and of baseness. Noble and mysterious triumphs which no eye sees, which no renown rewards, which no flourish of triumph salutes. Life, misfortune, isolation, abandonment, poverty, are battlefields which have their heroes; obscure heroes, sometimes greater than the illustrious heroes.

Strong and rare natures are thus created; misery, almost always a step-mother, is sometimes a mother; privation gives birth to power of soul and mind; distress is the nurse of self-respect; misfortune is a good breast for great souls.

There was a period in Marius' life when he swept his own hall, when he bought a pennyworth of Brie cheese at the market-woman's, when he waited for nightfall to make his way to the baker's and buy a loaf of bread, which he carried furtively to his garret, as if he had stolen it. Sometimes there was seen to glide into the corner meat-market, in the midst of the jeering cooks who elbowed him, an awkward young man, with books under his arm, who had a timid and frightened appearance, and who, as he entered, took off his hat from his forehead, which was dripping with sweat, made a low bow to the astonished butcher, another bow to the butcher's boy, asked for a mutton cutlet, paid six or seven sous for it, wrapped it up in paper, put it under his arm between two books, and went away. It was Marius. On this cutlet, which he cooked himself, he lived three days.

The first day he ate the meat; the second day he ate the fat; the third day he gnawed the bone. On several occasions, Aunt Gillenormand made overtures, and sent him the sixty pistoles. Marius always sent them back, saying that he had no need of anything.

He was still in mourning for his father, when the revolution which we have described was accomplished in his ideas. Since then, he had never left off black clothes. His clothes left him, however. A day came, at last, when he had no coat. His trousers were going also. What was to be done? Courfeyrac, for whom he also had done some good turns, gave him an old coat. For thirty sous, Marius had it turned by some porter or other, and it was a new coat. But this coat was green. Then Marius did not go out till after nightfall. That made his coat black. Desiring always to be in mourning, he clothed himself with night.

Through all this, he procured admission to the bar. He was reputed to occupy Courfeyrac's room, which was decent, and where a certain number of law books, supported and filled out by some odd volumes of novels, made up the library required by the rules.

When Marius had become a lawyer, he informed his grandfather of it, in a letter which was frigid, but full of submission and respect. M. Gillenormand took the letter with trembling hands, read it, and threw it, torn in pieces, into the basket. Two or three days afterwards, Mademoiselle Gillenormand overheard her father, who was alone in his room, talking aloud. This was always the case when he was much excited. She listened: the old man said: 'If you were not a fool, you would know that a man cannot be a baron and a lawyer at the same time!'

2. *Marius poor*

IT IS WITH MISERY as with everything else. It gradually becomes endurable. It ends by taking form and becoming fixed. You vegetate, that is to say you develop in some wretched fashion, but sufficient for existence. This is the way in which Marius Pontmercy's life was arranged.

He had got out of the narrowest place; the pass widened a little before him. By dint of hard work, courage, perseverance, and will, he had succeeded in earning by his labour about seven hundred francs a year. He had learned German and English; thanks to Courfeyrac, who introduced him to his friend the publisher, Marius filled, in the literary department of the book-house, the useful role of *utility*. He made out prospectuses, translated from the journals, annotated republications, compiled biographies, etc., net result, year in and year out, seven hundred francs. He lived on this. How? Not badly. We are going to tell.

Marius occupied, at an annual rent of thirty francs, a wretched little room in the Gorbeau tenement, with no fireplace, called a cabinet, in which there was no more furniture than was indispensable. The furniture was his own. He gave three francs a month to the old woman who had charge of the building, for sweeping his room and bringing him every morning a little warm water, a fresh egg, and a penny loaf of bread. On this loaf and this egg he breakfasted. His breakfast varied from two or four sous, as eggs were cheap or dear. At six o'clock in the evening he went down into the Rue Saint Jacques, to dine at Rousseau's, opposite Basset's the print dealer's, at the corner of the Rue des Mathurins. He ate no soup. He took a sixpenny plate of meat, a threepenny half-plate of vegetables, and a threepenny dessert. For three sous, as much bread as he liked. As for wine, he drank water. On paying at the counter, where Madame Rousseau was seated majestically, still plump and fresh also in those days, he gave a sou to the waiter, and Madame Rousseau gave him a smile. Then he went away. For sixteen sous, he had a smile and a dinner.

This Rousseau restaurant, where so few bottles and so many pitchers were emptied, was rather an appeasant than a restorant. It is not kept now. The master had a fine title; he was called Rousseau the Aquatic.

Thus, breakfast four sous, dinner sixteen sous, his food cost him twenty sous a day, which was three hundred and sixty-five francs a year. Add the thirty francs for his lodging, and the thirty-six francs to the old woman, and a few other trifling expenses, and for four hundred and fifty francs, Marius was fed, lodged, and waited upon. His clothes cost him a hundred francs, his linen fifty francs, his washing fifty francs; the whole did not exceed six hundred and fifty francs. This left him fifty francs. He was rich. He occasionally lent ten francs to a friend. Courfeyrac borrowed sixty francs of him once. As for fire, having no fireplace, Marius had 'simplified' it.

Marius always had two complete suits, one old 'for every day', the other quite new, for special occasions. Both were black. He had but three shirts, one he had on, another in the drawer, the third at the washerwoman's. He renewed them as they wore out. They were usually ragged, so he buttoned his coat to his chin.

For Marius to arrive at this flourishing condition had required years. Hard years, and difficult ones; those to get through, these to climb. Marius had never given up for a single day. He had undergone everything, in the shape of privation; he had done everything, except get into debt. He gave himself this credit, that he had never owed a sou to anybody. For him a debt was the beginning of slavery. He felt even that a creditor is worse than a master; for a master owns only your person, a creditor owns your dignity and can belabour that. Rather than borrow, he did not eat. He had had many days of fasting. Feeling that all extremes meet, and that if we do not take care, abasement of fortune may lead to baseness of soul, he watched jealously over his pride. Such a habit or such a carriage as, in any other condition, would have appeared deferential, seemed humiliating, and he braced himself against it. He risked nothing, not wishing to take a backward step. He had a kind of stern blush upon his face. He was timid even to rudeness.

In all his trials he felt encouraged and sometimes even upborne by a secret force within. The soul helps the body, and at certain moments uplifts it. It is the only bird which sustains its cage.

By the side of his father's name, another name was engraven upon Marius' heart, the name of Thénardier. Marius, in his enthusiastic yet serious nature, surrounded with a sort of halo the man to whom, as he thought, he owed his father's life, that brave sergeant who had saved the colonel in the midst of the balls and bullets of Waterloo. He never separated the memory of this man from the memory of his father, and he associated them in his veneration. It was a sort of worship with two steps, the high altar for the colonel, the low one for Thénardier. The idea of the misfortune into which he knew that Thénardier had fallen and been engulfed, intensified his feeling of gratitude. Marius had learned at Montfermeil of the ruin and bankruptcy of the unlucky innkeeper. Since then, he had made untold effort to get track of him, and to endeavour to find him, in that dark abyss of misery in which Thénardier had disappeared. Marius had beaten the whole country; he had been to Chelles, to Bondy, to Gournay, to Nogent, to Lagny. For three years he had been devoted to this, spending in these explorations what little money he could spare. Nobody could give him any news of Thénardier; it was thought he had gone abroad. His creditors had sought for him, also, with less love than Marius, but with as much zeal, and had not been able to put their hands on him. Marius blamed and almost hated himself for not succeeding in his researches. This was the only debt which the colonel had left him, and Marius made it a point of honour to pay it. 'What,' thought he, 'when my father lay dying on the field of battle, Thénardier could find him through the smoke and the grape, and bring him off on his shoulders, and yet he owed him nothing; while I, who owe so much to Thénardier, I cannot reach him in that darkness in which he is suffering, and restore him, in my turn, from death to life. Oh! I will find him!' Indeed, to find Thénardier, Marius would have given one of his arms, and to save him from his wretchedness, all his blood. To see Thénardier, to render some service to Thénardier, to say to him – 'You do not know me, but I do know you. Here I am, dispose of me!' This was the sweetest and most magnificent dream of Marius.

3. *Marius a man*

MARIUS WAS NOW twenty years old. It was three years since he had left his grandfather. They remained on the same terms on both sides, without attempting a reconciliation, and without seeking to meet. And, indeed, what was the use of meeting? to come in conflict? Which would have had the best of it? Marius was a vase of brass, but M. Gillenormand was an iron pot.

To tell the truth, Marius was mistaken as to his grandfather's heart. He imagined that M. Gillenormand had never loved him, and that this crusty and harsh yet smiling old man, who swore, screamed, stormed, and lifted his cane, felt for him at most only the affection, at once slight and severe, of the old men of comedy. Marius was deceived. There are fathers who do not love their children; there is no grandfather who does not adore his grandson. In reality, we have said, M. Gillenormand worshipped Marius. He worshipped him in his own way, with an accompaniment of cuffs, and even of blows; but, when the child was gone, he felt a dark void in his heart; he ordered that nobody should speak of him again, and regretted that he was so well obeyed. At first he hoped that this Buonapartist, this Jacobin, this terrorist, this Septembrist, would return. But weeks passed away, months passed away, years passed away; to the great despair of M. Gillenormand, the blood-drinker did not reappear! 'But I could not do anything else than turn him away,' said the grandfather, and he asked himself: 'If it were to be done again, would I do it?' His pride promptly answered Yes, but his old head, which he shook in silence, sadly answered, No. He had his hours of dejection. He missed Marius. Old men need affection as they do sunshine. It is warmth. However strong his nature might be, the absence of Marius had changed something in him. For nothing in the world would he have taken a step towards the 'little rogue'; but he suffered. He never inquired after him, but he thought of him constantly. He lived, more and more retired, in the Marais. He was still, as formerly, gay and violent, but his gaiety had a convulsive harshness as if it contained grief and anger, and his bursts of violence always terminated by a sort of placid and gloomy exhaustion. He said sometimes: 'Oh! if he would come back, what a good box of the ear I would give him.'

As for the aunt, she thought too little to love very much; Marius was now nothing to her but a sort of dim, dark outline; and she finally busied herself a good deal less about him than with the cat or the paroquet which she probably had. What increased the secret suffering of Grandfather Gillenormand, was that he shut her entirely out, and let her suspect nothing of it. His chagrin was like those newly invented furnaces which consume their own smoke. Sometimes it happened that some blundering, officious body would speak to him of Marius, and ask: 'What is your grandson doing, or what has become of him?' The old bourgeois would answer, with a sigh, if he was too sad, or giving his ruffle a tap, if he wished to seem gay: 'Monsieur the Baron Pontmercy is pettifogging in some hole.'

While the old man was regretting, Marius was rejoicing. As with all good hearts, suffering had taken away his bitterness. He thought of M. Gillenormand only with kindness, but he had determined to receive nothing more from the man *who had been cruel to his father*. This was now the softened translation of his first indignation. Moreover, he was happy in having suffered, and in suffering still. It was for his father. His hard life satisfied him, and pleased him. He said to himself with a sort of pleasure that – *it was the very least*; that it was – an expiation; that – save for this, he would have been punished otherwise and later, for his unnatural indifference towards his father, and towards such a father; – that it would not have been just that his father should have had all the suffering, and himself none; – what were his efforts and his privation, moreover, compared with the heroic life of the colonel? that finally his only way of drawing near his father, and becoming like him, was to be valiant against indigence as he had been brave against the enemy; and that this was doubtless what the colonel meant by the words: '*He will be worthy of it.*' Words which Marius continued to bear, not upon his breast, the colonel's paper having disappeared, but in his heart.

And then, when his grandfather drove him away, he was but a child; now he was a man. He felt it. Misery, we must insist, had been good to him. Poverty in youth, when it succeeds, is so far magnificent that it turns the whole will towards effort, and the whole soul towards aspiration. Poverty strips the material life entirely bare, and makes it hideous; thence arise inexpressible yearnings towards the ideal life. The rich young man has a hundred brilliant and coarse amusements, racing, hunting, dogs, cigars, gaming, feasting, and the rest; busying the lower portions of the soul at the expense of its higher and delicate portions. The poor young man must work for his bread; he eats; when he has eaten, he has nothing more but reverie. He goes free to the play which God gives; he beholds the sky, space, the stars, the flowers, the children, the humanity in which he suffers, the creation in which he shines. He looks at humanity so much that he sees the soul, he looks at creation so much that he sees God. He dreams, he feels that he is great; he dreams again, and he feels that he is tender. From the egotism of the suffering man, he passes to the compassion of the contemplating man. A wonderful feeling springs up within him, forgetfulness of self, and pity for all. In thinking of the numberless enjoyments which nature offers, gives, and gives lavishly to open souls, and refuses to closed souls, he, a millionaire of intelligence, comes to grieve for the millionaires of money. All hatred goes out of his heart in proportion as all light enters his mind. And then is he unhappy? No. The misery of a young man is never miserable. The first lad you meet, poor as he may be, with his health, his strength, his quick step, his shining eyes, his blood which circulates warmly, his black looks, his fresh cheeks, his rosy lips, his white teeth, his pure breath, will always be envied by an old emperor. And then! every morning he sets about earning his bread; and while his hands are earning his living, his backbone is gaining firmness, his brain is gaining ideas. When his work is done, he returns to ineffable ecstasies, to contemplation, to joy; he sees his feet in difficulties, in obstacles, on the pavement, ill thorns, sometimes in the mire; his head is in the light. He is firm, serene, gentle, peaceful, attentive, serious, content with little, benevolent; and he blesses God for having given him these two estates which many of the rich are without; labour which makes him free, and thought which makes him noble.

This is what had taken place in Marius. He had even, to tell the truth gone a little too far on the side of contemplation. The day on which he had arrived at the point of being almost sure of earning his living, he stopped there, preferring to be poor, and retrenching from labour to give to thought. That is to say, he passed sometimes whole days in thinking, plunged and swallowed up like a visionary, in the mute joys of ecstasy and interior radiance. He had put the problem of his life thus: to work as little as possible at material labour, that he might work as much as possible at impalpable labour; in other words, to give a few hours to real life, and to cast the rest into the infinite. He did not perceive, thinking that he lacked nothing, that contemplation thus obtained comes to be one of the forms of sloth, that he was content with subduing the primary necessities of life, and that he was resting too soon.

It was clear that, for his energetic and generous nature, this could only be a transitory state, and that at the first shock against the inevitable complications of destiny, Marius would arouse.

Meantime, although he was a lawyer, and whatever Grandfather Gillenormand might think, he was not pleading, he was not even pettifogging. Reverie had turned him away from the law. To consort with attorneys, to attend courts, to hunt up cases, was wearisome. Why should he do it? He saw no reason for changing his business. This cheap and obscure book-making had procured him sure work, work with little labour, which, as we have explained, was sufficient for him.

One of the booksellers for whom he worked, M. Magimel, I think, had offered to take him home, give him a good room, furnish him regular work, and pay him fifteen hundred francs a year. To have a good room! fifteen hundred francs! Very well. But to give up his liberty! to work for a salary, to be a kind of literary clerk! In Marius' opinion, to accept, would make his position better and worse at the same time; he would gain in comfort and lose in dignity; it was a complete and beautiful misfortune given up for an ugly and ridiculous constraint; something like a blind man who should gain one eye. He refused.

Marius' life was solitary. From his taste for remaining outside of everything, and also from having been startled by its excesses, he had decided not to enter the group presided over by Enjolras. They had remained good friends; they were ready to help one another, if need were, in all possible ways; but nothing more. Marius had two friends, one young, Courfeyrac, and one old, M. Mabeuf. He inclined towards the old one. First he was indebted to him for the revolution through which he had gone; he was indebted to him for having known and loved his father. '*He operated upon me for the cataract,*' said he.

Certainly, this churchwarden had been decisive.

M. Mabeuf was not, however, on that occasion anything more than the calm and passive agent of providence. He had enlightened Marius accidentally and without knowing it, as a candle does which somebody carries; he had been the candle and not the somebody.

As to the interior political revolution in Marius, M. Mabeuf was entirely incapable of comprehending it, desiring it, or directing it.

As we shall meet M. Mabeuf hereafter, a few words will not be useless.

4. *M. Mabeuf*

THE DAY THAT M. Mabeuf said to Marius: '*Certainly, I approve of political opinions,*' he expressed the real condition of his mind. All political opinions were indifferent to him, and he approved them all without distinction, provided they left him quiet, as the Greeks called the Furies, 'the beautiful, the good, the charming', the *Eumenides*. M. Mabeuf's political opinion was a passionate fondness for plants, and a still greater one for books. He had, like everybody else, his termination in *ist*, without which nobody could have lived in those times, but he was neither a royalist, nor a Bonapartist, nor a chartist, nor an Orleanist, nor an anarchist; he was an old-bookist.

He did not understand how men could busy themselves with hating one another about such bubbles as the charter, democracy, legitimacy, the monarchy, the republic, etc., when there were in this world all sorts of mosses, herbs and shrubs, which they could look at, and piles of folios and even of 32mos which they could pore over. He took good care not to be useless, having books did not prevent him from reading, being a botanist did not prevent him from being a gardener. When he knew Pontmercy, there was this sympathy between the colonel and himself, that what the colonel did for flowers, he did for fruits. M. Mabeuf had succeeded in producing seedling pears as highly flavoured as the pears of Saint Germain; to one of his combinations, as it appears, we owe the October Mirabelle, now famous, and not less fragrant than the summer Mirabelle. He went to mass rather from good-feeling than from devotion, and because he loved the faces of men, but hated their noise, and he found them, at church only, gathered together and silent. Feeling that he ought to be something in the government, he had chosen the career of a churchwarden. Finally, he had never succeeded in loving any woman as much as a tulip bulb, or any man as much as an Elzevir. He had long passed his sixtieth year. When one day somebody asked him: 'Were you never married?' 'I forget,' said he. When he happened sometimes – to whom does it not happen? – to say: 'Oh! if I were rich,' it was not upon ogling a pretty girl, like M. Gillenormand, but upon seeing an old book. He lived alone, with an old governess. He was a little gouty, and when he slept, his old fingers, stiffened with rheumatism, were clenched in the folds of the clothes. He had written and published a *Flora of the Environs of*

Cauteretz with coloured illustrations, a highly esteemed work, the plates of which he owned and which he sold himself. People came two or three times a day and rang his bell, in the Rue Mézières, for it. He received fully two thousand francs a year for it; this was nearly all his income Though poor, he had succeeded in gathering together, by means of patience, self-denial, and time, a valuable collection of rare copies on every subject. He never went out without a book under his arm, and he often came back with two. The only decoration of the four ground-floor rooms which, with a small garden, formed his dwelling, were some framed herbariums and a few engravings of old masters. The sight of a sword or a gun chilled him. In his whole life, he had never been near a cannon, even at the Invalides. He had a passable stomach, a brother who was a curé, hair entirely white, no teeth left either in his mouth or in his mind, a tremor of the whole body, a Picard accent, a childlike laugh, weak nerves, and the appearance of an old sheep. With all that, no other friend nor any other intimate acquaintance among the living, but an old bookseller of the Porte Saint Jacques named Royol. His mania was the naturalisation of indigo in France.

His servant was, also, a peculiar variety of innocence. The poor, good old woman was a maid. Sultan, her cat, who could have miauled the miserere of Allegri at the Sistine Chapel, had filled her heart, and sufficed for the amount of passion which she possessed. None of her dreams went as far as man. She had never got beyond her cat. She had, like him, moustaches. Her glory was in the whiteness of her caps. She spent her time on Sunday after mass in counting her linen in her trunk, and in spreading out upon her bed the dresses in the piece which she had bought and never made up. She could read. Monsieur Mabeuf had given her the name of *Mother Plutarch*.

Monsieur Mabeuf took Marius into favour, because Marius, being young and gentle, warmed his old age without arousing his timidity. Youth, with gentleness, has upon old men the effect of sunshine without wind. When Marius was full of military glory, gunpowder, marches, and countermarches, and all those wonderful battles in which his father had given and received such huge sabre strokes, he went to see Monsieur Mabeuf, and Monsieur Mabeuf talked with him about the hero from the floricultural point of view.

Towards 1830, his brother the curé died, and almost immediately after, as at the coming on of night, the whole horizon of Monsieur Mabeuf was darkened. By a failure – of a notary – he lost ten thousand francs, which was all the money that he possessed in his brother's name and his own. The revolution of July brought on a crisis in bookselling. In hard times, the first thing that does not sell is a *Flora. The Flora of the Environs of Cauteretz* stopped short. Weeks went by without a purchaser. Sometimes Monsieur Mabeuf would start at the sound of the bell. 'Monsieur,' Mother Plutarch would say sadly, 'it is the water-porter.' In short, Monsieur Mabeuf left the Rue Mézières one day, resigned his place as churchwarden, gave up Saint Sulpice, sold a part, not of his books but of his prints – what he prized the least – and installed himself in a little house on the Boulevard Montparnasse, where however he remained but one quarter, for two reasons; first, the ground floor and the garden let for three hundred francs, and he did not dare to spend more than two hundred francs for his rent; secondly, being near the Fatou shooting gallery, he heard pistol shots; which was insupportable to him.

He carried off his *Flora*, his plates, his herbariums, his portfolios and his books, and established himself near La Salpêtrière in a sort of cottage in the village of Austerlitz, where at fifty crowns a year he had three rooms, a garden enclosed with a hedge, and a well. He took advantage of this change to sell nearly all his furniture. The day of his entrance into this new dwelling, he was very gay, and drove the nails himself on which to hang the engravings and the herbariums; he dug in his garden the rest of the day, and in the evening, seeing that Mother Plutarch had a gloomy and thoughtful air, he tapped her on the shoulder and said with a smile: 'We have the indigo.'

Only two visitors, the bookseller of the Porte Saint Jacques and Marius, were admitted to his cottage at Austerlitz, a tumultuous name which was, to tell the truth, rather disagreeable to him.

However, as we have just indicated, brains absorbed in wisdom, or in folly, or, as often happens, in both at once, are but very slowly permeable by the affairs of life. Their own destiny is far from them. There results from such concentrations of mind a passivity which, if it were due to reason, would resemble philosophy. We decline, we descend, we fall, we are even overthrown, and we hardly perceive it. This always ends, it is true, by an awakening, but a tardy one. In the meantime, it seems as though we were neutral in the game which is being played between our good and our ill fortune. We are the stake yet we look upon the contest with indifference.

Thus it was that amid this darkness which was gathering about him, all his hopes going out one after another, Monsieur Mabeuf had remained serene, somewhat childishly, but very thoroughly. His habits of mind had the swing of a pendulum. Once wound up by an illusion, he went a very long time, even when the illusion had disappeared. A clock does not stop at the very moment you lose the key.

Monsieur Mabeuf had some innocent pleasures. These pleasures were cheap and unlooked-for; the least chance furnished them. One day Mother Plutarch was reading a romance in one corner of the room. She read aloud, as she understood better so. To read aloud, is to assure yourself of what you are reading. There are people who read very loud, and who appear to be giving their words of honour for what they are reading.

It was with that kind of energy that Mother Plutarch was reading the romance she held in her hand. Monsieur Mabeuf heard, but was not listening.

As she read, Mother Plutarch came to this passage. It was about an officer of dragoons and a belle:

'The belle *bouda* [pouted], and the *dragon* [dragoon] – '

Here she stopped to wipe her spectacles.

'Bouddha and the Dragon,' said Monsieur Mabeuf in an undertone. 'Yes, it is true, there was a dragon who, from the depth of his cave, belched forth flames from his jaws and was burning up the sky. Several stars had already been set on fire by this monster, who, besides, had claws like a tiger. Bouddha went into his cave and succeeded in converting the dragon. That is a good book which you are reading there, Mother Plutarch. There is no more beautiful legend.'

And Monsieur Mabeuf fell into a delicious reverie.

5. *Poverty a good neighbour of misery*

MARIUS HAD A LIKING for this open-hearted old man, who saw that he was being slowly seized by indigence, and who had come gradually to be astonished at it, without, however, as yet becoming sad. Marius met Courfeyrac, and went to see Monsieur Mabeuf. Very rarely, however; once or twice a month, at most.

It was Marius' delight to take long walks alone on the outer boulevards, or in the Champ de Mars, or in the less frequented walks of the Luxembourg. He sometimes spent half a day in looking at a vegetable garden, at the beds of salad, the fowls on the dung-heap, and the horse turning the wheel of the pump. The passers-by looked at him with surprise, and some thought that he had a suspicious appearance and an ill-omened manner. He was only a poor young man, dreaming without an object.

It was in one of these walks that he had discovered the Gorbeau tenement, and its isolation and cheapness being an attraction to him, he had taken a room in it. He was only known in it by the name of Monsieur Marius.

All passions, except those of the heart, are dissipated by reverie. Marius' political fevers were over. The revolution of 1830, by satisfying him, and soothing him, had aided in this. He remained the same, with the exception of his passionateness. He had still the same opinions. But they were softened. Properly speaking, he held opinions no longer; he had sympathies. Of what party was he? of the party of humanity. Out of humanity he chose France; out of the nation he chose the people; out of the people he chose woman. To her, above all, his pity went out. He now preferred an idea to a fact, a poet to a hero, and he admired a book like Job still more than an event like Marengo. And then, when, after a day of meditation, he returned at night along the boulevards, and saw through the branches of the trees the fathomless space, the nameless lights, the depths, the darkness, the mystery, all that which is only human seemed to him very pretty.

Marius thought he had, and he had perhaps in fact, arrived at the truth of life and of human philosophy, and he had finally come hardly to look at anything but the sky, the only thing that truth can see from the bottom of her well.

This did not hinder him from multiplying plans, combinations, scaffoldings, projects for the future. In this condition of reverie, an eye which could have looked into Marius' soul would have been dazzled by its purity. In fact, were it given to our eye of flesh to see into the consciences of others, we should judge a man much more surely from what he dreams than from what he thinks. There is will in the thought, there is none in the dream. The dream, which is completely spontaneous, takes and keeps, even in the gigantic and the ideal, the form of our mind. Nothing springs more directly and more sincerely from the very bottom of our souls than our unreflected and indefinite aspirations towards the splendours of destiny. In these aspirations, much more than in ideas which are combined, studied, and compared, we can find the true character of each man. Our chimæras are what most resemble ourselves. Each one dreams the unknown and the impossible according to his own nature.

Towards the middle of this year, 1831, the old woman who waited upon Marius told him that his neighbours, the wretched Jondrette family, were to be turned into the street. Marius, who passed almost all his days out of doors, hardly knew that he had any neighbours.

'Why are they turned out?' said he.

'Because they do not pay their rent; they owe for two terms.'

'How much is that?'

'Twenty francs,' said the old woman.

Marius had thirty francs in reserve in a drawer.

'Here,' said he, to the old woman, 'there are twenty-five francs. Pay for these poor people, give them five francs, and do not tell them that it is from me.'

6. *The supplanter*

IT HAPPENED THAT the regiment to which Lieutenant Théodule belonged came to be stationed at Paris. This was the occasion of a second idea occurring to Aunt Gillenormand. She had, the first time, thought she would have Marius watched by Théodule; she plotted to have Théodule supplant Marius.

At all events, and in case the grandfather should feel a vague need of a young face in the house – these rays of dawn are sometimes grateful to ruins – it was expedient to find another Marius.

'Yes,' thought she, 'it is merely an erratum such as I see in the books; for Marius read Théodule.'

A grand-nephew is almost a grandson; for want of a lawyer, a lancer will do.

One morning, as Monsieur Gillenormand was reading something like *La Quotidienne*, his daughter entered, and said in her softest voice, for the matter concerned her favourite:

'Father, Théodule is coming this morning to present his respects to you.'

'Who is that – Théodule?'

'Your grand-nephew.'

'Ah!' said the grandfather.

Then he resumed his reading, thought no more of the grand-nephew who was nothing more than any Théodule, and very soon was greatly excited, as was almost always the case when he read. The 'sheet' which he had, royalist indeed – that was a matter of course, announced for the next day, without any mollification, one of the little daily occurrences of the Paris of that time; that the students of the schools of Law and Medicine would meet in the square of the Pantheon at noon – to deliberate. The question was one of the topics of the moment: the artillery of the National Guard, and a conflict between the Minister of War and 'the citizen militia' on the subject of the cannon planted in the court of the Louvre. The students were to 'deliberate' thereupon. It did not require much more to enrage Monsieur Gillenormand.

He thought of Marius, who was a student, and who, probably, would go, like the others, 'to deliberate, at noon, in the square of the Pantheon'.

While he was dwelling upon this painful thought, Lieutenant Théodule entered, in citizen's dress, which was adroit, and was discreetly introduced by Mademoiselle Gillenormand. The lancer reasoned thus: 'The old druid has not put everything into an annuity. It is well worth while to disguise oneself in taffeta occasionally.'

Mademoiselle Gillenormand said aloud to her father:

'Théodule, your grand-nephew.'

And, in a whisper, to the lieutenant:

'Say yes to everything.'

And she retired.

The lieutenant, little accustomed to such venerable encounters, stammered out with some timidity: 'Good morning, uncle,' and made a mixed bow composed of the involuntary and mechanical awkwardness of the military salute finished off with the bow of the bourgeois.

'Ah! it is you; very well, take a seat,' said the old man.

And then, he entirely forgot the lancer.

Théodule sat down, and Monsieur Gillenormand got up.

Monsieur Gillenormand began to walk up and down with his hands in his pockets, talking aloud, and rubbing with his nervous old fingers the two watches which he carried in his two waistcoat pockets.

'This mess of snivellers! they meet together in the Square of the Pantheon. Virtue of my quean! Scapegraces yesterday at nurse! If their noses were squeezed, the milk would run out! And they deliberate at noon tomorrow! What are we coming to? what are we coming to? It is clear that we are going to the pit. That is where the descamisados have led us! The citizen artillery! To deliberate about the citizen artillery! To go out and jaw in the open air about the blowing of the National Guard! And whom will they find themselves with there! Just see where jacobinism leads to. I will bet anything you please, a million against a fig, that they will all be fugitives from justice and discharged convicts. Republicans and galley-slaves, they fit like a nose and a handkerchief. Carnot said: "Where would you have me go, traitor?" Fouché answered: "Wherever you like, fool!" That is what republicans are.'

'It is true,' said Théodule.

Monsieur Gillenormand turned his head half around, saw Théodule, and continued:

'Only to think that this rogue has been so wicked as to turn carbonaro! Why did you leave my house? To go out and be a republican. Pish! in the first place the people do not want your republic, they do not want it, they have good sense, they know very well that there always have been kings, and that there always will be, they know very well that the people, after all, is nothing but the people, they laugh at your republic, do you understand, idiot? Is not that caprice of yours horrible? To fall in love with Père Duchesne, to cast sheep's eyes at the guillotine, to sing ditties and play the guitar under the balcony of '93; we must spit upon all these young folks, they are so stupid! They are all in a heap. Not one is out of it. It is enough to breathe the air that blows down the street to make them crazy. The nineteenth century is poison. The first blackguard you will meet wears his goat's beard, thinks he is very clever, and discards his old relatives. That is republican, that is romantic. What is that indeed, romantic? have the kindness to tell me what that is! Every possible folly. A year ago, you went to *Hernani*.[110] I want to know, *Hernani!* antitheses! abominations which are not written in French! And then they have cannon in the court of the Louvre. Such is the brigandage of these things.'

'You are right, uncle,' said Théodule.

M. Gillenormand resumed:

'Cannon in the court of the Museum! what for? Cannon, what do you want?

Do you want to shoot down the Apollo Belvedere? What have cartridges to do with Venus de' Medici? Oh! these young folks nowadays, all scamps! What a small affair is their Benjamin Constant! And those who are not scoundrels are boobies! They do all they can to be ugly, they are badly dressed, they are afraid of women, they appear like beggars about petticoats, which makes the wenches burst out laughing; upon my word, you would say the poor fellows are ashamed of love. They are homely, and they finish themselves off by being stupid; they repeat the puns of Tiercelin and Potier, they have sackcoats, horse-jockeys' waistcoats, coarse cotton shirts, coarse cloth trousers, coarse leather boots, and their jabber is like their feathers. Their jargon would serve to sole their old shoes with. And all these foolish brats have political opinions. They ought to be strictly forbidden to have any political opinions. They fabricate systems, they reform society, they demolish monarchy, they upset all laws, they put the garret into the cellar, and my porter in place of the king, they turn Europe topsy-turvy, they rebuild the world, and the favours they get are sly peeps at washerwomen's legs when they are getting into their carts! Oh! Marius! Oh! you beggar! going to bawl in a public place! to discuss, to debate, to take measures! they call them measures, just gods! disorder shrinks and becomes a ninny. I have seen chaos, I see a jumble. Scholars deliberating about the National Guard, you would not see that among the Ojibways or among the Cadodaches! The savages who go naked, their pates looking like shuttlecocks, with clubs in their paws, are not so wild as these bachelors. Fourpenny monkeys! they pass for learned and capable! they deliberate and reason! it is the world's end. It is evidently the end of this miserable terraqueous globe. It needed some final hiccough, France is giving it. Deliberate, you rogues! Such things will happen as long as they go and read the papers under the arches of the Odeon. That costs them a sou, and their good sense, and their intelligence, and their heart, and their soul, and their mind. They come away from there, and they bring the camp into their family. All these journals are a pest; all, even the *Drapeau Blanc!* at bottom Martainville was a jacobin. Oh! just heavens! you can be proud of having thrown your grandfather into despair, you can!'

'That is evident,' said Théodule.

And taking advantage of M. Gillenormand's drawing breath, the lancer added magisterially: 'There ought to be no journal but the *Moniteur* and no book but the *Annuaire Militaire.*'

M. Gillenormand went on.

'He is like their Sieyès! a regicide ending off as a senator; that is always the way they end. They slash themselves with thee-and-thouing, and citizen, so that they may come to be called Monsieur the Count, Monsieur the Count as big as my arm, the butchers of September. The philosopher Sieyès![111] I am happy to say that I never made any more account of the philosophies of all these philosophers than of the spectacles of the clown of Tivoli. I saw the senators one day passing along the Quai Malaquais in mantles of violet velvet sprinkled with bees, and hats in the style of Henri IV. They were hideous. You would have said they were the monkeys of the tiger's court. Citizens, I tell you that your progress is a lunacy, that your humanity is a dream, that your revolution is a crime, that your republic is a monster, that your young maiden France comes from the brothel, and I maintain it before you all, whoever you are, be you publicists, be you economists, be you legists, be you greater connoisseurs in liberty, equality, and fraternity than the axe of the guillotine! I tell you that, my goodmen!'

'Zounds,' cried the lieutenant, 'that is wonderfully true.'

M. Gillernormand broke off a gesture which he had begun, turned, looked the lancer Théodule steadily in the eyes, and said:

'You are a fool.'

BOOK 6: THE CONJUNCTION OF TWO STARS

1. *The nickname: mode of formation of family names*

MARIUS WAS NOW a fine-looking young man, of medium height, with heavy jet black hair, a high intelligent brow, large and passionate nostrils, a frank and calm expression, and an indescribable something beaming from every feature, which was at once lofty, thoughtful, and innocent. His profile, all the lines of which were rounded, but without loss of strength, possessed that Germanic gentleness which has made its way into French physiognomy through Alsace and Lorraine, and that entire absence of angles which rendered the Sicambri so recognisable among the Romans, and which distinguishes the leonine from the aquiline race. He was at that season of life at which the mind of men who think, is made up in nearly equal proportions of depth and simplicity. In a difficult situation he possessed all the essentials of stupidity; another turn of the screw, and he could become sublime. His manners were reserved, cold, polished, far from free. But as his mouth was very pleasant, his lips the reddest and his teeth the whitest in the world, his smile corrected the severity of his physiognomy. At certain moments there was a strange contrast between this chaste brow and this voluptuous smile. His eye was small, his look great.

At the time of his most wretched poverty, he noticed that girls turned when he passed, and with a deathly feeling in his heart he fled or hid himself. He thought they looked at him on account of his old clothes, and that they were laughing at him; the truth is, that they looked at him because of his graceful appearance, and that they dreamed over it.

This wordless misunderstanding between him and the pretty girls he met, had rendered him hostile to society. He attached himself to none, for the excellent reason that he fled before all. Thus he lived without aim – like a beast, said Courfeyrac.

Courfeyrac said to him also: 'Aspire not to be a sage (they used familiar speech; familiarity of speech is characteristic of youthful friendships). My dear boy, a piece of advice. Read not so much in books, and look a little more upon the Peggies. The little rogues are good for thee, O Marius! By continual flight and blushing thou shalt become a brute.'

At other times Courfeyrac met him with: 'Good day, Monsieur Abbé.'

When Courfevrac said anything of this kind to him, for the next week Marius avoided women, old as well as young, more than ever, and especially did he avoid the haunts of Courfeyrac.

There were, however, in all the immensity of creation, two women from whom Marius never fled, and whom he did not at all avoid. Indeed he would have been very much astonished had anybody told him that they were women. One was the old woman with the beard, who swept his room, and who gave Courfeyrac an opportunity to say: 'As his servant wears her beard, Marius does not wear his.' The other was a little girl that he saw very often, and that he never looked at.

For more than a year Marius had noticed in a retired walk of the Luxembourg, the walk which borders the parapet of the Pépinière, a man and a girl quite young, nearly always sitting side by side, on the same seat, at the most retired end of the walk, near the Rue de l'Ouest. Whenever that chance which controls the promenades of men whose eye is turned within, led Marius to this walk, and it was almost every day, he found this couple there. The man might be sixty years old; he seemed sad and serious; his whole person presented the robust but wearied appearance of a soldier retired from active service. Had he worn a decoration, Marius would have said: it is an old officer. His expression was kind, but it did not invite approach, and he never returned a look. He wore a blue coat and pantaloons, and a broad-brimmed hat, which always appeared to be new; a black cravat, and Quaker linen, that is to say, brilliantly white, but of coarse texture. A grisette passing near him one day, said: There is a very nice widower. His hair was perfectly white.

The first time the young girl that accompanied him sat down on the seat which they seemed to have adopted, she looked like a girl of about thirteen or fourteen, puny to the extent of being almost ugly, awkward, insignificant, yet promising, perhaps, to have rather fine eyes. But they were always looking about with a disagreeable assurance. She wore the dress, at once aged and childish, peculiar to the convent schoolgirl, an ill-fitting garment of coarse black merino. They appeared to be father and daughter.

For two or three days Marius scrutinised this old man, who was not yet an aged man, and this little girl, not yet a woman; then he paid no more attention to them. For their part they did not even seem to see him. They talked with each other peacefully, and with indifference to all else. The girl chatted incessantly and gaily. The old man spoke little, and at times looked upon her with an unutterable expression of fatherliness.

Marius had acquired a sort of mechanical habit of promenading on this walk. He always found them there.

It was usually thus:

Marius would generally reach the walk at the end opposite their seat, promenade the whole length of it, passing before them, then return to the end by which he entered, and so on. He performed this turn five or six times in his promenade, and this promenade five or six times a week, but they and he had never come to exchange bows. This man and this young girl, though they appeared, and perhaps because they appeared, to avoid observation, had naturally excited the attention of the five or six students, who, from time to time, took their promenades along the Pépinière; the studious after their lecture, the others after their game of billiards. Courfeyrac, who belonged to the latter, had noticed them at some time or other, but finding the girl homely, had very quickly and carefully avoided them. He had fled like a Parthian, launching a nickname behind him. Struck especially by the dress of the little girl and the hair of the old man, he had named the daughter *Mademoiselle Lanoire* [Black] and the father *Monsieur Leblanc* [White]; and so, as nobody knew them otherwise, in the absence of a name, this surname had become fixed. The students said: 'Ah! Monsieur Leblanc is at his seat!' and Marius, like the rest, had found it convenient to call this unknown gentleman M. Leblanc.

We shall do as they did, and say M. Leblanc for the convenience of this story.

Marius saw them thus nearly every day at the same hour during the first year. He found the man very much to his liking, but the girl rather disagreeable.

2. Lux facta est [112]

THE SECOND YEAR, at the precise point of this history to which the reader has arrived, it so happened that Marius broke off this habit of going to the Luxembourg, without really knowing why himself, and there were nearly six months during which he did not set foot in his walk. At last he went back there again one day; it was a serene summer morning, Marius was as happy as one always is when the weather is fine. It seemed to him as if he had in his heart all the bird songs which he heard, and all the bits of blue sky which he saw through the trees.

He went straight to 'his walk', and as soon as he reached it, he saw, still on the same seat, this well known pair. When he came near them, however, he saw that it was indeed the same man, but it seemed to him that it was no longer the same girl. The woman whom he now saw was a noble, beautiful creature, with all the most bewitching outlines of woman, at the precise moment at which they are yet combined with all the most charming graces of childhood – that pure and fleeting moment which can only be translated by these two words: sweet fifteen. Beautiful chestnut hair, shaded with veins of gold, a brow which seemed chiselled marble, cheeks which seemed made of roses, a pale incarnadine, a flushed whiteness, an exquisite mouth, whence came a smile like a gleam of sunshine, and a voice like music, a head which Raphael would have given to Mary, on a neck which Jean Goujon would have given to Venus. And that nothing might be wanting to this ravishing form, the nose was not beautiful, it was pretty; neither straight nor curved, neither Italian nor Greek; it was the Parisian nose; that is, something sprightly, fine, irregular, and pure, the despair of painters and the charm of poets.

When Marius passed near her, he could not see her eyes, which were always cast down. He saw only her long chestnut lashes, eloquent of mystery and modesty.

But that did not prevent the beautiful girl from smiling as she listened to the white-haired man who was speaking to her, and nothing was so transporting as this maidenly smile with these downcast eyes.

At the first instant Marius thought it was another daughter of the same man, a sister doubtless of her whom he had seen before. But when the invariable habit of his promenade led him for the second time near the seat, and he had looked at her attentively, he recognised that she was the same. In six months the little girl had become a young woman; that was all. Nothing is more frequent than this phenomenon. There is a moment when girls bloom out in a twinkling, and become roses all at once. Yesterday we left them children, today we find them dangerous.

She had not only grown; she had become idealised. As three April days are enough for certain trees to put on a covering of flowers, so six months had been enough for her to put on a mantle of beauty.

We sometimes see people, poor and mean, who seem to awaken, pass suddenly from indigence to luxury, incur expenses of all sorts, and become all at once splendid, prodigal, and magnificent. That comes from interest received; yesterday was pay-day. The young girl had received her dividend.

And then she was no longer the schoolgirl with her plush hat, her merino dress, her shapeless shoes, and her red hands; taste had come to her with beauty. She was a woman well dressed, with a sort of simple and rich elegance without any particular style. She wore a dress of black damask, a mantle of the same, and a white crape hat. Her white gloves showed the delicacy of her hand which played with the Chinese ivory handle of her parasol, and her silk boot betrayed the smallness of her foot. When you passed near her, her whole toilet exhaled the penetrating fragrance of youth.

As to the man, he was still the same.

The second time that Marius came near her, the young girl raised her eyes; they were of a deep celestial blue, but in this veiled azure was nothing yet beyond the look of a child. She looked at Marius with indifference, as she would have looked at any little monkey playing under the sycamores, or the marble vase which cast its shadow over the bench; and Marius also continued his promenade thinking of something else.

He passed four or five times more by the seat where the young girl was, without even turning his eyes towards her.

On the following days he came as usual to the Luxembourg, as usual he found 'the father and daughter' there, but he paid no attention to them. He thought no more of this girl now that she was handsome than he had thought of her when she was homely. He passed very near the bench on which she sat, because that was his habit.

3. *Effect of spring*

ONE DAY THE AIR was mild, the Luxembourg was flooded with sunshine and shadow, the sky was as clear as if the angels had washed it in the morning, the sparrows were twittering in the depths of the chestnut trees, Marius had opened his whole soul to nature, he was thinking of nothing, he was living and breathing, he passed near this seat, the young girl raised her eyes, their glances met.

But what was there now in the glance of the young girl? Marius could not have told. There was nothing, and there was everything. It was a strange flash.

She cast down her eyes, and he continued on his way.

What he had seen was not the simple, artless eye of a child; it was a mysterious abyss, half-opened, then suddenly closed.

There is a time when every young girl looks thus. Woe to him upon whom she looks!

This first glance of a soul which does not yet know itself is like the dawn in the sky. It is the awakening of something radiant and unknown. Nothing can express the dangerous chasm of this unlooked-for gleam which suddenly suffuses adorable mysteries, and which is made up of all the innocence of the present, and of all the passion of the future. It is a kind of irresolute lovingness which is revealed by chance, and which is waiting. It is a snare which Innocence unconsciously spreads, and in which she catches hearts without intending it, and without knowing it. It is a maiden glancing like a woman.

It is rare that deep reverie is not born of this glance wherever it may fall. All that is pure, and all that is vestal, is concentrated in this celestial and mortal glance, which more than the most studied ogling of the coquette, has the magic power of suddenly forcing into bloom in the depths of a heart, this flower of the shade full of perfumes and poisons, which is called love.

At night, on retiring to his garret, Marius cast a look upon his dress, and for the first time perceived that he had the slovenliness, the indecency, and the unheard-of stupidity, to promenade in the Luxembourg with his 'everyday' suit, a hat broken near the band, coarse teamsters' boots, black pantaloons shiny at the knees, and a black coat threadbare at the elbows.

4. *Commencement of a great distemper*

THE NEXT DAY, at the usual hour, Marius took from his closet his new coat, his new pantaloons, his new hat, and his new boots; he dressed himself in this panoply complete, put on his gloves, prodigious prodigality, and went to the Luxembourg.

On the way, he met Courfeyrac, and pretended not to see him. Courfeyrac, on his return home, said to his friends:

'I have just met Marius' new hat and coat, with Marius inside. Probably he was going to an examination. He looked stupid enough.'

On reaching the Luxembourg, Marius took a turn round the fountain and looked at the swans; then he remained for a long time in contemplation before a statue, the head of which was black with moss, and which was minus a hip. Near the fountain was a big-bellied bourgeois of forty, holding a little boy of five by the hand, to whom he was saying: 'Beware of extremes, my son. Keep thyself equally distant from despotism and from anarchy.' Marius listened to this good bourgeois. Then he took another turn round the fountain. Finally, he went towards 'his walk'; slowly, and as if with regret. One would have said that he was at once compelled to go and prevented from going. He was unconscious of all this, and thought he was doing as he did every day.

When he entered the walk he saw M. Leblanc and the young girl at the other end 'on their seat'. He buttoned his coat, stretched it down that there might be no wrinkles, noticed with some complaisance the lustre of his pantaloons, and marched upon the seat. There was something of attack in this march, and certainly a desire of conquest. I say, then, he marched upon the seat, as I would say: Hannibal marched upon Rome.

Beyond this, there was nothing which was not mechanical in all his movements, and he had in no wise interrupted the customary preoccupations of his mind and his labour. He was thinking at that moment that the *Manuel du Baccalauréat* was a stupid book, and that it must have been compiled by rare old fools, to give an analysis, as of masterpieces of the human mind, of three tragedies of Racine and only one of Molière's comedies. He had a sharp singing sound in his ear. While approaching the seat, he was smoothing the wrinkles out of his coat, and his eyes were fixed on the young girl. It seemed to him as though she filled the whole extremity of the walk with a pale, bluish light.

As he drew nearer, his step became slower and slower. At some distance from the seat, long before he had reached the end of the walk, he stopped, and he did not himself know how it happened, but he turned back. He did not even say to himself that he would not go to the end. It was doubtful if the young girl could see him so far off, and notice his fine appearance in his new suit. However, he held himself very straight, so that he might look well, in case anybody who was behind should happen to notice him.

He reached the opposite end and then returned, and this time he approached a little nearer to the seat. He even came to within about three trees of it, but there he felt an indescribable lack of power to go further, and he hesitated. He thought he had seen the young girl's face bent towards him. Still he made a great and manly effort, conquered his hesitation, and continued his advance. In a few seconds, he was passing before the seat, erect and firm, blushing to his ears, without daring to cast a look to the right or the left, and with his hand in his coat like a statesman. At the moment he passed under the guns of the fortress, he felt a frightful palpitation of the heart. She wore, as on the previous day, her damask dress and her crape hat. He heard the sound of an ineffable voice, which might be 'her voice'. She was talking quietly. She was very pretty. He felt it, though he made no effort to see her. 'She could not, however,' thought he, 'but have some esteem and consideration for me, if she knew that I was the real author of the dissertation on Marcos Obregon de la Ronda, which Monsieur François de Neufchâteau has put, as his own, at the beginning of his edition of *Gil Blas*!'

He passed the seat, went to the end of the walk, which was quite near, then turned and passed again before the beautiful girl. This time he was very pale. Indeed, he was experiencing nothing that was not very disagreeable. He walked away from the seat and from the young girl, and although his back was turned, he imagined that she was looking at him, and that made him stumble.

He made no effort to approach the seat again, he stopped midway of the walk, and sat down there – a thing which he never did – casting many side glances, and thinking, in the most indistinct depths of his mind, that after all it must be difficult for persons whose white hat and black dress he admired, to be absolutely insensible to his glossy pantaloons and his new coat.

At the end of a quarter of an hour, he rose, as if to recommence his walk towards this seat, which was encircled by a halo. He, however, stood silent and motionless. For the first time in fifteen months, he said to himself, that this gentleman, who sat there every day with his daughter, had undoubtedly noticed him, and probably thought his assiduity very strange.

For the first time, also, he felt a certain irreverence in designating this unknown man, even in the silence of his thought, by the nickname of M. Leblanc.

He remained thus for some minutes with his head down tracing designs on the ground with a little stick which he had in his hand.

Then he turned abruptly away from the seat, away from Monsieur Leblanc and his daughter, and went home.

That day he forgot to go to dinner. At eight o'clock in the evening he discovered it, and as it was too late to go down to the Rue Saint Jacques, 'No matter,' said he, and he ate a piece of bread.

He did not retire until he had carefully brushed and folded his coat.

5. *Sundry thunderbolts fall upon Ma'am Bougon*

NEXT DAY, Ma'am Bougon – thus Courfeyrac designated the old portress-landlady of the Gorbeau tenement – Ma'am Bougon – her name was in reality Madame Bougon, as we have stated, but this terrible fellow Courfeyrac respected nothing – Ma'am Bougon was stupefied with astonishment to see Monsieur Marius go out again with his new coat.

He went again to the Luxembourg, but did not get beyond his seat midway of the walk. He sat down there as on the day previous, gazing from a distance and seeing distinctly the white hat, the black dress, and especially the bluish light. He did not stir from the seat, and did not go home until the gates of the Luxembourg were shut. He did not see Monsieur Leblanc and his daughter retire. He concluded from that that they left the garden by the gate on the Rue de l'Ouest. Later, some weeks afterwards, when he thought of it, he could not remember where he had dined that night.

The next day, for the third time, Ma'am Bougon was thunderstruck. Marius went out with his new suit. 'Three days running!' she exclaimed.

She made an attempt to follow him, but Marius walked briskly and with immense strides; it was a hippopotamus undertaking to catch a chamois. In two minutes she lost sight of him, and came back out of breath, three quarters choked by her asthma, and furious. 'The silly fellow,' she muttered, 'to put on his handsome clothes every day and make people run like that!'

Marius had gone to the Luxembourg.

The young girl was there with Monsieur Leblanc. Marius approached as near as he could, seeming to be reading a book, but he was still very far off, then he returned and sat down on his seat, where he spent four hours watching the artless little sparrows as they hopped along the walk; they seemed to him to be mocking him.

Thus a fortnight rolled away. Marius went to the Luxembourg, no longer to promenade, but to sit down, always in the same place, and without knowing why. Once there he did not stir. Every morning he put on his new suit, not to be conspicuous, and he began again the next morning.

She was indeed of a marvellous beauty. The only remark which could be made, that would resemble a criticism, is that the contradiction between her look, which was sad, and her smile, which was joyous, gave to her countenance something a little wild, which produced this effect, that at certain moments this sweet face became strange without ceasing to be charming.

6. *Taken prisoner*

ON ONE OF THE LAST DAYS of the second week, Marius was as usual sitting on his seat, holding in his hand an open book of which he had not turned a leaf for two hours. Suddenly he trembled. A great event was commencing at the end of the walk. Monsieur Leblanc and his daughter had left their seat, the daughter had taken the arm of the father, and they were coming slowly towards the middle of the walk where Marius was. Marius closed his book, then he opened it, then he made an attempt to read. He trembled. The halo was coming straight towards him. 'O dear!' thought he, 'I shall not have time to take an attitude.' However, the man with the white hair and the young girl were advancing. It seemed to him that it would last a century, and that it was only a second. 'What are they coming by here for?' he asked himself. 'What! is she going to pass this place! Are her feet to press this ground in this walk, but a step from me?' He was overwhelmed, he would gladly have been very handsome, he would gladly have worn the cross of the Legion of Honour. He heard the gentle and measured sound of their steps approaching. He imagined that Monsieur Leblanc was hurling angry looks upon him. 'Is he going to speak to me?' thought he. He bowed his head; when he raised it they were quite near him. The young girl passed, and in passing she looked at him. She looked at him steadily, with a sweet and thoughtful look which made Marius tremble from head to foot. It seemed to him that she reproached him for having been so long without coming to her, and that she said: 'It is I who come.' Marius was bewildered by these eyes full of flashing light and fathomless abysses.

He felt as though his brain were on fire. She had come to him, what happiness! And then, how she had looked at him! She seemed more beautiful than she had ever seemed before. Beautiful with a beauty which combined all of the woman with all of the angel, a beauty which would have made Petrarch sing and Dante kneel. He felt as though he was swimming in the deep blue sky. At the same time he was horribly disconcerted, because he had a little dust on his boots.

He felt sure that she had seen his boots in this condition.

He followed her with his eyes till she disappeared, then he began to walk in the Luxembourg like a madman. It is probable that at times he laughed, alone as he was, and spoke aloud. He was so strange and dreamy when near the child's nurses that everyone thought he was in love with her.

He went out of the Luxembourg to find her again in some street.

He met Courfeyrac under the arches of the Odeon and said: 'Come and dine with me.' They went to Rousseau's and spent six francs. Marius ate like an ogre. He gave six sous to the waiter. At dessert he said to Courfeyrac: 'Have you read the paper? What a fine speech Audry de Puyraveau has made!'

He was desperately in love.

After dinner he said to Courfeyrac, 'Come to the theatre with me.' They went to the Porte Saint Martin to see Frederick[113] in *L'Auberge des Adrets*. Marius was hugely amused.

At the same time he became still more strange and incomprehensible. On leaving the theatre, he refused to look at the garter of a little milliner who was crossing a gutter, and when Courfeyrac said: '*I would not object to putting that woman in my collection*,' it almost horrified him.

Courfeyrac invited him to breakfast next morning at the Café Voltaire. Marius went and ate still more than the day before. He was very thoughtful, and yet very gay. One would have said that he seized upon all possible occasions to burst out laughing. To every country-fellow who was introduced to him he gave a tender embrace. A circle of students gathered round the table, and there was talk of the flummery paid for by the government, which was retailed at the Sorbonne; then the conversation fell upon the faults and gaps in the dictionaries and prosodies of Quicherat. Marius interrupted the discussion by exclaiming: 'However, it is a very pleasant thing to have the Cross.'

'He is a comical fellow!' said Courfeyrac, aside to Jean Prouvaire.

'No,' replied Jean Prouvaire, 'he is serious.'

He was serious, indeed. Marius was in this first vehement and fascinating period in which the grand passion commences.

One glance had done all that.

When the mine is loaded, and the match is ready, nothing is simpler. A glance is a spark.

It was all over with him. Marius loved a woman. His destiny was entering upon the unknown.

The glances of women are like certain apparently peaceful but really formidable machines. You pass them every day quietly, with impunity, and without suspicion of danger. There comes a moment when you forget even that they are there. You come and go, you muse, and talk, and laugh. Suddenly you feel that you are seized! it is done. The wheels have caught you, the glance has captured you. It has taken you, no matter how or where, by any portion whatever of your thought which was trailing, through any absence of mind. You are lost. You will be drawn in entirely. A train of mysterious forces has gained possession of you. You struggle in vain. No human succour is possible. You will be drawn down from wheel to wheel, from anguish to anguish, from torture to torture. You, your mind, your fortune, your future, your soul; and you will not escape from the terrible machine, until, according as you are in the power of a malevolent nature, or a noble heart, you shall be disfigured by shame or transfigured by love.

7. *Adventures of the letter U abandoned to conjecture*

ISOLATION, SEPARATION from all things, pride, independence, a taste for nature, lack of everyday material activity, life in oneself, the secret struggles of chastity, and an ecstasy of goodwill towards the whole creation, had prepared Marius for this possession which is called love. His worship for his father had become almost a religion, and, like all religion, had retired into the depths of his heart. He needed something above that. Love came.

A whole month passed during which Marius went every day to the Luxembourg. When the hour came, nothing could keep him away. 'He is out at service,' said Courfeyrac. Marius lived in transports. It is certain that the young girl looked at him.

He finally grew bolder, and approached nearer to the seat. However he passed before it no more, obeying at once the instinct of timidity and the instinct of prudence, peculiar to lovers. He thought it better not to attract the 'attention of the father.' He formed his combinations of stations behind trees and the pedestals of statues with consummate art, so as to be seen as much as possible by the young girl and as little as possible by the old gentleman. Sometimes he would stand for half an hour motionless behind some Leonidas or Spartacus with a book in his hand, over which his eyes, timidly raised, were looking for the young girl, while she, for her part, was turning her charming profile towards him, suffused with a smile. While yet talking in the most natural and quiet way in the world with the white-haired man, she rested upon Marius all the dreams of a maidenly and passionate eye. Ancient and immemorial art which Eve knew from the first day of the world, and which every woman knows from the first day of her life! Her tongue replied to one and her eyes to the other.

We must, however, suppose that M. Leblanc perceived something of this at last, for often when Marius came, he would rise and begin to promenade. He had left their accustomed place, and had taken the seat at the other end of the walk, near the Gladiator, as if to see whether Marius would follow them. Marius did not understand it, and committed that blunder. 'The father' began to be less punctual, and did not bring 'his daughter' every day. Sometimes he came alone. Then Marius did not stay. Another blunder.

Marius took no note of these symptoms. From the phase of timidity he had passed, a natural and inevitable progress, to the phase of blindness. His love grew. He dreamed of her every night. And then there came to him a good fortune for which he had not even hoped, oil upon the fire, double darkness upon his eyes. One night, at dusk, he found on the seat, which 'M. Leblanc and his daughter' had just left, a handkerchief, a plain handkerchief without embroidery, but white, fine, and which appeared to him to exhale ineffable odours. He seized it in transport. This handkerchief was marked with the letters U. F.: Marius knew nothing of this beautiful girl, neither her family, nor her name, nor her dwelling; these two letters were the first thing he had caught of her, adorable initials upon which he began straightway to build his castle. It was evidently her first name. Ursula, thought he, what a sweet name! He kissed the handkerchief, inhaled its perfume, put it over his heart, on his flesh in the day-time, and at night went to sleep with it on his lips.

'I feel her whole soul in it!' he exclaimed.

This handkerchief belonged to the old gentleman, who had simply let it fall from his pocket.

For days and days after this piece of good fortune, he always appeared at the Luxembourg kissing this handkerchief and placing it on his heart. The beautiful child did not understand this at all, and indicated it to him by signs, which he did not perceive.

'Oh, modesty!' said Marius.

8. Even the Invalides may be lucky

SINCE WE HAVE PRONOUNCED the word *modesty*, and since we conceal nothing, we must say that once however, through all his ecstasy, 'his Ursula' gave him a very serious pang. It was upon one of the days when she prevailed upon M. Leblanc to leave the seat and to promenade on the walk. A brisk north wind was blowing, which swayed the tops of the plane trees. Father and daughter, arm in arm, had just passed before Marius' seat. Marius had risen behind them and was following them with his eyes, as it was natural that he should in this desperate situation of his heart.

Suddenly a gust of wind, rather more lively than the rest, and probably entrusted with the little affairs of spring, flew down from La Pepinière, rushed upon the walk, enveloped the young girl in a transporting tremor worthy of the nymphs of Virgil and the fauns of Theocritus, and raised her skirt, this skirt more sacred than that of Isis, almost to the height of the garter. A limb of exquisite mould was seen. Marius saw it. He was exasperated and furious.

The young girl had put down her dress with a divinely startled movement, but he was outraged none the less. True, he was alone in the walk. But there might have been somebody there. And if anybody had been there! could one conceive of such a thing ? what she had done was horrible! Alas, the poor child had done nothing; there was but one culprit, the wind; and yet Marius in whom all the Bartholo which there is in Cherubin was confusedly trembling, was determined to be dissatisfied, and was jealous of his shadow. For it is thus that is awakened in the human heart, and imposed upon man, even unjustly, the bitter and strange jealousy of the flesh. Besides, and throwing this jealousy out of consideration, there was nothing that was agreeable to him in the sight of that beautiful limb; the white stocking of the first woman that came along would have given him more pleasure.

When 'his Ursula', reaching the end of the walk, returned with M. Leblanc, and passed before the seat on which Marius had again sat down, Marius threw at her a cross and cruel look. The young girl slightly straightened back, with that elevation of the eyelids, which says: 'Well, what is the matter with him ?'

That was 'their first quarrel'.

Marius had hardly finished this scene with her when somebody came down the walk. It was an Invalide, very much bent, wrinkled and pale with age, in the uniform of Louis XV, with the little oval patch of red cloth with crossed swords on his back, the soldier's Cross of Saint Louis, and decorated also by a coat sleeve in which there was no arm, a silver chin, and a wooden leg. Marius thought he could discern that this man appeared to be very much pleased. It seemed to him even that the old cynic, as he hobbled along by him, had addressed to him a very fraternal and very merry wink, as if by some chance they had been put into communication and had enjoyed some dainty bit of good fortune together. What had he seen to be so pleased, this relic of Mars? What had happened between this leg of wood and the other ? Marius had a paroxysm of jealousy. 'Perhaps he was by!' said he; 'perhaps he saw!' And he would have been glad to exterminate the Invalide.

Time lending his aid, every point is blunted. This anger of Marius against 'Ursula', however just and proper it might be, passed away. He forgave her at last; but it was a great effort; he pouted at her three days.

Meanwhile, in spite of all that, and because of all that, his passion was growing, and was growing mad.

9. An eclipse

WE HAVE SEEN how Marius discovered, or thought he discovered, that Her name was Ursula.

Hunger comes with love. To know that her name was Ursula had been much; it was little. In three or four weeks Marius had devoured this piece of good fortune. He desired another. He wished to know where she lived.

He had committed one blunder in falling into the snare of the seat by the Gladiator. He had committed a second by not remaining at the Luxembourg when Monsieur Leblanc came there alone. He committed a third, a monstrous one. He followed 'Ursula'.

She lived in the Rue de l'Ouest, in the least frequented part of it, in a new three-storey house, of modest appearance.

From that moment Marius added to his happiness in seeing her at the Luxembourg, the happiness of following her home.

His hunger increased. He knew her name, her first name, at least, the charming name, the real name of a woman; he knew where she lived; he desired to know who she was.

One night after he had followed them home, and seen them disappear at the *porte-cochère*, he entered after them, and said boldly to the porter:

'Is it the gentleman on the first floor who has just come in?'

'No,' answered the porter. 'It is the gentleman on the third.'

Another fact. This success made Marius still bolder.

'In front?' he asked.

'Faith!' said the porter, 'the house is only built on the street.'

'And what is this gentleman?'

'He lives on his income, monsieur, A very kind man, who does a great deal of good among the poor, though not rich.'

'What is his name?' continued Marius.

The porter raised his head, and said:

'Is monsieur a detective?'

Marius retired, much abashed, but still in great transports. He was getting on.

'Good,' thought he. 'I know that her name is Ursula, that she is the daughter of a retired gentleman, and that she lives there, in the third storey, in the Rue de l'Ouest.'

Next day Monsieur Leblanc and his daughter made but a short visit to the Luxembourg; they went away while it was yet broad daylight. Marius followed them into the Rue de l'Ouest, as was his custom. On reaching the *porte-cochère*, Monsieur Leblanc passed his daughter in, and then stopped, and before entering himself, turned and looked steadily at Marius. The day after that they did not come to the Luxembourg. Marius waited in vain all day.

At nightfall he went to the Rue de l'Ouest, and saw a light in the windows of the third storey. He walked beneath these windows until the light was put out.

The next day nobody at the Luxembourg. Marius waited all day, and then went to perform his night duty under the windows. That took him till ten o'clock in the evening. His dinner took care of itself. Fever supports the sick man, and love the lover.

He passed a week in this way. Monsieur Leblanc and his daughter appeared at the Luxembourg no more. Marius made melancholy conjectures; he dared not watch the *porte-cochère* during the day. He limited himself to going at night to gaze upon the reddish light of the windows. At times he saw shadows moving, and his heart beat high.

On the eighth day when he reached the house, there was no light in the windows. 'What!' said he, 'the lamp is not yet lighted. But yet it is dark. Or they have gone out?' He waited till ten o'clock. Till midnight. Till one o'clock in the morning. No light appeared in the third storey windows, and nobody entered the house. He went away very gloomy.

On the morrow – for he lived only from morrow to morrow; there was no longer any today, so to speak, to him – on the morrow he found nobody at the Luxembourg, he waited; at dusk he went to the house. No light in the windows; the blinds were closed; the third storey was entirely dark. Marius knocked at the *porte-cochère*; went in and said to the porter:

'The gentleman of the third floor?'

'Moved,' answered the porter.

Marius tottered, and said feebly:

'Since when?'

'Yesterday.'

'Where does he live now ?'

'I don't know anything about it.'

'He has not left his new address, then ?'

'No.'

And the porter, looking up, recognised Marius.

'What! it is you!' said he, but decidedly now, 'you do keep a bright look-out.'

BOOK 7: PATRON MINETTE

1. The mines and the miners

EVERY HUMAN SOCIETY has what is called in the theatres a *third sub-stage*. The social soil is mined everywhere, sometimes for good, sometimes for evil. These works are in strata; there are upper mines and lower mines. There is a top and a bottom in this dark sub-soil which sometimes sinks beneath civilisation, and which our indifference and our carelessness trample underfoot. The Encyclopæ-dia, in the last century, was a mine almost on the surface. The dark caverns, these gloomy protectors of primitive Christianity, were awaiting only an opportunity to explode beneath the Cæsars, and to flood the human race with light. For in these sacred shades there is latent light. Volcanoes are full of a blackness, capable of flashing flames. All lava begins as midnight. The catacombs, where the first mass was said, were not merely the cave of Rome; they were the cavern of the world.

There is under the social structure, this complex wonder of a mighty burrow, – of excavations of every kind. There is the religious mine, the philosophic mine, the political mine, the economic mine, the revolutionary mine. This pick with an idea, that pick with a figure, the other pick with a vengeance. They call and they answer from one catacomb to another. Utopias travel under ground in the passages. They branch out in every direction. They sometimes meet there and fraternise. Jean Jacques lends his pick to Diogenes, who lends him his lantern. Sometimes they fight. Calvin takes Socinius by the hair. But nothing checks or interrupts the tension of all these energies towards their object. The vast simultaneous activity, which goes to and fro, and up and down, and up again, in these dusky regions, and which slowly transforms the upper through the lower, and the outer through the inner; vast unknown swarming of workers. Society has hardly a suspicion of this work of undermining which, without touching its surface, changes its substance. So many subterranean degrees, so many differing labours, so many varying excavations. What comes from all this deep delving? The future.

The deeper we sink, the more mysterious are the workers. To a degree which social philosophy can recognise, the work is good; beyond this degree it is doubtful and mixed; below, it becomes terrible. At a certain depth, the excavations become impenetrable to the soul of civilisation, the respirable limit of man is passed; the existence of monsters becomes possible.

The descending ladder is a strange one; each of its rounds corresponds to a step whereupon philosophy can set foot, and where we discover someone of her workers, sometimes divine, sometimes monstrous. Below John Huss is Luther; below Luther is Descartes; below Descartes is Voltaire; below Voltaire is Condorcet; below Condorcet is Robespierre; below Robespierre is Marat; below Marat is Babeuf. And that continues. Lower still, in dusky confusion, at the limit which separates the indistinct from the invisible, glimpses are caught of other men in the gloom, who perhaps no longer exist. Those of yesterday are spectres; those of tomorrow are goblins. The embryonary work of the future is one of the visions of the philosopher.

A fœtus world in limbo, what a wonderful profile!

Saint Simon, Owen, Fourier, are there also, in lateral galleries.[114]

Indeed, although an invisible divine chain links together all these subterranean pioneers, who almost always believe they are alone, yet are not, their labours are very diverse, and the glow of some is in contrast with the flame of others. Some are paradisaic, others are tragic. Nevertheless, be the contrast what it may, all these workers, from the highest to the darkest, from the wisest to the silliest, have one thing in common, and that is disinterestedness. Marat, like Jesus, forgets himself. They throw self aside; they omit self; they do not think of self. They see something other than themselves. They have a light in their eyes, and this light is searching for the absolute. The highest has all heaven in his eyes; the lowest, enigmatical as he may be, has yet beneath his brows the pale glow of the infinite. Venerate him, whatever he may do, who has this sign, the star-eye.

The shadow-eye is the other sign.

With it evil commences. Before him whose eye has no light, reflect and tremble. Social order has its black miners.

There is a point where undermining becomes burial, and where light is extinguished.

Below all these mines which we have pointed out, below all these galleries, below all this immense underground venous system of progress and of utopia, far deeper in the earth, lower than Marat, lower than Babeuf, lower, much lower, and without any connection with the upper galleries, is the last sap. A fear-inspiring place. This is what we have called the third sub-stage. It is the grave of the depths. It is the cave of the blind *Inferi*.

This communicates with the gulfs.

2. *The lowest depth*

THERE DISINTERESTEDNESS vanishes. The demon is dimly rough-hewn; everyone for himself. The eyeless I howls, searches, gropes, and gnaws. The social Ugolino[115] is in this gulf.

The savage outlines which prowl over this grave, half brute, half phantom, have no thought for universal progress, they ignore ideas and words, they have no care but for individual glut. They are almost unconscious, and there is in them a horrible defacement. They have two mothers, both stepmothers, ignorance and misery. They have one guide, want; and their only form of satisfaction is appetite. They are voracious as beasts, that is to say ferocious, not like the tyrant, but like the tiger. From suffering these goblins pass to crime; fated filiation, giddy procreation, the logic of darkness. What crawls in the third sub-stage is no longer the stifled demand for the absolute, it is the protest of matter. Man there becomes dragon. Hunger and thirst are the point of departure; Satan is the point of arrival. From this cave comes Lacenaire.

We have just seen, in the fourth book, one of the compartments of the upper mine, the great political, revolutionary, and philosophic sap. There, as we have said, all is noble, pure, worthy, and honourable. There, it is true, men may be deceived and are deceived, but there error is venerable, so much heroism does it imply. For the sum of all the work which is done there, there is one name: Progress.

The time has come to open other depths, the depths of horror.

There is beneath society, we must insist upon it, and until the day when ignorance shall be no more, there will be, the great cavern of evil.

This cave is beneath all, and is the enemy of all. It is hate universal. This cave knows no philosophers; its poniard has never made a pen. Its blackness has no relation to the sublime blackness of script. Never have the fingers of night, which are clutching beneath this asphyxiating vault, turned the leaves of a book, or unfolded a journal. Babeuf is a speculator to Cartouche; Marat is an aristocrat to Schinderhannes. The object of this cave is the ruin of all things.

Of all things. Including therein the upper saps, which it execrates. It does not undermine, in its hideous crawl, merely the social order of the time; it undermines philosophy, it undermines science, it undermines law, it undermines human thought, it undermines civilisation, it undermines revolution, it undermines progress. It goes by the naked names of theft, prostitution, murder, and assassination. It is darkness, and it desires chaos. It is vaulted in with ignorance.

All the others, those above it, have but one object – to suppress it. To that end philosophy and progress work through all their organs at the same time, through amelioration of the real as well as through contemplation of the absolute. Destroy the cave Ignorance, and you destroy the mole Crime.

We will condense in a few words a portion of what we have just said. The only social peril is darkness.

Humanity is identity. All men are the same clay. No difference, here below at least, in predestination. The same darkness before, the same flesh during, the same ashes after life. But ignorance, mixed with the human composition, blackens it. This incurable ignorance possesses the heart of man, and there becomes Evil.

3. Babet, Gueulemer, Claquesous and Montparnasse

A QUARTETTE of bandits, Claquesous, Gueulemer, Babet and Montparnasse, ruled from 1830 to 1835 over the third sub-stage of Paris.

Gueulemer was a Hercules without a pedestal. His cave was the Arche-Marion sewer. He was six feet high, and had a marble chest, brazen biceps, cavernous lungs, a colossus' body, and a bird's skull. You would think you saw the Farnese Hercules dressed in duck pantaloons and a cotton-velvet waistcoat. Gueulemer, built in this sculptural fashion, could have subdued monsters; he found it easier to become one. Low forehead, large temples, less than forty, the foot of a goose, coarse short hair, a bushy cheek, a wild boar's beard; from this you see the man. His muscles asked for work, his stupidity would have none. This was a huge lazy force. He was an assassin through nonchalance. He was thought to be a creole. Probably there was a little of Marshal Brown in him, he having been a porter at Avignon in 1815. After this he had become a bandit.

The diaphaneity of Babet contrasted with the meatiness of Gueulemer. Babet was thin and shrewd. He was transparent, but impenetrable. You could see the light through his bones, but nothing through his eye. He professed to be a chemist. He had been bar-keeper for Bobèche, and clown for Bobino.[116] He had played vaudeville at Saint Mihiel. He was an affected man, a great talker, who italicised his smiles and quoted his gestures. His business was to sell plaster busts and portraits of the 'head of the Government' in the street. Moreover, he pulled teeth. He had exhibited monstrosities at fairs, and had a booth with a trumpet and this placard: 'Babet, dental artist, member of the Academies, physical experimenter on metals and metalloids, extirpates teeth, removes stumps left by other dentists. Price: one tooth, one franc fifty centimes; two teeth, two francs; three teeth, two francs fifty centimes. Improve your opportunity.' (This 'improve your opportunity', meant: get as many pulled as possible.) He had been married, and had had children. What had become of his wife and children, he did not know. He had lost them as one loses his pocket-handkerchief. A remarkable exception in the obscure world to which he belonged, Babet read the papers. One day, during the time he had his family with him in his travelling booth, he had read in the *Messenger* that a woman had been delivered of a child, likely to live, which had the face of a calf, and he had exclaimed: *'There is a piece of good luck! My wife hasn't the sense to bring me a child like that.'* Since then, he had left everything, 'to take Paris in hand'. His own expression.

What was Claquesous ? He was night. Before showing himself, he waited till the sky was daubed with black. At night he came out of a hole, which he went into again before day. Where was this hole? Nobody knew. In the most perfect obscurity, and to his accomplices, he always turned his back when he spoke. Was his name Claquesous? No. He said: 'My name is Nothing-at-all.' If a candle was brought, he put on a mask. He was a ventriloquist. Babet said: *'Claque-sous is a night-bird with two voices.'* Claquesous was restless, roving, terrible. It was not certain that he had a name, Claquesous being a nickname; it was not certain that he had a voice, his chest speaking oftener than his mouth; it was not certain that he had a face, nobody having ever seen anything but his mask. He disappeared as if he sank into the ground; he came like an apparition.

A mournful sight was Montparnasse. Montparnasse was a child; less than twenty, with a pretty face, lips like cherries, charming black locks, the glow of spring in his eyes; he had all the vices and aspired to all the crimes. The digestion of what was bad gave him an appetite for what was worse. He was the *gamin* turned vagabond, and the vagabond become an assassin. He was genteel, effeminate, graceful, robust, weak, and ferocious. He wore his hat turned upon the left side, to make room for the tuft of hair, according to the fashion of 1829. He lived by robbery. His coat was of the most fashionable cut but threadbare. Montparnasse was a fashion-plate living in distress and committing murders. The cause of all the crimes of this young man was his desire to be well dressed. The first grisette who had said to him: 'You are handsome,' had thrown the stain of darkness into his heart, and had made a Cain of this Abel. Thinking that he was handsome, he had desired to be elegant; now the first of elegances is idleness: idleness for a poor man is crime. Few prowlers were so much feared as Montparnasse. At eighteen, he had already left several corpses on his track. More than one traveller lay in the shadow of this wretch, with extended arms and with his face in a pool of blood. Frizzled, pomaded, with slender waist, hips like a woman, the bust of a Prussian officer, a buzz of admiration about him from the girls of the boulevard, an elaborately-tied cravat, a sling-shot in his pocket, a flower in his button-hole; such was this charmer of the sepulchre.

4. Composition of the band

THESE FOUR BANDITS formed a sort of Proteus, winding through the police and endeavouring to escape from the indiscreet glances of Vidocq 'under various form, tree, flame, and fountain', lending each other their name and their tricks, concealing themselves in their own shadow, each a refuge and a hiding-place for the others, throwing off their personalities, as one takes off a false nose at a masked ball, sometimes simplifying themselves till they are but one, sometimes multiplying themselves till Coco Lacour himself took them for a multitude.

These four men were not four men; it was a sort of mysterious robber with four heads preying upon Paris by wholesale; it was the monstrous polyp of evil which inhabits the crypt of society.

By means of their ramifications and the underlying network of their relations, Babet, Gueulemer, Claquesous, and Montparnasse, controlled the general lying-in-wait business of the Department of the Seine. Originators of ideas in this line, men of midnight imagination came to them for the execution. The four villains being furnished with the single draft they took charge of putting it on the stage. They worked upon scenario. They were always in condition to furnish a company proportioned and suitable to any enterprise which stood in need of aid, and was sufficiently lucrative. A crime being in search of arms, they sublet accomplices to it. They had a company of actors of darkness at the disposition of every cavernous tragedy.

They usually met at nightfall, their waking hour, in the waste grounds near La Salpêtrière. There they conferred. They had the twelve dark hours before them; they allotted their employ.

Patron-Minette, such was the name which was given in subterranean society to the association of these four men. In the old, popular, fantastic language, which now is dying out every day, *Patron-Minette* means morning, just as *entre chien et loup* [between dog and wolf], means night. This appellation, Patron-Minette, probably came from the hour at which their work ended, the dawn being the moment for the disappearance of phantoms and the separation of bandits. These four were known by this title. When the Chief Judge of the Assizes visited Lacenaire in prison, he questioned him in relation to some crime which Lacenaire denied. 'Who did do it?' asked the judge. Lacenaire made this reply, enigmatical to the magistrate, but clear to the police: 'Patron-Minette, perhaps.'

Sometimes a play may be imagined from the announcement of the characters: so, too, we may almost understand what a band is from the list of the bandits. We give, for these names are preserved in the documents, the appellations to which the principal subordinates of Patron-Minette responded:

Panchaud, alias Printanier, alias Bigrenaille.

Brujon. (There was a dynasty of Brujons; we shall say something about it hereafter.)

Boulatruelle, the road-mender, already introduced.

Laveuve.

Finistère.

Homer Hogu, a negro.

Mardisoir.

Dépêche.

Fauntleroy, alias Bouquetière.

Glorieux, a liberated convict.

Barrecarrosse, alias Monsieur Dupont.

L'esplanade-du-Sud.

Poussagrive.

Carmagnolet.

Kruideniers, alias Bizarro.

Mangedentelle.

Les-pieds-en-l'air.

Demi-liard, alias Deux-milliards.

Etc., etc.

We pass over some of them, and not the worst. These names have faces. They express not only beings, but species. Each of these names answers to a variety of these shapeless toadstools of the cellars of civilisation.

These beings, by no means free with their faces, were not of those whom we see passing in the streets. During the day, wearied out by their savage nights, they went away to sleep, sometimes in the parget-kilns, sometimes in the abandoned quarries of Montmartre or Montrouge, sometimes in the sewers. They burrowed.

What has become of these men ? They still exist. They have always existed. Horace speaks of them: *Ambubaiarum collegia, pharmacopolæ, mendici, mimoe;*[117] and so long as society shall be what it is, they will be what they are. Under the dark vault of their cave, they are for ever reproduced from the ooze of society. They return, spectres, always the same; but they bear the same name no longer, and they are no longer in the same skins.

The individuals extirpated, the tribe still exists.

They have always the same faculties. From beggar to the prowler the race preserves its purity. They divine purses in pockets, they scent watches in fobs. Gold and silver to them are odorous. There are simple bourgeois of whom you might say that they have a robable appearance. These men follow these bourgeois patiently. When a foreigner or a countryman passes by they have spider thrills.

Such men, when, towards midnight, on a lone boulevard, you meet them or catch a glimpse of them, are terrifying. They seem not men, but forms fashioned of the living dark; you would say that they are generally an integral portion of the darkness, that they are not distinct from it, that they have no other soul than the gloom, and that it is only temporarily and to live for a few minutes a monstrous life, that they are disaggregated from the night.

What is required to exorcise these goblins? Light. Light in floods. No bat resists the dawn. Illuminate the bottom of society.

NOTES

For reasons that rapidly become obvious there exists at present no critical edition of *Les Misérables*, in French or in English: fully to annotate Hugo's text would generate a second (and possibly a third) volume that would in all certainty be considerably longer than the novel itself. As a result many editions duck the issue by providing no annotation at all. The present edition will not attempt to gloss all the references and allusions that are to be found in *Les Misérables*. It aims rather to account for the most important networks of references, the most significant clusters of allusions, and especially to bring out their ideological force. In the process it will try above all to indicate the directions in which Hugo is seeking to steer our reading of a text that becomes increasingly allusive as it develops. It is hoped in addition that the Historical Note to be found at the head of the Introduction will contribute to the reader's understanding of the topical background to *Les Misérables*.

1 (p. 10) *entered the souls of all* It is part of the democratic dimension of Hugo's enterprise that his text welcomes all local dialects and all social idioms. This will be taken to its furthest extreme much later with the incorporation into the novel of working-class Parisian argot.

2 (p. 15) *the writer of this book* Even if this genealogy is in all probability fanciful, it underlines from the beginning how present Hugo is in the texture of his novel and how actively involved he wants to be with its message.

3 (p. 18) *Gaspard Bès* an outlaw who had been executed at Aix-en-Provence in 1781

4 (p. 21) *Pigault-Lebrun* the author (1753–1835) of a series of highly popular, slightly risqué and somewhat anti-religious novels. A fondness for Pigault-Lebrun connotes post-revolutionary middle-class tastes and attitudes. No surprise then that he should be one of Thénardier's favourite authors.

5 (p. 22) *God is good for the people* The senator's facile scepticism accumulates a whole series of ill-digested references to authors who at best have probably only been half read. Only the last sentence of this long confession of faith is intended by Hugo to be taken seriously.

6 (p. 25) *an unknown light* This chapter, in which the bishop talks with and is blessed by a member of the National Convention, caused considerable offence in Catholic circles: the Convention was the revolutionary assembly that governed France through the bloodiest years of the Revolution, between 1792 and 1795. The deliberate contrast between the ridiculous senator of Chapter 8 and the admirable *Conventionnel* of Chapter 10 should be seen as especially scandalous.

7 (p. 29) *Louis XVII* the young son (1785–95) of Louis XVI and Marie-Antoinette, the so-called Orphan from the Temple [prison] whose fate still remains mysterious. The juxtaposition of the pretender to the French throne with Cartouche, a celebrated bandit, would again have seemed particularly offensive to royalist readers.

8 (p. 30) *over the dragonnades* The dialogue between the two men is here drawing a parallel between the violence of the Revolution (Marat clapping at the guillotine) and that of the *ancien régime*: the dragonnades were the persecutions

by military force (royal dragoons) of protestants in the seventeenth century and
the forced conversions that resulted. The following paragraphs reinforce the
point by contrasting two groups of people: perpetrators of violence in revolutionary and prerevolutionary times.

9 (p. 35) *Louis XVIII* This scornful attitude towards Louis XVIII and the
Restoration in general is characteristic of that of the republican opposition (see
Historical Note). The 'three toads' stand mockingly for the Bourbon fleurs-de-
lys.

10 (p. 37) *Majesty* A savage attack on the dangers of confusing success with
genius backed up by a string of references. Hugo's criticism is valid for all times,
Louis-Napoleon's Second Empire included.

11 (p. 60) *a loaf of bread* Claude Gueux is the hero of Hugo's book of the same
name (1834).

12 (p. 78) *The year 1817* This chapter accumulates an avalanche of references
that are all intended to underline the superficiality of Restoration institutions
and society. Precise identification of insignificant events and long-forgotten
figures thus matters less than the (critical) direction in which Hugo is seeking to
steer our reading: the fact for instance that the now unknown Marchangy and
d'Arlincourt were in 1817 more popular as writers than Chateaubriand or . . .
Hugo says it all.

13 (p. 88) *with the Druids* Hugo's evocation of the stuffiness of the Restoration
gerontocracy is now contrasted with the freshness and *joie de vivre* of the young.
It is a mood that is encapsulated in the Spanish song quoted later ('I am from
Badajoz. Love calls me. All my soul is in my eyes because you are showing your
legs') and in the visit to the nineteenth-century Disneyland which concludes the
chapter.

14 (p. 89) *père de Gand* a reference to Louis XVIII, who had fled to Ghent
during the Hundred Days (March–June 1815) of Napoleon's first return from
exile

15 (p. 90) *the Carmagnole* The *joie de vivre* of the Parisian working classes here
takes on a more menacing note that will find its full voice later in the novel: the
Carmagnole was one of the anthems of the French revolutionaries.

16 (p. 91) *the wisdom of Tholomyès* Tholomyès, Fantine's lover and Cosette's
father, is the typical 'old student of the old style' (p. 84). His pompous speeches
are full of learned references and pretentious puns that are intended to impress
his listeners rather than to be understood by them; to gloss them would be to run
counter to Hugo's intentions.

17 (p. 94) *Les pères . . . leur argent* The workshop song, 'void of sense',
translates more or less as follows: 'The father turkeys gave some money to a
policeman so that Mr Clermont-Tonnerre might become pope on St John's day;
but, not being a priest, Clermont could not be made pope; so the angry
policeman returned the money.'

18 (p. 96) *this melancholy strophe* translates as follows: 'She belonged to a world
in which carts and carriages have the same fate; and, like other nags, this nag has
lived for just one morning.' Tholomyès's verse, a clever-clever parody of
Malherbe's famous Consolation for M. du Périer, provides an ironic foretelling
of Fantine's destiny.

19 (p. 98) *The dinner is paid for* The students' hypocritical letter celebrates all

the bourgeois values that will be rejected in the body of Hugo's novel. Félix Tholomyès will shortly exit the plot to become a July-Monarchy lawyer and the embodiment of *louis-philippard* morality (p. 101).

20 (p. 105) *stupid novels* The sort of trashy romances that Hugo had read during his childhood, later also to be devoured by Flaubert's Emma Bovary.

21 (p. 108) *Madeleine* perhaps from the name of the repentant sinner, *Marie-Madeleine* (Mary-Magdalen)

22 (p. 116) *Joseph de Maistre* a right-wing polemicist (already quoted by Hugo, p. 12) who advocated the divine right of the monarch. In his thinking and that of his followers, the 1789 Revolution was seen as a just punishment visited by God on a degenerate France. Javert as the representative of the Restoration justice system would have been seen as the symbol of this school of thought.

23 (p. 129) *and an elector* During the Restoration (and indeed afterwards) only those male landowners paying a certain amount of direct tax were allowed to vote.

24 (p. 136) *of Laennec* one of the leading contemporary tuberculosis specialists (1781–1826)

25 (p. 183) *the Quotidienne and the Oriflamme* These under the Restoration were royalist newspapers opposed to Romanticism ('this perverse literature'). The 'story of Théramène' mentioned later is to be found in Racine's *Phèdre*, the epitome of French classical tragedy.

26 (p. 200) *the Drapeau Blanc* another rabidly royalist and anti-Bonapartist newspaper

27 (p. 207) *Waterloo* Hugo visited the site of Waterloo between 7 May and 21 July 1861 in order to research this section of *Les Misérables*. Frequently seen as a monstrously irrelevant digression in the novel, the description of the battle was in fact viewed by the writer as central to his purposes; the Introduction to the present edition argues this case.

28 (p. 213) *by Charras* One of the historians (later editions of the novel cite others) who had provided an account of Waterloo; a friend of Hugo's, he had followed him into exile after Louis-Napoleon's *coup d'état* (1851). Despite the extraordinary abundance of details, Hugo's stance is not that of the objective historian. Rather he seeks to provide an epic evocation of war and to place the battle in the broad context of nineteenth-century French history. 'Waterloo', Hugo writes later, 'is not a battle; it is the change of front of the universe' (p. 225). The two objectives, poetic and interpretative, do not always sit happily together.

29 (p. 216) *Salvator Rosa, not of Gribeauval* Salvator Rosa was a seventeenth-century painter, Gribeauval an eighteenth-century military strategist. Hugo's point is that the artist (painter, poet or novelist) is more likely to draw inspiration from Waterloo than the strategist.

30 (p. 223) *Veillons au salut de l'empire* 'Let us guard the destiny of the empire', a line from a patriotic anthem, then as popular as the *Marseillaise*

31 (p. 230) *French bullets* Ney was condemned to death after the fall of Napoleon and executed on 7 December 1815.

32 (p. 232) *the hinge of the nineteenth century* in the sense that Waterloo marks both an end and a beginning, the end of *ancien régime* France and the beginning of modern France

33 (p. 232) *'Merde!'* Most but perhaps not all non-French readers will know that this corresponds to English 'Shit!' Hugo was, unsurprisingly, heavily censured for including in his text what has become known in the folklore of French history as 'Cambronne's word' (*le mot de Cambronne*). Cambronne's expletive, like Waterloo, marks a break with the past 'in the name of the Revolution' (p. 234). For Hugo the inclusion of a down-to-earth (*misérable*) lexicon goes hand in hand with the presence in his novel of working-class (*misérable*) characters: hence later the disquisition on Parisian slang.

34 (p. 234) *England has Byron* and France has . . . Hugo

35 (p. 237) *a postilion . . . on the throne of Sweden* Murat, the son of an innkeeper, was made King of Naples and Bernadotte, in 1789 a sergeant-major, King of Sweden. Foy, mentioned a few lines later, was wounded at Waterloo; after the fall of Napoleon he became a leading left-wing politician. His funeral in 1825 triggered a popular uprising similar to that brought about later by the death of General Lamarque.

36 (p. 238) *Père Elysée* Louis XVIII's doctor. Louis XVIII was old and infirm: hence the description of him as 'the good old tottering invalid'.

37 (p. 238) *the 8th of July . . . of the 20th of March* 20 March 1815 was the date of Napoleon's return to Paris from Elba, 8 July that of Louis XVIII's return from exile.

38 (p. 238) *Trestaillon became famous* During the Empire Trestaillon was the nickname of Jacques Dupont, one of the leaders of the royalist resistance in Southern France. White (contrasting with the revolutionary tricolour) was the colour of the insignia of the newly restored Bourbons; the chapter accumulates details of other transformations through which Louis XVIII sought to buttress the new regime.

39 (p. 239) *the King of Rome* Napoleon's son (Napoleon II to the Bonapartists) who was exiled in Schoenbrunn, Austria

40 (p. 239) *article 14* the article in the constitutional charter that allowed the monarch to take exceptional (and extra-constitutional) measures in times of crisis

41 (p. 240) *sic vos non vobis* from Virgil and literally 'thus you but not for you' – the idea being that Waterloo is famous for the battle although the battle did not really take place at Waterloo

42 (p. 244) *the Gazette des Tribunaux* The *Gazette*, which published accounts of famous trials, was not founded until 1825. For the *Drapeau Blanc*, see Note 26. The article quoted (like that of the *Journal de Paris* later) is of course fictitious but the attributions add to the realism of Hugo's novel.

43 (p. 245) *De Savoie . . . par la suie* a quotation from *Le Pauvre Diable* by Voltaire ('the patriarch of Ferney')

44 (p. 245) *Villèle* leader of the ultraroyalists and prime minister under the restored Bourbons

45 (p. 247) *Fodit . . . nihilque* The two lines are translated at the end of the preceding paragraph. They may have been made up by Hugo.

46 (p. 249) *the Spanish War* A French expeditionary force intervened in Spain in 1823 under the command of the Duc d'Angoulême, son of Charles X. Hugely unpopular in France, the Spanish War represents an attempt by the restored Bourbons to emulate Napoleon's military successes. The failure of this intervention is seen by Hugo to prefigure the revolution of July 1830.

47 (p. 257) *the Champ d'Asile* A French colony implanted in Texas in 1818. It had been settled by a group of exiled liberals, republicans and Bonapartists.

48 (p. 275) *Monsieur Laffitte* a banker and politician who played an important role under both the Restoration and July Monarchy

49 (p. 279) *the Courrier Français* a liberal newspaper of the period

50 (p. 291) *the solitary pedestrian* An avatar of Rousseau's *promeneur solitaire*, this solitary pedestrian, like the earlier wanderer on the field of Waterloo (p. 207), clearly stands for Hugo himself. Writer and reader now come to Paris where they will remain until the end of the novel.

51 (p. 293) *in the style of a melodrama* Louis Ulbach was executed in September 1827 for the murder of a young girl of eighteen. Hugo's evocation of Paris is from the outset associated with notions of crime, love and death.

52 (p. 294) *the Orleans railway* today's Austerlitz station. Hugo reviews the history of Paris from the perspective of the writing present.

53 (p. 302) *was in Paris* Hugo is absent from Paris at the time of writing, in exile in the Channel Islands. The paragraph that follows presents a nostalgic evocation of a lost Paris.

54 (p. 304) *De Goblet . . . vend des Carreaux* roughly translatable as follows: 'This is the factory of Goblet son: come here to choose jugs and ewers, flower pots, pipes and bricks. Here the heart sells window panes [diamonds] to everyone.'

55 (p. 323) *Petit Picpus* The convent and the religious order that inhabits it are invented by Hugo. The convent is based on an historical establishment in the Rue Neuve-Sainte-Geneviève on the left bank of the Seine.

56 (p. 326) *Martin Verga* actually Martin de Vargas, a Spanish Cistercian reformer who died in 1446. The details that follow are a mixture of fact and fiction.

57 (p. 334) *Nemo . . . externis communicabis* 'No one should disclose our rules and institutions to strangers.'

58 (p. 334) *one of the most elegant women of Paris* a discrete tribute to Hugo's mistress, Juliette Drouet, from whose convent diary the writer freely borrows

59 (p. 337) *Imparibus . . . tua perdas* The Latin translates as follows: 'The bodies of three men of different merit are hanging from the branches: Dismas and Gesmas and, between them, the power of God. Dismas aspires to heaven; the unfortunate Gesmas thinks of trivial things. May the supreme power protect us, us and our possessions. If you say these lines, you will not be robbed.'

60 (p. 339) *Post corda lapides* 'After the hearts, the stones'

61 (p. 343) *Hic . . . viginti et tres* 'This is my tomb. I died aged 23.' The epitaph is authentic.

62 (p. 343) *Joseph de Maistre* See Note 22 above.

63 (p. 345) *kislaraga* the head of the black eunuchs in the Constantinople seraglio

64 (p. 346) *In the past* Hugo sees the convent as one of the many reactionary and regressive forces that are blocking the path of progress and preventing the birth of a better future. His 'parenthesis' (p. 343) on monasticism is thus in fact central to the ideological thrust of the novel.

65 (p. 349) *a metaphysical school at the North* The allusion is probably to Schopenhauer, to his treatise on *The World as Will and as Representation* (1819), and to the pessimistic current of thought they embody.

66 (p. 352) *Deo erexit Voltaire* 'Built for God by Voltaire' was inscribed on the church in Ferney, Voltaire's home town. Like Voltaire's church, Hugo's novel is built to the glory of God.

67 (p. 352) *whoever is self-exiled seems venerable to us* including the author of *Les Misérables* . . .

68 (p. 362) *Stat . . . volvitur orbis* 'The cross remains steady whilst the world turns.'

69 (p. 362) *with the loquacity of an opened mill-sluice* The mother superior's sermon is full of biblical and historical references; it is intended as a pastiche of theological rhetoric, as a parody of the techniques of the preacher.

70 (p. 368) *the monk Austin Castillejo* a writer who appears to have been invented by Hugo

71 (p. 374) *Qui dormiunt . . . ut videant semper* The Latin translates as follows: 'Those who sleep in the dust of the earth will awaken; some in eternal life, some in torment, their eyes open for ever.' The formulae that follow are taken from the burial service.

72 (p. 383) *the Chouan party* The Chouans were a Breton counter-revolutionary group. The mention of the Chouans and the presence of 'this Vendean assignat' (p. 383) as part of the furnishings contribute to the sense of historical irrelevance that Hugo associates with the convent.

73 (p. 389) *Parvulus* 'the very small one'; further down '*Homuncio*' = 'the small man'.

74 (p. 389) *the gamin of Paris* The Paris *gamin* (the term is untranslatable), later to be identified as Gavroche, is one of the mythical figures of Hugo's novel. The chapters that follow define the myth of 'this pale child of the Paris suburbs' (p. 391).

75 (p. 391) *Adamaster* the giant-hero in Camoens's *Lusiads*

76 (p. 392) *those singular Places* These are all locations on the periphery of the city, shabby and dilapidated, neither town nor country, ambiguous and mysterious. The 'wall of Grenelle' was used for the execution of court-martialled soldiers.

77 (p. 394) *a little work entitled Claude Gueux* by Hugo himself . . .

78 (p. 395) *Samson* The Sanson family provided a succession of public executioners between 1688 and 1847. The Abbé Montès was a prison almoner during the Restoration and July Monarchy. The lines that follow provide a list of [in]famous criminals who had been condemned to death for a variety of offences.

79 (p. 395) *a gigantic pear* Louis-Philippe's face was said to resemble a pear. Many contemporary caricatures play on the resemblance.

80 (p. 396) *Poquelin* the real name of the seventeenth-century dramatist Molière. Mentioned at the end of the chapter, Bara was a thirteen-year-old republican activist shot by the royalists in 1793.

81 (p. 397) *Paris is the expression of the world* The paragraphs that follow provide a mythical representation of Paris with great rhetorical force and an extraordinary wealth of allusions. Hugo presents a myth of Paris as the cosmic (p. 398) synthesis of all cultures and of all civilisations, of the French capital as a syncretic blend of all periods and countries. Once again the precise significance of each of Hugo's references matters less than their overall value when taken in combination.

82 (p. 397) *quis properantem me prehendit pallio?* 'who is stopping me, as I hurry along, by holding my coat?' The quotation is from Plautus.

83 (p. 398) *Contra . . . id est seditionem oblivisci* 'Against the Graccii we have the Tiber. To drink the Tiber is to forget the insurrection.'

84 (p. 398) *red perukes* The fool in popular theatre wore a red ribbon in his hair. Paris is the capital of both genius and foolishness.

85 (p. 399) *on the Pyramids* The preceding paragraph presents a pot-pourri of heroes and freedom fighters, of thinkers, writers and politicians, all associated with the mythical vision of Paris that Hugo is adumbrating.

86 (p. 400) *Fex urbis* 'dregs of the town'. The expression is Cicero's and leads implicitly towards Hugo's exploration of the parallel realities of slang and sewer.

87 (p. 401) *Little Gavroche* Hugo's theoretical analysis of Paris and of its underclasses culminates in the presentation of an archetypal representative, Gavroche.

88 (p. 406) *rue Quincampoix* the centre of financial speculation in the eighteenth century. Old Gillenormand stands for many of the outdated *ancien régime* values that the novel rejects.

89 (p. 409) *An old salon* The emphasis should be on the adjective: everything in old Gillenormand's way of living is meant to smack of irrelevance and outdatedness.

90 (p. 409) *Refoncez . . . l'drapeau blanc!* lines that translate as follows: 'Put back into your trousers the piece of shirt that is hanging out. Let it not be said that the radicals are displaying the white [i.e. royalist] flag.' The lines quoted later play on equally anti-revolutionary sentiments.

91 (p. 411) *'a brigand of the Loire'* a pejorative term in a royalist mouth, denoting those troops who remained faithful to Napoleon after the emperor's defeat and who sought refuge south of the Loire. Marius's father is one of these.

92 (p. 415) *Requiescant* 'Let them rest in peace.' The formula is taken from the burial mass. It denotes ironically how much the world of old Gillenormand is a world from beyond the grave. It is a world peopled by reactionary priests and aristocrats. Marius will define himself against this background.

93 (p. 419) *after the 8th of July* i.e. badly. July 8 (1815) saw the second return to Paris of Louis XVIII after the Hundred Days; on 5 September (1816) the strongly pro-royalist parliament was dissolved.

94 (p. 423) *He read . . . Count H* Louis Hugo, the writer's uncle, who had fought in the Napoleonic Wars (see p. 415). The *Moniteur* (*universel*) mentioned earlier was France's official newspaper. The *Mémorial de Sainte-Hélène* is the account of Napoleon's exile on Saint Helena. Marius's attitude to Napoleon is similar to that of Stendhal's heroes, Julien Sorel (*Scarlet and Black*) and Fabrice del Dongo (*The Charterhouse of Parma*).

95 (p. 434) *The Friends of the ABC* In his representation of this association of radical young men Hugo provides a fictionalised image of the group of young Romantic writers and artists (the *cénacle*) who rallied around him in the late 1820s and early 1830s.

96 (p. 434) *Tugendbund* a German patriotic secret society that was dissolved in 1813. The Cougourde was a Provençal secret society under the July Monarchy.

97 (p. 438) *highway robbery of 1772* the date of the division of Poland between Russia, Austria and Prussia

98 (p. 438) *Benjamin Constant* a liberal political thinker and writer, the author of *Adolphe* (1816)

99 (p. 439) *the bloody tumult of June 1822* in reality of 5 June 1820, when Parisians had gathered to protest against the killing of the young student Lallemand

100 (p. 445) *Jean-Jacques turned them forth* Jean-Jacques Rousseau is said to have abandoned the children he had with Thérèse.

101 (p. 445) *Initium sapientiae* 'the beginning of wisdom'

102 (p. 446) *the tun of Heidelberg* This was a barrel in Heidelberg that was said to contain 263,000 litres of wine. Grantaire's (drunken) speech is full of untranslatable puns and cryptic allusions. The effervescence of the medium is here more important than the flashy erudition of the content.

103 (p. 446) *Incitatus* the name of Caligula's horse (literally 'At the gallop') that had been made consul

104 (p. 449) *at Staub's* Staub was a famous Parisian tailor, frequently mentioned by Balzac.

105 (p. 449) *the famous Touquet Charter* Touquet, a militant printer, disseminated copies of Louis XVIII's charter in all sorts of different forms.

106 (p. 450) *an Article 14* See Note 40 above. The measures that Charles X took in July 1830 under cover of this article precipitated the Revolution of 1830.

107 (p. 451) *'Quia nominor leo'* 'Because I am called a lion' (from Phaedra's *Fables*)

108 (p. 453) *Res Angusta* 'the meagreness of their fortune' (from Juvenal's *Satires*)

109 (p. 455) *Marius needy* The representation of an impoverished Marius in this and the following chapters is based closely on Hugo's own experiences in the early 1820s.

110 (p. 466) *Hernani* The uproar caused by the first performances of Hugo's drama in February 1830 marks one of the highpoints of the battle for Romanticism. Old Gillenormand's dislike of *Hernani* is a further indication of his conservatism.

111 (p. 467) *Sieyès* Abbé Sieyès (1748–1836) was a politician during the revolutionary period and the Empire who voted in favour of the execution of Louis XVI: hence the description of him as a regicide.

112 (p. 470) *Lux facta est* 'And there was light': the biblical revelation becomes for Marius an amorous one.

113 (p. 475) *to see Frederick* The reference is to Frédérick Lemaître, the leading actor of the Romantic period; *l'Auberge des Adrets* was a hugely popular contemporary melodrama and the (théâtre de la) Porte-Saint-Martin the boulevard theatre where melodramas were principally staged.

114 (p. 481) *in lateral galleries* Amongst the 'miners' who are excavating human societies Hugo lists a whole series of thinkers from different times and countries. The metaphor of society as a mine is made to work for Paris as well as for civilisation in general.

115 (p. 481) *the social Ugolino* Ugolino was a thirteenth-century Italian tyrant mentioned by Dante in his *Inferno*.

116 (p. 483) *Bobino* Bobeche was a famous clown of the period, Bobino a comic theatre.

117 (p. 485) *Ambubaiarum . . . mendici, mimae* from Horace's *Satires*: 'Troupes of flute players, of drug sellers, of beggars and comedians'. The idea is that such gangs have always existed, at all times and in all societies.